ON THE EDGE OF LIFE

PROPHECY

M. BLACKTHORN

authorHOUSE®

AuthorHouse™ UK
1663 Liberty Drive
Bloomington, IN 47403 USA
www.authorhouse.co.uk
Phone: 0800 047 8203 (Domestic TFN)
       +44 1908 723714 (International)

Published by AuthorHouse 08/30/2019

ISBN: 978-1-7283-8784-0 (sc)
ISBN: 978-1-7283-8785-7 (hc)
ISBN: 978-1-7283-8786-4 (e)

She cried desperately, "He is your son! You kept him locked in that accursed place for long enough. Now that he has finally found his way out, you want to stuff him back there again? Just let him live. You don't have to give him his titles back, and you don't have to welcome him into the family, but don't make him suffer in those terrible dungeons."

"Let him live?" Rabolii laughed. "And how do you imagine he'll utilise his new-found freedom? He will seek revenge. He'll try to overthrow me and take my crown. Arkenel has hated me ever since he was a child. All he ever did was hurt me and my interests. Need I remind you that if it hadn't been for him, I wouldn't be a corpse now?"

"Arkenel was four years old when you died. What are you talking about?" Ravena reminded him.

Rabolii made a tragic face, as if the very memory of the dreaded past could make him cry. He replied in a dramatic tone, "That's not what I meant! Do you remember the apogee of my discoveries, the day I managed to brew the potion which could revive me? And what did Arkenel do? He broke the flask— because he hated me! Don't even try to defend him. He has always been my enemy, and that will not change. He will return to the prison where he belongs."

CHAPTER 1

BETWEEN SOLEYA AND ASLANIA

The day was lovely and warm—not a cloud in the sky. The sun lit up the green expanse, and its rays felt like a tender embrace. Although autumn was emerging, these lands knew neither cold nor frost. The Order of Sorcery had gathered for their usual meditation. The eldest priestess was at complete rest, when something troubled her. She felt a sudden fright in her heart. The shadow of a fearsome enemy flashed in front of her eyes. She could smell death and blood. The vision lasted for a mere second, but it startled her. When she began to scream, her friends rushed to her aid and gave her a bouquet of herbs to smell so she'd feel better. Such an occurrence was so frightening and unusual! It had to be brought to the queen's attention at once!

The blonde queen Flinaya Lumeris was in the throne room, where she stretched on her throne. She was swirling a few raindrops around her finger as she gazed idly through the window. Soleya was a peaceful country. The lands were fertile, and the queen's counsellors did most of her work. She didn't have a care in the world. Her only duty was to make sure it rained often enough, as she was a sorceress who controlled the element water. She was surprised to see her priestess so frightened. When her servants rushed into the hall, she asked, "What happened?"

"The Reverend Elerya had a vision! She saw a shadow!" one of the other priestesses yelled dramatically.

Everyone began gasping and chattering. Some guards turned around to hear what was happening. Something extraordinary seemed to be going on.

This frightened Flinaya, and she asked, "What kind of shadow? Is something threatening Soleya?"

Elerya seemed unwell. She swayed and said hoarsely, "Deadly danger. I feel Krumerus rising."

When they heard something about Krumerus, everyone went crazy. Elerya didn't know she was going to bring all this attention to herself, but for the rest of the day she was carried everywhere to explain to everyone—queens, counsellors, nobles, and so on—exactly which shadow she had seen.

Flinaya was worried. Krumerus was the neighbouring country to the north-west, but its fearsome inhabitants had not attacked for years. The sinister nation was renowned for its dark magic. Those living there were known by the contemptuous name of erebi. It was unclear if they were alive or dead. Flinaya had tried to keep her distance over the years, avoiding conflict with the strange creatures. She hadn't always been successful. Soleya would always remember the necromancer's assault on the capital city.

Flinaya was deep in thought over those distant events, when something dark and sinister moved behind her. At first she was startled, but when she turned, in front of her stood none other than her son, who was blinking at her with an innocent expression.

"Illy, my darling, don't you have lessons?" she asked him tenderly after her fright had passed.

Ilinar was about seventeen years old, but he was short and feeble with a childlike expression, so a stranger would think he was younger than his age. However, there was something else about him which made him stand out—and not in a positive way. His skin was sickly pale, with permanent black circles under his eyes and colourless lips. In sunny Soleya, most people had golden locks. They were cheerful and radiant. The dark-haired youngster differed drastically from the bright landscape. Had he not been the queen's son, the peasants would have beaten him to death so he wouldn't spread any strange diseases. According to some people, he had nothing positive about him apart from the fact that he was the prince.

"Mother, I'm worried. I heard something about a shadow," Ilinar said. He'd always found a way to keep up with all the gossip in the castle.

Flinaya pulled him gently into her embrace and stroked his dark hair. Her face was void of expression.

"Sweetie, Revered Elerya simply had a strange vision, but

you don't have to worry. Soleya is strong; there is nothing we cannot handle."

It could be argued whether that statement was true or not. After all, Soleya was currently a country of happy peasants, most of whom couldn't hold a sword.

Ilinar wasn't done interrogating his mother. He continued staring at her and asked, "Is it true that Rabolii is alive and is gathering armies? I heard some servants say that a man had seen living skeletons along the border."

Flinaya bit her lip. How was it that her son was always better informed about rumours like that than she? Not wanting anyone to panic for the time being, she mumbled, "Rabolii has been dead for nearly eighteen years. You know that."

"I have heard that he has risen. If anyone has seen living skeletons, that must be true, mustn't it?" he continued to insist.

Oh no. If Ilinar was so excited and full of questions, the royal council would probably be just the same. Flinaya was thinking of rehearsing a speech, and if she was successful at calming her son with it, it would probably work on the citizens. She put on a beaming smile and answered in a calm voice, "Darling, don't believe every rumour you hear. The necromancer Rabolii paid with his life the last time he dared set foot in Soleya. I'm not even sure someone has seen skeletons. People are just excited about Elerya's vision, which is not necessarily related to Krumerus. Within a few days, I promise no one will even think of this!"

That turned out to be an unfortunately inaccurate prediction. Flinaya rarely sent spies to Krumerus because the flora and fauna there were so unforgiving that it made her wonder how those lands could be populated by anything—even by skeletons. There were huge bugs, strange humanoid beasts, and so many abstract demons that most species hadn't even been recorded. Soleyan scouts who had managed to return reported some unusual activity in this land of nightmares. Large erebian detachments gathered in the wilderness, and they were marching across the country.

The Krumerians, referred to as erebi by the southerners, were strange people. Pale like corpses, they were known for their ability to see in the dark. However, Soleyans had a lot more to say about their appearance. According to some, the erebi were not really alive; they were corpses raised by evil spells. According to others, they had rotting flesh and no doubt ate children. It wasn't clear what they were, but they were known for their aggression. If they were gathering an army, Flinaya had to prepare her people. The best way to deal with a potential attack was by turning to her consort.

The Soleyans celebrated the god of fire and light. The golden cities rose high and strong. The sky was always bright blue and cloudless. However, Aslania, the country to the east, was dark and desolate. It was infinite and icy, and life there was harsh. The two nations were different, but the threat which Krumerus posed brought them together. Flinaya would seek help from Aslania.

Ilinar wasn't very pleased to hear this. He knew the Aslanian prince, Eslir. They had spent their entire childhoods fighting, pulling each other's hair, and arguing about who would be the better king. Eslir was five years older than Ilinar, and he was taller and more robust than most people his age. His mother had been a Soleyan princess, so Ilinar and Eslir were cousins, but they seemed to have nothing in common. The two boys had met whenever their families exchanged visits, and the little time they did spend together was filled mostly with childish quarrels. Ilinar thought Eslir to be boastful and unpleasant, and he didn't wish to lay eyes upon him.

A few days later this glorious meeting took place. Everyone in Soleya was thrilled to see the foreign guests from those strange, icy lands. Indeed, the royal family looked as outlandish and incredible as everyone had hoped. They arrived in a carriage made of crystals and icy-looking glass. It was pulled by huge horses with very smooth long fur. They stopped in front of the castle gates. The Soleyans gazed with amazement as the carriage doors opened, and out stepped the great king Treris Falnir, wearing his ornate armour, which was made of aluminium just for the show. It gleamed magically and looked impressive on the strong body of the ruler. Next to him stood his proud son with his platinum-blond hair, wearing similar attire as his father. That was Eslir. He was glancing upon the crowd in front of him with such superiority as if he were the god of the world.

Ilinar seemed like a dark spot when compared with all the whiteness and shine the Aslanian brought. He was looking around with a nervous, distrustful expression. He expected Eslir to begin teasing him immediately.

The queen welcomed the honourable guests and led them to the castle. Ilinar tried to follow them and greet them, but Eslir walked past Ilinar as if he were a statue, all the while talking about how he'd save Soleya from the skeletons.

One of the Aslanian guards noticed Ilinar and immediately sounded the alarm. "Your Majesty! Be careful! There's an erebius behind you!"

The rest of the Aslanian guards started swinging their icy swords, preparing to defend the Soleyans. Flinaya needed a second to understand that the guards were trying to arrest her son. Eslir observed this scene with an expression that suggested he hadn't burst out laughing only for the sake of decency. The queen threw herself in front of her dear son and began explaining that he was the prince. The guards began apologising and mentioned they'd been close to the border and had seen erebi who looked exactly like Ilinar. King Treris stepped forward, flushed with shame, and said, "Forgive my guards, Your Majesty. I forgot to warn them that you had adopted a baby erebius out of the goodness of your heart."

"Ilinar is my own son. I was pregnant with him at the time of the last erebi attack. I was struck by a black curse, and it is a real miracle that my son and I survived. Rest assured, Ilinar's heart is pure like spring dew, though his skin is grey because of the necromancer's spell."

"Of course. Forgive me." The Aslanian king smiled at her. He had heard so many stories about why Ilinar looked so strange and why he resembled a dark-haired corpse. Sometimes he'd forget what the official story was and whether the prince was Flinaya's real son or not.

Ilinar was pouting. How long would he need to live in this world in order for people to stop acting so shocked when they saw him? He turned and walked away from all these people, who kept teasing him. As he was leaving, he heard Eslir speaking, "Have you tried dying his hair and face, maybe?"

Ilinar returned to his bedroom, which was his safest place in this cold world. The room was overstuffed with all sorts of items like decorative swords, mannequins with different armour, and large bookshelves. Some of the volumes looked antique. In the middle of the room there was a large table with a drawing of a map like the ones generals used to reflect on their battle strategies. Ilinar loved the stories of battles and soldiers. He was constantly reading something on the topic, and he believed he would become a very successful king and general one day. He dreamed of the day when Soleya would see him as a hero and not as a skinny erebian boy.

"I knew I'd find you here. Nice monastery," a tentative voice called, pulling Ilinar out of his dreamland. He turned abruptly and saw that Eslir stood at the door and stared at him.

"Did no one teach you how to knock in Aslania, or do you have no doors in those igloos you live in? And my room is not a monastery!" Ilinar replied angrily.

"You live in it, and you're a nun, so why not? Do you have anything interesting here? What's this?"

Eslir picked up an old soldier's helmet. Ilinar pulled it from his hands and snapped, "Careful with that. It used to belong to Hreles Soleyan!"

"What is this garbage?" Eslir continued walking around as if he were at home. He picked up an old, shabby book. He laughed. "Oh, I remember that they were also reading to me the tales of Emanrylii Prehorian when I was eight."

"Give me the poetry collection. It's an original manuscript from two hundred years ago, and it's priceless!" Ilinar launched forward to defend his treasure.

"Do you have anything in this room that's not garbage? Are those swords on the wall real?" Eslir reached for a weapon stand above his head. "Can you fight with a sword? Or has Mommy forbidden you so you don't hurt yourself?"

"I haven't been trained to brawl and wrestle like a mere foot soldier, I will be a king! Or is it all the same in Aslania and you all fight side by side against the penguins?" Ilinar said angrily.

"I won't allow my future ally in my fight with the erebi to be a wimp," Eslir answered, throwing one of the swords for Ilinar to catch.

The Soleyan prince got startled and jumped away, letting the weapon fall on the ground. Eslir shook his head and noted, "Poor Soleya. It will get taken over on the very day of your coronation. Come with me into the courtyard and learn to fight instead of sitting here and being a baby."

Ilinar gritted his teeth and picked up the sword from the ground. He didn't want to deal with Eslir, but he did want to be brave like the characters in Prehorian's books. As the two were leaving, the younger prince kept trying to hide the sword with some silly movements every time some servant passed them in the corridor. As they went out into the courtyard, Eslir began to pose with the weapon. He explained: "The way you stand is the most important thing during fencing. Stand slightly to the side with your leg forward and with a straight back, holding your weapon with—" Ilinar struggled to keep the sword in the air because it was too heavy. Eslir sighed with condescension and added, "Preferably with your right hand. Now charge at me."

"But what if we hurt each other?"

"Aslania will melt before you hurt me," Eslir replied mockingly. "And now imagine that I am Rabolii and attack me!"

Ilinar gripped the handle of his sword, feeling as if he needed to jump off a cliff. He lunged forward ungracefully, only to fall flat on his face because Eslir had tripped him up somehow. The Aslanian stood over him, not sure if this was incredibly funny or tragic enough to ruin his mood for three days to come. Finally he decided it was the former, so he waved his hand, announcing, "The longer you lie there, the greener your trousers will become, and your mother will notice that you've been rolling in the grass. Get up."

Ilinar got up. His face had turned a strange purplish colour, which was his version of blushing. He ran his fingers through his messed up hair and complained, "My sword weighs too much!"

Ilinar felt like just tossing this sword and announcing he'd never deal with this nonsense again, but something in the Aslanian's cold gaze fixed him in his place. He'd feel stupid if he just left, so he clutched his sword again and attacked like a mad ram. The training continued until Ilinar had a floral sample in his hair from each flower bed where he had fallen.

It appeared that the two young men had made too much noise as Flinaya swiftly noticed something horrific was taking place in her gardens. With a squad of servant girls, she rushed to stop this violent encounter and to pick out daisies from her son's dark hair while Eslir watched him mockingly.

"Illy, how many times have I told you not to ..." Flinaya started with a soft, reproachful voice. Eslir felt he'd burst out in laughter when he heard "Illy".

"Ladies, I shall take my leave," said the glamorous blond warrior. He casually left the garden while Flinaya was chiding her son.

"Mother, you embarrass me. Just let me do what I want!" Ilinar snapped. He then pulled himself away and ran back to his monastery to find comfort in the poems of his beloved Prehorian, who was probably the only one who understood him.

Ilinar didn't know how long he'd need to suffer Eslir's presence and when that annoying visit would end. Over the last few days he hardly saw his mother because she spent all her time with that large snow-headed king. Whenever he was here, she'd forget about everyone else. On the fifth day of the visit, a royal council gathered. Ilinar and Eslir were also invited. The two sat next to each other just so they could kick each other under the table. They stopped when Flinaya stood up and started talking.

"Thank you all for coming. I gathered you to discuss the hostile activity of our enemies in the north." The blonde queen picked up a few letters from the table. "These are the reports from my scouts. They report that they have seen large armies patrolling Krumerus, concentrating mostly on the western and eastern border. My people have confirmed that the necromancer Rabolii Remedor is still the ruling monarch."

"Impossible!" Treris Falnir slammed his fist on the table. "When this monster broke into Soleya, he got stabbed over a dozen times. My close friends confirmed this. How can he still exist decades later?"

Flinaya sighed and smiled bitterly. "Krumerus is the land of the dead. Personally, I am not surprised by this. The fact remains that the necromancer gains strength, and we have no information about his intentions."

"I propose to gather soldiers and attack the wretched corpses before they attack us!" Eslir waved a fist heroically. Ilinar rolled his eyes with annoyance. It seemed that the dimwitted Aslanian thought that beating Rabolii would be as easy as punching a seventeen-year-old prince in the courtyard of the castle.

"I don't deem it wise to attack now," Flinaya replied. "Mortelion's season is upon us. Now that the corpses are stronger, we would be at a disadvantage."

Each of the four gods on this continent had its own ninety-one-day season, and during that time the sorcerers who belonged to the gods, as well as the creatures they'd created, were most powerful. In the autumn, when many animals and plants died, the god of death, Mortelion, was gathering strength, and his subordinates became much more dangerous.

"We couldn't afford to be idle after hearing those troublesome reports. That is why Queen Flinaya and I have decided to strengthen our kingdoms and make them even more united and powerful!"

"Yes. If we sacrifice you in honour of Mortelion, he will commit suicide in terror, Ilinar!" Eslir began to whisper mockingly.

"Or if we give you to the necromancer, Eslir, you can ruin his whole country just by existing," the young prince answered instantly.

"The lovely Queen Flinaya and I have decided get married!"

The king spread his hands in a festive manner. This announcement dropped like a bomb in the hall. The two princes would have been less shocked if Rabolii himself had materialised in the castle wearing a gown. They could do nothing but sit there, staring in shock, crushed by the terrible event. The king apparently decided to reinforce the effect and shouted, "And you two will be brothers from now on!"

"This is all *your* fault, you insane northerner with a frozen brain!" cried Ilinar. He threw himself at Eslir.

Flinaya was terrified by this outburst of malice by her little boy. She ran to stop the fight while Treris was laughing at the scene. He remembered how he'd play like this with his brothers. That's how they expressed their love for one another. He was sure it was the same with these two. He wanted for Eslir to have brothers, but unfortunately, with his huge torso, the boy had killed his mother during birth. For a time, that ended the king's dream for a bigger family, at least until now. Now he had met Flinaya, who was such a wonderful, kind-hearted woman. She had suffered pain and woes, but she was still taking such good care of her country and her child, even after the mad necromancer had killed her husband.

This marriage had been organised in order to bring the two nations together, but for the princes it had the opposite effect. Ilinar wasn't sure where he even stood any more. Was he still the heir to the throne, or would Eslir usurp his country? The prince of Aslania was also discontent because he wanted to go home to be with his friends, but he had no idea if that would happen soon. Both of them were nervous; the future was uncertain.

Darkness was falling over the silent city. The sky was cloudy; there were no stars in sight. A deathly chilling wind was blowing from the north, reminiscent of the horrors lurking in the lands of the necromancer. Ilinar sat alone in the garden of the castle, blankly staring into the night. He was deep in thought about his precarious life. He heard someone approaching him with a quiet step rustling in the dried leaves. Eslir sat beside Ilinar on the bench and said, "You'll sit here all night to wait for me? You know our sparring session is in the morning."

Ilinar grunted in reply. Eslir turned to him and said, "Are you seriously going to be angry at me? You do realise our parents' wedding wasn't my idea at all."

"I don't know," Ilinar replied.

"What don't you know? Who would want to be a brother of someone like you?" Eslir snapped, crossing his arms.

Ilinar sighed and said, "You know what, Eslir, you are my least problems. I'm worrying more about Krumerus. Rabolii is known to be capable of … unspeakable things."

"Yes, I heard about … what happened here," Eslir mumbled with a faint trace of sympathy in his voice.

"He penetrated the very castle here in Lumis!" Ilinar waved his hand towards the tall golden towers. "Can you imagine! How did he find a way to get in without being detected by anyone? He had attacked my mother. They told me about the battle. When the guards came to her aid, he fought them off like they were nothing. He used death spells to kill dozens at a time. Amongst them was my father, who found himself surrounded by the animated corpses of his own people. And soon after he himself joined them. It is a miracle that Mother survived. Over a hundred other people gave their lives fighting Rabolii, until they finally brought him down. And now it seems like all the sacrifices were in vain: he's risen again."

Eslir listened to this story with a serious look on his face. Rabolii Remedor was a legend all over the continent. It was said that he was the most powerful sorcerer of this age. Eslir had heard tales about entire legions of skeletons which the necromancer could control all by himself. After a short silence, Eslir noted, "Soleya is not ready to fight such an enemy. These two decades of peace have made you weak. But don't worry. Now that you have a competent ally, things will be much easier."

"Just because we've been at peace with our neighbours doesn't mean we're stupid," Ilinar snapped. "I have read books about warfare and fighting since I've learned the alphabet. Have you ever even looked at one in your life?"

Eslir turned his icy gaze towards Ilinar and said with a smirk, "You sure love your fancy books in Soleya, don't you? Perhaps if you actually spent time training your soldiers well instead of having them read books, you'd still have a king." After this cruel statement, he stood up and added, "Now, if you'll excuse me, I'm going inside."

Ilinar remained on the bench, staring into the darkness. He didn't believe that the Aslanian presence would lead to anything good. The foreigners could be here to protect Soleya or to control it. Maybe Ilinar had more enemies than he suspected.

The young prince continued to sit in the silent garden, deeply concerned about his own existential problems and those of his country. As he was sitting there deep in thought, he heard a distant tumult. He looked around. The noise came from somewhere in the direction of the city gates. He rose and went to find out what was going on. In principle, his mother didn't let him walk around the city without ten guards, but he was feeling rebellious these days, so he went alone.

The citizens were lighting candles and peering through the windows of their large, rich houses to see who was making noise in their peaceful city at night. Soldiers walked along the street in golden armour, leading some strange, terrifying creatures. Ilinar could get a good look at them despite the faint light. At the front walked two captives wearing black leather armour stained with mud, blood, and dirt. Matted dark hair hung in front of their faces and covered them. Behind them walked several foul creatures that looked like dug-out dead bodies with bones covered with little more than shrivelled brownish skin. Ilinar had not seen a living corpse before. He looked away, feeling sickened. Still, his curiosity about this whole situation prevailed, so he followed the soldiers.

It was quite uncommon for someone to wake Their Majesties in the middle of the night. In this case, it was for an extraordinary event. Very soon, Flinaya and King Treris, as well as their dear children, found themselves in the throne room to inspect the captives. Forward stepped a man and a woman with extremely pale faces and colourless cheeks. Their hair was black, and their eyes were whitish blue like a raven's. To the poor Soleyans, they looked terrifying. Eslir grinned and started poking Ilinar. He whispered to him, "Shrimp, is that your brother? The family resemblance is uncanny."

"Yes, and that's your girlfriend next to him. You've been staring at her like a hungry wolf from the moment she entered," Ilinar hissed.

The captured woman had some vampiric beauty to her. She was slender with bright red lipstick. But Eslir wouldn't admit that she was attractive. He replied, "I prefer girlfriends who have a pulse, thank you very much."

Flinaya stepped forward and addressed the captives, saying, "Krumerians! You were caught crossing the border between Vern and Soleya. Would you like to explain why you were invading our territory with an armed squad?"

The two erebi looked at each other with a hint of annoyance. The man turned to the queen and said, "I was just walking

11

my skeletons through the woods. I had not noticed the subtle difference between the Vernian forest and the Soleyan forest."

"Our relationship with your country is not a peaceful one. I have no choice but to send you to prison until I get the correspondence from your ruler with the conditions for your release."

The Krumerian man burst out laughing. He lifted his piercing blue eyes and said, "You listen to me now, doll face. My conditions for the release are the following: you will rattle your silver keys, and you'll unlock these ridiculous shackles. Then I will take my skeletons and I'll be on my way without causing you any more headaches. But if you decide to play dumb prison games with me, I'll turn your whole ridiculous colourful town into a pile of rubbish, and your gorgeous body will take an honourable position in my humble army. Do I make myself clear?"

Their Majesties started gasping while this hailstorm of ugly threats was pouring down on them. Although the words had come from the mouth of a chained, dirty Krumerian, they echoed ominously in the silent hall. Treris Falnir was the first to raise a voice of indignation. He stepped forward and waved a fist, sized like a head of a baby. He yelled, "You wretched creature! How dare you speak this way to the queen of Soleya! You are currently in her possessions, and you depend on her mercy!"

The Krumerian shook his head, casting back his matted hair, and said, "And I am Malior Remedor, the heir to the kingdom of Mortelion. So, if the thought of hurting me even crosses your wooden heads, then demons, undead, and monsters will begin pouring in your cities. And they will want your blood. So if you value your useless lives and those of your stupid peasants, do what I tell you, or you will experience things that will make your nightmares seem pleasant."

The king and the queen exchanged glances. They didn't know if they should take these threats seriously. They also didn't know whether the one who stood before them really was the son of the fearsome Remedor family. It was extremely difficult for Soleya to get spies into Krumerus, so everything that was happening there was covered in mystery. Eslir apparently didn't think the threat was serious, so he answered with a grin, "Oh, is that how it works? Krumerus decides to attack us and to bring demons and nonsense, and this puts an end to our civilisation? What stopped you from doing it until now? Maybe because your great Rabolii is useless and rotten and because you win your battles relying on fear, not strength. We won't be intimidated by you and your absurd threats, Malior Remedor."

The Krumerian continued to grin, then his face changed and became serious and sinister. He replied, "I don't think I was clear enough, Aslanian. I'm not threatening you with our armies alone. I threaten you with myself. I know it's unlikely that your snowmen spies have told you rumours of my reputation, but if you were aware of it, you would be afraid. I give you one last chance to let me go and save your hides."

Flinaya and Treris glanced at each other again. Then the woman said, "Malior Remedor, you will be locked up, and I will discuss your release and your suspicious crossing of the border with your master. If all of us cooperate and Rabolii Remedor accepts my terms, you will be released."

Malior raised his eyebrows with an insolent expression and said, "So is that how it's going to be? Too bad. I tried to negotiate as if you were normal people, but you're not. I'm well aware that once I set foot in your prison, I may end up there for a very long time. I'm a busy man." He smiled dangerously, his entire eyes turning a grim black colour, as he added, "Good night, sunshines."

As soon as he spoke those words, the great throne room began to darken. There were a lot of torches in it, and huge crystalline chandeliers hung from the ceiling, but all these flames seemed to drown in the darkness. Their light couldn't penetrate the black veil. The Soleyans began to panic as the bony hands of the skeletons reached out for them. Several of the guards tried to find the king and the queen in the dark to get them out of the throne room, but they couldn't find their way through the hall. There weren't any other sorcerers to defend the royals.

Flinaya didn't know how to use her water magic to attack foes she couldn't see. Ilinar crouched down and slipped away from the fray. He stared at the darkness, and he could see what was happening. He did have night vision just like the erebi, but he kept it a strict secret so no one would mock him for it. He could see Malior step away from the fight carelessly. He reached out with one of his chained hands and managed to pull a dagger from the belt of one of the soldiers. Then he turned towards the confused monarchs. Ilinar was horrified when he realised what was going to happen. He yelled and charged at the Krumerian. Malior easily dodged this weak attack. He moved away from Ilinar's path and pushed him towards the wall. He then drew his blade across the queen's neck. The Soleyan prince rose just in time to see that. The sight pierced him as if he had fallen victim to the blade. Time ceased to exist at this moment. The raging skeletons, the flying bolts of death magic, the spilled blood, and all the elements of this nightmare were swirling in front of his eyes, and it seemed like it would never end.

Ilinar barely noticed that at some point the darkness broke. He didn't see that the battle was over. He continued to sit with a traumatised look and couldn't move. The dead were carried away. Some cleaners came to wipe the blood off the floor. At some point Eslir came and sat down next to Ilinar and spoke out: "They are dead ... Our parents are dead ... Do you understand what this means?"

Ilinar couldn't answer. He felt as though he were crushed. He couldn't think straight, and right now he was definitely not pondering about the future. Eslir stood up and kicked with all of his strength some helmet which had been left on the floor after the fight. He shouted angrily, "They were two people and a handful of carcasses, and you let them kill the monarchs of two countries! Inside your goddamn castle! Are you Soleyans idiots, or are you infants?! You claim to be the children of the god Flalirion, the great sorcerer of the light! The cursed erebi just blew out your candles and slaughtered you like sheep. I couldn't care less about all of this, but why did this idiocy have to cost my father's life? He died because of your helplessness and incompetence."

Ilinar was still sitting there with the same dead expression on his face, staring blankly ahead. Eslir was infuriated by this behaviour. He grabbed the Soleyan by his collar and shook him. He yelled at him, "Good morning, *Your Majesty!* Would you like to do something? Would you like to get your royal ass out of bed one day, or will the other two erebi who got lost in your territory take over this stupid country?" He pushed Ilinar back and groaned. "I cannot believe how calm you are."

A man with greyish blond hair came up to Ilinar. He appeared to be in his late fifties. He started to help him get up and spoke to him: "Your Highness? Are you hurt? Come with me."

Eslir glared at him and snapped, "And who are you supposed to be?"

The Soleyan shot him a surprised gaze with his eyes, which were black like olives. He replied, "My name is Eley. I am Lord Ilinar's private tutor. Now if you would excuse us."

He took the prince away to his chambers. Eslir watched them

as they left. He shook his head with a desperate look. For the first time he really noticed how helpless the Soleyans were. He had listened to his father speak about the importance of the friendship between the two nations, saying that they were stronger against the common enemy. However, Eslir wasn't sure any more whether this alliance would turn out to be a burden. Now the hard decision whether to help Soleya was up to him. He didn't want to be the prince who would ruin the union as soon as the previous monarch died. But the thought of defending a nation made up of several million Ilinars was even worse.

Over the next few days, Ilinar couldn't function normally. He shut himself in his room and barely managed to go out to attend his mother's funeral. He was too traumatised to think about the country, about his reign, or about anything else. He stayed indoors, hugging his books which he loved so much, and explicitly ordered that no one let Eslir near him, because he wouldn't be able to handle his remarks and accusations.

In the meantime Eslir was in a much darker part of the castle, an underground laboratory dedicated to researching the erebi. There, on some stone tables, were placed the bodies of the Krumerians, tied with leather straps. They were motionless. One of the scientists spoke with a competent tone: "Those four bodies there have obviously been resurrected with magic. They stopped moving when she died." He nodded towards the body of the Krumerian woman. "This suggests that she was the necromancer who moved them, and she was probably a living human."

Eslir was inspecting the bodies with a disgusted look. He answered, "I didn't know Krumerus was inhabited by living humans."

"I know, right? Incredible!" the Soleyan scientist answered in an excited tone. He pulled the cover off the woman and began to point out various wounds and scratches. "Here's where she suffered an abdominal injury and the main artery was cut. The Krumerian has died of something as simple as a loss of blood, just as it would have happened to any normal person."

"What about him?" Eslir nodded with hatred and contempt towards Malior.

"He was also human," the scientist said. "He was stabbed in the chest, so his lungs filled with blood and he choked."

Eslir turned his gaze towards the darkness and said, "So the necromancers are no less vulnerable than we are. How many are out there? Sorcerers of all kinds are generally rare. If we hit Krumerus at the right spot, maybe this battle will not be so difficult after all. I'll make them regret slaughtering my father."

The Soleyan scientist gazed at him for a moment, not knowing how he felt about this. He asked, "What would you recommend we do with the corpses?"

"Perform whatever experiments you want on them, then burn them," said Eslir, before going out with a manly gait, his silver cloak waving behind him.

Mortelion's season was unfolding with all its terrifying power. The sky was clouded; a cold chill came from the north. Soleya's capital, Lumis, was quiet. People were weary. Silent voices whispered rumours of the return of Rabolii Remedor, the most fearsome sorcerer of all time.

Ilinar was in bed. He had pulled the blanket over his head, creating a small, cosy tent, and was concentrating on flipping through the same old book he'd read dozens of times. He found comfort in the familiar things. Books helped him escape from his tragic life. Unfortunately, reality always finds a way grip us mercilessly, so the prince heard some quarrelling in front of his door sometime near noon. Some people were shouting outside. One of the guards came in and spoke to the lump packed in the bed: "Your Highness, Prince Eslir is outside and wishes to speak with you. I told him you were indisposed, but he insists."

"Tell him to go away!" Ilinar cried.

Eslir didn't want to suffer such refusals, so he walked in. He looked around and stated, "You can't be serious. Your whole country is panicked and shaken while you lay wrapped in bed like a cocoon!" One of the Soleyan guards tried to stop Eslir from approaching, but the prince raised his hand and yelled, "Don't even think about touching me. I am the king of Aslania!" He then turned back to Ilinar, feeling a bit awkward as he was seemingly speaking to the blankets. He continued chiding him, "Yes, I understand. You're upset and you're scared, but you can't afford to act like this. You're this country's monarch now."

Ilinar emerged from under the blanket. His hair was shaggy; his eyes, red and puffy. He resembled some sort of mad zombie. He barked at Eslir with a hoarse voice, "My mother is dead, and I am incapable of taking her place! I can't win this war. Rabolii has defeated us."

Eslir clenched his teeth angrily and grabbed Ilinar by the collar. Some of their guards began to fight each other, while others were trying to stop the princes from fighting. The

Aslanian prince snarled, "Listen to me, you whiny little child! Had our parents actually gotten married, I would have a right to your throne, and I would have taken it from you with a snap of my fingers. I would do it to save this country from you. Unfortunately, this never happened, so instead I have to work with you. Thus I expect you to wash yourself, get dressed, and show up to your own coronation, then take some responsibility for the people who depend on you. It won't be too hard. You will not be alone. I will be there. Your mother's counsellors will be there."

Ilinar stared at Eslir with a mad gaze. It wasn't clear if he'd start fighting him or if he'd just cry. In this dramatic moment, Eley, the precious mentor of the Soleyan prince, came in. He managed to squeeze between the guards and began to speaking to Ilinar: "Your Highness, please listen to Eslir. The country needs you. The people are afraid. They want to hear from you that everything will be fine. Be brave and show that you can overcome all this."

Eslir rolled his eyes. He couldn't believe that it took several people to come and plead with Ilinar just so he'd go out of his room and pretend to be a king for a bit. He pushed Eley out of the way, put his hand on Ilinar's shoulder, and said, "Hey, you know what? Forget the people. Don't you want to avenge your mother? The cursed erebi butchered her like she was nothing. Don't you hate them? Don't you want to make them regret ever setting foot in your territory? We're capable of this together. We have the armies and the power to defeat them."

"Sweet Ardor," Eley muttered with annoyance.

Ilinar remained silent for a second or two. Then he spoke in a weak voice, "I'll get dressed and attend the council meeting, then arrange my coronation. I will protect my people from the erebi. But I'm not going to start an all-out war with them; it's not what my mother wanted."

Eslir, restraining himself from groaning or showing annoyance in another way, patted Ilinar on the shoulder and congratulated him. "I'm glad to hear that. We have a meeting with the council at three, so try to come on time."

Having said that, Eslir walked away with his shimmering guards, who were dressed in bluish armour decorated with icy crystals. Ilinar gazed after them with a sad face and sighed. "How is he capable of managing so well? How can he think about the nation and the wars after what happened to us?"

Eley sat on the bed beside Ilinar and replied in a velvety

voice, "Your Highness, he was raised in a different way. Your mother always protected you from the evils of this world, so it is normal for you to feel lost without her. She was a wonderful woman, and she'd want for you to carry on. I will help you achieve this. In these precarious times, I'm your best friend. I'll make sure nobody harms you."

"Of course, Eley," Ilinar replied quietly.

Eley had been close to Ilinar for a long time. He had tried to get himself in the prince's closest circle of people in order to benefit from his generosity. Eley had been trying to raise his family from the ruins of the moral degradation of his drunken parents, who were now sick and helpless. For him, Ilinar was very a comfortable solution to many problems. He would do everything he could to keep him in power.

Ilinar walked to the council hall with a dead expression. He needed to go there and pretend to be a king. Some time ago he had been so eager to attend these meetings, but his mother had not allowed him in. She had said it would be boring. Ilinar was now prepared to feel this boredom to its full extent.

At first, the counsellors exchanged a few words about the recent tragedy and offered condolences to the princes. Afterwards, Eslir stepped forward as if he were in charge of this meeting, and said, "Ladies and gentlemen, thank you all for being here! We have a lot to discuss today—funerals, coronations, wars. I suggest we make a start. First of all, I have exciting news! I want you to welcome a very special guest who may very well decide the outcome of this war."

As Eslir spoke, his guards entered the council room, dragging a woman in. Ilinar rose to his feet, shocked by the sight. The captive was pale and black-haired, obviously a Krumerian. She wore expensive clothes with lots of lace and glossy threads in it, as well as heavy, gorgeous jewels. It seemed like she'd been beaten. Her head swung forward, and her mouth was bloodstained. She was unconscious. Ilinar felt that it was too soon for him to see more erebi after that horrible incident. He turned to Eslir and barked angrily, "What is the meaning of this? Can you explain what you've done? Didn't you see what happened last time you brought monsters into my castle?!"

"Don't be alarmed by her. My specialists have examined her and confirmed that she isn't a sorceress," Eslir responded with a vicious smile. "She's my catch of the century. Her presence here is most fitting. After all, Krumerus did bereave us of our queen. It only seems right that we return the favour."

CHAPTER 2

DEAD MAN'S WOES

Far to the north, a grim fortress was rising amongst the jagged black mountain peaks. It looked like a ruin, forgotten through the ages. A bluish mist concealed the details of the landscape. Only the rising, sharp towers were visible. They stabbed the thick clouds like blades; from their sharp tips, an eerie teal energy flowed upwards. Like a wandering spectre, it moved slowly towards the clouds to feed the master who was ever so hungry for it. Spiky climbing plants embraced the old stone buildings. The place was bleak and inhospitable. If one were to observe it from afar, it would look completely abandoned.

Traces of life could be noticed beyond the tall, serrated fortress walls. The fortifications housed estates of tiny, scruffy houses which huddled in the darkness and mist like mice in a hole. The living people, as well as the dead, walked those streets, and that didn't seem to bother anyone. Stalls of rotten wood stood there, and strange goods were sold: large game, skeletons, and all sorts of smaller trinkets. Beggars and tramps emerged from every corner. Skinny and pale, they resembled those raised from the grave. Perhaps they wished for their own death.

Krumerus, the land of nightmares, home to monsters and dead men, the domain of Mortelion. Those who glanced at these lands for the first time would be shocked by what they saw. The locals, however, dwelled in the darkness and felt it as a comfortable protection. For some, this gulf full of monsters and death was paradise. It was an ocean of opportunity, a vast land on which to build their towers of gold.

At the outskirts of the city was a magnificent building—the royal castle. It looked old but opulent. The ornaments were abstract with stony spikes and horns protruding. Somewhere in the undefined shapes a demon or skull could be distinguished.

In the depths of the castle was a gloomy room, its windows covered with thick velvet curtains that had been gathering dust for decades. The air smelled of rotting flesh. A dozen vampires hung from the ceiling, quietly drowsing, as their master scribbled on some papers, devoted to intellectual labour. The room was too dark for a normal person to write or read, but this wasn't a territory inhabited by normal people.

"Master, I come bearing an important message!" An overly excited erebian servant invaded the necromancer's lair.

Rabolii raised his head with an angry, critical expression. His long grey hair hung from the sides of his face, and his thin, curved eyebrows seemed constantly raised, giving him a resting, lofty, and displeased expression. But, incidentally, he did feel that way at the moment. He responded with a clear, indulgent voice which echoed in the room: "Evidently I failed to teach you how to use a clock—either you or anyone else in this castle! Between the hours of three and six I have a vampirism research session, and you interrupted me. Get out! Seek me again after six."

"But, Master! It's about the fortress Aldur. There's been a jailbreak. Hundreds of criminals are at large, roaming our lands," the servant announced, agitated.

Rabolii stood up with a furious look, rising up tall and looking threatening. He began yelling, "Sometimes I just have a look around to get the impression that Mortelion is punishing me. I am sitting here and studying alchemy, and all of you are pouring into my chambers and flooding me with bad news. Why didn't you tell this to my stupid children for a change? Day in and day out they argue about who should succeed me, but whenever something requires the king's attention, who takes responsibility? Me! As always! You make me so angry. Leave my chambers at once! I will deal with this nuisance after my vampirism session, and if someone else dares to disturb me before six, they will become a subject of research themselves."

The servant slowly stepped back and vaporised from this place. It wasn't his idea to come here; he was just getting pushed around. He had first gone to Queen Ravena Remedor, who wasn't as unpleasant as her husband. However, she made him go to Rabolii anyway. Nobody liked talking to the necromancer. It was a well-known fact that since he'd died, he didn't do anything but sit in his room and explore new ways to make himself feel alive.

Potions, spells, curses—Rabolii was doing all he could, but this effort occupied all his time.

Those who didn't know Rabolii wouldn't assume that he had been killed. Seemingly he had no wounds. His skin wasn't rotting. However, he was still not whole. He was merely haunting his own corpse. His death was like a sickness from which he could never recover. He could only suppress the symptoms. If he didn't drink his precious potions, his limbs would become stiff, he'd start to rot, and his organs would start to fail one by one. As a matter of fact, he simply kept his own body from falling apart with magic, but he wasn't exactly connected to it, at least not the way he used to be. He was like a sailor in a boat from which he could fall at any moment if the waves shook him. No one was like him in this world. No one understood what he was going through every day.

Ravena was still in the capital, Kranium, not suspecting that Eslir was about to capture her. Still, there was no peace in her life because she had to deal with her husband. She waited till the clocks struck six, and she knew he had finished his vampiric research session. She went to visit him. She carefully pushed the heavy, ominous doors. They opened with a wailing creak. Ravena stepped into the dark chambers. She seemed too young and pretty to be Rabolii's wife. She was in her forties, and she wore glamorous velvet dresses and plenty of jewels crafted of a black metal. Rabolii glanced at her and mumbled, "What do you want?"

Ravena was used to this attitude. The necromancer was never in a good mood, not even when his closest friends came to see him. She spoke to him in a sweet, calm voice, "I didn't mean to bother you, Rab. I guess you heard about what happened in Aldur."

"It failed to escape my attention since some malapert stormed in here yelling on the topic and completely ruining my research session."

Ravena approached him and said, "Rab, Arkenel is amongst those prisoners."

The necromancer rolled his eyes as if he were going to die from annoyance. He said carelessly, "I'll send an armed force to take care of their riots. I won't let them roam around unchecked."

"Dear, please." Ravena reached out to him, but Rabolii pushed her hands aside as if she were contagious. She cried desperately, "He is your son! You kept him locked in that accursed place for long enough. Now that he has finally found his way out, you want to stuff him back there again? Just let him live. You don't have to give him his titles back, and you don't have to welcome him into the family, but don't make him suffer in those terrible dungeons."

"Let him live?" Rabolii laughed. "And how do you imagine he'll utilise his new-found freedom? He will seek revenge. He'll try to overthrow me and take my crown. Arkenel has hated me ever since he was a child. All he ever did was hurt me and my interests. Need I remind you that if it hadn't been for him, I wouldn't be a corpse now?"

"Arkenel was four years old when you died. What are you talking about?" Ravena reminded him.

Rabolii made a tragic face, as if the very memory of the dreaded past could make him cry. He replied in a dramatic tone, "That's not what I meant! Do you remember the apogee of my discoveries, the day I managed to brew the potion which could revive me? And what did Arkenel do? He broke the flask—because he hated me! Don't even try to defend him. He has always been my enemy, and that will not change. He will return to the prison where he belongs."

"Rab, that's cruel. You haven't even met him during all this time. I've spoken to him. He's seen the error of his ways," Ravena pleaded with her unforgiving husband.

Rabolii slammed his fist on the desk and roared like a tiger, "Did he now?! He would tell you anything just to soften you and get your help. He is not my son. I don't want to hear his name ever again. I will send an army west to Aldur, and I don't care who surrenders and who dies."

"Rabolii!" Ravena cried desperately, her eyes watering. "I beg you, just talk to him. Give him a chance! I can't bear to watch you two at each other's throats!"

Rabolii didn't seem touched by any of this. He only raised his long-nailed hand to quiet his wife. He said, "I'm not happy to see how zealously you defend a traitor, Ravena. But why am I surprised? I'm the last person you care about. Arkenel! May Arkenel be well, and I can go die for all you care. I can't make anyone happy. Everyone is always so discontent. You just keep taking and taking from me. Why would it matter to you? I'm nothing but a corpse to you."

So it had come to this. Rabolii was once again complaining about being an unloved corpse. Ravena listened to him with tearful eyes, unable to believe how horrendous her husband was. In fact, she was the only person in this world who was still surprised every time. To some extent, she lived with the memories of the person he had been twenty years ago. Back then he wasn't a bitter old man. And now every time he behaved like one, it broke her heart. It was because of those memories that she found the strength to forgive him every time he acted like a madman. She'd convince herself that he could be better and that he'd change his mind when he was calmer. She thought that his outbursts were a spontaneous thing that happened rarely, but generally he was a good man. She had hoped for too long that he'd realise he had been unfair with Arkenel and would accept his son back into the family. It was a hope she still had despite all the time the situation hadn't changed.

While Rabolii continued complaining, Malior entered his chambers. He was wearing his usual black leather armour. He looked jaunty and smug.

"Father, I heard about what happened to Aldur. Would you like me to lead some troops to the east and resolve this?"

"No, Son, I have a different task for you," he replied. "Our enemies surround us on all sides. The Vernians to the west are a menace and destroy defenceless villages. They're just a rabble, and they will stand no chance against your elite forces."

Malior nodded and made an exit. Ravena was still shaken because of her husband's bad temper. She noted, "You're kinder to your son-in-law than to your own children."

"Maybe it has something to do with the fact that my son-in-law acts better than my own children," Rabolii replied with a frown as he scribbled with a black, shabby feather. He looked up at his wife as if he were very surprised to see her and said, "Are you still here? I said all I wanted to say. I will not change my mind about the damned Arkenel. He left our lives seven years ago when he tried to kill me. He's dead to me."

Ravena kept looking at her husband and was wondering what was wrong with him this time. She knew that Rabolii was often in a bad mood because he was a corpse. However, today she was unable to shrug off this inconvenience and act like nothing was wrong. She clenched her fists and stormed out of the room. If Rabolii wouldn't take care of their son, she would.

It was true that Arkenel was a very disobedient and mischievous child. He had disappointed his father from the moment he was born, because Rabolii had really wanted strong sons gifted with magic. This dream never came true. Arkenel didn't see himself as royalty or an heir to the throne; he just sought ways to have fun. His activities had indirectly undermined Rabolii's relationship with other important families. Arkenel had caused trouble many times, and at best he didn't care. He thought Rabolii didn't do anything all day long other than stand like a scarecrow in his room and yell at everyone, so the young prince sometimes teased him on purpose. Ravena had seen this behaviour as childish games, while Rabolii had thought that Arkenel was most deliberately sabotaging him because he hated him. And so it came to pass that the seventeen-year-old Prince Remedor was shipped to the filthiest and most disgusting prison in the country. Ravena had tried to fight against this, but it wasn't easy to argue with the greatest sorcerer of the century. She had been mediating for hours between both of them, trying to make them see each other's point of view. She somehow managed to get Arkenel to understand he had behaved badly, but Rabolii was still very much convinced he was correct. He had no intention of treating his son as anything other than an escaped convict.

Ravena rushed into the royal bedroom, which had been used only by the queen during the last eighteen years. Ever since Rabolii died, he couldn't sleep in the same way he used to, so he didn't go in there any more. The woman started packing her luggage with feverish, panicky movements. She stuffed everything she thought she might need into large cases.

"Greetings, Mother! Have you spoken to Father?" a sweet voice sounded from the doorway.

Ravena was startled by this intrusion and turned around to see her daughters. She felt a certain relief because she knew she could trust them with this terrible problem.

"Yes, she has spoken to him, and evidently she's decided to go live on another continent," the other daughter spoke. Her name was Traneya, and she looked grim and somewhat bored. Patterns of tattooed demons and monsters twisted around her entire arms and her neck, all the way up to her cheeks. She wore heavy rings that looked like they could break someone's jaw if their owner decided to throw punches.

"Father didn't agree to make peace with Arkenel, did he?" said the younger sister, Salina, sighing. She seemed unusual for a Krumerian. Her skin was pale but not deathly greyish green like the others'. Her hair was a unique hue of a desaturated blonde.

"Girls, I'm afraid your father will kill Arkenel given the chance. I cannot let that happen. I have to go and find your brother," said Ravena as she continued packing her bags.

Traneya suggested casually, "Do you want me to go? The corpse will notice if you disappear."

"I won't let you refer to your father like that," Ravena said chiding her twenty-six-year-old daughter as if she were a child. "I have to be the one to go. I have friends who owe me favours. Maybe I'll convince some of them to shelter Arkenel. Of course, your father will be very angry if he learns, so please cover for me. I will be gone for no more than a few days. Make sure he does not notice that I'm missing."

"Do you think he'll even notice if we all go live somewhere else?" Traneya muttered.

"Don't worry, Mother. I'll cover you," Salina said readily.

"Thank you," Ravena answered warmly.

Salina and Traneya helped their mother to pack her things and made sure she left unnoticed. That was a very complicated task as Rabolii had eyes everywhere. He had reanimated most of the skeletons in Krumerus so that he would notice anything that was going on. Ravena escaped the city escorted by a small number of men and skeletons, these controlled by a different necromancer. Salina and Traneya watched her depart. The older daughter, frowning, noted, "I don't understand why this is all happening this way. Arkenel is our brother and the rightful heir to the throne, and we're treating him like a criminal."

"Well, we have to convince Father somehow to change his mind." Salina sighed.

Traneya looked at her younger sister in disbelief and exclaimed, "I don't get it. How can both you and Mother believe that we can carry on dealing with this issue like this? Didn't you both spend the last seven years convincing him? Where has that gotten us? We have to make a more serious statement and enforce our opinion somehow. He's not the only person in this world!"

"He is the king of Krumerus." Salina sighed.

Traneya rolled her eyes. She saw Rabolii neither as a father nor as a king. To her he was some despotic entity who wouldn't spare any means to enforce his opinion. The term *king* didn't really describe the almighty necromancer any more. He had all the political power. He was the one to decide on everything that was going on in Krumerus. He had no counsellors, and he was in control of the lesser lords. The sad truth in this land was that the strongest sorcerer had it all. Even if all the people of the land disliked his rule, they couldn't do much against the legions of skeletons he controlled himself.

Over the next couple of days, everyone was busy with their assignments. Ravena was searching for her wayward son. Malior went off to fight the Vernians to the west. This caused the movement of armies, which alarmed the Soleyans. They didn't even suspect that all these troops marching back and forth had nothing to do with them and Aslania. Rabolii had had a hard life and was always busy with something, such as locking his son in prison.

A strange feeling of malice had gripped the gloomy castle in the capital city of Kranium. Rabolii unintentionally emanated evil magic which drove everyone insane. He couldn't help it. He felt like he was surrounded by stupid people and that he had to prevent everything bad from happening all by himself. He was remembering dark events from the past, namely the occasion which drove him to imprison his own son. As a rule, Rabolii thought of himself as a very caring parent, but this boy had crossed a line. It had happened on one of those days about seven years ago when Mortelion guided the necromancer's hand to make the very potion of immortality. Rabolii had long studied these mixtures, even before he had died, but after that happened, he grew a lot more curious about vampire blood. In Krumerus, centuries ago, there were sentient vampires who had fed on blood and lived forever despite serious injuries. But after various incompetent sorcerers experimented on them, the vampires had lost their souls. They couldn't think any more, and they behaved just like any other animated corpse. Rabolii knew that if he injected himself with their blood, he would lose his soul and in fact would end up more dead than he was right now. That's why he was trying to synthesise pure vampire blood like that of the past and recreate an extinct species. Currently he had to make hundreds of different potions—one to start his heart, one to stop his muscles from getting stiff, one to keep his brain working. Without his priceless flasks, he would fall apart. However, if he were to succeed in recreating the blood of a pure vampire, all these efforts would be over. He'd just need to feed, and that wouldn't be difficult. And he did brew the potion after much trial and error. It had happened not because his precise calculations were a success but because he had spilled a few flasks while swinging his hand to chase away a fly. The liquids mixed and happened to look exactly the way the blood was described in the thousand-year-old books created by the oracles of Mortelion. Rabolii was overjoyed. The only thing left for him to do was to leave the potion out in the moonlight for the night. However, it was right then that those menacing children Arkenel and Traneya had decided to brawl in the yard and somehow managed to break the flask! Rabolii had felt as if this murdered him all over again. He screamed, he frightened the whole town, and he cursed random unfortunate souls. Had Ravena not come to soothe him in time, he would have caused the end of the world. Traneya was frightened by this cataclysm and hid away somewhere, but Arkenel wasn't so lucky. When his insane father got his hands on him, he could have died on the spot if it weren't for Ravena's convincing her raging husband to have mercy.

And so Arkenel found himself in the dungeon, from which he had managed to escape. Rabolii had no choice but to continue his vampire research and hope he'd get the mixture correct once more. He had begged Mortelion to give him a recipe, but apparently the god had little interest in the necromancer's destiny.

Rabolii pulled a box from beneath his chair, placed it on his desk, and got ready for work. He rubbed his hands together, getting the hungry, anticipating look he always had when he was about to kill something. As he removed the lid, some deformed baby demons his servants had collected from the caves moved inside the box. The creatures were still blind. They shuffled, whimpering and spreading mucus with their tiny hands. Their appearance caused more excitement than was necessary. The vampires which hung from the ceiling sniffed the air then dropped down with wild screams like sacks of potatoes, attacking the prey. The necromancer frowned indignantly and waved a ragged book, trying to chase them away. How could he have forgotten to feed them today? They would wreck everything now!

The demon babies suffered an unfortunate death. Rabolii's entire desk was covered in mucus, blood, and filth. The vampires squealed triumphantly and stammered gleefully. After they were done making a mess, they flew back to the ceiling. And it was at that disgusting moment that somebody else decided to inconvenience Krumerus's lord.

The heavy door was set ajar as Salina peered into the inhospitable room. She found the almighty necromancer standing like a monument behind a desk that was covered with all sorts of filth. Not that this was a rare sight. For a moment the girl seemed to forget what she had come in for. She asked, "Is everything all right, Father? I hope I'm not interrupting anything?"

Rabolii shook his head like an angry goat. Was it just him, or was she trying to mock him? Sometimes people treated him as if he didn't have important things to do in his room. Anyways, he decided not to yell at Salina, because she was his favourite daughter. He gave the warmest welcome he was capable of: "Actually, I'm a bit busy. What's wrong?"

"Father, something terrible has happened!" Salina cried.

"Yes, I know. Arkenel has broken out of prison. Worry not, I've sent an army," the necromancer replied casually as he lifted papers off his desk with a disgusted look on his face.

"It's not that," Salina replied, handing a letter to her father.

Rabolii unfolded it with his dirty hands. His eyes glanced across the paper. He said, "Oh, Malior has been captured and killed by the Soleyans."

"Yes!" the girl exclaimed in an upset tone. "It seems the Vernians were prepared for his attack, so he needed to retreat. After having gotten lost in the woods, he went too far south and stumbled across a Soleyan patrol. That's terrible. I don't know how to tell Traneya that her husband is dead."

"It's really is terrible," mumbled Rabolii. "This is written by some Eslir Falnir, who claims to be the new king of Aslania. He writes that during a fight, Malior killed his father and Flinaya. This makes our political situation complex."

Salina was crying as she spoke. "Malior was the chosen successor for the crown. What are we doing to do now? And Usera was with him. She must be dead as well."

Rabolii glanced at her, feeling slightly uncomfortable. He wanted to stop his daughter's suffering somehow, so he handed her a book. "There you go. Here you can read practical uses of light sorcery inside Krumerus. It's quite intriguing, and it will stop you from thinking about Malior. Go on now; get out. I need to clean up in here."

Salina barely had time to realise what was going on before Rabolii shooed her out and closed the door. The necromancer didn't like long encounters with people because they would cause him a headache.

Krumerus was losing power. Its territory was shrinking. It looked like a dying civilisation, kept alive only by magic, just like its master. However, the fall of one nation gives rise to another. Far to the west, the lands looked very different. There were lush forests. Heavy green vegetation made everything look wild. There were no traces of human activity from afar. This was where the kingdom of Vern rose. The buildings there were sheltered so well amid the greenery that they seemed to be part of the forest. If one was to explore these woods, one would behold incredible sights. One would see a civilisation that had found out how to progress by unleashing the powers of nature. These lands were blessed by the goddess Vernara. She was the one being worshipped by the locals, along with another very important person in these lands – the queen. Her fortress was in a remote location, and few people had the privilege of seeing her in person. She was the character of many legends. Her palace was the rarest miracle on the continent. It rose with all its crystal grandeur in the crown of a giant tree, so much so that the two appeared to be inseparable. It rose higher than the ancient forests and emitted a calm splendour. The interior was a magnificent harmony between the walls and the furniture of the building and nature. Massive branches made their way through the halls; the floors were covered with soft grass. Rivers flowed through some of the chambers, but they were crystal clear without a speck of dust in them. These were the halls of the almighty Krementa, who owned all of this. She was the queen of Vern, and under her care the lands flourished. Her power was to care for nature. Earth and life were her elements.

However, Krementa didn't spend too much time slaving over Vern's needs. The people in this country were different from those in Soleya. They didn't need a monarch all that much. Every society cared for itself, gathered food, and made its own laws. Krementa interfered with their lives only when something extraordinary was happening in Vern.

Sometimes Krementa became extremely bored in her crystal palace. Once again she was strolling around the library while her maids were looking for books they had not yet read to her. It was then that she heard music. The sounds were enchanting and beautiful; the piano's sound was breathtaking. However, to her this was just noise. She felt annoyance because she knew what it meant. She gestured to one of the maids to keep looking while she followed the sound of the piano. Without knocking, she burst into a room, hissing, "Valenis, I see you've given yourself a break from your magic lessons. Does this mean you're done for the day?"

A pair of cold, purple eyes, just like hers, fixed their sight on her. Her son was about twenty-five, and he looked different from the other Vernians. They were people with shiny, colourful skin, often covered in different patterns. Krementa herself looked very special. She was a light green colour, and her dress was made of living plants, so perfectly merged with the rest of her form that it seemed they were a part of it. Her greenish hair merged into the foliage, which seemed like a natural continuation of it. Her son looked nothing like her. He was pale and colourless. Although that wasn't strange on its own, as people in Vern were very diverce, he still assumed he was adopted. He didn't see the resemblance to his parent, nor did he feel much maternal love.

"Forgive me, Mother. I've spent so much time on these books that I already see energy currents in the air. I wanted to rest my mind for a while," he answered in a calm, well-mannered fashion.

His black hair was long, reaching his elbows, tied in a ponytail on his back. His clothes were expensive and so perfectly clean that it was almost unreal. However, his mother never saw him as flawless as he was trying to appear. She crossed her arms and exclaimed, "That's a good thing! First you will see them, then manipulate them. Do you have any idea how difficult it is to get you all these books and teachers? I bought you everything, and you don't want to learn! Won't you leave this piano alone? If I hear it once more in your room, I'll have it removed! You know you will never really need it in this life."

"Of course, Mother," Valenis replied, still not showing any emotion.

"I don't want to limit your freedom, but that's for your own good. You can't imagine how powerful you can become if you practise. One day you will be the lord of Vern. You must be prepared," she spoke with a softer voice.

While she was lecturing her son on the importance of hard work, a party of guards walked towards her. They were led by a pale Krumerian-looking man.

"You called me, my queen?"

"Mm, yes." She smiled at him pleasantly. "You've become indispensable to me when it comes to obtaining intelligence from Krumerus. There's a lot you can provide me."

"Of course, my queen. Vern is the only homeland I serve," he replied.

"I'm happy you feel that way. You are the only person I can send amongst the Krumerians because you don't stand out. You're a real gift from the gods." She turned to her son again and said, "Darling, go back to your lessons. I want you to read the two new books I gave you by tomorrow morning, if you want not to be useless one day."

Having said that, she walked away, her long dress waving behind her. Valenis looked at her coolly then pulled a book from his desk. Of course, it wasn't related to magic. It was another exciting novel full of darkness and blood-soaked romance, the kind he loved the most.

Meanwhile, there were problems in the capital city of Kranium. Large quantities of refugees were pouring from the west, looking for a new home because of the Vernian raids. Rabolii clenched his jaw as he watched the raging madness of the crowded city square and wondered when Ravena would come out to deal with it. The necromancer hated it when people were noisy. Such acts were punishable. At some point he noticed that the situation wasn't under control, so he decided to inconvenience himself by going there to deal with it.

Salina was amongst the crowd, desperately scrutinising long lists as her hands shook. She spoke to a woman who didn't even look like she was wearing actual clothes but was rather wrapped up with some filthy bed sheets. "Currently we're renovating the abandoned barracks at the outskirts of the city. We're turning it into residential area, but it will take us three weeks to chase off all the man-eating bats and to furnish the premises."

"*Three weeks?*" the woman yelled. "I have seven children. Should I have them live in the streets?!"

The princess blinked with a sad, frightened face and began to dig through the sheets to see if she could offer something different. Meanwhile, Traneya was fortifying the large door made out of iron bars. She turned to her sister and shouted, "How's it going, Salina?"

"I don't believe we can handle this!" Remedor's youngest daughter cried out.

Traneya shrugged and continued to fortify the gates with wooden planks as filthy hands with black nails reached between the bars. It was as if the people outside were bloodthirsty zombies. At this sublime moment, the crowd made way for Rabolii. Everyone was moving out of his way because he was intimidating. He scanned his surroundings with his critical pale grey eyes. In his hand he held a heavy metal staff with a horned skull on its top. His mantles were long and opulent, almost reaching the ground. The necromancer was a terrific sight. The screaming people became silent when he arrived. They turned to gaze at him with awe.

"Why are you all here? Don't you have anywhere else to be?" Rabolii growled inhospitably.

"They tried to go to the fortress of the Skeletal Wall," Salina explained to him. "However, all the refugee camps were already full there, so Uncle had to send all the newcomers away."

Rabolii was considering whether to do the same. However, he knew that if he sent these tramps away, they'd just go make a mess somewhere else, and then it would still be his job to deal with them. He looked around and asked, "Where is Ravena? I'm surprised she's not here to resolve all this."

Salina and Traneya exchanged worried looks. The younger daughter said, "Mother has a headache and is sleeping in her room."

"Go to wake her up then. Someone has to deal with this chaos." Rabolii waved his hand towards the crowd.

"I don't know. Maybe we should let her rest." Salina frowned.

"Now that I think about it, I have not seen your mother in the last two days. I thought she had a schedule and reserved hours to come in my chambers to bother me. She must be really feeling unwell. She was in her room, you say?" Rabolii had decided to be a caring husband at the worst moment possible.

The two daughters kept staring in shock. Salina spoke again, wondering how to distract the necromancer. "Father, can you tell us the story of how you met Mom?"

Having said that, she smiled sweetly as if there was nothing in the world she'd rather know. Rabolii was about to open his mouth and announce he had no time for nonsense, but Traneya chuckled and answered, "I can imagine. It must have been an arranged marriage. No mentally sane woman would agree to this!"

OK, that was gross defamation, and Rabolii felt obliged to protect his good name, but that would mean speaking about the past and other irrelevant things! How could he win?

"Maybe it will be better if you ask your mother. She will describe to you the more emotional version," Rabolii mumbled.

"We are more interested in how you remember it!" Salina smiled.

Rabolii rolled his eyes. "Well, it was a long time ago. My power had become enormous, and I had taken over Krumerus. I was scouring the lands to kill off the last of the Snake King's troops and to slaughter all those who remained loyal to him. I'm sure you know how dangerous a necromancer is around the battlefield. Even if I don't do much during the fight, I raise the corpses afterwards and make them serve me so that my numbers are constantly growing. Here and there I would find some stronger corpses, which I turned into vampires—more robust than ordinary skeletons, but soulless just like them. I demolished everything in my path, and the mere mention of my name caused fear in my enemies' hearts. At one point I reached the last fortification held by the armies of the defeated king. I charged at them with all my might. They had no chance against my armies. I demolished them without even sacrificing many of the skeletons.

"The few living soldiers in my army went on to enjoy the spoils of war they had gained. At first I didn't intend to interfere with their raiding and looting. Still, I found myself a little bit disturbed when they tried to force themselves on a girl who seemed not much older than fifteen. I wondered if I should intervene or just move someplace where I wouldn't look at them. To my surprise, that girl was actually fighting them off. She stabbed a knife in the temple of my best general, and that's when I stepped in. I got my soldiers to restrain her and tie her up. I needed her so I could test my new poisons on her.

"However, when we were alone in the tent, I didn't feel like doing that. My head was aching because during the battle everyone was screaming, and that kind of noise irritated me. She didn't look like she was afraid of me. On the contrary, she told me to poison her faster before my soldiers get a hold of her again. I told her that I was very sorry for not being able to fulfil her wish, saying that my head hurt so badly that I didn't want to be conscious at the moment. She told me that the people in her area knew how to deal with such pain and said that she could help me if I would untie her. I laughed and cut her ropes.

I was expecting her to attack me and try to kill me. I really wanted to see her try to choke me with her bare hands, since back then I was, as I still am, invulnerable. But instead she just put fingers over my brows and, with slight pressure, began to rub my forehead. Within a few minutes the headache was gone. That surprised me very much.

"I asked her what other tricks she knew. She began explaining things about points on the body and said that if you massage them, you relieve pain. The setting was very ... intimate. However, I continued the conversation as if I was unaffected. I was still suspicious of her.

"My soldiers were surprised to see the girl alive the next morning. I told them she had a rare resistance to poisons and that I would try to sell her blood as an antidote for people bitten by snakes. She laughed when she heard this. It had been a long while since someone found me funny.

"I spent more time with her, and my confidence in her grew. I began letting her outside, partially expecting her to escape, but she didn't. She stayed with me and helped me with whatever she could. Starting a relationship just felt wrong. She was fifteen, and I was thirty-five.

"Time went by, and our friendship developed into something more. Two years later we were married and had children." He paused for a moment and sighed. "I thought our reign would last forever. But fate is merciless. Only seven years had passed. Ravena was pregnant with our sixth child when everything reached its end. My life was over. Nothing was the same after that. I'm no longer the fearsome Rabolii, just that corpse in the tower. Look at this town! It looks like a cemetery! It seems like everything around me has died!"

This story had become very dramatic way too suddenly. Traneya shook her head, realising yet again how young and innocent her poor mother had been when she married this madman. Salina desperately wondered how to calm him, so she began to speak: "Father, that isn't true! It is a real gift to us that you are still amongst us. I was young when all those horrible events took place, but I still remember ... I remember how we all prayed for you. We couldn't believe we'd lost you! So when we saw you standing up again, we really ..."

"Salina, stop it!" Rabolii snapped. "You don't remember how things were before. I feel isolated. I'm like no one else. Your mother must be wondering why she stayed with me at all. At twenty-three she could have escaped and found a man who wasn't a corpse, but she was afraid I'd kill her if she dared. Nothing is the same any more. I cannot think of anything other than what kind of potion to brew so I don't begin to rot! And then I hear how some halfwits tell stories about my nose falling off and other idiocies like that. How am I supposed to live this way?! And why are we having his conversation anyway? So you can snicker behind my back? Because I'm a *corpse*? Get out of my sight! You both made me so angry today! I'm off to send a letter to my uncle, after which I'll go to my chambers. And if anyone disturbs me with their whims, they will be fed to the vampires."

Having said that, the terrible necromancer departed so he could spread hatred somewhere else. Traneya felt like she'd burst out laughing. She enjoyed seeing him angry, and now she intended to make fun of him for being a corpse. Salina stared after him with a painful gaze. She felt guilty for bothering her father, but somehow she was also pleased with herself for having distracted him from seeking Ravena.

"I would have imagined that after being a corpse for eighteen years, the thought would have somehow settled his mind and he wouldn't whine so aggressively," Traneya said.

Salina looked at her and realised her sister was too cheerful. She probably had not heard of what happened to Malior. God knew in which basement she'd been smoking this time. She must have missed the news. That was a trait they shared with Arkenel; they never cared about what was happening in this country and were always behind on any news. Salina signed and went to instruct the guards on what to do with the refugees. She needed to take Traneya somewhere quiet and update her.

While Kranium was trying to sort out its refugee crisis, Ravena was facing her own problems far to the east. In general, when she was travelling, the biggest threats to her were the large beasts in these lands. Krumerus was home to bats so large that they were kidnapping children, but sometimes they attacked bigger prey if they were together in a large colony. Giant centipedes wandered the wilderness. Their shells were so hard that killing them was a special craft. The wild marshes were inhabited by feral corpses that had been animated by the natural concentration of magic in these lands, not because some necromancer had raised them. There weren't wolves, bears or anything so mundane. Instead there were deformed demons which looked like scaly, deformed monstrosities. The worst, perhaps, was the Krumerian troll, standing over four metres in height. It was famous for chasing and eating lone travellers.

Ravena kept her eyes open for signs of such creatures, while her carriage, pulled by four-legged demonic skeletons, was making its way east towards Aldur. Half a dozen living soldiers walked along with it. They had almost arrived when hundreds of men wearing heavy steel armour charged from the side of the road and attacked the Krumerians, screaming ferociously. Ravena's guards cried and fled like frightened rats. Only the good, loyal skeletons remained to defend their queen. Ravena sighed with desperation and pulled a knife out of her belt, preparing to defend herself. She never got the chance to use it. The Aslanians grabbed her and restrained her in such a way that she wouldn't be able to defend herself. One of them stepped forward and removed his helmet. His skin and hair were so pale that he resembled an albino. In fact, most Aslanians looked like this. The man said, "Would you look at these fascinating erebi!" He touched the lace on Ravena's dress and said, "I can't imagine someone unimportant would walk around so dressy in a rotten country like this. Who are you?"

"Go die in a hole!" Ravena spat angrily, trying to break free from the soldiers who were holding her.

The Aslanian turned and nodded at one of his men who had captured one of the Krumerians. Seeing this gesture, the soldier pulled a knife and stuck the blade under the nail of the erebius, who started screaming, "She's Ravena Remedor, the queen! Please let us go. We are not important!"

"Mrs. Remedor!" The eyes of the pale man lit up, and he stared at the woman in front of him. "Prince Falnir will be delighted. Chain her. We'll take her to him. Kill the others."

Ravena started moving desperately in an attempt to squeeze out from the Aslanian's grip. This was the last thing she wanted to have happen to her! Her son's life depended on her finding him before the armies of Rabolii did. Besides, if the necromancer were to notice that she was missing, he would somehow find out where she was and what she had been doing, and he would probably be furious. Maybe he would try to rescue her, maybe not. Rabolii didn't like to be disturbed, and if saving his wife required him to make some effort and cause himself inconvenience, maybe he wouldn't.

So that's the story of how Ravena got captured by the Aslanians at the worst possible moment. Ilinar watched her with pure, genuine terror as Eslir was boasting like a fisherman who'd just caught a 15 kg catfish.

"Her being here is dangerous. We know Krumerus is gathering armies. Now we've just given them a reason to attack us," Ilinar noted with a trembling voice.

Eslir lifted his finger in the air and denied this statement. "Or we have a valuable hostage who could probably provide us with information about the enemy. She is their damn queen after all. She knows why they are gathering armies and what they plan to do with them."

Ilinar still seemed unsure about this. Eley approached him and began to whisper to him that maybe the idea was good and that if he took Eslir's advice, they would have the upper hand over Krumerus.

Eslir was eager to start harassing his new prisoner, so he went to her, grabbed her by the shoulders, and shook her roughly until she opened her eyes. Ravena looked at him hatefully, which seemed to amuse him. Ilinar decided to note, "Perhaps we shouldn't hurt her ... if we want a ransom or something."

"I don't want a ransom. I want information," said Eslir. "I have heard that the erebi are vulnerable to the magic of life because such energy is so foreign to them. It makes them feel dizzy and confused, so she's more likely to talk. Do you have a life sorcerer in this country?"

Ilinar frowned. There were wizards of light and fire in Soleya. After all, they did draw their energy from the god Flalirion, the patron of those elements. He shrugged and said, "Perhaps you should search in Vern. They respect the energy of life there. Also, how are you so well aware of how different types of magic affect the erebi?"

"Oh, in Aslania we sometimes execute them publicly by exposing them to the energy of life for days," Eslir answered casually.

"That is rude and uncivilised," Ilinar protested.

"What's your problem? They're animals." Eslir turned to his soldiers. "Hey, you there! Go explore the city to see if they have a sorcerer of life here."

"We have one, Eslir," Ilinar replied with annoyance and impatience. "Her name is Estrella, and you'll find her in Flalirion's temple. Call her if you want, but don't torment the erebius too much. The last thing I need is for others of her species to come seeking revenge."

Eslir dragged Ravena into a dark dungeon to torture her. The woman didn't seem all too frightened. She had an unimaginable resilience after all since she'd survived a marriage with Rabolii for nearly thirty years. She couldn't imagine that this ridiculous man with white eyebrows would cause her something more painful than watching her beloved man turn into an evil corpse.

Ilinar walked in silently. He had put on the antique helmet of Hreles Soleyan just so people would know he was not kidding around. Next to him stood the aforementioned sorceress Estrella. She had bushy brown hair and dark skin, contrasting with her very bright emerald eyes. The skin on her bare shoulders was marked by interesting green patterns which resembled those on the wings of a butterfly. She looked too beautiful to be real. Eslir stared at them two, incapable of deciding what to do first, whether to mock Ilinar or to start hitting on the sorceress. When he finally made his choice, he smiled widely and reached for Estrella's hand. "It is a pleasure for me. I am Eslir Falnir, king of Aslania. You look unique. You aren't local, are you?"

"Thank you, Your Majesty." Estrella smiled at him sweetly. "I was born in Soleya, but my father was a Vernian. That's why I don't look like the locals and I can control the magic of life."

"This is amazing! I've never been to Vern. Do you maintain a relationship with your relatives from that area?" Eslir continued the conversation.

Ravena groaned with annoyance. She wanted these kids to get out of her hair faster so she could enjoy the silence of the dark cell. She said, "How interesting. A Vernian, an Aslanian, and a Krumerian have gathered to interrogate me in Soleya. Is this the opening to some joke?"

Ilinar instantly took a defensive stance and shouted, "I'm not Krumerian!"

"Is that so, my boy? Look at me and look at everybody else in this country," Ravena continued to tease him. "Who do you look like?"

"My appearance is the result of a curse that the evil Rabolii Remedor cast on my mother when she was pregnant," Ilinar argued.

Ravena stared at the boy with a hateful gaze for a few seconds and then asked, "When is your birthday?"

Eslir tried to intervene because he didn't want the erebius to ask questions; the opposite was supposed to be happening. He stepped forward and said, "Why? Are you baking him a cake? Don't speak to him! I want to know from you why ..."

"When is your birthday?!" Ravena screamed this question again.

Ilinar got frightened and decided to answer before got hit with another curse, which would turn him into Rabolii. He whimpered, "Fifty-ninth Flalirion's."

There were ninety-one days to each season in this land, and fifty-nine Flalirion's was in the middle of the summer. Ravena stared at Ilinar for a few seconds with a cold, piercing look, then she groaned deeply as if she had come to some insight. Once again Eslir attempted to take control of this event. He pushed Ilinar back and announced, "Those were enough distractions! Erebius, you were caught dangerously close to the border with an armed detachment, which is far from being the first we've noticed. We need to understand why you are mobilising armies!" Eslir demanded.

Ravena gave out a slight smirk and said, "So Krumerus has no right to have soldiers on his own territory?"

"Nobody is arming soldiers for no reason. I want you to explain where you've been travelling to," Eslir barked, waving his finger with a threatening look.

"I have no more information for you," Ravena said coldly.

That was what Eslir had been waiting for. He replied, "Too bad. I was expecting we would reach this moment. If you don't agree to speak, I will have to force you. Estrella, hit her with the energy of life."

"Your Majesty, are you sure you want me to do that?" Estrella said. "I'm still learning, and I don't know my own strength. I wouldn't want to kill her by mistake. She is an erebius after all. She is very fragile when it comes to life sorcery."

"Don't worry about her. Just hit her!" Eslir waved his hand casually.

Ilinar shut his eyes, unwilling to witness this. Estrella sighed and raised her hand. A ball of magical energy, shining in bright green, formed in her palm. She sent it flying towards Ravena. When it hit her, it exploded and sputtered around the room the way old dust would if one was to blow it. Everyone in the room felt some inconvenience from the collision with this energy, and Ilinar straight out fainted. Bafflingly, Ravena remained sitting up as if she hadn't felt a thing. Eslir and Estrella exchanged glances. He said, "I think you need to hit her a little harder than that."

"Try something other than glitter, dear," Ravena teased her. It was so much fun. She had thought something horrible would happen to her, but these children didn't even know how to torture their prisoners.

"That should have worked," Estrella mumbled, forming a bigger ball of energy in her hand. But this one was as efficient as the previous one.

"You should aim better. Look who you struck instead," Ravena continued to tease her and nodded towards the unconscious Ilinar.

"He's a wimp. He faints because of random things a few times a day," Eslir said. "Estrella, are you sure you're even trying? Maybe that doesn't hurt at all. Shoot me."

"You can't be serious!" she exclaimed. "Your Majesty, I can't! What if I hurt you?"

"I want to see if it works. If I feel it, that horrid creature should also!"

Ravena rolled her eyes with annoyance. Estrella gently touched Eslir's chest with a shimmering finger, which caused him to jump away from her and exclaim, "Holy gods, that shook me! But it felt pleasant in a strange way. Do it again!"

This whole event was baffling. Ravena had no idea what had happened here and why she was immune to the spell. Finally she came to the conclusion that this was a weak sorceress whose magic couldn't hurt anyone. Could there be any other explanation?

After this torture session had failed, Estrella was worried that there was something wrong with her spell casting, so she went back to the temple to get examined. Eslir offered to escort her there, and Ilinar was carried away on a stretcher. Ravena stared at them and chuckled as they walked away. It was ridiculous to imagine what would have happened if Rabolii were captured instead of her, especially if his magic was depleted and he couldn't use it to defend himself. At times like this, she admired nature, which somehow balanced him to be so physically weak but so powerful with magic. His skin was very delicate, and if, God forbid, he were to rub it somewhere, it would bruise very dramatically, as if its owner had suffered a beating. She remembered this one time when Rab tripped over his dress-like mantles and fell down the stairs. Afterwards, for an entire month, he hobbled with a tragic expression on his face. He had black bruises and unexplainably messed-up hair, as if the hair itself had broken from the impact.

Ravena also remembered another event which happened when her husband was out with the armies. Some wild animal had bitten one of the soldiers, who contracted an insanity disease, so he burst into Rab's tent. The necromancer was so shocked by that invasion that in this moment of fright he set half the camp on fire. In such moments of recollection, Ravena was glad that she'd been captured, not her dear husband, for it would upset him so much that he would indirectly depress all the countries around him by emitting black magic.

Meanwhile in Krumerus, Salina was reading a huge book of spells and was trying to practise. Her element was light. Rabolii had sensed she was gifted with magic the moment he first saw her. Perhaps that's the sole reason which made him take her under his fatherly wing. Salina wasn't Ravena's child. During one of his wanderings, Rab experienced some unexpected things, the result of which was this little treasure. At first, the necromancer thought about keeping this a secret and not telling anyone because he thought Ravena would make an unnecessarily big deal out of it, and that would annoy him. However, as soon as he realised that Salina had a talent for magic, he became very enthusiastic and decided to keep her. Rabolii returned with her to Krumerus in such a manner as if it would be completely illogical for Ravena to be angry about such a gift of fate.

"Is this what you do when you go off to war?!" Ravena had yelled at him, trying to sound angry rather than hurt.

"So what? It happens to all of us. And I'll advise you not to scream. I've been with this baby all day long, and she's done enough screaming already. My head is about to explode." Rabolii had acted with the same self-importance when he was alive. He noted, "I think she is the most perfect child I've ever created. She controls magic. With a teacher such as myself, she can perfect it. It would be illogical not to raise her. Actually, I'm very happy I have her. But don't worry, we can always tell everyone she's ours. Didn't you give birth a few weeks ago? We can just tell people she is Arkenel's twin."

And despite its many imperfections, this story became "the truth", and all who disagreed ended up as skeleton servants. Only Ravena and Rabolii knew the truth about Salina. And now the young girl was sitting in her chambers in the castle, feeling as if she belonged only there and nowhere else. She was learning about spells from the heavy book. She turned her gaze to the wall on which hung a valuable memory from the days when Rabolii wasn't a corpse. Many, many years ago, they had made a calendar together. Her father had delineated a circle into four sections and had let Salina paint the four seasons embodied by the four gods and the magical elements they controlled. The girl was just learning about the gods and sometimes got the elements mixed up. All she knew back then was that their god was Mortelion and that his elements were death and darkness. Now she knew a lot about magic and knew that some elements are polar opposite to each other and can't exist together. It was strange that she was a sorceress of light, which is the polar opposite element of darkness. She was in fact the only light sorceress in Krumerus. Her father had told her it was a small miracle, but he had not explained more about how she inherited such a gift. Salina did get along with her father. She was making a lot of effort to please him, and he was more inclined to like her because his dream had been to have magic children.

Just as Salina was thinking about how much she liked father, someone began banging on her door. The girl turned her head, wondering what was going on. The maids usually knocked on the door so quietly that sometimes she didn't even hear them. Salina put the book aside and opened the door to see Rabolii towering over her, evil and terrifying. His expression resembled an approaching thunderstorm. Somewhere behind him lightning flashed. Salina instantly realised that the worst had happened.

"I demand answers! Where is your mother?!" Rabolii yelled horrifically.

Salina didn't know what to say or how to escape this. She hated lying to Papa in general, and now the whole situation was horrible. It seemed that Traneya had heard that the apocalypse had begun and stepped out of her room. She imitated Rabolii with a thick, hoarse voice: "Where is your mother? Maybe she finally came to her senses and left this stupid family."

Rabolii turned to her with the face of a confused bull that couldn't choose whom first to stab with his horns. He snarled, "Are you going to speak to me normally someday?"

"Speak to you normally ..." Traneya raised her arms with a shocked look, as if she couldn't believe what he had said. "Won't you first tell me why Malior died in Vern? The great Rabolii Remedor couldn't send an undead raven and scout the lands where you're sending your heir instead of throwing him into an enemy ambush?"

"Oh no, I don't want to start this conversation with you right now," answered Rabolii, but he continued speaking on the same topic anyway. "If you want to blame someone for bad intelligence collecting, blame Usera. She was also a necromancer. She could have sent a raven and could have looked at the territory herself. Also, Malior didn't die in Vern. He died in Soleya, because he got lost in the woods! I don't see how you can blame me for all this! Now don't you want to talk about how your mother has run off somewhere, and you both have covered for her? Don't you dare deny it. I noticed how the other day you were trying to distract me when I asked where she was. She has gone to look for your no-good failure of a brother, and now they are torturing her in Soleya."

Having heard all this, Traneya forgot to complain about Malior. She shook her head and said, "You cannot know all this. You're not powerful enough to send an undead raven to Soleya."

Rabolii was offended by this statement. He was powerful enough to send a whole army of ravens beyond Soleya without moving an inch from the tower, but these days he was using about 70 per cent of his strength at any given time to keep the most important corpse—his own body—in good shape.

"I didn't learn this with a raven. I felt tension on the surface of the shield of death and located the anomaly far to the south, perhaps in their capital city, Lumis," Rabolii said.

Traneya and Salina exchanged unintelligent glances. Their father was able to speak in a super confusing way about magic. Right now they didn't even want to discuss this in detail. The younger daughter said, "We didn't know that Mother was in danger. We really regret that we had to lie to you, Father. Please, do something to save her. She never wanted to betray you or ..."

"Of course. I won't leave her in the hands of those Soleyan beasts." Rabolii amazed everyone with this answer. "Letting them have my wife would make me look weak, and I would become a mockery." This sentence cleared the confusion about Rabolii's ulterior motives. "I will start preparing my army, and we will march upon Soleya's capital. They'll be sorry they were ever born."

"I'm coming with you," Traneya announced instantly. Ever since she was young, she'd been wild and untamed, so she loved hanging out with the armies and fighting other people—or animals. Whichever was on the front line.

"How about no? Now that Malior has died and Arkenel ceased to be a part of this family, you are the lawful heir to the throne, so act like it unless you want me to write a will in favour of

Salina," the necromancer responded, then began wondering if he should actually do that instead of just threatening.

After he decided on this action plan, the necromancer went to pack all his priceless potions in large, cushioned boxes and prepare them for the journey. When he was young, he had travelled a lot, but now he couldn't afford to leave his tower because there were always too many things he had to take. There was one good thing about this whole trip to Soleya—he would remind the world that Rabolii Remedor was the most powerful sorcerer. And he would frighten everyone so that they'd think twice before deciding to invade his lands.

CHAPTER 3

COLLISION

Rabolii was still preparing to leave for Soleya when the southerners sensed the danger. During some meditation, the Reverend Elerya fainted. Then she woke up screaming and predicting the apocalypse. This time she had not seen just the one cloud; she'd seen a few, so a state of emergency was declared. The news spread like wildfire, and the priestess was immediately taken to the king's castle.

In the meantime, Ilinar and Eslir were trying to rule a country. They sat next to each other in the throne room, and after a short war, Ilinar was placed on the queen's throne. The two youngsters sat there without being absolutely sure of what they were supposed to do now. Eslir had been more interested in managing the country, and he had spent time with his father, but he had no idea what was happening in Soleya or whether there was something specific he needed to do. Eley came to them to hand them a huge folder with papers. He opened his mouth to give instructions, but Eslir chased him away with annoyance. "I don't need every single person in the castle to stand next to me when I work! The kid and I can manage."

"But you are not even aware of half of these..." Eley said, trying to explain himself.

Ilinar turned towards him and snapped, "Yes, get out. We don't need you! We can do it ourselves!" Usually Ilinar would never talk that way to his beloved teacher, but right then he wanted to show off in front of Eslir and wished to appear as a self-sufficient, independent, magnificent ruler.

"Way to go, kid!" Eslir displayed his approval.

Ilinar was very proud of himself. Eley had something to say, but some guards pulled him out so the young majesties could work. Eslir turned to his cousin and asked, "Now, what are we doing here?"

"I don't know, some kingly things." Ilinar shrugged.

"Why did I even ask you this question?"

"Your Majesties, Senper Dravis wishes to address you in regards to the recent robbery of his house," a guard said, having led in an unknown citizen.

Eslir and Ilinar exchanged looks as if they were silently asking each other if this rang any bells.

"Please tell me the investigation has made progress!" the man said. "I finally heard that objects resembling mine were discovered but that the guards were still identifying them."

"Um, maybe his case is outlined in one of these folders?" Ilinar murmured quietly, nodding to the papers without touching them, as if he was afraid they'd overburden him with too much terrible information.

"Pff, sure, let me see ... Do you remember his name?" Eslir muttered.

"As if! Do I look like I have so little to do that I'll remember random people's names? Ask him to say his name again," Ilinar protested.

"Yes, so I'll look like an old lady with dementia? You ask him."

Of course this conversation could be heard by everyone standing nearby. The guards and Senper Dravis exchanged glances, wondering what kind of an outcome to this situation they could expect. Eslir and Ilinar started digging into the pile of papers, pretending they were working on the case while still hissing at each other, but since they had shaky hands, they pushed the pile of papers to the ground. Then they looked at each other again. Ilinar offered, "Let's call Eley. He'll know what to do."

"I don't need that boring loser. He will throw my country into chaos!" Eslir yawned.

"Sure, but all of this is boring for me, so let him do it!"

When Ilinar put his things this way, Eslir agreed. "That sounds great. Guards, call that Eley fellow we chased away just now!"

That's how their day went—the two kings were meeting people who had some problems, and they made Eley deal with it while the two of them were snickering about some entirely unrelated things and not paying attention to what was happening.

At some point two of the guards entered and announced,

"Your Majesties, the high priestess wishes to speak with you urgently."

"She can queue up then. Everybody wants to talk to me." Eslir waved his hand. "I am doing something else right now. I need to figure out where to send the armies. Maybe towards the border, for example. They don't seem to be very busy."

Eley clenched his teeth. He tried to speak out: "The high priestess may have received a new vision of an overcasting shadow."

"She brings the weather forecast—lots of clouds," Eslir announced. He started grinning with Ilinar.

"She believes an invasion is upon us, Your Majesty!" stated one of the guards who had spoken to the priestess. When he said those words, all fell silent. He continued, "We assume it'll be Krumerus."

Eley expressed his opinion: "If you want to secure the borders, maybe the north is a good place to start. Perhaps all this is happening because of the erebius we captured. I would suggest you lock her someplace where they won't find her. Then continue interrogating her."

Eslir was silent for a moment, then he waved his hand and said, "I know all this! Do you think me a fool? I mentioned securing the border before you did!"

"We have to protect Soleya somehow. They will level every village to the ground if they decide to loot for corpses," said Ilinar.

"I told you what I think needs to be done," said Eslir. "But maybe it would be a good idea for me to go back to Aslania to make sure my people are safe."

Ilinar turned to Eslir with a shocked expression and said, "What? Now? No, please stay. Soleya is in terrible danger. We know they will hit here! They want their erebian queen. I need help with this."

Eslir thought about it for a second without seeming concerned in any way by the thought that it was he who'd brought the erebius here, which led to an army following her. He waved his hand and said, "All right, my armies and I can stay for a while. If we withstand the erebian attack, we may be able to stop them from resurrecting our dead and they won't advance."

For the first time the young monarchs got down to work and began giving some reasonable orders to fortify their defences. They would position whatever troops they had on the border. They couldn't retreat and wait for the attack on Lumis because the necromancer would probably destroy all the defenceless villages along his way to add corpses to the army. The wars with Krumerus had always been severe because the kingdom of the dead gained strength after every collision. They didn't sacrifice humans, and every enemy soldier who died would join their ranks.

Once Eslir had addressed the problems of this country, he went out to talk to his soldiers. As soon as he was gone, Ilinar suddenly felt nervous. He noticed that Eley was looking at him with disapproval, and he realised that he would nag at him as soon as they went somewhere more private.

He wasn't wrong. Despite Ilinar's skilful attempts to escape unnoticed, eventually Eley managed to ambush him in a corridor. "Excuse me, Your Majesty, may I speak with you urgently?"

"Not now, Eley. I'm sleepy," he whined, in an attempt to save himself from an annoying conversation.

"Then allow me to accompany you to your chambers and help you prepare since you're so exhausted at seven in the evening," Eley told him, leading him down the corridor.

As soon as they were in the king's chambers, they started talking about the topic Ilinar expected.

"Have you not learned to accord your actions with me? Did it never occur to you that Soleya can make it without Eslir's aid? We could have resolved this situation ourselves. Why would you ask him to stay? Do you not see he's incompetent about everything? But still you insisted that he manage Soleya's defence!"

"Well, he's my ally and my friend," Ilinar said.

"With all due respect, my lord, there cannot be two kings in a country! Eslir doesn't need you. He does not see you as a friend, and he may try to get rid of you. Do you want that to happen?"

"He wouldn't do that."

"Are you certain about that? Maybe he will not if you continue to act like he's your superior and you're not worthy of your throne. What would your father say if he could see you now?"

Ilinar blinked with a sad expression, not knowing what to answer. It was clear to Eley that the prince felt abandoned and orphaned after his mother's death, and now he was looking for another dominant person under whose wing he could hide. Eley wanted to be the one to take this role, but it seemed that Eslir had succeeded instead.

Rabolii went south with his glorious army, planning to attack

Lumis directly without dealing with any distractions along the way. He had prepared potions for five days, which was enough time to get to his destination, take over the city, and return. He believed that this amount of time would be enough. The wretched Soleyans would probably be begging him to take Ravena and go away. They would bow to his power.

Even though he was weakened by his death, Rabolii was still a powerful necromancer. As long as he was close to his skeletons, he could control them efficiently. He had the ability to see the world through any one of them, but he didn't give them individual commands; rather, he encoded some behaviour which they would stick to even if he wasn't around them. He ran them not as individuals but as a flock. They were a perfectly synchronised army that knew no pain or fear. They would fight as long as they were in an approximate whole, and only shattering them to pieces would stop them.

Rabolii felt discomfort and disappointment when he saw that Soleya's border was guarded. It was such a shame. Why did these people ever make an effort to resist him? The necromancer groaned with annoyance and entered his portable tent, which was carried by skeletons. He would lie there in peace so he could better focus on the battle. He took his large, heavy staff in his hands and laid it upon himself, resembling a stone statue on a sarcophagus. He closed his eyes, feeling the chaotic energies. His skeletons began to attack the border troops, charging ahead like rabid dogs, and were barely hurt by any blows. Each soldier who perished rose and joined the troops of Rabolii.

Whichever soldiers survived, they retreated back to Lumis to report their overwhelming defeat. Rabolii had swept them away like a hurricane in the field, which they couldn't have fortified in any way. They reported that they had seen the Krumerians carry horrifying siege equipment and towers made of bones that moved by themselves with the help of the necromancer. The people in Lumis were frightened. As the skies clouded and darkened, panic ensued.

Eslir stood on the fortress wall, staring at the horizon. Ilinar ran in circles around him and whimpered about how we was too young to die. Estrella appeared next to the Aslanian and tweeted, "That's so scary! I don't remember the last time we've stood against such an enemy. We are so grateful that you are here to defend us, Your Majesty."

Eslir, feeling like the hero of this helpless nation, swelled with importance. He put his hand on Estrella's and said, "I promise to keep you safe at any cost, my lady." Then he thought for a moment, looked back at the horizon, and added, "Actually, are you capable of fighting skeletons?"

Estrella didn't like that change of tone. She preferred to be kept safe at any cost. She answered hesitantly, "I ... I am able to immobilise a few, maybe a dozen at the most, but I don't think I can do too much against Rabolii Remedor's army."

"A dozen will be enough." Eslir smirked. "I don't need to fight the whole army. I just have to cut off the serpent's head."

Ilinar and Estrella stared at Eslir in disbelief. The Soleyan king said, "You want to set an ambush for him? But this is dangerous. If you fail, you will be killed on the spot. At least send soldiers to do it instead of risking your own life."

"I cannot expect my soldiers to die for me if I wouldn't do the same for them," Eslir stated proudly in a loud voice, so that the listeners would start applauding and whistling. "If I succeed, we will not have to spill blood today, and we will deal a huge blow to Krumerus."

Estrella still didn't seem very pleased with all this. She loved purity and beauty, so she was afraid of carcasses because they were nasty, unnatural, and stinky. Ilinar considered this plan and gave his blessing. "I remember a ravine described in Prehorian's writings. According to him, it was well-concealed by the foliage, so a small party of soldiers could hide there without getting spotted by scouting ravens. As soon as Rabolii's army passes you, you can attack him from behind. The necromancer will be somewhere in the back lines, so you can capture him."

"Who said anything about capturing?" Eslir grinned.

Ilinar raised his finger in the air and gave a warning: "We don't know anything about the Remedor family. It is possible they have a young, powerful son who will simply replace his father. I don't want that incident in the forest with Malior Remedor to become an endless revenge war."

Eslir rolled his eyes. To him it seemed these foolish Soleyans were so soft that they didn't want to kill anyone, not even Rabolii Remedor himself. He replied, "We'll be in the middle of the battlefield. We'll see what happens and whether I'll be able to bring him to you on a silver platter. As for you, just keep an eye on the battle and on the erebian queen."

After giving his orders, Eslir lead Estrella and a small number of soldiers towards the discussed destination to ambush corpses. Ilinar took Ravena out of her cell so she could be nearby if he found himself in a situation where he needed to bargain for his own capital city.

The skeletons rushed across the field towards Lumis. Arrows and boulders were hurled at them, but they had little effect. The sorcerers of fire and light had taken positions on the fortress walls and attacked this scourge in any way they could. They were not very effective. After all, the skeletons had been raised by the energy of death, its polar element was life, and Estrella was the only sorceress in this town who controlled life. Rabolii's creatures began climbing the wall and charging at the heavily armoured soldiers. Ilinar wasn't on the wall; he was nervously watching what was happening from a terrace on a high tower. His guards and Ravena stood beside him. The woman, also observing what was happening, said, "I hope you understand that they are here for me."

"Yeah, and just handing you over to Rabolii will make him leave, right?" Ilinar snapped. "I don't know him. I don't know what to expect from him."

Ravena shrugged. In fact, nobody knew what to expect from Rabolii, not even her. She thought she would witness a dramatic, blood-soaked battle, but to her surprise, after no more than one hour, the skeletons stopped moving and attacking and fell to the ground like rag dolls. The soldiers below began to wail in astonishment, crying out loud, "Rabolii Remedor was captured! The battle is won!"

Ilinar seemed overjoyed, and Ravena just groaned with annoyance. It looked like they'd have a whole family reunion in the dungeons of Lumis. It was hard for her to believe the battle had been lost so easily. Why was she surprised though? She should have known better than anyone that Rabolii couldn't do much in a direct surprise attack. He was so terribly uncoordinated in a stressful situation. However, getting captured was another thing. What could have happened? Surely he was guarded! What could have penetrated his defences?

Soon all questions were answered when everyone gathered in the throne room. Several living Krumerian soldiers were walked in, along with Rabolii. They were led by Estrella. Ravena sighed heavily. Of course! The sorceress of life could have immobilised Rabolii's personal skeleton guards and resisted some of his most fearsome death spells. Even if Estrella had failed to torture Ravena with sparkles, she had managed to complete the harder task.

Eslir walked proudly next to the captives. He opened his

mouth, intending to tell everyone about his cunning strategy with Estrella and how they both had sneaked in behind the army and captured the necromancer, but he didn't get the chance. When Rabolii and Ravena were faced with each other, they had to show their love. He shouted, "You! How are you not ashamed of yourself? Look what happened because of your stupid ideas! I expected a little more."

"Shut up, Rabolii!" Ravena yelled back at him. This time she also had multiple reasons to be angry with him. "This is not the biggest issue we have right now. How about we talk about the actual reason you died on that day?!"

"That has nothing to do with this situation. And if you intend to reproach me for being dead …"

"No, I just wanted to point out the beauty of the life you created and then how you died in the process," she yelled at him. Then she turned to Ilinar, who still held the end of her rope, and blinked innocently. He hadn't expected to witness such an ugly family fight.

This utterance silenced everyone as they stared at the young king with open, motionless mouths like that of a fish. Rabolii was the first to recover. He tried to speak: "This is ridiculous. I …"

"He's exactly seventeen years old, born three seasons after your visit to Soleya. Just look at you two. He's a chip of the old block, isn't he?" Ravena said angrily.

Perhaps that was a conversation for another time. Eslir had a facial expression as if he had been kicked in the chest by a horse. He approached Ilinar and asked in a soft, velvety voice, "Ilinar, is that true?"

The Soleyan, who seemed surprised by these unexpected accusations, looked around in shock and began to babble: "What? No, this is not possible! Eslir …"

The blond king, however, wasn't in the mood for conversations and explanations, so he pulled out a mighty sword and announced, "I'm sorry, but if you really are an erebius, I'll have to kill you."

Eley had been staring no differently than all the witnesses to all this, but now that he saw that an execution was under way, he jumped in front of the Aslanian and yelled, "Your Highness, let's not be rash! I'm certain that they are playing a scene to distract us!"

"What scene? Just look at him! When I saw him for the first time, I told you he was an erebius, but did anyone listen?!" Eslir roared ferociously.

"So is he capable of using any magic?" Rabolii stretched his neck to have a better look at the trembling Soleyan.

"Rab, I'll tear your head off!" Ravena shouted.

This was a particularly noisy and unpleasant situation. Everyone was yelling again. That instantly annoyed Rabolii, who would have killed everyone present, but it would have been too exhausting. It would cause discomfort to him. His nails were already blackened because he had animated so many skeletons, so he couldn't handle much more of this. Ravena was shaking with anger, and Eley was trying to save Ilinar from suffering a horrible death. It was in this tense, fundamental moment that something unexpected happened. The glass ceiling over everyone's heads was shattered, and the pieces fell upon everyone in the hall. Estrella barely managed to respond in time and get a hold of the flying pieces, delaying their fall with magic. They landed softly on the ground without hurting anyone, but it took too much of her strength, so the exhausted sorceress fainted and fell into the arms of one of the guards.

From the hole in the ceiling, ropes were thrown so that a large group of men could make an entrance. The Soleyans immediately cried out in panic, recognising that the newcomers were Krumerian. That was the only plausible suggestion. Who else would be wearing black leather armour with bones attached to it? However, neither Ravena nor recognised them as anyone they had employed as a guard or a soldier. These men were shabby, sullen and fierce. They charged at the soldiers without making a pause. Chaos ensued. Even Eslir noticed that something was happening while he was pulling Ilinar's foot in an attempt to get him out from underneath a table. He glanced in confusion when a crazed Krumerian hit him in the jaw with his fist then threw him to the ground. Ravena watched them and thought that whoever these people were, as long as they were attacking the damned Soleyans, they were her friends. And then, most unexpectedly, the one who had knocked Eslir turned to her. A wide smile blossomed on his face, and he greeted her: "Long time, no see, Mom!"

Ravena was stunned, wondering if it was possible. The man looked filthy. He was covered in scars and wounds, and one of his eyes was whitish and probably blind. His hair was hanging in clusters, its length uneven. She could hardly recognise her handsome boy. When Eslir recovered from that hit, he tried to retaliate. He raised a sword, preparing to impale the enemy. Ravena gasped in horror, predicting an ugly end to all of this, so she was surprised when Arkenel spun around with lightning speed and crossed his two blades, blocking the sword. Then the two of them engaged in a fearsome duel. Arkenel continued to laugh, mocking his opponent and jumping around him in order to exhaust him. He seemed like the most skilled fighter Ravena had seen in a while. His friends were not doing much worse. There were several huge men who were cliving the heads off their opponents with axes. They had barricaded the doors of the hall so that no reinforcements would be able to come in.

Ilinar was looking at all the terror from afar. He was sitting in a corner, clutching his little fists in front of his face, whimpering silently. What was even happening here? He couldn't see all the grandeur of the battle that Emanrylii Prehorian had described. This was a filthy slaughter, a waste of human lives. And everything was happening so close. Eslir was trying to continue fighting, but Arkenel was moving too quickly to get hit by anything. At some point when Eslir swung his sword, Arkenel managed to catch the Aslanian in a vulnerable posture. He broke his balance, then threw him to the ground. Arkenel got on top of him, holding a dagger to his neck. He looked around, grinning widely, waiting for the rest of the people to calm down and pay attention to him. When this happened, Arkenel declared loudly, "I heard that a snowman in some aluminium armour had captured my mother, so I came to check out what was going on. Who would have thought that my whole family would gather here? You made it very easy for me to enter, by the way. While you guys were playing with some skeletons in front of the city, me and my men came in from the back."

Having said that, he shot a devilish look at Rabolii. The necromancer had already freed himself from his chains, so now he was just standing aside, where he wouldn't be affected by the fight, and pouting. Arkenel continued, "I didn't come here to kill anyone." He glanced with his only eye at all the slaughtered soldiers and added, "Whoops. I just want to get my mother, and then we'll go."

Eslir couldn't accept such a defeat. He had captured so many members of the royal family; he wasn't about to let them go. He pulled away from Arkenel and broke free from his hold, then attacked him again. That might have ended badly, but Rabolii stepped forward and separated them with an invisible energy shield. Arkenel turned to him for the first time today, and addressed him: "Do you mind? If he wants to be stupid, I'll kill him. And if you also want to die, get in line."

"You will not kill anyone, Arkenel." Rabolii snorted. "You didn't need to come here. I had the situation under control." When Ravena heard this, she gave out the heaviest sigh her lungs were capable of. That was such a shameless lie. "Soleya is not our enemy." Oh, here's another one! Maybe we're creating a whole book of them here. "Let's not forget who our real enemy is."

Arkenel raised his eyebrows, putting the daggers back on his belt. He replied, "Excuse me for not being aware of all the political gossip. I have been cut off from the world for seven years! Still, since Soleyans kidnapped my mother, I think it's fair to say they still are the enemy."

A tall man with a short black beard came up to Arkenel and began to poke him. "When do we kill the corpse?"

Arkenel raised a hand to shush him and turned to his father.

"You missed a lot," Rabolii replied calmly. It looked like he was going to play diplomat now. "Do you know what's going on to the west of here? Vern is on the move and is trying to establish world domination. Their armies have been flooding over our borders and have already struck our unprotected villages. A wise ruler would rethink if such an enemy deserves more attention."

As he said this, he turned his gaze to Eslir, who was sitting by the wall, wiping blood from his mouth. When Eslir noticed that the necromancer was speaking to him, he snapped, "Vern is a peaceful nation. Only you can anger them so much that they'd start a war. They are not my problem."

Rabolii smiled all-knowingly and replied, "Every nation, even the most peaceful one, could become a monster to its neighbours, as long as it is poisoned by the ambitions of an insane, powerful ruler. She wants to take over the world, and even if Aslania is too far away, Soleya is in the way. Your western border is exposed."

"That's so stupid. Soleya is at peace with Vern!" Eslir snapped, trying to get up.

"Regardless, think about it. If I really wanted your annihilation, I would have let Arkenel kill you on the spot. But I don't want anyone's death. I only came to free my wife. Now I will leave without any more confrontation. Moreover, I want to offer you a temporary alliance, at least until we solve the problem with Vern. If we don't unite forces, we run the risk of perishing."

"How could I unite anything with you? You are disgusting!"

cried Eslir, wondering how anyone could offer him such unacceptable terms.

"You don't have to like me to save your people!" Rabolii grinned. "I offer you something that will be profitable to both of us. Of course, I can imagine that all this is too sudden and you cannot make a decision on the spot. But I will suggest something else to you. Why don't you think about it? Maybe send some scouts to the west. If you see that the threat is real, you may change your mind. No one wants to fight on two fronts, young prince. Now, if you'll excuse me, I wish to go back now."

"You're not going anywhere! My army has been gathered. They have this hall surrounded. You won't be able to sneak out," yelled Eslir, standing up on his feet with a sway.

Rabolii groaned. Some people were so interesting. Why did they think he wasn't capable of dealing with the whole army? The necromancer just glanced at the present Krumerians, stopping his gaze at Ravena. He told her, "You know how concentrating death energy affects me."

"How can I forget?" she muttered. She got to her feet and went to him.

After he melted her chains, she took hold of him. He collapsed in her arms and began his famous meditation, during which he emitted death magic, causing harm to anyone nearby. It made people fall over and feel terribly sick. It would affect anyone who wasn't Krumerian, because the northerners were used to such energy charges. Arkenel sighed and went to help his mother carry away the corpse man as he was clearing the way. Eslir slumped helplessly to the ground and could only watch them motionlessly as they were escaping. He felt enraged. This wouldn't be the end of it!

After the storm was over, everyone who remained in the hall felt very uncomfortable about what had just happened. Ilinar wasn't affected by Rabolii's spell, so he stormed out from underneath the table and stood up next to his fallen cousin. He began to rebuke him. "Really, Eslir? Would you really kill me because of the crazy necromancer's lies?"

"No, erebius, get away from me," the Aslanian snarled, gargling his own blood. He had still not recovered from the spell and didn't fully realise what was going on.

"You sicken me! I tried to get along with you, but you're insane!" Ilinar yelled at him. "You let this happen in our castle! You'll bring my country to ruin."

Eslir shot him an indignant look full of disbelief. He exposed his bloodied teeth as he groaned, "I didn't see you make any effort to secure the country!"

"You know what, I changed my mind. I no longer want you in Soleya! All our troubles are your fault! Just leave!" Ilinar ordered. He crossed his arms.

"Yes, sure, because you're going to be excellent at protecting Soleya? You're the son of that corpse!"

"*I'm not his son!*" Ilinar cried hysterically, seeming like he would kill anyone who dared to contradict that statement.

"I think we are all too upset to be making important decisions." Eley dived between them and pulled Ilinar back by his shoulders before a fierce battle could begin. "Perhaps we should just clean up and take care of ourselves and the wounded men?"

Eslir wiped his mouth with the back of his hand, still glaring at Ilinar hatefully, and snapped, "Wonderful! Grab the rag and start scrubbing! I will go someplace where there are no madmen."

Having said that, the blond king went out, walking proudly as if he were moving amongst creatures lower than slugs. Eley gritted his teeth and nudged Ilinar. "Your Majesty, come on. We need to help the wounded guards."

"Eley, what am I going to do? Now everyone will think I'm the son of an erebius." The boy began to whimper.

"It is very important for us to be the first to present this story to the people. We'll give them our point of view. The last thing we need is restlessness amongst the citizens," said Eley with his usual rigor, this time with a tiny pinch of concern.

"It's all so terrible. I want to crawl in a hole and die," continued Ilinar, gazing around. He saw only puddles of blood, ruin, glass, and wounded soldiers. How was he to handle all of this, especially since Eslir had turned against him?

"What happened today wasn't so bad, Ilinar. Things could have been worse. We could have been taken over by an army of skeletons. It'll be difficult for the people regardless, so you have to be in a position to calm them down. I will help you. Come with me."

Afterwards Eley started dealing with pretty much all the problems arising from the unrest in the city. He was involved in the funeral ceremonies of the fallen warriors, the repair of the ceiling that Arkenel had broken, and the care of the wounded. He wrote condolence letters. Of course, all of this was done on behalf of Ilinar, intended to make it look as if the king was the one attending to all these details. At the end of the day,

Eley brought him some documentation and told him almost commandingly, "I think I managed with everything. If you sign this, we will be able to send people to deal with the repair of various damaged structures, but of course we will have to pay for their labour and the building materials. The sum is about five thousand gold coins."

Ilinar took the papers. He unfolded them and noticed that Eley had planned to play one gold coin per hour to each worker. The young king scratched his head and remembered that his mother would give him up to five gold coins just as pocket money. It seemed a lot, but maybe that was what workers usually received? Eley was biting his lower lip as he watched the prince take a pen and sign the document. His eyes gleaming, he picked up the papers and rushed off somewhere. Ilinar watched him as he left, feeling quite content that there was someone who was sorting out all the difficult issues after Eslir had abandoned him.

Meanwhile the Krumerians fled to the north, before Soleya could dispatch any troops after them to finish them off while they were weakened. Ravena held her husband, who didn't walk but was just being dragged. His eyes were whitened. He seemed completely unresponsive. His hair had lightened even more as if he had aged ten years today alone. Arkenel was holding him on the other side when Rabolii turned to him with a monstrous look and roared, "Ravena! Don't let this creature touch me!"

Arkenel tilted his head to one side. It was hard for him to believe what he had just heard. His friends began to encircle Rabolii in a threatening manner. It seemed like they were preparing to lynch him. Ravena felt that trouble was coming this way. She yelled, "No, please, don't start fighting again now! We are a family and we are still on hostile lands."

"Nice family, throwing their son in jail," said the same tall, bearded man, who then stepped forward with his sword drawn.

"Mavarius, we can speak about this later," Arkenel said, trying to calm his friend.

"He's the one who shut us all in that stupid prison," another of the men noted.

"Let's kill him while he's weak," a third one suggested. The crowd roared in approval.

Rabolii's soldiers stood around him, preparing to defend him, but they were too few compared to the hundreds of prisoners. Arkenel smiled faintly and stepped forward. He said, "Yes, it's true. Rabolii is to blame for many things. The prison wasn't pleasant, but while I was there, I had a lot of time to think. I am not flawless myself." He turned to his friends and told them, "None of you are! We were in Aldur for one reason or another, and we didn't free ourselves to keep behaving like beasts that must be put down. I set you free because I believe that we all deserve a second chance." He turned to his father and said, "Listen, Dad, I know we've had our differences. Sometimes I didn't understand what it was I'd done to make you angry. Sometimes it seemed that you were being unfair. I wanted to be allowed to do anything, and I didn't realise my actions harmed you in some way. I'm sorry about this, and I'm sorry about the potion. But I've changed now. Now I know how to take responsibility, I know how to think about the consequences. I want to prove to you that I can be the son you always wanted."

Mavarius listened to this speech with a puzzled, shocked expression. He groaned, "Arkenel, your crappy father locked you in prison and you're apologising?"

"Mav, it's all right. Trust me." Arkenel nodded to him with a quiet smile.

Ravena was overjoyed and relieved to see Arkenel reasoning just the way she had encouraged him to do. Apparently she had managed to get through to him. She glanced at Rabolii, hoping he wouldn't act like a stubborn donkey so they could all go back home as a family. However, the necromancer hated peace, so he shook his head like an angry horse and said, "Arkenel, your insolence is legendary. You dare show up after all these years and demand my forgiveness? After all that you've done to me? And now that you don't even resemble a human being any more? Just look at yourself. I have corpses in the army who look neater than you."

"Rab, he's been in the most terrible prison on the entire continent for seven years. How do you expect him to look!" Ravena rebuked him.

Arkenel showed great patience and continued speaking: "Father, I can't change the past. The only thing I can do is tell you I'm sorry for everything that's happened and that I've changed. I will no longer be the annoying kid who ruins your potions and messes up your political marriages. I just want to be part of this society again and do something good for myself and the others."

Rabolii couldn't stand to look at this shaggy, ragged creature who was so dirty that the colour of his skin was unrecognisable. His movements were chaotic as if he had been drugged and intoxicated. It was extremely difficult for Rabolii to humiliate himself and address Arkenel, but he sensed that if he were to keep the hostile tone, his son's ugly buddies would get involved and tear the necromancer apart in a very short amount of time. He gritted his teeth and answered, "All right, Arkenel! I will try to accept the fact that you exist, and I will not shut you and your scum back in jail unless you break the law again. However, I don't accept you back in the family, and you will not get any of the privileges or power a prince would have. I can allow you in Kranium, but don't set foot in my castle!"

Arkenel shrugged, accepting this as some kind of victory. He said, "Call me what you want, but I will always be your son, and you will always be my father. I won't try to claim my titles. I just want to do something for Krumerus, to be of some kind of service. After all, my friends and I need to make a living somehow. Many of them have been in prison for over fifteen years. They will find it hard to get a job just like that. Can we be a part of your army? According to what I've heard, we have problems with Vern, and their sorcerers are effective against skeletons."

Ah, the skeletons ... Rabolii felt pain when he remembered that he had animated over ten thousand of them and taken them into Soleya, but now that his powers were drained out, he couldn't raise them again to bring them back to Krumerus. Such a waste!

"It wasn't so difficult to get along now, was it?" Ravena said.

Arkenel grinned and called to his men, "Let's get up and start going! Kranium awaits us!"

The former prisoners started cheering and swinging their swords in the air. With immense effort, Rabolii began reviving as many skeletons from the fields as he could so there would be someone to pull his carriage of potions. Ravena didn't want to sit with him and coddle him any more. She went to see how her son was doing. Arkenel used to be pretty as a picture, but now he was all covered in wounds and dirt. As he sat on the ground and tried to tie his boots, which were falling apart, she moved a lock of hair out of his face and asked, "What has happened to your eye? What are these wounds on your face?"

Arkenel looked up at her, grinning widely, and said, "Oh, that's nothing."

"How is it nothing? Did someone cut you? What about this?"

It seemed she wanted to address every single wound on her son, but he had no time for explanations. He stood up and announced, "Just a bunch of scratches. Let's go to Kranium before the sunflower men chase us."

Ravena was amazed at how casual and calm he was. She had expected that when Arkenel and Rabolii met, there would be fights, screaming, and blood. As a matter of fact, the necromancer's son did plan something similar a while back.

He had been thinking about whether he wanted to kill his father, torture him, or destroy his miserable life first and let him suffer forever. But over the years, these feelings faded. Arkenel hardly even acknowledged how much he'd grown and matured in that prison. He had forgotten how difficult it was when he first found himself there. He had forgotten how he cried and screamed when he was sentenced to life imprisonment— and not just anywhere, but in Aldur. He couldn't believe that his transgressions were so terrible that he deserved such a fate. Ravena did all she could to dissuade Rabolii, but begging, arguments, and exhortations simply didn't work on him. So, within a few days after spilling the priceless potion, Arkenel and Ravena found themselves in a caravan on their way to the dark fortress. The boy felt like he was going insane. He hadn't even been aware that he was capable of screaming so loudly as he was doing at that point.

"You didn't even try! You almost *agreed* with him! How can you do this to me?!"

"My son, don't say that. I did try, but ..." Ravena responded in tears.

"Yeah, right! Are you not the queen? How is it so hard for you to save your own son from the damn prison?! Can't you just lose me on the way? Bribe the guards so they let me go?! Or just tell that dumb geezer I'm dead, for God's sake!" Arkenel kept screaming.

Of course, this conversation was loud enough for everyone who travelled with them to hear. All the guards were listening to them. If Arkenel were to disappear, they would instantly tell the necromancer what they had heard here, hoping to be generously rewarded for their good service. Ravena knew that. No one could be trusted with information like this. But how could she tell her child that she was absolutely helpless to save him from prison?

"Arkenel. He controls the element of death. Do you think he won't know when his own son dies?" Ravena said, "This is terrible for me as well. Don't think I'm not sympathetic to you."

"Just kill me," Arkenel cried out, feeling defeated. "It's over for me. Life in Aldur is not a life at all. They'll treat me like a doormat there. I don't want such a future."

He didn't think he'd survive prison. Though he was skilful with blades and quite agile, Arkenel wasn't very strong psychically. He was short like his maternal relatives, and he didn't know how he'd defend himself.

"Don't talk like that!" Ravena told him, "No matter how bad it is, it is not the end of the world. I will continue to talk to your father. I may convince him to let you go. During this time I will visit you frequently to help you in any way I can. One of the Aldur prison guards is my friend. I will tell him to watch out for you and to make sure that nothing terrible happens to you. We'll be fine, you'll see."

Arkenel continued to think that this was a nightmare. Still, knowing that there would be a friend amongst the guards was some comfort. Arkenel imagined that the man would keep him away from the other prisoners. Maybe he'd even excuse him from spending time in the mines, where they made convicts work like slaves. Maybe they'd smuggle in some normal food for him and they'd let him sleep in the rooms of the guards, where he wouldn't have to deal with rats, tuberculosis, and sewage water.

Ravena's friend Aveus did seem like a good man. To Arkenel he was like some kind of providence. He was tall with broad shoulders and wavy black hair. He comforted Ravena as she explained to him how unfair things were and how Arkenel was too young and innocent to experience prison.

"Aveus, promise me that you'll take care of him." Ravena was sobbing. "Promise me you will not let those animals torture him."

"I will do my best, Mrs. Remedor," the man said in a solemn tone with just a slight hint of sympathy. "I'm sure the boy will get used to the environment."

Arkenel was trying to be brave and not cry, even at the moment when he was dramatically torn from mother's arms and dragged into the darkness and filth of the prison where everything was rotting, wretched, and repulsive. As he was led down the corridor past the other cells, terrifying eyes of disgusting men were peering out through the bars. Many were missing half their teeth, and their nails were black. Some had horrendous wounds on their arms and faces. Arkenel had not seen such ugly people before. Compared to them, he was a mythical creature, flawlessly clean and innocent. Perhaps that's how they saw him as well. They slobbered over him and watched him hungrily like he was a piece of meat. Some of them stood there making gestures that he didn't know what they meant, but he felt as if he didn't want to find out.

"I am a prince, Aveus!" Arkenel hissed, shaking from everything that he had witnessed there so far. "You can't just leave me with these people! Just look at them! Please, don't let them near me."

"I won't always be around to hold your hand, my prince." The man grunted. "I have a job to do. Also, it's a kind of a rule that the guards don't interfere with prisoners' affairs. They have their own communities and gangs here. It's not our job to play God and to take sides. My advice for you is to get friends. You will not survive down here alone."

Arkenel shuddered and turned his eyes to those monsters that inhabited this place. How would he become friends with any of them? He couldn't even perceive them as human!

"Will I be alone in a cell?" Arkenel murmured.

"Actually not. I chose a friend for you," Aveus said. "I would advise you to get close to him and not to mention in front of anyone that you're a prince. You are not a prince down here. Here you are not even human. I will be doing you a favour by not leaping to your rescue all the time and treating you in a special way. That would only make the others hate you, and it would make things harder for you. Oh, look, we've come to your cell."

They stopped in front of one of the doors so that Arkenel could face his next nightmare. There sat his so-called "friend", whom Aveus had chosen. This was the most dreadful man Arkenel had ever seen! He was huge, a whole mountain of muscles. His arms were strong and firm as if he could crush skulls with his hands alone. Half of his face was tattooed. He looked more like a troll than a man.

"What is this? What have I done to deserve all this?" Arkenel murmured. He was already too tired to get frustrated any more.

"He's called Grazedrii," Aveus replied. "He's locked up here because he killed five men with his bare hands." Arkenel turned and shot the guard a frightened gaze. Aveus added, "Because they killed his nine-year-old son. I'm doing you a favour by putting you with him. If there is one person in this prison who can intimidate others with his presence alone, it would be him ... if you befriend him, that is."

Arkenel bit his lip. He stepped hesitantly into the cell, standing stiff like a wooden bar when the door slammed behind him. Grazedrii shot the newcomer a disinterested look and went back to carving a piece of driftwood which resembled nothing at this point.

"Um, hello. I'm Arkenel," said the boy, deciding not to mention his family name.

"Graz," the huge man introduced himself briefly.

"Is this ... a piece of wood? What are you making? Can I watch? I'm not good at such things at all. The last time I tried carving something, I almost lost a finger."

Grazedrii didn't answer; he just continued working. Arkenel approached him cautiously and sat at a respectable distance to avoid being irritating. He didn't know whether to keep talking to the huge man or to remain silent. He was afraid that whatever he decided to do, the big guy would spontaneously get up and beat him up. He didn't get the feeling he was building a valuable friendship at the moment.

—✺—

A very, very long day had passed. Arkenel hadn't been able to sleep. Grazedrii had snored so loudly that people across the border probably heard him. The air stank. Some huge bugs around the cell made buzzing sounds. One was annoying enough to actually jump in Arkenel's bed. It scared him so much that he woke up screaming. As soon as he realised where he was, he shut up and froze in terror. He thought the big guy would get up and break his face for screaming in the middle of the day. However, Graz didn't seem to be disturbed by this. He only shifted a bit and continued to snore thunderously.

Arkenel felt like he had slept for just a few minutes when some horrible guard started walking down the corridor and rattling a tin can to wake everyone, shouting loudly like a market trader.

The prisoners were taken out to eat. The common breakfast room was spacious with numerous long tables. Arkenel followed Graz like a puppy, feeling as if terrible things would happen if he were to lose him. The young Remedor continued to attract all the perverted gazes from the other men. He was terrified to find out they had given him female names and were using them to refer to him. They must have been dreaming about him all day.

Arkenel wasn't sure what the breakfast was, but it looked revolting. While Grazedrii gulped with appetite the contents of his bowl, Arkenel was poking his own food with an offensively filthy wooden spoon and cried out, "What is this, slug stew?"

"You wish, kid." Aveus laughed. He was overseeing the prisoners to prevent any spontaneous fights from breaking out. "Slugs actually contain meat. I think these are some sewer plants. Regardless, I would advise you to eat. You will need strength."

Arkenel turned green when he heard that. He just pushed aside his bowl and crossed his arms. This was an insult to his personality. Still, he wanted to gain at least something from this whole situation, so he poked Grazedrii and offered, "I'm really not hungry. You can eat mine too if you want to."

The huge man just shrugged and took the bowl of his buddy. They were in prison; resources were scarce.

After breakfast, the prisoners were lead to the mine. The work was debilitating. The pickaxe seemed incredibly heavy for Arkenel. After just a few blows he felt overwhelmed. How would he be able to do this all day? Every once in a while a guard would walk near him and would kick him so he'd work harder. There weren't all too many guards. They went off to patrol somewhere else. As soon as they disappeared, everyone stopped working immediately. Today was very special, and the prisoners were excited because of the interesting newcomer. Arkenel was instantly surrounded by some punks who were grinning dangerously. He tried to stand on his feet, squeezing the pickaxe as his last weapon. He had never felt less capable of defending himself.

"Hey, sweetheart! Why didn't you come and introduce yourself?" One of the men came forward, grinning with a foul, toothless mouth. "We've been waiting to greet you all evening."

"Come to Daddy!" Another one was slobbering; he was so filthy from the coal that his facial features were unrecognisable.

Every single one of them was revolting and uncivilised. Arkenel was shaken with fear, but he tried not to let it show. He just smiled politely at them and answered, "The name's Arkenel. This is a nasty place, eh? Do you guys have bug nests in your wall too?"

They must have been a little surprised that he was actually talking to them. They had thought he would start screaming like a little girl. Well, it wasn't too late to make him scream, but one of them actually answered the question. They weren't all too brave anyway when the huge Grazedrii was so close by. Arkenel tried very hard to keep that conversation going and kept asking questions to make sure it did. Every once in a while Graz glanced in Arkenel's direction to make sure no one was being violated. Arkenel himself couldn't believe that he was doing so well.

It only took a few months for Arkenel to merge with this community. Soon he was just as filthy as everyone else. There was no trace of his royal manners. It was as if Arkenel himself had forgotten he was royalty. He even got used to the disgusting food. He noticed that there was something special about it. Never before had he felt so energetic after eating something. After breakfast, he would have so much stamina that he could work in the mine for hours without feeling tired. Several times he had fainted, seemingly from exhaustion, although he didn't feel it coming on at any point. Aveus informed him that there was a drug in his food so he wouldn't feel fatigue, but he could still die of the strain, so it was a good idea to take breaks when no guards were overseeing the workers. People did die of exhaustion in this mine, so they had to be careful. Grazedrii was still nontalkative, so Arkenel didn't know how their friendship was advancing. That didn't worry him too much because he did make friends with other prisoners.

It was just another day of mining in the damp underground. Arkenel felt like he was going to burst out laughing at any moment. That was due to his magical breakfast. He was entertained by everything. Even the way the rocks crumbled seemed funny. The guard who was overseeing this corridor went out to go somewhere else. The prisoners immediately dropped the pickaxes and proceeded to sit there and rest. Arkenel looked around, wondering where his friends were. He couldn't see them anywhere. Maybe they had been sent to dig elsewhere? Regardless, he wasn't left bored for too long. Some huge man with copper rings in the piercings all over his face came over, accompanied by his buddies. He made his way to Arkenel. While Arkenel sat there innocently, the unfriendly character pushed him by the shoulder and barked, "And just who do you think you are? You've been here for, what, a couple of days and you think you're in charge of everything? You're not. I am the boss here. I paid the guards so they would move your dumb friends to another corridor. Who'll save your ass now?"

"Oh, hello," Arkenel grunted, smiling brightly. "I've heard of you, Copper Face."

Clearly Arkenel wasn't sober after breakfast, so it didn't occur to him that he was in danger. He was faced with the biggest monster in this prison and called him by his mocking nickname. The man, of course, widened his nostrils, exhaling air like an angry bull, and swung his fist to break the face of his new enemy. Arkenel had not endured all those painful fencing lessons in Kranium so that he'd get punched so easily. He dodged the blow, rose quickly to his feet, and grabbed his pickaxe. Copper Face and his friends started grinning. They didn't feel threatened at all. Arkenel just swung the pickaxe and snapped a rope that passed next to them. This made a wooden platform up on the ceiling collapse, and various rocks dropped on top of the vile foes. The other inmates in the corridor stared with amazement. After a brief reflection, they seemed very pleased with the outcome and began to clap and cheer. Arkenel grinned at them and waved the pickaxe. He had handled this problem more easily than he'd expected. Although this didn't kill the fearsome prison warlord, it did win more friends and followers for Arkenel, which made life easier.

Arkenel smirked as he remembered all this. He had been fighting with quite a lot of people in those early days of prison, but later on some of them had become his friends. Life was so volatile!

The whole day had passed on the road, and Ravena had not even glanced in Rabolii's direction. This was very unusual for her. On most occasions when she argued with her husband, she was the first one to try to make peace, even if he was at fault. This was the case now as well, but still she was avoiding him. She only sat with Arkenel and spoke to him about his adventures. At some point he ran off somewhere to play with his buddies, and she was left alone. Rabolii watched her from a distance as she sat deep in thought near the campfire during the morning. Rabolii puffed with annoyance. He got up and went to her, determined to deal with her whims and to resolve whatever was wrong. He wanted to get that out of the way so he could freely ask her for help if he needed something from her in the near future.

The necromancer sat next to his wife, waiting for some attention, but she acted like he was invisible. It irritated him, and he said angrily, "Is this how you plan to treat me from now on? Why are you angry with me about something that happened eighteen years ago? It's not important any more, so stop it."

"I thought we had a good, strong marriage, at least back in the day, Rab," she said quietly, staring at the fire. "I thought we had something real, and I was ready to forgive you one slip or two, but it seems that cheating on me was a habit for you."

He rolled his eyes, irritated by what he saw as unnecessary drama. He replied, "I didn't sleep with that sorceress because I wanted to."

Ravena looked at him for the first time that evening, surprised at how cheeky he was.

"Oh, I'm sorry! How did I not realise you were a victim of rape?" she exclaimed.

Rabolii got angrier because it was hard for him to continue the conversation in the way he had intended. He wanted to set things straight faster then change the subject and make Ravena massage his soft body, some parts of which hurt because of that long carriage ride.

"No, it's not like that. I was just ... seeking immortality." He dropped this strange answer.

Removed from any context, which was lacking here, by the way, this statement sounded ridiculous. Ravena suppressed the flame of anger in her soul and stayed patiently silent, hoping to find out exactly how sleeping with various women makes a person immortal. Rabolii continued, "A long time ago, at the very beginning of our acquaintance, I started learning how to communicate with the gods. Occasionally strange things happened around me. These were signs. I was reading messages in them. Mortelion was showing me the way."

Oh, that was very intriguing. Perhaps Mortelion had told him to commit adultery. It couldn't have been anything else. Ravena restrained herself from expressing her opinion. Her husband continued to speak in such a voice as if it were a very painful and difficult story for him to tell but he was trying to be brave. "One day there was chaos in my room." Once again Ravena exhibited heroic self-control and didn't ask why that was exceptional. "I had acquired a baby troll, but it broke free from its chains, bumped into my desk, and spilled a painful number of valuable potions on the floor. One of them was black. It was the Thick Fog potion that I made from an extract of leeches."

Ravena stopped listening. There was a detailed description of what kind of potions there were, what they looked like, and what they were made of, and Rabolii was telling all about it in such a voice as if to imply that now his wife had to gasp and recognise the divine will in all this. Rabolii continued blabbing: "At first I didn't see the pattern that was formed by the colours, but then something unbelievable was revealed in front of my eyes: for no apparent reason the eight coloured fluids whirled around, forming a circle. It was perfectly round. They swirled faster and faster until they finally disappeared, evaporating into the air. The floor remained perfectly clean."

"Oh, it's great when at least Mortelion helps you clean your floor," Ravena told him.

Rabolii stared at her with an open mouth as if he couldn't believe that statement. He barked, "Didn't you hear me?! They formed a *circle!*"

"I don't understand why we're talking about all this," she muttered.

"The potions were black, teal, blue, brown, green, yellow, and orange, and one was transparent!" He continued to speak with excitement, not knowing how anyone could fail to see how unbelievable this was. "Just like the magical elements themselves, Ravena! A circle is the symbol of circularity, of infinity—of immortality, according to the oldest writings known to man. Mortelion was trying to tell me something. He showed me the way to ... my greatness. He wanted me to somehow combine the essence of all elements, but I wasn't sure how."

"And that's why you decided to have a baby with each type of sorceress? How logical," Ravena mumbled.

Rabolii got angry. He was trying very patiently to explain his innocence to this stupid woman, and she wasn't even listening!

"Please withhold your inappropriate comments, Ravena!" he snapped. "I am trying to explain something of cosmic importance to you! Of course the babies are not the key to my immortality! But you are too illiterate on magical subjects to understand! I needed something else, something to protect me. I know of a magic that is capable of shielding you from its polar energy. I control the element of death, so I was able to apply to myself a shield that defends me from the pure energy of life. I didn't do it just for myself. I have created such protection for you and our children. This is how I found you when you were kidnapped. I felt your shield was under pressure. I felt where you were and came to rescue you."

Ravena blinked. She did think it strange that the sorceress of life couldn't hurt her, but she had not even suspected it was because of the tender protection of her caring husband. She had forgotten about that shield. Rabolii had cast all kinds of spells on her two decades ago and she hardly knew what they all were.

Rabolii noticed that his wife had gone quiet, so interpreted that as his victory. He swelled with importance and continued rambling: "Such a shield is a unique kind of magic that is special in terms of its application. It is generally done for people who are ... necessary for you in some way." This was probably the sweetest love proclamation that had ever come out of Rabolii's mouth. "When I saw how those potions mixed, I pondered a lot. I concluded that maybe that was it. I had to get a shield from every kind of sorcerer. You can imagine that not every single one was excited by the thought of performing such a spell on a stranger, even less a necromancer. I had to become really good friends with some of them, and we kept in touch until ... until ... you know. Others, especially some of the ladies, needed more persuasion. I couldn't convince each one I approached, but fortunately no sorcerer is unique. I would find someone else with the same element. And in the end, my fantastic collection was complete."

Ravena remained silent for a few seconds, then she asked quietly, "It wasn't the shields, was it?"

"No." Rabolii sighed. "Flinaya was the last one. The water shield was the final one I needed. However, when she raised it around me, nothing changed. I didn't feel any different, and I realised this wasn't the will of Mortelion. I had misinterpreted his signs. It was all so absurd. I was meant to receive invulnerability on that night, and instead I was slain!"

Afterwards he went tragically silent. Ravena didn't really know how to treat him at this point. She was still a bit angry with him for cheating, but she could never keep that mood for very long, especially when he was so wretched and unhappy. She put one hand on his shoulder and pulled him closer, saying, "Maybe you'll know one day, Rab. Nothing's over."

"On the contrary!" the man grunted. "I have no idea what Mortelion's message was! There are so few ways in which different types of magic interact! I could think of nothing else but the spell with the shields! My last hope was to find out how to make that extract from vampire blood, but what's the point of hoping? Even if I manage to create it again by pure chance, Arkenel is in the very convenient position to kick the cauldron again."

"I hear my name accompanied by a squealing voice, and it's annoying me!" Arkenel shouted while he was lying down a bit further away.

Ravena opened her mouth to tell them to stop arguing, but Rabolii yelled first, "You don't have the right to speak, not after you ruined my life, you ungrateful boy! I am your father, and you ..."

Arkenel got up, leaned on his elbow, and cast his father a look full of disbelief. He had forgotten how daft that man was.

"Maybe I really should kill him," Arkenel noted.

"Take this. You'll feel better," said one of his friends, who handed him some dirty cigarette full of unknown herbs.

Arkenel took it and inhaled from it, rolling his eyes back with delight, and said, "You know, I think I owe my life to the miner's spice. I wouldn't have survived in Aldur had I been sober."

The other prisoners began to chuckle. Rabolii shot them a critical look. This was what he had to deal with—a filthy gang of drug addicts! They had been bouncing all over the place at night, they screamed and yelled like madmen, and then when the drugs were wearing off, they were grumpy, moody, and inadequate. As a matter of fact, they were always inadequate.

"I just want to get home already," mumbled Rabolii.

"What are we going to do with all the newcomers once we get home?" Ravena asked. The nearby prisoners raised their heads and listened. In fact, they were also wondering about that.

"It's not my job to deal with this!" The necromancer folded his arms, looking offended.

"You'll give us houses somewhere in the city, that's what you'll do!" Arkenel said. "You don't want us to be running around the streets, do you? You can shelter us anywhere. I'm sure you can find five hundred or so properties. We're not picky. We can share houses if need be."

Rabolii turned his head to his insolent son. His eyes were full of indignation, and his eyebrows were cocked so high that they were almost hitting his receding hairline and merging into it. He had all that trouble with the refugees, and on top of that he'd have to deal with more annoying homeless men. He yelled angrily, "*Five hundred?! Seriously?!* I see no more than fifty on this field. How dare you be so impudent?"

"Um, yes. We're about fifty over here." Arkenel shrugged. "However, there are still more of us in Aldur, and I'd rather keep them close to me. We have loads of plans with them. If you can't accommodate us, I guess we'll all have to go back to Aldur."

"You know what?" the necromancer yelled. "Perhaps that would be best! I don't want you living where I am! Go to the damn Aldur and live there with your despicable tramps whom you set free."

"It sounds like a wonderful idea." Arkenel shrugged his

shoulders casually. "I had the good intention of keeping a normal relationship with you, but ..."

"But it's impossible because you're a failure! Even before spilling my potion, you were such an unpleasant boy. You walked around the castle as if everything belonged to you. You thought you were some sort of a god and that you had the right to everything just because you were my son! No aspirations, no ambitions! You thought you could have what you wanted just by ordering someone to bring it to you! You thought you'd have it all after I died. It's outrageous. I can't believe I failed so badly at making a man out of you. Look at what you've become! You're a wreck. I guess you'll just die in your thirties because you're infected with all manner of diseases that you've gotten from your filthy companions."

All this left Arkenel speechless. He did remember that Rabolii was just way too gobby and that he would say whatever he thought of without caring. Arkenel did know how to talk back to irritating individuals, but this was too much. He remained in silence for a few seconds while his tortured brain was trying to make up an answer, then he just waved a hand and mumbled, "Gosh, why am I talking to you at all? Just go to bed. I hear that sleep reduces crankiness."

"I thought he didn't sleep?" One of the other prisoners yawned.

"Oh, right." Arkenel laughed. "That's eighteen years of crankiness because of no sleep."

"I think it's time for everyone to fall asleep." Ravena frowned. The last thing she needed was arguing.

Arkenel glanced at them, leaning against one of the trees. He wished he were able to relax and fall asleep normally, but he had lost that joy a long time ago. He was used to always being aware of where he was and what was happening so that he would be able to defend himself if someone spontaneously decided to kill him.

It had been awhile since Ilinar and Eslir had had a cockfight, but now it was happening again. And the worst part was that nobody could now tell them to stop arguing like two babies. Eley tried, but he was rudely ignored. The Soleyan king was upset by the fact that his cousin was slandering his good name and claiming Ilinar was Rabolii's son. As for Eslir, he was watching his cousin's every move with hateful eyes, convinced that as soon as he looked away, Ilinar would rush to the aid of the mad necromancer.

Eley noticed that the situation was serious. He thought the only thing that would help Ilinar in this case would be the support of the Soleyans. So he continued to propagate the claim that the king had been vindicated and that he wasn't the son of Rabolii—that all of that was a filthy lie. Many of the people couldn't put two and two together and just believed the one who shouted the loudest. That happened to be Eley, the spokesman at the rally. But some others had suspicions, saying that everything did fit together. They were spreading rumours, so something had to be done to counteract that.

"I don't know how to make everyone like me," Ilinar murmured.

"Try harder then," said Eley. They were having another meeting in the king's room.

"Try harder how? They doubt me! They think I'm an erebius! And I don't know how to convince them I'm not!" cried Ilinar.

"Just make sure you oppose Krumerus openly. If you don't show kindness to the necromancer, and if you maintain your mother's policy, then all of this will blow over," Eley answered. "I'll take care of your campaigns."

Ilinar lowered his eyes, feeling some relief from the fact that he wouldn't be burdened with everything. He said thankfully, "I'm in your debt, Eley. I don't know how to repay you for all the help."

"Two hundred gold coins would be a good start," Eley replied casually.

Ilinar glanced at him with confusion. He had not expected such a spontaneous demand for a material reward. And this was hardly the first time Eley requested money as if he didn't have a salary already. His parents were to blame for this as they had gotten in debt, larger than the castle in Lumis. As a good son, Eley was trying to get his family out of debt, and draining money from Ilinar seemed to be doing the trick.

Meanwhile, Salina and Traneya had been left in charge of Krumerus. In fact, on days like these, they remembered that this was a country that stretched far beyond Kranium. All the peasants were angry because the skeletons had been drafted for war, so much of the manual labour had become difficult to do. There was no one to pull the wagons, carry the heavy bags, or take care of the households. One of the few skeletons that was left behind was the one which belonged to Regel and Dregel, the twin sons of Rabolii. They had smuggled one skeleton from the call to arms, and now it wasn't even doing anything useful. The brothers dragged it around and used it just to irritate everyone. At one point, they lost control over it, and it jumped in the middle of the road, scaring some horses that started jumping around, overturning the carriage they were pulling. Whinnying hysterically, they trampled the unfortunate man who was trying to drag himself out of the carriage. They stomped all over the market and escaped to their salvation. Regel and Dregel ran to the scene of the accident and stared blankly at the mess.

"That was so weird," bellowed one of the twins.

"I know, right? I haven't seen horses in years. Where did they come from?"

Yes, there were very few horses in Krumerus. On the whole, plants were in very limited supply in this dead land, so no grazing animal could survive. The skeletons were doing the hard work anyways. And talking about skeletons ...

"Oh no, it's broken!" Regel exclaimed with disappointment when he pulled a smashed skull from underneath the carriage.

"That sucks!" whined Dregel. "Who is this idiot who killed our skeleton?!"

Everyone on the market had already gathered round to find out the answer to that question. Regel pulled the man out of the carriage. Blood flowed from his head. He was dead. The townspeople started asking each other if they knew him. It was as if no one had ever seen him before. With so many refugees in this city, this man was just another unfamiliar face. They all thought he was a trader. He was wearing some unusual clothes, and he had horses. He was certainly not from here.

"Whatever. Let's take him to the castle and give him to the necromancers to animate him." Dregel shrugged. He couldn't leave such a valuable resource as a dead body to be wasted.

"He is not ours. He must have a family who wants to animate him for themselves," replied Regel.

"Who cares? We killed him, so he's ours now."

Afterwards they both dragged the corpse away to boil his meat off and make him a skeleton. Since he had a hole in the forehead and wasn't pretty, they stuck a glass eye there, hoping that it wouldn't affect his qualities. After all, they had seen skeletons with all kinds of damage like missing fingers, but their owners kept them because they didn't have money to get better ones.

A few days later Rabolii arrived back at Kranium with his jolly company. He was greeted by cries and anguish. The townspeople were mortified to see that he was returning with only a handful of skeletons when he had gone out with nearly ten thousand! This valuable resource—gone! How would they survive now? At least the return of Ravena and Arkenel was a bit of a distraction from the tragedy. Many of the townspeople had dreamed of the day when the prince would return, but no one imagined seeing him like this. He was so shabby and scarred, he seemed somewhat crazy. He always had that weird smile, and it made people wonder what to expect.

Traneya and Salina came to greet their family, and they were really surprised to see Arkenel and Rabolii in one place and in one piece. Traneya was overjoyed to see her brother; she leapt into his arms and hugged him while chattering, "Is this really you? Brother, you look terrible. What's with the eye? Oh God, I didn't think I'd see you again out of that cell."

"Ouch, ouch. Happy to see you too, but I have a cracked rib over here," he complained while trying to loosen her iron grip on his sore body.

"How did you escape?" she asked him excitedly.

"Long story. We'll have to sit down somewhere and I'll tell you." He laughed. "Where's the rest of this family? Won't they come to salute me as well?"

"Forget about them. Regel and Dregel are playing with some dumb skeleton. Malior's dead."

Arkenel's smile faded. This city would feel empty without his best friend. He wondered how many things had changed since he left. Salina bit her lip. She held no illusions that this would be a happy family reunion, and she was right. Now they would sit down and talk for a few days about who had died. Rabolii clenched his teeth, somewhat jealous that he wouldn't be the subject of this conversation. Announcing that he'd go read in his room, he picked up a small sack with two vials and dragged it up the stairs with loud puffing as if he were carrying a mountain, while his servants loaded the skeletons to deliver the remaining potions up to his tower.

The city was full of refugees. It would be difficult for Arkenel to find a place to sleep for himself and all his companions. Kranium was a large city, but most of it was ancient ruins that looked like they were from another age. There was a network of underground tunnels; some were so old that no one had set foot in them for centuries. The prisoners were housed in an underground area which looked like it'd been used for blood sacrifices for Mortelion. It was damp and stuffy, but it looked a bit more comfortable after some beds and cupboards were brought in. Salina and Traneya helped their brother to settle there. The younger sister noted, "This place is disgusting. Was there really nowhere else for you to stay?"

"I don't know. Weren't you in charge of the whole accommodation crisis?" Traneya asked.

"Hey, it's all right as long as we're not in grave danger!" Arkenel grinned carelessly as he lit torches on the walls. In the underground rooms like this, it was too dark even for the Krumerians.

"I'm sure we can find you a house or a room somewhere, you're not sleeping in this cursed basement!" Traneys exclaimed.

"I'll stay with my men, it's fine." Arkenel replied casually. He had always planned to stick with this group instead of clinging to his rich relatives and getting comfortable."

"I'll look for something better tomorrow," Salina offered them.

The men began making themselves comfortable on the simple furniture. Aveus was amongst them, sitting a little farther away from the prisoners. They hadn't massacred him when they broke out, but he wasn't one of them regardless. Graz was leaning against the wall, drowsing. Arkenel sat down on some blankets and said, "So, do tell! What else has happened in this city while I was away? I can't believe that Malior is dead. How did Rabolii allow that to happen? Had he not adopted him and made him his heir?"

"Yes, that was the case." Salina sighed.

"I don't know what happened," said Traneya, sitting down beside her brother. "He could have done so much to save him, but he didn't life a finger. And then he started screaming at me because I dared speak about it."

"Pff, what a father," Mavarius said with a grim look. He exhaled a large cloud of cigarette smoke. He was the only person who remained very moody even after he had smoked the miner's spice. He was just so used to it.

"Mav wants us to kill him." Arkenel nodded towards his friend with a cheerful smile.

"Me too," Traneya groaned.

Mavarius made a gesture with his hand towards Traneya, as

if that was the perfect answer and a decision had been made. Arkenel smiled and said, "Yes, I know that Rabolii is a tosser. I did want to screw him over for a long time. But now we have a chance for something better. We can start building our lives outside that damn prison. We can prove that we are useful, reasonable people. I don't want to mess up my chances of doing this because of vengeance. We can start clean with Rabolii."

Mavarius made a face as if he had heard that too many times and couldn't be bothered to start arguing. Salina looked at the hairy, toothless people around her, thinking that even if Arkenel's sanity questionably had survived in Aldur, the same didn't apply to most of the people present. Perhaps the fact that so many people had escaped from a heavily guarded prison was actually a terrible thing.

"So, how did you escape? Do tell!" Traneya tried to start a conversation which wasn't about Rabolii.

"With my mad smithing skills." Arkenel grinned.

His sisters stared at him, expecting a clarification. They didn't know what sort of forging might have taken place in a prison. Arkenel chuckled and thought about his glorious escape from the prison, which had taken place just a couple of weeks ago.

In fact, this escape wasn't something that just happened overnight. Of course, ever since they first entered Aldur, everyone had tried to find some way out to their freedom. However, even when they weren't locked and chained, prisoners were guarded by too many armed men. The guards were cruel. They sometimes broke up petty fights by killing the people involved. Maybe the inmates would try to organise a prison break, but a place like Aldur drained all their desire for freedom and life. They stopped perceiving themselves as people and had no energy for anything. Arkenel didn't have too many ideas about how he could change this situation. So far he had enjoyed little victories. For example, on occasion he managed to sneak in some normal food or alcohol with Ravena's help.

Once again, he was lying in the pile of rags in his cell, staring lazily at the ceiling as Grazedrii continued to carve yet another piece of wood. In moments like this one, Arkenel was envious that his friend had found something to do in the long hours of boredom. He asked, "You were a sculptor before they stuck you in here?"

"Blacksmith," he said tersely without looking up.

"What did you forge? Weapons? Armour?"

"Yeah, that."

"Hmm," Arkenel grunted. "It's almost ironical. We mine iron and coal all day long. You can probably craft something with this raw material."

"I don't have a furnace or tools," Graz noted.

"I guess... It's not like you can forge a sword for everyone so we can fight our way out of this hole. The doors are all locked, and when we're out, we're always in chains."

"We can break the chains with pliers."

"We don't have pliers. Though you can probably forge those too, can't you?" At this point, Arkenel raised his gaze and asked, "Provided you have all the tools, what exactly can you make?"

At first that seemed like a very vague idea. It was ambitious even to talk about liberation. Prisoners forging a sword in Aldur seemed like a fairy tale. Arkenel began planning and solving each problem, one at a time. On days like this one, the dirty, nasty mines just smelled of freedom. A group of prisoners noted that they had found a hidden corridor where they would sneak in and hide so they wouldn't have to work. Since the supervising guard was too lazy to even use his eyes, he didn't notice some of his subordinates were disappearing every day.

The hidden corridor looked like a good work area. Soon all sort of materials were stored there—coal, metal ore, hammers, rags, and whatever else Grazedrii wanted. Prisoners could smuggle in some small objects when they bribed the guards. There was a specific guard who was willing to break a lot of the rules to fill his own pockets. A chimney was drilled so that once the forge was lit, people in the corridor wouldn't be choked by the smoke. The top end of the chimney pierced one of the cell floors, but it was actually very convenient and didn't bother anyone. In those hours when the forge was lit and smoke came out, everyone was downstairs in the mines. No one could even be sure where the smoke came from.

The guards did notice something was off. Prisoners would disappear for hours at a time. A lot less metal and coal was gathered from the mines every day. There seemed to be a smoky smell in a particular part of the prison, and no one knew why. A few times Aveus led Arkenel away and cornered him to have "a very serious talk". He asked him if he was doing anything irregular. However, Remedor had become a great liar and cast away any doubts.

Grazedrii got his own work area with an improvised forge. There he taught Arkenel and a few more people how to smith so they'd get more work done. They did make a lot of noise, but their mates outside covered that up by smashing their pickaxes on the rocks extra loud. Of course, there were those who feared this whole plot would turn sour and the prison break would be drowned in blood. They couldn't imagine such a huge undertaking would go unnoticed, and even if it did, there would still need to be a fight, which the prisoners could lose. History remembered other courageous attempts of drugged madmen to escape, and it always ended badly. Some men tried to kill Arkenel to make sure they didn't end up suffering, but he handled them. He would always state that he preferred to take the chance instead of spending the rest of his life in that dump. Fortunately, even those who opposed him never told the guards. They all had a sense of prisoner's honour and wouldn't snitch. They'd try to solve such problems themselves as they really didn't trust that the guards would solve them fairly.

As a matter of fact, there was this one guard who knew about it all. He was the one who accepted the bribe of the century to unlock the cells at the decisive moment. After the armed prisoners charged out and started fighting for their freedom, even Aveus was surprised. He survived just because of Arkenel's mercy. Aldur was drowned in blood, both the prisoners' and the guards', but it was the former who triumphed. They conquered the entire fortress of Aldur. The son of Remedor was so proud that under his command something like this had happened. He and his friends had done something very difficult when they were hungry, beaten, and powerless. He was now dreaming of a beautiful future and imagined he would achieve more. He believed that he would win again and again, until one day he would be the son his father had always wanted.

Chapter 4

POISON

Kranium definitely felt the presence of a gang of drug addicts in the days that followed. The men were noisy and disgusting. Most of the time they didn't know what they were doing or why. They moved in large, threatening groups around the city and were always looking for something to steal and someone to beat up. Arkenel seemed to be the only one with a drop of sanity left, so he tried to control them and save them from the rage of the almighty necromancer. Because of them and all the refugees, a constant state of chaos gripped Kranium. Too often the necromancer heard news about houses someone broke into, valuables which had been stolen, and fights which ended in death. It was usually the skeletons that acted as militia, but since they were gone, the city was engulfed in chaos. The necromancer was just wondering how to discreetly kill all those who caused problems and made noise under his window when Ravena walked into his room. She greeted him, "I hope you're OK, Rab. The last few days were exhausting."

"Every day is exhausting, now a little more than usual," mumbled Rabolii. He glanced at the window, from where unpleasant shouts could be heard.

"Give them a few days to settle in," Ravena told him. "Thank you for making peace with Arkenel. I always knew you two could get along."

"It would seem so to you." The necromancer sighed. "Arkenel is a sycophant; he's trying to use me. He thinks of me as an old fool who will be softened by tales of fatherhood and so on. He is hypocritical, Ravena. He's up to something."

Rabolii's wife wondered why she had ever thought that the legendary argument between her husband and her son would end so easily. She said, "Rab, trust him. He is sincere. He just wants your acceptance; he wants us to be a family again."

That seemed too cheesy and impractical to Rabolii. He couldn't believe in such a scenario. Yet he knew that if he were to start arguing with his wife again, the conversation would last for a few hours. Fortunately, something distracted them. The big, dusty clock began to count to midnight. The man sighed and murmured, "It's time for my daily potions which I need to take in so I don't rot—because I'm dead."

The drama and the tragedy were heartbreaking. Ravena got up from the desk, walked around it, and stood beside her husband as he took all manner of bottles out of his cabinets and carefully arranged them on the desk like it was some sort of ritual. The woman decided to enquire about all this. She asked, "What's the green one for?"

"I use it to control my brain function," Rabolii replied with a sour face. "I'm trying to develop a new formula as there are imperfections."

"What about the blue one?"

"This is a concentrate of crushed forest moss with river salt additives. It helps me keep my pulse. It is very weak." The necromancer continued to mumble in such a tone as if he were saying some very sad things, and then rolled up his sleeve. His arm was whitish, and the veins were purple and well outlined under the thin skin. Ravena couldn't help but notice a needle attached to her husband's arm.

"Um, Rab, what is that?" she asked.

"Well, I always keep a needle in because my skin is delicate and shouldn't be punctured every night," he announced, every following word sounding more tragic than the former. "My veins would swell. My wounds wouldn't heal. I would start bleeding regularly. I can't take anything through by mouth because my stomach stopped working eighteen years ago ..."

"My poor darling!" Ravena pulled him in an embrace as he was attaching a syringe to the needle in his hand, sniffing all the while.

"Will you pass me the concentrate of crushed forest moss?" Rabolii asked with an expression of a man whole life had been broken.

Ravena looked around and handed him the blue bottle. Apparently this is what their quality time would be like— injecting potions. Rabolii carried out every movement with such harsh sighs and a mournful expression that listening to him could break your heart. In general, he managed somehow to keep calm in such a moment of remorse and suffering, but now he had an audience, so he was trying to create more emotion. Ravena couldn't bear to see him so unhappy, so she suddenly decided to change the mood. As Rabolii was injecting the last potion, his wife cleared the desk with one movement of her hand and sat down on it, putting her legs around her husband. The necromancer stared at her with an outraged look and groaned with discontent. "Can you be more careful? What if you spill something!"

"Don't think about it, Rab," she replied, making an attempt to hug him while he was pulling away with a stubborn face.

"You're just reproaching me for being a corpse. You already know I can't do such things any more." He continued to fight her.

"You know there's a potion for that," she said, pulling a bottle out of her pocket. "Besides, you're not a corpse to me."

"Oh no, don't come close to me. I'm hideous. You don't have to demean yourself like that. I look shockingly bad without clothes on. I don't want you to be disgusted by me."

"Shush, stop protesting," answered Ravena as she sat in his lap.

Rabolii didn't know why his wife bothered with this struggle every one or two years. He knew he used to be handsome and desirable in his youth, but now there was nothing left of that. He was old, scarred, and abominable. He couldn't imagine that someone would still find him attractive. Ravena, who seemed to have no problem with his flaws, continued to kiss him. Rabolii began to recall what people who weren't a corpse were capable of doing, when someone started banging on his door. A voice came from the other side, "Yo, Dad! I heard you called for me?"

"Arkenel! I shall smite you where you stand. Leave at once!" the necromancer squealed as he buttoned up his clothes and Ravena got up from him. Rabolii had completely forgotten that he had called for his failure of a son to give him some work outside the city.

Arkenel paused for a second, wondering what had caused this hatred now. He addressed the first thing he thought was the problem, "Er, I won't spill any potions, I promise. Did you need me to do something about Vern? Is it a bad time?"

"It's never gonna be a good time. Drop this," another voice sounded from outside.

Rabolii already looked decent enough, Ravena stood beside him, regretting that they had been interrupted. It was so hard for her to get any sort of tenderness from such a husband; she literally had to fight for it.

The necromancer answered, "Oh, yes, of course. Vern. Come in. And calm your trembling limbs. I don't want you to break everything in my room."

The door opened, and Arkenel stepped into the lair of his fearsome father. It seemed that he had tried to look less like an escaped convict. He was a lot cleaner, and his hair was nicely combed, mainly because he had finally succumbed to the pressure of Salina, who was very insistent on dealing with his hair. But his buddy who was accompanying him hadn't put forth the same effort. Mavarius was just as shabby as in his days in prison. He now stood with his arms crossed and shot suspicious glances towards everything around. He seemed so discontent that a person might think he was related to Rabolii. He was a tall, skinny man in his thirties, so he did fit the profile of the necromancer's bastards. The old Remedor, narrowing his piercing blue eyes when he saw the stranger, mumbled, "Arkenel, what is that?"

"Oh, this is Mavarius. He's my friend." The son shrugged casually.

"And why is he here?"

"To make sure you don't smite anyone where they stand," the man growled.

"Ha, ha. Let's not start the acquaintance like this, shall we?" Arkenel tried to take control of the conversation. "So, you needed us for something?"

"I'll tell you what I need you for!" answered Rabolii. "I have a vital political plan, and I have given you the honour of participating in its implementation. I want you to murder a whole squad of Vernians and bring them to me. However, you mustn't just kill them in any way you see fit. If you fight them in battle, I want their wounds to be easily concealable. I don't want anyone scorched or with obvious wounds like cut hands or missing eyes!"

"Won't it be easier to poison or drown them?" asked Mavarius.

Rabolii opened a huge mouth to scream. "Good luck with this! These are not wretches like the Soleyans, into whose capital you can walk in without anyone seeing you. The Vernians are like animals. They smell their enemies for dozens of miles away! They'll probably smell you specifically from a hundred! How are you going to get close enough to poison them unnoticed?!"

"I ain't talking about getting close. We find where they get their water, and we dump the poison there. I'd think a guy like you has some sort of poison which doesn't stink or taste weird," said Mavarius.

Rabolii had at least a million things to say about why this plan would be a total failure, but Arkenel said, "It does seem difficult right now, but this is Mavarius we're talking about. He was raised by Vernians. He knows their ways as well as anyone. I think he would be irreplaceable in this mission. So, Daddy, do you have such a potion?"

Mavarius just looked down at his friend and raised his eyebrows.

"Daddy? My lord, Arkenel!"

"How else should I refer to him? Your Majesty?"

"You want suggestions on what to call him?"

"Shut up!" the necromancer yelled at them. "You there, the filthy one! Let's say I will agree with your foolish idea. I have a poison that we could use for that purpose. I can have it ready for tomorrow. Arkenel, I'll give it to you. Just get your tramps out of my town. They're a catastrophe that's going to destroy the bloody capital! You shouldn't be alone on the mission anyway. You will need men to load the carcasses into carriages. Also, I'll give you the Never Rot potion so you can inject them with it and deliver them fresh to me. This is essential. I need them intact!"

"Um, I don't suppose you'll tell us what you need them for?" Arkenel asked.

"You know, 'cause the Vernian soldiers are mostly women. He'll pick a lover from the other corpses." Mavarius slammed this mortifying statement.

Arkenel did everything in his power not to burst out laughing. He just covered his mouth with his hands then stuttered, "I ... I don't need to know, really. I'll go tell the men we're going."

Rabolii was so shocked by this ugly slander that he couldn't even kill these two with flames. He just sat there staring as Mavarius shot him another angry glance. He put his hand on Arkenel's shoulder and led him out through the doors.

Ravena couldn't remember the last time that someone had dared to make such a statement. She decided to distract her husband before he started an apocalypse. She took a potion from his desk and said, "Rab, you forgot to inject this one. What is it for?"

Ravena spent another hour or two dealing with Rabolii, then she went to take care of the rest of her family. So far she hadn't had a chance to spend much time with Arkenel. She found him in the underground corridors. The place was filled with clouds of smoke and scruffy people, and empty bottles were rolling on the floor. Her son was sitting next to Mavarius, the two exchanging a blunt. Ravena felt pain when she saw her boy surrounded by such friends. She said as if with some difficulty, "Son, can you accompany me to the castle? We need to speak."

"I get invited in the castle twice a day now? And there I thought I wasn't allowed in it." Arkenel grinned dizzily as he handed the blunt back to Mavarius.

"It's OK. Come with me. Your father didn't mean that."

"Just as he didn't mean to imprison me," Arkenel noted as he got up and walked towards his mother. Mavarius shifted uncomfortably, wondering whether to follow his friend or not. Remedor shot him a look and smiled. "It's fine, man. My mom won't let them gut me."

Ravena continued talking as she walked with her son. "I didn't imagine you were in such a bad state. I'm sorry I couldn't visit you over the last year. Had I known you were planning an escape, I would have helped you."

"I guess it's for the better that you didn't get involved. Just imagine if Rabolii had found out." Arkenel grinned.

"He'll take you back in the family, you'll see," answered Ravena.

Arkenel exhaled heavily, wondering if he wanted to start an argument over this statement. Eventually he replied, "I'm sceptical. You kept saying this throughout the whole time I was in prison, but according to my sisters' letters, Rabolii didn't seem to show a hint of guilt or regret. He would have never changed his mind about this."

That wasn't how Ravena saw things, though. She tried to put her opinion in words as she had done many times before. "Darling, please remember that your father is under a tremendous amount of stress. He carries the fate of the whole country upon his shoulders, and his very existence has been extremely painful and inconvenient ever since he died. He's told me he can't even get proper sleep but can only snooze for a few hours a day. He feels so dreadfully tired and unhappy all the time, so it's very difficult for him to show love and compassion. I know him better than anyone. I remember what he was like twenty years ago, and I know he has it in him to be a wonderful man and a true father. Right now he keeps working on improving his potions so he can feel better and become more of the man he used to be. We just need to be patient with him."

Arkenel raised his gaze to meet his mother's eyes and asked, "Is he making any progress? How's that vampire potion going?"

The two of them spoke about that as Ravena led her son into a large closet with various outfits. She told him, "Let's find you something nicer to wear. I can't look at you in these rags."

While she was going through the hanged clothes, he put his scratched hand on hers and told her, "Mom, please. My friends will call me a fag if they see me dressed in something like this. Do you have any leather armour? Preferably in large quantities so the rest of the men can get some too? Other than that, just give me some money, and I'll get clothes from the marketplace. I don't want to look too royal all of a sudden."

Ravena thought he was too adorable. He'd always speak and think about "the rest of the men" whenever she was visiting in Aldur and trying to smuggle some goodies into prison. Arkenel seemed never to think of just himself. She turned to him and looked at his gashed face, feeling deep pain for seeing him like this. She told him quietly, "I never wanted all this to happen to you. I knew that you would never be the same again. I can't imagine what you went through in that place."

Arkenel smiled a bit, put his hand on his mother's shoulder, and said, "I'm not saying I'm happy all of this happened. My time in Aldur wasn't pleasant. I got beaten a lot, and sometimes, honestly, I didn't know if I would live to see another sundown. However, all that made me stronger. I rose amongst people who would be considered uncontrollable. I found real friends. I can put my past to rest. I just want to take home the best of my time in Aldur and carry on."

Ravena looked at him with pain and worry. He could say he was fine, but she had a hard time believing him. She said to him insistently, "You know you can talk to me about anything that happened to you there. I'm your mother, and I'll support you no matter what you've been through."

Arkenel smiled brightly at her and said, "Mom, I wasn't helpless there. I wasn't the victim of the big, strong men. I had friends, I had allies, and the others respected me. I didn't simply survive. I triumphed. It was the first victory of many to come."

Ravena really wanted this to be true. It seemed unreal that Arkenel took seven years in prison so positively. Maybe he was a very strong person; who could know. How was it possible that he not only wasn't complaining about his ruined life but also was thinking so much about a bright future? Well, he'd definitely get the opportunity to achieve his many victories on the battlefield as Rabolii was causing plenty of fighting with the other nations.

The secret, mysterious plans of Rabolii were not clear to anyone. Still, whatever he was doing, the seeds of doubt were cast in Soleya. Ilinar had gathered his advisors and held a very noisy meeting where no one agreed with anyone. Eley had given his opinion about how Ilinar should behave so the others would like him, but it didn't seem the young king had heeded those words.

"I think it would be unwise for us to do nothing when we've been warned of potential danger," Ilinar said.

Eslir sighed so heavily that he almost exhaled his lungs whole. He answered with annoyance, "The damned Rabolii told you such a stupid and obvious lie. Why do you ever listen to him? Is it not evident what he's trying to do? He wants you to move the armies to the western border, and while you defend yourself from Vern, you are exposed to attacks from the north."

"Your Majesty, that really is possible." Eley tried to intervene, unable to believe he agreed with Eslir on any subject.

"I don't think Krumerus is capable of hurting us at present," Ilinar replied. "My men gathered thousands of skeletons from the battlefield. The necromancer lost so many. What could they possibly attack us with?"

"Oh, I don't know, maybe with demons?" Eslir spread his arms. "My grandfather has been running a ten-year campaign against Krumerus, and their demons are the main soldiers. Also, we don't know how many skeletons they have in total. That may have been only a fraction of their army. Suppose that things are the way you imagine them! If Krumerus is weakened, we must attack, not protect another border from imaginary enemies."

Most of the council members seemed to agree. Ilinar clenched his teeth and answered, "Our western border is not nearly as well fortified as the northern one. If the Vernians attack us, they will easily make their way here without anyone stopping them."

"You mean like Rabolii did a few days ago?" Eslir replied. "Who would you defend your country from, an army of monsters or women with spears? I'm sorry, but this is ridiculous."

Ilinar noticed that everyone was against him, and he felt confused. Indeed, there was no reason for Vern to attack him, but perhaps the necromancer knew something the Soleyans didn't? Finally he tried to make a compromise and announced, "In that case I want to go west with a squad of a hundred people. I will judge the situation, I will try to contact Queen Krementa and ask her if there is a reason for the necromancer to make such claims. During that time, the rest of the army can stay here or at the northern border."

"Your Majesty, you can't go there personally!" exclaimed Eley.

"Why not? Apparently Eslir here and everyone else thinks that Vern does not pose a threat. What is to stop me from going to the border then?" Ilinar answered him.

The Aslanian king couldn't imagine anything more stupid. He didn't know why this nation was still obeying Ilinar given that he was an erebius. Eslir wondered if his younger cousin was exposing the country to his daddy on purpose, but then he thought that a hundred soldiers wouldn't make much difference in a more serious battle anyway. He waved his hand and said, "Whatever. If you don't want to take advantage of the situation, I will. I have my own soldiers, so I will go through the passage connecting Lumis and Kranium to attack the capital. They suffered a heavy loss here. I will not give them time to recover."

"I won't stop you," Ilinar said. "Attack them if you want. My point is that we have no information about the forces they have and marching into their land can be dangerous. I intend to protect my country instead of attacking."

"Good luck with that," Eslir said briefly, and rose from his chair.

Ilinar looked at him as the Aslanian left, hoping he wouldn't cause more trouble. So far his initiatives had been devastating. Eslir saw things in black and white and was pretty sure he knew exactly who was an enemy and who was a friend. Ilinar wasn't so certain. He had the feeling that there was no sufficient information about anything, that everything was confusing, and that every choice could be wrong.

He and Eslir were very different, but did that mean they'd always fight? Maybe their differences would make them stronger and mutually complementary. Ilinar thought it was quite possible. After all, that was exactly what happened with Felis and Arelius in his favourite book *Between Fire and Death* by Emanrylii Prehorian. The young king had read it at least a dozen times, but since he liked repetition, he decided to look through the story again and see how the characters behaved at first and at which specific moment the hardships brought them together.

Ilinar shivered with excitement just as he saw the golden letters of the book's title on the expensive leather cover. It was his favourite Prehorian book because the main character, Felis, somehow reminded Ilinar of himself. They were both young, quiet boys who preferred their books to the noisy games and fights their peers engaged in. But still, they both liked to learn about military strategy and to play out imaginary battles with their little toy soldiers. It was like a more elaborate game of chess. Ilinar's gaze slid across the first lines of the book:

> Autumn had come. The bright colours and the pleasant, warm breeze of the dying summer brought a special kind of emotion. The green meadows were now replaced by a colourful carpet of leaves. There was no nostalgia for the scorching days that had passed, for the upcoming ones would be just as enjoyable and carefree. The open windows graced the walls on which hung paintings created by a master of art who had portrayed magnificent landscapes in fiery and golden colours. From dawn till dusk children's voices and laughter did echo. The young boys chased each other and dived into heaps of dry leaves. The girls gathered autumn flowers and twined wreaths made out of them. Autumn was just another adventure to them.

Ilinar sighed. Prehorian had always used such beautiful language and described magnificent scenes that seemed to be too magical to exist in the real world. The young Soleyan kept reading, silently dreaming about somehow meeting this incredible author by way of some unknown magic that would close the gap between the two centuries which lay between them.

On the next page, there was a description of the meeting between Felis and Prince Arelius, who was wild and outrageous at the time just like Eslir. The two families had gathered to discuss their uncertain relationship with the country to the south.

Felis had been acquainted with the members of the royal family, and he had mixed feelings about seeing them again. His reasons for being nervous were mostly confined to the personality of King Vanerius's firstborn son, whose twentieth birthday was soon approaching. Arelius had earned his nickname "the Fiery Disaster" because of his unsurpassed magical abilities and impetuous character. He had caused countless incidents and was somewhat of disgrace in Felis's eyes since he behaved like a foolish demigod child who thought he owned the whole world. One could only imagine that the peaceful Felis found the meetings with his distant cousin agitating. Fortunately, at least Arelius's sister would be there to make it all more bearable. Her name was Eneya. She possessed a lively character that seemed to be a family trait, but she combined it with maturity and wisdom. That made her a person of strong will and rationality, which was rare for a girl of her age. Felis was eager to see her again. There were rumours that the king and the general planned to wed them to each other when they were old enough. The information wasn't official, but Felis was hopeful it was true. Never had he met another girl he'd gotten along with so well. Perhaps that was the reason why Arelius was being unbearable around Felis—he was irritated this would be his sister's husband.

Ilinar wasn't even sure if Eslir was worse than Arelius. On the one hand, he didn't control destructive magic, capable of burning entire cities, but on the other hand he was swinging around his huge army, which could technically do the same thing. Arelius didn't look very serious about destroying stuff anyway.

"Here you are, Felis!" Arelius appeared most suddenly like a rain cloud, overcasting the sun. He was tall. His golden hair hung down to his shoulders. A few stands hung in front of his face as if there had been a heavy wind. A constant flame did burn in his eyes, predicting that the young man was crafting new ways to irritate everyone and begin a cataclysm. "I've been waiting for you all morning. Did you bring me another humorous poem?"

That was a reminder of their previous encounter. Arelius had once found the poems of Felis and had not liked them. He was still ridiculing his cousin to this day.

"Of course, dear friend. Would you like me to read them to you, or are you capable of accomplishing it yourself?" Felis felt obliged to retaliate, still keeping his voice down so he wouldn't offend King Vanerius upon his arrival.

"How unkind. I'm wounded!" Arelius grinned. Agitating a peaceful person such as Felis was so delightful to him.

"Stop it, the both of you! Would you act this way on every occasion?" Eneya appeared like an embodiment of the word *salvation* to remove her irritating brother from sight. She turned to Felis with a warm smile and asked, "Did you enjoy your journey? You must be exhausted."

Ilinar began to laugh. He thought Felis had a very sophisticated and intelligent sense of humour, and he loved to see him collide with savages like Arelius. He would learn from him and try to talk back to Eslir in the same way every time he said something stupid. There, even in such desperate moments, Prehorian's books gave Ilinar the strength and wisdom to cope with his life.

Meanwhile, Arkenel was working on preparing his squad for their trip to Vern. It was a laborious task that took several days. The first hurdle was the fact that he and Mavarius smoked too much and fell asleep in a basement for an entire night. When they finally woke up, they could hardly remember who they were, and they were getting visions of Mortelion. Once they felt better, Arkenel went around town to look for his other friends. Once he found them, he took them to dress them and arm them. Throughout that time some spontaneous fights would start for no reason at all. Rabolii watched what was going on out of the window with a disgruntled look and wondered if it was too late to cancel this mission since he had already given Arkenel the poison for the Vernians. These men seemed so unreliable; maybe he should have given the task to someone else.

Arkenel and his men left Kranium and headed towards the west. Soon they crossed the Skeletal Wall. That was just a natural phenomenon, a special formation of whitish rocks which enclosed part of the Krumerus valley quite nicely, acting like a fortification. And of course, since Rabolii had always been inspired by everything that had to do with death, he had hired construction workers to polish the stones and carve the bone-shaped and skull formations on top. The wall was reliable, but everything that remained beyond it would be vulnerable to Vernian attack.

Mavarius appeared to be as moody as ever. It would seem that was just a part of his character. His abstinence crises were worse than anyone else's for this reason. He was a grim person on his better days, and that combined with a drug deficiency made for a scary combination. Soon people started gazing at him, which made him nervous. He was supposed to lead the group on their search for Vernians, but he wasn't sure if he even wanted to.

Arkenel came up to him and said, "Well, the southwest is covered by forests and mountain ranges. Do you think it would be a good idea for us to pass through there as we'll be easier to spot in the open fields?"

"You think it's gonna be a good idea to drop this dumb plan and go back to Aldur?" Mavarius growled. "The geezer is setting us up."

"He needs corpses after leaving behind thousands in Soleya. He's just trying to make up for his losses." Arkenel shrugged.

"Yeah, right! A whole squad of Vernians, and he needs them whole. He just wanted us to fight them while trying not to hurt them so they would get to kill us. You saw how angry he got when I suggested poison. He hates us and wants us to die," Mavarius continued to protest.

Arkenel sighed and glanced at the other men, who were listening to all of this and seemed a bit confused and worried. It was already hard to control them; he didn't want them to lose their trust in his leadership. He turned to Mavarius and said, "Maybe I know my own father a bit better than you do. How's that? Even if he doesn't care if I live or not, he wouldn't just send me to die for Ravena's sake. Don't be so negative about all of this. If we're useful to him a few times, he'll start trusting us more."

"You're an idiot," stated Mavarius.

"No, just think about it! Regardless of what happened, I'm

still Rabolii's son. And even if we've been in a bad state until recently, now we actually have the chance to be a part of society! We will be an elite squad, not a bunch of nobodies!" Arkenel continued to speak with excitement.

"Not happening. The geezer will kill us off." Mavarius continued to glow with optimism.

"Come on, don't think about it now. Let's get on with our work. And once we return victorious to Krumerus, things will be different. Trust me, Mav. Our situation will be much better soon."

Mavarius groaned with annoyance. He announced, "There's a light wind from the west. We can get going. The Vernians won't catch our scent. We'll pass through the forest; that's where their camp's gonna be. Arkenel and I will sneak up on them to poison them, and the rest of you have to stay further quietly."

Arkenel nodded. They all continued their trip to the west. They had faith in Mavarius to execute the whole plan flawlessly. He was well known for the fact that he'd been raised by Vernians, so everyone figured that no one knew them better than he did. In fact, he had not seen much of Krumerus other than Aldur's dungeons. Arkenel was surprised that his friend had agreed to participate in a mission for exterminating the nation which raised him.

While they were travelling, Rabolii's son began a conversation: "I understand you don't want to be dealing with this, Mav. People like them did bring you up after all."

"It was a long time ago, and it's not the same people," Mavarius growled, his gaze fixed ahead.

"You're not using this mission as an excuse to travel back to Vern and then ditch us once we're there, are you?" Arkenel asked him the worrying question.

"What sort of a dumb-ass question is that?" the man said grimly.

"I want you to know I'm not stopping you. If you want to see your family, or if you don't want to kill Vernians, I won't order you anything different. I just want you to keep me in the loop with what you're up to and not to ... run away or something." Arkenel smiled at him.

Mavarius looked away from his friend and went silent. That statement made him feel like an open book. Sometimes he was annoyed by the fact that Arkenel had suddenly become the master of the prison and behaved as if everyone else was his subordinate. He really was thinking of escaping from him and not having to deal with stupidities and with the almighty "father". But after this conversation he couldn't do anything like that. He didn't know what to answer, so he just continued walking in silence. Speaking wasn't amongst his strengths anyway.

—◆◆◆—

Meanwhile, in Vern, there was trouble and misfortune in the Crystal Castle. For a few weeks now Krementa had not received any letters or news from the man she had sent to spy on Krumerus. She should have received some sort of a bird carrying reports by now. They'd usually use pigeons or ravens—anything really. The Vernians found it easy to make friends with animals; they could even communicate with them. The queen already suspected something bad had happened to her spy. She couldn't get in touch with him. She had no idea that he had fallen victim to Regel and Dregel, who were now waving around his animated skeleton and playing with it. Of course, the nobles weren't happy with this situation at all; they were all mumbling that it was important to have information about the enemy right now when war was under way. Krementa tried to fix the situation by shouting, "Enough of this! I know my agent has delayed his last report, but he's always been trustworthy. He'll probably send letters soon."

Everyone had gathered in one of the vast gardens of the palace. They were sitting on grass-covered benches. The place was overflowing with greenery.

"Regardless, if he's dead or captured, there's not much we can expect," one of the Vernian representatives said. She was a woman wearing a huge, overly decorated dress. It had so many plants on it that she could hardly pass through doorways without damaging the leaves.

"It's a little difficult to find a replacement! I'll send a message across the forest saying that I'm looking for a person who resembles a Krumerian, but I don't know how soon I'll find one."

"That may take months. And Krumerus is currently leading campaigns against us," some other pretentious nobleman said. He had live petunia plants sprouting from the shoulders of his vest to show how much he respected nature and the goddess Vernara. "But on the other hand, your son looks sufficiently enough like a Krumerian to deceive our enemies."

Krementa was shocked. She had never wanted to imagine that her dear Valenis would leave her protection. She immediately screamed, "On the contrary! My son is not at all capable of doing anything like that! He is our prince. We cannot risk his life just like that and throw him into the hands of those monsters!"

"I think it's a great idea," another of the nation's representatives said. She had all sorts of tangled weeds in her braid. "After all, Valenis will be much more capable than any spy. He's smart enough to trick the enemy, and his magic can save him from some other situation from which a normal person wouldn't escape."

"He's the heir to the throne! I will not put him in harm's way!" Krementa continued screaming.

"Perhaps it'll be a good opportunity for him to become a man," spoke the man with the petunias. "Who would want a ruler who has spent his entire life in a tower with his books and who has no practical knowledge of anything? This will help him mature."

Krementa was furious. It was obvious to her that everyone was against her precious son and wanted to throw him like a piece of meat to those insane Krumerians! Being a sorcerer didn't help him that much. His element was earth, and it couldn't protect him against the deadly spells of the Krumerians. He could use it to demolish buildings or throw stones at his enemies, but it wouldn't be as useful as the element of life, for example.

Broken and miserable, Krementa went to Valenis's tower to tell him what the mad nobles had requested of her. As she rushed into his room without knocking, she found him sitting with a book about magic raised to his eye level. What she couldn't see was that inside of it there was a smaller one opened, and that was the one Valenis was actually reading. As soon as he saw his mother so anxious and frustrated, his first reaction was to wonder if he was responsible for something horrible again. He blinked innocently as she sat next to him on his piano and started wailing, "Valenis, my sweet boy. You cannot imagine what the noblemen forced me to do. I didn't want to agree with them, but I don't want to spoil my relations with them and lose the support of all the provinces." Valenis was just looking at her seriously, wondering where this conversation was going and how to close the books so that Krementa wouldn't get to see what he was actually reading. "We believe our spy in Krumerus has died. He has not sent us letters for too long. And since goddess Vernara has given you a ... different look ..."—Valenis clenched his teeth. He didn't want to be reminded of his appearance and that he was grey and ugly, unlike normal people—"they all stated that you would fit amongst the undead and that you could be our spy there."

Valenis was a bit surprised. Oh great, that was the only thing he hadn't heard yet, that he looked like one of the undead! He had not seen a Krumerian in his life apart from the Vernian spy, but the spy was a mixed race. He had heard that Rabolii's people were very ugly and had spots of rotting skin and that worms ate them as they walked. Krementa noticed that he wasn't happy, so she pulled him in an embrace and continued crying.

"I'm extremely unhappy about this too! I told them that as soon as I let you out on your own, something will kill you. If only you could at least use magic well, but that's not the case! The others think you are mature and reasonable. I lie to them every time and tell them that you are, but I know you'll mess everything up."

"Oh, Mother, calm down." Valenis finally moved the books to the side and patted his poor parent on the back. He had never seen her so concerned about him. "I think I should be able to handle something like that."

"This is exactly the problem! You know nothing about Krumerus; you don't know what their lifestyle is like, how to behave. You'll be so obviously different, and they will immediately recognise you as an intruder! You're not reliable enough, but I don't know what to do. Someone needs to keep an eye on those beasts."

"It can't possibly be that difficult. I'm just going to merge with the crowd." Valenis shrugged. "I will listen to the gossip and report."

Krementa rose to her feet, tearful and agitated, and stomped with her foot, saying, "No! I will not allow this! You're not going anywhere! I'll talk again to the nobles. We will think of another way. Concentrate on your studies, and don't distract yourself with nonsense like the piano. Goodbye."

Afterwards she just walked back out. Valenis looked at her grimly. Frankly, that irritated him a bit. Why would he be so unreliable? How hard could it be to spy on the Krumerians? He would probably manage well enough. His mother didn't trust him with anything. He had already become a grown man and had seen nothing but the interior of this castle. Sometimes he felt like he would just die without ever having lived first. He would spend his time alone with the books here, in the tower, and one day his light would just dim and go out. He would see no one else but his mother because she didn't want him to be surrounded by fake friends who'd attempt to use him. The thought of being away from his cosy life was frightening but also somewhat exciting. He would find a whole new world, and he was ready to take risks. So he got up and followed his mother. If he told her in the presence of the nobles that he was accepting the task, Krementa wouldn't have the right to argue. She would probably want to kill him, but he was prepared to withstand such an inconvenience.

Mavarius and Arkenel were making their way through the woods. It was just the two of them. They had left the other Krumerians at camp a bit farther away because if too many of them tried to approach, the Vernians would detect them. The tall man stepped silently like a cat and listened carefully, crouching each time he heard a noise. Arkenel followed him clumsily, looking around, in no way demonstrating that he knew how to sneak. Once again he stepped on some loud branch, which snapped noisily. Mavarius turned to him and scolded him, "You dumb tosser, do you want the whole forest to hear you?! Stop stomping!"

"Hey, I know this is just the way you talk, but you don't have to snap at me for everything," Arkenel replied calmly. He hardly remembered the last time he'd actually had a quarrel with anyone. When he became the leader of groups of uncontrollable, overdosed people, he had acquired the incredible skill of keeping calm whatever he witnessed and no matter how he was spoken to. Shouting back simply didn't help.

"Arkenel, you irritate me so much these days!" Mavarius continued, mumbling. "This is such a dumb plan! That old boar sent us to die. Forget about this. Let's just leave."

"So you don't trust him?" Arkenel asked him calmly.

"Of course I don't trust him!"

"Do you trust me?"

Mavarius just sighed heavily, as if silently admitting his defeat in this dialogue, and muttered, "I'm helping you just 'cause I know you'd do this even if I weren't here. And you'd die like an idiot."

"I appreciate it," Arkenel replied to him sweetly.

They continued to make their way through the woods. They found Vernian troops a lot farther to the west than they had expected. It seemed that the enemy didn't know whether it was safe to stroll around the land of the necromancer, so they had set up camp near the border. And what a camp it was! There were as many objects and tents on the ground as there were in the trees. Strange people with colourful spots on their skin were perched on the branches, overlooking the area as they chattered. Mavarius and Arkenel watched them from behind some rocks. They had been rubbing moss and dry grass on themselves and their clothes so that the crazy Vernians wouldn't smell them from afar. The weather was relatively cool, and that prevented the smells from being carried too far. The two Krumerians scanned the terrain with their eyes, then hid away to further discuss the plan.

"I know there are some caves nearby where water dips through the walls. Perhaps they drink from there," Arkenel whispered when they had found themselves far enough that no one with superhearing could detect them.

"Yes. Seeing how well they've settled down, they've been here for a bit. Got the poison?"

Arkenel felt his pockets. His face darkened, and he cursed, "Dammit, I think I left it in Kranium."

An unfamiliar grimace that the people who knew him knew was a smile appeared on the face of Mavarius. He punched Arkenel's shoulder. Similar jokes were so common that they could no longer deceive each other that they were serious. He reached out to take the bottle from his friend, and that spoiled his mood again. It contained five grams of liquid.

"Is that father of yours deaf or dumb? Did he miss the part where we'll be poisoning a whole water supply, not some castle lady's drink?"

"Perhaps the potion is very potent?" Arkenel shrugged.

"And how do I make sure they drink it? I'll pour it in the water, and it may drain away without killing anyone."

"Dilute it somehow. Come on, Mav, we should at least try." Arkenel put his hand on his friend's shoulder. "We might get lucky."

"Nobody talks about luck here. The question is, will I be able to sneak into their cave, or will they gut me before I get close? At least we've got one thing that's better than what they have—we see in the dark. I can try to sneak in at night."

"I hope we sort this fast," Arkenel said. "Whatever food we brought with us, you ate it, so now I'm not feeling too well."

"I can catch some sort of animal. What can I do? It has come to this. I have to feed you!" Mavarius snapped.

"Thanks, dear!" Arkenel replied with a wide smile, which earned him a slap behind his neck. It would be a miracle if the

Vernians hadn't heard them chuckle and argue just over one hundred metres away from their camp.

When night fell, Mavarius sneaked away quietly to the Vernian camp. He walked around the Vernians and headed straight towards the caves, still careful not to be noticed. Of course he was going alone. Arkenel was hopeless. He would make so much noise that he would wake the dead. He'd been raised in Krumerus after all, and raising the dead was what they did there.

As soon as Mavarius reached the rocks, he knew where he needed to go. There was a muddy path which definitely led to a cave. However, it was guarded by some men who, unfortunately, were awake. It would be difficult for him to slip past them unnoticed. So he decided to include Arkenel in this part of the plan, letting him do what he did best, namely make some noise nearby and then run away. When the guards took that bait, Mavarius slipped inside the cave and sought out the source of the water. He wasn't afraid of stumbling over sleeping people in the dark. If anyone had decided to sleep here, they would have lit a fire or had some other kind of lighting, but it was pitch-black in there.

Soon he found himself in a big hall. All around him was the sound of water dropping. Soon he felt that the floor was wet under his feet. He looked around, and it soon became clear to him where he needed to drop the poison. It was as if Mortelion himself was pointing at the place. It was like a big bowl, naturally formed and protruding from the rocks. The cave's ceiling had a small opening over it, and a few moonlight rays were casting light over the formation. The bowl was filled with water. Judging by the many footsteps left in the mud, it was the place where the Vernians drank. Mavarius opened the bottle and dropped a few drops of the poison into the water. That would do for now. He didn't want to pour it all in all at once because the bowl was slowly overflowing with water, so he didn't want all the poison to end up dripping on the ground.

Feeling proud of a job well done, he headed back to the exit, thinking that his adventures had come to an end. However, he hadn't guessed right. Seeing the crossed spears outlined at the opening of the cave, he realised that the guards had come back, and now there was no way for him to get out without being noticed. He was trapped.

"And if we put a little pollen from Night violet, we get a very good powder that will dull the skin colour, so we could send any of our people to spy on the Krumerians." Krementa was speaking before the nobles and making various flowers grow on the table. She picked them to demonstrate how to make this revolutionary make-up recipe.

"That would be helpful, but our eyes are also different from those of the Krumerians. What kind of pollen can fix that?" asked some dandy with such a splendid flower bed on his head that he was gathering bees.

"Our agent can wear a hood so his eyes can't be seen." Krementa spread her hands as if what she'd just said were obvious.

"By this logic, we can just cover someone from top to bottom with clothes so they don't even need make-up," answered another representative with annoyance.

"I don't see why not."

Everyone started arguing again. It seemed like they'd talk about nothing more until this was resolved. The argument would possibly last a very long time, but Valenis appeared suddenly to resolve it. As soon as he stepped into the enclosed garden, everyone looked at him. Usually he'd attract attention because he didn't have enough living plants in his clothes and in his hair. He had tried to include some in his outfit, but they always dried out and died. People would say that happened because the goddess Vernara despised him. However, right now the pompous nobles were glad to see him, hoping he would end this dispute. Well, that was the case.

Krementa stared at her son and shouted, "Valenis, did I not give you books to read?! You are not progressing with learning magic as fast as I did when I was your age, and I'm disappointed. Go back to your room; here we talk about important things."

"Mother, I was thinking about the ... problem with Krumerus and the spying." Valenis gathered all his courage and offered, "I think it would be a good idea for me to do it."

This caused a great many cries and screams. Each of the attendees loudly expressed agreement with Valenis several times. Krementa climbed on the table so they could see her better while she was screaming at everybody like a madwoman without pronouncing any specific words. Valenis blinked in fright and stepped back. He sensed that he wouldn't go to Krumerus now for sure, because his mother would kill him as soon as she finished screaming. He decided to fortify himself in his room and wait for the storm to pass.

The next few days, right before leaving, Valenis did feel a lot of strain. Krementa was in such a mood that she would either be screaming that he'd done something stupid or be hugging him and bathing him in her tears because she loved him so much. In a fit of the latter, she ambushed him in his room, sitting down beside him as he prepared his luggage. She began touching him with wet hands, sobbing, "I wish you all the best on the way, my dear. I hope everything will go well and that you will be coming back soon. I will miss you very much."

"Mom, I don't want you to worry about me." Valenis felt guilty about leaving the poor woman in such a vulnerable state. He hugged her, hoping she'd calm down.

"How can I not worry? You've never left my sight your whole life!" she exclaimed, squeezing his hands. "My baby, you're the only precious thing in my life, and if there was any other choice, I wouldn't let you go. I want you to be in constant contact with me. Do you know what this is?" She opened her hand and revealed a platinum amulet with a clouded stone deeply glowing. "It's a rare necklace that allows sorceresses of the earth element to communicate with each other. I have one just like it. This is for you. I want you to speak to me every day so I know you're OK! If you feel that I'm calling you, answer immediately. I may have received omens of danger from the goddess Vernara."

"Oh, thank you, Mom." He had thought that if he could escape a hundred kilometres from here, he could at least get a break from Krementa, but that didn't seem to be the case.

She continued to hover around him all the way up to his departure. She checked him a thousand times to see if he had everything he needed, deciding on what he was going to wear and so on. They'd found him some tatty black clothes that sort of looked like a normal Krumerian outfit. The colour black was their favourite because it helped the population blend in with the darkness. All the time before his departure seemed to last forever. Valenis couldn't believe that one day he would be done with all the preparations and farewells. The whole of Vern had gathered to bless him and wish him luck. They followed him to the edge of the forest. All the while Krementa was crying as if she were at his funeral. He would have wanted this whole thing to happen more quietly and with less publicity.

At last it was over. When he stepped outside to the open

field, he was alone. Everyone he'd ever known was now behind him. The landscape was so different here; the mountains to the east rose high and ominous. Valenis took a deep breath and walked forward. Yes, it would be dangerous, but despite the danger, he was very eager to experience something different than the inside of his room.

Rabolii was digging through a cupboard in his room. He was trying to find some old notes he had buried there somewhere. He was inside the drawer halfway to his waist and was likely to dig his way out to the other side of the world and drop somewhere in Mortelion's domain. It was then that his fingers felt something he couldn't recognise. He pulled it out to check what it was. He knew all his belongings and remembered where each one was. Well, it turned out to be a family portrait. A drunken artist had tried to draw him, Ravena, and her parents soon after they'd met. It was a terribly annoying experience.

Her parents were nobles who had managed to stay out of the civil war, which they didn't approve of. That's why they were shocked to see their daughter hand in hand with the usurper necromancer who'd taken the throne from the Snake King. Ravena had put her foot down and declared that he was a wonderful man, saying that they wanted to be together. Rabolii snorted while looking at the skinny faces of her parents in the portrait. Even the drunken artist had been able to depict their pouting. He remembered how he'd found himself obliged to stay in the home of those horrible people while the portrait was drawn.

"So, Master Remedor, how old did you say you were?" the prospective father-in-law had said, turning to him.

"My age is insignificant in comparison to the immeasurability of cosmic infinity," Rabolii had mumbled. At that time his skin was much smoother, and his hair was still black with just a few stray grey hairs.

Ravena grasped his hand and turned to her father. "Dad, that's not important. He is a very successful man. I think he will be a great king. He is blessed by Mortelion himself!"

"My dear, are you sure he is the kind of man who will take care of you, instead of just going out to war?" the mother-in-law whimpered as if Rabolii wasn't present.

"Stop it, Mother. I don't care if you like Rab or not. We love each other, so we're going to live in Kranium together," Ravena had said with a tone which suggested she wouldn't accept any objections.

That statement had dropped like a bomb in the dank manor of the unfortunate people. They had begun to yell and protest, threatening and bargaining, but no one could contradict the new ruler of Krumerus. Ravena's parents were against all this, but they couldn't enforce their opinion. Ravena really had been a piece of work back then. She was just like those silly young women who think they knew everything, and she would jump head first into unwise relationships, which would end with more tears than at a funeral. Anything associated with Rabolii felt like a funeral anyway.

Well, Ravena never really regretted her choice because Rabolii had been such a caring and loving husband. He didn't allow his in-laws the pleasure of smack their daughter with an "I told you so." The problems in the marriage began only after Rabolii died.

The necromancer chuckled and put the portrait back into the cabinet as someone knocked on his door. Oh, who dared to disturb him again! It was nice that at least Arkenel and his drunk friends had left, so they wouldn't cause him headaches, but Ravena was probably coming in to annoy him in all possible ways.

"What do you want? I'm busy!" he barked. The vampires on the ceiling were disturbed and started shifting.

"Father, it's me. I was wondering if we could talk," Salina's voice came from the other side of the door.

Gods, what was her problem now? Rabolii groaned deeply, stepped out of the drawer, sat in the chair behind the desk, and shouted, "Oh, fine. Come in."

The heavy door opened with a dull squeak, and the younger daughter of the necromancer stepped into the room. She looked excited in some strange way; she had a blush to her face. Rabolii hated happy people. They were too unpredictable. He raised his head majestically to be more impressive and urged her, "So what do you want to talk to me about?"

"Father, I was just thinking. I'm already twenty-four. I'm not a little girl any more, and most of my friends are ... married."

At that moment, Rabolii's eyebrows raised up and struck his hairline. Oh no, that's what this was about! He didn't want to deal with anything such as this. He yelled, "Salina, this is outrageous! You know perfectly well that you will marry when I decide! And this will happen once I find you a good partner and see that you get along well with him! I'm not going to proclaim that I'm looking for a suitor for you, because that will attract untrustworthy liars who only want you because of your wealth!"

Every trace of cheerfulness vanished from the face of the girl. She had suspected that Rabolii wouldn't burst with joy when she spoke to him, but she had not expected such a harsh reaction. She tried to argue: "But, Father ..."

"No buts! You know I want the best for my daughters," barked the necromancer. "When I find someone worthy of you, I will let you marry, but in the meantime I don't want to hear more about it. You are distracting me from my work. Leave!"

Salina departed with defeat as Rabolii stared at her majestically. In fact, he couldn't imagine a man who would deserve Salina. Even if Malior were alive and wasn't wed to Traneya, he wouldn't be good enough. He could be too insensitive to women at times, and that would be a problem for Rabolii's young daughter. She needed someone caring, classy, and intelligent, and above all the man she married would need to be a sorcerer so they'd have powerful children. She needed someone like Rabolii himself. However, he was a miracle, something which nature created only once. And that being the case, he would prefer to keep his daughter forever instead of giving her to a fool who wouldn't be able to develop her skills with magic and would ruin them.

Somewhere far to the west, Arkenel was sitting in some shrubbery, wondering where Mavarius was. The sun had risen high in the sky and was shining dazzlingly. The Krumerians usually slept during the day because the light was irritating, but the young Remedor couldn't close his eyes. He was nervous. He began to dig in his rucksack with trembling hands and a dry mouth. He began rolling a blunt filled with the miner's spice. This plant had been named that because in Aldur the guards would put it in the prisoners' food. It gave them a burst of energy which allowed them to work in the mine much more efficiently.

Arkenel had eaten and smoked the miner's for seven years and was desperately addicted to it. If he were to spend half a day without it, he would become extremely irritable, nervous, and paranoid. Sometimes he'd even see things. For these reasons, he would always make sure he smoked it regularly just to feel sort of normal. The maniacal fits of laughter and excitement had become a part of his personality; he couldn't imagine his life any other way. His mind was seldom clear, and his consciousness was loud.

Arkenel inhaled the smoke from the cigarette eagerly, feeling rejuvenated already. The trembling of his hands stopped, and he closed his eyes to rest them from the bright sunlight. He felt like he was finally ready to sleep and was contemplating if he should do that or maybe look for Mavarius. Ultimately he'd get to do neither.

"Don't move, you wretched creature!" a voice sounded unexpectedly close to Arkenel.

The young Remedor exhaled a cloud of smoke and slowly turned towards the source of the voice. From the brush beside him peeked out Vernian women with long, sharp spears pointed at him. The women looked very unusual. Their skin was tinted with pink, lilac, and even bluish shades. They seemed to be shimmering. Some of them were spotted with different colours. Their hair was two-coloured with various flowers entangled in it. Arkenel smiled at them as if he'd been very pleasantly surprised by them. He wasn't scared. He was accustomed to seeing all the deformed and ugly faces in Aldur, which made these colourful women seem like a pleasant dream.

"Good afternoon, ladies," he greeted them casually, not bothering to stand up. "Am I arrested?"

The Vernians exchanged glances as if they were asking each other how to interpret such calm behaviour. One with lilac skin and black hair coloured at the edges stepped forward. She stated in a serious tone, "He must be a Krumerian spy who has come to monitor us. Bind him. I want to interrogate him."

Three different sexual jokes occurred to Arkenel after he had heard this statement, so he got confused and didn't know which one to say. The Vernians surrounded him and wrapped liana ropes around his wrists. He continued to grin as he let them take him away. He knew they wouldn't keep him as a hostage for long. He was sorry that he had been given the task of poisoning such fairies. Rabolii was horrible for giving him such a job.

"You will answer all my questions," said the purple woman seriously.

"Arkenel, at your service." He stretched out one of his tied-up hands, offering it to her.

The Vernian pulled a knife from her belt with a lightning-fast motion, touched the tip of the blade to Arkenel's neck, and snapped at him, "Listen to me, abomination! You may think us a joke! However, just because we're not demons or undead monsters doesn't make us any less dangerous, especially when you are tied up in our camp. Nothing pleasant will happen to you! You'll be tortured for information, and when I squeeze everything out of you, I'll lay you in the ground."

"What is your name, babe?" Arkenel asked.

The Vernian slapped him across the face because she felt disrespected. This didn't erase Arkenel's cheeky smile. He was still having a lot of fun with this situation. He had always wanted to see the Vernians, but Rabolii had watched him like a hawk to make sure his son didn't leave the country and didn't ruin his political relationships with anyone.

"Do you really think he is a spy, General Evena?" one of the women asked.

"Of course he is," said the purple woman. "I'm going to make him feel sorry for setting foot near our camp."

Meanwhile Mavarius had stuffed himself in the most secretive hole in the cave. He would even stop breathing whenever Vernians came in to collect water. When were these people going to die?

Chapter 5

AMONGST THE RUINS

Arkenel was pushed into General Evena's tent, which fortunately happened to be situated on the ground. Otherwise they probably would not have managed to get their prisoner to climb up one of the trees, especially since he was tied up.

"Can you manage to deal with this creature on your own, General? Should we stay with you in case it uses evil spells?" asked one of the Vernian women.

"No need. I can handle the situation," Evena replied, watching Arkenel with her yellow-green eyes like those of a predator. After the other women went out, she began to walk around the bound captive and talk: "So! I expect you to tell me what manner of beast you are and why you were snooping around our camp."

Arkenel's brain was overwhelmed by too much smoking, so he felt free and calm as if he were with an old friend. He kept acting casually and simply gave the answer which he thought would probably not result in his execution.

"Your camp is in Krumerus, is it not? Why are you surprised that you came across a Krumerian?"

"Your kind avoids us. What made you decide to approach?" Evena hissed.

"I wanted to see you guys!" Arkenel stretched a sweet, dizzy smile. "I've heard so much about the mysterious Vernians in the forests, about your way of life and your customs."

That wasn't a lie. In the days when Mavarius felt talkative, he had shared a sentence or two about how he lived in Vern. Evena stopped striding around, turned to Arkenel, and decided to test that story. She said to him, "Excuses! Anybody could lie about that. What exactly did you hear about us that sparked your interest?"

"A friend of mine lived in Vern," said Arkenel. "He told me that the people here look very different and that some of you even have feathers."

As a matter of fact, knowledge of the feathered people wasn't so well-spread. Evena thought about what to do with this unusual captive. She asked again, "What are you? You can't be just a normal person."

Arkenel reached out to her with one of his tied hands and said, "I'm not an undead, if that's what you're asking. You can check; I do have a pulse. You will notice that it is the same as yours. Perhaps the only difference between us is that I don't have your beautiful skin."

Evena felt his wrist with her fingers to make sure he wasn't an animated corpse. Then she raised her yellowish eyes towards Arkenel and asked, "So you think I'm beautiful?"

She couldn't remember if anyone else had dared to continue flirting with her after so many slaps. Arkenel seemed so unperturbed that it began to entertain her. He slid his finger over the skin on her shoulder, feeling some fine pappus. He smiled, thinking about how unusual this encounter was, and said, "I may have only one eye, but it works perfectly, and I am very grateful about that right now."

If Arkenel knew anything about the Vernians, it was that they were quite straightforward, physical people. He'd often be surprised by how unsubtle and blunt Mavarius was.

Evena smirked, grabbed Arkenel, and pressed him against the wall of the tent. She told him, "Hmm, I think you just want to seduce me so I'll set you free."

"Well, to be fair, I don't wanna be free right now." He grinned at her.

The Vernian seemed to think that this was enough talk, so she grabbed his collar and began kissing him roughly, undressing him without bothering to untie his hands. Maybe she liked him better that way. Arkenel kissed back without any hesitation. He hadn't even touched a woman since Aldur, so all of this was really thrilling to him.

The two of them spent several hours in the tent, performing various activities. After they had fed their passion, they talked a bit about life in Vern, the animals there, and so on. The two of them were so different from each other, as if they'd come from separate worlds. They had countless incredible stories.

Evena had been taught to hate the beasts of Mortelion, but this particular one appealed to her. It was like a strange, wild creature. She wanted to tame it and take care of it. She was just imagining how she would take Arkenel to Vern and begin to teach him to hunt when a voice came from outside, saying, "General Evena, how are you? We bring you fresh water."

"Thanks a lot. Come in!"

A Vernian woman slipped into the tent to find Evena and Arkenel barely clothed, lying on top of some wolf pelts. The woman looked confused, not commenting on all this, and handed Evena a large jug of water. Remedor looked around, realising that the poison was in that jug. He moved his gaze from one Vernian to the other, feeling a crushing sense of guilt. He had killed people before—it was a mundane thing in prison—but this felt different.

"Thanks. I needed that," Evena said, taking the jug of water.

"Another thing. Perhaps you'll want to examine the sick people. They say the pain in their abdomens has increased," added the Vernian.

Yes, that was also the poison's fault. Arkenel was instructed that the Vernians would die a slow death, so he'd get the chance to inject them with the potion against decay while they were still alive but weakened. The potion needed to spread all throughout their bodies in order to be effective, and that was unachievable without a pulse.

"Yes, I'll check on them," said Evena. "They probably caught some Krumerian disease."

Having said that, she raised the jug to drink from it. At that moment, without even thinking, Arkenel spontaneously knocked the jug out of the woman's hands. It fell in their laps, spilling on their bodies and the wolf pelts. Evena looked at Remedor with surprise and shouted, "Have demons eaten your brain? What did you do that for?"

Arkenel opened and closed his mouth several times, wondering whether to say that a flea from the pelts had bitten him, causing him to jump; whether to drop a statement that he likes wet women; or whether to just admit that demons had eaten his brain. He didn't need to reply, however, because the other Vernian woman who had brought the jug wriggled painfully and fell to her knees. Evena rushed to her aid, when some painful screaming was heard outside.

The general ran out to see why suddenly everyone in her camp was in agony. Arkenel felt that the game was over and that his real reason of being here was uncovered. He began pulling his trousers up and looking around for his boots. He had barely managed to dress when Evena returned, deadly and terrifying. She grabbed him by the collar and yelled, "Can you tell me what on earth is going on with all my soldiers?! We've been here for two weeks now, and as soon as you appeared, all of this starts happening."

Without realising it himself, Arkenel glanced at the spilled jug. Evena noticed this. She pulled out a knife, pressed the blade to the Krumerian's neck, and continued yelling: "You put something in the water, didn't you? Explain what you have done *immediately*!"

Arkenel continued to feel overwhelmed by all of this; he expected to get killed. At that moment, to his surprise, someone slammed the back of Evena's head, which caused her to collapse. Behind her stood Mavarius, holding a thick wooden rod. He approached Arkenel and began to examine him for any new injuries he didn't already have from prison. He mumbled, "Um, what happened? Why are you in here?"

"They found me and brought me in," Arkenel replied, feeling shaken by everything that had happened to him.

Mavarius cut off his ropes and said, "Yeah, it's all right. You're fine. Let's call the other idiots."

Arkenel nodded stiffly. Both of them returned to the camp where they had left their companions. Together they brought in the wagons into which they'd had to load the Vernians after injecting them with the Never Rot potion. Remedor, trying to control his drugged subordinates, explained to them, "The Vernians should still be alive. Once you inject one of them with the potion, load her on the wagon so we'll know she's processed, and..."

However, the men weren't interested in what Arkenel had to say. They started walking around and looking at the agonised women with utmost interest.

"Look at that! You think she's purple everywhere?" one of them said with amazement.

"This one's hot. Just look!" another voice sounded.

Arkenel saw that everyone was getting too distracted and tried to establish some order. "Hey! We're just injecting them with a potion, OK? Leave them as they are. Rabolii wants them intact."

"Beat it!" One of the former prisoners pushed him roughly, throwing him back a few metres into and Aveus's grasp.

"Do you now understand how I felt when I was trying to stop you all whenever you were doing something stupid?" Aveus asked as he stood next to Arkenel.

"They're scum. What do you expect?" Mavarius sighed as he pulled out various syringes from the bags in the carts. "Haven't seen women in years."

"We found a naked one!" a voice came from farther inside the camp.

Arkenel stood up and tried to go and stop what he believed was happening, but Aveus put a hand on his shoulder and told him, "Don't start fights over dead women."

Arkenel was feeling more and more upset by the minute. He mumbled, "We shouldn't have done this. This was too much. I should just stick to killing tossers."

"Just 'cause they're women don't mean they ain't tossers." Mavarius shone this divine wisdom upon Arkenel as the former was starting to pull bodies onto the carriage and inject them with the Never Rot potion.

This didn't help Arkenel too much. He felt uneasy about what had happened. He mumbled, "But we sat together for so long. She told me all those stories about the animals in Vern."

"You never gave a damn about the animals in Vern," Mavarius noted. "Just pick a syringe, will you? We're doing this for Daddy, remember?"

Arkenel sighed and got down to work. Maybe he'd need to keep doing things he disliked until he was in some position of power himself. He wondered how it was so easy for Mavarius to do something like this given that the Vernians literally raised him.

Darkness was descending when Arkenel's mates finally calmed down. By then the Vernians had been injected with the potion. Most of them had passed away. Some were still twitching in mortal spasms. The young Remedor felt unhappy after all this, so he decided to fight his emotional trauma by rolling a thick blunt with trembling hands. He'd stop caring if he was drugged.

"Hey, tossers, don't forget to cover the wagons with sheets after you load them! Rabolii ordered us to bring them covered up in Kranium," Arkenel shouted at the men as he was rolling his cigarette.

"Yeah, right. 'Cause Kranium will be shocked to see corpses," muttered Mavarius as he loaded the last body onto the wagon.

"Who knows, maybe someone will fight us for them in the

wilderness and try to steal them." Arkenel shrugged. It wasn't uncommon for someone to try to steal a corpse in Krumerus. Once its meat was burned off, it was hard to tell who the deceased was. Of course, Rabolii could make a mental connection with the corpse and ask if it had been stolen, but often he had a headache and didn't hassle himself, so he would reanimate the body for whomever paid him without asking questions.

"Am I the only one who wonders why Rabolii needs all this crap?" mumbled Mavarius.

"Oh, I don't know, maybe because we lost ten thousand corpses at Lumis?" Arkenel said. He inhaled deeply from his blunt.

"There must be a better way to get corpses," replied Mavarius. "This was all so dumb."

"Take this. You'll feel better," Arkenel told him, handing him a bottle of strong alcohol.

After an unnecessary amount of time, the Krumerians finally set off on their way back to Kranium. They were drunk and drugged, so they could barely walk in a straight line and moved incredibly slowly. Various noisy songs and screams echoed in the night. While all this was happening, Arkenel was sleeping peacefully in one of the wagons. After all, he had been up all day, and that was a rare occurrence in his world. His bliss didn't last for too long, however, because Mavarius began poking him in the ribs. He looked like a hunting dog that had sniffed some game. He hissed, "Look over there by the horizon. Is that fire?"

"This is very strange. Do you think someone has set a camp in the middle of the field?" Arkenel replied, stretching lazily.

"Whatever. If there's something dumb over there, I'll gut it," said Mavarius, unwilling to spend too much time on this. He was very distrustful and was ready to fight everything.

The squad approached the fire quietly, and soon a small camp with a sleeping man revealed itself before them. Mavarius stared at the stranger viciously and hissed, "Man, let's see if he's got coin."

"Chill out. Once we go back to Kranium, we can get anything we need from my father. We don't have to rob people in the field," Arkenel whispered.

"Sod off with your father. I don't want him giving me a goddamn thing," Mavarius replied.

"Let's at least wake this guy and check if he's a tosser. If he is, we can rob him." Arkenel came to an agreement.

The men ran out of their hiding spot and approached the

stranger. He was sleeping so deeply that he didn't feel any danger until the very moment someone started shaking him. Then he got startled and woke up. He was faced with dozens of monstrous men with hideous facial scars and black matted hair. Their vicious eyes reflected the moonlight just like the pupil of a cat.

"Who do you think you are lighting a fire, huh?" Mavarius greeted him. "And are you stupid for sleeping at night?"

The suspicious man with the fire was Valenis. He had travelled through the open field without ever thinking that he might get into trouble. Now some terrifying people had gathered around him. He opened his mouth uncertainly and replied, "I ... wandered around after the Vernians demolished my village. I didn't know where to go. I'm exhausted as I have been on the move for so long."

"He's such a princess." One of the escaped prisoners grinned, stepping dangerously close to Valenis. "He smells of a forest bouquet!"

"Look at his girly ponytain! Wanna bet I can knock him out with a single punch?" another one added.

Arkenel crossed his arms. He would try to save this innocent man from a pointless beating, so he took control over the conversation. He asked, "How long ago was that? You look too tidy for someone who has survived a raid."

Valenis realised that perhaps this was their leader, so he decided to address him. He said, "I ... I didn't get involved in a battle. I just tried to get away. It was horrifying."

"So, what, you left your brothers to fight while you ran off into the wilderness?" Arkenel raised his eyebrows. If he had found a whole group of refugees camping in the field, he would have believed such a story, but since it was just one man from a whole village, it was a bit suspicious.

"I don't have any family." Valenis forced a painful expression on his face. "I'm an orphan. I had only one grandmother, who didn't want to leave the house when I told her we were in danger."

"I see. And where are you off to now?"

Valenis shrugged, wondering how to look more innocent. He said hesitantly, "I was hoping to find refuge somewhere behind the Skeletal Wall. There I could start a new life and save myself from the Vernians."

"Travel with us if you want." Arkenel shrugged. "It will weigh heavy on my conscience if I let you set fires in the wilderness and attract bandits who'll kill you."

"Thank you very much for your kindness." Valenis felt the need to tell them something nice, but that just made the men snicker because they thought he was speaking like some dandy. He didn't understand what he had done to deserve such a reaction, so he decided to add, "Um ... where are you going?"

"Well, we'll go beyond the Skeletal Wall. We are on our way to Kranium," said Arkenel.

Mavarius groaned and pulled his friend away while fussing, "For God's sake, why don't you tell him your life story! He's dodgy. Just let me gut him."

"He's a Krumerian citizen seeking shelter, Mavarius," Arkenel replied with the sort of tone expected of a young prince.

"You don't know what he is." Mavarius crossed his arms and glared at Valenis.

"It's fine. Let's get back on the road." Arkenel waved his hand.

Valenis looked at the wagons behind the Krumerians. They were covered with sheets, but he could still see an arm or a leg hanging out, so he realised what was inside. He was sickened by this and felt burning hatred for these terrible, ugly men who were massacring his people. However, he knew he couldn't afford to appear suspicious by showing emotion. He knew that the Krumerians were always surrounded by corpses, and if he reacted somehow, it would become clear he wasn't from around there. He smiled politely and said, "Of course."

Mavarius kept leering at him. He was suspicious. In his eyes Valenis resembled some young aristocrat. He was way too clean; his hair was smooth and shiny. His story wasn't really convincing, but whatever the truth was, maybe he wasn't a threat anyway. Maybe he was lying to avoid getting robbed.

Rabolii was brewing potions with a grim face, but he was calm and happy on the inside for being able to do his own thing undisturbed. But that wouldn't last for long. Someone knocked on his door. He raised his head, his eyebrows cocked to the middle of his forehead, and barked, "Who are you, and what do you want?!"

"Dad, we have problems at the border!" said a voice from the other side. "Can I come in?"

The necromancer sighed with infinite annoyance. These people didn't want to leave him in peace.

"Fine, come in!"

Traneya entered the room. The necromancer once again felt anger when he saw her. He was under the impression that she had gotten all those tattoos to make the statement that he didn't control her life. Rabolii crossed his bony fingers in front of his face and urged her, "Speak. Which border am I to deal with this time?"

The truth was that he didn't wish to deal with anything; he just wanted to quickly figure out what the problem was so he could send Ravena to deal with it. Traneya said to him, "It seems the south has decided to attack. An army is marching through the western pass. They are headed this way."

"Is that so? Do you think they will attack Kranium? When will they be here?" he asked coldly. He didn't seem at all worried that his city could fall under siege.

"In two or three days, perhaps?" Traneya shrugged. "According to our scouts, the army contains about eight thousand men; their armour seems to be Aslanian."

"That's so interesting. I'm ready to bet that it's led by the blond fool who fought me in Soleya when I went to free Ravena."

"Fool or not, he has enough soldiers to be a problem," Traneya said gloomily. "We have so few skeletons here; the people are still protesting that we didn't return the ones we took. What forces do we use to defend the capital?"

"I don't intend to let it go that far," the necromancer answered mysteriously, a dangerous spark flashing in his grey eyes. "Traneya, how capable are you of sneaking in the Aslanian encampment and slaying that petty fool?"

The woman raised her eyebrows as if she couldn't believe she'd been given such a task. She said, "Wow, how desperate you must be."

"If we get rid of their leader, they won't dare to attack. I don't want them in front of my gates. Do whatever needs to be done so we don't get attacked."

Traneya shook her head and said, "I really don't know if I can."

"Why not? Ever since you were young, you have constantly gotten on my nerves with how you want to be a fighter. I paid the most exotic teachers in this country to make you an elite killer. Why did I waste so many resources if you aren't even going to use your talents? I would find someone else to do the job if time wasn't pressing me, since I can see you don't desire to be useful."

Traneya was sickened as she realised that her father knew hardly anything about her. She gritted her teeth. "Arkenel is the elite assassin-type killer. He's crazy about daggers and stealth and whatnot, though I always told him that was girly. I'm trained to use a two-handed sword. My brother would be much better suited to assassinate someone. Perhaps he'll return before the Aslanians do."

"I'm monitoring him with a raven. I don't think he'll be back in time." Rabolii dismissed that proposal. "I have no one better than you at the moment. I'll give you all the poisons and weapons you might need. Just do what I told you."

Traneya didn't seem to like that idea. "Kill the king! Just like that!" She preferred fighting at the front line; playing assassin and sneaking around was just not like her. She knew it was just a job for Arkenel, who was very good at striking at the right time without even getting in a fight in order to kill someone.

Traneya went out. The necromancer just followed her with his gaze, then he turned his cold eyes away from his potion onto the scribbles on his desk. He was looking at a very special map. It resembled the continent, but very few of the cities were labelled. The borders were vaguely outlined. Instead, there was a large number of complicated drawings and mathematical formulas scattered with different densities on the paper. There was a cluster around East Krumerus, and near there Rabolii had drawn a large red circle. It seemed important, but it was just another super-secret thing. Only he knew what it was about.

The sun was high in the sky, illuminating East Krumerus. Arkenel's pals were all sleeping. The men were almost as motionless as the corpses. This morning they had gotten mighty drunk in a nearby town and had become so loud and crazy that they were chased out into the field. Valenis sat next to one of the wagons, playing with the platinum amulet. He was thinking that maybe he shouldn't mention to his mother that the Krumerians had found him in the field. She would lose her mind. But maybe he did have to tell her about the dead Vernians Arkenel was carrying away.

Valenis was deep in thoughts, so a sudden movement from the wagons startled him. Something was fidgeting in there, sobbing and squealing, getting louder by the second. The prince rose quickly and went to remove the sheet which covered the cart. He was surprised to see that one of the women was alive. She looked confused. Then she noticed she was naked and that some strange grey man was watching her. She started making some miserable attempts to escape from him. Valenis raised his hand and tried to shush her. "No, no, don't scream. They're sleeping now. I am a friend. I am from Vern."

The surviving woman was Evena. She tried to remember what had happened to her. She could remember Arkenel. She remembered that everyone in the camp had begun to agonise in pain and that eventually someone had hit her on the head. Confused, she shrunk into the carriage and muttered, "Where am I? What has happened? Are those my soldiers?"

Mavarius, who was accustomed to being always alert in case some tossers came, began to fidget in his sleep. Valenis looked up worriedly and said, "You're in danger here. You have to get out. Vern lies to the west, in that direction," he said, pointing. "Your soldiers are all dead."

After saying this, he handed her his cloak so she could cover herself. Evena took it with shaking hands. She was still dizzy and didn't understand what was going on. Valenis helped her out of the wagon. The woman gazed upon her surroundings. In the meadow at least fifty Krumerians slept, and there were three wagons with dead Vernians.

Evena fled to the west, noticing that her body hurt and it was difficult to walk. She began to realise what had happened. Arkenel wasn't the only enemy around their camp. There were others, and they had poisoned the water. She didn't know why he had stopped her from drinking it. Maybe he wanted to keep her alive both to interrogate her and for whatever other uses he had for her. However, she didn't remember how she'd become completely naked. She realised that the poison had worked on everyone else—they had been killed—and while she was unconscious, the Krumerians had stripped her and had their way with her. She detected a foreign scent on her skin and felt pain from their rough touch. These thoughts enraged her to the core of her soul. She was furious by the thought that she could have killed Arkenel so easily when she caught him. Instead, she had believed his lies and had allowed him into her bed so that he could seduce her and then throw her unconscious body to his soldiers. She was angry with herself for being so gullible, but she was a lot more furious with him. She thought him a liar and a monster. Only the thought of forcing a blade between his ribs brought her some satisfaction.

Eslir was cheerful and happy, as if he wasn't on a dangerous march but rather on a walk in the woods. He had taken Estrella with him because of her gifts of life magic. She wasn't pleased with this at all. She didn't have the option to refuse Eslir. She was pouting with a grim expression as she watched the jagged peaks of the Krumerian mountains come closer. From the north, she felt a deathly chilling breeze and noticed that it carried a rotten stench. The landscape changed by the hour. The ground blackened and clouds clustered in the sky as the white hands of the dense fog choked the passengers.

"When will we stop for a break?" she murmured.

"It's still daytime," said Eslir, who was boasting on his gleaming horse and was shining like the sun itself.

"How can you tell? All I see are clouds in the sky. The sunset could have been two hours ago. Maybe we didn't even notice," she continued to protest.

Eslir turned to her to see why she was angry. It was sort of cute to him, especially since he had the power to please her and show her what a great man he was. He turned back to his troops and waved his arms. "All right, men, we'll stop here for the night." Then he turned to Estrella with a cheeky smile and said, "Madam, may I assist you with your luggage? If it's too much to unload, you can spend the night with me."

She was angry with him, so she snapped, "I'll unload my luggage myself, thank you very much. Servants! Set my tent! A little farther that way if you will!"

Estrella started setting her tent as far away from Eslir as possible as he stood there looking confused like a pigeon which had had its bread chunk stolen from right under its beak. He tried to figure out what had disturbed her inner world and why she was angry, but he couldn't think of anything, so he just shrugged and went to talk to his generals and look at some thirty-year-old Kranium maps.

No one even suspected that at that very moment Traneya was sneaking through the camp. She watched the people as if they were prey. She would wait for a few more hours for the darkness to fall and would use her advantage of seeing in the dark. For now, she just watched the Aslanians and paid attention to where the guards were, planning her path into the camp.

It was strange to her that she was doing a task for Rabolii. Maybe it was the first one in many years. It was no secret that she didn't like the necromancer and disagreed with almost everything he did. She was dismayed every time she'd notice how Ravena and Salina were breaking their backs to please him. They both suffered so much for him, and he still treated them like belongings which only existed to serve him. Traneya didn't perceive him as a father but as a monster controlling the lives of everyone. For these reasons she rarely talked to him and tried to avoid him. The necromancer treated her in the same way, so they had somehow found a way to coexist.

The darkness descended like a dome upon the Aslanian camp. The flames flickered in the night, casting a dim light on the tents and the people moving between them. In spite of the darkness, Traneya could see just fine. She wrapped herself in her cloak, merging with the night. It was called Nightwind and it wasn't made of just any cloth. It was enchanted with the energy of darkness, so in dim light its owner was almost invisible. Moving like a shadow, Traneya slipped into the Aslanian camp. She searched for the king's tent. She wasn't very well oriented but assumed she had found the right place. It was surrounded by guards; they encircled the tent. There was no way to get in there. The necromancer's daughter remained hidden in the shadows, waiting for someone to move so she could get some opening to strike. The hours passed. They were long and tiring, but nothing changed.

"Can you check if Estrella is asleep?" Eslir popped his head out to talk to his guards.

"Sir, it's 1 a.m.," one of the soldiers said.

Traneya began digging in her pockets with trembling hands to find something to throw at Eslir. She felt the small bag with the blades, pulled one out, and threw it clumsily. It hit somewhere near the entrance to the tent without hurting anyone. The Aslanians didn't notice.

"Yes, whatever. Go wake her up. Tell her I have champagne," Eslir answered in a cocky tone.

Traneya prepared another blade, but before she got a chance to throw it, Eslir went back in the tent. One of the guards asked, "Where is this Estrella?"

His buddies pointed at another tent, and he went to search for the sorceress. Traneya thought that the name Estrella rang some bells. Ravena had mentioned her when she spoke about the time she'd gotten captured. It was becoming clear that Traneya wouldn't be able to kill Eslir, but if she eliminated a key sorceress, it would still be something. She quietly followed the soldier and found the tent of the woman in question.

Of course, Estrella declined the invitation for champagne.

119

Then, offended and angry, she went back to sleep. Traneya waited for about half an hour, and as the area went quiet, she slipped into the unguarded tent. It was strange how many ornaments and how much white lace there was inside. The sorceress herself lay in a luxurious large bed, her dark wavy hair spread over her pillow. She seemed so serene and peaceful. Traneya stood and watched her for a few seconds, holding a dagger in her hand. This picture somehow seemed too perfect to be spoiled with blood on the white lace blankets. The Krumerian woman looked around, thinking that maybe Rabolii would want the sorceress alive. Surely she was valuable to Soleya. They had hardly anyone who could control the element life. She could be used for a ransom. Guided by these thoughts, Traneya pulled a sleeping potion from her pocket. She hoped the sorceress would be worth it, because carrying her all the way to Kranium would take great physical effort.

—∭—

Rabolii's door opened with a bang, which caused him to jump and throw papers into the air in shock. He raised his head, and his eyebrows jumped into the heavens in horror and indignation. He wasn't accustomed to people daring to invade his chambers without even knocking. He thought everyone in this town was aware of this rule! All his perplexity disappeared when he saw that Mavarius was holding the door handle, and Arkenel was coming in behind him, looking around unintelligently. It seemed like there was always someone new in town unaware of the rules.

After recovering from this insulting invasion, the necromancer noticed the obvious traces of a fight on the faces of the two men. A big bruise swelled around the blind eye of his son, and the other man's mouth was smeared with blood as if he had eaten somebody alive. Rabolii clenched his teeth with disgust and snapped, "How did you manage to get hurt this time? Were you fighting with the Vernian corpses?"

"Oh." Arkenel and Mavarius looked at each other as if this was the first time they'd noticed something had happened. Rabolii's son answered, "No. I think we slapped each other a bit a little while ago in the corridor."

Rabolii realised that was true because he had heard voices of simpletons outside and the whole floor had shaken as if cattle were running, but naturally he had thought that it was just Regel and Dregel doing something stupid again. He was used to the nuisance they caused, so he had restrained himself from going out and killing everyone with hatred. He waved his hand and urged them, "Well? Why were you fighting?"

The two of them glanced at each other again with unintelligent faces and shrugged. Arkenel mumbled, "God, I don't remember what I had for breakfast today, and you ask me stuff like this."

"Tosser, the thing with the corridor was sooner than breakfast," said Mavarius.

Rabolii watched them with a grimace of annoyance and raised his eyebrows as if he smelled something abominable, but he was trying to be civilised about it and trying not to demonstrate his true feelings. He laced his fingers in front of his face and said, "I hope you remember at least why I sent you to the west. Do you?"

The two noisy subjects once again directed their attention towards their master. Mavarius answered, "You think I'm daft? You sent us to kill them tramps because you didn't want us in your city."

"Did you bring them all? Covered in sheets, not rotten, and with no injuries?" The necromancer continued to ask vital questions.

"Yes, we did it all, Dad. We're not idiots," Arkenel answered.

"All right. I just don't want the news that I'm collecting corpses to spread. Do you understand me?" He told them solemnly, "I'm trusting you with this, and if you disappoint me, I won't give you another chance."

"Yeah, fine, whatever. Can we go now?" Mavarius was pacing around nervously.

"Chill for a second." Arkenel nudged him. "Dad, my men still have no homes in this city. We can't sleep forever in that underground."

"Talk to Salina. She's the one dealing with the homeless," Rabolii answered hastily in an attempt to get rid of this annoyance.

"Oh, there's something else!" Arkenel said.

"Gods, what else is there?" muttered Mavarius. He shared Rabolii's desire to end this meeting.

"We found some weird dude roaming around in the field. He said he was Krumerian," continued Arkenel.

"You've found a Krumerian in Krumerus? I will hand you a medal for bravery." Rabolii was mumbling.

"Yes, but there was something off about this guy." Somehow

121

Arkenel found the strength and the desire to continue, even though everyone around him was complaining. "He had some weird clothes like ... he was a nobleman or something. He seemed way too neat, and the story he gave me ..."

"I cannot deal with this *now!*" yelled Rabolii, who was growing anxious as he watched Mavarius walk around his room and touch his things. "You've finished your job with me. If some wanderer is so upsetting to you, take him to your mother. She'll notice if anything's off with him." Turning his attention to Mavarius, he roared, "Don't touch that!"

Mavarius had grabbed a bursting explosive mixture in a glass bottle and waved it casually. When Rabolii screamed at him, he got startled and dropped it, forcing the necromancer to perform a heroic jump to catch the bottle before it hit the ground. Only two moments later, Mavarius had found another way to be harmful. He was leaning over the complex top-secret diagrams on the desk and was trying to read the one which resembled a map: "Cos-cosmic e-energy charge. Whaaa? Is that a flying fart you painted over Aldur? Are you hinting that we smell?"

At that moment Rabolii made a horrifying face. His pupils shrank, he bared his teeth, and on the whole, he got such a raging and dangerous expression that even the most clueless person could tell that this was the apocalypse. The voice that came out of those breathless lungs chilled the two men to the bones as he screamed like a banshee: "Stay away from my documents, you wretched creature! Out! And if you come near my desk again, I'll burn your body and tear your soul apart. Leave!"

Arkenel and Mavarius had frozen in place after that reaction. When they recovered from the shock, they stepped back before all those threats got implemented. Rabolii leered at them with vicious eyes then forced the doors to slam behind their backs so violently that dust fell from the ceiling, making the vampires clap their wings and shift wearily.

Once he was alone, the necromancer sat there breathing heavily, still shooting murderous glances at the closed door. Then he reached over, grabbed the diagram from his desk, and pressed it defensively against his chest. He had a feeling that these people just didn't take it seriously when he said he was dealing with top-secret matters in this room and that some of the vital information he had could change the fate of the whole continent if it were to fall into the wrong hands. Regardless of all that, some idiotic addict would dare to peek at his papers and read them? Unbelievable! Rabolii wondered why Mavarius was still alive. It was some damn misunderstanding.

Meanwhile, Valenis was hanging out with Arkenel's comrades. He looked around stunned, realising that never in his life had he seen a place which looked so ... evil. So dead. Bones were used for ornamentation here. Skulls were visible between the bricks of the houses. Massive ribs of large animals formed the fences; they hung from the roof's ledge. Skeletons wandered around, carried goods, and dug through the gardens. Everything was grim and black.

Valenis didn't know where he needed to go now. His original idea was simply to disappear somewhere around the city and avoid anyone he had already met, but suddenly he didn't have the guts to do that. This city looked so monstrous that he doubted he'd survive without a group. Luckily there was an angel in Kranium who took care of the homeless and unfortunate. That was Salina, who had to deal with the housing of Arkenel's men.

As soon as she came to them, she immediately noticed the one who looked too clean and decent to be a part of the gang. She approached and said to him in a sweet voice, "Are you the stranger my brother found?" Valenis suddenly felt a hand on his shoulder and turned around. He gazed at the girl standing in front of him, not knowing what to say. Salina looked so different from anything he'd seen before. There was a little more colour on her face than the other greenish grey Krumerians. Her hair was a desaturated shade of blonde. She looked like a spot of light and colour which stood out in this dead, dark landscape.

"Um, yes. I'm sorry for the hassle. I didn't want to disturb the whole city with my very arrival. You don't need to ... greet me," he mumbled frantically, wondering how to end this meeting and remain unnoticed.

"Oh, don't worry, it's no problem." Salina smiled at him kindly. "It's my job to look after the citizens of Krumerus. That's what the princesses are for!"

"If I knew I'd be greeted by a princess, I would have come a long time ago." Valenis made a painful attempt at a joke, feeling his mouth become completely dry. He wondered how to behave to avoid suspicion. He had a feeling that all of this would end miserably, that they'd take him to Rabolii, who would instantly recognise him as a spy, skin him, and turn him into a skeleton servant.

"We have many refugees coming from the west. Maybe you'll meet some of your friends here!" Salina told him cheerfully.

Valenis stopped breathing in horror but decided to follow her and not act suspicious. He would be forever grateful to Vernara if he survived the following days here. He dragged his feet after Salina, wondering how to act naturally. At first he tried to get rid of the wrinkle of disgust on his nose. It would appear there involuntarily because everywhere it smelled of carcasses and there were swarms of bugs, though no one seemed to mind.

It was at that moment when another weirdness ran past the shocked spy. Regel and Dregel stomped in a nearby area and played a game of chase with their skeleton. Valenis turned to stare at them, getting a very strange feeling for the first time. He tried not to stop and just continued walking down the street as if he were in his own country. He needed to get this spying work done right. If he were to fail, he would need to go back to Krementa, who would yell at him. And nobody wanted such a thing in their life.

Ilinar needed a few days to ready his small squad and go to the western border. He didn't believe something would actually happen, but as a responsible ruler he couldn't simply ignore a warning of an attack. Prehorian's wise books had taught him that every nation was as peaceful or as aggressive as its ruler. This was obvious in the case of Eslir. In general, the Aslanians were guided by the philosophy that the important things are eternal and that there is little purpose for a man to take up arms and fight against anything. After all, their goddess, Glacera, was the mistress of the air and water elements, which were in fact eternal. To Ilinar, this ideology was a little abstract, and he chose not to ponder upon it too much. Instead, he loved to delve into his favourite book about Felis and admire how brilliant he was. The main character was the son of a general, and he had a great memory and a very sharp mind, which helped him create brilliant military strategies. Ilinar had always dreamed of getting into a situation where he could use some of Felis's ideas and receive a tumultuous ovation for his quick thinking.

"Your Majesty, would you like to talk to your generals?" Eley asked, poking his head into Ilinar's tent. He found him rolling in his bed with some thick books. That might have excited any other teacher, but Eley knew all too well that these were not learning aids full of knowledge.

"Sure, in a moment," Ilinar replied.

He got up eagerly and started putting his boots on, getting ready to go see his generals to discuss combat strategies, all while imagining how he was being smart just like Felis and how his ideas would be great. According to Ilinar, he and the book's character were similar in every way except their appearance. While Ilinar resembled the young Rabolii (interestingly), Felis was described as a sixteen-year-old boy with golden hair the colour of dry hay and sky-blue eyes.

"The Vernians are coming!" Some overly excited scout burst into Ilinar's tent.

This startling news shocked the young king. For a moment he could do nothing but stare in bewilderment. He asked, "How come? Have they sent soldiers?"

"The others and I came across a large armed detachment. I hardly managed to escape and warn you," the scout said, still breathing heavily after having rushed to the camp.

Ilinar was still astounded. He had come to the western border out of caution, not because he had expected someone to attack him. He ran out to talk to his generals and see where they would make a stand. They had to protect the villages somehow.

The Soleyans had no time to dig trenches or prepare a proper defence. They couldn't raise the palisade or do anything else before the Vernians appeared. Without any warning or explanation, they took out their bows, and a cloud of arrows flew over the village. As the soldiers hoisted their shields and were preparing for battle, Eley pulled Ilinar behind one of the houses and hissed, "Your Majesty, it's too dangerous here. You need to get back to Lumis immediately."

"But I cannot leave my soldier. What kind of a king would I be if I did that?" Ilinar cried out, trying to sound brave.

"You would be smart and, most importantly, a living king," Eley replied. If Rabolii would have heard that, he would have been offended. "We will tell the council that the west is under attack and that reinforcements are needed at this border."

Ilinar felt suffocated by all that. It was a very unsuitable time for this to happen! Eslir had taken his entire glorious army to Krumerus, and who knew how long he'd stay there? Even if he did take the capital and kill Rabolii, perhaps that wouldn't leave him with enough soldiers to defend the west.

"Maybe I can catch up with Eslir and tell him not to attack Kranium," Ilinar said. "Rabolii knows something about Vern. He warned us they'd attack."

"Ilinar, you won't reach Eslir unless you leave right now! We have to warn Lumis about all this."

"Go ahead and warn them," Ilinar told Eley. "I have to stop my crazy cousin from starting a war with every country out there."

It was debatable whether Eslir was starting a war or simply continuing the one that already existed, but in any event Ilinar didn't want to deepen any conflicts. He took some of the soldiers with him and headed north. Perhaps if he rode without rest, he would catch up with the Aslanian and try to conduct some normal negotiations between rulers. Deep on the inside, Ilinar had some interest in Rabolii without even realising it. He saw that he and the necromancer had some things in common. After all, they were both labelled as monsters. Still, his only meeting with Rabolii had taken place because Eslir had captured his wife. One does not have to be a monster to charge into a city and protect his family. Maybe they were both made out to be worse than they really were? Maybe it wasn't impossible to negotiate with Rabolii?

Meanwhile, the Vernians had problems not related to Ilinar. Krementa was walking around the castle and complaining that Valenis had left two days ago and hadn't called her even once. She was just about to try contacting him herself when her servants brought the disturbing news that one of her generals had come back in a poor state and wanted to talk to her. Krementa went to her throne room, wondering what might have happened. It was rare for her people to approach her for anything.

In front of her stood Evena. She looked shabby and bruised, wearing some clothes that seemed too big to be her own. She seemed to have been through some sort of trauma. Krementa gave her a worried look and asked, "General Evena, you were on a mission in Krumerus, if I remember correctly. What happened?"

Evena clenched her fists and tried to give a regimental reply: "At first, everything happened according to schedule. We had cleansed three villages, and we had made a camp in the woods near the border. About a week later, we caught some creature that had sneaked near our tents." Evena wrinkled her nose in disgust as if the memory itself would make her vomit. "It was repulsive, all covered in scratches and scars. It had one eye missing, and its hair ..."

"Was it a Krumerian or an undead?" Krementa asked.

"It was a Krumerian," Evena snarled, lowering her wet

eyes. "I ordered my soldiers to capture him. I tied him up and interrogated him about what he was doing near our camp, but he admitted nothing. On the next day, my people started to suffer from stomach aches. They were squirming in agony. I figured the creature had done something, and at first I didn't understand how. I had kept it bound the whole time! Somehow he had found a way to poison my people. Soon I discovered he wasn't alone. He and his friends overcame me and began molesting my body in disgusting ways. They kept me alive only so they could prolong my suffering."

Evena started to sob. She didn't want to tell Krementa what actually had happened, because if she admitted she'd slept with Arkenel instead of instantly killing him, she probably wouldn't get too much sympathy, and people would state that it was her foolishness which killed her troops. Krementa was gasping in dismay, indignant at the Krumerian savagery. She said to Evena in a warm, velvety voice, "I am heartbroken to learn of your misfortunes, my child. Don't cry. Wash away the dreadful touch of those beasts, and train for battle harder than ever before. Vernara whispers to me that you will soon get a chance for revenge against the monsters that disgraced you."

Evena nodded and wiped her tears. She proceeded to the river streams to wash herself. She stared at her reflection in the water and threw a stone at it with an angry gesture. She couldn't believe that something like that had happened to her. She felt so humiliated and filthy. One single thought kept her from falling apart at that moment: she wanted to find Arkenel and cause him all the pain of this world before killing him. She didn't know anything about him, but she would recognise him even if she were to see him twenty years from now. She muttered under her breath an oath—Arkenel would regret everything he'd done to her.

Ilinar was crossing the northern border for the first time. If this were happening under normal circumstances, he would be frightened by Krumerus, he'd be shocked by the appearance of the withered trees, and he'd get startled each time something larger than a man flew over his head. But right now he was too busy thinking about Rabolii and about Soleya. He turned to one of his soldiers and asked, "Is that the way to Kranium? A path is hardly visible through this shrubbery; I thought there was a passage through the Thorny Wood?"

"This is the passage, Your Majesty," replied one of the soldiers.

Ilinar realised there was no point in asking them questions. This place was as unfamiliar to the soldiers as it was to him. The five of them continued to the north, holding torches to break the unforgiving darkness of Krumerus. There were so many thick dark clouds in the sky. It seemed to be covered by a blanket. On both sides of the road rose black trees, spreading their sharp branches like a witch's fingers. A feeling of despair grasped the soul. The black landscape melted away into the mist.

Something was stirring in the darkness. Various trees began to bend and break down, making way for a great creature with thundering footsteps that shook the whole ground. Ilinar turned towards the source of the noise and stared at a huge, grotesque face covered with warts, upon which there was moss growing. As soon as the Soleyans had set foot in this accursed place, they happened to stumble across a Krumerian troll. It wasn't the worst thing one might encounter there, but still, if they wanted to defeat him, they would have to assemble a group of fifty fighting men. Ilinar cried, "Sweet Ardor! *Run!*"

Ilinar and his soldiers spurred the horses and galopped away. They were forced to manoeuvre and avoid various blows and the trees being thrown at them. They dived in the Thorny Wood with the hope that the dead vegetation would slow down the monster. And indeed, after a while, the creature gave up on the chase. Unfortunately, by that time, they had gotten completely lost and had no idea where they were. After some time they tried to get back to where they had been, but they couldn't navigate in this accursed place. Some plants resembling huge, thorny tentacles blocked the road. The woods seemed so confusing as if they had swallowed their very footprints.

"Nothing seems familiar," Ilinar said. "I could swear we had not passed through here."

"But that's the direction we came from," replied one of the soldiers.

"I think I would have remembered seeing that on our way here!" Ilinar said, waving his hand in the direction of some ruins engulfed by black vegetation.

"Maybe we just didn't notice it." Another soldier shrugged.

The sun was setting. Maybe it was only about five o'clock,

but the darkness was beginning to thicken. Ilinar noted, "I don't want to be wandering at night. Let's explore the ruins. Maybe we'll find a shelter."

In Krumerus every nice thing a man could encounter in the wild was a double-edged sword. Food, water, and shelter attracted weary travellers and wild beasts alike. The soldiers had to kill some small black demons that inhabited the ruins. Ilinar was very impressed to see such beings. As his men were setting the fire in the main hall, he sat and down and examined one of the demons. It was as big as a rabbit and was just as thorny as the plants outside.

"Perhaps it would be a good idea to explore the rest of the place," suggested one of the soldiers. "If there are more creatures here, it would be better to kill them now than to get a surprise attack while we sleep."

"I'll come with you," Ilinar offered them.

The five began to walk around the creepy ruins with their torches. There were huge holes in the walls and ceilings, through which the branches of the thorny forest were creeping, grasping the building like fingers. Skulls and bones were inlaid in the walls of the building, forming some patterns which had been destroyed by the passage of time.

"I think I see some kind of glow," Ilinar remarked, staring into the darkness.

When the rest of the Soleyans approached, they also noticed it. At the bottom of the temple there were black, damp tentacles that emitted a gloomy, spectral light. They looked like something from another world. Ilinar stared at them and said, "I think they're holding someone."

He approached and lightly touched with his fingertips a hand which was sticking out of the entangled tentacles. Once that touch had taken place, the fingers of the captured person twitched. Ilinar remarked in surprise, "Could he be alive?"

"Sir, we are in Krumerus. Many dead things move here," said one of the soldiers.

"Yes, but still. See if you can cut the tentacles," Ilinar ordered.

The men drew their swords and began chopping. Green juices started squirting. The tentacles moved with painful screeching and, in some inexplicable way, got sucked in between the bricks of the wall. The man they were holding fell to the ground helplessly. He was unconscious. Locks of blond hair fell in front of his eyes. He looked like a Soleyan. Ilinar gazed at him curiously, realising

129

that he was probably as old as he was. He put his fingers on his neck and said, "I can feel a heartbeat. Take him next to the fire."

Ilinar's mother had told him stories of how Mortelion would steal naughty boys with his tentacles and drag them to Krumerus. Who would have thought that this story would come to life like this!

Within a few hours the young blond man began to show signs of life. He moved helplessly as he lay by the fire. He opened his deep blue eyes and began to look curiously at the people who had gathered around him. They stared at him, expecting him to explain what he was doing in the midst of the Thorny Wood in some ruins, held by tentacles, and how he managed to remain alive. He blinked innocently and said, "I regret to disappoint, but I don't have any recollection as to what happened to me. I don't remember anything." He thought about it for a moment and bit his lower lip with a serious expression. "Absolutely nothing."

"What's your name?" Ilinar asked, a seemingly simple question.

The stranger continued to stare solemnly into the fire as if looking for some universal secrets in the flames. He replied, "I cannot recall it."

"You can talk, so it's not like your mind has completely melted away," Ilinar said to him. "Check your pockets; see if you can find anything which will help you remember."

The stranger dug his hands into his pockets, searching for belongings. He found a piece of paper which looked fragile, scuffed, and antique. He unfolded it; his blue eyes ran through the written lines.

Hello, Agelik!

I am so excited. I want you to know that I was thinking a lot about the things you told me, and I believe your every word. It seems to explain everything—my dreams, my visions ... You risked so much for me, and I thank you. I want to meet you. I won't make you come to Krumerus for me again; I think they're looking for you. Meet me at the border, and don't forget to bring me that delicious green thing.

See you soon,
R. R. Remedor

20 Mort. 11299

The Soleyans exchanged glances. It was obvious that something very interesting had happened here, but by the looks of it there was no one to explain. Ilinar noted, "Well, well. What an interesting letter from two centuries ago."

"I think in fact my name was Agelik." The stranger decided to shock everyone with this statement. "It sounds familiar to me somehow."

"You can't be the same Agelik who is mentioned in that!" Ilinar replied, nodding towards the letter.

"What year is it now?" asked Agelik.

"The year is 11550. We celebrated the great anniversary of Holy Ardor this summer," Ilinar replied as if it was something that everyone knew.

Agelik continued to look puzzled. The name Ardor also rang some bells, but he had already chosen what he wanted to be called. He glanced around and said, "This place is rather unpleasant. Would you like to tell me who you are and what your destination is? I'm afraid I don't have any interesting stories of my own."

Ilinar shrugged and began to tell his life story. He rarely received such an invitation and had to make the most of it. He and the young man spoke for a few hours, and then when everyone was tired, they made themselves comfortable around the fire to sleep. Tomorrow was going to be a busy day. In fact, Ilinar was so excited that he decided to read *Between Fire and Death* before bedtime. He was just reading about the moment when Felis's girlfriend Eneya suspiciously went missing, and he had gone looking for her with a small group of soldiers. The dark scenery in the book seemed too real with its feeling of upcoming danger as Ilinar lay in the ominous Krumerian ruins.

Thick and grey were the clouds in the sky. The darkness seemed too dense. It was no later than five in the afternoon. Still the soldiers found the need to light their torches. The surroundings seemed lifeless and inhospitable. Soon the men saw a strange shape on the path; it was probably the same thing that had left the bloody marks they had seen earlier. The soldiers and Felis unmounted the horses and proceeded to examine the body. It was all so bizarre. The man was

131

unknown to them; he was dressed as a peasant. His skin was grey and colourless; his eyes, glassy blue and somewhat protruding. However, the most peculiar thing was the blood which dripped from his mouth. It was black, completely desaturated, without any tint of red in it.

"Merciful Flamis, what is that?" one soldier mumbled.

"Never have I seen such a thing before. He appears to be a victim of some dark curse which wiped all colour away from him." The red-headed Destalia sighed. "I don't know of any spells which could have done this."

Felis had one idea. He remembered the ancient legends of the god of death, Eratius, who could disfigure people in such a way. The wars with him were bloody and severe; the rivers would run red. It was believed that the evil god had been defeated and that his demon troops had been obliterated by Ardor Skyfire many centuries ago. The very thought that the monster might have survived made Lord Lucera and the problems associated with him seem like child's play.

"And what are petty creatures such as yourselves doing in my domain?" spoke a low, vibrating voice that startled the Flemitrians.

Two terrifying eyes watched them from the darkness. They were but a light-blue glow that cast peculiar, sinister light over everything they touched. Below them the mouth of the beast was outlined in the dark. Long, sharp teeth protruded, glowing in the same fashion as the eyes.

"What are you?!" Destalia immediately jumped to her feet and drew her sword as she stood guard in front of Felis.

"My name is Lethius, you wretched fool. I am the son of Eratius, and the sole reason for my existence is to bring him glory. He lusts for blood, which he shall receive. It shall be your blood."

Destalia felt this was the time for her to attack. She formed a ball of fire and cast it at the beast. This didn't bring any desired effect other than setting fire to some nearby shrubbery.

As the flames cast their light, for the first time the soldiers saw their foe. The creature known as Lethius was enormous. He had a long head upon which grew two pairs of horns which were curved down, angled, and edgy. He wasn't covered with skin or hair; upon his four-legged body were scales of rigid, stern matter. His legs seemed thick and robust, ending with hooves. The beast waved a pointed tail as if it were a whip. When the flames struck him, Lethius gave out a fearsome laugh and attacked the soldiers, striking one with his horned head. He grunted, "A demon stands before you. Immortal and eternal, I shall be the one to overthrow your pathetic nation. And as you bathe in blood and bones, you shall realise that your souls have always belonged to Eratius, the one true god."

Yes, Prehorian wasn't famous for any meek and pleasant books that didn't include a monster in the first twenty pages. Ilinar shuddered. While he was lying in a place like this, the story of an immortal demon seemed very plausible to him, even though many experts argued that it was biologically impossible for such a beast to exist. Ilinar himself didn't know if Prehorian had attempted to achieve verity. On the one hand, Saint Ardor was vastly believed to have existed, but on the other hand the names of the cities, countries, and gods in his book didn't correspond to anything in reality.

Not long afterwards, Ilinar put away the books and got ready to sleep. Agelik lay facing the darkness of the ruins. He stared forward without blinking. He kept the letter in his hand and read it over and over. The words seemed to carry some huge meaning that he simply couldn't grasp.

Chapter 6

UNDER SIEGE

The doors of a foul-smelling room opened, and Salina choked for a moment. As the smoke cleared away, she saw Arkenel and his buddies scattered lazily across the floor, smoking like chimneys. Today they had chosen to camp in a former dining room in the castle that was no longer used since it was infested by rats. That didn't seem to bother these people.

"Um, Arkenel? Have you seen Mom?" Salina asked.

She was still dragging Valenis around with her; he was trying not to look like a kid who had gotten lost in the woods, but he was failing at that. Arkenel raised his reddened eyes at them and grinned. "The two princesses. I knew you'd get along!"

"What's with your eye?" Salina asked.

It took Arkenel a few seconds to realise she meant the bruise, since there were plenty of other things wrong with his eyes. He looked at Mavarius, and they both shrugged again. They had forgotten. The second one mumbled, "Was it the corpse who hit you? He was angry or something."

"Oh no, you haven't angered Father, have you? What did you do?" Salina asked wearily, trying to assess the damage.

"Beats me. We just looked at some piece of paper on which he'd drawn a fart over Aldur, and then he snapped and started doing things like ..." Mavarius waved his hands around in the air as he didn't have the words to describe the devastating attack they had suffered.

Salina gave them a look of annoyance. It seemed to her that there was no point in explaining to them why it was a very bad idea to annoy Rabolii. She decided to take care of the damage. She sent Valenis to Ravena and then went to the chambers of the necromancer, the deadliest place in the castle. She knocked

134

on the heavy, ominous doors and called out, "Father? May I come in?"

There was no reply. She bit her lip. How was she to interpret this? Either Rabolii had forgotten to drink the potion of steamed snails and had gone deaf, or he was so insulted that he didn't want to talk to anyone. She decided she couldn't leave things that way, so she opened the doors and stepped into the room.

As the heavy doors opened in front of her, she gasped. The chambers were empty. The necromancer wasn't behind his faithful desk, and the room looked like an empty abyss without him. Salina looked around and walked in, wondering if he might be standing in a corner or behind a curtain. Rabolii leaving his room was an event that took place once every two years, and when he did leave it, everyone would hear about it. How could he disappear just like that?!

"Father?" Salina called again, checking behind the desk to see if he had fallen.

Something on the desk caught her attention. On top of the other papers was the one with the fart near Aldur which had excited Mavarius so much. She glanced over the parchment; the scribbles had much more meaning for her than for the uneducated man. Salina recognised that this was a map of magical charges in the vicinity. In Krumerus, the charges of darkness and death were concentrated; in Soleya, light and fire were prominent. Such maps were not rare; they were collected and put together by powerful sorcerers so they could monitor the strength of their opponents. There was something out of place on this map, though. There was a charge which she didn't recognise. There were only eight elements, and cosmic energy wasn't one of them. What could it be? She touched with the tip of her finger the red cloud over Aldur. She wondered if she should ask Rabolii what it was, but she was a bit anxious he'd get angry.

Meanwhile, Traneya had returned to Krumerus, carrying the unconscious Estrella. She looked around and noticed the town had been thrown into chaos again. There were too many refugees who were gathering in the streets and making noise. A number of her father's soldiers were trying to mobilise those skeletons that were too cracked or deformed and hadn't been taken to Lumis for that reason. Remedor's daughter carried her hostage to the castle and first sought out her father to update him on her mission. To her surprise, the necromancer was gone. Everybody was dismayed. Where could he be?

135

—ɯɯ—

Somewhere to the south, Ilinar woke up and shuddered from the cold. He could see the sky through the cracked ceiling. It was as bright as it could possibly be in Krumerus. He looked around, noticing that his soldiers were still asleep, but Agelik wasn't around. Ilinar jumped to his feet and ran out to seek out his new acquaintance. He found him in front of the entrance to the ruins, leaning against the ancient stone wall and staring at the gloomy forest.

"I am sympathetic to the fact that as a young king you have plenty of tasks which occupy your time and attention," Agelik said without turning around. "Still, I was wondering if you would be able to possibly find the time to assist me in finding out more about myself. Somewhere deep on the inside I remember I was in the midst of an important task, but I don't recall what it was." He turned his eyes to Ilinar. Something in his intense gaze weighed heavily, making it hard to argue with him. "I feel as if I have a mission."

Ilinar found all of that to be really strange. He stated, "It seems we all have a mission, Agelik. It will be hard for me to help you right now. You have no memories of anything. We don't even know if that is your real name. I'll see what I can do, but first I have to deal with Eslir."

"Of course," Agelik told him, turning his gaze back to the forest. "I'm not sure Krumerus holds the answers I'm looking for. Nothing here seems familiar to me; I don't believe my place is here."

"Come with me if you want. After dealing with Eslir, I will return with his army to Soleya to the south. It will be safer if we travel together," Ilinar said.

"I don't need an escort. I shall make my way to Soleya now." Agelik dropped this strange statement.

Ilinar was surprised by such an answer. He noted, "Didn't you just ask me to help you? How do you expect me to do that if you run off into the woods? Besides, you don't carry food, and you are unarmed. The border is one day away from here—and that is if you find a way out of this strange forest. It is absurd to think you would survive alone!"

"I'd rather spend the next few days investigating my past instead of venturing deeper into Krumerus. Don't worry about me. I will find my way," Agelik answered.

"We just freed you from some tentacles. I cannot assume

you're in the right frame of mind to make decisions." Ilinar tried to be the responsible one here.

Agelik turned to him with a smile as if he found that statement endearing in some way. He said, "I'm touched. I don't remember anyone taking such care of me." That was meant to be a joke, but Ilinar was too nervous to notice. "Farewell, my friend."

Having said that, Agelik just left and started walking through the woods. Ilinar couldn't believe what was happening. He turned to the inner side of the ruins, where his soldiers were still asleep, then back to Agelik, who kept walking so calmly like he was in his own back yard. Ilinar felt fuming on the inside because he really wanted to be a good person today and save a young man from Mortelion's tentacles, but he wouldn't be able to. He went back inside to wake the other Soleyans, knowing he had to lead them to the north again so they could catch up with Eslir. That was his priority.

Clouds overcast the dark sky over Kranium. Fearsome birds with red eyes let out bone-chilling screams. Thunder roared. The town suddenly went silent as the main gate opened with a bang. A flash of lightning illuminated the tall, slim figure of an undead and his skeletal servants. Everyone went silent. Even Regel and Dregel's idiotic laughter faded away. Rabolii had returned. He looked skinny and horrifying; his face was more grey and colourless than ever. The black shadows under his eyes were monumental. Without muttering a word to anyone, he made his way through the city, hoping to reach his tower without being immediately overwhelmed with useless matters. Everyone was moving out of the way, as if he would explode if they touched him. He had already crossed the city, moving forward with a majestic gait and an impervious facial expression. He had reached the steps of the castle when his worst nightmare came true.

"Father! I was looking for you all day!" Salina said, ambushing him. She just couldn't miss being the first person to attend the glorious return of her father. "I want to talk to you about something!"

"Hey, I came back from that mission you sent me to. Come here!" Traneya peeked out of a window. She wanted to tell the necromancer what had happened when she infiltrated the Aslanian camp and suspected Rabolii would kill her for failing.

"Rab, where have you been? Have you forgotten to take your potions?" Ravena was also quick to greet him with her concerns.

"Uh, Dad, I think one of my men caught the plague. Got anything for that?" Arkenel had also appeared, holding a dirty bottle in his hand. He looked too cheerful to be reporting such news.

The head of the poor necromancer felt like it had instantly exploded. He wanted to smite all these monstrous people. He thought that he couldn't take two steps outside without everyone attacking him mercilessly with their absurd whims. He had an idea why they were doing it: they were trying to remind him that he was dead and that he wasn't a good ruler like before. They were trying to dishearten him so much that he'd end up leaving for feeling unwanted. They did it every time. He glanced around furiously like an owl struck by torchlight. He was so disturbed by all this menace that he didn't even know whom to shout at first. All of them kept talking to him:

"Come on, you'll do your vampire study things later. This is really important."

"Rab, are you OK? You seem very pale."

Rabolii waved his hands with blackened nails as if chasing away a swarm of flies. He had almost decided to kill everyone for annoying him when suddenly he noticed a new face which seemed a bit lost in the screaming crowd as if its owner had no idea what he was doing there. There was something different about him—an aura. A great necromancer such as Rabolii noticed it immediately. For a moment he became deaf to all the voices around him. He pushed everyone aside to make his way to this intriguing individual. The person in question was Valenis, and from his point of view the situation was more terrifying than Krementa's worst tantrums. First of all, the necromancer was making such a frightening entrance, and then everyone in the city surrounded him as if to irritate him. Now when their glances met, Rabolii just stared at Valenis with eyes which stabbed his very soul. It was as if the necromancer saw right through him and knew who he was. It became even more horrifying when Rabolii began making his way towards the young man, until he was standing right over him. The old Remedor spoke in a hoarse voice, "You ... you're not from here. Who are you?"

"Um, my name is Valenis," he replied in a raspy, weary voice.

He thought for a moment that he should have probably used a fake name. The one he had didn't even sound Krumerian.

"Come with me," the necromancer urged him briefly. Without paying any attention to anyone else, he opened the wide gates of his sinister castle and merged with the darkness inside.

All those who had been screaming for his attention watched this in shock. It wasn't uncommon not to understand what the necromancer was doing and why, but this was too much.

Traneya was the first to voice her indignation: "So this is how it's gonna be. First he sends me off in the middle of an Aslanian army to kill a king, and then he doesn't even want to find out what happened. Great job, Dad!"

"Dimwitted geezer," stated Mavarius as he appeared next to Arkenel. He wasn't aware of what was happening; he just took the opportunity to insult Rabolii.

"Come on, your father is tired. You can see that he has had a very difficult trip," Ravena said, trying to speak up for her husband, but no one thought it was a good enough excuse.

"Fine, let's go back inside. Wait for him to rest. We'll talk later," suggested Arkenel.

"That's the damn problem. He's been resting in peace for a century now," answered Mavarius, causing mixed reactions of admiration and disapproval from the people around.

Inside, Traneya crossed her arms and began to walk around her room nervously. It was all too much. Why would Rabolii not care about the fact that the entire Aslanian army would be storming the gates in a few hours? Was there really something so important that he could be doing in his stupid room? That was unlikely.

Estrella had awoken and was gazing around with swollen eyes. She had figured out that the Krumerians had somehow kidnapped her, and now she couldn't even imagine what would happen to her.

Rabolii walked along the corridor, followed by Valenis, who felt like he'd burst with horror and agitation. Had the necromancer recognised what he was? How could he? What could have given him away? Valenis didn't know what to do. He also didn't know whether he'd be interrogated and tortured. He thought about attacking the necromancer as he walked behind him. Even though, the corridor was empty, he wouldn't dare. He had heard of Rabolii's inhuman power.

They went to the sorcerer's tower. It was rather uncommon for a stranger to be admitted there. Valenis stepped in cautiously with a worried look on his face. This seemed to be the heart of evil and darkness in all of Kranium. He couldn't imagine a more dreadful and sinister place. It was full of murderous potions, secret formulas, and the unholy, monstrous exploitation of dead flesh that could kill enemies just by the sheer horror it caused. Despite all of that, this was home to Rabolii. He fit in perfectly in this eerie setting and was like its crown jewel. He sat down behind his desk and fixed his pale grey eyes on Valenis, who stood in the middle of the room and knew neither where to put his hands nor where to sit—or even how to stand. The necromancer spoke first: "You can't possibly be unaware as to why you attracted my attention. Why haven't I heard about you before?"

Valenis was chilled to the bone. Was it possible that Rabolii had recognised him as Krementa's son from one glance alone? How could that be? Krementa had kept him a secret from most people. Few Vernians outside the castle knew he even existed. She wanted to protect him from everything. The necromancer couldn't have known. Valenis tried not to give himself away any further or to start panicking. He replied briefly, "I wasn't a particularly charismatic person within my town. I was never one to attract attention."

"Even so," the necromancer answered, not breaking the intense eye contact. "When a sorcerer appears somewhere, people are swift to stick to him like leeches, especially if it is a sorcerer like you, especially in Krumerus."

Valenis blinked. The deathly thought that he had been recognised as a spy began to fade. The necromancer was just speaking about sorcery, which was a nice, neutral topic of conversation. He gave another undefined reply, trying not to give anything away: "Yes, I have my talents. I was trying to develop them. However, I haven't been all that useful to the rest of the people in town."

"How can you underestimate a talent like yours? Perhaps your family was ignorant and never told you what you are. I don't know how you lived for so long without noticing it yourself. Do you know how rare it is for a sorcerer to have a secondary sphere?"

This was all very strange. Valenis continued to gaze innocently, wondering how he had impressed this man with his pathetic magical talents. He found the element of earth to be sort of impractical, so he'd never put too much effort into mastering it.

"What do you mean by secondary sphere?" Valenis asked.

"I don't know what sort of magic lessons you've had so far, but the reason why one is a sorcerer is because one has some type of elemental energy in his or her soul," Rabolii began explaining. He took out diagrams showing what souls look like. "The energy is in the shape of a sphere that clings to you so you can use it to cast spells. As a rule, it's rare for anyone to have a magical sphere, but having two is almost unheard of. I would understand if you were unfamiliar with such a phenomenon. It's only been encountered in the Remedor family. I control both death and fire. I never thought I'd meet someone like this outside my family."

Valenis continued to feel very stupid. He could hardly control one element, and suddenly this man was telling him he had a second one! He was starting to think that Rabolii was probably just too old and confused and his senses were failing him. There was no other explanation. He didn't even know how to answer such a statement. He mumbled, "Yes, I do control earth, but I've never felt anything else."

Rabolii gave him a smile and said, "It's not possible that you have never felt it. Your secondary element is death. It seems strange to me that you haven't realised it before. In a place like Krumerus, there is plenty you can achieve with such a gift."

Valenis was stunned. It was something he had never suspected, but now that he knew about it, he realised that there had been some signs in the past. Krementa must have been aware and had kept him away from any dead flesh. She had not let him go to funerals, not even in the kitchens where they prepared freshly killed rabbits and deer. On the whole, he seemed to have never encountered dead things unless they were well-cooked.

Valenis still didn't know how to answer Rabolii. He could imagine that being a necromancer in Krumerus was a thing which would be noticed in early childhood. He answered cautiously, "In fact, I suspected it. When I was young, I played with a lot of ... dead things, and I made them move. But my grandmother forbade me from doing that and told me that people would never leave me alone if they knew I could do such things. She said I'd not be at peace."

Rabolii watched Valenis with a serious expression and thought that what he'd just said didn't make a lot of sense. Why would anyone waste a talent like that by hiding it? He stated hesitantly, "Being a necromancer is burdensome sometimes, but it's a safe and secure way to make money and rise up in society. If you control two elements, your parents must have been powerful sorcerers. How come they didn't care enough to develop your talents? Actually, at one point in time I knew most of the necromancers in these lands. By what names are your parents called? Perhaps I know them."

That question slapped Valenis painfully as he realised he didn't know what lie to come up with. Even if he said he was an orphan, it would be hard to convince the necromancer that he had no idea who his parents were. He was wondering what to say when fate saved him. Someone began banging on the necromancer's door. Voices were coming from outside. "Rab! I'm sorry to bother you, but the city will be under siege in a few hours."

The necromancer looked up with annoyance. He was tired of incompetent people who insolently invaded his private space so often that he couldn't ignore them no matter how hard he tried. Apparently he would have to get down to business. He turned to Valenis and handed him a book. "Learn more about your element. Here you can read some common things about it and learn the most basic spells, but at this stage it will suffice. I want to keep in touch with you. There are not a lot of necromancers in this country. I would like to keep track of your development."

"Thank you, my lord." Valenis nodded and took the ragged book, then assumed the statement was synonymous with "goodbye", so he stepped back and added, "I'll ... we'll meet later on."

Valenis went out of the room, his heart pounding wildly in his chest. He passed by Ravena, who gave him a strange look. Rabolii tried to save himself from nuisance and called to his wife, who stood at the door, "Leave me alone, Ravena. I have work to do."

"Work more important than protecting Kranium? Rab, come out. We need you on the wall."

"I've already done all I could. Now leave me," he snapped.

Ravena was shocked. She knew that her husband was obstinate and unfriendly, but this was unbelievable. What exactly did he care about? He'd disappeared from the city without giving any explanation, after which an Aslanian army marched in. It occurred to her that perhaps he had gotten himself into some sort of trouble and had been chased by the soldiers, but she didn't even dare to ask the question. It would only frustrate the necromancer, who would feel like he was being blamed. Regardless, she felt like there was no point in talking to him further, so she left and walked down the corridor. Salina appeared at her mother's side and suggested, "Should I try to talk to him?"

"There's no need. Let's go help your sister on the wall. Hopefully he will come out at some point."

"What did you tell him? Did you talk to him?" Salina kept asking.

"He said he has taken care of things. Let's trust him. He may have defended us again in some way without telling us. He does that from time to time."

Salina nodded, casting a worried glance back at the heavy, dusty door of the necromancer. She didn't know what to expect.

It was unbelievable how hardships like this brought Ravena and Salina together. It was as if they were both alive to serve Rabolii, to entertain him, and to distract him from the fact that he was a corpse. It was natural for one of them to get exhausted and frustrated by this occupation at times, but then the other one would take over. They trusted each other that they would do fine. Even though they were not a real mother and daughter, their mission brought them together and made them closer than Ravena was with her biological children.

Meanwhile, Arkenel and Traneya walked along the fortress wall and tried to prepare for the siege. The walls and gates were not in a great condition. The necromancer's daughter noted, "Look at these holes in the wall! This is a tragedy."

"Did you really notice this only now, right when Aslanians have come to besiege us? What have you been doing for these seven years while I was in prison?" Arkenel answered angrily. "It never occurred to anyone to fix this?"

"Rabolii doesn't care and likes to spend money only on himself." Traneya shrugged.

Arkenel rolled his eyes and muttered, "I'll get my men to do some repairs on the wall and the gates." He turned to Traneya. "I will do what I can, but I don't think this city is in a good position to withstand an attack for too long."

Various peasants ran around in panic, carrying bones and human remains, hysterically stuffing them into chests in their houses to protect them from the call to arms. Only the lamest and most crippled skeletons had remained in Kranium. Now they would also be taken away. Traneya shot the panicking peasants an unimpressed look and continued to walk along the fortification and shout at anyone who was seemingly not doing anything useful. Mavarius was one of them; he was sitting on the wall with a blunt in his mouth, just staring into the Krumerian wilderness. Arkenel walked past him and pushed a sword into his hands. His companion shot him an offended look and mumbled, "Get lost. Do I look like I'm in the mood to fight jerks?"

"You have that option, or you can go hide with the women and children. But I don't trust you. You'll drive them crazy. So get up!" Arkenel said.

"I'm not fighting." Mavarius shifted angrily and crossed his arms as Arkenel continued to poke him with the sword.

"Tosser, come on! I also have more enjoyable activities to be doing this morning, but as you can see, I'm trying to make myself useful. What else should we do, just lie down, die, and let those losers take the castle?"

"So how's the geezer helping, eh?" Mavarius asked as he cast a glance at Rabolii's tower.

"Oh, he's not doing much, you know. Just animating half the army we're using." Arkenel shrugged. "Come on, I want to see you ready to fight. Otherwise I'll break something in your head, so move. *You there!* This applies to you too!"

Arkenel's other soldiers mumbled their discontent and started grabbing random objects to arm themselves for the battle. One of them got a lid for a garbage bin and held it like it was a shield. Another armed himself with a shoe, because in his drunken logic the people who were laying siege would look as tiny as ants while at the bottom of the fort, so he could probably just kill them as such. Arkenel couldn't stand to look at the men so drunk and inadequate. He groaned desperately and yelled at them, "Men, get in shape and stop drinking! I'll try to get you more miner's. In the meantime, get ready."

Half of Arkenel's soldiers were lazy and irritable, but those who had smoked until recently were running around energetically but without doing anything useful. One of them began to run in circles around Mavarius and to poke him in an annoying way. "Hey! Hey! What are you drinking? Mavi, give me some!"

This didn't seem to delight the other man, who just stood up, gloomy and dark like an upcoming storm, and punched the annoying man so hard that he changed his face. He swung his fist to strike again while yelling, "Go call your mother, Mavi, you dumb-ass freak!"

Arkenel was startled by this outburst of aggression. He jumped between the men to break up the fight. He didn't want everyone in his army to kill each other before the Aslanians even got there.

Everyone in Kranium was panicking and running around. Valenis took advantage of all the chaos and slipped out of sight. He hid in some ruins outside of town, pulled out his platinum amulet, and activated it. He had been in such a hurry to finally make the call, and he was nervous because he'd never had the opportunity to do so. He'd been trying to get down to this at the first possible moment. By that time he had almost forgotten what sort of conversation this would be. Krementa's figure appeared before him, cloaked in mist; she seemed nervous and agitated as always, which vaporised all his excitement about speaking with her.

"Valenis! I thought you were *dead!*" she yelled the moment she saw him. "Didn't I tell you that I want you to call me *every* day?! Do you know how much time has passed? An entire week! Day in and day out I wonder what to tell the council members when they ask how your mission is progressing. I feel like a fool who can't establish communication with her own son! Do you know what it's like for me to send you off so far away and then you don't even call me for a month?! How are you not ashamed of yourself for causing me such stress?"

The whole tirade would have taken much longer, but Valenis decided to interrupt because he had already planned on what to say. He said, "Calm down, Mother. I'll explain everything. You will not believe what happened to me. During the first days right after I left, I found a Krumerian patrol looking for refugees from the destroyed villages. I introduced myself as one, so the local authorities not only took care of me but also ..."

"I told you not to get noticed!" she barked, apparently not listening very carefully to what he was talking about; she just wanted to say everything she had planned. "You'll thank me one day for not making it a known fact that I have a son. You think I'm ashamed of you, but my only thought has always been to keep you safe. Unfortunately you just had to go to a place where I can't protect you. You could at least think about how I'm feeling and try to call me and let me know you're alive."

"Mother, I was just trying to explain all that. Ever since I found this patrol ..."

"Yes, you are always full of excuses! You make it sound like the patrol in question followed you around everywhere so you didn't have five minutes to call me. You're not telling me what's actually going on. Have you been captured, Valenis? Are you being held as a hostage? Let me know right now so I can go ahead and send the army to rescue you."

"Mother, I'm fine!" Valenis answered with annoyance. "I'm not captured. I'm in Kranium, and I'll soon be sending you messages about what Krumerus is planning and ..."

Krementa had started crying, so her son paused and patiently waited for her to calm down. He knew that this conversation simply couldn't be done differently. Krementa would always be extremely worried. She would cry, and she would shout. It was up to him to try and calm her. He tried to speak out again, as he didn't know how much time he had left in the cramped shack where he had hidden. Unlike Rabolii, he was aware of the fact that there was going to be a battle here, so he wanted to be safe when it all started instead of suffering the fate of everyone else in the town.

"Mom, I'll be fine. I know you're worried because it's the first time you've sent me so far from home and I'm in enemy territory, but I have not felt a hint of hostility here. Nobody even notices me; to them I'm just like the rest of the refugees."

"Are you remembering to wear your cloak? I don't want you to get cold." Krementa sniffed with a sad expression.

"I wear it, Mom."

"What do you eat over there? Merciful Vernara, they'll poison you there with their disgusting food!"

"I do manage to get decent food." Valenis shrugged. That was a lie. Realistically he had not eaten anything since that one time when Mavarius dropped a piece of moss bread on the ground twice and decided to generously give it to Valenis.

"Promise me you'll take care of yourself!" cried Krementa.

The queen of Vern continued questioning Valenis on what he ate and what he wore. Finally, when he got tired of all this concern, he changed the subject and told her what he had found out: that Rabolii was eternally upstairs in his tower. Even now, when Aslanians were marching at his gate, he seemed like he didn't care about anything that was going on in his town. Krementa was quite intrigued and surprised by that news. After asking Valenis numerous times whether he was sure of what he was saying, she smiled with contentment. Now that was some good news she could present to the council. It seemed to her that Rabolii wasn't in the right mental state to fight any more and that he had given up. Who knew, maybe she wouldn't need to send Vernara's children off to war after all; perhaps the Aslanians would finish off the wretched necromancer. She ordered Valenis to hide somewhere during the battle or find a way to leave Kranium if things got too intense. As a sorcerer of earth, he would be able to raise and demolish stone walls and carve any passages which suited him.

Estrella sat in Traneya's room, all tied up with a rag stuffed in her mouth. She had been in this pose for hours and was going insane. She didn't know what the Krumerian beasts would do to her, and that uncertainty was killing her. Her heart skipped a beat as the door opened with a loud bang, and in came two of the dreaded erebi. One of them was shaggy; wounds split his face, and one of his eyes seemed whitened and blind. Beside him stood a tall woman whose arms were covered in tattoos all the way up to her neck. The two Krumerians fixed their pale eyes on her.

"Is that her? She looks unusual," noted Arkenel.

"I don't know what to do with her. I was going to ask the corpse, but it's too difficult to get a hold of him," replied Traneya.

"If she's their only sorceress of life, it may be harder for them to attack without her. However, I still don't think they'll cancel the whole attack just because of her," said Arkenel.

"Then what do we need her for?" Traneya crossed her arms.

"We can send a message to Aslania and suggest such a deal anyway," Arkenel replied. He walked up to Estrella and removed the rag from her mouth. He noted, "We can't keep her tied up like this."

"We also can't let her walk around," Traneya protested.

"Yes, that's why the wise men have created locks on the doors," said Arkenel.

From Estrella's point of view, he was probably the friendliest Krumerian she had seen up to now, so she started pleading with him, "I beg of you, offer me back to the Aslanians for a ransom. They will agree. They need me."

"Sure, dear." Arkenel granted her a wide grin and noted, "Let's hope they show some common sense."

Having said that, he led her away to find a room where he could lock her in. He felt guilty enough for killing a whole squad of Vernians. He didn't want any more pretty women to suffer in this war.

The anticipation of the battle seemed to be worse than the clash itself. A skeleton was sent to deliver a message to Eslir about Estrella's ransom. The Krumerians demanded that the Aslanians withdraw his army or else the woman would die.

147

However, an answer never arrived. The skeleton had probably suffered a horrid fate.

Clouds began to gather in the sky. Thunder echoed over the tall towers of Kranium. It suddenly became overwhelmingly cold. Traneya stood on the wall with the skeletons and watched the approaching soldiers grimly; their white armour contrasted with the black earth beneath them.

The earth shook. Aslanian voices echoed. The wind was howling; it carried the echo of the battle cries and brought it to the indifferent skeletons which stood at the wall. Traneya watched the army below, realising nothing could stop them from taking over Kranium. The fortress wall was old and fragile. Nobody had taken care of this place for decades, so it was hardly strong and reliable against the enemy forces. Valenis was watching the event while sitting on a cliff which overlooked the city. He had called his mother so he could update her on what was happening. The amulets they shared let Krementa see only him and not his surroundings, but that was enough for her. She was glad he was safe.

"The whole plain below has turned white," Valenis commented. "There are probably seven or eight thousand men down there." He shook his head. "I don't know how Krumerus will defend this city."

"That makes our job much easier. What is going on? Has the attack begun?" Krementa was overjoyed by the situation.

"No ... I mean yes. I see fire in the distance. Now it's gone. It just started raining."

Amongst the thousands of Aslanian soldiers stood a tall woman with eyes as deep as the ocean. She had raised her arms to the sky, looking as if she were hypnotised. Clouds were gathering above her. The echoing thunder suddenly sounded a lot closer as torrential rain began pouring down. The Krumerians had prepared oil and fire traps for their enemies, but none of that would be very efficient in the rain.

"Tosser! Tosser! Smack that bitch!" sounded the noble voice of the renowned leader of men Mavarius, who had successfully spotted the culprit for the rain catastrophe. He had the best eyesight as he was used to relying on it when hunting rabbits in the field, and seldom did he burden his eyes with unnecessary activities such as reading.

Arkenel also saw the sorceress amongst the soldiers. He took out a bow, readied an arrow in it, and tried aiming. This weapon felt so alien in his hands, he knew he wouldn't be able to hit his target. He noted, "I've always been bad with the bow. I haven't even touched one in seven years."

"Lemme try!" Mavarius said. He pulled out a bow as well and began aiming.

Arkenel watched with admiration the precise movements of his friend's hands as he readied the bow. Mavarius's arrow struck like thunder, piercing right through the sorceress's chest. Remedor's son began cheering with excitement while Traneya looked at the sky and noted, "The storm hasn't stopped."

"Well, don't you remember what the corpse taught us about magic?" Arkenel replied. "It's just like with fire. Once you use a spell to set it, it'll burn for a while regardless if the sorcerer lives or not. Give it some time; it'll go away."

Arkenel and Traneya would be the ones leading the defence. Salina wasn't there since her light spells would do more harm to the Krumerians, who enjoyed the dark.

Wooden towers were being rolled towards the fortress and seemed to be approaching way too fast. Heavy hooks were shot in the air; they attached to the wall and were used to raise ladders for the Aslanians to climb.

"Cut the ropes!" yelled Traneya. She turned to her brother. "Arkenel, I need you for this!"

"Awesome! Morons, come on!" he called to his loyal brethren, who ran after him. Graz stomped so heavily that the wall threatened to collapse just because of him.

Meanwhile Rabolii was still sitting in the same pose he had kept for a few hours now. He had dug his fingers into his hair, staring blankly at the stained surface of his desk. Painful visions and unclear shapes raced in front of his eyes. He couldn't recognise them. They burned him, tortured him. His throat felt dry. Many people didn't even acknowledge the severity of his condition. The fact that he had died brought him horrific pain. Every time he made an effort for another complicated spell, he used energy which he needed to sustain himself. And despite of all of that, he felt like he was still responsible for everything. He couldn't trust anyone with his important tasks; they were just not sorcerers like him. He felt all of this was so unfair that he just wanted to lie down and die, but he couldn't even do that.

At this tragic moment of loneliness and misery, his door creaked open. He didn't have the strength even to raise his eyes and see who was coming in to annoy him. He just sat there, metaphorically burying his head in the sand like an ostrich, refusing to recognise the existence of anything in this world except the desk he was leaning on. The next thing he felt was a pair of hands on his bony shoulders, gently squeezing him. Only one person in this world could touch him that way, almost making him forget that he was a miserable corpse. Ravena was there not to tell him once again that there was a fight out there, as if he were some kind of imbecile who hadn't even noticed. She wasn't there to reproach him or to shower him with a flood of words he didn't wish to hear. She just sat beside him without speaking, quietly demonstrating that she acknowledged something was wrong with him and that she wanted to help him somehow, even by just sitting with him. She wasn't going to ask him why he was in such a petty state, what had angered him and exhausted him this time. She just wanted him to feel like only he was important. This approach upset Rabolii. His first reaction was to flinch at her touch as if he'd been stung; he thought that corpses like him didn't deserve such attention. However, he didn't want to fight her, so he just continued staring blankly at his desk. He must have done something right in his life if Mortelion had gifted him with such a loyal and understanding wife.

Although time seemed to have stopped in Rabolii's life, the siege was becoming fiercer by the hour. Arkenel and his friends were running across the wall like headless chickens, trying to stop the enemy from raising ladders or bringing their towers closer, but a hundred people were not enough to protect a fortress. The skeletons were stupid and disorientated. They would stop shooting with the bow only if they were told to do so explicitly. They wouldn't switch weapons even if someone was attacking them directly. Traneya was trying very hard to monitor what every unit of her army was currently doing and to command the skeletons.

The whole wall shook. The Aslanians were trying to break down the gate. It was a matter of a few moments before that would happen. Traneya remembered how once that fiction of literature, the Kranium militia, had decided to uphold public order for the first time in decades by throwing a drunken peasant out of the city. Fat and furious, he had managed to break the gate himself and entered again. Rabolii was disturbed by this occurrence and had bought a stronger gate which could keep the drunks out. Still, this upgrade wouldn't keep a battering ram at bay for too long. Traneya grabbed a bow and leaned over the wall, trying to aim at the people who operated the ram.

"Reinforce the gate!" Traneya yelled. She turned around to

spit out another command. "Arkenel, quickly! Bar it with the planks we have."

"Me?!" shouted Arkenel, who with a couple of other men was fighting off a whole tower filled with Aslanians which had successfully arrived by the wall. Hundreds of enemies were pouring out of it.

"Anyone! Am I alone on this wall?!"

At that moment, Traneya felt pain in one of her arms and dropped the bow. An arrow had pierced the leather armour, and it stabbed her just below the elbow. Arkenel rushed to his sister's aid while Mavarius was chasing after him, telling him to stop running around in such a chaotic manner and to be careful.

"You have to go back inside. You can't fight like this," Arkenel began telling her.

Traneya was breaking off the parts of the arrow which were sticking out of her arm without taking it out completely. She turned to her brother and snapped, "My tattoos are gonna be fine. Now go bar the gate!"

Arkenel didn't know if there was a point in insisting. He turned to Grazedrii, who held two soldiers, one in each hand, and was hitting their heads together.

"Graz! The gate!" Arkenel called to him.

An arrow flew in their direction and would have probably hit someone, but Mavarius managed to deflect it with his sword. Arkenel was about to praise his incredible skills, when his friend said, "Hey, how about you go back inside as well? It's getting nasty out here."

"It's nasty all right, but we can't all just go back inside. Come on, we have to deal with those towers," Arkenel replied.

The city didn't provide any protection. There was no place to escape. It was a real disaster, and in Traneya's opinion it was all Rabolii's fault. She thought that if there was a single person who could make a difference in this battle, it would have been him. He didn't even try. He wasn't even there. She couldn't imagine any possible reason why her father was just sitting in his tower refusing to come down. Did he not know that they were under attack and that the city could fall? Did he not care that everyone he knew was in very real danger of dying? Or maybe since he was a corpse, he didn't care about anyone else being alive. Did it matter anyway? They would all be corpses by the end of the day.

Eslir was gazing at the fortress wall with fire in his eyes. He yelled commands at his subordinates; he wanted to see the

151

city fall. His soldiers were excited. News spread that Rabolii wasn't even participating in the battle. As a rule, Rabolii was the biggest reason fights with Krumerus were so terrifying. The dreaded necromancer would raise the Aslanians' own dead against them. However, most of the fallen warriors remained on the ground. The skeletons seemed disorganised and confused; they were hardly holding on. It was the inferior necromancers who were participating, but they couldn't do together what Rabolii could achieve all by himself. That encouraged Eslir even more. The fortress seemed like an easy target now. Its last defences would bend and break like a twig very soon.

Rabolii had laid his head on his wife's chest as he sat in front of her on the dusty old bed on which no one slept any more. As hard as he was trying to avoid listening to the fray outside, the noise was still getting on his nerves. He was grim and moody, feeling the reproach and the indignation everyone felt towards him. He was sure the whole town was wondering where he was and why he wasn't defending them, but he couldn't make them understand. Worst of all, he didn't even know if he cared about the outcome of this battle. He imagined that the city would fall, then the Aslanians would engulf it like a disease and eventually make their way up to his tower. He sighed heavily and shifted in Ravena's arms. He wanted to say something to her, but in that moment it seemed like there wasn't a single thought important enough to be voiced. His wife knew that even though it seemed like Rabolii didn't care, deep inside he was just feeling helpless and desperate. She pulled him closer and said softly, "Rab, I don't want you to think we're blaming you for not being out there."

"Don't lie to me; you know that's not true," Rabolii mumbled.

"Darling, it's OK." She rubbed his shoulders gently. "Even though I don't know what's troubling you, I can see you're tired and you have no strength for any of this. You probably just think you wouldn't be of any help in the battle. Is that it?"

"First of all, I don't think it's my job to single-handedly win entire wars. And secondly ..." He sighed heavily again with an angry look and said, "I don't think I can win this one anyway."

Ravena contemplated his words. She was trying to discover the actual problem. She was aware that Rabolii's death was a sensitive issue to him, and he was always ready to throw a lot of responsibility to the side if he was upset. However, over the years he had never neglected the general safety of his country even if his rule had been a bit sloppy at times. Now it seemed like he had just given up. What could have changed things so suddenly for him? She struggled to find the right thing to say in a time such as this. She asked him, "Why is this battle different for you, my darling?"

Rabolii moved a bit, stretching his arms forward, and stared at his hands with a tragic expression. He let out another heartbreaking sigh. His palms were covered with brown spots, and his purple veins were outlined and protruding under his skin, which seemed wrinkled like old parchment. Ravena knew what those symptoms meant. Rabolii had recently used a lot of magic and was exhausted. She wasn't sure if that was a good thing or a bad thing. At least she had discovered the real reason the necromancer remained in his tower—he didn't have enough strength to participate in the battle. That made her wonder where all his magic had gone and what he had been doing. She hugged him again and told him, "It's all right, Rab. Whatever you used your magic for, I'm sure it was of great importance and it has benefited us all. I'm sure we'll work our way around this. Where's your staff?"

"My staff is an amplifier. It won't be efficient." Rabolii groaned.

"We can still open the sarcophaguses." Ravena suggested. "I know they have historic value, but this is their intended purpose. Come on, I'll accompany you!"

The necromancer shot her a miserable glance. Sometimes he wondered how she could talk about things in such a simple yet enthusiastic way. He didn't know how she had the will to do anything other than disintegrate and sink through the wooden slats in the floor.

The sarcophaguses were special artefacts, kept in Kranium's underground catacombs. They were historical treasure, which was to be used in the direst times. It seemed like the occasion was suitable. Each time a powerful necromancer would die in Krumerus, his remains would be sealed in a special coffin, made from an anti-magical mater which resembled foggy glass. He would rot away in there, his death energy would be kept contained like an emergency reserve for other people to use. Rabolii glared at the different coffins, wondering which one to unseal. Consuming this ancient magic would give him a short boost of strength. He hoped it would be enough.

The fighting went on. Eslir had already climbed up on the wall, smiting erebi in a heroic and impressive way. The skeletons didn't pose a great threat to him. He swung a heavy flail and crushed them with ease. However, someone stepped in to ruin his fun. Out of nowhere someone dropped down on Eslir's shoulders, pulled his helmet off, and threw it aside. The next thing the Aslanian would feel would be the cold stab of a blade in his neck, but he managed to grab one of his attacker's legs and throw him to the ground. That turned out to be Arkenel. The two of them stared at each other for a moment, realising they know each other. Eslir stood up, boastful and proud, and stated, "So we meet again, you son of a corpse. During our last encounter, you survived with your family thanks to pure luck, but that won't happen again. Now, will you face your death standing on your feet, or will you keep on rolling on the ground?"

Without waiting for the answer, Eslir stomped towards Arkenel and swung his flail. The Krumerian rolled away swiftly, and then the two engaged in a fierce duel. The Aslanian was heavily armoured, which made things more difficult than the last time. He swung his weapon around, smacking some random people who happened to be nearby without noticing. Arkenel decided take advantage of the fact that his opponent wasn't very smart. He moved to an archery tower nearby and stood near the wall, almost allowing Eslir to hit him. Arkenel ducked at the last moment, which caused the chain of the flail to get wrapped around an iron torch holder protruding from the wall. As the Aslanian struggled to free his weapon, Arkenel attacked him again, targeting the unarmoured head and neck of his opponent. Surprisingly, Eslir drew a dagger from his belt at the last moment and stabbed his enemy with the blade.

Black blood splattered. Arkenel stood there unable to make a sound, his eyes...eye - wide open. He was so surprised that he couldn't even feel the pain. He coughed, realising that he felt as if he were drowning. The scene in front of his eyes blackened. The smeared outlines of the fighting men, the raging flames, and the pouring rain was the last thing he saw before he passed out.

CHAPTER 7

THE FATHER

In bygone days, when Krumerus still rose in all its morbid glory, devastating forces were at work, fulfilling Mortelion's desire for bloodshed and gore. The bored god was always looking for a way to start new quarrels amongst the mortals, to find new ways to enforce his will upon his subordinates so they'd conquer their enemies, spill blood, and make sacrifices in his name. The necromancer Vegnorii used to be one of his favourites. He'd travel around Soleya dressed as an old traveller, bringing disease and death wherever he went. Once he had come across a southern princess and had offered to read her fortune by looking at her hand in his hut. On that night, when his fingers had touched hers, her skin was strewn with rotting stains, and she succumbed to a terrible disease which finished her off in just a few days. He was hardly the only individual with similar macabre talents. Ekvanor the Soulshredder was famous for his legendary ability to tear through the very fabric which created his victims. Krumerus was full of all sorts of fearsome characters that had roamed these lands. Each generation had new and different ones. The neighbouring nations didn't know if they should try to eradicate such vile beings or just stay away.

The goddesses Glacera and Vernara usually kept their children away from Mortelion's creations, but not on this day. Eslir was storming around the battlefield, smashing one skeleton after another, feeling not a drop of mercy or fright. The skies had opened above him; divine light shone over him. He felt with every fibre of his being that today would be the day he would vanquish this vile nation. Not only would he level this wretched fortress to the ground, but also he would raid every house and cave and would slaughter all erebi—the women, the children,

155

and the elders too. Today would be the day. That would be the magnificent happening which had been set up for such a long time. The end of every kind of tyranny looked exactly this way. After so many centuries and generations saturated with blood and suffering, someone would take up arms, lead strong forces up to the very heart of the evil, and have the good luck of finding it in a vulnerable state. This was exactly what was happening now. The wounded giant Krumerus was on his knees, screaming in pain, ever since the day Rabolii foolishly sacrificed his armies at Lumis and set the beginning of his own end. After many long years in which he had barely been living in his hideous mountain, he was now powerless enough to be overwhelmed.

The storm was raging, the wind was howling, and the pouring rain was enough to sink through armour and clothes, chilling a man's very soul. The mountains were shaken by the titanic collision; huge pieces of Kranium's fortification were collapsing and slamming down with a thunderous sound. The lifeless fortress was succumbing to the Aslanian forces; the men felt that they were destroying the final defenders. The skeletons were too few, and Traneya was struggling to keep the wounded under control. She was losing her grasp on what was happening on the wall. She had not taken care of her arm, which hurt with every movement, but she couldn't imagine abandoning the fight to take care of herself. She didn't want to be like the whiny Rabolii, who made it known worldwide whenever he was experiencing the slightest inconvenience. Her sword was seeming to weigh more and more after every swing, her wound hurt, she was soaked by the rain, and her very body was failing her. The sounds around her seemed somewhat muffled and distant. Somewhere there amongst the fighting men, she thought she heard a familiar voice she used to love so much. It said, "Come on, men, this is our final push! If we overcome this last squad, the rest of their soldiers will flee!"

She blinked with a confused expression. She could see Malior in the crowd. He slaughtered the Aslanians with his long black sword, killing off entire groups of them while remaining untouchable. His dark magic messed with their minds and terrified them. He turned to Traneya with a teasing smile and told her, "The battle is over, my princess. Get back inside."

She used to get so irritated when he called her that. It reminded her that she was related to Rabolii, and that was one of the worst things in her life.

Traneya shook her head, trying to reconnect with reality.

Malior's image faded without disappearing completely. Remedor's daughter felt that she couldn't get away from her visions. She felt like she was slipping away to a place from which she wouldn't be able to return. Her legs finally gave out on her, and she fell to her knees as the battle continued to rage all around her. She was torn apart with anger and frustration. If she were dying for a battle which she knew they'd win, she'd shut her eyes with a sense of accomplishment. Instead she was sinking in darkness, knowing she had failed. At this difficult moment, she raised her eyes towards the overcast sky and mumbled an indistinguishable prayer to Mortelion. It was rare for her to ask him for anything, but there wasn't anything else left for her to do.

The sky began to darken before Traneya's eyes. At first, she thought she was just going to faint, but then she realised that the people around her also noticed the change. The clouds clumped up, ominous and dank, as if they were sucking all the light around. Surprised, she turned her head towards the castle inside the city. Her breath stopped when she saw a very special delegation on the inner wall surrounding the palace. All the darkness sorcerers were rallied together and seemed to be performing some complex combined spell with someone very special. Leaning on a heavy staff crafted out of black steel, Rabolii stood in front of them, tall and pale. His eyes seemed to be greyed out like a blind man's. His hair had paled significantly, and overall he seemed like a thing of nightmares. His mantles waved back as if the wind itself was aiming to make him seem more impressive. No matter how bony and skinny he seemed at that moment, he looked as if he were the master of death, which wasn't his burden at that moment but a weapon. Whenever he would appear in battle, he made a special effort to merge with his element and show only the terrifying power to the enemy without any hint of his inner weakness.

The Krumerians turned and stared at him in surprise. They couldn't believe that this was the same sour old man who could only complain and snap like a disgruntled mother-in-law. He now resembled the necromancers of old legends. The sorcerers of darkness continued draining away the light as this was the perfect setting for a Krumerian to win a fight.

Rabolii hovered over the wall like a ghostly apparition. There was a whirlwind of the energies of death around him. He rolled his eyes back, reaching all the way into another dimension. Together with the other sorcerers of darkness, he did what none of them could accomplish alone. They summoned demons from Mortelion's realm. Grotesque and disfigured, slimy creatures began to emerge amongst Eslir's army beyond the city wall, where they attacked like rabid dogs. The ranks were thrown into chaos. The Aslanians stopped climbing the wall and had to focus on defending themselves.

Rabolii smirked as he watched this happen. He extended his bony hands forward, feeling all the dead flesh on the battlefield. He could hear it. It spoke to him. Its consciousness was primal and confused—a mess of thoughts that once belonged to the souls who inhabited these bodies. Rabolii didn't have strength for much, but he simply couldn't resist animating corpses, because that was his favourite thing in the world.

"Rise up!" Rabolii ordered. His voice thundered over the whole mountain, double-pitched, echoing, and unreal. It made every other sound fade. The clash of the war faded, and the storm was silenced. "Rise up and obliterate the hypocritical Aslanian race. This world will be ruled by the dead."

Eslir felt a chill go up his spine as he was looking upon the unexplainable whirlwind of magical energies above the city. Rabolii's voice startled him and distracted him from finishing off Arkenel. He had not expected the necromancer to end up participating in the battle. He'd thought him weak and defeated. He clutched the handle of his flail, trying to remain unaffected, and was just about to yell to his soldiers to carry on attacking when all the muddy, blood-soaked bodies of the fallen began rising around him. Their mouths were open, their eyes empty like windows of an abandoned house. Their movements were like a puppet's, driven by nothing but magic. Only the voice of Rabolii, their perfect master, sounded in their minds, and they would do everything for him at that moment. They would attack the very same men they had fought side by side with just a few minutes ago.

Rabolii was watching over this chaos, feeling as if he was hardly breathing. His lungs ached and his limbs trembled, but he wouldn't let that feeling take away the thrill of the moment. He liked to feel powerful, untouchable, and divine. Once this intoxicating feeling had followed him no matter what he was doing. He'd feel powerful as he was stretching out in his bed in the morning or when his children would admire him. He'd feel magnificent as the whole of Krumerus trembled at his feet every time he left the castle and walked amongst the crowd. And now, as the energies were chasing in a whirlwind around him, when thousands of dead consciousnesses were in awe before him, when the Aslanians cowered before his majesty, he felt as divine as he once was. He enjoyed that immensely.

While Rabolii was performing the light show, Mavarius finally made his way to Arkenel. Eslir had abandoned the crime scene to smite more vile foes. Remedor's son lay all alone on the ground, barely twitching in some spasms. It seemed that he was trying to cough but didn't have enough strength to do so. Mavarius fell to his knees beside him, not knowing what to do. In prison he had seen open throats, gutted bodies, broken skulls, and whatnot, but for some reason what he was looking at right then felt so much worse. He began to nudge Arkenel and talk to him, "You're fine. Get up!"

Remedor didn't respond. Mavarius looked around helplessly, not knowing how to handle this. He picked up Arkenel carefully and carried him towards the castle to revive him there. He was familiar with a variety of herbs in Vern, and he was good at stitching wounds, but such a deep stab wasn't something he could treat.

Inside the castle, he met up with Traneya, who had finally been dragged away from the battlefield since she could no longer stand on her feet. Salina was accompanying her while two skeletons supported her. Mavarius approached them. The two young women gasped when they saw their brother in such a state. The four of them made their way towards the clinic and were welcomed by some ancient doctor. He looked like a mummy that had survived for several centuries. He sat there examining Traneya's hand for fifteen minutes with such an intense, competent look, as if healing it with the strength of his mind alone. Mavarius was pacing around nervously. When his patience ran out, he grabbed the old man by the shoulders and snapped at him, "What's there to look at on that arm? Don't you see your other patient has nearly kicked the bucket? Look at him, why don't you?"

"Oh, I'm afraid his wound is very serious," said the doctor.

"Your wound will be serious in a minute. You didn't even look at him!"

"Mavarius, don't kill him. We don't have another healer in this city," Salina said softly.

"So, what, we'll let the prince of your stupid country die? Do you have herbs here?"

Mavarius began to rummage through the racks and take out some bottles of liquids he had never seen before. They smelled of death. He turned to the mummified doctor and asked, "Is there anything against infections, or should I get alcohol? What's this crap?"

"Those are medicines for skeletons," the strange doctor said.

Mavarius gritted his teeth, feeling the strong urge to kill everyone. How was it that skeletons were getting better healthcare than the people in this country?! With an aggressive gait, he came up to the doctor, grabbed him by the collar, and snarled, "Listen to me, you freak!"

"Mavarius, he won't help," Traneya said in a weak voice. "I captured a sorceress of life last night. Bring her over. Maybe she can heal us. We didn't get to use her in a trade with the Aslanians, but maybe she'll still be useful somehow."

Mavarius wasn't sure if that was a good idea as he was suspicious of sorcerers, but currently he didn't see a better alternative. He brought Estrella, who still looked frightened and stunned as if she were walking through some nightmare. She started speaking wearily, "Did you send letters to King Eslir with conditions for my ransom? What did he reply?"

There was the crash and rumble of smashed buildings outside. Traneya waved her hand in the direction of the noise and said, "That's his reply!"

"And that." Mavarius nodded towards Arkenel's bed.

Estrella felt a sickening sensation in her abdomen as she recognised the only person in Krumerus who had showed her some kindness. Traneya ordered her, "Heal him!"

"What? But I'm not specialised in treating wounds. I've only ever cured diseases."

That shouldn't have come as a surprise since Soleya had been at peace with its neighbours for more than a decade. Estrella hadn't encountered many wounds—mostly scratches on children's knees.

"How come you can't heal?!" Mavarius raised his hands with annoyance. He remembered his time in Vern. The sorceress of life they had in their tribe was like a goddess amongst mortals. People sought her out for all sorts of problems—minor things like tick bites or serious issues like severed limbs. She could bring people back from the brink of death.

"How about you at least try?" Traneya answered.

"I can pour a bit of life energy that will prevent him from dying anytime soon, but he will need a real doctor and medication to be treated properly," Estrella explained.

Mavarius was still pacing around nervously. He was thinking of all those herbs they had used to treat wounds in Vern. He felt like there was something he could do, but not with Krumerus's vegetation, which was all thorny, dead, or poisonous. He sighed with desperation and went back to digging in the skeleton medicine cabinet in case something useful had actually gotten lost in there.

—ᴍ—

Seeing himself in a tight situation because of Rabolii's involvement, Eslir withdrew his soldiers for a bit to regroup and assess the damage. They backed farther away from the fortress, killing off whatever demons chased them. Eslir looked at the faces of his men. Many of them were startled, insecure, nervous. Some of them whispered that this was a retreat and that there was a monster in Kranium that couldn't be slain by ordinary soldiers—the devastating necromancer Rabolii Remedor. However, Eslir didn't want such thoughts crossing their minds. He stood up, seemingly proud and unaffected by the setback, and said in a loud, clear voice, "Men, I won't deny it, Kranium is holding their ground. They withstood us for longer than I would have expected their weak skeletons to last, but we are on the verge of victory. Let us not forget that their famous necromancer is very old and worn out, and he has just used a lot of his strength. I can tell he's nearing the end of his power as he didn't even attempt to press the attack while we were retreating. I know that in your eyes, Krumerus is a monster of another world, and the fact that it's ancient makes you think that it's always been here and can never die. But that is not the case. Now it's more vulnerable than ever. It's demolished like an old memory, like a ruin. Our suffering ends here because today is the day when we will decapitate this ancient serpent and start a new era in which valour and light shall reign! An era in which there will be no evil beings, monsters, or hatred! This is our legendary day, and nothing will take it away! Take care of your wounds, my brethren. Regain your strength. Once we charge again, we shall level this vile stronghold to the ground! I give you my word!"

The men roared with excitement. They saw a flame in the eyes of their king, such patriotism and determination, that they really felt on the eve of a new era; something revolutionary and great was happening. It was inspiring for them to imagine

161

they were destroying something as enormous and powerful as Krumerus. Suddenly it all seemed real and achievable.

Rabolii watched the retreating Aslanians and barely managed to keep his facade of an almighty sorcerer. He was breathing heavily, a pain in his chest tearing him on the inside. Maybe his heart was giving up on him. Since the enemies were gone and he didn't need to intimidate anyone any more, he stopped hovering in the air and landed on the fortress wall. He leaned against Ravena, feeling weakened.

"I shouldn't have used so much of my strength. For a moment there I forgot that I'm merely a corpse and should boast less, but goddam ..."

"You were amazing, Rab," Ravena said softly. "But this is not over yet, and you're exhausted. We still have vampires, but almost nothing remains of the skeletons."

"I knew that my involvement wouldn't change a thing. Maybe I could have won this doomed battle had I been younger, but now I just can't."

In this line of thought, Rabolii felt a burning hatred for their children because they were so useless and weren't powerful sorcerers like him. He wondered whether he should tell Ravena that all of this was her fault because she had not birthed some decent heirs for him. The necromancer raised his hands to the level of his eyes and sighed desperately. His skin was covered in age spots, his nails were very dark and rough, his knuckles were bony and protruding, and his skin was very thin and frail. This had happened to him before. After using so much magic, his body would dry out like a raisin; he'd look like he had aged a whole decade in just a few hours. He started complaining, "My teeth are shaking. My hair is white, isn't it? This is disgusting."

"I will prepare your potions, my husband. Let's go inside." Ravena led him gently to the castle to spoil him and restore his mental comfort.

As the two of them walked towards the castle, Rabolii's paled, critical eyes scanned the destruction which reigned. The Aslanians hadn't penetrated very deep into the city, but their catapults had still done sufficient damage to the buildings. The necromancer started wailing, "We'll lose this town. And of course it's going to be all my fault. Why couldn't I single-handedly kill ten thousand Aslanians? Why am I not more powerful! You all think that I'm nothing more than a useless corpse."

"Come on, no one thinks that." Ravena tried to calm him.

"As if!" Rabolii grunted. "I know how things are. You expect me to always magically fix everything. However, I'm powerless now. I used up the energy I absorbed from the sarcophaguses. If I take more, I may destroy myself. I don't know how we'll survive once they attack again."

Ravena bit her lip with a grim expression. They didn't have the resources to deal with this situation. She couldn't imagine that the fortress would fall, but she didn't know what to do to prevent it from happening. She suggested, "I'll see if I can mobilise more peasants. There are plenty of men in the caves."

Rabolii didn't know what to offer. He was enraged that he needed to deal with something like this at his old age. He had some plans and hopes for how to deal with his enemies, but nothing had worked the way he had intended it. He couldn't escape. The caves were a dead end, so even if he hid there, he wouldn't survive without his potions for long. His only option was to defend the stronghold in any way he could.

Arkenel shifted lazily, having been awakened by some grumbling voices. He could tell Mavarius and Salina were arguing about something. He felt a numb pain in his chest. He was dizzy and hardly knew where he was. He began moving around, trying to get up and figure out what was going on.

"Tosser, quit moving. I'm elbows deep in your guts," his friend murmured in cheerful greeting.

"He woke up?" Traneya stood up and looked at the bed.

"Arkenel! Are you OK?" Salina screamed. She appeared next to him. As she came too close to Estrella, the two only looked at each other and bristled like hostile cats, then quickly looked back at the wounded man. "When I saw your wound, I thought we'd lost you."

"I'd think you'd lost me anyway. After all, look who's operating on me!" Arkenel answered. A light grin appeared on his pale face.

"Shut it or I'll shank you," Mavarius ordered him as he stitched Remedor's wound.

"Oh, this is hopeless. I heard we have no skeletons left!" Salina continued chattering.

"How's everyone?" Ravena walked into the room and examined the situation. Her gaze fell upon the bed of her wounded son, and she sighed. "When I heard a sorceress of life was captured, I suspected it was her. Do you think we can trust her and leave Arkenel in her hands?"

"Oh, I trust her all right," growled Mavarius, baring his teeth and staring at Estrella. She was pale and had the feeling that she would faint from all this negative tension.

"Will my son be safe with you, Mavarius?" Ravena asked seriously. "I need my daughters. Our situation is very difficult. We have to figure out a way to save the fortress."

"Yes, ma'am." The man nodded with a grim expression.

"Come on, ladies!" Ravena waved her hand. "Let's meet with your father."

Traneya and Salina got up with moody expressions. Mavarius looked down at his wounded companion, his face strained with anger; he punched the wall, which startled the anxious Estrella.

"We can't defend the fortress, they say! Idiots! It's like I broke out of that dumb prison with skeletons and bullshit. It was a gory fight with blood and guts flying everywhere, but we won. How many people do we have in this dumb town? If we arm everyone with a shovel or a rod or whatever ..."

"Man, this is Kranium we're talking about," Arkenel replied in a deathly voice. It was difficult for him to talk. He didn't feel like explaining to Mavarius in too much detail how in Krumerus everyone thought they were too cool to fight because the soldiers were always skeletons. "Nobody here knows how to hold a sword."

"How come?" Mavarius asked, surprised. "It's not some tricky science. You just swing the damn thing! Hiding in the caves and waiting to get slaughtered isn't exactly better."

"Tell that to my father," sighed Arkenel.

"We'll all bloody die. All of us!"

"Stop whining!"

"Tosser, I'm serious! We're in all sorts of trouble. And I'm not sorry for anything except that ..."

He got up and turned his back to the bed. Estrella shifted timidly. She was witnessing some very intimate scenes at the enemy camp, and she didn't know what to think. Arkenel remained silent in anticipation. Mavarius continued, "Except that I'll have to leave you here to die."

"No one's dying, man."

"No, you know we're screwed. That wall will fall before the morning, and this graveyard of a town will be levelled," replied Mavarius gruffly, still standing with his back turned to Arkenel. "I won't stay here to see it. I'm out."

Arkenel tried to get up from the bed, but the pain cut him through the torso and he couldn't. He made a tortured face, then slumped back and said, "Oh, come on! We'll manage somehow. You'll see. My father's Rabolii Remedor. That's gotta count for something."

"I won't sit here and wait for the Aslanians to gut me," Mavarius mumbled without turning around. He went to the door and pulled out the large, rusty key. He looked down as if talking to the lock and said, "I'd also prefer it if you survived, but ..."

"Don't waste your breath, you disloyal tosser!" Arkenel snapped. He lay back on the pillow and stared at the ceiling. "Don't even bother coming back once you hear we've won the battle."

Mavarius clenched his teeth, and without looking back he walked out, locking the door. Arkenel once again stirred uneasily, realising with whom he was sealed in the room. He slowly moved his eyes towards Estrella, and the two of them stared suspiciously, each expecting the other to perform some deadly manoeuvre. Without blinking, the sorceress stepped back as silently as a spectre and crouched in a corner, not breaking eye contact with her patient. Arkenel looked at her, thinking she was probably harmless. She looked like one of those women who wouldn't even kill a cockroach because she was either afraid, disgusted, or too compassionate. If he were feeling a bit better, he'd strike up a pleasant conversation with her, but right then he was sick and in pain, so he just chose to be silent and rest.

Rabolii sat on his throne, his fingers laced in front of his face as he stared ahead, deep in thought. He didn't seem like a proud and strong ruler; he resembled one of those tragic characters from a dramatic Krumerian play which ends with everyone's death. He couldn't remain at rest for too long because everyone started coming into the throne room to seek his wisdom. Traneya seemed pale and grim; Salina, emotional and agitated; and Arkenel's companions, drunk and confused. Rabolii gazed at the faces in front of him, knowing that they would start asking him questions which he couldn't answer.

"I managed to mobilise another fifty people from the caves," Ravena said. "It was difficult to gather even that many. Most were hiding with hoods and capes and tried to pretend they were old women."

This would have been funny if Kranium weren't facing imminent destruction. Traneya noted, "We should never have been left so exposed. We became easy prey."

Rabolii turned to her and told her, "As for you, dear daughter of mine, why did you fail to assassinate the Aslanian king? I don't know why I even entrusted you with such a task. I should have known you'd fail spectacularly."

Traneya raised her eyebrows in surprise and asked, "Oh, you're actually aware of that? I didn't know you cared about anything that was going on."

The truth was that Rabolii could spy on everyone through his skeletons, but he decided to play it cool, so he replied, "Death speaks to me in a way which I cannot ignore, so I'm aware of things of similar magnitude even if I miss the gossip about the insignificant affairs in this castle."

"I hope Death told you Arkenel's nearly dead. Or is this also an insignificant affair?" Traneya taunted him.

Rabolii's facial expression didn't change at all. Without demonstrating a single emotion, he asked, "Arkenel's been injured?"

"They just pulled his guts out through his throat—nothing to write home about." Traneya shrugged while Salina moaned as if she were going to faint.

"Where is he?" Rabolii asked casually.

"In my room. I left some people to tend to him."

"Let's go see him. I'm curious to see if he's going to die. The rest of you, go see if you can fix up some of the broken skeletons. It's easier than raising new ones, at least for me."

Ravena sighed and nudged Salina, who was wondering whether she should accompany her father. The two of them went to tend to the skeletons.

Traneya found the key to her room on the outside of her door and was surprised to see that Mavarius was gone. Estrella was still sitting in the corner, and Arkenel lay in bed, his eyes and mouth wide open. Not a muscle on his face moved, and he displayed no signs of being alive. Rabolii just shot him a disinterested look, then pointed at the sorceress and complained, "That's the Soleyan. What is she doing here?"

"Ask Death to tell you," Traneya scoffed.

"Don't mock me, girl!" the necromancer snapped.

"Well, when you sent me to kill kings, I found myself incapable of infiltrating a camp with ten thousand men to stab their leader. So I just took what I could. I figured they either would not attack without the sorceress of life or would want to ransom her in exchange for something. I sent them letters, but they didn't answer."

"How did it occur to you that they'd just drop the whole battle because of one sorceress?" Rabolii asked. "Never mind.

"Since they've shown no willingness to negotiate, they can kiss her goodbye."

Estrella listened to this, so horrified that she couldn't even start crying. It was a nightmare. She had always heard stories about how terrible, evil, and ugly Rabolii was, but what she witnessed exceeded all tales. Traneya frowned and said, "What's the use of killing her? She is not a threat. Also, she takes care of Arkenel."

...The same Arkenel who just lay there drooling on his pillow, but because of this lively discussion, no one paid any attention him. Rabolii replied, "I didn't say I would kill her. But I won't give her back to them. They didn't show any intention to behave, so we'll keep her here and find some use for her."

Estrella didn't know if that was even worse than death. She had hoped for Arkenel to recover so he could put in a good word for her and say she saved his life, but such an outcome seemed unlikely. Traneya crossed her arms and mumbled, "Also, it's good to see that you're touched by your son's condition. At least I expected you to be happy to have a new skeleton."

Rabolii turned towards the bed and replied casually, "Oh? Don't worry about him. He'll be fine."

Traneya looked at her brother again, noticing that flies were starting to swarm around him, and exclaimed, "What? I don't even know if he's alive right now! How can you know that?!"

Rabolii looked at her with superiority, raised his head boastfully, and replied, "Death told me, Traneya. Now, if you'll excuse me, I need to have my potions so I'll be in shape for our last stand."

"How can you still think we'll win this miserable battle?" Traneya sighed.

"Death told me that as well." Rabolii raised his eyebrows mysteriously.

The wind blew cold air over the Krumerian ruins. The mist was thickening, but even with the limited visibility, one could still see the Aslanians were coming back. They were marching in formation; their sorcerers were prepared to protect them from enemy spells. Rabolii appeared on the fortress wall and scanned the army with his eyes. He focused on exploring what remained of his strength, trying to estimate if he had enough to raise any more corpses. He felt like he was cursed. He could never use all his power on animating soldiers or else he would lose control over his own body. He'd always had a lot of energy, but he had to use it on himself, and that infuriated him. Traneya and Ravena walked up to him and stood by his side. He looked at them critically and murmured, "Why are you not in the castle? This is no place for women."

Traneya laughed. He made it sound like their gender was the problem. He should have just said, You're not dead enough to be here. Ravena put a hand on his shoulder and said, "Rab, you know we would never leave you to fight this alone and let something happen to the fortress while we're stitching embroidery inside."

Salina walked up to them. She considered this a good time to panic, but she could see that Daddy was being brave, so she'd try to be like him. The four of them held each other's hands (Rabolii did so unwillingly) as they watched the approaching horde. They wondered how many Aslanians there were down there. Even if the bold assessment were to be made that a third of them had died in the last battle, which probably was not the case, the number was still too great. The last skeletons stood on the wall, cold and motionless; the vampires were perched upon the nearby towers, awaiting a command so they'd dive down. The whole of Kranium looked like a cold, bleak ruin. However, for its residents it was a ruin with soothing darkness, fresh cave air, and yards with sickly plants which could also turn into a decent meal provided they were handled correctly. The streets were full of scattered children's toys made out of bones. The attics hid treasures from ages ago when Krumerus had been through many rises and falls. All of this was home to so many. That's why no one from the Remedor family could believe this would come to an end or that they'd need to leave it all behind in order to survive.

Every second dragged on seemingly for an eternity. The Aslanian drums of war and their battle songs echoed amongst the mountaintops, sounding apocalyptic. Any moment now arrows would fly in the air again and ladders would be raised so blood could be spilled. Rabolii never did show much excitement in situations like this, but he did feel a nervous anticipation. He was somewhat inpatient. He was so preoccupied with thoughts about battle strategies and possible spells he could use that he almost didn't notice some turmoil in the enemies' ranks.

The Aslanians marched all the way to the fortress wall. The drums of war went quiet, and the songs faded. No one was attacking. The army was standing still, seemingly awaiting commands. That moment of nervous expectation seemed to Rabolii to last a century. Ravena and her daughters shifted a bit. They started casting glances at the necromancer as if silently asking him if he knew what was going on. He said nothing. Instead a victorious grin stretched across his face, and his eyes lit up. He resembled an evil genius who had triumphed by way of his perfectly executed plan. The expression became even more apparent when he received a request from the Aslanian army for an urgent diplomatic meeting. The rest of the Remedor family couldn't believe it. Ravena asked, "Could this be a trap? Maybe they just want you to leave the fortress. There's no reason for them to negotiate now."

"Oh, I think I know what this is about. Don't worry about me. I'll be back soon," her husband replied with the same contented smile on his face.

Rabolii made his way down, walking proudly like some legendary winner. He couldn't wait to see the faces of his enemies. When he stood in front of them, he realised this would be even more satisfactory than he imagined. Eslir stood in front of the army with a discontented, angry look and crossed arms, and only a few metres from him was a squad of men in golden armour. Those were the Soleyans, led by Ilinar Lumeris, who shot his cousin discontented looks. When Rabolii appeared, both young kings stared at him; Eslir was trying to kill him with his eyes alone. The Soleyan hardly recognised Rabolii. Was this truly the same man who had invaded Lumis mere weeks ago? He looked decades older!

"Your Majesties, how pleased I am to see you together!" exclaimed the necromancer with a contented smile. "Ilinar, I wasn't expecting you. What are you doing so far north in this cold weather?"

"I had to come immediately to discuss some important things after we had a surprise attack from the west," Ilinar said, getting straight to the point.

"Why am I not surprised?" Rabolii raised his eyebrows and cast an all-knowing gaze at Eslir, who seemed even more furious and hateful, if that was even possible.

"And naturally, some of us immediately decided to focus on the wrong enemy," snapped the Aslanian king. "But why am I surprised, Ilinar? You *are* an erebius after all!"

"Shut up, Eslir!" Ilinar replied, unamused. "I didn't come here to save Krumerus. I just think that our political situation is more complicated than we expected. I'm against the idea of undertaking huge military campaigns to the north while we're being attacked from the west."

Rabolii observed that conversation with a smile. He was so proud of himself as everyone was right where he wanted them to be. He was glad he had made such an impact on Ilinar that he'd come all this way to stop Eslir's army. What he planned to do afterwards was to continue reinforcing the idea that Vern was the more dangerous enemy. And if Ilinar believed that, it would be the end of all problems for the necromancer.

Ilinar wasn't happy to be in Krumerus. He wasn't sure if it really was a good idea for him to have come to this godforsaken place. It was too cold and dark. Everything about it seemed threatening. But what else could he do? If it weren't for him, Eslir would start a war with the entire continent. Even if Krumerus was weakened and could be an easy target, Vern surely wasn't.

The kings were led into the fortress with a small escort of soldiers. Eslir couldn't stop leering around and mumbling with discontentment. He was outraged by the architecture, which made every building look like a catacomb. He saw more skulls there than he had seen in his entire life. Ilinar looked like he might faint at any moment now; he was hardly walking in a straight line. This place was so depressing. It was as if death was around every corner. The smell of rotting flesh was everywhere. Rabolii noticed the nervousness of his guests and felt very good about himself. He led them into his throne room and sat on his magnificent throne, stroking the huge bones from which it was made. Everyone else remained standing. Eslir glanced around, his lips curling into a dissatisfied grimace. He was the first to raise his voice: "All right then! Now that we've all gathered here, would someone please explain what we're doing exactly? I think I was very clear when I stated that I am against any peace talks. Ilinar Lumeris, why did you interfere?"

"Yes, Ilinar, tell him!" said Rabolii in such a manner as if had he not given his permission, the young king wouldn't have spoken. He liked to feel as if he were the one controlling the conversation.

"I'll tell you what I'm doing here. I came all the way here to inform you of what's happening on our western border," exclaimed Ilinar. He seemed more confident and authoritative when he spoke than he usually was, and he was casting glances at Rabolii, monitoring his reaction. "Maybe this will shock you, but we did get attacked from the west. And it was the Vernians!"

"That's not possible. Vern hasn't declared a war," Eslir grumbled.

"I don't know how else to explain their raid then. I left the battle early, but I saw them. Our attackers were definitely Vernians with bows and spears. I can't even begin to imagine what happened to that poor village which they surrounded. I only had a hundred soldiers there to defend it."

Rabolii made himself comfortable on his throne with a satisfied look on his face. He enjoyed observing this conversation. It was as if he was watching a play. Eslir continued arguing, "I'm sure there's another explanation for all that!"

"What other explanation do you want for armed Vernians who just attacked the border? They didn't talk to us. They didn't try to avoid a collision. They just charged head first!"

"Maybe they were bandits. We have no evidence that they acted by order of their queen," stated Eslir.

"Sure, of course! And Rabolii somehow predicted we'd be attacked by hundreds of bandits who would charge at the royal troops! Do you hear yourself?" Ilinar was enraged by Eslir's suggestions. He couldn't believe his ears.

"So what? Soleya was attacked by Vern. How is this stopping Aslania from obliterating Krumerus?" Eslir spread his arms.

"I thought that the alliance between Soleya and Aslania was unbreakable and that if my country was in danger, you'd come to help. Instead, you're throwing your armies against another country which is hardly doing anything to us now," Ilinar snapped.

Eslir's eyes opened wide in outrage and disbelief. He raised his arms in a furious gesture and barked, "You really think they're harmless? *They* killed our parents! Just a few weeks ago they invaded our land with an army of corpses!"

"And whose fault was that?" Ilinar raised his voice. It didn't seem like he was trying to be polite with his ally any more. "I didn't want to raise this issue before, but everything that has gone wrong for us recently was your fault. You just *had to* kidnap their queen! Every time you made a decision, it was a wrong one."

"I will tell you what the only correct decision is. It's to kill these freaks!" Eslir gestured towards Rabolii. "Do you think that our ancestors have been at war with them for thousands of years out of boredom? This place births only monsters and abominations. It's like a disease. If we give them a chance, Mortelion will create his next champion, who will be the death of us all. For as long as one of them survives, there will always be a chance for there to be another Rabolii, another deranged sorcerer, another monster! This is our opportunity to end it once and for all! Why would you stand in my way?!"

"Because I believe that a large army belonging to a country in a good state is more dangerous than a single monster," said Ilinar. "Vern's attack was shocking; we know nothing about their intentions. And I believe Krumerus is more experienced in fighting them. Perhaps they have some answers for us."

"You suggest I work with them?" roared Eslir with outrage, starting to pace back and forth like a caged lion.

"I suggest you throw your armies at an actual threat," Ilinar answered coldly. Rabolii's eyebrows cocked up. He found that statement offensive. The young king turned to him and said, "This is not an attempt on Soleya's behalf to save you. I will not bear a provocation on your part, but at this point I have prioritised my enemies. I don't know if I can trust you, but you have a reason to keep a good relationship with us. Otherwise you will be at war with all your neighbours."

"I'm aware of that, Ilinar," Rabolii answered with a thin smile, watching how Ilinar shuddered a bit when the necromancer referred to him by his first name. "Was I not the first one to propose a truce? Your Majesties, I am already an old man. I don't have the same fighting spirit as I once did. I don't aim for bloodshed and battles. I'm just trying to secure my country's well-being. I know Krumerus has a terrible reputation, but things change. I'm open to the idea of peace and alliances."

"I don't trust him," Eslir snorted, crossing his arms.

"You don't have to trust him. It's in his interest not to fight with us, don't you think?" Ilinar said to him. "This discussion is over. Soleya has reached a decision. I recommend that Aslania do the same, and then help with strengthening the western border and establish communication with Vern."

"That's your own war. Deal with it." Eslir grunted, turned around, and headed towards the exit. He said, "Aslania will proceed to fortify its northern border. It won't be the first time we'll be invaded by erebi."

Ilinar looked at him, slightly startled. "That's your own war"? What was that supposed to mean? Did Eslir have no intention of helping him if things with Vern escalated? Things weren't looking too good. He'd resume negotiations with him after he had calmed down a bit. Eslir had already reached the chamber's doors when he turned around and yelled, "And before I forget!

What exactly did you do with the sorceress of life you stole so insolently from our camp?!"

Rabolii opened his mouth to respond to this, but Traneya stepped forward and replied before he got the chance. "Why do you even ask? Didn't I send you letters telling you to withdraw your soldiers or else the woman dies? I thought I was perfectly clear!"

Ilinar shuddered. He had known Estrella all his life. Even though they weren't close friends, they sometimes talked. He'd see her almost every day. Lumis would seem empty without her. He wasn't sure whom to blame for her death, the Krumerian who had slit her throat or Eslir, who evidently had made no attempt to bargain for her life.

"Murderers!" Eslir roared, pointing a finger at his vile foes. "You won't get away with this! With or without Soleya, I will crush you. Mark my words!"

Having said that, Eslir disappeared from the scene, leaving behind an ominous silence that contrasted greatly with the shouting voices which had echoed mere seconds ago. Ilinar's mind was blank, and he didn't know what to think. He turned to Rabolii, feeling stiff and uneasy. He wasn't sure what he felt. There was something about the necromancer which made him feel so insignificant, like a fly faced with something it just couldn't comprehend. He felt a kind of awe. It was the emotion that had helped Rabolii conquer Krumerus a while back, and he still inspired it.

"Soooo, about Vern...," Ilinar stuttered.

Rabolii put on a polite smile and answered, "Come now, there's no need to get down to business upon your very arrival! Here in Krumerus we are more hospitable than that. Come, I'll introduce you to my family and show you around the castle. At dinner, we'll discuss Vern in more detail."

Ilinar blinked in fright as he watched how Rabolii got up and descended from his throne. He stood in front of the boy, tall and dreadful, with an all-knowing smile on his face. It looked like he had some plans for bonding.

Meanwhile Arkenel was starting to come around. He felt as if he were returning from the afterlife. He was covered in cold sweat and could taste blood in his mouth. He hardly remembered anything that had happened to him in the last day or so. Half awake, he mumbled, "Hey ... hey, Mavarius, got any booze?"

He heard someone move in the room, so he opened his eyes... his eye. In front of him appeared a face far too pretty and clean to be Mavarius's. Arkenel's smile widened and he said, "Tosser! You've finally showered!"

"Your friend is not here, Your Highness," Estrella said. It was a relief that her patient was alive. Maybe she still had a chance to justify her presence in Krumerus and prove she could be useful.

Arkenel's smile dimmed as he returned to reality. He moved nervously and said hoarsely, "Oh yes, it's all coming back to me now. Help me get up!"

He started moving around, which pulled his stitches. Bloodstains appeared on his bandages. Estrella was horrified. She had put so much time and effort into nursing him to health; she wasn't going to watch him ruin it all as soon as he woke up. She held him down by the shoulders, trying to restrain him, and said, "Where do you want to go? You were badly injured. You can't get up!"

"Where has that idiot gone to? He can't leave the city! The Aslanians are everywhere." Arkenel grunted. He continued to fight for his freedom with the power and might of a turtle flipped on its back.

Estrella overpowered him and pinned him down to the bed, still holding him by the shoulders to make sure he wouldn't try to get up again. Arkenel turned his gaze towards her. A pale, tortured smile stretched across his chapped lips. He said, "Milady, don't get me wrong. I love it when women lie on top of me. But in this case I really need to find my stupid friend and bring his smelly self back to a place where no one will break his head. So will you help me?"

"What would you possibly do? The door is locked," Estrella said.

Arkenel stopped struggling. He laid his head back on his pillow and exhaled wearily. He muttered, "That's just great. Dammit, why am I injured while battles and all sort of stuff is happening outside? Oh well, since we're both already here, how about we get to know each other?" He turned his attention to Estrella once again, trying to grant her a charming smile, but his missing eye and bloody teeth didn't help create that impression. "You don't need to get all formal with me. Just call me Arkenel. And what's your name?"

Estrella was used to being courted by all sorts of men. She decided to just answer politely so hopefully a peaceful conversation would distract him from trying to get up again.

"I ... I'm Estrella Galiviar."

"Estrella. What a beautiful name. I think it means 'star' in some southern dialect." Arkenel continued the secular conversation.

"Is that so? Nobody has ever told me that."

Arkenel smirked. During the time spent in prison, he had forgotten all the useless knowledge his teachers had stuffed into his young head, but now as soon as he beheld his father's shrivelled face, he was suddenly overwhelmed by all kinds of memories of things he thought he had lost a long time ago. Words from the southern dialect were just one of those things. Estrella asked him, "What about 'Arkenel'? Does it mean something in any northern dialects?"

"It does, as a matter of fact. As far as I know, there was some order of sorcerers called Arcans. So my father just named me after them because he couldn't even imagine I wasn't going to be a sorcerer myself. At least that's my mother's theory. I do want to mention that in some lakes we have some massive leeches with fins. They're called *arkanels*. Maybe my father thought I looked like one of those, so he gave me that name!"

Estrella took that too literally. She exclaimed, "Do the babies of the ereb—of the Krumerians—resemble leeches when they're born?"

"They do in Rabolii's eyes." Arkenel shrugged. "He has too many kids. He must be sick of us."

"Why? How many of you are there?"

"Um, five. What about you? Got any siblings?"

The woman sat by the bed to make herself a little more comfortable and started telling Arkenel about her family. He would nod and reply. Any kind of a light conversation was a nice distraction from the currently reality full of war and uncertainty.

Meanwhile Ilinar was accepted as an honorary guest in Kranium. He and his soldiers were given rooms with clean water and soap. The young king sat on the bed, which was covered by a heavy velvet blanket, and looked around. The castle was richly decorated in various peculiar ways. Everything in it looked old and ominous—the skull-plated wallpaper, the artificial knit webs, the grim portraits of creepy people framed by antique blackened silver. All furnishings and fabrics seemed centuries old. The room felt stuffy as if no one had aired it out in years. It was very strange for Ilinar to be in a place like this.

The diplomatic dinner in question took place at a ridiculous time, between eleven and twelve o'clock at night. It was in the big dining room where Rabolii had not set foot in a long time, but now he would have to cause himself this inconvenience. There was an excessive number of candles so the Soleyans could see their plates. Rabolii turned to Ilinar and told him, "I hope the lighting is sufficient."

"I don't need the light to see," Ilinar replied drily as he was poking the contents of his plate with a fork which seemed to be made of some sort of bone. "I hadn't even told that to anyone before."

Ravena was sitting next to her husband. She seemed moody and didn't even want to look at Ilinar. She was annoyed because she felt this was more than a diplomatic meeting between monarchs and was wondering if she'd end up having to adopt another child. Salina looked worried. Traneya was just sitting there frowning at her plate. She still thought that Rabolii hadn't done much to help the city, but he was now boasting as if he had saved it all by himself. Arkenel was also sitting with them, even though everyone had told him to lie down and rest. He couldn't accept that the fate of his nation would be decided here and that he wouldn't be there to witness it. He looked as pale as a ghost with whitened lips like he might spontaneously die at any moment. The necromancer pretended that he wasn't noticing anyone's discontent. He turned to his guest with a pleasant smile and said, "I'm glad to hear you're comfortable. Because of our good eyesight, we don't use much lighting here, but you are obviously fit for that. Tell us about yourself, Ilinar! What do you do in your free time?"

Ilinar raised his eyes from his plate of suspicious food, wondered if he had heard that right. He wasn't sure why Rabolii was asking him that. He almost instinctively gave the same response he did every time: "I have soldier figurines and use them to reenact the battles described by Emanrylii Prehorian in his books."

Ravena started coughing. When she'd first seen Ilinar, she thought him to be somewhat dumb and childish; that was the impression she got. Now when she found out he played with toys, she felt like her suspicion was warranted. Rabolii, smiling as if he were very interested in Ilinar, stated, "I do respect Prehorian very much. He was a remarkably intelligent man with ingenious battle strategies and a very strong means of expression. Looking at armies' compositions is a useful activity."

Ilinar was somewhat surprised by that answer. The only other person who had ever seemed genuinely supportive of his hobby was his mother. Eley had repeatedly told him that his games were nonsense and that reading the same outdated book would make him stupid. This encouragement made him more talkative, so he added, "Well, yes. I also have sword replicas like the ones they used in the Prehorian age."

"That is very interesting," Rabolii stated. "You seem to know a lot about armaments and the way an army functions. You must be an excellent general. Tell us how you handled the attack of the Vernians? I'm curious about what strategies you have implemented."

Arkenel shifted in his chair. This was the first time he'd heard that Soleya had been fighting with the Vernians. Ravena nudged Salina under the table, and the two exchanged glances. They were both thinking the same thing—Rabolii wasn't known to be this nice to a person he wasn't trying to use. The necromancer knew how to act so people would like him. Back in the day he'd often use that skill to get what he wanted. Ilinar was getting more comfortable and continued to chatter, "We were surprised they actually ended up attacking us. The scouts carried the news minutes before their troops appeared. We weren't very well prepared, and I had to retreat in order to chase Eslir and ask for aid."

"That was a good idea. A wise ruler should know how to prioritise his enemies and how to distribute his forces to minimise losses." Rabolii nodded with approval. "Have you been in other battles before?"

Ilinar blushed a bit. He didn't want to admit he hadn't even taken part in this battle. He had escaped as soon as the first arrow was shot. But he didn't want to embarrass himself, so he said, "Actually, it was my first battle. Soleya has been at peace with everyone so far."

"It really is a bit frightening." Rabolii tilted his head to one side, his piercing eyes fixed on Ilinar. "Peace and comfort can end in a single moment, and while death and destruction rage all around you, you feel powerless. In moments like that, it's important to keep your friends close and to always know what you're up against."

"Lord Remedor." Ilinar turned to him. "Is it true? Are you really not hostile towards Soleya? Eslir thinks you're lying, and I don't know whom to believe."

Rabolii watched him carefully and patiently, then said, "I have more than one reason to be honest with you, Ilinar. First of all, I'm a man of integrity and I stand by my word. And furthermore, you really are my son. You could become the bridge between Soleya and Krumerus, securing a brighter future for everyone. If there is a single person on this continent who could achieve peace, it would be you. Both of us want it. Let's help each other achieve it."

Ilinar sat there staring. He hadn't expected his family relationship with the necromancer to be brought up so soon, but perhaps it was inevitable. It did feel like that topic was an elephant sitting next to them on the table that they were all trying not to acknowledge. The moment Ilinar saw Rabolii for the first time this day, he had felt some really strong emotions for him. He had the sudden urge to make up for all the time he had lived without a father. Ilinar had always considered his father dead, but now here he was. At first it was shocking for him when he learned the fearsome necromancer of legend was his dad, but after the thought had settled in his mind, it somewhat excited him. Perhaps Rabolii would be the strong shoulder on which he'd lean for support; he'd be the protection he felt he lacked. He needed a dreaded monster on his side which would vanquish his nightmares. Ilinar felt like telling Rabolii all of that, but he was afraid of how he would react. So he just blinked a few times, trying to remember what they were talking about before this frenzy of thoughts passed through his head. He just nodded stiffly. "I ... I also want peace. However, I need to know more about Vern's agenda and why they attacked us. Have you spoken with them?"

Rabolii sat back in his chair, placed his hands on the table, and said, "If you want to understand Vern, you must first gain familiarity with their queen. Her name is Krementa, and although she's older than me, she appears youthful because of her close relations with Vernara. Perhaps she's even immortal. She is a very powerful woman and a bored one at that. She lives in a very remote location, so our nations are a lot more bizarre and alien to her than Krumerus, Soleya, and Aslania are to each other. The technology in Vern is not as developed as in our countries. Much of the knowledge about construction, agriculture, and medicine is unknown to them. The easiest way for Krementa to get what she wants is through war. She spreads something which Vern has never known before—greed and aggression."

Ravena frowned while listening to this. She wasn't sure if those were in fact real reasons. She was just left with the impression that for decades Krementa and Rabolii had been at each other's throats and were mercilessly trying to destroy each other. Both sides have had their ups and downs, but it was the necromancer's forces that had prevailed over the years. Now Krumerus was stretching far beyond the Skeletal Wall to the west. Any captured Vernians would just be turned into skeletons, adding more cheap servants and making the country rich. Ravena had noticed all of this and was left with the impression that Rabolii was the real aggressor and was waging war because it was profitable. Krementa wouldn't be so aggressive if she didn't have to fight for her life. But if that really was the only reason, why was the Vernian queen adding to her troubles by attacking Soleya now?

Arkenel was thinking something similar, his blood-drained brain trying to process all the information. He might have had a little more knowledge about Vern than most Krumerians as he had spent time around Mavarius. He was aware that the locals to the west hated Mortelion's nation and viewed it as a race of monsters and abominations. However, based on what he knew about Vern, it made no sense for them to attack Soleya when they were already at war with Krumerus.

"If she's so interested in material goods, perhaps we could trade." Ilinar shrugged. "I don't see why we can't be civil about this."

"I wish it were that easy." Rabolii sighed. "It may seem that she hates all of us the way Eslir hates Krumerus. Most Vernians cherish life, so they tend to be peaceful, but she's turned them against us. She tells them how Krumerus is a mockery of life itself and that in Soleya no one values nature. The fact that we don't worship trees is her excuse to wage war, but she has other reasons. She expects us to be easy prey because Krumerus and Soleya are not united and Aslania is too far away to provide solid help."

Traneya scoffed quietly. It was unbelievable anyone would think of Krumerus as easy prey, especially people who used wooden bowls. She found it funny how anyone could depict those tree-lovers as an aggressive nation. Arkenel continued rethinking the whole situation when suddenly he was shaken by an insight. He finally figured out why he had been tasked with bringing a whole squad of nonrotten Vernian soldiers to Krumerus in complete secret. Rabolii had reanimated them and sent them to attack Soleya. None of the southerners had noticed the deception, so now they thought Krementa was sending troops, which made her look just as crazy and evil as Rabolii made her out to be. Arkenel shook his head in disbelief.

On the one hand, he felt a bit sorry for the poor Soleyan boy who was getting entangled in this web of lies, but on the other hand he was very grateful to the necromancer for pulling this off. If it hadn't been for Ilinar's interference, Eslir would have levelled the whole fort by now.

"I don't know how to handle this. If I do sign a peace treaty with you, Eslir will most likely turn his back on me. He doesn't share a border with Vern, so he cares less what happens," Ilinar continued rambling nervously.

"Let's think of Eslir later," Rabolii said with a pleasant smile.

And so the dinner continued. Salina and Ravena were paying attention to Rabolii's every word, trying to guess what he was hiding and plotting. Every once in a while they'd nudge each other and whisper something. Ilinar decided to make this dinner even more useful and to investigate Agelik. The whole mystery surrounding that guy wouldn't leave Ilinar's mind. He casually dropped into the conversation, "Master Remedor, as you may have noticed, I have a great interest in history. As far as Krumerus is concerned, however, my knowledge has always been limited to stories of the battles my ancestors have had with you. But recently I came across a name, and I was wondering what that person was involved with."

Rabolii gave Ilinar an all-knowing look and answered, "I've always been fascinated by history myself. Which name has attracted your attention?"

Ilinar took a deep breath, knowing that it was unlikely he'd receive information after providing so little of it himself, but he continued, "I'm not sure of the full name, but it was abbreviated to R. R. Remedor, and the person lived in the 113th century. I know that's not very specific, but I thought that maybe if he was someone famous ..."

"Oh!" Rabolii's eyes lit up. "I think you mean Renya Raylii Remedor. In fact, she wasn't all that famous in comparison to other members of our great family. What have you read about her?" Rabolii replied, feeling proud for knowing all about any of his ancestors which could be mentioned in Soleyan literature.

Ilinar didn't want to give away any information he wasn't supposed to. His mouth felt very dry as he answered, "I ... I think she had something to do with Soleya. She was mentioned in someone's journal."

"It's not impossible. She was a talented sorceress. She possessed a rare combination of the death and light spheres. In fact, such energies burdened her more than they were actually useful to her. She was quite sickly and often had hallucinations. Perhaps her fragile health and emotional state is what prompted her to heresy."

Ilinar frowned and asked, "What is considered heresy in Krumerus?"

"Worshipping the other gods, of course," Rabolii replied instantly. "It's forbidden for anyone here to perform rituals or have amulets for anyone but Mortelion. If our god detects heresy amongst his subordinates, he will punish the culprit and everyone around them. There have been cases of entire villages being demolished this way. Renya was exposed as a heretic when she was about fifteen or sixteen years old, and Mortelion's cultists caught her while she was trying to escape to Soleya. Of course, the punishment for this was public execution."

Arkenel made a painful grimace. He knew that those "public executions" were a manifestation of all the hatred and malice of the Krumerians. Some people were so angry about their own lives that they would rejoice at the opportunity to take their anger out on a helpless victim. The heretics or the so-called "lightmongers" experienced a series of the most terrible torture techniques before they were finally killed. He felt angry that someone would do such a thing to a fifteen-year-old kid.

Ilinar frowned at this answer. That didn't really grant him a lot of insight. He would have thought that Agelik was a friend of Renya and that he had persuaded her to escape to Soleya, which led to her getting captured and executed. But how was it possible that this was the same Agelik as the one in the ruins? It made no sense for Mortelion to coddle him and keep him safe and alive for two centuries. Maybe the soldiers were right and Agelik was dead without realising it? Nothing was certain.

It was apparent that Ilinar would be a dear guest in Kranium for at least a few days while he was getting to know his family and conducting all the necessary negotiations. As he was settling down and preparing to sleep in his new chambers, Rabolii was trying to retreat to his own chambers but was being attacked by Ravena and Salina, who wanted an explanation for his strange behaviour.

"Come on, when will you tell us what you're plotting?" Ravena was trying to get him to talk. "How much of what you told your 'son' is true? What did you lie about? And how on earth do you know the intentions of that Krementa so well?"

Rabolii turned to them with a fearsome face. His eyes were whitened. Deep wrinkles cut through his face, which had never looked so old before. It was such a nice change when he was acting all friendly and pleasant for Ilinar, but everyone was prepared that it wouldn't last for long. The necromancer started fussing, "Is this how it's going to be? I've been leading battles all day long. I endangered my life and health, negotiated with all sorts of people, and missed my vampirism sessions, and instead of letting me catch up, you attack me! But why should you feel any empathy for me? To you I'm just that corpse that's supposed to make everyone's wishes come true. I'll answer your billions of questions another time. Now if you'll excuse me ..."

Rabolii placed his bony hand on the heavy iron handle of his huge door, which was almost too heavy for him to push these days. The moment he entered, he felt as though the air itself was different. He began sniffing and looking around, then his eyes fell on the mess on his desk. Rabolii was not legendary for his pursuit of perfect order, but all the scattered papers and smashed flasks hinted that this was the work of someone else.

"Merciful gods!" He gasped as if he were witnessing his own death. He threw himself at his desk, looking around at his messed-up possessions with insane eyes.

Ravena and Salina approached uneasily, waiting for a further reaction. Rabolii turned to them, looking like a madman with a few snow-white clusters of hair that fell in front of his eyes. He wheezed, "I left this tower when Ravena and I joined the battle. You and your sister were on the wall. Arkenel and his hooligans were too. All the civilians were evacuated in the caves. Who was left in this castle? Who could have entered?!"

"What were they looking for? Have they taken anything?" Ravena asked as she came up to her husband.

Rabolii was already digging frantically amongst the sheets of paper, looking for a specific one. He knew exactly on which messy corner of the desk he had left it, but it was gone. He had to admit the terrible truth: "It's not here. The map of the elemental concentration is gone!"

Ravena didn't know what that meant, and she felt very uninformed. She waited patiently to be enlightened about this mystery. Rabolii kept rambling, "Whoever took that map knew exactly what they were after. They understand magic, and that's very dangerous. I will investigate the sorcerers with whom I prepared it. Leave me alone. I need to think ... There are not many people in this city who fit this description. I'll get to the truth, find the one responsible, and make them wish they were never born!"

"Um, OK then, tell us if you need anything," answered Ravena. She stepped back.

The two women left the necromancer's lair because they knew it was a bad idea for them to be around him when he was in such a foul mood. While they walked down the corridor, Ravena asked, "Can you tell me which map frustrated your father so seriously, and why?"

"I think he was talking about the map showing the concentration of magical energy on the continent," Salina replied.

"And what's the problem? I thought they had maps like that in every country? Why is it suddenly so valuable?" Ravena shrugged.

"I don't know. I think Father has discovered something that other sorcerers might not know," Salina replied hesitantly, remembering that there was something written about the cosmic charge on that map. She didn't know what it was.

Such maps usually showed magical charges generated by temples where gods were worshipped and by undead armies or living sorcerers. Different countries prepared such maps in order to pinpoint locations where their enemies had magical resources. Salina wasn't sure what to think about this map in particular.

—m—

When Ilinar entered his room, he found an unexpected visitor inside. Eley was sitting on his desk, staring him down with a solemn expression. He was still wearing his passenger clothes, which meant he must have arrived just now. He didn't seem happy at all, and it was little wonder why that was. He began talking, "You must be asking yourself why I am here, Ilinar. Of course I had to follow you to make sure that everything would go smoothly and you wouldn't make any uninformed decision. It seems I'm too late."

Ilinar folded his arms and began to explain: "I took the decision I had formally announced. I told you we need the armies of Aslania to deal with Vern, so I stopped the clash with Krumerus."

"Kranium has been on the verge of collapsing!" Eley spread his arms angrily. "I spoke to the Aslanians. They told me that they had barely a hundred undead and living people to defend the wall! Eslir could have conquered the capital of this damned country and killed Rabolii, but you've stopped him! How could you make such a decision?"

"Well, Rabolii and I were discussing diplomacy and all. We're both worried about Vern."

"We all are, Ilinar." Eley rose up and began pacing around the dark room. "However, you haven't thought this through. Don't tell me that you really believe that an alliance with Krumerus will be useful to Soleya!"

"He's not lying to me, Eley!" Ilinar cried emphatically. He was emotional as ever. "He just doesn't want to fight anyone but have peace on the continent. Why can't we all work towards that goal?"

"Because this is Krumerus we're talking about!" Eley said like it was the most obvious thing. "Their entire economy was built on bloodshed and raids. War is a way of life for them."

"That's not true. Krumerus hasn't attacked anyone in the past ten years," Ilinar said.

"Is that what you think? The erebi simply avoided Soleya over the last decade because we were not an easy target, but they never stopped fighting Vern. How can you try to make up excuses for them? Their lies are so obvious!" Eley continued rambling.

"What if Vern is to blame for that? They attacked us without warning or provocation. How do you know they are not doing the same to Krumerus?" Ilinar maintained his position.

Eley took a breath as if trying to be very patient with an infinitely stupid child. He started, "Even if we are to assume Rabolii is innocence incarnate—that he's indeed too old and tired for plotting and that his intentions are honest—we still cannot accept his peace. Eslir Falnir is too hurt by the whole situation, and there's no way he'd approve of such an act on Soleya's behalf. The worst possible outcome would be him terminating our alliance if we were to establish a diplomatic relationship with Krumerus."

"Why would he do that?! Soleya and Aslania have been allies for centuries!" Ilinar exclaimed.

"I think he made his position very clear. There is no need to ask why any more," Eley said coldly. "To me it's obvious how things are: Vern is a potential threat, but their aggression is mostly directed at Krumerus. You have to choose with whom to unite—with the erebi or with Aslania. I think that's no choice at all."

Ilinar paused. It was clear that what Eley thought was

right. The young king looked down, staring at the stone floor, pondering for a moment. Finally he just nodded and said, "I see."

"Do you understand that Aslania is a much more reliable ally?" Eley continued to insist.

"Yes."

"Is it clear that an alliance with Krumerus will be dangerous to Soleya and will cost us Aslania's friendship and support without offering anything in return except for a small amount of information about Vern?"

"Yes, it's clear."

Eley looked at him suspiciously. He knew him too well to know that this wasn't the end of the story. Whenever Ilinar agreed with him like that, he'd usually go and do what he wanted anyway. But this time Eley wouldn't let him. This was too important; the young king simply couldn't mess it up.

The two of them turned in to bed. Though it was quite late at night, Ilinar was overexcited and couldn't keep his eyes closed. There was so much to think about. He realised that Eley had presented him with the most reasonable solution—to keep Aslania as an ally and, even if he wouldn't attack Krumerus, at least to step out of the way and let Eslir fight with them and obliterate a nation which had been nothing but a source of monsters and nightmares. On the other hand, Ilinar couldn't shake the feeling that it wasn't the right decision. Rabolii seemed reasonable and intelligent; he didn't strike Ilinar as a mad, bloodthirsty monster. Ilinar was convinced the necromancer was sincere and wasn't just faking friendliness to survive. He didn't know how to keep things from escalating until he could make a mature decision himself, a solution which wouldn't suit just Soleya but the whole continent altogether.

While the Soleyans were preparing for bed, the Krumerians were feeling quite awake. Traneya entered her room and was once again surprised to see people in there. She had forgotten she was housing them. Arkenel had already left and gone to bleed elsewhere, but Estrella was still locked inside. Remedor's daughter looked at her and said, "Oh, you're still here. My father was asking for you. He wanted to do some experiments."

"What? No, please don't let him!" Estrella replied instantly. She began looking around, frantically thinking about ways to save herself. "I ... I was useful to you. I saved your brother ..."

"I hope you know you will never leave this place," Traneya replied coldly as she unfolded her bandages to check her wounds. "I would personally prefer to die if I was the captured one."

Estrella bit her lip, wondering what they would do to her. She sat stiffly next to Traneya, paying attention to her wound, and remarked, "I don't know much about medicine, but I think this bandage needs to be changed."

She raised her bright green eyes to the Krumerian and said, "I'm sure you can find a lot of applications for my corpse, but I would be much more useful to you alive. You could use my magic."

Traneya smirked a bit and ran her fingers through her short hair, wondering how to explain to this poor girl that this country would be horribly merciless to her. She noted, "Life magic isn't our favourite thing in Krumerus."

"And yet it was helpful," said Estrella. "I could do even more than that. I could ... clean your room, sew dresses for you. Please, just give me a chance!"

Traneya laughed. She rarely felt the need to wear dresses, maybe just once or twice a year on a formal occasion. She thought that it was almost cute that the poor southern woman wanted to live so badly. The necromancer's daughter asked, "Are you begging me? Is that how you do things in Soleya? OK then, I'll let you stay here and you can clean my room. I can't promise you a long and happy life, but I'll keep you away from Rabolii for now."

Estrella sighed and lowered her gaze. It seemed that she'd need to sit here and live day by day in hope that at some point she'd be saved by someone's army. Traneya was watching her carefully, after which she stretched out her wounded arm towards the sorceress and told her, "You can start being useful by sorting this."

The sorceress was really sorry she'd never learned more about healing wounds. Their very odour disgusted her, and she didn't want to get near them. She barely touched the Krumerian's arm and decided to distract herself with a casual conversation. She started asking if the tattooed faces, hands, and tentacles expressed something specific. Traneya started telling her stories about the illustrated demons and fictional characters on her arm. If anything, Krumerus was full of many interesting stories about monsters and martyrs.

On the night after that, Salina went out on an important mission, bravely leaving her guards behind. Dressed in commoner's clothing, she trusted she wouldn't attract attention, and even if she did, she could defend herself with light spells. It had occurred to her what might have happened to the map

186

of magical energy. After all, Rabolii had shared with her in great confidence that the strange newcomer whom Arkenel had found possessed two magical spheres and that he had never seen anyone with such a strong talent outside his own family. It was too much of a coincidence that such a powerful sorcerer would appear out of nowhere and then, a few days later, a map with information about magical energy would disappear. The young woman knew it was only a matter of time before the necromancer remembered the man in question. And if he suspected he had stolen the map, the interrogation wouldn't be pleasant. Salina thought that Valenis seemed nice, and she didn't want him to die a terrible death because of vague suspicions. It occurred to her that if he had stolen the map, he'd probably escaped with it already, but she still decided to look for him in the house Ravena let him share with three other refugees who had come from the west. If he was guilty, she didn't expect to find him there, but she could still check to see what things he left had behind and search for clues as to where he'd gone.

When she entered, she found Valenis in the house, sleeping. To a Krumerian, sleeping at four o'clock in the morning seemed very strange. Salina decided to attribute it to the fact that he was exhausted after his village had been destroyed, but it was time to adjust to the normal regime. She began waking him. "It's a wonderful night, Valenis! Don't sleep through it!"

He opened his eyes with a confused look as if he had no idea where he was or what he was doing there. He focused his gaze on Salina and tried to construct a meaningful sentence. "Forgive me, madam. Can I help you with something?"

She smiled and said, "Yes, I know it's strange. I don't usually go to people's houses like this; I just wanted to check to see whether the refugees are feeling comfortable."

There was no point in asking her how she'd gotten in. This trampy house didn't even have a lock.

"Don't you have social workers for that?" Valenis muttered, still too sleepy to be able to think properly.

In fact, they didn't. Rabolii didn't want to pay anybody to do such nonsense. Salina decided not to give that blunt answer, so instead she explained, "It's important that princes and princesses know the lives of each kind of people in the country. Otherwise we will never be able to manage it properly."

That was well said. Valenis nodded in silent agreement. He realised that he had no idea how Vernians lived outside the castle. He had heard something about tree houses, but he had

187

never entered such a building. Krementa kept him away from nature so he wouldn't get bitten by a snake. He thought that maybe Krumerus wasn't as dangerous and that princesses could walk where they wanted.

"Do you have everything you need in here?" she asked, starting to walk around him and examining what was in his room by picking things up which could be concealing the stolen map.

Valenis shuddered as he watched her rummaging through the place, but he kept a calm expression on his face and answered, "Pretty much. I'm really grateful for the help the authorities provided. I am getting a chance to start a new life."

"I'm glad to hear that," Salina replied automatically without looking at him. She continued to glance all over the room. "I'm sorry that you had to encounter another war as soon as you arrived here. What did you do during the siege?" She realised something and noted, "My mother and I evacuated all the citizens in the mountains. I don't remember seeing you there though."

"I ... I have a fear of confined spaces," said Valenis. "I also evacuated, but instead of going in the caves, I climbed on some rocks which overlooked the city and watched the battle from there."

If Mavarius were here, he'd probably curse Valenis viciously for being some super rare type of sorcerer but still not helping at all in the battle. Salina didn't want to start that conversation, so she just asked him, "Did you get a good view of the area? Can you take me where you were? We've been meaning to build a watchtower over the city for months; maybe you've found a good spot."

Valenis shrugged. He didn't see why not. He led Salina towards his camp which overlooked the city. She kept asking him questions, casually making it seem like a pointless conversation. She thought that if she could learn exactly what he was doing during the battle with the Aslanians, she could decide for herself if he had had the opportunity to steal the map. However, she was getting the feeling that he had nothing to do with that whole thing.

Valenis felt that this meeting had some underlying purpose. He thought he had raised suspicion, so he tried to switch to some neutral topic of conversation, but he couldn't think of anything. What casual conversations could Krumerians have anyway? They started talking about magic and messing around with their elements and laughing. While they were doing that, a metal chain shimmered on Valenis's neck and caught Salina's attention. It seemed odd that a poor man would have jewellery, so she asked, "Hey, what's that around your neck?"

Valenis felt like he'd been struck by this heavy question. He stuttered, "Nothing, just a pendant ..."

"Can I see?" Salina asked with an insistent tone of voice, as if telling him she would look at it whether he wanted her to or not.

Valenis considered his options. He could do one of two things: push Salina from the high rocks or get caught in possession of a very curious object. At that moment of doubt in which he wondered whether he had enough physical strength to do the former, Salina pulled a platinum amulet with an opaque stone from beneath his shirt. She gasped. She had heard of such things only in books, but she knew what it was. The two of them looked at each other. Her eyes were inquisitive and suspicious. He remained calm; his expression, inscrutable.

"Do you use this to talk to someone I should know about?" she asked firmly.

"No," he said briefly, giving himself some time to make up an answer.

"Is that so? That's not how my father will see things if I tell him I've found this amulet on you! It can only be used to communicate with sorcerers of earth. You could be reporting our actions to our enemies with it."

Valenis sighed sadly, and without breaking eye contact with Salina, he started lying shamelessly. "This amulet is as lifeless as the communication it once hosted. My brother had another one. He was the older one, and he took care of me after our parents were gone. We used the pedants to speak to each other when he left the city. But one day he just never came back. I still keep this with the absurd hope that it will connect us again someday."

Salina listened to that, seeming like she was moved by the story, and said, "I didn't know. I'm sorry. It was insensitive for me to intrude like that."

"It's OK." Valenis faked a bitter smile. "You couldn't have known."

"When did this happen?" she asked quietly.

The Vernian stared at the rocky path below their feet and said, "Eight years ago. I should have moved on by now, but the very fact that I never found out what happened to him doesn't allow me to have peace. Maybe I should have tried harder to find him ... If you don't mind, let's talk about something else. I don't want to remember all this now."

Salina felt guilty for having touched on a painful topic for him, so she tried to change the subject. "Of course. So you were going to show me that place ..."

"Yes, it is farther up that way." Valenis nodded towards the rocky path and led Salina forward.

Meanwhile Rabolii was too depressed to even think of putting Valenis on his list of suspects. He sat with a dramatic look in front of some books and pondered. In fact, he didn't know what to think about first—the war, the diplomacy, Vern or Aslania, or the cosmic energy and its importance ... Ravena was once again the uninvited guest who insisted on being in there. She stood like a tower behind Rabolii, who was trying to ignore her because he was too important to acknowledge her, but still occasionally he dropped a heavy sigh to show that he was feeling discomfort. Ravena decided to interrupt at some point and said, "All right, I think it's time to talk, Husband. Can you tell me what's going on? I have the feeling that there's a lot you're hiding from me."

"For the last time," the necromancer grunted, "I'm terribly sorry that Ilinar was born because of my horrid crimes twenty years ago. I thought this topic of conversation had been exhausted!"

"That's just one of the problems!" Ravena raised her voice. "And it seems like it's not even the most important one to you. I want you to finally explain to me what the cosmic charge is and why you got so upset over it. Obviously it's very important to you, but you never told me why."

Rabolii sat back in his chair with the look of a wise man recalling the essence of bygone centuries to speak words of eternal knowledge. He began with a deep, velvet voice, "Most people know about the four gods and their eight elements. Over the years, we have worshipped them, lived for them, and enjoyed their gifts. Their wars were ours, and although most of us have not heard their voices, we somehow know their ideals and aspirations. Their elements complement and neutralise each other; they form integrity and balance, which has brought us security."

Ravena patiently waited for the introduction to this historical novel to end so they could reach the important bit. She knew Rabolii liked to be theatrical. He stared blankly ahead, as if the secrets of the universe were being revealed in front of him, and he continued quietly, "We mapped the magical charges to keep track of this balance and to guess what's happening with our gods to read their commandments, to know what strength we have ourselves. From time to time when we create these maps, we get data about something we don't understand. There are nodes of energy that don't class as any of the elements. Most other energies are connected to a temple, an artefact, or a sorcerer, but these ones just seem to be loose in the world. Their exact location is difficult to pinpoint; their structure is strange; and we don't know why they are there. Many sorcerers have looked for them before. Some have even captured them. To the surprise of their discoverers, however, these spheres seem to serve no purpose. They don't give their owners new powers, and they don't make them feel different. That's why the energy is called the null charge.

"Very, very few people have found how to use these spheres. Those who were clever and persistent enough to understand the power they possessed were also rewarded. They found ways to manipulate matter, to gain a new understanding of magic, but that only happened if they lived a long time and spent all their time in studying the phenomenon. It became clear to them that this is not a 'null' energy at all. It is much more than that. It was then called 'cosmic energy', and its very existence raises many questions: When does it appear? Who can master it? Where does it come from? Is there a god associated with it? Imagine the possibilities."

Ravena nodded. It was a long story, and yet it didn't answer the main question here, so she decided to ask again: "What kind of powers did people get after absorbing that energy?"

"It's very difficult to find a pattern." Rabolii sighed. "For most people, it didn't make a difference, and others experienced many unexplainable events. Over the past five hundred years, there has been only one Krumerian sorcerer who supposedly mastered it, and that's Ekvanor the Soulshredder. He had the fearsome power of tearing souls apart and killing enemies without even touching them. No necromancer could do that. So we formed a theory that souls are composed of cosmic energy and that its power over this new element is what made his deeds possible. There are others who have discovered the cosmic energy in more recent years, one in Vern and one in Aslania, but as you can imagine, their countries haven't agreed to share any knowledge of this phenomenon. We've sent spies to report on what these individuals were able to do. Intelligence has brought us scarce information, most of which hasn't made its way to us over the centuries, but the most shocking thing one spy reported is that the Aslanian control three spheres."

"Three spheres?" Ravena repeated in dismay. "You mean, including the cosmic one?"

"I mean air, water ... and fire," Rabolii said grimly. "We could never explain that. We could only speculate. Maybe the null charge could adapt and become an existing element? We would have accepted it as a theory, but it's unheard of for a single sorcerer to control both fire and water and be that powerful. Normally opposing elements would tear a sorcerer apart and few would survive into adulthood. We don't know what to think. There isn't enough information."

At that point, Rabolii made another strategic pause so he'd look wise, thoughtful, and tired. Ravena was thinking frantically and was trying to assess the situation. Finally, she summed it up: "So we have a large deposit of cosmic energy just past Aldur? Who else knows about it? You sensed it. Maybe the other nations did too. Is that why they're at our borders? Why haven't you done anything about this? Since someone stole the map, it means people out there are looking for it. We need to find it before our enemies do."

The necromancer gave out another heavy, tired sigh like a punctured bagpipe. He seemed like someone who had a very good reason not to do what Ravena had told him to do, so she sat patiently, ready for his reply.

"Yes, that sounds like the most logical thing to do, does not it? At least for someone who has no idea of the structure of magic. Elemental energy is different. It is stable, and its behaviour is constant and predictable. The sphere a sorcerer uses rests on the knot joining the soul and the body. When that is broken, the magic bursts out and spreads across the universe, making as little difference to the overall charge of the environment as a candle trying to warm the night. However, the cosmic charge is quite different. Its structure is unstable, and it is susceptible to decay. It forms spontaneously in some places. It feels saturated and aggressive. When it merges with a person, it connects to the body itself, and we think it's the heat that keeps it in place. But if the owner dies, the cosmic energy will not disperse like elemental magic does. It gets passed on to the closest living being. If no one is around, it will linger for a while, and only then will it disappear. Usually if it randomly appears somewhere, if it's just left alone, it will scatter within a few weeks and there will be no trace of it for a couple more centuries."

"I understand. You don't want to introduce such an unstable weapon in the war. You want to wait for it to disappear, but we won't have that luxury," Ravena replied firmly. "Someone is already looking for the energy. It will be found, and I'd rather it was us, don't you think?"

"This is not a gift of power and might, Ravena. It's a double-edged sword," Rabolii snapped. "If I take this energy, I'll become a target of more attacks than I can handle. Everyone will want to kill me to get the cosmic energy."

"Why would it need to be you then? Can't you make someone you trust collect it and then guard that person?"

"It's still too risky." Rabolii sighed. "The person may still get compromised or turn against me. The possibilities are endless."

"And what will happen to us if Vern or Aslania takes it away instead of us?" Ravena insisted. "Even if you don't want to use it, at least defend it until it disperses so it won't cause problems."

"That's actually a good idea," Rabolii said slowly. "I'll send troops there. They'll cover the area, and they won't allow anyone to pass until the energy is gone."

This could turn out to be quite the adventure. Rabolii felt nervous about the whole situation. He wanted the cosmic energy to go away. Maybe that would even make the other countries attack him less. However, a voice at the back of his mind whispered bleak words, making him think that perhaps nothing would be that easy. He could only sit there and wonder how to avoid disasters for his country.

CHAPTER 8

PEACE

Arkenel and some of his comrades were hanging around in some dusty, abandoned parts of the city. Kranium was huge; some of its parts hadn't been renovated for decades and just stood as ruins. New buildings were built from scratch because it was easier for the skeletons. They were better at just starting a new project instead of mending old things, as they couldn't assess how to do it. Arkenel wasn't in the best condition to be taking walks, but his mother and his doctors weren't around to stop him. He had sweetened his life with some miner's spice, so he felt no pain anyway. He walked past the cold forges and the ruins beside them. He crossed his arms and muttered, "Just as I remember it. Everything is a wreck."

"They probably haven't forged a single blade in decades," Aveus replied as he examined the ruins. He felt like an explorer of ancient civilisations. He expected Kranium to be a thing of magnificence, but even Aldur seemed nicer at the moment.

"I know there are some blacksmiths in the castle, but they work in a small area. We won't be able to fit more than five people in their basement of a workshop, and my father won't let us in anyway. We'll make do with what we have. Maybe if we remove these beams, we'll get more working area." Arkenel looked at the rubble enthusiastically.

Graz started shifting the heavy beams. Some of the other men helped him. They had all been through a bloody battle quite recently, so their movements were slow and lethargic, but Arkenel wasn't too discouraged by that.

"Do you think there's metal left around here somewhere?" the young Remedor asked. "If we're to gear up, we'll need the raw material for it."

"Steel is an expensive resource; do you think they'll leave it lying around?" Aveus muttered.

"There's a mine nearby," Arkenel said. "Do you want to see what's in there? Aveus, here's the last of my money. See what you can get from there. Graz and I will clean up here and see if we can scavenge something from this place."

Aveus smirked a bit and took the money. He didn't quite know what he felt as he observed Arkenel's enthusiasm. Sure, it was very nice to have goals in life, but this boy was trying to make soldiers out of a gang of miserable drunkards and drug addicts who were little more than beasts. They were not interested in anything; they lived for the day and fought and stabbed each other over nothing. Aveus didn't understand how anyone could believe such men weren't a lost cause. Regardless, he went to check the mine.

Arkenel perched himself upon the ruins and pulled out some papers to draw armour sketches on them. Grazedrii continued moving rubble as his friend chattered. "I have not decided yet: would light armour suit us better, or would heavy armour be best? Maybe leather would be better against the Aslanians since they use maces and flails against our skeletons."

"Hmm." Graz grunted as he struggled with the obstacles in the environment.

"But we'll need at least some chain mail to protect us from arrows, right?" Arkenel shrugged and started scratching on the papers. "Where can we find cheap leather in this city? We can try to catch some animals in the wilderness outside the city limits. I'll hire hunters." He frowned as he said that, then slammed his fist against the old stone wall. "The damn tosser would have been perfect for this if he was still here."

"Uhhhh." Graz threw a huge beam to the side. It landed with a wild clash, causing a bunch of mice to flee the scene, squeaking in panic.

Arkenel grunted and continued, "I still can't believe Mavarius ditched us like this. I take this personally, you know. This shows that my people doubt my judgement. They don't feel safe with me in charge. They prefer to run off. And it was he who did it, out of all the people. I have started to wonder if the others consider me as a leader, if they're willing to share my ambitions. After all, for Mortelion's sake, we won our freedom so we could show we're good people and we can be useful to this country! I don't want everyone bluntly demonstrating I'm the only one who believes that. We may have lived in holes, and we may have eaten raw rats for too long, but that changes nothing for me. I'm still a Remedor. So I want the power to put in order the lives of those who believed in me enough to storm Aldur with me."

Arkenel glanced down at his sheets of paper and began scribbling on them again, thinking about the hardships of life. Graz cast a gaze at him, chuckled a bit, and stated, "You're doing all right, kid. You give us something to do."

"Yes, thank you! That's what we all want, isn't it? To have some purpose in life. There's so much I want, and I believe the tossers will follow me where I lead. We'll put some life in this dead city, and we'll make cemeteries of the stupid southern countries! Thank you for your support, Graz. Talking with you is always great."

The giant smiled slightly as he moved the last beam to the side and uncovered the furnace. He buried his fingers in the cold ashes and felt as if he had been reunited with an old friend. It was good that after so many twists and turns of fate, he had returned to what he was good at. Arkenel looked at him, chuckled, and said, "I also missed smiting things. Graz, I never got the chance to thank you for what you did for us in that prison. We would have never broken out of that place without you. The crowd should have carried you as the liberator, not me."

"You're easier to carry," Graz said. He and Arkenel started laughing. With the help of the miner's spice, the murky ruins of Krumerus seemed like a place of joy and friendship.

Meanwhile Rabolii was angry. He was trying to explain to his general where to position the vampires and which area to guard, but the man was asking too many unnecessary questions. The necromancer was trying not to mention that this was all about the cosmic charge, but avoiding the topic of what the actual mission was, was hard. The general stood in front of his master's throne like he was being punished, while the undead creatures circled around him, displaying a disturbing interest in him.

"Um, excuse me, my lord, but what do they eat?" the general asked. He knew he would spend a lot of time alone with the vampires, and he didn't want to suffer some accident.

"They hunt their own prey. Don't worry about them. Now, unless you have more questions, I suggest you go." Rabolii waved his hand majestically as he sat like a matron with crossed legs and a magnificent posture on his throne of bones.

"I just want to confirm the location I'm supposed to guard."

The general looked down at his map. "Fifteen kilometres north of Aldur? You want me to build a fence around it? Is there anything important there?"

"Do you think I would send you to guard it if it wasn't important?" Rabolii snapped. He thought this was ridiculous. It was as if this man wanted to know what he was being sent to do! The last thing Rabolii needed was for the general to get captured by the Aslanians and tell them about the cosmic energy.

"Father, maybe we should send a sorcerer with him," said Salina.

Rabolii made a painful grimace. It was so hard for him to keep something secret in this castle without everyone around him constantly spitting clues which gave away everything. And right then Arkenel entered, so the chaos in the poor necromancer's life became absolute. Once again Arkenel looked dizzy and was tottering at his feet. His eye was reddened, and he looked like he wasn't sure where he was or what he was doing there. It had become part of his character. Rabolii tried to ignore him, but he addressed his annoying enquiries anyway: "Hey, Pa! We will need some money. Me and the guys were thinking about making armour and renovating the barracks. It will help with the public order in the city. Right now we have fifty silver coins after gambling in the pub and winning this and that, but now we need another three hundred and ..."

"You! Leave my presence at once!" Rabolii yelled at him and pointed at him with a long, bony finger crowned by a curved nail. "You cannot set up the barracks with 350 coins! All you want is money for booze and drugs, so don't take me for a fool!" Ravena tried to get involved, but her husband shot her an angry look. "I'm not letting you give him money either. He needs to learn to make his own money." Turning to the general, the necromancer said, "As for you there! Get going. You were given a task."

"You're sending him off to Aldur?" Arkenel asked.

Rabolii was feeling more and more enraged by the second. It was apparent to him that any news of what he was doing spread with lightning speed around here. He said through his teeth, "Where did you get that idea?"

"I heard you screaming it just now; your voice echoes all over the castle," Arkenel replied casually. Then he looked at the general and his supposed army. "You don't intend to send him there with only a handful of vampires, do you? He'll get massacred once he gets there."

The general gulped with fright. His worst fears had come true. Rabolii rolled his eyes with annoyance for having to deal with all this. He replied, "My vampires don't attack people unless they're ordered to do so."

"No, I don't mean them," Arkenel replied with the same casual tone. "North of Aldur is at the border of the demon territory. If you send small dispatches to that area, they'll get eaten. The prison guards would sometimes throw prisoners out in the field just for the fun of it, and they'd listen to the beasts tearing the men apart."

Rabolii looked bored. He hated it when he was trying to get something done but everyone was getting in his way with some problems they'd gotten from God knows where. He had to dig through his memory, namely in the section for useless information. "The last thing I heard about this was that the demons seldom leave their caves and no one's seen them in a long while."

"Dad, you haven't lived in that place ..."

"And neither have you! You haven't as much as peeked outside for seven years. You couldn't know what's going on. Who knows what you heard, what you understood, and how sober you were when it happened," the necromancer snapped.

"Whatever you say!" Arkenel raised his hands. "Whatever it is you're protecting near Aldur, it can't be important since you're sending five vampires to do the job. I just came to ask you about the armour and the barracks, so I will leave you now."

Rabolii shifted on his throne, watching with superiority as Arkenel and his general left. Then he returned his boastful glance to Ravena and Salina as he told his daughter, "By the way, I wanted to let you know that I have not forgotten the conversation we had earlier. I haven't been idle on that matter. It may indeed be fitting for you to get married soon, so I chose the right man. The son of Lord Fresner Remedor is a sorcerer your age. He's smart and dependable, and a relationship with him would improve our friendship with the northwest region."

Salina and Ravena exchanged glances as if they were checking whether they had heard correctly. It was typical for Rabolii to do something spontaneous like this, but they hadn't imagined he'd set up a wedding in these precarious times. Or maybe he really wanted a strong friendship with the Northwest Provinces? But the surprises didn't end there. Rabolii snapped his fingers, and a skeleton opened the door to one of the rear rooms.

"Ladies, this is Morelii Remedor, Salina's future husband.

He is a very powerful sorcerer of darkness, a master of his element. He's a virtuoso with the sword and an extremely desired match. Lord Fresner Remedor visited us when you were about three years old, Salina. I think you liked him back then. He remembers you and asks how you've been doing. Now you and Morelii can get to know each other. I have work to do."

While the skeleton was still opening the doors, someone else threw them open from the other side, smashing the poor undead and making it fall apart. In came a young man, grinning and gesturing like he was being applauded by a whole town of people. His shoulder-length hair was neatly cut in a straight line. He wore shiny dark purple plate armour and velvet clothes underneath. He stood in front of Salina with a boastful and proud expression. He took her hand and kissed it, saying, "It is a pleasure to meet you, Princess. I am Morelii Remedor. The tales of your beauty fade in comparison to your actual image."

Salina blushed a bit and looked away, mumbling, "You're too kind, Lord Remedor."

"Please, do call me Morelii! Would you care for a walk? I'm looking to explore the legendary city of Kranium."

Having said that, he dragged her outside. Salina could just look around, casting an expression of confusion and uncertainty at Ravena as she was led out of the throne room. Rabolii was perched upon his throne with a satisfied look and a sense of a job well done after he had taken care of everything in Krumerus. Ravena looked at him and began, "Rab, how finalised is your decision that Salina is to marry this man? They just met."

"I think they're a splendid match. They're both sorcerers," the necromancer said confidently. "Lord Fresner has been discussing it with me for some time. We have signed some agreements that are profitable for both of us, and we have arranged most details about the wedding."

"Yes, but I want Salina to be happy in her marriage, and Morelii is a bit ..."

"He's perfect for her." Rabolii waved his hand dismissively. "He's noble, well mannered, and extremely clever. He'd never get her in trouble. He will respect her, and together they will learn about magic for hours, which is a great bonding experience for partners. Of course, if they're being ridiculously stubborn for whatever reason and they don't want to marry, I will cause myself the embarrassment and shame in front of Lord Fresner and cancel everything, even though I don't see one reason why anyone would have a problem with this."

Ravena sighed. So this was how it was going to be. Rabolii would act like he respects Salina's opinion, but if she did decide not to marry, he'd groan, complain, and reproach her until she agreed, only to restore peace. Ravena had visited the northern Remedors before, and she was under the impression that Morelii was spoiled and disrespectful. She didn't think too highly of him, but it wasn't she who was marrying him. She remembered how her parents always had an opinion on whom she should marry; they'd always nudge her towards men they liked. But when she brought in Rabolii, they were one step away from banishing her from the family. Ah, the memories!

There was a time when Rabolii was a very different man. He was somewhat wilder and thirstier for life, for conquest. He couldn't stay in the same place for too long. She remembered how he carried her in his arms around the military camp. His smile was dangerous, and his eyes burned. Everything he did was so exciting to her. Even back then he was a bit arrogant and pompous, but it somewhat became him. His soldiers were all loyal to him.

The day he met her parents was unforgettable. A dozen of his horsemen escorted him to the town at the far western border, passing like a royal delegation on the streets, attracting everyone's glances. The neighbours stared at them and could hardly recognise their little Ravena. She was now riding behind a tall man in black armour, shiny and exquisite. It looked decorated and ornamental. This impressive delegation stopped in front of Ravena's house, while servants were running in to tell their masters that their daughter had come home. As the parents appeared on the doorstep, they were startled by the sight. Ravena was smiling brightly as she sat behind this man who watched them like he was a god of some sort; from the saddle of his horse, several severed heads hung by chains.

"Darling, are you OK?" her mother had immediately exclaimed.

"Ravena, who is this man?" her father had said uneasily.

The girl jumped from the saddle and sank into her mother's embrace, then turned her gaze, full of adoration, towards Rabolii, waiting for him to introduce himself. He watched her with a subtle smirk. Without uttering a word, he raised in the air one of the severed heads. It hovered over his hand ominously, threads of magical energy wrapped around it. It rose to the level of the necromancer's eyesight. Its bottom jaw dropped down helplessly, and the voice of its former owner echoed all around: "His name is Rabolii, Rabolii Remedor. Never have I felt such a powerful magical charge in a living man before. He is guided directly by the hand of Mortelion himself, and he's here to conquer Krumerus, bathing it in blood and raising the dead amongst us. None of us will have peace again."

Ravena's parents stared at him as if he had crawled out of the most abhorrent demon hole. They were even more shocked when their daughter announced this was the man of her dreams. He treated them the whole time with a polite mockery, as if he knew perfectly well that they didn't like him, and he ridiculed them for being powerless against him. He was subtle enough not to irritate Ravena, but he got his message across. She was aware this would be a strange marriage and that she would be powerless against the aspirations of the necromancer. She knew he was a dangerous man, but she refused to believe that it would affect her personally. She was so fond of him that not even his death changed that. After his "resurrection", she continued to see him in the same way; for her he was unchanged. He was just somewhat sorrowful and bitter. She thought he needed just a little nudge to return to his inherent grandeur and to transform into that demigod she'd married. According to many people, he was far from being a perfect husband, but it was her choice, and she still believed she had done the right thing. Now she wanted Salina to get the same right to choose, so she'd try to make that possible.

Meanwhile Salina was sitting with Morelii in an inner garden full of black trees and with tame demonic birds which spread their fleshy wings, made croaking noises, and casually tried to murder each other. It was a peaceful place where people would read or relax. Morelii began talking: "I'm quite proficient at throwing knives, you know. I was the champion at it in Fort Blackwind. I could outdo anyone. Behold!"

Before Salina got the chance to say anything, Morelii pulled out a small blade from his belt and threw it at one of the birds. It was struck, but it didn't die immediately. It fell on the grey granite tiles, screaming dreadfully, splashing in its blood, and tumbling all over. The other birds began attacking it to eat it, but Morelii casually chased them away. He picked up the catch and gave it to a skeleton servant. "Hey, you! Take this to the finest goldsmith in the whole of Krumerus and task him into crafting a fine necklace from its skull and bones for the lovely Princess Salina."

Salina was still a bit shocked from this display of knife

throwing. In general, she didn't like bone jewellery; it was too macabre for her. She tried to protest, "It's really not necessary, Morelii."

"You're right! A tiara will be better." He grinned at her and handed the skeleton a heavy purse of gold which could probably feed a family of five for a few years.

The skeleton went on to gather its buddies and go to the goldsmith because it would surely be robbed out there. Morelii sat next to Salina closer than what she was comfortable with and carried on talking: "As a matter of fact, I excel in all manner of pursuits. You should have come to last year's sorcery tournament. Men from all over were competing for a huge money prize and a night with the most beautiful woman from the east. Her hair was as white as snow. I won, of course. But not even her beauty could measure up to yours."

Having said that, he started playing with a lock of Salina's hair. She felt a bit awkward, but because of politeness, she asked him more questions about the tournament. It looked like this was Morelii's favourite topic of conversation anyway. He told her all about the competitions he'd been in and how he'd won every one, mentioning who he has killed and what women were interested in him. Some time passed. Salina kept casting glances at the huge pendulum clock which was a bit farther under a marble shelter which looked like a mausoleum. She realised it'd been forty minutes since she'd had the chance to speak, and it didn't look like things were about to change. Morelii was going on about the special sword which was crafted for him. Salina grew a bit annoyed by this. She felt like he didn't really care about her as a person, so at some point she interrupted him and stated, "Apologies, Morelii. Your story is fascinating, but I'm feeling a bit unwell. I'd like to rest in my chambers for a bit."

"I could accompany you and make sure you have everything you need." Morelii grinned at her with his perfect white teeth.

Salina couldn't believe he'd just invited himself to her bedroom. She thought she must have misunderstood him, so she just said, "Thank you, but I'd rather remain alone. I'll see you later."

Having said that, she got up and began walking to her room. She felt upset. She didn't like this man. He was so self-focused and shallow. The only time he'd speak about her was when he'd compliment her beauty. She was sure that Rabolii thought Morelii was perfect. In her father's opinion, if a man was a sorcerer, won competitions, and had good fencing skills, it meant he was amazing and would be a good husband. She didn't know if Morelii would be just as bad as she thought or if she'd be given an option to decide whether to marry him at all.

It was at that moment when a melody sounded across the dead corridors of the dark Kranium. Salina had heard nothing like it before. It was a whole symphony of sounds flowing like a river. It captivated the soul in a way the girl had never felt before. Who could be capable of such art? The local pianists were useless. There were a few in the castle, but they knew only a few pieces, and they were discouraged from practising more because noise gave Rabolii a headache. Enchanted by the music, Salina followed the sound to one of the guest rooms. She sneaked in quietly so she wouldn't disturb the mysterious musician. He was facing away from her, but to her surprise, she still recognised him. It was Valenis. He was wearing the same ragged clothes, but despite this he had certain nobility to him. His perfectly smooth black hair was bound in a neat ponytail, his back was upright, and his fingers ran across the keys with exquisite ease. The piano had come to life in his hands. Salina lost track of how long she stood there, listening to him in daze. Even a few seconds after he had stopped, she didn't move a muscle. Eventually she said softly, "You never told me you played ..."

Valenis turned to her with a light smile as if not surprised to see her there.

"I'm sorry, I didn't mean to intrude. I just came in to ask one of the lords if I could be assigned to a job in the castle ... I need an income. I came across this piano. Music was always been one of my passions, and it was just sitting here dusty and forgotten."

"We could hire you to play for us," Salina suggested. "We definitely need this type of entertainment here."

She lowered her eyes. She didn't seem happy at all. Valenis rose from the piano bench and walked over to her, trying to meet her gaze. He asked cautiously, "Princess Salina, is everything OK?"

"Yes ... Actually, no ... But I don't want to burden you with my problems."

"On the contrary, my princess. It would be my pleasure to listen about your worries."

"Let's sit down," she mumbled, feeling like she might burst in tears. They sat down on a large black leather sofa decorated with vertebrae around the armrests. Salina took a deep breath and told this stranger about her biggest problem: "My father has decided to marry me off. He never involved me in choosing the husband, and he has selected someone who is not right for me at all."

Valenis raised his eyebrows and suggested, "Perhaps you ought to trust your father. He has chosen a person he found fitting. Allow yourself more time."

"Yes, Father chose someone whom he likes, not whom I like. The man just murdered a bird in front of me for no reason!"

"Did he now?" Valenis exclaimed.

"He just went on for hours about what a great sword he has, what women he's slept with, how he terrifies people to death with his fearsome darkness magic, and all sorts of other things," Salina explained.

Valenis wondered whether this was something sociably acceptable in Krumerus. After all, if he was trying to make a positive impression on a young woman, he wouldn't talk about terrifying people to death. It occurred to him that in this country something like this may be a thing to boast about, but it was just Salina who was sensitive enough to find it disturbing. It was ... sweet that she'd grown up as kind as she was in a monster hole like Krumerus.

"Have you met this man before? Or was it the first time?" Valenis asked.

"I hadn't. I knew he existed. He's Morelii Remedor from the north. I'd just never met him."

Valenis frowned and asked, "Aren't you two related then?"

"Gosh, no. Not really." Salina shook her head. "It's a bit difficult to follow, but my grandfather and Morelii's mother had grandparents who were brothers."

Valenis seemed a bit confused for a moment and asked, "If his mother was a Remedor, how is he one as well?"

Salina smiled and began explaining: "The family name Remedor is the only one which gets passed on by both men and women. It's the oldest traceable bloodline in Krumerus, going all the way back to Mortelion's wife and son. I think it's amazing."

The two of them continued chatting for a long time. After they had exhausted the topic of family trees and demigods, there was more piano playing, more tales, and more stories, so Salina ended up spending much more time with Valenis than she had with Morelii, but she hardly felt the hours as they passed since this time she led an actual two-way conversation and no more birds were killed in her presence. By the time they had to part ways, they were already close friends.

A skeleton in a formal suit arrived in Arkenel's den. It carried an official letter with the royal seal on it. The young Remedor sat in the smithy with his friends, most of them drugged out of their minds. They had decided to make work more fun with the miner's spice, so some of them were now fighting. Others were throwing stones, and the more joyful ones, like Arkenel, entertained themselves with the very shape of their hands or something similar. Aveus was the only sober one, as always. Sometimes he still felt like the overseer of these hopeless creatures, and it was somehow his job to keep them from killing each other. He was the first to notice the overdressed skeleton and nudged Arkenel. "I think it's a personal message. Do you want me to read it to you?"

"Why is the skeleton wearing a suit?" Arkenel burst into laughter, gazing around like a dimwitted child.

"All right, I'll read it to you," answered Aveus. He took the letter. After all, he knew the skeleton was busy, and he didn't want to keep it waiting. He unfolded the note and read, "Arkenel, I decided to take into account your semisober reports about the area around Aldur. I wouldn't imagine the creatures there are a threat, but rather a natural result of the magical concentration in the region or a creation of your tortured imagination. However, I still consider the safety of that area to be vital, so I'm inclined to take your jabber into account. I give you permission to gather your men and catch up with my general and assist him in defending the perimeter." Aveus finished reading and noted, "It's from Rabolii."

Arkenel had a look of struggle on his face; he'd get it every time he wasn't sober and he was expected to think. Aveus didn't expect him to produce a meaningful decision in this state, so he urged him, "I think it's a good idea for us to go. I'll escort you there. And then please drop me off at Aldur! I have a family there whom I have not seen for weeks. They must be worried about me, and I'm not calm either knowing what you unleashed on those streets."

Arkenel shushed him with a hand gesture, then he stood up and stumbled towards the papers he used for sketching armour. On the back of one he didn't intend to use he scribbled an answer to his father and then began attaching the paper to the skeleton. Aveus gritted his teeth again and intervened in this insanity. "Arkenel, you didn't write anything."

"Uh, what? I told him we're going," mumbled Remedor with a confused look.

"No, you just wrote three squiggly lines, and they mean nothing in either alphabet. So you do want us to go? I'll tell him in person, and you ... just sober up a bit and then start preparing for the trip."

Overall in Kranium a specific feeling of nervous anticipation had seeped in. The entire fate of the country was uncertain. Rabolii kept many secrets; not even Ravena knew what he was doing. Of course, Ilinar had no idea that he had been lied to. He had forgotten that Soleya needed a ruler and other details like that. Most of the time he was busy hiding from Eley, who would make him do something boring. He preferred to explore the castle. He felt he had to touch everything. He was fascinated by the bones inlaid in the wall. He watched the undead skeletons secretly and followed them as they did their daily duties. He wondered if they had souls, if they felt pain, and what the force which kept them alive was. He had always been curious. He hoped to meet Rabolii and talk to him about the skeletons. Poor him, he had no idea that there was no chance of randomly "finding" the necromancer in some corridor. He was in the room, as always, and was enjoying another session of vampirism studies during normal hours. However, Ilinar wasn't familiar with that schedule, so he decided to just walk up to the necromancer's tower.

As the heavy doors of Rabolii's chambers creaked, the necromancer looked up from his work with a maddened expression. Was it possible that there was a person left in this castle who wasn't aware that it was strictly forbidden to disturb the king at these times, and that the punishment for doing so was sometimes death depending on how irritated Rabolii happened to be? Seeing that the invader was Ilinar, he realised that there would always be someone unaware of the vampirism session. The necromancer didn't know how to shoo him out or what to do now. He was often faced with such madness, which he simply didn't have the strength to deal with.

"Good afternoon, Master Remedor!" Ilinar greeted him cheerfully. "How are you today?"

In all honesty Rabolii felt dreadful. His clothes were too loose because he had lost weight in the last few days, his whole body hurt, and his vision was so blurred that he could hardly see his own desk. Still, he tried not to mention his unearthly suffering, at least not to Ilinar. He would complain thoroughly to Ravena later, but for now he only replied, "Busy as always, Ilinar." That was a hint.

"Really? What are you doing?" The young Soleyan drew a chair closer with a curious face and stared at him.

Rabolii was shocked. He had not faced such insolence since his daughters were young and were playing tea party with their dolls and his priceless potions which they'd steal. After he roared at them a few times for doing that, they had stopped. He felt like implementing the same approach in this situation, but he was still trying to be friendly with Ilinar. He responded drily, "I'm having a vampirism experimentation session."

There was just a single vampire left in the chambers, and he was sitting beside the desk. He wore a miserable expression, and there were a dozen different drains attached to his hands and neck. Some were infusing potions; others were draining blood for the necromancer's studies. Ilinar looked curiously at the vampire and asked, "Does he feel pain?"

"Most dead men don't. I am the only one to experience this unique inconvenience as I'm the only one to retain my soul," he replied in his typical melodramatic tone he used every time he declared he had died. He was probably not even aware he was doing it.

Ilinar was fascinated by all this. He continued spilling questions: "So vampires have no souls? Are they clever?"

"They are but animals," Rabolii said casually. "Their reasoning ability is quite primitive. It's reduced to instincts. What distinguishes them from ordinary corpses is that there is a chemical in their bodies that protects them from rotting and makes them eternal. Some of their bodily functions still work. In order to preserve themselves, they need to feed regularly—on blood."

Ilinar looked curiously at the vampire. It was the first time he'd seen a creature like this, and it seemed very strange to him. It had something animalistic in its face even though it looked like a man at first glance.

"I could have sworn I saw flying vampires the other day," the Soleyan noted.

Rabolii rose from his desk, walked up to the object of his research, and grabbed one of his arms, lifting it up into the air. Once that was done, a magical membrane of light blue energy flashed between the limb and the vampire's body, extending like a wing. The necromancer explained, "Vampires are much lighter than a normal person, and these 'wings' help them fly."

"I see. And why do you study them?" Ilinar continued to enquire.

This conversation was irritating Rabolii. He was reluctant to tell people about his work because he was paranoid people would steal his discoveries. The only person he discussed such matters with was Ravena, and she needed to feel special about hearing of his potions. Wanting to change the topic, Rabolii answered briefly, "Mostly curiosity. Now tell me how you feel, Ilinar. Do you like the city?"

"Oh yes, it's full of interesting things!" Ilinar exclaimed. "I was walking around the castle. It all seems very strange, but in a good way."

"Why are you not asleep at this late hour?" asked Rabolii.

"Why should I be asleep at four in the afternoon?"

"Oh yes, I forgot. You sleep at night in those light-worshipping countries."

"It's a little difficult for me to sleep anyway. I have a lot to think about." Ilinar sighed.

Rabolii looked up at this delicate boy in front of him, wondering how his weakness could be used. He smiled lightly and began to weave lies: "Ilinar, I remember how things were when I was a young ruler. I had so much to worry about. The solutions were never simple, and I was always under pressure to do the right thing. So, if it brings you any reassurance, I understand how you feel."

"Thank you for the kind words. Sometimes I want someone to give me the answers I can't reach myself. I just don't know how I could keep peace with Krumerus and an alliance with Aslania." Ilinar sighed.

Rabolii walked past his son and put his bony hands on his shoulders. He leaned forward and said softly to him, "Still, despite the difficulties I encountered, I have always found the answer to every situation. Do you know why, Ilinar?" The Soleyan turned his big innocent eyes to his father and shook his head. Rabolii smirked and answered, "Because I did what I believed was right. The others have tried to impose their views on me and dissuade me, but I have always stood my ground and fought for my beliefs. You are my son. I am sure that you are capable of the same. What do you believe in, Ilinar?"

The young king was looking at him with astonishment, absorbing every word. He answered hesitantly, "I believe that peace is all we have to strive for and that negotiations and cooperation will lead us forward instead of meaningless battles and quarrels. Now that I am the king, I have to put people's well-being as my priority."

"That's a beautiful way to see the world," Rabolii said. "You seem to know what you're aiming for. You just have to make it happen."

As he said that, Rabolii materialised as if out of thin air a few heavy parchments of old, expensive paper, and thumped them in front of Ilinar. It was a peace treaty between Krumerus and Soleya, already filled with conditions. The young king began to shift nervously in his chair and stuttered, "I ... really want that, but the situation is very complicated. Aslania ..."

"Aslania has a different opinion on this issue, but why do you have to submit to their lead, Ilinar? What makes them better than you? If you sign this, do you think they will just declare war on you and send their armies to your land? What's the worst they are capable of? Eslir Falnir boasts like as an irreplaceable ally, but what has he ever done for Soleya? On the other hand, if you sign this and stop your military aid to Aslania, it will make it harder for them to invade Krumerus, and they will need to be more careful. This will give both of us the freedom to deal with Vern."

Ilinar listened to him with the face of a young child who was being told his favourite story. He was fascinated by how smart and thoughtful Rabolii was. He exclaimed, "That's the decision I was looking for! I'm just going to sign the peace treaty, and I'll present everyone with a fait accompli. Once I do, Aslania will have to follow my example. Otherwise it will make their wars difficult."

"You are so young, and yet you act as a true monarch. I'm proud of you," Rabolii said with a thin smile and patted his shoulder.

Ilinar shook with excitement. As if he were under a spell, he took the quill handed to him by his father and put his wonky signature on the precious paper, and then he stared at his creation. It was hard for him to believe he had done something like that. It was magnificent. For the first time he felt like an actual ruler.

Meanwhile Salina was walking around the gardens of the castle. They were filled with strange plants, most of which were prickly, their colours greyish, and they seemed dry and dead even though they were blossoming. Shrubs with black roses grew everywhere. She touched one of the flowers with her fingertips, and a dreamy smile appeared on her face.

"They are beautiful, aren't they?" she said.

Valenis appeared next to her and said, "I'm used to living farther to the west. We have different flowers there. But, yes, these gardens also have their charm."

Salina turned to him and asked, "Really? I would very much want to see the flowers from your homelands."

Valenis smirked. An idea came to him, and for the first time he was grateful for his annoying magic lessons. He raised a hand, around which specks of dust from the earth and air began to gather and form. They took the specific shape of a solid object. He handed his work of art to Salina. It was a perfect stone orchid in white and purple colours. The young woman gasped. A smile blossomed on her face.

"It's beautiful!" Salina exclaimed. "I didn't know you had so many talents!"

"You are yet to discover them," Valenis answered with a mysterious smile.

She didn't known if it was because of some strange earth magic, but that gaze made the princess's knees feel weak. She could only keep gazing at Valenis with her large, innocent eyes, admiring him. The moment didn't last as long as she would have liked because, like a black plague, they were attacked by an unholy evil. Someone grabbed Valenis by the shoulder out of nowhere and turned him around to punch him in the nose. As it happened, Salina saw that it was Morelii, whose mad eyes were flashing furiously. He barked, "How dare you perform such indecency with my beloved whom I will marry? Your insolence will cost you your life!"

Salina was stunned by this display. She turned to Morelii and hardly managed to mutter, "Indecency? What are you talking about? Valenis is my friend. Please don't hurt him!"

"Take this sword and die like a warrior instead of being a worm!" Morelii tossed an ordinary steel sword at Valenis and drew his, a shiny black blade with white bones on its hilt. One would ask oneself why Morelii was walking around with two swords and if he spent his day-to-day life looking for people to fight in the streets. Such presumption would happen to be correct.

"There is really no need," Valenis tried to protest, although this cocky brat had irritated him like few people do.

"I see you choose a humiliating death, then!" Morelii swung his sword to decapitate his victim.

Valenis quickly reached for the steel sword and managed to

block the hit at the last possible moment. Then a vicious duel began. The Vernian knew that he shouldn't display his power by fighting too well or else it would be suspicious. He tried to defend himself rather than attack. As that was happening, black tendrils which looked like they were composed of thick mist shot out of the ground towards Valenis. This surprised him, and he sliced at them, but to his dismay, the blade just went right through them. In his mind this looked like an entire tentacled sea monster rising for him from oblivion.

"Valenis, it's an illusion. Don't look at it!" Salina yelled at him. She was well aware of how darkness magic worked, and she knew what it did to the mind. However, it didn't look like Valenis was in a state to hear her, so she raised her hand and sent light blasting across the whole garden, dispelling the nightmares.

Morelii was just standing behind his rival, ready to finish him off, and was infuriated by this involvement. He turned to Salina and roared at her, "You! You assisted him? What sort of loyal bride are you, you lying, cheating ..."

At that very moment, Valenis bashed his head with the hilt of his sword and sent him into the world of dreams. Salina didn't seem to mind. She rushed towards the Vernian and cried, "Valenis, are you hurt? I'm so sorry about this."

The man swept some blood from his nose and answered, "I'm OK. Thank you for intervening. Let's just leave and hope that he doesn't remember anything when he awakes."

The two of them ran towards the castle. They wanted to spend some time in a place where no one would come in and disturb them, so they went to the attic of one of the highest towers, where probably no one had been in months. Salina walked around the dusty room, looking at the portraits of her ancestors. She noted, "I love coming up here. It's full of ... history. I like to look at the clothes in the wardrobes."

"Hmm, I'm curious. What do they look like?" asked Valenis. The truth was that he was barely acquainted with Krumerus's current fashion, and he had no idea what the clothes looked like fifty years ago.

"I will show you," Salina said enthusiastically. She ran to one of the closets. When she opened it, small bats flew out, screaming. She ignored them as if they were something mundane, but Valenis jumped away, startled.

"Traneya and I loved looking at these gowns when we were young. However, Mother never let us remove them from the coat hangers. She said we'd damage them."

When she turned to Valens, he again gave her a carefree, charming look, as if the bats hadn't shattered his masculinity in any way. He looked at the dress Salina held by the hanger and said, "You know, this one may fit you."

"It's so strange." Salina smiled. "When I was a child, they seemed huge to me, but now they may be my size. Perhaps I can try it on."

"That would be lovely. While you do that, I could play you something. I do remember a sonata which you might like," Valenis answered. He sat by a dusty piano which sat there, forgotten by the years. Salina had brought him up here especially because of the piano.

She stood behind him and began changing her clothes. She was enchanted by the music. It was no accident that Valenis had chosen the most romantic piece he could think of. And it achieved its intended purpose. At one point, Salina stepped next to him, dressed in the old-fashioned dark blue dress which once belonged to one of her grandmothers. Valenis looked at her, dazed, and said, "It's as if it was sewn just for you. I'd recommend you keep it."

He stood up from the piano. His hands found Salina's. He drew her closer. She felt like she would melt in his arms. For the first time she felt as if she had found someone who was really worth being with. If that moment could last for eternity, it wouldn't bore her for a second. Maybe they would have kissed, but just before that could happen, Valenis pulled away and said, "Oh, I'm sorry, Salina. I just remembered, I have to meet somebody this evening. I had agreed to … help him with something. I'm probably late already."

"And will you leave me just like that? So suddenly?" she asked, disappointed.

"No one regrets this more than I do. Forgive me for ruining the moment, but I promise to make it up to you." He added, with a slight smile, "I adore your company. I'll see you soon, Salina."

Having said that, he rushed out like his coat was on fire. Salina looked at him in wonder. She thought he probably had a good reason to rush out, and she could only hope to see him again soon. She smiled, looking down at the enchanted stone orchid on the piano. She took it and her dress then walked towards her room, feeling excited like never before.

Looking around frantically as if he was being chased, Valenis disappeared in the darkness of the corridors. He walked out onto a balcony, shutting the door behind him. His trembling hands reached under his shirt so he could pull out the platinum amulet. It felt so hot to the touch that it was painful for him to hold it. He finally managed to answer the call. The semitransparent silhouette of Krementa appeared before him, and she started screaming immediately: "I've been trying to call you for five minutes. Why are you not answering?"

"Mother, I was in front of people. I had to go out first."

"You've lost weight. Have you remembered to eat while you're there? Do you still have the supplies I sent you with?" She kept shooting questions.

Valenis didn't have the heart to tell her that the supplies in question had finished days ago because Arkenel and his buddies had discovered them and didn't leave anything for him afterwards. Regardless, he just nodded and said, "I manage them reasonably, Mother. I already have connections here, and I'm receiving money, so I won't struggle any more," Not that this was a lie. Salina had indeed hired him to play the piano in the castle. Who could have known that this hobby of his would bring him money? If he were to learn to raise skeletons as well, he would become a millionaire.

"I'm so happy to hear that! You're so clever, my dear child! You'll make Vern proud."

Valenis blushed, looking down bashfully. It was extremely rare for Krementa to compliment him in any way. Maybe she missed him a lot. Or perhaps she was so happy to see him every time because it was a pleasant surprise he was still alive.

"Valenis darling, what was the outcome of the battle? Did Kranium fall?" Krementa asked her next question.

Her son looked around and said, "As a matter of fact it didn't. I'm not exactly sure what saved them. I heard rumours, I think Soleya intervened and interceded for Krumerus."

The Vernian queen said in surprise, "How so? According to our intelligence, Soleya is also at war with Krumerus."

"Yes, but recently they have had a change in rulers. The new one may run things differently. He has been a visitor at the castle for several days. I've seen him. He looks exactly like a Krumerian, and it is rumoured he's a son of Remedor."

Yes, Valenis was aware of all the gossip because of Salina. She had not forgotten to mention the annoying kid whom Father had been paying too much attention to.

"This is bad news for us! The last thing I need is to have to fight Soleya in order to destroy the necromancer!" Krementa raised her hands in an annoyed gesture.

"Everything about Soleya aside, there are hundreds of kilometres of land between Vern and Kranium and the Skeletal Wall. Rabolii wouldn't be an easy target. He has not only soldiers but also some very powerful magic. Attacking him on his land would be very difficult."

"On his land, you say?" Krementa answered, deep in thought, then added, "I have an idea forming, but it will be difficult to achieve."

Valenis raised his eyes with interest and asked, "What is it?"

"No, maybe it's a bad idea. If you attract too much attention, they will surely find out who you are and kill you."

"You underestimate me, Mother! Tell me what you're planning, and I'll let you know whether I can do it or not," Valenis answered emphatically.

"It will only work if you befriend someone important in this city, if not Rabolii himself. But you've always been a bit unsociable. I don't know if you can do it."

Valenis cocked his eyebrows and said confidently, "Hmm, as it happens, I've already done that. I'm good friends with one of the princesses. Perhaps I could reach Rabolii through her as well."

Krementa gasped. "Valenis! That is too risky! I told you to try to be inconspicuous. I would have otherwise been very unhappy with this. But in this case it will work out in our favour. This is what I have in mind: If this princess trusts you, you could convince her to take armies out and attack us. If we set a good ambush, we can turn things around in our favour so that we can deprive Krumerus of an army and maybe even have a valuable hostage. Once we have her, we can dictate the rules and ask anything from Rabolii, even propose that he switch places with her."

Valenis listened to the plan and realised he wasn't exactly comfortable with it. He stuttered, "I ... Mother, I don't know if they would send their armies someplace just because I asked them to."

"You think you can't achieve this? Valenis, we're all counting you! I don't know how else to approach Krumerus, especially if Soleya's backing them," Krementa exclaimed.

"Uh, no, I'll manage all this ... I just need ... more time to earn their trust," Valenis muttered.

"I believe you will succeed. Vernara will support you all the way, my sweet son." Krementa smiled lovingly. "Keep me updated on what you're doing, and don't forget to call me regularly."

Afterwards Valenis was left alone with his thoughts. He sat in a corner of the terrace, hugging his knees and staring at the ground. During the whole time he had spent here, he had not forgotten who he was or why he was in Krumerus. He knew where his loyalty lay, but he still hated the idea of leading Salina into a trap. He couldn't bear the thought of her discovering he was a spy and an enemy. But what if she didn't get involved in all this? It would be enough to convince her and Rabolii that it was a very good idea to take a strong army to the west. The princess didn't need to be there personally. Another one of Remedor's sons or some valuable, experienced general would be just as suitable as a hostage. If Salina weren't present, she might never even learn that Valenis was an enemy. He would be just another missing man, most likely killed, and it would be better for her to think him dead than to know the truth.

It seemed like the plan was made.

CHAPTER 9

THE TWO SONS

A few days had passed. During that time Arkenel and his friends were preparing for a trip. It was very difficult for them to gather all their things and organise themselves. There had been frequent fights that Graz had to break up. And somebody had always forgotten something. While they were hanging around, Arkenel decided to go say goodbye to Rabolii and pay him a last visit before the trip because he missed him. As he walked up, he came across a ridiculous scene which was unfolding right at the castle stairs for everyone to see.

"Father, this is a mockery. I demand that this situation be remedied at once, or I'll leave and never return." Morelii was croaking and stomping like an angry toddler.

Salina stood there with Valenis by her side. Fresner Remedor turned to the young woman and began yelling, "Your behaviour is disgraceful! I have given you my son in good faith, but it looks like you're unworthy. I can't have him marrying someone so ... promiscuous."

Valenis couldn't stand listening to that, so he stepped in. "How can you speak of her like that? She's never done anything to deserve this."

Salina wasn't looking forward to a marriage with Morelii at all, but she would try to keep arguments from escalating in case he turned out to be her future husband after all. She didn't want to get off to a bad start. And she wanted her father to learn about this ordeal even less. She tried to speak out, "Gentlemen, this is a misunderstanding. Valenis is but a friend. I do want this marriage very much."

"Good!" Morelii stated. "However, after all of this, you'll need to earn my trust. I demand that you have your virginity tested. I am to be present when that happens. And after it's done, we can start planning the wedding and begin conceiving children at once as I need at least five sons."

Valenis couldn't listen to this, so he turned to Salina. "Don't do this. This man is repulsive. If you marry him now for the sake of peace, you'll be miserable for the rest of your life."

"But, Valenis, this was decided by my father!" Salina exclaimed. "If I don't marry Morelii ..."

"Marry me instead," Valenis told her so spontaneously that it shocked everyone.

Morelii started yelling. He began stomping and throwing a tantrum, trying to attack Valenis with punches. His father was just as outraged and yelled, "That's it! I'll tell Rabolii that our agreement is off. There shall not be a wedding."

He stormed off into the castle, his son following. Salina glanced around for a moment and chased after them, shouting, "Please, wait. Don't bother Father. I'm sure we can come to an agreement."

Valenis went after her as he didn't want her to be alone in such a terrible moment. Arkenel was observing this with an expression of mild surprise as if he'd seen something similar every day. He followed all of them towards Rabolii's tower. That's where he was going anyway.

The necromancer was sitting at his desk, absent-mindedly gazing at his notes. For the first time in a while he felt some sort of peace. True enough, Vern was aggressive. Also, he had lost thousands of skeletons in Soleya, and moreover his failure of a son had returned. However, Rabolii still felt like he could take a breath from all of that, happy about the fact that Ilinar had signed a peace treaty with him. His bliss ceased when his doors opened with a loud bang and the enraged Lord Fresner and his screaming son burst in. Both of them started croaking like crows, describing their horrible problem. They were so loud and overexcited that only they knew what they were actually saying. Rabolii and his tormented brain barely managed to make out what they were talking about; still, he caught a few words and understood that Salina had refused to marry Morelii.

It was his turn to raise his voice, which would silence everyone else. He stood up and slammed his fist on his desk, yelling, "All right then! Obviously, you have so little respect for me, my personal space, and my free time that you dare to just barge in here and scream at me! Who do you think you are? Could you not find a more sophisticated way to bring this issue to my attention?" Then he turned his fearsome glare at Salina, which caused her to die a little inside. "As for you, I thought you were a little more sensible than this! First you wanted to get married, but when I arranged it, you decided to make me look like a food! Don't tell me that Morelii disappointed you so bitterly during your brief acquaintance that you just decided to call everything off! I already told you what's at stake and how important this marriage is, but obviously Krumerus's welfare is not at all important to you, and neither is the stability of our relations with the Northern Provinces. I don't want to hear anything more about the whims of any of you. Sort this between yourselves. I won't force you to make certain choices. You can decide by yourselves what's best for this country, if you care about it at all."

Valenis was silent. He didn't dare stand up to Rabolii. He and Salina just stood there looking at the floor in a defeated fashion while their villains were triumphing. Arkenel watched this scene while leaning against the doorframe. He saw an opening to speak, so he stepped in. "Father, I have to agree with you on some things. Indeed, our relations with the Northern Provinces are very important. It's nice to maintain them, but is an arranged marriage really the only way we can achieve this? We are one country. We don't need to take such measures. It's not like we're trying to keep a fragile peace so that we need to resort to weddings."

"How can I have a good relationship with a man whose daughter rejected my son?" the lord roared.

"I really want to think my sister is not a unit of exchange, Fresner," Arkenel replied, walking around the room with his arms folded. "If we are so keen to use her to improve relations and make peace, I'd think marrying her to a foreigner would do us more good. Not that I would insist on it if she doesn't want it."

"No need to worry. She decided to marry him!" Morelii barked and pointed at Valenis with a stiff, crooked finger.

"I don't know why it's so important for us to marry her off right here, right now," Arkenel said. "She barely knows either of you two, so maybe it's unwise to jump into something like this. Marriage is ... It is a privilege and a wonder to bind your fate with someone else's till the end of days, so frankly, it annoys me how carelessly you make these decisions. Grant this honour to your best friend, someone you already accepted with all their ... stupid quirks, strange habits, and irritating sides. Not the first person you see when you decide you want to marry."

"Arkenel, I'm not a child. I know what I'm doing." Salina sighed.

"I hope you do! Still, I would recommend you give yourself some time. Get to know both of them before you decide. Who knows, you may not change your mind about Morelii, but during that time you might find a million reasons why a marriage with doll face is a bad idea. Does this plan of action please everyone?"

"No! I would suggest ..." Fresner tried to object.

"I thought so!" Arkenel raised his voice, not taking notice of this protest, and waved his arms as if he were chasing away geese. "Now if you don't mind, go away before you kill my father with your drama. Anyway, I came here because ..."

Before he got to finish his sentence, Arkenel turned to Rabolii. However, since he wasn't a sober man, he couldn't stand firmly and bumped into the desk. That shook the shelves that were fixed on one side, and some flasks that were sitting on them to fell onto the desk, shattering, the contents spilling out. Until then everyone in the room had been murmuring and protesting, but after this ugly incident they all shut up, mute like fish and could only wait for the necromancer's reaction. Arkenel was paralyzed and anticipated his death. He still remembered what had happened last time he spilled a potion, so he was ready to say his prayers and write a will. Several of the bottles lay broken on the desk, their liquids mixed, dramatically dripping into a cauldron that was left beside the desk. As if things weren't terrible enough already, the mixture created some bizarre reaction. It began to smoke aggressively, emitting red steam, which began to settle on the floor and splattered in the form of blood. The room was filled with a low, rumbling, fearsome voice that uttered some incomprehensible words. It all finished as quickly as it had started; the illusion of blood vanished, and the surface of the potion in the cauldron calmed down. It became dark red.

Now all the glances turned to Rabolii. He sat there like a stone sculpture in a chair, a terrible grimace frozen on his face. His eyebrows were close to hitting his receding hairline. Without saying a word, he stood stiffly and went to the cauldron to inspect the damage. Arkenel, terrified and confused, began to whimper, "Gosh, Dad, I'm so, so sorry! I don't know why that fell ... I hope it wasn't important ... Please don't be mad ... It was an accident. I will, er ... I'll buy you another flask. I'll glue this one together if you want me to."

Rabolii fixed his pale eyes on his son and said hoarsely, "I can't believe it. This was actually the right formula. I could never get the serum to be the right consistency, but this is it! Which potions mixed? Did you manage to see?"

Arkenel thought he was being attacked, so he raised his hands to defend himself. "No, no, nothing mixed. I hope I didn't mess up your potion. I ..."

"Leave my presence at once, you fool! And thank the gods that your stupidity wasn't fatal on this day!"

Arkenel didn't need to hear that twice. He dashed out of the room, grateful to Mortelion that he was still wearing his own skin. Everyone else also left. Salina and Valenis walked a bit faster so they could get away from the lord and his spoiled son. The Vernian asked, "Um, can you explain to me what happened just now? What was that potion?"

"If that's what I think it is, it's incredible!" Salina exclaimed. "I think it is the vampiric potion that will grant Father immortality! He could never quite get it right for years, but it seems that by breaking those bottles, Arkenel dosed it correctly. Isn't it unbelievable?"

"The gods act in mysterious ways," Valenis replied. He didn't even want to imagine Krementa's reaction when she learned Rabolii is immortal now.

"Valenis, I'm so happy! Now that this has happened, I'm sure my marriage with that awful man will get cancelled. It's so exciting. And ... I know I didn't answer your question. Valenis, my answer is yes!"

He stared at her in dismay. At this point he actually regretted having asked her. He'd find himself engaged to a woman whom he'd need to betray, whose country he would need to destroy, and whom maybe he would need to indirectly kill. He had no idea what spontaneous emotion made him act that way, but he'd beat himself up for his stupidity later. At this stage he just looked at Salina with a sweet smile and replied, "This is wonderful, Salina! Let's celebrate!"

In the meantime, Rabolii knelt by the cauldron and couldn't believe the perfect mixture in it. It was the ideal base for the potion he needed. During all these years, he had never been so close to completing it. It was somewhat ironic that no one else but Arkenel had made this happen. Obviously, Mortelion loved to play such jokes on the poor necromancer. Regardless, there was no time for more thinking now. Rabolii started pouring the potion into different flasks. He'd try to complete each portion separately to make sure he didn't mess up the whole mixture all at once. It was all so wonderful! Something positive had finally happened in his tragic life.

Over the next few days, everyone went back to their tasks. Arkenel and his men left the city and began their journey towards the land near Aldur which Rabolii wanted them to guard. No one knew what was so special about that land or how it was threatened. The snow had made the paths muddy, but that didn't seem to bother Arkenel, who was too wounded to walk anyway. He had mounted the huge skeleton of a four-legged demon and was riding it with an absent-minded expression. He was quite comfortable as long as no low-hanging branches slapped him across the face. He listened to the sounds of the forest, and every once in a while he'd grin, seemingly for no reason. His mind was flooded by memories. A mere month ago, his friends and he had travelled on this same road after they escaped Aldur. He was in such an elevated mood. To him the whole world shone with glamour, beauty, and warmth, although he was surrounded by nothing but thorns, beasts, and death. He could only remember himself running around like a loose animal that'd never been outside before.

"You want every beast in this damn wood to hear you? Sure looks like it. Shut up for a second," Mavarius had said, trying to silence him.

"But look how spacious and open it all is!" Arkenel had answered with excitement while swinging from the branch of a tree.

Mavarius had rolled his eyes and walked up to his friend just to kick him down from the tree. That didn't ruin the mood of his young companion, who fell into a pile of leaves. Arkenel paused for a moment, listening to the sounds around him, and noted, "Do you hear that crackling noise? These are the centipedes."

"Such a dumb place. Do you have any game here?" murmured Mavarius as he tried to discern any traces on the ground. But he didn't get to do so, because Arkenel ran over it like a herd of cattle, elated by the next sound he heard.

"And that other sound is from a troll. It groans in such a funny way."

"How's that a troll? It sounds dumb, like some sort of lamb," Mavarius protested.

"Aw, looks like the great forest specialist has stumbled across animals he doesn't recognise!" Arkenel started mocking him while running in circles around him.

"Give me a break. How could I have learned about anything in Krumerus by sitting in some prison for ten years?" Mavarius snapped at him and tried to hit him, but his younger friend was too quick.

Arkenel continued to annoy him without noticing what was around them. At one point, Mavarius spontaneously pulled out his sword with a lightning move and swung it at his friend. Remedor was surprised by such a fierce attack, but he ducked in time. Behind him, a beheaded vampire dropped to the ground, twitching dreadfully. Arkenel turned to Mavarius with reverence and said, "Oh ... thanks, tosser."

"I know your animals well enough. They die. There's nothing else to know," Mavarius summed up the situation and wiped his sword on the vampire's cloak.

Arkenel remembered all of that with a smile, which started fading. They were passing by the same place where the vampire had died. There was nothing left of him other than pieces of his cloak. The beasts had eaten all his remains. The forest looked unchanged, but at the same time it had none of that glow like a month ago.

Arkenel didn't even realise they had nearly arrived. He was dozing off in the saddle of his skeleton. The darkness was soothing. There wasn't a single sound. It was then that he picked up a familiar scent. He opened his eyes... his eye. The pupil reflected the moonlight. He glanced around and said, "Hey, tossers, do you smell that?"

"Yes, it's blood," one of the men yelled.

"Idiots, is it someone's time of the month?" someone else answered him.

"Your mother's." A small war seemed to be forming.

"Go drown in manure, you stinker!" Devastating swears echoed around.

Arkenel tried to hush the men. He was sleepy and dazed, but he was still aware it wasn't safe to be making noise here, not until he knew exactly what had died and what had killed it. He got out of his saddle and stumbled forward. His stitches were pulling at him in an uncomfortable way. He spotted the source of the smell. He fell to his knees next to a corpse. Its hair was smooth and tarry black, the skin yellowish. The mouth of the dead man was bloody. Sharp canine teeth protruded from it. He was a vampire. Arkenel gestured quietly to the others to come to him.

"Who is this cretin?" one of the men asked.

"I think he's one of Rabolii's vampires. That's not good," said Arkenel. "He had sent a few here to guard something, and now we've found a dead one."

"Er ... more than one," Graz said, looking ahead.

Arkenel raised his gaze and gasped. A little farther in the dark grass he noticed dozens more bodies. Something had definitely gone wrong. Remedor waved his hand, and his company moved forward. Who could the vampires have fought with? And for what reason? There wasn't anything in sight worth dying for. In such moments, Arkenel really wished Rabolii would tell him at least from time to time what's happening.

The darkness was thick and somewhat heavy. For the first time in his life, Arkenel felt his vision limited. The farther he walked in the meadow, the worse he felt. And this time it had nothing to do with the wound. He felt his body become somewhat stiff when he saw something move in the dark. It was a massive dark silhouette that passed the men without even paying attention to them. He carried an enormous sword from which blood dripped. Arkenel opened his mouth to speak. The words came out with some difficulty. "Hey ... hey, you! Wait!"

The silhouette slowed down without turning. He responded with a voice that sounded strange, as if coming from everywhere, "What do you want from me, stranger?"

"I ... I'm Arkenel, son of Rabolii Remedor. I was tasked with guarding this area, and when I arrived, I found my father's other guards slaughtered. You ... do you have anything to do with this?"

"Yes," the voice whispered unceremoniously. It was low-pitched and ominous. It caused a nervous feeling, implying that it was a bad idea for anyone to keep talking to this individual, but Arkenel wasn't that easy to intimidate after having handled Copper Face and other similar villains.

"Yes? How calm you are for killing subordinates of the Crown! If you surrender now, you'll be punished, but if you don't, we'll kill you on the spot," Arkenel threatened. Some deep instinct he had was screaming that this was a bad idea, but he wouldn't just turn around and leave, although many of his men had started to cower and step back.

"You? You will kill me?" the stranger exclaimed amazedly. "I'm tired of arrogant men like you. You have no idea in whose presence you stand. I am the one who can crush your bones with a mere glance. I shall not suffer your threats."

After saying that, he turned, only to cause more panic and

confusion. He had no face. His whole head was wrapped in a dark cloth, leaving only his eyes uncovered. They were emitting some unearthly light in a spectral teal colour. It dripped out of his eye sockets like heavy smoke. Arkenel was startled by this, but he still didn't move. The next thing he felt was his mouth filling with blood, and despite his attempt to swallow it, he choked on it as it poured out of his nose and mouth. As he watched the enormous man walk towards him, he realised that he had encountered something very powerful that he didn't understand and that would cost him his life. His enemy, towering over him, fearsome and sinister, just snorted and said, "You are so pathetic you sadden the gods. I will show the mercy of ending your suffering."

He raised his sword to the sky and sent a devastating shock wave in every direction. It threw everyone in the meadow back. They dropped unconscious so quickly that they didn't have time for any last thoughts or pleas. The darkness thickened. The smell of blood was overwhelming, swallowing the whole place.

Meanwhile, in another part of Krumerus, Rabolii was also having problems. Valenis was causing him such inconvenience. He called the young man over to his "office". Salina sent him there with many tears as if he were going to a slaughterhouse. This didn't improve morale of the Vernian, but he tried to stay calm in this worrying situation. After all, he had left Rabolii's room alive before. He stood in front of the necromancer, wondering whether that really was him. Rabolii looked rejuvenated. Last time Valenis saw him, the necromancer was wrinkled and shrivelled because reviving all those Vernian corpses had been exhausting. But after he had some rest and a whole lot of potions, he was handsome and flawless again, not looking a day over sixty-two, which was his actual age. Little did Valenis know that this was also because the necromancer had been draining energy from people and corpses. After this boost he looked like his normal self again.

Without waiting for an invitation, Valenis pulled up a chair and sat opposite the necromancer, waiting for his attention. Rabolii was writing down things with a competent look to demonstrate he was very busy. Once he thought he had already made the necessary impression, he looked up at his visitor. He crossed his fingers, laying his elbows on the desk, and said, "I thought I'd see you again, Valenis. I just imagined I'd be asking you how you are progressing with the study of your sphere and trying to find out if you have any good ideas about how the elements earth and death can combine. Now we have such different issues to discuss. How things have changed!"

Valenis decided not reply at this stage. The less he spoke, the better it would be for him. Rabolii watched him with a critically raised eyebrow, then continued to talk: "You obviously want to get involved with my family in a very personal way. It was at the very moment when I finally decided to marry off my daughter. Do you realise that you are an obstacle at the moment?"

"I think I'm just one of many reasons why Salina decided against marrying Morelii," Valenis said coolly.

"Oh, really? You know everything about marriages, right? I would say I have a little more experience than you on these matters. If it weren't for you, Salina would be more enthusiastic about her future engagement. She would have tried to get to know Morelii. They have a lot in common; they would fit well together. But how can we expect this to happen while you're here! She may think she loves you, but how could you be her husband? What can you bring to this family? You expect me to just give my daughter to a nobody?"

Valenis found that a bit offensive. He didn't enjoy being belittled, especially since he didn't make much effort to hide the fact that he was educated and intelligent. He didn't like being called a "peasant" or a "nobody".

"I am sorry to have caused an inconvenience. I knew Princess Salina before her engagement. Perhaps it would have been successful if it weren't for me, but getting rid of me at this stage won't improve the situation."

Valenis himself didn't know where he'd gotten all this bravery from. He never dared to voice his opinion in front of Krementa like that. However, now he felt he had a good reason to pursue his goals. During a sleepless night of reflection, it had occurred to him that if he actually were to marry Salina, he could at least save her from his mother's wrath and take her away from the dying Krumerus. After all, there was no reason for Krementa to dislike Salina. She was so quiet, sweet, and kind-hearted that no arguments would ever arise. So in a way, this marriage could be life-saving.

Rabolii raised his eyebrows when he heard Valenis's reply and asked, "And what do you suggest? You just want me to give you my daughter? How have you deserved to become a part of my family?"

"You'll need to ask Salina that question," Valenis answered

calmly. "I think I will be a good husband and I will make her happy. I believe she thinks so too."

A grimace appeared on Rabolii's face. It was supposed to be a smile, but it didn't give out joy or happiness. It was just an indication of his terrible thoughts. He stood up from his chair and began to pace and circle around Valenis like a shark while staring at him with fearsome eyes. "The problem is that we know very little about you, Valenis. We can't even trace where you came from. Your city is 'destroyed' and everyone who knew you is 'dead', so there's simply no way of knowing anything about your past. You could lie to me about everything; I have no way of checking."

The Vernian looked down nervously. He knew he had plenty to hide indeed, so he felt anxious. Maybe the necromancer noticed something about him that gave him away? Rabolii continued talking: "I want to talk to you about something I used to have until it disappeared mysteriously. It was important for the balance of magic in these lands, so if it were to fall into the wrong hands, the results could be catastrophic. However, only a sorcerer could utilise it. Is that why you came here, Valenis? Was that your goal the whole time?"

Rabolii watched his victim with a stone-cold gaze, waiting for any signs of lying or hesitation. Both seemed present. Valenis shuddered in his chair, staring at his hands in his lap, and said, "I don't know what you're talking about, Master Remedor."

"Is that so? I have ways of finding out. If you have the common sense to cooperate with me and tell me what you did with my map, maybe I'll have the mercy of throwing you out of the city without killing you. Being stubborn doesn't bond well with you."

Valenis looked up at him and repeated, "I haven't taken any maps."

"Don't lie to me!" Rabolii roared. He put his hand on Valenis's forehead.

The necromancer's nails dug into the skin. His hand glowed ominously. Valenis couldn't make a sound. He felt a monstrous force penetrate his mind, and it began fumbling around, causing him pain with every movement. He tried to push it away with everything he had. Rabolii snarled at him. "Stop fighting. It's pointless. Your whole life lies bare in front of me!"

Valenis struggled helplessly. He felt strangely paralysed and couldn't escape. He realised that Rabolii was in his thoughts, and he was terrified of everything he could see there. He would find out that Valenis was a spy, that he planned to harm him, and that he was telling Krementa everything he found out there. He didn't know how to defend himself.

Rabolii loosened his grip, looking at the man in front of him with an incomprehensible expression. Silence dropped like a heavy ball of lead. Valenis continued to feel petrified and was awaiting his execution. He felt like the necromancer knew everything about him. Rabolii was the first to break the silence with a surprising statement: "You seem to know nothing about the map. I'm sorry for being rough with you. The mistake was mine."

Valenis blinked in confusion and couldn't produce a coherent reply. "I ... I don't know ... the map ... What map? ... I'm not ..."

"Yes. I know. You don't." The necromancer began to caress his shoulder as if he were consoling an upset maiden. "You are not to blame for anything."

"I'm not?" Valenis stuttered.

"You are not." Rabolii smiled at him kindly and cheerfully, like no one had seen him do for a long time. Then he touched with his finger the chain around the young man's neck and said, "You have an interesting amulet. Can I have a look?"

Valenis could barely understand what was being said to him. He was still bewildered that he had managed to survive something like that and had even kept his mission a secret while doing so. Perhaps the necromancer had not seen all his thoughts but was just looking for something related to the map and didn't find anything. He handed over the amulet with a stiff movement. Rabolii gave him another concerned look and said softly, "Perhaps you should get some rest now. We'll talk later."

Valenis rose, still confused and shaken, and without waiting for a second invitation ran off from the chambers of the fearsome necromancer. Rabolii cast him a cold, judging look. He had seen Valenis's thoughts in all their detail. He understood that he was a Vernian spy who had been sent to monitor Krumerus and lead its troops to certain death. Rabolii didn't want to demonstrate that he had learned everything because he preferred to think about how to make use of the situation. Simply capturing Valenis and asking for a large ransom wasn't necessarily the best decision. Something like that would enrage Krementa and make her even more aggressive. Rabolii thought it was a better idea for now to simply watch the prince and serve him only such information he'd want him to learn. And of course, he'd fight with everything he had to make sure Salina didn't end up marrying the enemy. He'd find a way to stop that from happening.

Rabolii returned his attention to the interesting amulet. Just like Salina, he could recognise what it was and what it was used for. The boy had used this to convey information. The necromancer realised that Valenis had been in Krumerus for some time and probably had some interesting stories to tell. Rabolii didn't know too much about Vernian artefacts, but it occurred to him that the amulet had memory and could repeat conversations that had taken place through it. The ruler of Krumerus wanted to know exactly what his enemy knew, so he began to poke around the amulet in an attempt to get it to work. He tried several tricks, then tried to invade it in the same way he penetrated a human being's consciousness. This definitely led to some results, though not exactly what he had hoped for. His hand clutched the amulet against his will, and he couldn't break away regardless of his efforts. He sensed strange fingers which seemed to be touching his very soul. Something unfamiliar and powerful had struck him like an infection, causing him to shake uncontrollably. Unable to get a hold of himself, the necromancer was stuck with his hand on the amulet as a loud echoing voice sounded in his head: "Rabolii Remedor, a withering wreck of a man poisoned by ill ambitions and buried by mistakes he's made in the past which he will pay for now."

Rabolii's jaw dropped. He couldn't understand who was talking to him. The voice didn't sound either male or female; it was ethereal and inexplicable. He barely managed to answer, "Who are you? What do you know about me, and what do you want?"

The voice continued to speak, "I'm trembling with anticipation ... because I know ... I know how Rabolii Remedor will perish. What disgrace and humiliation he will endure ... It's all he deserves for disgusting everyone with his malice."

"Who is disgusted by me?" he insisted, trying to make this into a dialogue, but it wasn't known whether the other party heard him at all.

"A horror will befall him like a winged storm, and his own family will destroy him. One son does he have who will see the will of the Divine. He will be his guardian and fight for his salvation. Another son he has who suffers in isolation, bitter and wounded. He will direct the aggression of the whole universe against Rabolii Remedor, and it will be the blade that shall cut his flesh for the last time and take his life again. His soul will not find salvation. It will visit whom it is promised. That will be the day when all of Rabolii's lies will bleed out through his open wounds and his broken oaths and promises will crush his bones. The story is written with his own black blood."

Rabolii stood there, stunned. He realised that the amulet was no longer holding him, so he pulled himself back. His shaking hands got a hold of a piece of parchment. While frantically dripping ink all over the page, he began scribbling down those words that had burned in his mind. He would probably want to ponder upon them later when he recovered from the shock, but at the moment he could only write without thinking. He didn't feel his own fingers while he was clutching the feather. His chest was ripped by the agonising pain of his heart that had probably stopped, but that didn't matter. The necromancer continued to write on the sheet. With trembling hands, he added the last words: "The story is written with his own black blood." The ink had become a strange texture, somewhat too watery, its blue colour replaced by a black one.

All this was unreal, just like a nightmare. Rabolii sat in his opulent, ornamented, velvet-coated chair, his chest still torn in pain. He rolled up his sleeve and injected a potion, then listened in silence. His pulse slowly began to return to normal. Rabolii looked down at the sheets where his fate was written with his own blood. He began to realise what had happened to him. He had received a prophecy. So many accusations, so much hate. He realised all too well what was happening and who was threatening him. His mistakes of the past were catching up with him. He knew that Krementa hated him, that wasn't anything new. Her hate for him was so soaked in this amulet that it burst out on him when he touched it. What he couldn't understand though is where this prophecy was coming from. Krementa wasn't powerful enough to see the future. So who was it then?

That's how Ravena found him. Perhaps he had not moved for two or three hours, and he had a bruise where he had leaned on the desk because he had soft and sensitive skin. He didn't even move when his wife came in. She looked at him suspiciously, wondering if this was a demonstration or if something was seriously wrong. She walked over to him and helped him sit up.

"Rab, what's wrong? Have you forgotten to inject your potions? You look terrible."

She began collecting bottles off his desk and giving him the syringes. Her husband was looking at her with a dead expression, then he bleated tragically, "What's the point? I am but a doomed corpse, and there has never been much chance for me!"

Ravena ignored him. He was probably feeling depressed again. He'd feel better after he got to vent and complain for a bit. So she prepared to listen to him so there'd be peace until tomorrow at the same time. She began to inject him with potions and told him, trying to sound sympathetic, "On the contrary, dear husband. Everything will be fine, you'll see."

"No, this time it's different!" Rabolii moaned.

"Did a potion go bad again, darling?" she asked. She was trying not to sound indifferent, but she was simply incapable of worrying about the same thing every day. She wondered how Rabolii could do it.

"No! You aren't taking me seriously!" the necromancer yelled.

"Tell me what's wrong." Ravena was simply in the mood for masochism today.

Rabolii opened a mouth as huge as a shark's and began spitting more words per minute than any other human could. Perhaps it was a record. He told in detail about the prophecy: what he had witnessed, what he'd been told, how he was afraid. He waved around the terrifying parchment with the black prophecy, then cried about how uncertain he was, how the whole world was against him and so on. For Ravena, all this was unbelievably surprising and startling information. After hearing all of this, she had a few questions. She began,

"Are we just going to take at face value something which comes from Krementa? She has every reason to want to scare you. Maybe she made up the prophecy entirely."

"No, I doubt it." Rabolii replied. "When she spoke, it sounded like she had no idea I'm listening. She spoke as if I wasn't there. It was something which I overheard."

Ravena sighed. She would need to try very hard not to show how unamused she was. It all just seemed so unlikely. Trying to sound optimistic, she stated,

"Rab, maybe we should look at this as an opportunity to change the course of events rather than see it as the end of the world. Imagine, all this would have happened without our knowledge, but now we are warned." "So what if we are?" Rabolii snapped. "Our fate is decided by the gods, and we are incapable of doing anything but floating down the stream of events ... The only thing left for me to wonder is how long I have until my second death ... which will be the final one!" he cried dramatically.

Ravena continued trying to see the good in this situation. "What about the two sons? I think it's a very good idea to support the one who will protect you and try to eliminate the one who will target you. Do you have any idea who they are?"

Rabolii snarled with hatred and hissed like an angry cat, "Who could they possibly be? It's obvious that the one who'll be defending me is Ilinar. He already did it once when Aslania could have finished us off. He also signed a peace treaty with Krumerus, which is probably the best thing that has happened to us for quite some time."

Ravena rolled her eyes. Typical. The most magnificent children Rabolii had were the extramarital ones. Feeling like she already knew the answer, she asked, "And who's the bad son?"

"I think that's also obvious!" Rabolii was fussing with contempt. "No one else is more 'bitter' and 'wounded' than the damned Arkenel! It's as if everything he's ever done was against me! Evil itself possessed him when he destroyed my way back to life the first time around! Now I'm very close to making the potion again, and he's back to finish me off!"

"Rab, that's enough. I think it's plain to see that Arkenel is not hostile." Ravena opposed this theory. "He is neither vindictive nor angry with you."

"Of course you'd say that. From my point of view, he fits the description perfectly." Rabolii snorted. "If he's pretending to be friendly now, he's just doing it to numb my vigilance. You'll see, he'll stab me in the back at the first opportune moment."

"You're overreacting, Rab," Ravena told him. "I don't want you panicked so much because of this one prophecy. Fates do change. Your sons are under control. I will make sure I watch them, and I won't let anyone kill you. And if you want to make sure that doesn't happen, I recommend you start treating your offspring a bit more fatherly. None of them will touch you if you're a good parent. And speaking of sons, I mean Regel and Dregel as well."

"You don't understand anything! Leave me alone!" Rabolii bleated with a tragic expression.

"Nonsense. Come with me. I want to take you outside a little bit. Clean air's good for you," Ravena replied.

The necromancer knew that the sooner he did what she wanted, the sooner she'd leave him alone. He got up with a sigh and dragged his feet after her."

—m—

Pain. It was something so typical, so constantly present in everyday life, that when the flesh was pierced once again, one would first experience annoyance and only then begin to realise how dreadful it felt. That was the mood Arkenel woke up in. He was lying with his eyes closed and trying hard to return to that silent state he had been in a short while ago. He was feeling sick, he was wet with his own cold sweat, and he was shivering. In fact, he was a little surprised that he was alive at all, but he didn't enjoy it at the moment. He felt movement near him; someone was poking around his wounded body. It occurred to him that perhaps he had not been unconscious for so long and that the masked monster was now checking him to see if he was dead. With a lightning-fast motion and unexpected precision, he squeezed the wrist that had been in his private space and tried to stand up and fight his attacker, but he could only collapse back on the hard ground. His vision was blurred, so he didn't know whether to believe his ears when he was greeted by a very familiar voice: "Quit moving, tosser. It was hard enough to stitch you up, so don't fall apart the second you wake."

"Tosser, what are you doing here?" Arkenel grunted. He was too sick and wounded to even feel something from this unexpected meeting with Mavarius.

"I will tell you later. Just be happy I found you when I did, OK? Dunevir would have split your head like a melon."

"Dunevir, huh? You mean that huge freak with the bandage on his head?" Arkenel snorted.

"Shut it! Don't talk like that while we're still here," Mavarius warned him grimly as he continued stitching up Arkenel, whose wounds were starting to open again because he'd moved too much.

"How are the rest?" asked Remedor.

"Better than you," Mavarius said briefly. "Won't you chill in one place just till your wounds heal? Why are you running around stupid places again?"

"My father gave me a job. He sent me to guard this place. I don't know why, but he said it was important. I've failed by the looks of it," Arkenel murmured. "I guess whatever was here, the big guy found it before I did."

"Pff, nothing was here, just some magic crap," Mavarius said, giving a tactical explanation of the situation.

"You see? Everybody knows what's going on here better than I do!" Arkenel groaned.

Mavarius bit the thread with which he had been stitching him up, then he met Arkenel's gaze. They both blinked awkwardly, wondering whether to discuss their last separation and say a couple of words about their feelings on this meeting, but apparently they decided not to and stared in different directions. Arkenel noticed that he was in some temple of Mortelion which he didn't recognise. The interior was made of tons of bones aesthetically arranged on the walls. They made the chandeliers, decorated the furniture with their ominous whiteness, hung from the ceiling, and formed different shapes. Most of the temples looked like this one. The huge number of bones helped the concentration of the energy of death, and this brought strength and glory to Mortelion.

"Where are we?" Arkenel asked hoarsely.

Mavarius glanced at him, realising that his companion would always have the energy to ask questions and seek conversation no matter how sick, wounded, and miserable he was. It looked like this talk wouldn't wait.

"It's a temple near Aldur, and there are cultists in it. They're some crazy priests—outlaws for all I know. They must have been well mad at you if they smacked you like this."

"One of them slew my father's guards. I couldn't have just told him 'bye' and then left." Arkenel shrugged.

"How about you start doing that, eh?" Mavarius snorted. "Look at yourself. You're a shrimp, but ever since I've known you, you've always had your little pissing contests with men much bigger and tougher than you."

"Aw, I thought you were happy to see me standing up to such men." Arkenel smiled sweetly and leaned towards him as much as his bruised flesh allowed him to.

"Sod off. I don't even know if they'll let you live or not."

"I don't know, are any of those people around here? We can ask them what they plan on doing with me and my friends. I won't just let them kill me."

"Well, yes, there are two of them by the door," Mavarius answered.

Arkenel raised his head with an inhuman effort and saw two hooded figures leering suspiciously at him about five metres away. He grunted and tried to remember if he had just said anything he didn't want them to hear, but he was in too much pain to think excessively.

The doors of the room opened with a creek, and in came a woman with long black hair and a dress of torn veils to the middle of her calves. Her skin looked ghostly white. Her footsteps were soundless. Arkenel stared at her as she approached him, thinking that this was probably the most beautiful person he had ever seen. Her light eyes were surrounded by smoky black make-up, and her lips were colourless.

"Oh … um … hi. I'm Prince Remedor." He began trying to sit up. Mavarius rolled his eyes with annoyance.

The apparition-like woman sat next to him and stared at him with a lifeless expression. She held a bowl in her hands. It contained some unknown food.

"My name is Halena. I live to serve Mortelion."

"Mm, is that for me?" Arkenel stared at the bowl. Halena pushed the food towards him and continued to look at him coolly. She didn't seem very talkative, but that didn't stop the young prince. He kept chatting her up. "Thanks for that. I was starving. I can't help but wonder though, why are you guys feeding me after trying to kill me? Where's that big guy, Dunevir?"

"He is busy. Lord Dunevir pardoned the lives of you and your friends after Mavarius stood up for you," Halena said with a blank face.

Arkenel moved on to the other important question: "There was something in this area that I was supposed to protect. May I speak to your Dunevir and ask him what happened to … the thing?"

"The master is busy," Halena repeated.

"Tosser, let's just go away," Mavarius suggested pleadingly.

"Hold it, man. How do you imagine this? Dad's sending me on a mission, and I'll just go away?" Arkenel turned to Halena and smiled charmingly at her. "Come on, you seem like a cool girl. I promise I won't take too much of your master's time."

"If you insist." She groaned and stood up. "Come with me. I'll check if he can see you."

"He … he seemed quite powerful to me. Do you know which family he's from?" Arkenel asked.

In Krumerus, all the sorcerers were a part of a famous family. It was known that the Aldur area was the domain of the Bloodred Skull family, but Arkenel knew all its members. Rabolii liked inviting them to dinners. None of them were so tall and muscular.

"Perhaps you will be given the opportunity to ask him this question," Halena gave a vague reply.

Arkenel frowned. He didn't like half answers and riddles. He wanted to know what sort of monster he'd be facing.

Mavarius helped him stand up, and the three of them walked through the dark temple. While they were moving through the bone-decorated corridors, Arkenel gazed at Halena in front of him. Her walk was graceful, and her figure was beautiful. He noticed a lot of scratches on her pale wrists. Some were white scars while others were still black and looked fresh. It wasn't uncommon for people to cut themselves in Krumerus for various reasons. Blood was used for rituals, and some even killed themselves to sell their corpse.

The main sanctuary turned out to be even more macabre. The walls were made of more bones than plaster. Femur bones were arranged artistically near the floor. Skulls formed pillars that rose to the ceiling. There was a fountain of blood which should probably dry out, but in a place like this, everything was enchanted to remain forever fresh. The altar was large and terrifying, and in the middle there was a sacrificial table with straps that were tied to a young Aslanian girl in a white dress. She was weeping with terror. Above her was the familiar massive silhouette holding a knife. Arkenel shuddered at this sight but knew it would be a bad idea to intervene. He clenched his teeth, stood by the door, and waited for this to finish. Halena watched the murder with the same blank expression, but now there was a shade of satisfaction. Arkenel noticed this and stepped away with a disturbed look. He had heard that all cultists were crazy. Perhaps it was true.

"In the name of Mortelion, our master and lord,
accept this gift, oh demon horde.
Bones to break, white, fragile, and light.
Blood may soak your lips with delight.
The soul shall scream in anguish as it's torn away.
It shall now do what the master will say."

Dunevir muttered his fearsome prayer, pulled out a butcher's knife from his belt, and began the sacrifice. That's what he needed—bones and blood. It's what the whole temple was built from. Arkenel himself didn't know why this woman was getting murdered, but when the time came for the flailing, he looked away. He always thought he had seen everything, but this was too much. He had to wait a painfully long time for Dunevir to finish massacring his victim and sorting all the pieces in the way he needed them. When he finally finished and turned to the door, he looked at the intruders and snarled, "What are you doing here?"

"I was just enjoying your work, Master. Also, I've brought to you one of the captives. He wishes to speak to you."

Arkenel hesitantly stepped forward towards the huge man who was now also up to the elbows in blood for an extra scary effect. Dunevir growled with a voice coming from an unknown direction, "Let him talk then. The rest can leave."

"How about no?" Mavarius gave a brief refusal. He didn't want to leave Arkenel alone with this beast.

Without discussing the subject any more, Dunevir swung his hand, causing the doors to slam themselves, leaving Halena and Mavarius outside. OK, now Arkenel was alone with a giant man covered in blood up to his elbows. He stared at the skin around his eyes, trying to imagine what the face would look like. It seemed dark reddish and uneven, as if it had been burned. Arkenel felt terribly uncomfortable in the presence of such an individual, but he tried to gather his wits and talk about what he had come for.

"So ... I need some answers. When my father, Rabolii Remedor, sent me to guard this area, I don't know what exactly was in it that was worth protecting. Did you find anything interesting here?"

"Of course, you ignorant creature," Dunevir replied, beginning to wipe his hands with a rag. "There was a huge deposit of cosmic energy here. But it seems to me that your father does not really trust you since he sent you to guard something without even telling you what it was."

Arkenel blinked stupidly. For the first time in his life, he was hearing of cosmic energy ... or not. He thought about it and managed to recall something.

"Is that the same as ... uh ... cosmic energy charge?"

"I believe that's what I just said," Dunevir replied coldly.

Arkenel strained his brain. He remembered how a few weeks ago he and Mavarius were punching each other in Rabolii's room. It was then that his friend dared to peep into the necromancer's papers and read something about a cosmic energy charge that was actually a flying red fart over Aldur. It was then that Rabolii had hit the roof in rage and had made Arkenel's life flash before his eyes.

"Um ... I think my dad was researching something about

this, but I was under the impression it was a secret," Arkenel continued, trying to make sense of what was happening.

"Many sorcerers have felt the charge," Dunevir replied. He turned around to sharpen his butcher's accessories, starting with the giant chopper that could probably cut spines.

"Aaaand?" Arkenel said. "My father really was very mysterious about all this, and I don't understand why, if it's such a mundane matter."

"What I said was that many sorcerers have felt the presence of the ninth element. But only Remedor and his oracles, through combined efforts, could determine its exact location. The other rulers and their oracles are too far away to achieve that accuracy. So without the map we had no chance of finding the place."

As he said this, Dunevir lowered his eyes to one of the desks where rolls of parchment lay. Arkenel traced his gaze. He couldn't help recognising that one of the parchments was the infamous map with the flying red fart over Aldur. He frowned and said, "Ah, I could have sworn that this was in Rabolii's room until recently. How did it get here?"

"Your friend brought it to us," Dunevir replied casually.

Arkenel choked on his own surprised cough. What kind of global conspiracy was this! How on earth had Mavarius decided to steal this rag? And why did he bring it to the one guy who was just waiting for this? It was a rather complicated story, and Arkenel didn't feel capable of resolving it right then. So he waved his hand and said, "You know what? I think my dad would be very happy to meet you. You look just like one of the things he has a huge interest in."

...Along with all the demon hatchlings, the baby trolls, the cocoons of man-eating ants, and the mucus of a hybrid flying frog. But Arkenel wouldn't mention that.

"My place is in the temple of Mortelion. Here I can read omens and fulfil his wishes," Dunevir blurted.

"Yes, that's exactly what you'll be doing there too. All my father does is try to guess what Mortelion wants. You'll be very useful to each other, I promise you. You will talk about magic and about all the things that are interesting to you both. If it doesn't work out, you'll always be able to come back here. We won't force you to stay."

Dunevir thought for a moment, pointing his inhuman eyes to the sparkling fountain of blood. He said hoarsely, "I suppose this is amongst the plans of Mortelion. If he didn't wish me to meet your father, you wouldn't be alive and on your feet to make that suggestion."

"Thanks, Mortelion," Arkenel mumbled, feeling blessed by the gods.

"Never forget that he is the one who decides our fates," Dunevir said. "And while you serve him faithfully, you have nothing to fear.

Arkenel nodded. He had the feeling that he didn't understand the will of Mortelion, and he understood Rabolii's will even less. He hoped the necromancer wouldn't go insane because someone had found his cosmic charge. But if he did, at least Dunevir would conveniently be there to take the blame, and maybe Arkenel would survive.

CHAPTER 10

THE TRAITOR'S BLADE

Ilinar was walking through the castle and sought out Eley. He had not seen him since the day the teacher had learned about the peace treaty the young king had signed. It was no secret what Eley thought on the matter, so he reacted just as expected. He was angry and thought it was a diplomatic mistake that would put Soleya in a very complicated and unpleasant situation. Ilinar hadn't bothered arguing with him about it. He let him protest and pout. However, now it was time to start going back to Soleya. Eley was nowhere to be found. Ilinar visited his room yet another time and found it empty as before. There were quite a few things scattered around. Ilinar decided to go through them to get a clue as to what Eley was doing. He noticed a sealed letter left on his bed. Ilinar thought it was strange for a letter to be lying there, so he picked it up and noticed it was addressed to him. Puzzled, he opened it, feeling his hands begin to shake as he read it.

"Ilinar, I'm sorry for what I have to do, but it's for the sake of our country. I want the best for it, and that's not you. Don't return to Lumis. There you will not find your throne and your subordinates. You're dead to Soleya, and if you decide to come back, you will be killed. If you know what's good for you, stay in Krumerus. Obviously that's the country you chose."

Ilinar read the message a few more times, wondering what to make of it. "You're dead to Soleya"? "If you come back, you will be killed"? How come? What had Eley done? How could one of his closest friends have left him a message like this? Ilinar was stunned. He grabbed the note and ran as if he were being chased down the corridors of the castle. He stumbled like a madman towards Rabolii's tower. Despite some servants' brave attempts to stop him and protect the necromancer's peace, Ilinar prevailed and barged into the fearsome ruler's lair. Just at that very moment Rabolii was holding a large jar of bugs and was reaching in with some tweezers to take out a select few, but this rude intrusion startled him and he just dropped the whole thing. The glass shattered, and the beetles flew out with angry buzzing. Rabolii was so discontent that his mouth turned the shape of a flipped letter C. He glared with deathly eyes at the door. Had anyone else done this instead of his blessed son, chosen to save him from evil Arkenel, there would have been death.

"Master Remedor ... Father ..." Ilinar stumbled towards the mighty ruler with shaking feet and a face like he would cry at any moment. "Something terrible has happened ..."

"I noticed that!" Rabolii snapped. "It took my servants years to collect one hundred speckled beetles from the wilderness." He turned to a few of the skeletons who were peeking through the door and ordered, "Hey, you! Collect whatever beetles you can find on the floor."

Ilinar could feel one in his hair. He shook it off into the hands of one of the servants and continued wailing, "No, I don't mean that ... One of my closest friends has stabbed me in the back."

Ilinar handed Rabolii the horrifying note. The necromancer glanced over it and frowned with a slightly confused look. He asked, "What does he mean? How are you 'dead to Soleya'? This is ridiculous. He can't just proclaim you dead because he doesn't agree with your politics. Who is this Eley fellow anyway? Is it that shrivelled, unpleasant Soleyan?"

"He was my teacher and my closest friend!" Ilinar bellowed.

Rabolii, still staring at the note, raised his eyebrows and shook his head, wondering what kind of person you have to be if you're a teenage prince and your closest friend is a grumpy, shrivelled Soleyan. Trying very hard not to drop some biting comment, Rabolii stated, "This isn't a death threat. He has something else in mind. He'll probably fake evidence to incriminate you of something so that not even your own country will want you back."

"But ... but ... I haven't done anything," Ilinar began stuttering.

Rabolii slapped the dreadful letter on his desk with an angry look and raised his voice, saying, "You haven't done anything?! What kind of king are you if you justify yourself like a guilty child?! Do you think *my* subordinates would dare raise a hand against me? If they were to as much as look at me in a way I didn't like, it would be off with their heads. And you've let some teacher try to dethrone you?"

Ilinar was about to cry. He didn't understand why all this was happening to him. He mumbled, "I ... I'm not as powerful as you, Master Remedor."

"And whose fault is that? Do you surround yourself with powerful guards and sorcerers who can protect you from anything? Do you execute publicly the betrayers and their entire families? Do you command fear and respect, or do you *apologise* to your enemies?"

Ilinar stared at the floor with a guilty look and didn't know what to say. Rabolii began pacing around his chambers and stated, "You do know I have no resources to help you right now? I have a few necromancers who survived the siege, and I have a few vampires, but they won't be able to sneak undetected, especially if your Eley friend catches up with the Aslanian army, which he has probably already done. They carry a very strong imprint of death energy, and the other sorcerers will detect them. A living assassin would do the job, but I have none of those now, do I? Not after my city was all but levelled to the ground!"

Ilinar started biting his nails nervously and asked, "An assassin? Do we want to ... kill Eley?"

"Letting him live is out of the question!" Rabolii exclaimed. "He deserves death for what he's doing, and we need to deliver it to him or else he'll slander you. He needs to die. And you have to be the one to kill him."

Ilinar glanced up at the necromancer in shock. Rabolii's wrinkled, stern face bore no signs of humour; this wasn't a joke. The Soleyan whimpered, "I've never hurt a single soul in my life! I'm not capable of this!"

Rabolii put his bony hand on Ilinar's shoulder and told him, "You have no choice. We have no one else to send on such short notice. You won't be detected by the sorcerers, and if you do get caught sneaking around before you've had a chance to strike, you won't be harmed and you'll have opportunities to act further. I'll support you in any way I can, but this is ultimately up to you."

"I can't kill a man!" Ilinar explained with a high-pitched, panicky voice.

Rabolii clutched his shoulder and said in a low, vibrating voice, "What kind of king do you want to be, one who makes the whole world tremble before him, or a doormat who's a mockery even to the lowest scum in his country? This will define you as a person. Slaughter the traitor and rise to your potential. You are my son. Greatness is within your blood, but I'll turn away from you if you choose to be weak and useless."

Ilinar felt crushed by the weight of this situation. He felt that killing Eley was the worst thing that had as much as crossed his mind. But did he really have a choice? Even though he didn't care as much about his pride as Rabolii cared about his, he did care very much about the fate of his country. If he let Eley spread rumours and dethrone him, Soleya's new king would likely follow Eslir in this pointless war, which would result in so many deaths. Wasn't it crueller to spare one person if that resulted in thousands of deaths? This was a terrible burden, but he had to take it upon himself as a ruler. He looked at Rabolii bravely and said, "I'll do it. Tell me how you can help me."

"Good!" Rabolii smirked with contentment. "I knew you had it in you to be a great ruler. Your biggest challenge will be to catch up with Eley as he has the head start. In my family we have a magical artefact which can help. It's a cloak called Nightwind, and it was woven by our most powerful sorcerers of darkness and air. It can make you move ten times faster, and when you step into the shadows, you become invisible. You'll be able to move right through the Aslanian camp unnoticed. Right now I think it's with my daughter Traneya. She used it last. Go and borrow it from her."

Ilinar nodded stiffly. He could hardly believe this was happening. Nothing would ever be the same for him after this day. Whether he were to succeed or fail, his life was changed forever, and it wasn't for the better.

Meanwhile, Arkenel and his friends, accompanied by the cultists, had started going back to Kranium. They had stopped for a break, and Mavarius was trying to change his wounded friend's bandages, but the blood had dried up and the wound had stuck to the cloth. Arkenel was voicing loudly his pain and discomfort, and that irritated his healer. "For God's sake, tosser, won't you stop moaning like some whore? Do this yourself if you're gonna be such a wuss about it."

"Oh, so now you don't want me moaning?" Arkenel grunted. "Can you explain why you do this at all? It hurts and it makes me bleed. Just leave it alone."

"What, you want this crust to merge with you?" Mavarius mumbled. "Don't teach me how to tend to tossers. I was doing it while you still wore diapers."

Both of them fell silent because they felt an evil, dreadful presence nearby. Accompanied by an aura of darkness, Dunevir walked past them. He stopped and stared at them with his missing face and with his hands on his waist. Mavarius gritted his teeth and continued to bind Arkenel as if this required all the concentration of the world.

"Weak creature. I hardly touched it, and it bleeds like a virgin," said the heavy man.

"In Mortelion's name, I don't wanna imagine what you do to your virgins," Arkenel muttered under his breath.

"Excuse me?!" Dunevir raised his voice, and the mountain trembled.

Mavarius poked two fingers in his patient's gut as a kind reminder that it wasn't a good idea to talk. Arkenel whimpered as his friend turned to Dunevir and said, "He was hurt before this. He fought for the glory of Mortelion."

"It pleases me to see that all sorts of people are serving him loyally," Dunevir announced, then went away.

Arkenel glared at Mavarius with an evil eye and was just about to tell him he was the worst nurse ever, but he got distracted by Halena, who was walking after Dunevir. In her hands she carried branches from some prickly plants. Remedor took interest in that activity and said, "Hey, Hali! Careful with those; they can prick you."

The moment he said that, he noticed that the young woman's fingers were already bleeding. Halena paused for a moment and replied, "I'm making wreaths of thorns for Mortelion's glory. Do you want one?"

Arkenel realised that the crown of Krumerus's kings was a metal thorn wreath with precious stones. He had never asked the question, but now it seemed to be the right time. He asked, "Why do we wear thorn wreaths?"

"You're not very religious, are you?" Halena smiled lightly and sat down beside him. She began to knit a wreath with her bleeding fingers and explained to him, "It not hard to love what is easy and pleasant, and then to cheat on it at the moment you lose the fascination. True love, however, is that which survives despite all the pain and suffering. Mortelion wants to know that we love him in this way, and that's why we carry thorn wreaths, to prove it to him. The most beautiful love is the love that hurts."

Saying that, she put one of the wreaths on Arkenel's head, then walked away. He began to turn around so he could stare at her as she was leaving. Mavarius removed the wreath from his friend's head and threw it away in disgust. He commented, "That was the dumbest thing I've ever heard."

As he noticed that Arkenel was still staring at Halena, he groaned and slapped a wet, bloody rag across his face.

"You are so very kind this morning," Arkenel replied, removing the rag.

"Listen here, tosser. You know I don't care that you look at bitches. Just not her," Mavarius hissed. "Just look at her. She's nuts! You'll see she's always doing something weird, and if that's not enough for you, I think there's something between her and the big guy. Imagine they're together and you try to ..."

"Yes, fine, I get it." Arkenel shifted with a displeased look. "I'm just looking at her, OK? And I wouldn't say she's nuts. She's fascinating."

Mavarius wasn't fascinated. He sat there pouting. He mumbled, "Why am I stitching you up, you halfwit! You clearly wanna die."

"I wouldn't cause you anything so heartbreaking." Arkenel grinned.

Mavarius wasn't very sure. They were in danger too often for his liking. He cast a glance at Dunevir, who was sitting nearby and might be listening to them.

"By the way, I never asked you something. What were you doing in the Aldur area?" Arkenel turned his attention to his friend.

"Where else could I go?" Mavarius shrugged.

"How come? What about Vern? Your family is there. They'd probably be happy to learn that you're alive!" Arkenel exclaimed.

"Or not." Mavarius looked away and stared into the distance.

"Come on, Mav. You know there's nothing to be ashamed of. The whole thing with the prison was quite dumb, but it's over. We can do what we want again. I can come with you if you like."

"Shut up. I'm not talking about it now," growled Mavarius.

Arkenel sighed quietly. It was difficult to talk to his friend about any personal matters. Mavarius was sometimes an impenetrable fortress, and it was possible for someone to know him for decades without actually knowing anything about him. It seemed like he didn't want to talk about his family either.

Less than a week ago, Eslir had left Kranium with many

confused thoughts. Ilinar standing up in his way like that was unexpected. He had thought it was clear as day that Krumerus had to be destroyed, and if Ilinar had seemed indecisive, it was more because of fear and uncertainty. It became evident, however, that the Soleyan wanted to explore the other part of his family and perhaps wouldn't want to fight his father, even if it was Rabolii Remedor himself, the monstrous necromancer of legend! Eslir didn't know what to do now. If he started a new campaign against Krumerus, would he have to battle Ilinar? These thoughts bothered him on the way back. He was travelling with his troops slowly towards Lumis. He didn't know what he would do once he got there. He would probably start collecting his luggage and then return to Aslania.

"Your Majesty, you have a visitor. He says he must speak with you urgently." One soldier put his head in Eslir's tent. A camp was set up for the night, and most of the soldiers were about to go to sleep.

Thoughtful, the prince merely waved his hand, inviting the newcomer to enter. He turned to look at him and was mildly surprised to see Eley. He scanned him with his eyes, wondering if it was really him, and mumbled, "Oh, I remember you. Why are you not with Ilinar? And what are you doing here?"

"I came as quickly as possible to bring you shocking news," answered Eley with a mournful expression. "Krumerus has stabbed us in the back."

This caught the attention of the Aslanian. He made himself more comfortable on the couch and nodded at Eley to sit at the table next to him. Eslir urged him, "Tell me what happened."

"From the very beginning, when Ilinar and Remedor met, I felt restless. The necromancer was trying to get the young king to do his dirty work," Eley answered with a frown.

"That does not surprise me. Erebi, always trying to be manipulative. Tell me the kid had a little more brains than this and he didn't agree," answered Eslir.

"At first, Ilinar was trying to negotiate for peace. He said he could persuade Aslania to discontinue the attacks on Krumerus, but Rabolii knew it wouldn't happen. He asked Ilinar to declare war and put you on your knees in front of Remedor. According to the necromancer, this is the beginning of the great alliance between light and darkness, between Soleya and Krumerus, and all those who disagree with their ideology will be smitten and destroyed."

A crease formed between Eslir's eyebrows. He sat quietly. A

feeling of weariness was forming in him because of the direction in which this story was going. Eley, looking worried and serious, continued, "Ilinar didn't agree. He said that such peace was not worth it if innocent Aslanian citizens had to pay for it and that he wouldn't fight you. Rabolii fell into a rage when he heard this. Ah, how I wish I'd been there when it was all happening. I felt something was wrong when Ilinar disappeared for a few days. I went looking for him. I slipped into the necromancer's tower just to find Ilinar's body on a table. I checked it for pulse. He was ice-cold and breathless ... dead. I couldn't believe that Rabolii had killed him. I couldn't see why. I didn't have much time for reflection. I heard footsteps and hid behind one of the cabinets. The necromancer had returned. He stood over the table and began to mutter some words in a language I didn't know. It was a curse of Mortelion. It made Ilinar's dead body move. I saw him standing on his feet ... There was no life in his eyes. It was scary just to look at him. Remedor watched his creation with satisfaction and said, 'We are now equal, Ilinar. Now you understand me, and you know why we have to destroy Aslania.' Ilinar just replied in a hoarse voice, 'Yes, Father. For the glory of Mortelion!'"

Eslir's shock was noticeable despite the icy indifference he always wore on his face. He shifted nervously on the sofa and said, "I can't believe this has happened ... but at the same time I am not surprised that the necromancer is capable of such a low blow. Soleya would have never known their king had been slain and reanimated as Rabolii's puppet. They could have destroyed us with this plan."

"Not that it matters now, but when I arrive in Soleya, I'll tell them the tragic truth: that Ilinar is dead and what walks under the sun is now nothing more than a body without its own mind, a shadow of what he once was. We won't let him into our territory. Our friendship with Aslania is too valuable. We will not allow the necromancer to destroy it," said Eley with a bereft look.

"Damn erebi, it's because of things like this that I want to exterminate them! They are not reasonable people. Every word they say is a lie, and the death of their own sons is a means to an end," Eslir stated angrily. "What will happen to Soleya now? The direct royal bloodline is lost."

"I know. We are in a very difficult situation." Eley sighed. "I hope the power vacuum won't cause fights and chaos between distant relatives. I'll try my best to prevent such happenings by reading out Ilinar's will as soon as I get to Soleya."

"The kid had a will?" Eslir raised his gaze. "How did he know he'd be dying so he'd write one?"

"This is a precautionary measure in Soleya; it is always a good idea for the last representative of the royal family to have a will in case something happens to them. There they indicate the next monarch to take their place. It was terrible that we had to get a seventeen-year-old boy to write a will, just to have it reviewed in a few weeks. But that's just another wound that Krumerus has left for us and another reason to hate them."

"Krumerus will regret this. Let's go back to Kranium! I still have my army. I will level that accursed city to the ground!" Eslir proposed immediately.

Eley realised he had other plans and wanted to get back to Soleya as soon as possible and have the entire Aslanian army and its monarch agree with his story. His preference was to stop this attack for now. He answered, "You left Kranium four days ago, Your Majesty. During that time Rabolii and his family have gone into hiding. And he's calling reinforcements to guard the capital while he's away. Attacking them now will accomplish nothing."

Eslir grunted with a displeased look. "The damn necromancer saw all this coming. It doesn't matter. I'll regroup in Aslania, and I'll investigate his new location."

Eley just nodded with understanding. Behind his mask of sadness he was feeling great satisfaction that Eslir had believed him. If he did, the rest of Soleya would as well. It was a bit unpleasant for him that he'd had to frame Ilinar like that, but all his dreams about a bright future overshadowed any feelings of guilt. Eley did believe he was doing the right thing, both for himself and for his country. For people like Eslir and him, the right decision was obvious—nothing good would ever come out of Krumerus. They knew that the mad god of the erebi only lusted for blood and destruction. Even if by some miracle a peaceful ruler were to sit on that throne, he wouldn't stay there for long. Mortelion would replace him with another champion who would bring him glory. Ilinar didn't seem to understand that Rabolii couldn't choose peace even if he wanted to and that he was just doing all this to win a temporary ally, only to betray him later. For Eley peace with Krumerus was a naive, childish dream that would tragically collapse at the worst moment. He couldn't allow Ilinar's blind idealism to cause the destruction of both Soleya and Aslania.

—*m*—

Arkenel had begun to regain strength. His stitches were holding, so he could once again pay attention to what was happening around him. The cultists were strange. Most were shrivelled and ugly, just like those people who'd steal children from the marketplace to sell their bones. Only Halena looked attractive, at least in appearance. She wasn't talking to anyone but Dunevir; she was always by his side. Sometimes the cultists would get together to arrange a circle of skulls and pray to Mortelion. Arkenel didn't know what the deal of these people was, but he'd try to figure them out later. He felt discontentment amongst his ranks. His people seemed disgruntled. Whenever he'd look at them while they were whispering to each other, they'd shut up as soon as they noticed he was looking. They'd been on the move for too long. They didn't get much money, they didn't have enough food, and their miner's was gone. One night, Arkenel was once again listening to the angry whispers of his friends. They had already begun to sit farther away from him during the breaks. Mavarius was the only one sitting beside him and listening. At some point he noted: "Man, you feeling the discontent?"

"Mm-hmm," Arkenel grunted. "They must be wondering why we're here right now. And what can I tell them? You see how Rabolii messes me around. I know as much about this mission as they do."

"Just act like you do. Or else each of these mongs will just sod off to somewhere. We didn't break out of Aldur to be roaming Krumerus like some nomads." Mavarius snorted.

Arkenel let out a heavy sigh. He'd rather not be dealing with this right now, but he needed to speak to his people if they had a problem. He walked past the nearest group of men. One of them was complaining about a wound on his foot which he had gotten from too much walking. Remedor sat casually beside him and suggested, "If it bleeds a lot, call Mavarius to bind you. I wouldn't want to keep him as a private nurse just for myself!"

The wounded man leered at him and said, "It would heal by itself, but I'm walking all day, aren't I?!"

"Well, yes. I feel the same way. Just look at this." He lifted up his shirt. The upper part of his stomach was wrapped in bandages soaked with blood and stained with other dirt.

"Poor you, you must be suffering so much on the back of that skeleton you ride," the man growled.

"Yeah, why can't we ride?" the other men started shouting.

"Because I bought it, tossers!" Arkenel spread his arms. "Next time we get to Kranium, just buy one."

"With what money? You're the one who's supposed to be paying us. We work for you!" said one of the ex-prisoners, pointing a finger with indictment.

"I'll give you more money when we get to Kranium!" Arkenel raised his voice because they had become very noisy. "But don't expect a full-time wage. Rabolii will only agree to a symbolic payment until you've gone through the barracks to train as proper soldiers."

"We hate your stupid Rabolii. He was the one who stuck us in that godforsaken prison," one of the men continued to protest.

Arkenel couldn't comprehend how anyone could argue about this at all. He stood up so more people could hear him, and stated, "Hey, as much as it may shock you, you'll have to work for your wages. It is a miracle that we're free and that we get to visit large cities without the militia chasing us to put us back in Aldur. You have only me to thank for that. I didn't release you so you'd get wages for nothing but because I thought you would be able to become a part of society again and take care of yourself without burdening anyone. It will be difficult at first, but if we continue to prove our worth and be useful, our lives will become much more enjoyable."

One of the prisoners walked over to Arkenel and pushed him back roughly, shouting, "You are the one who does nothing around here, and you act like you're better than us. Is there another prince whose friends are just roaming around in the field and dying in battles?"

"How about you watch yourself?" Mavarius came between them and shoved the aggressive man.

This obviously angered prisoners, who were annoyed already, so they started a fight, not with Arkenel but with whomever was closest. Mavarius slipped out of the fray and stood closer to his friend. The young Remedor seemed concerned and asked, "Am ... am I doing bad as a leader? Man, I don't know how to help them or what to do."

"What do you care? They're all idiots. Let 'em fight and waste energy. It will do them good," Mavarius replied casually.

"Can you check out this area and look for some miner's maybe?" Arkenel suggested.

"Sure," Mavarius responded. He walked out amongst the spiky trees. As a rule, it wasn't quite safe for a man to wander alone in the Krumerian wilderness, but this one could fend for himself.

Dunevir watched the fight and enjoyed it immensely. Blood made him happy. He glanced at Arkenel, wondering whether Mortelion had some sort of a plan for this weak creature who had appeared at such an interesting moment.

Somewhere far to the west in Kranium, Traneya was on her way back to her room. She slipped out of her sweat-drenched sweater. The training in the barracks always exhausted her, but that wasn't much of a bother these days because she had taught Estrella how to massage her very nicely. She found Ilinar in front of her door. He was standing there obediently. At first Traneya completely ignored him because she thought he was one of the skeleton servants who also stood there. She started unlocking her door. Ilinar decided to attract her attention and started talking: "Um ... um ... apologies, Princess Traneya."

She finally noticed him and shot him a frowning glance. She hated it when people referred to her that way. She said, "Go away, Princess Soleya."

Ilinar was sometimes shocked by the lack of manners in Krumerus. He tried to keep talking. "I ... your father sent me to you so you'd give me a cloak."

Traneya opened her door and looked around the room with a serious expression. She called, "Estrella?"

Ilinar looked around and asked, "Is Estrella here?"

"Apparently not," Traneya mumbled, turning to one of the skeletons. "Hey, you! Do you know where Estrella is?" The numb skeleton nodded his head. Traneya urged him, "Take me there at once!"

Ilinar started walking after her and talking: "I'm sorry, but I really need to do something very important, and I need Nightwind, so if I can first ..."

"Shut up!" Traneya snapped at him with annoyance. She could tell the skeleton was leading her to Rabolii's room, and that worried her.

The three of them stopped in front of the necromancer's sinister cloister. Despite the heavy doors, they could hear noise and tumult. Traneya decided not to knock. She went straight in to witness a ridiculous scene. Rabolii was standing on his desk, waving a long broom. He was trying to get his last surviving vampire off the ceiling all whilst yelling, "Get down from there at once, you wretched beast, and return to me the memorials for the magic from the sixth era! *No!* Don't chew on them, you feral corpse!"

As the door slammed, Rabolii froze with the broom in his hands and stared at the intruder with his pale eerie eyes. He started barking at Traneya: "*You!* How many times must I tell you to knock before you barge into my room?"

"Am I interrupting your flying lessons?" Traneya couldn't help herself, knowing this could well cost her her life.

Ilinar covered his mouth with his hands, not knowing whether it was funny or that she behaved disrespectfully towards his father. Rabolii didn't consider that statement humorous, so he tossed the broom at Traneya and yelled so loud that he broke a window with his voice: "Unbelievable! Not only do you dare charge into my room, but also you speak to me in such a disrespectful tone. I'll give you fifteen seconds to explain why you came in, and if I don't find your reason good enough, I shall feed you to the vampire!"

Traneya walked around the room, finally noticing Estrella, who was passed out on a couch. A few drains were stuck into her arm, pouring in suspicious liquids. Remedor's daughter rolled her sleeve up and displayed some bloody bandages.

"I need the sorceress."

"We all need her. I'm doing some experiments on her. Don't touch her," Rabolii ordered.

"Lord Remedor, please! Estrella is my friend!" Ilinar also began whining.

"You heard that, Lord Remedor," Traneya repeated ironically. "Do you want to ruin your peace with Soleya because of your experiment?"

"Ilinar, this is not your concern," Rabolii snapped at him. But when he saw those demanding, stubborn faces in front of him, he surrendered and said, "*All right!* Take her then. It's probably not important to you that her concentrated blood could lead to an improvement in my metabolism and might prevent clots in my veins."

"Mm, yeah, trifles. Bye, Dad," Traneya said unceremoniously. She picked up Estrella and carried her out.

Rabolii was shocked at how badly he was being treated. Ilinar bit his lip and followed Traneya out. He hoped she would now be grateful enough to give him the cloak without other delays. But Remedor's daughter continued to ignore him; she began talking to Estrella. "Hellooo! Are you alive? Do you know what the corpse injected you with?"

Estrella was slowly coming around. She opened her eyes dizzily and cried, "They ... they just dragged me to him. I couldn't fight all of them."

"I'll change the door lock. Are you OK?"

Estrella began to complain about how Rabolii's guards had pulled her hair while they were leading her to him and how she had lost one shoe. Traneya watched her with a thin smile that was both sympathetic and a bit ironic. Ilinar began to poke her again. "Excuse me, can I get the cloak Nightwind? I really need it."

"Yes. Stop pestering me. God!" Traneya told him with annoyance.

"Oh, hello, Your Majesty." Estrella turned to him.

Ilinar nodded stiffly. If he didn't kill Eley soon, he wouldn't be a majesty at all.

After getting his cloak, Ilinar left immediately to chase the armies. It wasn't difficult to trace their tracks, and thanks to his speed, he managed to avoid Krumerus's aggressive creatures. He often stumbled because he barely controlled his movements, which were faster than his own thoughts. He began to slow down when he reached a camp near Soleya's border. He groaned desperately. It seemed that Eley had already caught up with the army and was probably accommodated somewhere amongst them just as he had feared. It was all too difficult, too horrible. Ilinar felt like just turning around and walking away from it all. But was he given such a choice? If he didn't act now, he'd never be able to return to his home. He took a breath, as if he were going to dive into a deep ocean, and sneaked between the tents. He had never thought he would be cursing the light, which now gave him away. He moved quietly in the shadows, sometimes needing to wait for hours for the opportunity to move further, all whilst checking each tent. None of the Aslanians noticed him. At some point Ilinar thought this was like a great game of hide-and-seek. He used to be good at that. He had the patience to stalk, to stay in place for as long as needed, despite how uncomfortable it was. He was good at avoiding detection. He was doing it now.

Yet another tent appeared in front of Ilinar. It didn't differ from the others in any way. He waited for a few chatting Aslanians to walk away so he could peek inside. His stomach fell when he found his victim, Eley. And there were another five sleeping men in the same tent! This task was becoming harder by the minute! Ilinar slipped inside to avoid being seen by a patrolling watchman. Once he was embraced by the darkness, it made him feel a bit safer. He walked slowly towards Eley's bed, his stomach turning into a ball of nerves as he asked himself, *Can I do this?* He gritted his teeth, took a dagger from his belt, and pressed Eley's mouth with his other hand as he slit his throat. Indeed, he did it without a single thought, without pondering over it, so he was almost surprised by the outcome. The man started shifting in panic, trying to defend himself somehow, while a fountain of blood erupted from his neck. Ilinar kept pressing his mouth so he couldn't make a sound. The sight was so ugly—the forced end of a life. What lay on the bed was no longer human. He was a dying victim, shaken by primal, animalistic dread, blind eyes staring into the darkness as his blood flowed out. The fatality of the situation was chilling. Right now no goodwill in this world could change things or undo this throbbing, ugly gash. Ilinar's hands were shaking. He watched Eley's last spasms and felt such an anger towards him. He had left him no choice.

Without warning, a flock of memories overwhelmed Ilinar, memories of much happier times, memories of good people he had left in the past—Flinaya, who was happy that her son was such a good and clever child, and his grandmother, who would tell him that his virtues and kind heart would make him an excellent king. There were so many people in his life who saw him as a kind, gentle soul, and right now he was betraying all of them. Now he was standing over the corpse of one of his closest friends. The irreparable had happened, and human life seemed like the most valuable thing in the world. It was priceless, but it still cost less than a crown.

Ilinar knew he had to get out of there, but he felt petrified. He continued to stare silently at the corpse as if he punishing himself. He put his bloody hand on the man's chest with one silent *I'm sorry.* He felt the rustle of paper under his shirt. What piece of parchment would be so important that one would go to bed with it? Without much enthusiasm, he pulled it out. His gaze slid along the lines, and his face remained cold and emotionless as he read his own will, according to which he was electing Eley as the next king. The text was written in Eley's handwriting, and the signature was a perfect copy of Ilinar's. So was that the plan? He'd declare the king for dead and sit on the throne? How would that work? Ilinar had but to return to Soleya and prove he was alive. Eley was smarter than that. What else had he planned?

A beam of treacherous light fell on Ilinar's back, illuminating the bloody mess he had created. Startled, he dropped the piece of paper and turned towards the entrance of the tent. There stood Eslir himself, gazing wide-eyed with shock. He gritted his teeth and snarled, "You ..."

He drew his sword and charged at Ilinar. The Soleyan hardly realised he had to dodge. He rolled away from the blade and stood between Eslir and the exit. He could flee at will, but first he hoped to get an answer to his questions. "So it's true!" Eslir hissed. "You've lost your mind indeed if you're roaming around my camp killing people."

"Just him. Because he was spreading slander about me," Ilinar said, trying to stop his voice from trembling.

"Is it slander that you've been resurrected by Rabolii and you serve him now?!" Eslir yelled. "What you did here just now proves it. Now come here so you can die for a second time!"

The other men in the tent had begun to awaken and looked around in astonishment. They'd figure out what was happening very soon, and they'd attack as well. Ilinar realised that the time for talk was over, so he turned and ran out of the tent. Behind him sounded horrifying shouts. The camp was alerted, and soon hundreds of men were chasing him. Without pausing, he continued to run until he finally sank into the darkness and became invisible. Once again, he was as fast as the wind. And even though the camp was far behind, he was still running. He realised he was leaving behind his whole life. Everything he had, everything he knew, had been taken away from him. Soleya no longer existed to him. Things had gone from bad to worse for him for a while, and now they had hit rock bottom. And the worst of all was that somewhere on the way he had lost himself. He was soaked with blood. He had become a murderer to protect a utopia which he'd lost anyway. Everything was in vain.

Ilinar slowed down only at the time he arrived at the gates of Kranium. He leaned against the stone wall to catch his breath, wrapped himself in his cloak, and burst into tears. He didn't know what he was going to do next. He had lost his way. The night was icy cold, and the shadows soon came to life. Ilinar's nightmares attacked him. They were full of reproach; they had the taste of blood and betrayal. It would be a really long night.

Rabolii's life was tedious, tiring, and full of stress caused by incompetent people. First of all, his project to improve his decoction of red coal was completely ruined because of Ravena's presence, who kept entering his room and pestering him with things. And as if that wasn't enough, Arkenel had the gall to return with his band of drug addicts. When Rabolii heard they were in town, he choked on his own tongue. What were they doing here?! They had probably gotten high and forgotten all about any missions they were sent to do. The necromancer knew he'd soon find out, so he didn't go out to greet them. Given the fact that his chambers were a magnet for nuisance, they'd come to him. In fact, as he thought all this, Arkenel and Mavarius were exchanging silent punches a little farther down the corridor.

"So, what, you're too ashamed to go to the great Rabolii Remedor if I'm there?" Mavarius was pouting.

"Tosser, don't go there," Arkenel pleaded. "I'm not ashamed, but this time you've made such a mess, and I don't want my father cleaving your head once he finds out."

"And what have I done to your holy father this time?" snapped Mavarius as he crossed his arms.

"What do you mean, 'what'? You stole the map with the flying fart! Obviously it was important, and you gave it to the big guy. We never got to talk about this alone. What were you thinking going through Dad's stuff and taking something? When did you do that, and why?"

"'Cause he sucks, that's why," Mavarius blurted out. "When Aslania besieged us and I left you, I came up here to get it. I wondered what he had buried there and why he roared like a wounded cow when I saw this for the first time."

"And what did you expect, gold and platinum? It's just his nerdy, stupid magic stuff," Arkenel replied excitedly.

"I noticed," mumbled Mavarius. "When I got there, Dunevir was digging around. Turns out he needed that map."

"Merciful Mortelion, what have you gotten us into?" Arkenel put his hand on his forehead.

"Ya, Mortelion did this. He decides your fates and all." Mavarius shrugged carelessly.

"Tosser, just go away." Arkenel pointed at the exit. "You'll say something stupid in front of my dad, and I won't be able to collect the pieces of you from the floor."

"Screw you, Arkenel. You don't tell me where to go," Mavarius replied with determination. He strode off towards Rabolii's chambers.

Fantastic, Arkenel would now have to run after him despite all his wounds. With the utmost effort, he managed to catch up with him and grab a hold of his shoulders just as they were in front of the massive doors of the necromancer.

"Stop making one mess after another. Take a break, will you?" Arkenel snapped at him.

"So, what, should I let you go in there alone? You're hardly standing. Who knows how the corpse will snap once you tell him someone took his fart," Mavarius yelled.

"Goddammit, I hate you!"

"I hate you too, you mooncalf!"

The two of them stared at each other like angry bulls, breathing heavily. Arkenel could appreciate that this was the greatest form of concern. He knew that Mavarius was trying to protect him and that he wouldn't back down even if it meant he had to knock Arkenel out to make sure he'd be safe. However, it was a bad time for such concern. With all their arguing and yelling, they had disturbed the necromancer, so the heavy doors behind them opened, revealing the most dangerous place of all. Now they had to go in. Rabolii was sitting behind his perfectly organised desk, exuding strength, authority, and beauty with his rejuvenated face, not a day older than sixty-two. Mavarius and Arkenel stood before his desk as the doors behind them slammed by themselves, raising dust and making a piece of the glass Rabolii had shattered with his voice fall to the floor. The necromancer looked at them coldly, realising that he was faced with the son who would kill him according to the prophecy. Rabolii had never harboured the warmest feelings towards Arkenel, but right then he simply hated him. He didn't know how he'd endure this meeting at all.

"Well? What are you waiting for?" The necromancer spread his arms, his long sleeves hanging down. His garment today was made of pure dark blue silk with spines embroidered over it. "Sit down and tell me how you failed this time and whether a possible execution would correct the damage you have done!"

"When has an execution undone anything?" Mavarius replied with a grim look.

Rabolii snapped at him,

"Don't annoy me with idiocies or I'll undo you! Now would you be so kind as to tell me why you're back in my city again? Do you remember I sent you somewhere? Or maybe, Arkenel, you were too intoxicated when I gave my orders and you suddenly sobered up somewhere in the field and decided to come back?"

Mavarius gritted his teeth again. This sarcasm was too much for him. There were a thousand things he could reply, most of which were limited to his regular set of swear words, but Arkenel spoke first: "We're not idiots, Dad. I know what your orders were. We arrived at the place you pointed out, but it was too late. Someone had already killed your general and the vampires."

"*Wonderful!*" Rabolii screamed, slamming his fist on his desk, which probably would leave a bruise for a few weeks, but now he wanted to demonstrate how angry and fearsome he was, so he ignored his hand, got up to his feet, and started striding back and forth. "Why did I think I could count on you for anything? I realised you didn't deserve such a task when I saw you hanging around the city for three days after I had given the order! But why would you cause yourself the inconvenience of rushing just because I said so? Let's ignore that corpse in the tower! If he won't give us money for nonsense, why should we do anything he says?!"

"You're bloody insane, you are!" Mavarius jumped up, pointing at the necromancer threateningly. Oh, no, the apocalypse had started. Arkenel tried to intervene, but his friend shoved him to the side. "Those tossers found your stupid charge a week before Arkenel arrived."

"*You!* How did you know about ..." Rabolii's eyes widened horribly.

"We asked them!" snapped Mavarius. "But you always wanna blame Arkenel. If you wanna take it out on someone, go argue with the one who took your magic crap. We've brought him here."

"The thief of my cosmic charge has simply come along with you?" Rabolii was hissing like a rattlesnake. "How did he discover it alone? He had the map, didn't he? Who took it to him? And then you'll tell me how loyal you are to me! How useful you want to be to Krumerus! You are constantly doing things like this behind my back."

"Dad, you're not even letting us explain," Arkenel pleaded like a sad beggar kid.

"I don't want to hear more excuses and lies!" Rabolii shook his head like a furious horse, then turned around and started digging in a cupboard, thundering and scattering things in a horiffic way. "I'll prepare for my meeting with the thief. Tell him to meet me in my throne room." He glanced at his son hatefully and snarled, "As for you two, just return to that abandoned kitchen where you get drunk and snort poison. You're incapable of doing anything different anyway."

Mavarius widened his nostrils like a bull, clenched his fists, and got up to kill Rabolii, but Arkenel grabbed him above the elbow and pulled him back to save the peace on the continent. Withholding his irritation, he replied, "OK, we'll tell him to meet you. Come on, Mavarius, let's go."

Rabolii leered at them hatefully as they left. This was too much for him. In his opinion Mavarius was overflowing with aggression, and in contrast, Arkenel was too patient and polite, though he must be thirsty for vengeance. With this line of thought, Rabolii realised that the prophecy was already happening. Obviously, his stupid son felt wronged and unappreciated. His dumb buddies must consider him to be such a big deal because he figured out how to get out of some prison. They probably planned treason. Things would soon be out of control. Rabolii decided he had had enough of this. He had given Arkenel a chance, and in his opinion his son had proven malicious. The necromancer decided it was time to get rid of these people. He was powerful enough to kill Arkenel in a million ways, but he'd need to be discreet or else he'd have problems with Ravena. He had to think of a way to cause his son's death without seeming to be involved.

Mavarius and Arkenel left Rabolii's chambers overexcited and in the mood to fight. The former was furious and was raging, "He'll execute us, he says! We can only get drunk and snort poison, he says. What a load of crap!"

"Come on, that's just the way he speaks. Don't take it too seriously," Arkenel was trying to calm him.

"I'm sick of self-important freaks like him treating me like a dog," Mavarius yelled. He pulled away from Arkenel, making aggressive movements.

"Tosser, how do you think I'm feeling?" Arkenel raised his voice. "I used to be a prince, you know, and now I'm in the same boat as you. But we're not going to change this by arguing with Rabolii and acting like madmen. I'm trying to fight for our good names. I try to look more representative, and I try to teach you guys to do the same. And all I get are whispers about how I've 'changed'. You think this is easy for me? I thought at least you'd help me here, but you won't even shower. How do you expect someone to take you seriously when you're wearing the same trousers in which you've been pissing the last twenty years?"

Mavarius was defeated by that statement; he could only stare with a wide-open mouth. His first impulse was to fight with Arkenel, but the truth of what he was told somehow made that reaction seem pathetic. Instead, he crossed his arms and mumbled, "Oh, the great leader with his brilliant ideas. I don't remember you giving us clean clothes and free soap."

Arkenel smiled softly, recognising a victory. He put a hand on his friend's shoulder, both as reconciliation and because he was struggling to remain standing, and said, "Come on now. We can do this now. And since I can see Rabolii's bugging you, let's kill two bats with one stone. You can shower in his private bathroom." Now that was an idea which Mavarius approved of. A rare smile appeared on his face; it was ominous and gloating. Both he and Arkenel laughed.

Ilinar returned to the castle after a sad, cold night. He dragged his feet down the corridors with a depressed expression and told every person he met that he needed to talk to Rabolii. Most of them advised him not to bother the mighty lord unless it was very important. Some of them directed him to the throne room, where there was an event taking place at the moment. Ilinar went towards that destination. He couldn't imagine how Rabolii would react when he learned his son has lost his crown tonight. When he entered, the throne room was a bit overcrowded. All the princes and princesses were there, as were Ravena, Rabolii, Arkenel's drunkards, and many other strangers. Ilinar stepped forward with a tragic expression, but Ravena caught him by his elbow and whispered to him, "Not now. Wait a minute!"

Then she shot Arkenel a warning glance as if telling him that if he was too high, he should go out instead of grinning loudly with Mavarius. Why were they in such a good mood on a day like this anyway? At least they looked clean. That was something new.

Rabolii was preparing to execute people. He sat on his throne with a fearsome expression, watching everyone below him as if they were petty bugs and he had the divine mercy not to kill them on sight. He spoke with an authoritative, loud, and clear voice, looking at the new faces in front of him, "So! I believe you know why I called you! One of you has obtained something of great value to me. One of you has not only acquired a magical energy that does not belong to you rightly but also had the boldness to kill my guards. Who had the gall to do so?"

The faces of the cultists were wrinkled, dull, and dry, most of them veiled and hooded. It was hard to distinguish individuals in this crowd.

"I think I'm the one you seek." Dunevir stepped forward, making his way through the crowd of people.

Rabolii got a slightly puzzled expression. It wasn't every day he saw a faceless man nearly two metres tall with strangely bright eyes. Generally, spectral blue was the colour of the pure energy of death, and now it was flowing out of the eyes of this man. With his appearance alone, Dunevir gave rise to so many questions that Rabolii didn't know where to start. Still, he put on a face of pride and superiority and asked, "You! What's your name?"

"The locals call me Dunevir," the man replied.

Rabolii tried to recall distinguished individuals with that name, but he couldn't remember any. He crossed his arms and replied, "So, Dunevir, what authorised you to go to steal resources and kill my guards?!"

"The magnificent and mighty master of our souls, Lord Mortelion, did," Dunevir said emphatically. Rarely did he seem excited, but if it happened, it was because of the god. "The cosmic charge was his gift to aid Krumerus in days of hardship. I could sense it would dematerialise, so I began my quest to seek it out."

"And what about my permission?" yelled Rabolii. He could normally tell if he didn't like someone within the first thirty seconds of the acquaintance. He definitely had a strong chemistry with Dunevir in all the bad ways. "Is my opinion of no significance? I thought the charge was dangerous! There isn't an experienced studious sorcerer in this country who would utilise the charge. I didn't take it, because it would make me a thorn in the sides of everyone. And for those reasons I wanted it to disperse. Why did you take it?"

"Because this is the will of our perfect master," Dunevir replied unceremoniously. He spread his arms as if it were obvious.

"And what makes you such an expert in what Mortelion wants?" snapped Rabolii.

"Because I hear him. He is in the last breath of my victims, the whisper in the darkness, the fury of the war. I understand his desires. I see the paths he draws for us, the plans he has in store. Mortelion is my life and my death, and his soul is in every action and decision I make. He intended for the charge to be found."

Rabolii shifted on his throne, lacing his fingers in front of his face. How interesting. Had he found an oracle? Generally, the Crown highly valued such people, and it was difficult to find powerful and sincere representatives of their kind. The oracles deciphered the signs of the gods. As a rule they were sorcerers, and they were very helpful to their rulers, because if people acted according to the will of the mightier beings, they were rewarded for it. But it was difficult to determine who was really an oracle and who was a shrewd bargainer who made things up for money's sake. Rabolii noted, "Hmm, perhaps this isn't as bad as I initially thought. You look strong and capable. Perhaps you will be able to utilise the charge without the danger of losing it to the enemy. And if you are the bearer and not me, I will not be the target."

"Everything I'll do with this charge shall be in Mortelion's name," Dunevir replied in the same tone.

Arkenel nudged Mavarius and whispered to him, trying not to burst out laughing, "Hey, tosser! Let's make it a drinking game. Every time the big guy says anything about Mortelion, we have a shot."

"Tosser, we'll be rolling under the table in an hour," replied Mavarius.

"You will soon be given the chance to prove your loyalty," said Rabolii, casting a deathly glance at the grinning Arkenel and Mavarius. Then he announced, "Hmm, and talking about feats, I believe it's high time I gave you some work as well! You've done nothing for a fantastic amount of time, and I'm convinced you're bored."

"Dad, are you for reals?" Arkenel shouted, disappointed. "We just got home today! My people are exhausted. Give us at least a week before you send us off to somewhere!"

"He wants to screw us over and kill us," Mavarius mumbled quietly. Arkenel struck an elbow in his ribs to keep him quiet.

"Yes, why not?" Rabolii waved his hand. "Just make sure you're not particularly noisy and destructive."

Bearing with them for another week would be a nightmare. Regardless, he did need to figure out where to send them to die. However, the decision appeared much faster than he'd expected. Valenis stepped forward, choking on excitement, and said, "Master Remedor, if you please ... I would be very happy if my home town was avenged. I know where the enemy troops are camping. We could ambush them and kill them when they least expect it."

Rabolii knew about Valenis's plan, so he was sure the

Vernians were the ones setting the ambush. It was perfect. He decided to make it even easier for fate to do its thing, so he replied, "Sounds like a good plan. Also, remind me to return the amulet to you. I had not planned to keep it for so long."

Valenis himself wondered how it could all be so easy. He had expected Rabolii to be suspicious, to ask questions and double-check every possible aspect of Valenis's story, and to finally see the terrible conspiracy. However, right now the necromancer looked as if he just wanted everyone to leave him alone. Maybe everything would go smoothly? Or not.

"Father, can I accompany them? I don't want to leave Valenis's side," Salina said. She stood by the Vernian. Recently they had been inseparable.

"I—" both Rabolii and Valenis yelled so aggressively that they surprised themselves. They exchanged strange glances, and then each of them started talking to her.

"I don't believe you have any business there. Aren't you busy? Have you already read all the formulas of light spells written by the Order of the Star Dynasty?" Rabolii scolded her critically.

"I haven't, but I believe I can be useful there," Salina mumbled.

"Darling, there really is no need." Valenis smiled softly at her. "I don't think it will be very dangerous, and I will come back quickly."

"OK, if you both insist." She looked down in disappointment. She was tired of staying in her tower while amazing things were happening outside, but she was somewhat accustomed to it.

Rabolii made himself comfortable on his throne and said, "All right, I think that's enough for today. If someone else wants my attention, they can visit me tomorrow. Now leave my presence."

Murmuring and snorting, the people began to exit the throne room. Rabolii looked at them critically and was pleased to see them leaving. He felt they were abusing his goodness. Shameless people! He didn't want to bother with them any more, so he was very dissatisfied and angry when one of them stayed and showed no intention of going out. On the contrary, he dragged his feet right towards his throne.

"King Ilinar, that includes you as well," Rabolii said through his teeth. Some people were just begging for trouble.

"I'm only Ilinar now," the boy said without looking up. He took his hands out of his pockets. They were still stained with dried blood. He threw the dagger at his feet, the weapon of yesterday's murder, then lifted his eyes and hit the necromancer with the short version of the story: "I did it. I killed Eley, but Eslir caught me doing it. He thinks I'm a murderous resurrected corpse, who serves you. They tried to hunt me down. I can never return to Soleya again."

Ravena, who was standing at the exit, heard this. She froze in place. She returned to Ilinar, grabbed him by the shoulders, and whispered to him as if he were a child who had behaved inappropriately, "This is a matter for another time. Come with me. Rabolii needs peace now."

The necromancer himself could hardly grasp the news. He froze on his throne with a face as if someone had just hit him with something heavy on the back of his head. He was too surprised and shocked to know how to react. Ravena led Ilinar out. Right now she felt even more uncomfortable around him. Until now, he was a potential ally and a diplomatic figure, and she could treat him accordingly. She knew he'd be gone in a few days. But after that night, everything had changed. Ilinar was reduced to be nothing more than Rabolii's bastard son, sent to exile in Krumerus. He'd probably expect to become a part of her family now.

—◊◊◊—

Excited, Valenis sought an opportunity to have alone time with his platinum amulet when he wasn't with Salina. He was breathing heavily from running up the stairs towards a dusty attic when the translucent silhouette of Krementa appeared in front of him.

"It's all set in motion. Rabolii has given me the opportunity to lead armed forces to a place we can ambush."

"Is that so? Darling, I'm so proud of you!" Krementa exclaimed enthusiastically. "I knew you could do it. I always believed in you!"

Valenis blushed bashfully. He didn't even know if that was true, but he decided not to spoil the moment. He mumbled, "Uh ... yes, I hope everything goes smoothly. The troops will be led by Arkenel Remedor. But this is far from being my most important news."

And then Valenis proceeded to tell his mother about the cosmic energy and the unusual man who found it and about the accidental creation of the vampiric potion. Both were disturbing news items. Krementa just nodded while listening to all of this.

They would definitely have more problems to deal with, but at this point she was content enough to have Arkenel fall into her trap.

Ilinar sat with a lifeless expression in one of the libraries, while Ravena and Salina paced around him and wondered what to do now. They had to figure out a way to help him reclaim his throne, but it was not an easy task.

"Can't we simply have him return? It should become apparent to everyone he is in fact alive." Salina shrugged. "A talking, nonrotting corpse needs too much energy to maintain, so if Ilinar is one indeed, he'll collapse within a week anyway."

"You can't expect them to come to such a conclusion," Ravena mumbled. "They know nothing about what a corpse can or can't do. We deliberately kept such knowledge a secret."

"There must be someone with high authority in Soleya who'd stand up for him," Salina suggested.

"Do you have such friends there?" Ravena asked Ilinar.

Ilinar only shook his head stiffly. Right then he felt like he didn't have a single real friend left in Soleya. He didn't know how people would react upon his return and how he'd be treated if he did.

"It's all very complicated. I think it would be best to wait and see who takes over Soleya's leadership and start negotiations with them," Ravena said.

"I'll never set foot in Lumis again!" Ilinar cried hoarsely. "They'll kill me before I get the chance to say a thing."

He slipped out of his chair and dragged his feet towards his room. He wasn't in the mood to talk about Soleya. He didn't wish to think about who ruled it or about Eley. If he could just hit his head and forget his whole life, it would be perfect. Ravena followed him with her gaze and groaned. There was no point in getting Rabolii's opinion on the matter. She knew what he would say. After all, according to the infamous prophecy, Ilinar is the saviour son, and he needs to receive help by any means necessary and get his throne back so he can defeat evil Arkenel.

"Losing Soleya as an ally—that was the last thing we needed," Ravena muttered.

"Krumerus has always been waging its wars alone," Salina noted. "Maybe not having allies is just the natural way for things to be."

"We could use allies right now." Ravena sighed.

Salina stared out the window. She shrugged, just saying a

short, disinterested "Hmm." Obviously she was thinking about things other than war now. Ravena, noticing this, directed the conversation to the thing which was on both their minds: "Sooo ... about that man Valenis. Are you seriously planning to marry him?"

Salina's face immediately lit up, and she responded enthusiastically, "He proposed to me. I didn't believe he would do it so soon, but it doesn't feel rushed to me. He and I just ... match in a way I didn't think possible. We spoke about organising the wedding once he's back from the mission with Arkenel."

Ravena nodded without visible emotion. It was kind of nice to see that her daughter was excited and had found someone she liked, but at the same time her mother was a little worried. She said, "You've known each other only for a short time. Is it not a bit soon?"

"Was it not too soon when you offered me as Morelii's wife before I met him even once?" Salina's smile disappeared, and she prepared to defend herself. She knew that this would happen—all of her well-wishers would start dissuading her and telling her that she had to wait and be careful.

"Come now, you know that dynastic marriages are a completely different thing. They are conducted for reasons other than mutual liking. Since there are no 'other reasons' here, I want to make sure that he is the right person," answered Ravena. The last thing she had ever wanted was to sound like her own mother when having this conversation with her children, but it was her words she was repeating right now.

"What's the matter with you and Father? What do you have against Valens? He is the most attentive, charming, and caring man I've ever met in my life!" Salina exclaimed. "You're just picking on him."

"Everyone is charming when you meet them for the first time," Ravena noted. "There is too much we don't know about Valenis. If he was a boy of a family I know and I was familiar with what sort of people they are ..."

"His family was slaughtered by Vernians. I understand it if he doesn't want to talk about his past," Salina snapped.

Ravena sensed that this would grow into an argument, so she just raised her hands and said, "All right, my daughter. I hope that you know best and that you will get lucky the way I did with your father."

"It's so hard for everyone to believe that I've met the love of my life." Salina snorted. She had been preparing for everyone to question her choice, so she was prepared to defend it.

Having said that, Salina went outside. She wouldn't allow others to spoil the best thing that had ever happened to her. For the first time she really felt alive and would fight in any way to keep Valenis.

CHAPTER 11

THE FATAL MARCH

The week came when Arkenel's men were preparing for the next march. Their young leader was trying to get his friends in shape and make sure everyone was content, fed, and rested before leaving again. Mavarius was chasing after his friend with a basket of bandages and herbs, and could only shout at him for fidgeting too much, which didn't help the wounds. However, cooling such enthusiasm wasn't easy. Arkenel had begun making friends with the people in the mine in order to get cheaper metal. He already had a few complete sketches for the armour he wanted to make, and he actively renovated the forge in whatever ways he could. He was hardly taking any rest. Rabolii pouted as he watched his son's attempts to take over the city. He could hardly wait to send him away. The necromancer's life was so difficult. On top of everything he usually suffered every day, he'd need to also coddle Ilinar now and act like a father to him. Realistically, he had no idea how to give him his throne back.

They had once again met in the necromancer's chambers, where the Soleyan could complain about how upsetting everything was as the necromancer just nodded with a bored expression, trying to perceive Mortelion's will behind all this. The best explanation he could come up with was that the god was mocking him again. Right then they heard a knock on the door, and Salina's voice called out, "Father, can I come in? I wish to return the book of the Solar dynasty. I read it."

"All right, come in!" he said lazily with a bored look.

Ilinar didn't interrupt his tirade for a second. At the moment, he was emphatically describing what Eley had told him during some history class about some war. According to some logic of his, this was vital information to the necromancer. Rabolii barely paid attention to Salina until she had come to his desk. As she was laying the book on his desk, the necromancer lifted his eyes lazily, and his face froze in a silent shock. He clutched his daughter's hand and muttered hoarsely, "Ilinar ... this is a fascinating conversation, but you have to ... go out. Now."

Ilinar and Salina blinked in surprise, but they dared not argue with this terrible person. The Soleyan slipped out of his chair and backed off. When he had disappeared from the scene, the necromancer's daughter asked hesitantly, "Um, Father, is everything OK?"

Rabolii continued to stare at her in a very disturbing manner. A few seconds passed, making the silence feel heavy. When he finally recovered, he squeezed her hand and said, "I was ... I was just surprised you're ready so soon, my daughter. Have you seen the extras in the back?"

Salina exhaled. Had he created all this tension just for the book? She knew as well as anyone that Rabolii loved to be dramatic, but this was too much. She nodded and said, "Yes, I saw the extras. I'm sorry I interrupted your meeting with Ilinar."

"No, no, on the contrary." Rabolii began blubbering and stuttering. "I ought to thank you for it. He was rather tedious. Please, sit by my side ... Did you enjoy the book? Is there anything you'd like me to clarify for you?"

Hmm, that was unusual. Rabolii had never spoken to her like that before. She replied suspiciously, "I believe I understood everything. Father, are you well? You look rather pale."

"Quiet, Salina." He pressed his fingers against her wrist to take her pulse. It seemed to be in order. He raised his eyes towards her with a petrified smile and asked, "Why don't you sit with me for a bit? We haven't spent time together lately."

Salina couldn't understand all this. Had Ilinar been so shockingly boring that he'd cause her father to have a nervous breakdown? That was the only logical explanation. Rabolii was acting just plain weird. He started talking about every single aspect of the book, then told her stories about the necromancers from hundreds of years ago. While doing that, he took some of her blood without properly explaining why and made her drink some potions without saying what they would do. Salina just accepted all this. She trusted her father and wanted to believe he was really interested in her. It just felt a bit out of the blue. He was acting like never before. She could only wonder about all that as she spent the rest of her day with Rabolii. It was so rare for him to be communicative that she didn't want to miss the opportunity.

About a day later, Eslir arrived in Lumis with a heavy loss and some heartbreaking news. He gathered a rally in the city square to make an important statement. He displayed the blood-soaked fake will that Eley had written. No one had cared about Eley at all until now, but all of a sudden everyone began recalling his great deeds and those of his family. Gifts of all kinds were gathered for his hulled house and his drunken relatives. Bards sang songs about how the saviour of this nation had fallen under Krumerus's blade. If Eley himself were to watch all this in some ghostly form, he would be hitting his head against some ghostly building, furious because he wasn't alive to enjoy being celebrated. Not that if he were actually alive, people would still care.

All the glances were focused on the luminous Eslir, who was giving a passionate speech: "He arrived late at my camp, bearing shocking news. I didn't want to believe my ears when he told me everything, but his words made sense and perfectly described Krumerus's treacherous nature."

Eslir proceeded to tell them Eley's story about Rabolii killing Ilinar. Gasps and screams sounded around. He also told them how the undead Soleyan had made his way through the camp of ten thousand Aslanians to find his former teacher and murder him before his words reached the ears of the public. There was a heartbreaking description of Eley's last words: "Glacera led me with her wisdom when she whispered to me to visit the tent of the Soleyan at night. Unfortunately, I arrived just when the irreversible had happened. Ilinar stood over the bleeding body of the man with whom he used to be inseparable. I tried to capture him, but he vanished in the darkness like a shadow. I knelt by Eley to see if I could his stop bleeding, but there was nothing I could do. He barely spoke. He told me: 'Soleya stands on the brink of a catastrophe. The royal bloodline is severed, and enemies surround us on all sides. Please take care of my people, Eslir. Don't allow them to meet the same end that I and Ilinar did.' I put my hand on his arm and promised him, 'I will put an end to this evil race, whatever the price. I swear it.' I hope that my words gave him some peace as he slipped away. He just closed his eyes and died in my arms ... His blood dripped softly on this sheet lying beside his bed." Having said that, Eslir waved around the bloody will. "He was the heir to Soleya's throne! He was elected by Ilinar while he was still alive to rule if something happened to the young king! Tonight we suffered two losses: that of the present and the future king! They are the people who ventured into Krumerus to fight for peace to negotiate to stop aggression, and this is what happened to them! This is a real tragedy for Soleya. However, I promise that the erebi won't celebrate another victory. Our next clash will be fatal to them. By uniting the armies of our two proud nations, we will be the greatest power on the continent! We will be the masters of these lands, and the erebi will tremble before us! For Glacera's glory! For Flalirion's fame!"

The square thundered from screams. Although the recent days had seemed uncertain and gloomy, the people were glad to see that someone strong and courageous like Eslir was in charge and promised to fight the monsters. Perhaps not everything was lost.

—⁂—

Arkenel and Mavarius were lying in one of the terraces on the third floor and were smoking fags they had rolled themselves. They seemed sleepy and bored. The former mumbled, "Tosser, how long have we been here?"

Mavarius shrugged indiscriminately and tossed the fag off the terrace. He replied lazily, "Beats me. Two days?"

"You think he'll soon notice?"

"As if. The old muppet doesn't shower."

"And then he complains about smelling like a corpse. I wonder why!" Arkenel began to snicker.

Perhaps they would soon fall asleep because they were bored, but the corridor was shaken by a shrill scream: "Ravena! What is this?!"

Mavarius and Arkenel pressed their mouths with their hands to muffle their laughter and peeked into the corridor to enjoy their mischief. Rabolii stood nearby in front of his shower door. He was dressed in a mind-blowing green bathrobe with a hood and black flip-flops decorated with tiny skulls.

"Rab, why are you screaming? What is it?" Ravena called from two floors down. These corridors were specially designed to have good acoustics so that if Rabolii found it necessary to yell, everyone could hear because it was important.

"Come and see what's happened to my bathroom. I'm sure your son is responsible!" The necromancer was yelling. He had crossed his arms, standing in a threatening pose.

The mischievous guys kept chuckling quietly. They had waited a long time to see the necromancer's reaction. After all, they did try their best to make the bathroom as dirty as possible. They had left there the old pair of Mavarius's trousers, which had collected biological material for twenty years, just to add insult to injury. Ravena arrived at the scene of the crime to see what extraordinary event had upset her husband this time. She glanced at the twigs and leaves taken out of someone's hair, the muddy footprints, the balls of hair, and all other wonders. She turned to Rabolii and said, "Yes. The bathroom is dirty. What do you want me to do? Call a maid."

"No, I just think this shows the attitude of your filthy failure of a son towards *me*!" Rabolii yelled.

"You don't even know if he did this." Ravena shrugged.

"*Oh, really!* Is there anyone else as filthy as him in this city?!"

Arkenel sniffed his armpit to check if this ugly accusation was as harsh as Rabolii made it sound. Mavarius felt like he'd die while he was trying not to laugh noisily. Ravena was obviously not having fun with this. She said, "Stop talking about Arkenel like that already. How about you start behaving more like a father to your children?"

"I spent half a day with Ilinar and the other half with Salina. I think my duty is fulfilled," he spat.

"Yes, I heard about Salina. How come you sacrificed your peace like that? Or do you suddenly love her very much because soon you'll marry her off and she'll leave us?"

Rabolii leaned against the wall. The beastly expression of his raging face disappeared, and he sighed sadly. After a short pause he replied, "Actually, yes. That must be it ... I don't know what the future has prepared for us."

Ravena noticed he was emotional, as always, so she suggested, "Let's sit somewhere while your servants clean the bathroom."

She took Rabolii a little farther down the corridor to one of the benches. Arkenel and Mavarius were discontent because they had been sitting there for so long, but their entertainment with Rabolii's reaction was too short. While walking, the necromancer continued to complain, "I ... I really want her to be happy. But this boy, Valenis ..." Rabolii realised he couldn't tell Ravena about his findings; otherwise she wouldn't allow him to send her dear Arkenel on a mission with a Vernian spy. So he decided to think of another reason why he didn't like the man. "Don't you think it's very suspicious how he came out of nowhere and started courting her? Perhaps he has hidden intentions. We don't know anything about him."

"Or he just fell in love with Salina, who is a beautiful girl," replied Ravena.

As they spoke, Salina herself appeared. She had heard her father's screaming and had come to see if he was alive—not that he was, but anyway. Rabolii didn't notice her and continued to speak, "Mark my words, nothing good will come out of this. Valenis has hidden motives and will hurt our daughter. If he returns from that mission, I will not let them get married."

When she heard this, Salina dived into the first empty room she saw in the corridor. Ravena and Rabolii cast a glance in that direction, detecting some movement, but she was already gone.

Ravena blinked in surprise, wondering why Rabolii was still insisting on this. She said in a hushed voice, "Rab, didn't we speak about this? I thought you agreed that the fertile land which Lord Fresner is offering you isn't worth Salina's happiness."

"May I remind you that it's no mere patch of land? It's the only place where demon's thorn grows, and that's an ingredient vital for most of my potions. If I had more of it, I wouldn't be suffering daily, but as I've very well noticed, all of you care little about that. I think I shall insist further that Salina marry Morelii, but in the meantime that other boy is out of the question."

Ravena watched him talk so confidently, so sure of himself and his own judgement. She couldn't understand. She pleaded once more, "Can you at least tell me what changed your mind? What is it about Valenis which has caused your distrust?"

"I owe explanations to no one, Ravena," the necromancer snapped, then turned his attention to a few skeleton servants who were walking by. "It sure took you long enough! Clean my bathroom at once."

Ravena continued trying to talk to him, but he wasn't having any of it. His decision was made, but he wouldn't tell anyone why. He was a bit annoyed at Salina for deciding to fall in love with the most unsuitable man in the whole of Krumerus and causing her father this inconvenience.

Salina stood leaning against the wall, breathing heavily. She couldn't believe what she had just heard. Why would Rabolii think Valenis would hurt her?! He was the best thing that had happened to her, and he was probably in danger. Rabolii apparently believed that the mission wouldn't be an easy one since he'd said "if he returns". Salina felt shaken by all this.

There was only one thing she could do, no matter how childish and foolish it was, but there was nothing she wouldn't do to stay with Valenis.

—m—

The week for resting was over very soon. The Krumerians prepared for their ambush against the Vernians, not knowing that the actual ambush was set for them. Rabolii was very eager to see them gone. He was keeping Salina in his room and wouldn't let her out of his sight. In the last couple of days he'd remained near her. She was biting her lip nervously, thinking she would enjoy all the attention on a regular day. However, now she thought she saw the hidden motive—her father wanted to keep her close while he safely arranged her marriage with Morelii.

But perhaps she'd get a window of opportunity to leave. Valenis was also interested in getting Rabolii out of his lair. He found a skeleton servant and dug into its mind, convincing the primitive creature that Dunevir was causing some chaos in the city and needed to be dealt with immediately. Shocked by this information, the skeleton started stumbling ungracefully towards the necromancer's tower to deliver the news at once. Just a few minutes later, Rabolii slammed his door open and rushed down the corridor, yelling angrily, "Unbelievable cretins! This city will not see peace! I just managed to send one malice away, but another one has replaced it in an instant. Salina, follow me."

Valenis stood behind some columns, so nervous that he was shaking. He also felt sad. Perhaps this was the last time he would see Salina, at least for some months to come. He would work on ways for them to get back together, but he had other important tasks he had to focus on. As the necromancer disappeared from the scene, Valenis left his hiding place and slipped into the necromancer's chambers. Of course, this invasion didn't go unpunished. Rabolii's last vampire charged at the intruder with wild screams to protect the land of his ancestors. Valenis wasn't prepared for this aggression, so he hit the creature on the head with the first object he could grab a hold of. It turned out to be some rusty fire irons, which broke the vampire's skull. This was enough to knock it out. Valenis shook a few stands of hair back with his bloodstained hand and looked around. He remembered what Rabolii's vampiric potion looked like, and soon he found it. It was on the balcony in a syringe under a glass dome, left to absorb moonlight. Without further hesitation, Valenis snatched the potion and rushed out of the room. He had been pushing his luck too much these days. It was a wonder that no one had caught him yet.

When Valenis finally managed to get out of town, Arkenel and his friends were already waiting for him. The young Remedor cast a curious look at the Vernian and noted, "Princess, why are you all covered with blood? I hardly recognised you."

"Why? Is it rare for someone in Krumerus to be stained with blood?" Valenis snapped. He was feeling aggressive after fighting vampires and was becoming increasingly annoyed by Arkenel and his mates for talking to him like that.

"You want a handkerchief?" Rabolii's son handed him a filthy, crusted rag, used for terrifying purposes.

"I want you to get your brains together so we can fulfil our mission," Valenis replied, ignoring this idiotic behaviour.

Arkenel and his friends started grinning. It was hilarious; the doll face was trying to act important and give commands! Aveus stepped forward and noted, "Arkenel, you know I can't go now. As I've been telling you, I need to go back to Aldur."

"Come on, tosser, you're like a mother to us. We can't go without you!" Arkenel replied, grinning dizzily. Once again, he was in an overly elevated mood and everything was funny to him because he'd had too much miner's.

Aveus wasn't happy when he was addressed like this. He had never wanted to be equal to the people in the cells. He was the one who was supposed to be in charge of them, but they didn't seem to think that any more. In all honesty, he was afraid of what they'd do to him if he decided to run away from them. He continued to bargain, "Come on now. When your family was in danger, you left Aldur, which you had just conquered, and ran to Soleya. Why is it so strange to you that I want to return to my children?"

"They're fiiiine. Stop freaking out!" Arkenel spread his arms with a carefree look. "My men aren't some savages. They don't eat children. I bet it's all cool. I promise to let you go after this mission. I promise! Just come with us! Please! Please! Please!"

Aveus rolled his eyes. Fate was a cruel mistress. He still remembered that frightened, miserable kid called Arkenel who had stepped into Aldur's dungeon for the first time seven years ago. He couldn't believe that he was faced with the same individual now. He sighed heavily, seeing no other option but to agree. He groaned, "All right then. I'll come with you again, but this mission better be the last. I have other matters to tend to."

"You got it, boss." Arkenel grinned, then waved his hands. "Tossers, let's get going! I want to make myself a necklace of Vernian skulls!"

In the meantime, Rabolii had actually discovered a problem in his city. He found Dunevir, who had settled in another temple of Mortelion and began dismembering people for sacrifices. The necromancer flew into a rage and yelled at him, "This is beyond words! How did it occur to you to sacrifice people from the streets? I spoke to the relatives. They told me you didn't even buy these men and women for their sacrifices, so now I owe the families money or skeletons. Just look at this mess. I can't reanimate this any more!"

"Our ubiquitous master needs blood and bones." Dunevir shrugged indifferently, handling his huge chopper as if he were boning a lamb.

"If your ubiquitous master has such desires, either buy victims from the market or go catch some foreigners! It's like we have few problems with our neighbouring countries," Rabolii yelled. "Why don't you try to be useful for a change? How does massacring my own citizens help me?"

Dunevir assumed a very fearsome look. He narrowed his eyes and slammed the chopper onto the table. He turned to Rabolii, casting a shadow over him. He responded with his surreal, ethereal voice, now sounding low and growling, "You dare doubt me and my ability to serve our supreme master?"

Rabolii inhaled air as if trying to bloat like a frog which was making itself larger and scarier. He snapped, "We need to serve both Mortelion and our country. Serve both of them, will you? I don't want to receive more news about you killing Krumerians." He stepped back, keeping his eyes on Dunevir, and called out, "Come on, Salina, we're going back to the tower."

But he didn't get an answer. When he looked around, he didn't see his daughter anywhere. He left the temple and continued to call for her, but she was gone. The necromancer turned to Dunevir and barked like it was his fault. "My daughter! Where is she?"

"Bored with your nonsense, she left fifteen minutes ago," Dunevir replied casually.

"*So where did she go?!*" Rabolii spat.

"Mortelion does not intend to enlighten us on this matter," the large man replied.

"You useless wretch! I'll find her myself!" the necromancer screamed. He stomped his feet down the stairs as noisily as he could so that everyone would notice he was irritated.

At least Arkenel's mates were having fun. When a bunch of people got high, it was impossible not to be cheerful. In fact, only Valenis and Aveus were sober, but the Vernian was avoiding the former prison guard. The last thing he wanted was to have a conversation with someone who had not completely lost his mind and could catch him lying about something. Instead, he focused his attention on the others in the group who ran in the field without any meaning, purpose, or organisation. Mavarius was equipped with a large basket and uprooted every other plant he saw. Without even bothering to remove the roots or cleaning them of soil, he'd put them in the basket. Arkenel walked past him to enquire about this unnecessary activity. He put his hands on his heart and gasped, "Flowers? For me? Mavarius, I am touched."

"Yeah, they're for you," the man mumbled, and began looking for something else he could uproot and stick in the basket of wonders.

Arkenel blinked in a confused way, wondering what to make out of that answer. Then he stepped back a bit and answered, "Erm, I was kidding. Flowers would be too much for me."

"I mean I'll cook them, you idiot," Mavarius replied sullenly.

"Phew," Arkenel replied with relief. Now he was able to digest this shocking information. He added, "Wait, what? That's food? Are you sure you'll feel the same when you're sober? That's some bush!"

"The locals call it 'earth apple'," Mavarius mumbled. "A bush is what you have in your pants."

Arkenel burst into laughter. In fact, he should have been used to this by now. Whenever he'd go out with Mavarius, he'd always start plucking plants and checking what's edible. Arkenel had no idea how come his friend knew anything about Krumerian plants since he had spent almost no time in the wild.

Valenis watched how everyone behaved in a simplistic, mindless way, shoving and insulting each other, and wondered what kind of society that was. Not even in Vernian high-security prisons did people behave like that. Apparently the culture, the upbringing, and the hygiene of the ordinary Krumerian was at a very low standard. He didn't get to ponder about that too much because Mavarius became weary and looked around like a frightened doe. Arkenel wasn't impressed, because he was used to such behaviour as well.

"I hear wheels. Something's coming. I'll check. You hold this."

He shoved his basket in the hands of Arkenel and sneaked in the tall grasses, going towards the backlines. Remedor just shrugged, bit off one leaf of the earth apple, and followed Mavarius casually to check which fallen twig had upset his feline hearing this time. They saw a small carriage making its way towards them from Kranium. It was towed by the skeletons of large, horned animals. When he perceived this as a nonthreatening occurrence, Mavarius stood up from his hiding place and stood beside Arkenel, who didn't bother crouching at all. The carriage stopped, and to everyone's surprise, Salina came out of it. Her brother raised his arms in a questioning gesture, but she didn't pay attention to him. She immediately threw herself into the arms of the confused Valenis and began to cry, "Valenis, Valenis, I'm so happy I managed to catch up with you! You can't imagine what my father decided! Recently he's been keeping me close at all times, and I was unsure why, but then I heard him telling Mother that you'd hurt me, so he won't allow us to marry! He wanted to make sure I didn't run away, but I took the first opportunity I had and came here!"

Valenis stood as if he were thunderstruck. His jaw dropped, and he couldn't think of a single word in response to this whole story. He could only keep opening and closing his mouth like a fish. When Salina paused for half a second to catch her breath, he managed to say, "Darling, I want us to marry more than anything, but why did you come here of all places!"

"Because I want to be with you!" Salina replied softly.

"I'm on a military mission!" Valenis exclaimed. He couldn't believe he had found himself in such a horrible position. "There will be no time for romance. It will be dangerous!"

"Don't think I haven't seen battles before! And how come it'll be dangerous? You told me that it would be a simple ambush and that you would finish quickly!" Salina continued protesting.

"Valenis! But I will die without you!" Arkenel screamed in a high-pitched voice, while handing Mavarius a bouquet of the earth apple with soil still falling from its roots.

"Sod off, Salina. Why did you come back? I just got rid of you," Mavarius replied with a similar high-pitched voice and with his hair tied in a short ponytail to better fit the image.

"But I love you! I don't want to marry Morelii!" Arkenel could have done a better job at impersonating his sister if he weren't about to burst out in laughter.

"Why on earth do you want me? At least Morelii isn't a lesbian." Mavarius dropped this devastating answer.

When he heard that, Arkenel just couldn't restrain himself any more, so he collapsed on the ground, laughing like crazy. Valenis watched them with thin lips and widened nostrils, imagining their heads on spikes. Then he turned to Salina and grabbed her by the shoulders. He opened his mouth to say something, but he paused, staring at her. When had she managed to tattoo her face? That disappointed him a little. He thought it was tasteless. It was a drawing of a strange rune or a symbol on her right temple. Finally he said, "What did you do to your face?"

Salina blinked and reached for her lips with her fingers. She didn't understand what he was talking about. Could there be some piece of food near her mouth? Or maybe she had gotten a spot? Oh no! She mumbled, "I don't know what you mean."

"How so! How could you miss getting something like this?!" Valenis exclaimed.

"I'm convinced I have nothing on my face," Salina murmured.

Arkenel walked past her, examined her, and stated, "There's definitely nothing on her face. Except for that spot on her forehead. If you are a connoisseur of art, you may be inspired by it, but ..."

Salina pulled away to the side, then blurted to Valenis, "I don't care what my father wants. I will not go back to Kranium. I'm coming with you. And don't think I'm defenceless. My spells of light are so strong that I could win that battle. And after we've done our job, we'll get married in a town away from my father. We'll go back to him as spouses, and there won't be anything he can do."

Valenis looked at her with pain. It was very difficult for him to see Salina excited about a dream life she couldn't have. He wanted to do more for her, but his job, his duty as a prince of Vern, was to defeat her people. The only idea which occurred to him was foolish and crazy, but maybe it would save Salina if no one else. His tortured facial expression broke into a smile, and he told her, "Why wait? We could get married in the very first city we find on the way."

Salina smiled brightly and hugged him around the shoulders. Valenis caressed her back, thinking frantically about his own strategies. He knew that Krementa would probably want to kill him for this, but he would need to marry without her consent.

He'd tell her he'd married the princess, so now the only way to go forward would be to treat Krumerus as a potential ally and to negotiate instead of fight. So maybe he would win whatever resources his mother had wanted and he would save Salina. After all, he was fighting for love and peace. He deserved to win. If the gods didn't aid him, what sort of gods could they be?

"My father will probably send people to look for me." Salina sighed, still hugging Valenis. "I don't know if we can keep ahead of them."

"Don't worry, my dear. I have an idea how we could delay pursuers," Valenis told her soothingly.

He laid his hands on the ground, causing it to shake under their feet. Salina gasped, watching a huge crevice open in front of them. It expanded as far as the eye could see, then remained like a bottomless abyss, completely cutting off the road to Kranium. She shook her head and said, "I never imagined you were so powerful. But this will hinder the trade of our country."

"I promise to close it as soon as possible." Valenis smiled at her. "Now let's not waste any more time."

He took Salina by the hand and proceed towards Vern. Arkenel staggered behind them, grinning at how the doll face created natural disasters. In no way did he suspect he was in danger. The carriage and the massive skeletons which pulled it were left on the other side of the crevice. Bringing along creatures reanimated by Rabolii would been a bad idea.

Meanwhile the necromancer raged around his castle, searching high and low for Salina. The whole city could hear him yelling, slamming doors, and breaking things. Ravena came to see what had upset him this time.

"Salina has escaped!" Rabolii roared angrily. "While I was dealing with stupidities, she was right next to me, and when I turned around, she was just gone!"

"What do you mean? Why would she run away? Maybe she's in her room?" Ravena asked, trying to calm her husband.

"Do you think this never occurred to me? That was the first place I checked. She's not there. Everybody in the city is looking for her!"

"Rab, why are you so worried? On most days you have no idea what your children are doing, and now that Salina is gone for a few minutes, you've raising search parties?"

"Are you questioning my judgement?" Rabolii yelled.

Ravena sighed, realising there was no point in asking

279

questions. She said, "I believe your judgement. I just can't help but notice you're worried. Is Salina in danger?"

"She will be if we don't find her, so start looking!" The necromancer nudged her. "I want every person in this city to be on the lookout for her! Also, I want to assemble troops to follow that scum Arkenel. I'm ready to bet she's with Valenis."

"But, Rab, why would she run away?" Ravena asked. She didn't understand Rabolii's thought process.

"Just do what I tell you!" he roared with protruding eyes like a madman.

Ravena hurried to leave and give the orders. She wouldn't ask more, because Rabolii was getting irritated. But now she was worried as well. She wanted nothing more than to find Salina.

Meanwhile, Arkenel's group were making their way to the west. Valenis was very quiet most of the time and felt guilty about what Salina would have to experience. Of course, he wouldn't let her die in the ambush, but that would be a small consolation for her. He didn't know how to prepare her, so he could only drop statements like, "Whatever happens, we'll be together" or "We'll find a way," even in conversations which weren't meant to be so dramatic. Moreover, Valenis was surprised to see that almost everyone around him had the same tattoo on their temples as Salina had, and they all behaved as if it didn't exist. Was it some fashion, something they all had but that nobody talked about for some reason? Or maybe the smoke of all the miner's cigarettes was intoxicating him and he was seeing things? Quite possible.

Mavarius often separated himself from the group to wander around. No one even noticed when he was gone. He would catch up with them after a few hours, and he would have brought something to eat. One night Arkenel was bored and decided to follow his friend on his wanderings. As he sneaked between the trees and looked around for god knows what, Remedor appeared behind him, thinking he would surprise him and scare him.

"Arkenel, you know I hear you, right?" said Mavarius without even turning around as he examined the trunk of some ordinary tree.

"Come on, tosser, you're no fun. What are you looking for, more roots? I'm tired of roots. Catch me an animal!" Arkenel came out of the dry bushes and sat by his friend.

"Look 'ere, you see where the bark is chewed off?" said Mavarius. "Maybe it was that stag I've seen. So if you don't make noise, I may catch it. It's rare for a stag to come so far east."

Arkenel put his hands on his waist. Catching animals was such a useless occupation when you were carrying supplies. Actually, he'd never hunted. Hunting should have been a fun pastime for a young prince, but Arkenel had missed those moments because he preferred to stay in Kranium and stop everyone from living peacefully.

"Will you teach me to track animals?" Arkenel asked unexpectedly. "After all, it could be useful."

Mavarius turned to him with a surprised look. He was too used to his friend making fun of him each time he mentioned the forest, the animals, and the plants. Arkenel would call him a druid, a forest wizard, and other unpleasant things. So he was justified in asking, "You wanna be a druid too then, eh?"

"I won't go that far. I don't want you to stop feeling special. Besides, while we roam, we can find miner's somewhere."

Oh, all right. It was because of the miner's. That made more sense. Mavarius shrugged and said, "Come then. It's all muddy because of the autumn rains, so it's easy to track beasts. We'll get the damn stag and miner's too if we're lucky. And maybe you should whisper rather than yell; you're always so noisy."

"As you say, Master," Arkenel replied in a quiet, velvety voice.

Mavarius slapped him on the back of the neck then nodded towards the forest. There was a lot for them to do. The experienced hunter looked for broken branches, more footprints, and any other signs the stag might have left. Arkenel became bored two minutes in and began chatting, "All right, so since you don't have houses in Vern ..."

"We do," Mavarius mumbled as he strode forward and looked around.

"You do? OK, so what do you have in a normal Vernian house?" Arkenel continued asking.

"Beds, tables, tools ... animal skins. Whatever we need."

"I don't know how you live like that," Arkenel noted. He had heard about how primitive the Vernians were, how they made everything out of mud and leaves. And if they bought metal dishes or weapons from Soleya, they felt like gods.

"What, you've not seen nastier places to live in than Vern? You people have slaves in your precious Kranium, so what are you on about?"

Arkenel made a grimace as though he didn't fully agree with that statement. He replied, "Now, they are not 'slaves'; they are just people who can't cope with their lives. And if they get drunk and pass out, someone can find them on the street and sell them to rich men."

Mavarius spread his arms with the unspoken question of how this could seem normal to anyone. In Vern, everyone took care of each other and stood together, and in Krumerus you got to sell anyone who was too drunk or defenceless to fight. Arkenel, after thinking about how to explain it to him, said, "The strong survive. It's like that everywhere, even in Vern."

"Yes, we die 'cause of sickness or hunting accidents, not 'cause the neighbour waits for us to pass out and put us in a sack," replied Mavarius.

"Well, we have fewer diseases in Krumerus because we don't sleep in the trees!" said Arkenel.

In fact, he didn't know how to compare the two ways of living since he hadn't experienced both. There was a time when Krumerus made perfect sense to him and he didn't need to ask why things were certain ways. He knew the strong survived, and that didn't seem unfair to him because he'd met such people in castles, in mines, and in the field. Few of them were sorcerers, but they had other talents. Rabolii had tried to teach him that starting at a very early age: he must prove his value as a person, and if he never accomplished anything worthwhile, there would be no point to his existence.

"My father was raising ravens this one time." Arkenel mentioned after a period of silence. "I remember how one of our birds had died and we had to hatch her the eggs ourselves. I was seven years old. My father could warm them with magic." He smiled as he remembered it. "It was so cool. Do you know the babies start making sounds while they are still in the eggs?"

"Yeah, they do that," Mavarius confirmed. He had discovered more than one bird nest in his youth, and he knew exactly what noises the eggs made when he'd start poking them.

"We had six, and half of them were dead. They didn't make sounds and didn't move, but the other three were all right. Traneya and I would whistle, and they would reply. We finally hatched two, but the third bird couldn't break the shell. Rabolii told me not to touch it because it had to do it on its own ..."

Arkenel's voice faded. Mavarius nodded, seeming to be a bit distracted, and said, "True. Makes them stronger when they break the shell."

"But it couldn't do it alone and was growing weaker. It would make sounds which were much rarer. It was dying inside the egg. The other two had already hatched two days ago! So I and Traneya, we decided to help it out. We broke the egg very carefully, but the chick seemed to be bloodier than the others. Rabolii was angry when he found out what we'd done. He said we were wasting energy and resources for an unfit creature and that we should have let it die in the egg. I protested and said we could raise it with the other two, but he didn't listen. He announced that he wouldn't tolerate weakness and inferiority under his roof, saying that even if his own child had been born poorly, he would have done the same thing. He gave the chick to one of his vampires to eat."

"Rabolii's a bastard. Nothing new there. He could have just let you try," said Mavarius.

"Yes, I thought so when I was younger," Arkenel sighed. "Rabolii often seemed so merciless and unreasonably cruel. After quite a long time I finally understood what he had wanted from me. Now I know that he was making my life difficult with his constant requirements because he wanted me to break the shell myself."

Mavarius couldn't convey in words how much he disagreed with all this. He didn't want Rabolii to be treated like a fair educator while he was actually a torturer. Mavarius thought that if there were people in this world who should support you all the same, those people would be your mother and father. He summed up his opinion in the following sentence: "What a bunch of crap."

"I understand that it was all a test," Arkenel continued to explain excitedly. "When I was younger, I was living with no purpose and I wasn't interested in responsibilities or goals, but now things have changed. You'll see. Once we win this fight and a few more after it, Rabolii will appreciate me. I'll make him proud to be my father."

Mavarius rolled his eyes with annoyance. It was beyond him how a yelling, murmuring old man could provoke such love and dedication in people. Arkenel, as well as Ravena and Salina, treated him as if he was precious. He was a god according to most Krumerians. This country was a mystery to Mavarius.

Kranium was overtaken by an overall tragic mood. Rabolii had sent birds to search for his daughter, and indeed they found her. He could only watch her travel farther to the west. He tried to intercept her along the way with whatever skeletons he had in the area, but he quickly lost control of them. As Valenis was closer, he managed to force his will upon them and take them as his own. What a horrible mistake Rabolii had made by giving educational literature to the spy! The Vernian used those as bribes for any villagers who had gotten the necromancer's word and tried to interfere with the army. Rabolii realised he could do nothing. He was furious at the whole world because, had he been younger and more powerful, he would just kill from a distance one of Arkenel's tramps, reanimate him, and make him tell Salina the truth, even if it meant ending the whole mission. But he couldn't, not in his tragic, undead state. He couldn't reanimate bodies so far away from him. He tried sending messengers and troops from Krumerus, but things became even worse when the patrols came back and reported that their way to the west was cut off because of some mysterious precipice that had appeared out of nowhere.

"The locals have begun building bridges, my lord. They ask for financial aid so that it can be done faster," one of the scouts said.

"A precipice ..." Rabolii shook his head with a look of disbelief. "I'll give you whatever you want to build a bridge on the main road, and I want it done tomorrow."

"But, my lord, the crevice is huge, and the earth is crumbly. The stonemasons said that ..."

"I don't want any excuses!" Rabolii roared with a fearsome, hoarse voice and slammed his fist on the throne's armrest. He was such a terrible sight that not even the bravest of his countrymen dared to even look at him. "I don't care what you'll build and what you'll do. *Fly* if you must, as long as you do what you're told. *Do you understand?!*"

The scout bit his lip, clutching his hands behind his back nervously, and responded, staring at the floor, "Master, the landslides have already taken two bridges built in haste. There is nothing we can do. We can't fight nature."

"Rab, this cannot be a coincidence. Such a crevice doesn't just open after a small earthquake," said Ravena, standing by her husband's throne.

"Do you think I don't know that?!" Rabolii snarled, baring his teeth. "It would be too much of a coincidence that Valenis, a sorcerer of earth, is with Salina and then suddenly we have an earthquake the likes of which no one has ever seen! He's doing it! He doesn't want us to catch up with them!"

"But why?" said Ravena. She was getting more worried by the minute.

Because he's our enemy and serves Krementa, Rabolii

thought, but he wouldn't say it aloud. He was pondering about how things had gone down, and he had no regrets he had used Valenis to get rid of Arkenel. He was only sorry that Salina had gotten involved in all of it.

"I'm tired. I'll go upstairs to rest," said the necromancer as he got up. "I'll think of something. I doubt some foolish urchin can cast a spell which would impede *me*, Rabolii Remedor."

Then he walked with a quiet step and waving robes in a ghostly manner towards his cloister. As he opened the door to his room, he realised he hadn't been in there since Salina disappeared. He had been preoccupied, but it seemed that he had overlooked something else. His vampire lay dead, and the balcony doors were wide open. Rabolii's whole body was petrified by this scene. He stepped forward, feeling his limbs were numb, and a cold chill gripped him tight. With a frozen expression of shock on his face, he walked up to the doors, slammed back and forth by the wind, and peered out. His syringe was gone. That was all the potion he had, the last two hundred milligrams, enough to revive but one person. And now it was gone. He fell on his knees by the empty stand, giving out a long scream which gathered all the hatred, bitterness, anger, and despair of someone who felt once again like he had lost everything in his life. A shock wave of deathly blue energy was scattered within a fifty-metre radius from Rabolii's tower, killing every living thing which had the misfortune of being nearby. Birds fell dead from the skies.

Valenis had caused a great deal of suffering to this poor old man, but he didn't feel the slightest amount of guilt. He hoped the earthquake would keep the pursuers away for a few days. His group were approaching a big city. Spiked and uneven rocks outlined their black shapes against the evening sky. They looked strange and resembled protruding ribs, spines, and skulls, as if a giant had died on the ridge. That was the Skeletal Wall. At its foundations was a large city with high towers and many houses scattered at the foot of the mountain. Salina noted, "That's where my cousins live. I would normally offer to pay them a visit, but my father has probably sent them ravens. They may try to apprehend me."

Valenis was quite nervous about this situation already. As if it wasn't enough that he was leading his enemies into an ambush, he also had to watch out for Rabolii's hirelings and corpses he kept sending. He asked, "Can we pass through somewhere else?

We are bound to get stopped in such a big city, and then your father's troops will take you away."

"Are we out on a war mission, or are we doing a secret wedding?" Mavarius snapped with annoyance. He had studied the route and he knew that going around the Skeletal Wall would add another day to their journey.

"Yeah, Sis, is this absolutely necessary? Can't you just stay in Kranium till we come back? I'm sure you'll resist a marriage with Morelii for a few weeks," Arkenel noted.

Valenis pondered for a moment, realising that if he didn't marry Salina now, he'd probably lose her forever. He felt like he had to go through with this and try to stick with her. So he protested, "We don't know that! Obviously Rabolii was trying to marry her off without her consent."

"Yes, such things are so typical of Father, unfortunately." Salina sighed. "Arkenel, I am so sorry for this whole mess. However, I can't allow myself to be captured."

"We can't wander around forever. We'll run out of food." Mavarius turned to Arkenel to protest.

Arkenel noticed that all gazes were turned to him for a decision. He could tell by his men's faces that they wanted to get all this over with as soon as possible. Still, he found some inner strength to be the patron of love today and announced, "Going around the Skeletal Wall won't take all that long. We can afford the detour. Besides, it will take us south into the deeper woodlands, and you guys can probably find miner's there."

He was truly proud of this amazing way to please everyone. The men started chattering excitedly. Only Mavarius still seemed discontent. In his opinion these missions were pointless, Rabolii was stupid, and if everyone minded their own business instead of playing generals, the world would be a better place.

The army marched south to avoid the wall. On the way they passed by a small village which had just a few houses and a temple. It wasn't an exciting place to visit, but since Valenis wanted to get married this instant, he nodded towards it and asked, "How about there?"

"Why not!" Salina smiled lovingly. "I've dreamt of my wedding ever since I was a little girl, but I never imagined it would be like this. I thought I would be surrounded by my relatives, that I would be in Kranium, that we would be overwhelmed by decorations and guests ..."

"Nothing will stop us from having a celebration once we're back," Valenis told her, feeling like something was clutching his throat. Painting a perfect picture wasn't the best thing he could do since he knew what was ahead of them.

"I had imagined the dress I would wear ... I was probably thirteen years old when I first started drawing it in the diaries," Salina continued. "But, you know, this is all so beautiful and spontaneous that I'm happy it turned out like this."

Valenis felt like he was melting. It was as if every word she said was just perfect. Salina wasn't pretentious and capricious; she could obviously enjoy the moment. Meanwhile, Mavarius and Arkenel watched the couple with mischievous faces. They'd made fun of them occasionally because they thought Valenis was a dandy, and the very thought that someone wanted to marry him seemed like a joke.

"Hey, tosser! You think doll face here also drew herself wearing wedding dresses in some diaries?" Arkenel whispered.

"Wonder what it looked like," Mavarius replied with a menacing look.

"Must have had a bare back."

"And high heels."

"And a veil!"

"For how much longer will you be picturing me wearing dresses?" Valenis snapped at them. He wished he could go deaf to the stupidities they were saying, but he couldn't.

Arkenel stared at him with a biting smile and shamelessly added, "And with cleavage down to the stomach."

"Doesn't your boyfriend get jealous when you talk like that?" Valenis asked mockingly.

Mavarius and Arkenel exchanged glances. Remedor flung his arm over his friend's shoulders and replied, "We're open-minded. We accept third parties."

"Valenis, don't listen to them. They like to joke." Salina grabbed her beloved by the arm and led him forward.

The young couple could still hear grinning and biting comments even as the time came for them to walk towards the altar. This nuisance didn't stop the wedding, which took place in the local temple of Mortelion. It was a brief, improvised ceremony. Traditionally, the Krumerian spouses exchange a bone amulet, often crafted from a beloved deceased relative. Since neither Valenis nor Salina had prepared bones for this spontaneous wedding, they had none. The priest gave them some old, cheap amulets they kept in the temple in case some poor homeless folk came to marry.

"He's complete. He has a girly pendant now," noted Arkenel.

"Say that again when you get a girly pendant yourself," Mavarius mumbled.

"Me? Get married?" Arkenel gave out a laugh. "Do I look like some loser?"

"Who knows? Aren't you a 'prince' now? You'll need to continue the royal bloodline and such." Mavarius shrugged.

"Nah, I'm not an heir, remember? Besides, it would be stupid and boring." Arkenel yawned. "I couldn't just sit in Kranium day in and day out dealing with bureaucracy and spawning children with the same aging woman. I want to be the kind of prince who conquers lands, kills weak fools, and is on the edge of dying every day!"

"You're doing a good job with the latter all right," Mavarius noted.

"How about you quiet down? The ceremony is not over yet," Valenis called over his shoulder.

Arkenel stuck his tongue out and made a grimace, demonstrating he didn't care about his opinion. Valenis turned away so he wouldn't have to look at him. He faced Salina and put the amulet around her neck. He smiled with nervous excitement. That could save her. His mother wouldn't want his wife to be treated as a mere political prisoner. Maybe there would be a chance for them after all.

Ilinar received a grim letter from one of the skeleton servants. It seemed like the Krumerian diplomats sent to Soleya hadn't been successful. Their heads had been returned in a box with a wrathful letter from Eslir. The Aslanian didn't wish to believe that his cousin wasn't a corpse and refused any communication. It didn't seem like the Soleyan ministers were all too willing to make contact either. They were probably exploring options for the next monarch. Ilinar decided to go on a risky mission. He had to talk to Eslir. He couldn't think of any other way to connect to his people. Perhaps if he could prove he wasn't a corpse and persuade his cousin to stand up for him, he would have the chance to get his throne back. That's why once again he set off for Soleya in the hope that Eslir would still be there and would listen to him.

The days at Krumerus resembled a prolonged twilight. The sky was shrouded by such a dense blanket of magic clouds that the sun couldn't break through. Between the greyish puffs, spectral light lingered, casting ominous shades on everything it touched. Ilinar walked confidently, shrouded by the Nightwind cloak. He wasn't all too fast during the day, but according to his calculations he would be arriving in Soleya while the night was still young.

Strange creatures peered between the spikes of the Thorny Woods. Some were free skeletons revived by Mortelion; others were slimy creatures with no eyes. Ilinar wasn't going to linger around and tried to avoid them. But something caught his attention. He thought he saw a light between the black trunks of the trees, smudged by the constant whitish mist. That was unusual for Krumerus. No one here used torches unless the darkness was pitch-black, too much for even the eyes of the erebi. Ilinar decided to approach very carefully. Perhaps he would encounter a lost wanderer or a trap set for one.

At the roots of a tree sat a young blond man with hair falling in front of his face. Ilinar blinked with a puzzled look, wondering if it was possible to come across this apparition for a second time in Krumerus. He felt nervous and stepped back without making a sound. Though he was utterly silent, the strange Soleyan turned to him casually, looking up from the old parchments he was holding, and said, "Well met, Ilinar! Do come closer and rest by my fire. There's no reason to be shy."

Ilinar clenched his fists nervously and stepped forward hesitantly. He was trying to think. He didn't know if he had a reason to be afraid. He asked with a dry mouth, "I thought ... you were going back to Soleya?"

"It's what I did indeed ... and now I have returned. I didn't come across a single soul who knew me or anyone by the name of Agelik." The blond young man glanced at his parchments, on which there were paintings of grotesque creatures. "I still don't know who I am, but one of my dreams brought me back to Krumerus, which probably hides the answers I seek."

Ilinar glanced at the parchment and recognised that these were the drawings of demons. He shuddered and asked drily, "What was that dream about?"

Agelik thought about it for a moment. He moved a few stands of hair from his face and replied, "He was a demon. I saw him kneeling and bloody, crushed by the ripping pain that made me wake up screaming. Since that happened to me, I've been trying to sleep again, attempting to make the connection, but something stops me, and I've found myself incapable. I didn't see much. I barely gazed upon the form of the creature, and I am unsure if it resembled a four-legged beast or a man. I felt somehow ... connected to him. It was as if I shared his pain. That's why I visited the most prominent Soleyan scientists, who shared with me these articles about the creatures of Mortelion. Now I am seeking the one who might know me."

Ilinar frowned as he listened. He asked hesitantly, "Agelik ... aren't you afraid of what you might find? Do you really want to know if you have been involved with a demon? Just come back with me to Soleya and start whatever life you want. Krumerus is not safe."

"I will not deny that the truth is frightening. For all I know, I may discover I'm a villain and that I've done terrible things with the demon. But uncertainty is heavier than any truth, and I promise to keep my morals no matter what my findings are. Deep inside I feel that I have a crucial mission. I need to remember what it is."

Ilinar thought all this was very strange. The whole story was teasing his curiosity, but he wasn't keen on exploring the danger. He preferred that Agelik remain an innocent boy without memories, instead of turning into an ancient ally of demons, exchanging letters with the Remedors two hundred years ago. He decided to address another important issue: "How do you expect to find a specific demon in Krumerus? It's not like you can get in their circle of friends and ask them questions. Most are wild creatures. I think you came back to these lands too soon. Give yourself more time to research everything."

"My task is not an easy one, I know. But during my short dream I learned the name of the creature. I hope at least someone here has heard it before," Agelik replied, gazing at the trees ahead.

"So ... what's its name?" Ilinar asked without knowing why he bothered. It wasn't like he was buddies with any demons so he'd know their names.

"Lethius."

Agelik uttered this one word, but it seemed as if it echoed around the whole forest and remained ringing in Ilinar's head. He felt his very soul drop like a ball of lead in his stomach, and he could do more than stare with a petrified expression. Agelik gave him a curious look, and when he didn't receive any attention in the following few seconds, he asked, "Do you know him?"

"I've heard the name before, but I don't know how it could be possible. Lethius is a four-legged demon described in the books of Emanrylii Prehorian more than two centuries ago." Ilinar looked around, thinking frantically, and asked, "Have you heard of him?"

Agelik got a confused look on his face and shook his head. Ilinar knew perfectly well that his beloved author had died at the age of seventy-three; he knew where he was buried. Prehorian was born about three centuries ago, so he was alive when that mysterious letter from R. R. Remedor was written. Ilinar didn't know which things were related and which were coincidences, but now that his beloved author was involved, this whole mystery suddenly became all the more interesting to him. He turned to Agelik and said, "The dispute about whether Prehorian's stories are historically accurate or not is very extensive. Some scholars believe that the facts in his books overlap with real events, but others argue that he has simply used actual people and locations to gain credibility and that his books are still fiction. I don't know if the demon Lethius you dreamt about is the same one from the book, but I think it is important for you to research Prehorian."

Agelik was nodding with understanding and asked, "Is Prehorian relatively famous in Soleya? It doesn't seem like the demon he described was."

"Yes. He has plenty of other books. *Between Fire and Death* isn't that well known, but I'm sure you can find a copy."

Agelik smiled lightly and said, "Then I shall honour your invitation to accompany you to Soleya. We can travel together up to a point and then take our separate ways."

"Yes ... up to a point. I have a long journey ahead of me and may not stay in Soleya for long. I do hope I meet you again."

They took the southern road together, engaged in lively conversation. Ilinar couldn't restrain himself, so he began retelling Agelik the story written in the book *Between Fire and Death*. He had read it so many times that he could recite it. He told him about how people had mysteriously disappeared, and when Felis went looking for them, he came across the terrifying demon Lethius who served the evil god Eratius. The boy would have probably died had he not been saved by a group of mysterious sorcerers called Equilits. They possessed an element unknown to anyone until then. They could use the energy of their own souls for spells. Agelik listened with interest as Ilinar spoke with excitement: "Felis didn't know anything about them, but he hoped they would help him defeat Lethius. They began teaching him to use their magic, claiming he had tremendous potential without even suspecting. And I think it's amazing. If that were true, it would mean that each of us could be a sorcerer!"

"Yet none of us is, unless we were born with an elemental sphere," Agelik said.

"Yes, but Felis was very talented and had an extraordinary soul, which made him a much stronger student. Maybe one needs to have a special kind of soul to master the craft?" Ilinar continued to chat with excitement.

When the two reached Soleya, it was already dark. They arrived later than Ilinar had planned, but he was happy things worked out this way. The two separated as old friends. Each went on to fulfil his mission.

—m—

Eslir was making himself comfortable around the castle in Lumis. He had begun to meet local noble families and members of the council. He was looking for ways to bind himself to this country because in his opinion he was the best person to rule it. After a long day of hard work, he strode towards his chambers. Since his mother was a Soleyan princess, he felt he had a claim. Since he had been here for a while, a lot of his possessions were here and he felt at home. When he entered his chambers, the lights were out and the windows were open. Eslir inhaled the cold air, which reminded him of his motherland. He lit the oil lamp near the entrance and was a little surprised when a silhouette suddenly appeared in front of him near the window frame. The light illuminated Ilinar, who sat on the ledge.

"You!" Eslir looked back, wondering whether to sound the alarm.

"You can call your guards, or you can shut the door and listen to what I have to say," Ilinar stated with an emotionless expression.

Eslir hesitated for a second. On the one hand, he wanted to be the one to control this conversation. He'd rather have his new foe disarmed and chained for this conversation, but he was too proud to call the guards. He clenched his teeth and slammed the door, then turned to Ilinar and said, "All right then! Speak! Who are you planning to murder in Mortelion's name this time?"

"Eslir, you don't understand how things are!" Ilinar hissed at him, getting off the window ledge but still keeping his distance. The last thing he wanted was for the Aslanian to knock him out. "Please understand that all that Eley told you is a lie! I'm not dead! I am alive. I am the same person! You can check me for pulse. My blood is the same temperature as yours, and ..."

"It doesn't mean you aren't dead. As far as I know, Rabolii also has a pulse," Eslir replied, following Ilinar with a suspicious gaze. "You can say whatever you want, but you are not the same person! You killed that annoying guy in the tent, Ilinar! Two months ago you couldn't even hold a sword properly, and now you're a killer. Did you feel so threatened by an old man that you would kill him in his sleep?"

"You see what he did to me!" Ilinar spread his arms. "He spoke all those lies about me, and now my whole nation considers me a monster! I regret more than anyone that I had to kill him, but did he leave me a choice?"

"You could have come to me. You could have told me your version of the story before slaughtering anyone!" said Eslir. "Now you're in a position where nobody can help you, and nobody wants to either. Because as soon as you sit on this throne, you will start pursuing these ridiculous peace negotiations with the maddest country ever to exist because you have *family* there."

"And what would *you* do? Sacrifice thousands of lives because you're thirsty for blood? How are you better than them?"

"Did I say I plan to be better? No. I just want to be victorious." Eslir bared his teeth. "I'll be the one to strike first. If I start wasting time with diplomacy, Krumerus will prepare to unleash something horrendous upon these lands. My duty is to protect my people in any way I can, and that won't happen with your foolish ideas of peace!"

"Peace is the moment when we all stop fighting. *This is peace!* Is it so hard just to do that, instead of sacrificing thousands of lives, destroying cities, and hating each other?" Ilinar cried desperately.

"Peace isn't an option for us." Eslir snorted. "The moment we trust Rabolii, we sign our own death sentence. He will use us, treat us as a friend while fighting Vern, and once he destroys them, he will turn on us. How can you not see that?"

Ilinar sighed heavily. He felt that only he knew Krumerus and Rabolii, and he didn't know how to argue with someone so biased. In a final attempt, he tried to speak, "But ... but that's not true. Krumerus doesn't want war. I meet Rabolii every day. We've talked about it many times. He wants peace as much as I do. He's preparing no campaigns against you. He's not gathering troops. His only enemy is Vern, and I'm sure he won't attack."

"Is that what you think?" Eslir said drily. "Don't forget that Rabolii is not all-powerful and isn't in charge of every decision. If Mortelion orders through his oracles that he wants another war, Krumerus will fulfil his command. I will protect these lands no matter what I have to do. And now, if you would be so kind, please surrender so I can decide with the authorities whether you really are alive and what to do with you."

Ilinar sighed. He really wanted to have some more successful talks, but obviously Eslir wasn't interested in whether his younger cousin was alive. He cared only about politics. The Aslanian wouldn't help him, not until Ilinar agreed to declare war on Krumerus. If he refused, it was entirely possible "the authorities" would conclude he really was dead, and he would be disposed of as an enemy. So, without any further negotiations, the Soleyan jumped out of the window and disappeared into the darkness. Eslir ran to the ledge and leaned out the window. There was no sign of Ilinar. The Aslanian looked around, worried, then went outside to inform the guards that a potentially dangerous erebius was wandering around the city, so everyone should be cautious.

Meanwhile, Arkenel and his army were already deep in no man's land and were out of Rabolii's reach. They kept going west, and according to their maps, they were about fifty kilometres away from the town that Valenis had pointed out to them. That was where the unsuspecting enemy troops should have been. The Vernian himself was very pale and unusually quiet. The closer they got to Vern, the more the dead grey landscape receded and was replaced by green shrubs and trees with large crowns. Mavarius was listening attentively to the sounds of the forest with an unusual interest. As he was silent for too long, Arkenel decided to wake him up by punching his shoulder and telling him, "Hey, tosser! Ravena used to tell me that when a baby goes very quiet, it's because it has wet itself. Is that what you've done?"

"No, it's just that a red robin said that." Mavarius tried to explain himself.

Arkenel wasn't all too familiar with the Vernian fauna. He had only hard about it from Mavarius's stories, but he figured out the robin was a bird, so he couldn't even finish listening to the sentence. He burst into loud, uncontrollable laughter, and the whole group had to stop and wait for him to recover from this humorous event.

"Do tell! What did the robin say?" Arkenel was cramping from laughter. "What mysteries of the forest did it reveal?"

Mavarius stared at Arkenel with contempt and slapped him on the back of the neck, sending him face first to the damp, muddy forest floor. He responded sullenly, "I didn't mean I talk to birds, you moron. I can just tell the sounds they use to warn of danger. Right now they're announcing idiots like you."

"Oh, so the bird is saying, 'Tosser! Tosser! Tosser!'" Arkenel continued grinning.

"Almost," muttered Mavarius. He looked around. "They warn each other about people. But these birds are too far. They can't be so bothered by us that they'd start chipping."

"Maybe you stink to them." Arkenel shrugged as he was getting up from the ground and brushing mud off his nose.

"Or maybe we're not alone here," Mavarius answered while glancing around. "You should set up camp here. I can scout around."

"Make sure you don't get lost!" Arkenel shouted after him.

"Don't get lost, he says. Dumb cretin ..." Mavarius was mumbling as he walked away from the group.

Led by the voices of the birds, Mavarius left the road, heading straight for the ambush of the Vernians who were so close that they could smell their prey. Mavarius walked slowly and sneaked between the grasses, trying to discern any traces of human activity. The red robins continued chipping in the same way, although the forest looked completely silent. The man got a feeling of dread deep in his stomach as it occurred to him the birds were seeing something he couldn't. He paused for a moment, straining all his senses to perceive everything in the woods around him. He could only hear the rustle of the leaves, seeing nothing but the sea of vegetation in front of him. And then, when the wind blew, it brought a scent he was all too familiar with: Vernians. By the time he realised he had walked into an ambush, it was too late. He ran back in the direction from which he had come. As if guided by a sixth sense, he tumbled forward, dodging a few arrows which would have hit him had he remained standing. A few Vernians attacked him from each side, trying to stab him. He avoided their blades by some miracle, and before they were able to surround him, he dived into the sea of plants. He knew they would chase him. There was no hope of outrunning the Vernians, who could trace him with their eyes closed just by the scent. He would try to get back to the army as fast of possible. Maybe they'd prevail if they stood together.

Meanwhile, the Krumerians were already trapped without even knowing it. On the contrary, Arkenel felt very much protected on the green meadow surrounded by tall trees, some of which seemed centuries old. He had never been this far west before, so this new landscape was refreshing and interesting to him.

"All right, men, we'll sleep here today. Set up the tents!" Arkenel turned to the group.

It was early in the morning, the perfect time for sleep according to Krumerians. Now that their guard was down, they were making themselves comfortable and preparing to sleep. The only two watchmen who got the first shift were half asleep. One of them had been on this post for two minutes, but he was already yawning and wondering when his shift was going to be over. He hardly realised what was happening when an arrow whistled out of the trees and stuck him in one of the eyes. His companion stared at him, shocked, but didn't even get a chance to shout out when another two arrows struck him as well. The Vernians emerged from the woods and charged at their defenceless enemies. The Krumerians were surrounded. Arkenel was stunned by how quickly things had gotten out of control. He picked up his weapon in an attempt to fight back, his enemies were too many and surrounded him. The next thing he felt was a blow to the chest by a blade. It cut his skin deep. Blood spattered. The hit made him drop his sword. Two Vernians grabbed him from behind and began chaining him. Arkenel gazed around in dismay, only to see Valenis standing in the middle of the fray with no one attacking him. He seemed somewhat sad and guilty but not the least bit surprised by what has happening.

"Dammit, doll face, how could you?" Arkenel mumbled as he was being chained up.

Whoever refused to surrender peacefully fell, slain. There weren't many who suffered such a fate because the Krumerians were drowsy and too lazy to fight, not at a ridiculous time of the day such as this. Salina was also neutralised and bound. She was fighting the ropes and screamed, so one of the Vernian women raised a hand to strike her. Valenis immediately appeared between them to stop any further fighting and snapped at the woman, "Enough. I'll be taking over from here. You won't be hitting the prisoners."

"Of course, Your Highness." The woman backed off.

Valenis wouldn't even dare to turn around and see Salina's face and her reaction to all this. She stared at him in shock, unable to believe what was happening. Arkenel was still struggling to set himself free, but it was in vain. He was cursing his own life. He didn't know what was worse, dying all the way out here in such a pitiful way or surviving, only to return to Rabolii, who would yell at him for being a loser. Arkenel's river of thought was stopped by a hand which gripped his hair and pulled his head back. An outstandingly ornamented sword was pressed to his neck. It had more flowers and butterflies on its handle than the entire Krumerus had.

"You! You wretched creature! You've fallen into my hands at last!"

Of course, it was General Evena. When she heard that an ambush was set up for Arkenel Remedor, she was the first volunteer for the event. Her captive felt like he collapsed mentally under her soul-shattering gaze full of hatred. He knew he'd get no mercy here.

"So it is you! You dare set foot in my lands again?!" She began beating him up, throwing punches and kicks with all the force she had. Valenis tried to intervene immediately, not because he liked Arkenel too much, but because he didn't want Salina to hate him even more if he let her brother get beaten up.

"I have orders from Her Majesty to deliver the prisoners unharmed, especially the prince and the princess."

"I still can't believe this creature is a prince. He's literally the worst of them all. He and his men are vile, horrible people. I'll have them killed for the humiliation they caused me."

"Wait, what?" Arkenel raised his bleeding head. He thought he was getting this beatdown because he'd killed her soldiers. He didn't know there was more.

"I need to deliver them to Her Majesty for questioning and as a bargaining chip. You're not killing anyone. I know they're animals. I know what they did to you," Valenis told her compassionately yet firmly.

"Oh, Evena," Arkenel muttered in pain. "I can guess what my soldiers did to you, and I really am sorry. I don't know if this is any consolation, but they didn't mean to. They probably thought you were dead."

Once again, Valenis had to get involved because Evena was about to run down the prisoner like a herd of wild cattle. He took her by the shoulders and told her, "Revenge won't make you feel any better."

Evena glared at him for a few seconds and then burst out crying on Valenis's shoulder. "I have no peace any more!

Whatever I do, I can only think about what happened! I can't carry on knowing that freaks like this are alive. *I hate them!*"

Valenis stood awkward and motionless as a dry log as she was crying on top of him. He didn't know if he should hug her, pat her on the back, or try to remove her altogether. Arkenel said, "Well, to be fair, what is there to think about? Weren't you, like, unconscious the whole time?"

Valenis cast him an angry look and snapped, "You'd best be quiet. You're in a whole lot of trouble, so give us a reason to keep you alive."

"Whole lot of trouble, he says!" Arkenel laughed at him, baring his bloodied teeth. "Gee, I knew you were a doll face. How could I have suspected you're a granny as well?"

Arkenel took another kick in the stomach, this time from Valenis. The Vernian felt like each time he had to speak to this guy, he disliked him more and more. As for Salina, she could only watch was happening, feeling like her heart was bleeding. All this was too dreadful. It was like a bad dream!

CHAPTER 12

THE GREAT STRUGGLE

"Just one more mission, Aveus. Once we're finished, you can go home, Aveus," the ex-prison warden muttered disconsolately.

"Hey, man, that's still the plan," Arkenel replied, walking with the other captured men.

"Oh yes, sure. I can imagine you have the confidence of an escape artist who can get out of any prison or captivity," Aveus murmured.

"Since they tied me up, I've been working on loosening my ropes. I'll be able to slip out of them soon. All I need to do is get my hands on that wimp's neck." Arkenel nodded towards Valenis, who was leading the group. "How much do you want to bet they'd do anything if he was in danger? He's their prince. Imagine that. Who would have guessed?"

"You're always daydreaming of impossible scenarios," Aveus snapped at him. "You have such high self-esteem that I don't know where you got it from. The Vernians outnumber us three to one if my count is correct. We're on enemy land. How do you see us getting out of this?"

"Fine, even if my plan doesn't work, let's not forget Mavarius wasn't captured. He's probably watching us from afar and waiting for a good time to strike," Arkenel replied.

"Oh, sorry, what did Mavarius do last time he was outnumbered? He just picked up his stuff and left you. He didn't try to get you out of Kranium—or anyone else, for that matter. He's naturally selfish, so I can't imagine him descending from the heavens as a saviour and delivering us with divine power. And even if he does try, he'll fail. He will be captured like everyone else." Aveus kept talking angrily.

"Oh, screw you and your pessimism!" Arkenel snapped.

"He'll come back for us, you'll see. We'll get out of this. I don't intend to die like this."

"You're not the one deciding," Aveus noted grimly.

Arkenel turned his gaze forward again. Instead of complaining, he preferred to figure out ways to escape. He continued to loosen his ropes. The fact that his wrists were swollen and bruised wasn't helping. Once the group stopped for the night, he barely slept. He watched the guards, their habits, their schedules. He tried to remember which ones fell asleep while on watch. He had the feeling that his brain had never worked so hard, processing so much information. It took the same amount of effort as carrying huge rocks up a hill. With each passing day Arkenel became more nervous and irritable. Of course, the Vernians had taken his luggage and hadn't given him miner's in days.

It was yet another evening during which Arkenel watched all movement in the camp nervously. This time Valenis seemed to be sitting much closer. He was more annoying than usual. He was hanging around Salina, so clingy and needy. He threw a blanket over his wife's shoulders, but she shook it off and looked at the man hatefully. She snapped, "Why are you even trying?"

"Salina, it gets cold at night," he said, trying to speak to her.

"I've survived cold nights without your care," she answered angrily.

"Please don't be mad at me."

"How do you want me not to be mad?!" she yelled at him. "Firstly you charmed me so I'd trust you. Then you married me. And you did all that just so you could capture me as a hostage. I don't even want to look at you!"

"You think I'm happy about all this?" he cried. He wanted to keep the personal conversations for when they were alone, but such a moment probably wouldn't present itself soon. "All this isn't a joke to me, Salina! It hurts me just as much as you—even more—because what we had was real. I married you because I wanted to, because I believed that in wartime it would save you and would make our parents stop fighting and have the peace we both want. It's not my fault I'm from Vern, but I'm trying with everything I have to make our relationship possible. I'm begging you, don't hate me ... Help me with what I started."

Salina stared at him for a few seconds. Her eyes were puffy; her cheeks, wet. But she didn't have the strength to cry any more. She replied, looking at him resentfully, "Oh, now you want me to believe you! You want me to believe your story while I'm bound like an animal, prepared for the chopping block. Is this how you fight for peace? Hasn't it occurred to you that after every conflict, after each sacrifice, peace becomes harder and harder to achieve? The bitterness of it all becomes more difficult to swallow. What you did killed the trust. If you were sincere, you could have told me about this before it was too late! We could have negotiated first, rather than start off with fraud and lies."

"Do you think this is my decision to make?" Valenis cried desperately, his voice breaking. "I too have a ruler to serve, and I can't just start doing whatever I please."

"That's why I don't trust you." Salina sighed. "You are weak-willed and helpless. Even at my execution you'd just shrug and tell me it's not your decision to make."

"This is not true!" he yelled with anger and despair. "I'll endure anything to keep you safe so we can be together."

Evena walked past Valenis and reproached him, "Your Highness, stop it. That's ridiculous. The soldiers are watching you."

Valenis turned around to reply, but a ghostly shadow grabbed hold of him from behind before he got a chance to do anything. Arkenel had finally slipped out of the sight of his wardens and had grabbed the prince from behind, pressing his chains against his neck harder than he needed to. There was a spark of insanity in his eyes, cold sweat on his forehead.

"Do I have your attention, scumbags?" he yelled at them. "So, how many of you want me to strangle this trash, and how many want to cooperate?!"

Inspired by this, the rest of the Krumerians also attacked their guards, trying to get whatever weapons they could. Chaos ensued. Evena was shocked by this outrage. She cried out, "Monster! Release His Highness right now, or I'll pluck out your last eye for this insolence!"

"Kiss my ass!" Arkenel snapped, clutching Valenis around the neck as the latter gasped for air.

Evena felt so angry that she was about to blow up. The conflict, however, was resolved as fast as it had started. Valenis finally managed to retaliate. With the last of his strength, he made several stones fly up from the ground and hit Arkenel, which made him loosen his grip. Valenis broke free and pulled away from his assailant. That's all Evena needed. She began punching and kicking Arkenel, and after she was done, she turned to Valenis, remembering to ask him, "Your Highness, are you all right?"

The prince couldn't speak. He had put his hands on his throat, which hurt him horribly after he'd almost been strangled. While he was recovering, the rest of the Vernians managed to restrain the rest of the captured men. Evena towered over all this mess and then spoke her heavy word: "These people are too dangerous to be left alive! We can't carry on leading them towards Vern. Who knows what may happen next time."

Valenis tried to speak, though his voice still wasn't his own. He sounded as if someone was still choking him. "We need them alive for questioning."

"Not all of them," Evena replied bluntly, taking out her overly ornamented green sword which looked like a spring garden. "I can imagine you won't let anything happen to your 'wife'. Since she's princess, I don't intend to offer her for execution at this stage. The same applies to him." She kicked Arkenel again. "He's suitable for interrogation. Besides, I don't plan on giving him an easy, quick death. But why do we need everyone else?"

The former prisoners began exchanging worried glances. Valenis adjusted his collar so that he wouldn't look like the distraught victim of a beating, and said, "Her Majesty ordered me to bring her people in for questioning. She didn't say anything about spontaneous executions."

"Her Majesty told me to make sure that the mission would go smoothly without endangering your life!" Evena stated imperatively. "But it still happened! As long as these people are together, they will feel brave enough to attack us and try to escape. Do you want to risk it?"

"I don't think I can't handle them. As you can see, I did just that," answered Valenis. He really didn't want to stain his hands with more blood. As Salina had said, peace was becoming more and more difficult to achieve after each act of violence.

"You forget who those men are!" yelled Evena, pointing at the captives with the tip of her curved sword. "They are lowly creatures, freaks, and abusers. This one," she said, turning to Arkenel. "Last time he obliterated all my soldiers with his presence alone."

"Enough! That's impossible. He is not even a sorcerer," Valenis said with a frown.

"Were you there to witness it? He poisoned my people even though he was tied up and I was keeping an eye on him. And how do you know he is not a sorcerer? Do you forget whose son he is? Can we deal with such magic and fifty prisoners at the same time?"

"Those are not our orders," Valenis said through his teeth.

"Is that so?!" Evena cocked her head with a look of superiority. "Where's your amulet, Your Highness? Why don't you contact the queen right now and tell her about the situation and let her decide if we need fifty extremely dangerous and useless prisoners."

Valenis groaned. He knew that if Krementa got involved, things would become more unpleasant. She would definitely agree with Evena if she was told that the situation was dangerous. So he just waved his hand and said, "OK, do whatever you want with them. I refuse to take responsibility for this."

Arkenel shifted and tried to sit up. He licked the blood off his lips and spat. "And what does that mean? You can't just kill fifty unarmed men like it's nothing."

"Just watch me," Evena answered boldly. She reached out for the closest person and slit his throat.

"No, no, no, you can't do this!" Arkenel rose from the ground, struck by shock and disbelief. "Are you insane? Leave them alone."

Evena shot him a mean smile. She stood by the next man and slaughtered him without any sign of hesitation or regret. She watched Remedor's expression with great satisfaction. He gritted his teeth and said, "You'll be sorry about this. Just dare to slit another throat and ..."

"And what, you wretch?" she taunted him, then slaughtered yet another man.

At this point, the Krumerians had already begun to panic. Apparently, this crazy Vernian wasn't joking. They started to struggle against their chains and try to flee, but they were kept in place by their guards. Salina turned to her husband and snapped, "Valenis, won't you do anything?"

He gave her a cold look and replied indifferently, "I didn't make this decision."

"You ... if you have a problem, bring it to me!" Arkenel was trying to kill Evena with his gaze. His tone was threatening and murderous, but it didn't matter. Three people were trying to restrain him as he fought with everything he had to break free.

"I have a problem with each of you." Evena grabbed hold of a screaming man and stuck her blade in his eye. "Every one of you monsters dared to lay hands on me and treat me like less than an animal when I deserved none of it. You're getting what's coming to you."

"Enough. Graz and Aveus never laid a finger on you! Leave my men alone!" Arkenel continued yelling.

The eyes of the condemned were directed only at Arkenel. Some people looked at him hopefully, and others with horror, but on Aveus's face there was only disappointment and quiet hatred. He wasn't the only one who felt that way. Many others felt angered and asked why fate had brought them here right when they thought they'd be free. They didn't feel they deserved to die like this. Arkenel gritted his teeth, realising that the responsibility for each of them was his, so he started pleading, "Come on, stop! Just ... just let them go. Take me and do whatever you want with me. I promise to answer all the questions you have about Krumerus, about Rabolii, about our magic. Just let them be!"

"You lying, pathetic creature." Evena stuck her sword into another man's neck. "You'll tell me everything either way. It'll be a pleasure for me to force it out of you."

"You're not gaining anything by doing this! You're just creating enemies!" he yelled at her.

"I believe I'm getting rid of enemies." Evena laughed.

And so they all died before his eyes. He would have done anything to stop what was happening. He screamed, he swore, and he pleaded, but Evena was just having fun with his reactions. The meadow was soaked in blood. One by one all those eyes were shut forever. Some were filled with horror, disbelief; others, with reproach. Arkenel was incapable of saving them. He could do nothing but watch.

And when the last neck was cut, when everyone was dead, Arkenel felt drowned in their blood. His own promises to them cut into his brain. He remembered how he had made such grand plans, how he had spoken of victory and success, of glory and greatness. And here was where all his promises had led to. He felt like a weak liar who couldn't do the simplest thing—keep his people alive. He had chosen those fifty who felt like his closest friends. Some of them had known him for the full seven years he'd spent in that prison. He owed his life to some of them. Some were like brothers. And they'd been taken from him just like that. It was like some nightmare. The reality was hard to comprehend. It was an entirely new world, filled only with pain, hysteria, horror, and disappointment. At that moment Arkenel couldn't remember who he was, why he was there, or what he had hoped to achieve. His dreams and aspirations were distant and soulless; they existed as a parody of himself, as a mockery.

The only real thing was death. And even though he wasn't lying with a sliced neck himself, a stabbing inner pain made him feel as if part of him had been torn off and had died with his friends.

Cold, shaken, and broken, he could only keep staring in the direction of the massacre, but he could no longer focus his gaze on what was there. Satisfied and menacing, Evena appeared before him, grabbed his head under the chin, and picked it up to meet his gaze. She asked him mockingly, "Well? How does the great prince feel now? What's it like when it's your people who are getting slaughtered?"

Arkenel looked at her coldly with little emotion on his face. He didn't think he could say anything to her to hurt her, but he'd try his best anyway. "You'd be smart to just kill me now ... because I won't speak. I won't give you even a shred of the information you want. But if I ever break free, I'll come back here with an army big enough to eradicate your whole damned Vern from the face of the earth. And I'll keep you alive so you'll get to see it all."

Naturally, this statement irritated Evena. She pushed Arkenel to the ground and snarled. "You won't speak? We'll see about that. I haven't even started with you. But firstly, why don't you tell me which one of these ugly freaks was your favourite? I'll chop of their heads and tie them around your neck. I wouldn't want to separate you from your friends after all."

"Maybe it will be a good idea ... That way you can also look at them and remember them when they come back for you," Arkenel replied hoarsely.

Very soon he would stop having the strength even to talk back. This was his end. These dreadful people would just play their cruel games with him for a few days, and then they'd kill him as well.

Apparently Rabolii and his foresight had been right, Arkenel thought. Apparently Rabolii had realised something about his son. He had seen him for what he was—a useless piece of meat—and that was his reason to be rude and reserved towards Arkenel. Perhaps it would have been better if Arkenel had never escaped from Aldur, at least for those who were now lying in their own blood on the ground.

Rabolii was fully devoted to the search for Salina lately. With each passing day, he looked increasingly sick and unhappy. Krumerus was experiencing a double mourning, both for the missing princess and for the stolen potion, so sobbing and weeping sounded throughout the dark night. Ravena was also worried, but she had no right to complain, because that would infuriate Rabolii and he'd feel like she was trying to burden him with her feelings. Instead, she had to comfort him while he was moaning, "Why do the gods punish me and take everything dear I hold? Why! Both my potion and Salina ... Now everyone will see me as a failed parent. I couldn't protect my own child and raise her up to a mature age ... I have never failed before. I've succeeded with whatever I've undertook."

The skulls hanging from the ceiling were grinning at this false statement. Ravena could also argue with that, but she didn't raise the subject. She put her hands on her husband's bony shoulders and began rubbing them gently and talking to him, not knowing on which subject to comfort him first.

"Rab, try to calm down ... Nothing is irreparable. Salina can protect herself. Show her a little trust. She'll be fine, and she'll be back soon."

"No! He will never come back!" the necromancer cried, crossing his arms. "And I will have to feel guilty about that. It's like I didn't care for her! It's like I didn't do everything that could be expected from a father! I raised her as a proper lady. I trained her to use magic and to unleash her potential, but all of this will go unnoticed because she decided to escape from me! I can't believe this."

Ravena would have never imagined that Rabolii would make even this all about him. That was a rare skill. But she decided not to say anything about it. Instead she let him complain, in the hope that while he was doing so he would drop a hint as to why he was so worried or if there was a particular reason he thought Salina was in danger.

The following days were gloomy. It seemed like everyone was living in a nightmare, especially Arkenel. On the one hand, Evena was trying very hard to make him miserable, and on the other, he hadn't had miner's for days. At first, this made Remedor just a bit tired and moody, but later it became torture. He was becoming anxious and paranoid. Any attempts he made to escape became more and more desperate. At some point he somehow managed to kill some of his supervising guards, and instead of trying to run, he charged at the middle of the camp to search for his luggage, where his miner's was. Evena immediately suspected that this was the source of Arkenel's witchy power and commanded that Remedor be kept away from his luggage at all costs.

Things only got worse for Rabolii's son. In a couple more days, either because of lack of energy or stubbornness, he stopped walking. They had to put him in one of the carriages with the luggage, though Evena fully supported the idea of tying him by the legs and dragging him. Valenis didn't agree to this so he'd seem kind-hearted to Salina.

"I'm sick of this disgusting creature." Evena snorted with disdain as she glanced towards Arkenel. "If he throws up again, I'll stop giving him water."

"Well, we do have to deliver him alive to Vern somehow." Valenis sighed. The trip back was dragging, and he couldn't stand it any more. "What's wrong with him anyway? Do you think he's ill?"

"I wouldn't be surprised," Evena answered confidently. "Look at him; he looks like a rat that is spreading the plague. I will pray to Vernara to protect me from his disgusting diseases."

One couldn't hear Evena say one sentence about Arkenel that didn't include the words *disgusting*, *wretched*, and *monster* and such. Valenis shrugged and said, "He'll be easier to interrogate now that he's weak."

"I can't wait." Evena cast Arkenel a gaze full of hunger and bloodthirst.

"I'm glad to see you planning 'peace' so passionately, Valenis," Salina called from behind as she listened to this conversation.

Evena rolled her eyes. She didn't want to witness another cheesy scene between the prince and the captive where he'd tell her how much he wanted peace, which would probably never happen. She let them talk and went towards Arkenel so she could hang over him threateningly like a bird of prey. Seeing him so pale and skinny gave her incredible joy. It seemed that he had lost another five kilos, if the skin stuck to his skeleton could spare so much.

"If you think you're suffering now, you slime, just wait till we get to Vern." Evena was grinning at him like a flycatcher plant. "We rarely torture our prisoners for information, but unfortunately for you I'll be in charge of your interrogation, and I'm willing to make an exception."

Arkenel couldn't focus his gaze. He was trying to understand what he was looking at. Once again he was hallucinating, so what he saw was something with monstrous teeth and horns. He didn't want to communicate with something so grotesque. Actually, he felt so sick that he didn't want to be alive right now, so he decided to invoke his own death and raised one middle finger. Evena screamed and attacked like an angry goose, flapping with her demonic featherless wings and spitting poison, at least according to what Arkenel saw. Unfortunately, a bigger monster overtook her, swallowing her whole, so it was too full to pay attention to Arkenel. It left whilst making grumbling noises.

The world had gone insane. Arkenel wasn't sure why he felt so bad. He'd gone without miner's for days before, but now he couldn't stand on his feet. His wounds hurt him horribly; they were probably beginning to fester. He didn't think of salvation and liberation any more; he just hoped for his own death. He didn't have anything left in this world he wanted to go back to.

After an eternity, everyone finally arrived in Vern. They got to the Crystal Castle, where Krementa acted all wise and formal in front of her soldiers, but as soon as she was alone with Valenis, she bathed him with tears, love, and drama. She was overjoyed to see he had survived all his perils.

"I'm so glad you came home!" she croaked like an excited magpie that had found a piece of bread. "See how well we work together when you listen to me!"

Valenis took a breath, planning to say something shocking which would probably kill all the joy of the moment, but he couldn't delay it. "Mother, I did follow your plan the whole time, but there's something I failed to mention."

"You keep secrets from me?" She immediately became alert and needed to know everything. She insisted on being informed on even the tiniest of issues, and she somehow felt this wouldn't be one.

"Um, yeah ... While I was in Krumerus, I met a girl."

"Valenis, dear!" Krementa exclaimed. "You know if you want to meet girls, you just have to tell me and I'll pick one for you! You don't need to deal with those tramps."

"She's not a tramp. She is the princess of Krumerus. And I married her. And in an unfortunate combination of circumstances, she is one of the captives I brought here," Valenis spat out the terrible truth.

There was a moment of silence that screamed louder than any voice. Only some cheeky crickets outside creaked to create extra drama. The next moment Krementa's voice tore the silence like a whip, demonstrating what demonic roars sounded like in Mortelion's slaughterhouse. "You've done what? How could you even think of this?! Is this some sort of protest against me? Where have I gone wrong with you? What have you done?!"

Valenis bit his lip and prepared to be strong. He hadn't expected anything different. Once he had made the decision, he knew a whole sea of yelling and crying would follow. He said calmly, "No. I married her because I love her."

"You love her, do you?! You don't know what love means! This is unbelievable. What will people say now?! We've been refusing the girl from the Violet clan every year because you weren't ready for marriage and a family. What will we tell her family now?!"

Valenis remembered the person in question. Her teeth were scattered in such a frivolous way as if they were the petals of a flower shaken for a few days by the winds of a vicious storm.

"Mother, just please think about what an opportunity this is," Valenis tried to speak again. "Once I'm married to Rabolii's daughter, we can negotiate for peace and ..."

"Rabolii's daughter." Krementa's eye started twitching. She forced a tragic smile on her face and said through her teeth, "Honey, I don't think you've thought this through."

"On the contrary, I have thought it through very carefully!" Valenis exclaimed fervently. He'd use every possible second to speak because he expected to be interrupted anytime now. "She's the woman for me! She is kind, caring, and fun. We have so much to talk about! And she could be the reason we'll have peace. If I'm married to her, Rabolii will stop attacking us."

"You want to be at peace with these monsters? Their very existence is an insult to Vernara!" Krementa yelled.

"It doesn't matter what they are as long as they keep their distance!" said Valenis emphatically. "Please, just let me do this! I'm sure we can stop the fighting, and then things will be better for both them and us."

Krementa turned her back on him, leaning on a bench all covered with plants. She usually never ran out of arguments; she'd bombard her interlocutor with them endlessly. Valenis wondered for a moment if she'd choked. When she turned, her face had a startlingly calm look, and she just asked, "And does your wife share this opinion? Or is she furious that you have involved her in a military expedition against her own country?"

Valenis was actually glad that he was asked this question.

"She was disappointed with me because she thought I had

married her just to betray her. But if she sees that I'm fulfilling my promises and that I'm sincere, she will forgive me, I'm sure."

"I'll think about it. Meanwhile, I'll deal with that so-called prince you brought me. Do you have any requests on how he should be treated? Will you claim to be his defender as well?" Krementa asked with the same unexpected calmness.

"Um, no," Valenis mumbled. If someone else called him doll face again, he'd start killing people. "Do what you want with him, just not in front of his sister. I don't want her knowing what's happening to him."

"Of course," Krementa replied with an expressionless face.

Valenis had the vague feeling that his mother was holding back from bursting out, and that was unusual for her. Could she have missed him so much that she tried not to scream at him? He felt so grateful that he felt he wanted to make her happy somehow. And, as it happened, he could. A mischievous smile blossomed on his face. He said, "By the way, I have something for you. Do you remember when I told you that Rabolii had completed the vampire potion to revive himself? Well, I managed to steal it from his room."

Krementa turned around, surprised, as Valenis handed her the syringe full of something that resembled blood.

"This is incredible! You've foiled his plans of resurrection. I never wanted to fight him in his full power, and it seems like I won't have to. I love you, sweetheart!" Krementa pulled him in a loving, gentle embrace.

Valenis smiled contentedly and added, "By the way, I know the reason that we took prisoners is to ask for a ransom or an exchange. Mind you, I don't believe Arkenel will be useful in that way. I was left with the impression that Rabolii is not very close with Arkenel. Salina, on the other hand ..."

Perhaps this would be the best thing for her. This way she would be able to return to Krumerus, and later she and Valenis could discuss their future. He hoped she wanted the same, but even if that weren't the case, he preferred to set her free, instead of holding her in Vern and ruining her life.

"Of course, dear," Krementa responded briefly, demonstrating that the conversation was over. Then she stroked her son and said, "I'm so proud of you. Now rest. You deserve it."

Afterwards Valenis proceeded to groom himself and dress up for the first time in a painfully long time with clothes which weren't rags covered with holes. He also put on shoes which weren't leaking. It was kind of nice to be in his room again and to find the piano and all his books exactly as he had left them. On any other day, he would have enjoyed the familiar atmosphere and peace, but at the moment he was too excited to pay attention to it. He wanted some closure to the situation with Salina. If the fighting did stop and if she forgave him, it would be a real miracle, a dream come true, a monumental victory. It was also unbelievable that Krementa had taken the news so well. Yes, she was a bit loud as always, but since the whole thing didn't end with her crying and stating she didn't want to see Valenis again, it meant that it had gone well. The prince trembled with excitement. Maybe he and Salina had a chance ...

Arkenel didn't even know what was happening when his guards dragged him off to somewhere. He wished they'd leave him alone and just let him die. Now he was taken to Krementa's throne room. Everything there was so bright and divine with birds flying around the tall room and waterfalls pouring in the middle of the hall. The throne itself was a bunch of stones covered in thick moss and ivy. On top of all this greenery, Krementa was sitting with a magnificent expression. She could hardly be seen because of all the flowers and plants she wore as clothes. The two guards who supported Arkenel pushed him to the floor. At least the fall was soft, because everywhere there was grass that was regularly mowed and fertilised. Remedor was dizzy and half unconscious, but he could hear Evena's shrill voice, so he knew she was nearby. That's why he made the effort to stand up. He didn't want to be helplessly lying down while that raging woman was there.

"There is the son of the great Rabolii Remedor!" Krementa cried mockingly. "What a weak creature, unable even to stand upright."

Arkenel didn't react. He stared at the ground, his jaw clenched painfully.

"What is happening right now is a court," Krementa announced. She added condescendingly, "If you have enough wit to know what I'm talking about at all. Your race has always been composed of halfwits. But it doesn't matter! You are trialled for crimes against Vernara and her children. Under your command, a detachment of Vernians who were simply sent as an innocent patrol were killed. Besides, you have caused unimaginable and disgusting things to happen to General Evena which not even the gods could forgive you for."

Evena raised her head dramatically with a face of undying bravery despite her perils. Outraged and sympathetic

311

exclamations sounded from the councillors, soldiers, and other generals who were in attendance at the event.

"And as if that weren't enough, you had the audacity to attack your guards after you were captured and create chaos by attempting to escape." Krementa kept talking. "Your deeds are unforgivable and outrageous. That's why you're sentenced to death. Your execution will take place in two days in the morning. May Vernara have mercy on your rotten soul. In the meantime, you'll be interrogated and you'll provide information on Krumerus's intentions. If you don't cause problems and give us information, we will have the mercy of making your last days relatively enjoyable. We will give you food and water, and we will accommodate you in agreeable conditions. But if you refuse to cooperate, you will be treated like the animal you are. I've put General Evena in charge of your interrogation and execution. I think she will best find ways to make you talk. Do you have something you want to say before this court before you are taken away?"

Arkenel clenched his teeth in a hateful grimace then forced a smile on his face and said, "Nice 'court', Majesty. I didn't expect any better from you. Do what you want with me, but I won't tell you a thing. I'm not afraid of pain, and I'm even less afraid of death. May you choke on my blood."

Krementa stared at him in disgust and said, "Just as I thought. Take him away!"

Evena pulled up his chains, but he began to resist and poke her in the eyes, not because he was expecting to make a miraculous escape but simply because he wanted to harm the Vernians as much as possible before they killed him. This only made his situation worse. Evena slammed him on the head and knocked him out. Then she stood up over him with a majestic face and pointed to the guards. "Take this slug to the prison, and place him behind the darkest and prickliest of plants. I'll begin interrogating him as soon as he awakes."

Valenis stood by his mother's throne, and as everyone was gathering around Arkenel, he told her quietly, "Hmm, are we actually executing him? I thought we'd interrogate him for longer than that."

"Actually not," Krementa replied casually. "I don't think Arkenel will tell me anything new after you spied on them and told me so much. But on the other hand, nothing would give me more pleasure than to hurt Rabolii by killing his heir."

Valenis frowned, realising there was something personal

going on here. He had no idea why Krementa would want to hurt Rabolii. He didn't even want to mention that Arkenel wasn't the heir and that his death probably wouldn't affect the necromancer much. He wouldn't want Salina to become the victim of some strange revenge scheme instead.

The so-called "prison" seemed very unusual. Arkenel thought he was hallucinating as he watched a tangle of spiky tree trunks. Most were as thick as his arm and formed a wall without many gaps in it. One of the guards touched the plants, his fingers glowing with brownish energy. This made them disentangle from each other and form a gap large enough for Arkenel to be pushed in. Then the trees once again wrapped around each other. The prisoner was lying on his back, staring into the blue sky above. He had never imagined it would all end like this.

Salina was in a similar enclosure. However, hers was more pleasant and looked like a garden. Birds fluttered and tweeted, and crystal clear streams flowed, but somehow it all failed to raise her mood. She sat down on a stone and reached into her bosom. She took out her wedding amulet and stared at it angrily. She had thought there was one real thing in this world, and it had turned out to be the biggest fraud.

"Uh ... hey ... I came to see how you're feeling," a voice sounded nearby.

Salina looked up indifferently and saw Valenis, who stood by the bushes with a forced, guilty smile.

"I don't know," Salina murmured, looking in the opposite direction.

"Please don't be mad at me! I am the last person in this world who wanted to see you in a cell, and I promise you it will not last long. I told my mother about us," Valenis began chattering.

"Oh no. How are you alive?" Salina exclaimed sarcastically.

"That's the thing. She didn't take it that hard!" Valenis continued talking emphatically. "She even asked what you thought about the whole situation. Perhaps we have a chance!"

Salina stared at him coldly and crossed her arms. She replied, "How can you still make plans?! You surrendered me to the hands of my enemy. How do you expect me to trust you again?"

"I can't blame you if you're angry with me and if you don't want to see me any more." Valenis looked down with a sad expression. "I just want to think that once our countries are at peace and the fighting has stopped, you can appreciate that without our intervention it wouldn't have happened."

Salina raised an eyebrow and answered, "If that time does come, I'll make a decision then."

A smile stretched across Valenis's face. He replied, "In that case, I will do my best to speed up the process, ma'am ... In the meantime, enjoy our birds. They are a rare breed!"

The two of them probably had more things to talk about, but the presence of the guards didn't predispose them to romantic chatter. Valenis found himself going back towards his tower. There was something he'd been wanting to investigate for some time now.

Evena came into Arkenel's cell made of plants to begin the interrogation sessions. He looked as if he were in a deep sleep. She decided to take advantage of this and began binding his wrists to the wall of plants. As she did this, she was plotting on how to hurt him so he'd be in a lot of pain but wouldn't die. She'd need to make the whip work for now. She had it prepared. As she moved and touched her captive, he began to shift. He found himself tied to his prickly jail, some of the spikes protruding only a few inches away from his face.

"Oh, look who's decided to wake up!" Evena said slowly. She buried her fingers in his hair then grasped a few strands and pulled his head back painfully. She stood behind him, threatening and vicious. "It's up to you how we'll do this. You'll either cooperate and get away with a few bruises, or you'll be difficult, so I'll whip you till you have no more skin left. You decide."

"You've already decided. Why are you asking me?" he mumbled. For days he'd known he was a dead man. There was no spark of hope, no dreams of surviving, no memories of a life more pleasant than what was happening to him now. So he was no longer trying to help himself. He wanted everything to end.

"Obviously you want it the hard way. This makes me very happy." Evena grinned and dragged the tip of her knife across her prisoner's neck. "It won't be 'fast and painless', monster. In your last days I'll break all your misunderstood dignity until the last of your humanity has left you. I won't stop hurting you until there's not a single spot on you which I haven't burned and cut. Let's see if your precious Mortelion will help you then! No one will save you from me. OK then! Tell me what sort of evil plot your accursed father is trying to entangle Soleya in?"

"Kiss my ass, Evena," Arkenel snapped at her in a weak voice.

"Wrong answer!" Evena yelled and tore the clothes on his back with her knife, then finished baring his back with her hands. "How many whips can you take before your spine begins to show?"

He didn't answer. His bare skin bristled, anticipating the blow. Evena slid her cold fingers along his spine, feeling all sorts of scars and small wounds scattered along the former prisoner's back. Then she landed the first strike upon her captive. Arkenel clenched his teeth. He would rather bite his own tongue off than make a sound. Evena would triumph at the sight of weakness.

"Is this how you want it to be? Will you not talk?" She shoved her knife into the sleeve of her captive and ripped it as well. "Why are you silent? Do you like pain?"

He continued to grit his teeth without making a sound. Evena finished tearing his top off, which left him naked to the waist. Arkenel clenched his fists and tried to find comfort in the fact that his execution was only two days away. They would be a really long two days.

The whip connected with his flesh again, this strike even more unbearable and shattering than the previous one. Evena continued screaming and whipping him. Arkenel took all of this stoically. He just kept repeating in his mind, *Two days, two days, two days* ... Death would be salvation. After all this pain, failure, and shame, he could be saved from himself.

Evena paused for a moment to rest. The back of her captive was torn in many places, all covered in blood. She wondered if she'd overdone it. Maybe Arkenel wouldn't be able to take everything she had planned for him. The Vernian pulled his head back by the hair and said through her teeth, "Answer me, wretched creature. What is your relationship with Soleya?"

While she was so close to his face, he thought of spitting on her. He realised that he was completely destroyed since he didn't do it. He split his dry lips to answer hoarsely, "We're at war with Soleya."

"Do you take me for a fool?" Evena hissed at him and pulled his hair back as much as she could. "We know about the Soleyan king who defended you. We know he's Rabolii's son."

Arkenel was in another world of pain. The landscape itself was smearing before his eyes. His thoughts were twisted and incoherent like in some strange dream. He wasn't capable of coming up with a decent lie in this state, so he repeated, "We're at war with Soleya."

He didn't say anything more, regardless of the questions

Evena asked. Covered in cold sweat, he couldn't stand the torture any more and lost consciousness, putting an end to the interrogation. In the last seconds before the world went black, the image of Rabolii appeared in front of him. He looked calm and gentle. He had kindness in his eyes and warm smile. At that moment Arkenel felt that his father was proud of him and supported him. This thought was the last spark of light for the young Remedor before he fainted.

Evena was disappointed that her game had ended so abruptly. She slapped her prisoner to try to revive him, but he wasn't coming around. Discontent, she let him lie naked and bloody in the mud. She signalled the earth sorcerer outside. He shifted the plants so that Evena could go out and do something else.

—ɷ—

Rabolii sat in the darkness of his room and propped his forehead on his laced fingers. He felt such heavy despair about everything that was happening to him. He rarely found himself in a situation where he could do nothing. He wished he could simply invade Vern with an army and retrieve his daughter, but he had already lost those resources when he invaded Soleya to rescue his wife. He was too exhausted to lead such an attack, and if he pulled out the rest of his forces, he'd leave the whole of Krumerus vulnerable. The only thing left for him to do was to bark at his enemies like an old, toothless dog. He knew that Salina was probably in the hands of Krementa by now. She was too far to the west for him to continue monitoring through undead birds.

The necromancer started taking papers out with trembling hands and began writing on them with a beautiful script so ornamented that it was sometimes hard to read:

Krementa,

I applaud you for your little plan to send me a spy who'd lead my armies into an ambush. I hope you're pleased and feel proud of yourself. Generally, I'm too busy to deal with such hooliganism on your behalf, but you decided to make this personal.

I know you are keeping my daughter hostage. Maybe I should expect your letters with conditions and blackmail. Or you'll probably just declare her death so you can get some petty revenge, right? I can tell you now that Krumerians are not afraid of death. You will have to be afraid of what will happen to you if you refuse to return my daughter, dead or alive. I don't make empty threats.

In recent years I have been preoccupied with other pursuits than undertaking a serious cmapaign, but if you oppose me on this matter, I will cause myself the inconvenience of burying you in the ground with all your people. I'm sure you can decide what's better for both of us. This is my last warning.

—Master of Krumerus, Supreme Necromancer and Champion of Mortelion, Rabolii Vargnarii Remedor

After writing this terrifying message, the necromancer sent it via an undead raven with orders to take it as far as the border. He didn't know what he was hoping for and realised that the Vernians would probably laugh at him for trying to be scary, but he didn't know what else to do.

Meanwhile, Valenis sat comfortably in his room beside his lamp full of fireflies. He had brought in some ancient books of magic that had been gathering dust in the library, forgotten and unwanted. These were volumes about Mortelion and the death sphere. Now Valenis flipped through them, but not because he was enthusiastic about learning master curses or anything. In fact, he was looking for something very specific. He wanted to know about that picture Salina and everyone in Arkenel's army had on their faces. He didn't know where else to look. These books were the only sources of information about Krumerian culture. He was looking at typical tattoos that sorcerers of death would get, scrolling through lists of old runes, and so on. From time to time he found something that kind of resembled what he'd seen. Valenis narrowed his eyes and studied it thoroughly, wondering if that's what he needed. What Salina had on her face was something written in an archaic alphabet. The letters were made to resemble bones. It was hard recognise a word in a language that he didn't know. Eventually Valenis felt too overburdened by so much new information, so he began to flip though the book lazily and just search for pictures. He was almost asleep when he turned to a page where there was a painted human face with exact the same tattoo on the temple above the right eyebrow. Valenis paused to see what the chapter was about.

"Mortelion is known for the way he causes fear and fatal predestination in his subordinates. He loves it for people to always remember that they aren't eternal and that every day they spend on this land is because of his brief mercy. That's why he marks those for whom life is over, writing the ancient rune of death on their foreheads. Only sorcerers of death are able to notice the so-called 'Sign of Mortelion', the symbol of fatal doom. As soon as the sign appears on someone's face, the person in question surely will..."—Valenis's eyes widened, and a horrendous pain spread throughout his chest as if his heart had exploded. There was a storm in his head—"...will die within days."

Dazed and shocked, he threw the book to the side, stood up, and ran down the stairs. He had only one thought—to go to Salina. He wanted to see that she was still fine, and then he would sit beside her and wouldn't move for the rest of his life. He wouldn't let anyone approach her. Pulsating pain and horror destroyed every sound thought. The only thing he wanted to do was find Salina.

During the night, Arkenel had been trying to set himself free. He managed to chew through the straps around his wrists and then tried biting and scratching the plants. That didn't help. If such a thing were at all possible, he made things worse, because when the plant got tired of him, it started smacking him with its thorny branches. There was no way out of here. Arkenel was lying on the ground face down. He was in too much pain to sleep. The world around him seemed surrealistic. It was very fragrant and green with lush shrubs and flowers, but it was still a hostile, murderous place. It was almost like a beautiful woman with the soul of a demon. Arkenel was trying to prepare himself morally for the last session of torture before he was killed.

The prisoner remained lying on his stomach, his breathing crackly in pain, staring with his only eye in the dark. Suddenly, he heard a silent rustle nearby, followed by the typical gargling of a slaughtered man in whose throat was bubbling blood. Arkenel stood up to see the guard thump dead in front of his cell, if all these weeds could be called a cell. A silhouette knelt by the prisoner, put his hands on the thorny plants, and whispered, "Arkenel! Arkenel, you all right?"

Beaten and miserable, Remedor reached out towards the bars of thorns. He could barely focus his gaze on the face in front of him, but when he did, he made a painful grimace and muttered in a weak voice, "Mavarius, is that really you? What are you doing here?"

"Shut up. I'm getting you out of here. Those freaking bastards, what have they done to you?!"

Mavarius glanced over the bruised, wounded body in front of him. He felt deadly rage and hatred for the damned Vernian beasts for treating his friend this way. The man gritted his teeth angrily and tried to tear or move the stems which blocked the way. Of course, the malicious plant shifted and tried to wrap around the hands that were attacking it.

"Careful with that. It's nasty," Arkenel warned him. "Listen, tosser, you can't get me out of here. I can't even stand."

"Nobody asked you what you think," Mavarius growled. He was trying to think strategically here, but his gaze was once again drawn to his friend's wounds, which made him furious. "Idiots. What have they done to you? ... The great worshippers of life! Filthy stinkers!"

"I saw a sorcerer of earth control the plant," Arkenel noted while Mavarius was combatting the thorny branches.

"Sorcerer, my ass," the other man replied, not giving any signs that he was about to quit.

Arkenel made a painful grimace. He didn't know how to explain to Mavarius that this was a futile rescue mission and that he should get out while he could. But they weren't given a chance to talk more. In front of them appeared someone who was as shocked to see them as they were to see him. It was Valenis, looking pale and panicked, shimmering with cold sweat. He knew they were trying to escape, but at this point he couldn't care less. He tried to continue towards Salina's cell. However, Mavarius didn't interpret things like that. He thought the tosser was rushing to alert the guards, so he grabbed the Vernian by the collar, turned him around, and slammed a fist in his eye. But that wasn't enough. He continued to punch his loathsome enemy in the stomach while growling at him, "Think you're so smart, do you, you freak? Thought you could just walk us in here. You're bloody dead, you hear me?!"

"No, release me. I have to see Salina!" Valenis was pulling away, trying to get to his beloved.

Mavarius punched him in the mouth again. Blood splashed everywhere. Then he pushed him in the bushes and snapped, "You're some stupid sorcerer, aren't you? Open this or I'll break your ugly head."

"I'll do anything. Just let me go," Valenis whimpered.

Mavarius glared at him commandingly with a cold, merciless look in his eyes, holding his sword against the Vernian's neck. Valenis decided to cooperate. It occurred to him that they were too busy escaping, so they would leave him alone. He didn't want to fight them; he had no time for it. He grabbed a hold of one branch of the plant and silently instructed it to open the way. Mavarius reached out, grabbed his friend by the shoulder, and pulled him out, then swung his sword. Valenis chilled from fright, but to his surprise, the Krumerian didn't hit him. Instead he hit one of the thick branches of the plant. It shuddered violently and perked up its thorny branches, grabbing hold of the nearest person to exact its revenge. It wrapped its branches around Valenis like tentacles and began tightening the grip.

"No, no, no, let me go!" the Vernian pleaded desperately.

Mavarius stared at him with burning hatred and slammed another blow on the plant to irritate it further. He replied, "Told you you're dead, you disgusting traitor."

Valenis screamed and used all his strength to try crawling away from the ruthless branches. No commands, no magic, helped him here since he was too panicked to execute them correctly. The grip of the branches became unbearable. The prince's ribs began to crack and dig into his lungs, and it was then that he realised he really was dead. His screams were muffled by the blood flowing from his mouth, which eventually drowned him. To his friend's surprise, Arkenel fell to his knees by the bush and tried to help Valenis. He exclaimed, "Tosser, what about my sister? She's still here. We need this loser to open her cell."

"No way, I can't free the whole prison. You're burden enough already," Mavarius mumbled, annoyed.

Arkenel watched helplessly as Valenis's eyes filled with blood as he was suffocating from the grip of the bush. He tried to talk to him, "Come on, you can free yourself. Think about Salina."

It seemed to be too late. The Vernian lay in the merciless embrace of the plant, broken and dead. Arkenel stood up and pleaded, "Mav, come on. Let's find Salina. We'll look for another way to free her. I can't go without her. Please."

Mavarius watched him with clenched, thin lips, and cold contempt. He cursed his own inherently kind soul on days like these.

"It'd be so much easier to dump you here, you stinker," Mavarius mumbled. He helped Arkenel up and dragged him between the cells to search for Salina.

Walking was hard. Both Krumerians hoped that Salina would be in a better state so she could carry them. After all, the Vernians had been feeding her and giving her water the whole time. Mavarius knew where to look for her. He had found out where everything was before he plucked up the courage to strike.

To their surprise, when they arrived at the cell, there were no guards, and the bushes stood open. A heavy feeling settled in Arkenel's stomach when he noticed that Salina lay in the open enclosure. He stumbled to her and began nudging her. "Sis, wake up! We have to run ... Salina?"

She lay with her eyes closed. Her body was stiff and firm. Mavarius stood behind him with an expressionless face and announced, "Ya, she's dead all right."

Arkenel turned to him with an angry look and snapped, "What? No, she couldn't have just died! The bloody doll face took care of her!"

Mavarius knelt beside Salina and turned her face up. There was a large bloodstain on her dress. Arkenel stared in shock. His dear little sister lay dead on the green forest floor, all covered with flowers and splashes of blood. He refused to believe what he saw. It wasn't possible she'd be killed. She was the loveliest being in this world, so caring and understanding and giving like no one else. Arkenel grasped her and stated firmly, "We have to take her with us."

"Are you nuts?" Mavarius snapped. "How do we just carry a corpse? It weighs and stinks. Everyone will sniff where we are."

"We can't leave her here. We'll get her back to Dad. He'll revive her somehow," Arkenel answered in an upset voice.

"She'll rot by then," Mavarius muttered disconsolately.

"No, don't say that. Help me pick her up." Arkenel was trying lift her, though he was barely standing on his feet.

Some yells and screams sounded nearby. It seemed Valenis had been discovered. Mavarius bit his lip, realising they had run out of time. Without any more bargaining, he grabbed Arkenel, threw him over his shoulder like a bag of potatoes, and carried him away. In times like these he was very happy to be much taller than him since he needed to carry Arkenel so often. Remedor began fighting and protesting, "No, tosser, we can't leave her. Please."

Arkenel continued to struggle helplessly as he watched them move away from Salina. He thought out loud, "Well, they are in Vern. Things like this are probably cured here. The sorcerers ... they'll heal Valenis, and he'll insist that they heal Salina as well."

Mavarius didn't say anything. He would let Arkenel believe that. He had lived in Vern long enough to know that the sorcerers were helpless. Indeed, they were able to prevent death when things seemed hopeless, like in the case of a difficult childbirth or the bite of a poisonous snake. However, they couldn't resurrect the dead. No one really could.

Mavarius knew that it would be like child's play for the Vernians to track and catch them. Arkenel smelled of blood, and the scent could be detected for miles. He didn't know what he was hoping for. For a long time Mavarius had gone without miner's spice. It wasn't a plant native to Vern. He felt that after every passing hour, his body screamed louder for the plant. It was only a matter of time before this need consumed him. Then he didn't know how he would take care of Arkenel. He hoped they'd get to Krumerus before things worsened.

It goes without saying that Krementa became hysterical. Maybe had the situation been different, she would have been a bit concerned that Arkenel had escaped, but now she couldn't care less. As soon as she learned what had happened, she immediately came down to the prison shrubbery, took her son out of the tangled branches, and carried him to the castle. While the heartbroken dwellers of the Crystal Castle were weeping, the sorcerers began to gather and assess the damage. Valenis was dead beyond doubt, his ribs crushed. He had bled out. Vernara's elder priestess, leaning over the young man, examined his injuries and rubbed his chest. She just turned to Krementa with a sympathetic expression and shook her head. The queen burst into tears again and squeezed her boy's hand. At that moment, everything else went out of focus—the escaped Arkenel, the rivalry with Krumerus, and the desire to kill Rabolii. None of these things had any importance compared to Valenis. It was heartbreaking for her to see him like that, blood-soaked, broken, crushed ... His eyes were still wide open in terrible horror, and the gaping emptiness in them was the most tragic thing of all.

"*Leave us alone!*" Krementa yelled at her subordinates.

She couldn't believe it. This was Vernara's country. Life was valued above everything here. And despite that, no one could do anything for the life of the most important person in the country—her son. For the first time, Vern's queen felt helpless in the face of something terrible that she couldn't handle. All her power and magical strength didn't matter. Fate seemed so cruel and unfair. This was her war, her battle with Krumerus, and her sweet young son had become the victim. Everything was so shocking and overwhelming that she could barely make sense of it.

It was at that moment that Krementa realised something. She still had Rabolii's vampiric potion. But for the sceptical Vernian queen this didn't mean "magic revival". Where was the guarantee that this potion would work? And even if it was useful for Rabolii, would she be able to utilise it herself? Did the body of the deceased have to be prepared somehow? Was it all part of a ritual? Krementa pulled out the syringe and stared at it, stopping her sobbing for a moment. Yes, it was a syringe, but did she just have to inject the potion into her son? And what good would it be since Valenis didn't have a pulse? How would the potion spread in his body? She had but one idea. With trembling hands, she opened her son's shirt and laid her fingers on his chest where his dead heart was. She put the tip of the needle on the spot, then pressed the plunger. She injected the potion into his heart, then pressed her ear to Valenis's chest. She had stopped breathing in burning anticipation of hearing a pulse again. Her son's skin was damp and cold, his chest stiff. Nothing was happening; there was no change. For a few minutes Krementa remained motionless like this, expecting something—anything—to happen. However, Valenis remained just as still, just as dead. Once she realised that the potion had not changed anything and that the chance was wasted, she burst into tears again and threw the syringe against the wall. She collapsed next to the bed of her son. She probably wouldn't move from there over the next few days. During that short night, she seemed to have lost everything.

Three Vernian pursuers ran through the forests, guided by the strong smell of blood. It was like another hunt for a wounded animal to them, but it was even easier because this one couldn't even run. Soon they found the one they were looking for. Arkenel was lying on his stomach on the ground covered by thick moss and the roots of a huge tree. He could only look up at them. He struggled getting up on his knees and took a short knife from his belt. He threatened them, "Don't come any closer."

They began grinning at him and walked towards him with mocking faces, as Mavarius came out behind them with a knife in each hand and thrust them into the necks of two of the Vernians. The third man attacked him, and after a short fight, the Krumerian grabbed a hold of his arm, twisted it around his back, and pressed a knife against his neck. He growled, "Is this all of you? Are other people looking for us?"

The Vernian stammered, "We ... it's just the three of us, but Queen Krementa will probably send more people soon. Please don't kill me ... If you let me go, I'll tell Her Majesty that I found Arkenel dead."

"Sure you will," Mavarius replied mercilessly as he cut his throat.

Arkenel looked away, feeling sick from this sight. Slaughter ... he couldn't look at it any more, not after Evena had opened the throat of each of his friends.

Mavarius began undressing the corpses and choosing which garments could be used and which ones would become rags and bandages. As he did that, he began to speak to Arkenel: "OK, we'll get a bit of head start. Listen 'ere: we can't outrun them. But if we wash you and bandage you, I can drag your bloody clothes all over the forest and confuse them as to where we went."

"Man, just forget about it," Arkenel grunted. He was covered with cold sweat, lying in a shapeless pile on the ground like a heap of melting snow. "You can't save me. It'll just slow us down, and they'll catch both of us."

"You think this is fun for me?" Mavarius grunted. "You make it even worse by whining. Here, have some water. Choke on it. I just don't wanna hear your voice."

As he said that, he tossed his friend a sack of water. Arkenel grabbed this treasure and drank it all at once. He couldn't remember the last time he'd had water. It made him feel a little better, but he still didn't believe he could survive this—and he didn't want to.

After Arkenel was watered and bandaged, they headed east. It was only about an hour's time before Mavarius found a hole he liked in the roots of a tree. He knelt to examine the find. He explained hoarsely, "Looks like it used to be a fox den. Large opening, marks of digging. Something's tried getting in here, and it looks abandoned. Maybe you can fit inside. Lemme see."

"What about you?" Arkenel asked huskily.

"No, I have something to do," Mavarius mumbled while he was digging around the entrance. "This oughta do. Get in."

Arkenel found it a bit difficult to get into a tight animal den, but getting captured by Evena was far worse, so he slipped inside. He dropped into an underground pit, the ceiling of which was tall enough for him to sit up and the top of his head brushed the old spiderwebs above him.

"It's unexpectedly wide ... and very nasty. I got entangled in something," commented Arkenel, struggling fiercely with some roots. He'd recently had negative experiences with evil plants and was traumatised.

"All right. Now I'll cover the entrance so that no one finds you. Don't make a sound, especially if you hear noises. I'll bring some useful junk and something to eat," instructed Mavarius like a mother who was leaving her child alone in the house for the first time.

"But what if the tossers find you?" Arkenel voiced his concerns.

"Screw them. They're not that smart," growled Mavarius. "Now get some sleep. You look like crap."

After this exchange of caringness and courtesy, Arkenel was left in the hollow, and Mavarius went to work. There were a lot of objects and tools the latter would need to take which he had hidden elsewhere. After all, he had been in the woods for more than a week and had settled in. He had escaped from the Vernians when he discovered their hidden ambush, but he didn't manage to warn the others in time. Once his friends were captured, he could only monitor things from a distance. During that time he used his own means to survive and collected things left by the group. He had watched what was happening, and he was constantly torn by conflicting impulses. Instinct told him he needed to get away from these hostile lands as soon as possible, but he just couldn't turn his back, not when he saw how the Vernian beasts were slaughtering the other Krumerians and were beating Arkenel. He did want to survive this himself somehow. However leaving his friend behind wasn't the way. When he escaped during Eslir's attack, he did feel restless. He wished he knew what had happened, he wished he had stayed behind. The same feeling would haunt him again if he left Arkenel. They had gone through six years of all kinds of hardship. It had created a bond which held them together.

Meanwhile, Evena and several of her soldiers stood next to Arkenel's empty cell and examined the traces. The general was furious that her evil enemy had escaped, but after the thought settled in, it began to excite her somewhat. She'd get a chance to chase him and capture him. The surrounding fifty metres smelled like him so clearly. The floor of his cell was like an open book that described where he lay, where he strode, and where he bled.

"He definitely had outside help," one of the soldiers noted, waking Evena from her daydreams about manhunts.

"They probably went east to Krumerus. The fugitive is injured. It won't be difficult to catch up with them," replied another.

"Yes, of course," Evena stated boastfully. "We will go east. I can pick up the smell of the little monster from miles away."

It really wasn't difficult. As they came out of the surroundings of the Crystal Castle, the first thing they found were the bodies of the three Vernians. Evena concluded, "He is definitely not alone. The puny creature wasn't even able to stand upright."

She began sniffing the air, trying to detect where the bloody trail was leading. She walked in one direction, following the trail. After a while, they reached a spot where some deep footprints could be seen.

"I don't know if these footprints were left by the fugitives. They were left by only one person," Evena noted. The smell was also slightly different. The bloody tint was still there, but there seemed to be something else.

"Perhaps the wounded one was carried. And why are the tracks are so deep?" said one of the soldiers.

Evena had to agree with his assessment, so they followed the trail. They found a camp with a burning fire. The ground had been cleared as if somebody had slept there. There was also a dead deer missing two legs, one of them having been cooked over the fire.

"They're here somewhere!" Evena hissed like a viper. "They're cooking meat. They'll probably come back for it! Hide!"

The treacherous robin nearby was chirping at them, announcing it had seen people. This made Evena feel only slightly uncomfortable, but she knew that Arkenel was very stupid and definitely didn't know the language of the birds.

The day rolled to an end, twilight fell, and the Vernian

soldiers became drowsy, but Arkenel wasn't returning to the camp. Evena got angry. Was it possible that the damned creature knew she'd be here? On the following morning they kept looking for tracks and found two sets of footprints. They were still apparent, leading towards a swamp. This was unbelievable!

"Filthy pigs! Have they really gone in there?!" Evena was outraged.

"Maybe they did so we'd lose their scent? Let's walk around the swamp and see where the tracks continue," one of the men suggested.

"Damn Krumerians! Profane Arkenel ... putrid creature!" She cursed him and started walking along the swamp. It was muddy everywhere. Slippery frog grass made it hard to see where the water was. Some frogs croaked festively. One made a spectacular jump in front of Evena. This startled the general, and she fell on her behind, spectacularly staining her beautiful green skirt. Her soldiers began to wander around her and wonder how to stand her up and clean her without touching her in the wrong way and offending her. The robins were still chirping loudly as if they were jolting them.

Of course, this whole circus was happening because Mavarius had trampled the region in his spare time and had left misleading tracks to trick the Vernians. He was about five kilometres south and carried all sorts of useful things. As soon as he swept the leaves from the entrance of the hollow, Arkenel immediately popped out of the opening and began to chide him: "Where were you, you dumb ass? You've been gone for two weeks. I was sure the freaks had caught you!"

"That's what you're best at. Come out. I've gotta treat your wounds because you're a wimp."

Arkenel looked around like a timid doe and muttered, "What about the tossers?"

"They are elsewhere now. Don't worry. I brought you food. Eat this crap slowly because it's an old stag. The meat is chewy, and your stomach is thin."

Arkenel didn't seem to listen. As soon as he was given the meat, he started gnawing on it like a starved dog. While he was eating, Mavarius sat beside him and began treating his wounded back. This was such an idyll for him! Living in the woods was so liberating and relaxing. It would have been perfect, but two things spoiled everything: (1) the crazy Vernians and (2) lack of miner's spice. Mavarius felt on the brink of his strength. He couldn't imagine he'd need to keep caring for Arkenel, carrying all the luggage, and walking for miles every day. He had no strength for it, and it felt like he would fall apart at any moment.

"You're walking by yourself today, mate," Mavarius announced. "I slaughtered two idiots today and took their clothes and shoes. If we keep changing every day, we won't smell like ourselves. This should warm you. It's wool."

"Yes, finally!" Arkenel took with gratitude a green sweater ornamented with pink flowers and blue feathers.

As soon as he put it on, Mavarius scanned him with an ironic gaze, raised eyebrows, and a curly smile. It was funny to see his buddy dressed like that, so he waved a hand and told him, "Nah, changed my mind. Take it off."

Arkenel slapped him with the gnawed stag bone in response. The two of them engaged in a fight and rolled in the grass, but that lasted only a few seconds.

"Crap, my wounds ..."

"Damn, my bones ..."

"I think I'm going to throw up ..."

The two men fell on their backs and stared at the crowns of the trees above them. Arkenel was still wearing the outrageous sweater.

"Everything hurts me," Remedor noted.

"I'm feeling sick."

"Me too."

"Why are we alive?"

The two of them exchanged glances. They were hardly functioning, against their own will. Everything seemed like a futile effort, prolonging the time until the inevitable happened. And every second they spent without miner's was simply torture. Mavarius rose first, announcing, "We'll have to die later. Go get out your junk. Let's go while those idiots are still in the swamp."

"Swamp?"

"Yeah. I'll tell you on the way."

Meanwhile, Krementa continued to cry over her son's body. She squeezed his cold hand and cursed the whole world. The room was gloomy. Clouds were swirling as if nature itself was suffering. The queen felt like she was losing her mind, and everything seemed surreal in its darkness. That's why she was mighty startled and jumped back when her son's fist suddenly clenched. Krementa stepped forward again and knelt on the floor with a shocked expression, batting her wet eyelashes. She stared at her son's motionless body. Had he really just moved, or was she going crazy? Not a single muscle twitched on his face, but his overall expression began to change. His wide-open eyes lost their look of surprise. It was replaced by a painful expression from the rough awakening. His lips, smeared with dried blood, broke open as he took a deep breath. The teeth shone in his mouth, and they appeared much longer than they were just hours ago. Apart from the expression, something else had changed in his eyes. Their purple colour backed away and gave way to a dark, bloody red. He was breathing again. His heart was beating again. But was he still Valenis after everything he had been through?

CHAPTER 13

DESPERATION

Have you ever faced a very important but somewhat overpowering task? In a moment like this, you may know how urgently you should do it, but for some reason you just don't start? Well, that was exactly how the exiled Soleyan king felt. Ilinar was sitting in the library and was lazily flipping through some volumes of Emanrylii Prehorian as if they'd speak to him and tell him how to return his throne. In fact, he wasn't even thinking about that. He was stroking the cover of the volume with one finger and remembering an almost identical book he had in Soleya. Eley had given it to him for his fifteenth birthday. It was a happy day. His teacher was in an unusually good mood. After the festivities, the two of them had gone into the wilderness to ride horses. Ilinar, still unable to believe that these times were hopelessly lost, cursed himself. Killing Eley hadn't helped anyone. He felt his hands constantly wet and sticky from his blood. It was a feeling that never seemed to go away.

At that moment the doors of the library opened loudly and an unusual company entered. Ilinar shot a glance towards the newcomers, and for a moment he forgot his thoughts. The only person he recognised was Ravena. Behind her were strange Krumerians with long mantles and hoods almost covering their faces. The Soleyan blinked, puzzled, as the necromancer's wife presented the strangers. "Hello, Ilinar. These are Mortelion's cultists who have been visiting us in the castle for the last few days. They have learned of your perils and have expressed a desire to help you with the return of your throne. I'll leave you alone to discuss their plans."

After saying that, Ravena just left. She was busy. She had to wipe away Rabolii's tears, since he couldn't get over the losses in his life, as well as be responsible for everything that was happening in the country. Ilinar gave her a pleading glance as if silently telling her not to leave him alone with these strangers. He didn't know how cultists would help him anyway. To his surprise, only one of the cloaked figures came into the room. She sat down at the table beside him and removed her hood. This was Halena with her usual mournful expression and abundant black make-up around her eyes.

"Ilinar, is it not?" she said in a voice that sounded somewhat weak as if she were trying to speak despite some serious illness. "We've heard a lot about you. It is a pleasure to finally meet you."

He stared at her suspiciously, still unable to understand what this meeting was about. He answered hesitantly, "Yes ... hard times."

"I spoke to Lord Remedor about you. He thinks that if you regain your throne, you will be of great benefit to the continent's peace," said Halena.

Ilinar sighed and looked at the table. He replied, "I ... I have no idea how I could get my throne back."

Halena smiled at him, still seeming cheerless. She said, "Soleya will soon realise it can't protect itself from Krumerus the way you can protect it. All you have to do is prove to your people that you still have the best intentions and that you can shield them from the monsters. We can help you make that impression."

Ilinar looked at her frowningly, unable to understand where this was going. He noted, "I can't protect anyone better than the whole united Soleyan and Aslanian army."

Halena stood up gracefully and began to walk around the table, gently brushing its surface with the tips of her fingers. Her footsteps were as quiet as those of a ghost. She started talking, "You have something much more precious, Ilinar. While you're here, you have information that your army has no way of getting. You can be a hero." She stood beside him, staring at him with her big blue eyes. "There's something specific you can do to protect Soleya. Have you heard of a demon named Stronius?"

Ilinar shook his head. The only demons he knew of were from the pages of the books of his favourite author, but he didn't know how true they were. He said, "What do I have to do?"

"The demon Stronius leaves his hiding place every few centuries to feast upon the souls of men," Halena said softly, her voice almost a whisper. "When he comes out, he can cause ruin and desolation few of us can imagine, and it can last for years. The demon doesn't choose his victims, and the only reason to attack foreigners is that we have weapons to fight him and we know his weaknesses. If we teach you how to defeat the monster in front of your terrified countrymen, they'll see your worth."

That plan sounded odd for several reasons. Ilinar immediately began shooting questions: "If something like happens only once every century, why haven't I ever come across records that describe it?"

"Stronius likes to raid countries other than Soleya. Most recently, he attacked Vern. I don't know when he was in your land. Do you really think you'd just find literature about attacks on some villages on the outskirts five hundred years ago or more?" Halena said softly.

"OK, supposing you're right." Ilinar continued, "I think it would be irresponsible on my part just to take some weapons from you and go fight the demon by myself. I'm not a great fighter, and if I'm defeated, my country will not be warned about this crisis and innocent people will suffer. We'll have to get in touch with people in control, arm soldiers, devise some plan …"

Halena halted Ilinar's rant as she approached him and put her ghostly white hand on his shoulder, staring at him insistently. She said to him, "You think they'll believe you? They will scoff at your warning and declare you a liar. If we send you or Krumerians to bring them weapons, they will probably attack. I understand you're afraid of failure, Ilinar, but you have not failed until now. You have succeeded in protecting your country from the Vernians, you've protected us from the Aslanian army, and you managed to take revenge on that traitor who tried to defame you. You will be able to get your throne back, I'm sure of it. Do you know why? Because the weakness of Stronius is shown when he sees someone stand up to him with immense bravery. Everybody usually flees in horror when they see him, but if you stand your ground, if you look at him in the eyes, it will confuse him enough that you'll have an opportunity to strike. You don't need an army. You'll succeed, and you'll be praised as a saviour by your people.

Ilinar stared at her without blinking. He felt strange that her hand was just resting on his shoulder. He was used to being a prince, with no one daring to touch him, so this was something new. He could only look at her whitish lips and her big bright eyes, realising that in his entire palace full of courtiers and noblewomen, he had never seen anyone with such a beautiful face. He felt dazed as he asked, "Do you think I'm really capable? That I can confront Stronius and defeat him? That I can win the love of my people?"

Halena smiled again. She slid her hand over his shoulder then stepped away and replied, "Winning someone's love should come easy to you. I'll help you. We'll organise everything together. Just trust me. I believe we are capable of achieving the peace that we both want."

Ilinar stared at her for a few seconds, then tilted his head down, embarrassed, and spat, "Oh ... yes ... of course. Tell me what to do."

Halena chuckled. She sat down next to Ilinar again and began describing her plan in detail. She seemed to be well informed of where the beast was going to attack, where he might be intercepted, and how everything should happen to allow more people to witness Ilinar's feat. He still felt a little uncomfortable that he was taking advantage of such a cataclysm to make himself a saviour, but he thought he was doing the smart thing. After all, he would create peace between Krumerus and Soleya. Such a great achievement would be worth the price.

—∿—

Evena was examining some footprints. They seemed suspicious. The search for Arkenel had become a farce. Capturing a wounded Krumerian who couldn't even walk by himself was supposed to be so easy, but they had not even gotten close to finding him.

"He has not gone from here!" Evena barked. "The smell isn't exactly the same!"

"With all due respect, General, it's not possible even for us to be sure of the smell of a man who may have gone through here days ago," replied one of the soldiers.

"To you, maybe not! But this is Arkenel, a man who has left me never-healing wounds! I can smell him from miles way! His stench is stuck to the insides of my nostrils!" Evena snapped. "And this"—she waved her hand towards the tracks—"is a mockery! I have the feeling that someone deliberately trampled all over the woods in the most incredible places so we'd follow the trail and end up in the filthiest swamps and thorny bushes."

"We have no better track to follow." One of the men shrugged.

"This is ridiculous!" she continued to complain.

She wandered off somewhere, but she stumbled and tipped over like a drunk. The soldiers immediately supported her on both sides and stared at her with a concerned and questioning look. Evena snapped at them, "I'm a little dazed. Big deal! It's just my time of the month, nothing shocking."

"Do you want to stop and rest, General?" a Vernian asked.

"No! Arkenel isn't resting!" Evena dropped this severely inaccurate statement, which was absolutely false for twenty-two hours of the day and night.

Brave and independent, she continued to stumble around as if someone had hit her on the head, when suddenly her foot found itself in a snare. The rope tightened and pulled the woman into the air, and she hung upside down from a tree.

"General!" the soldiers screamed, dashing around.

"Get me down from here *immediately*!" Evena screamed, jerking around in the air.

The general was hanging about five metres above the ground. The tree to which her rope was bound didn't have any low branches to aid climbing. In fact, as the men inspected the tree, it seemed like all low branches had been chopped off recently. The resin was still sticky. How unfortunate! Actually, the very same branches were burning in Mavarius's campfire. The pine always burned so well exactly because of the resin. Keeping a fire lit wasn't a good idea in general when you were trying to remain unnoticed, but now the two Krumerians had settled in a cave around which there was enough greenery to conceal the smoke. Arkenel was lying wrapped in a stolen blanket and looked very comfortable. Even though he knew he was being pursued by a mad Vernian and was in enemy territory, he felt safe. Most of his wounds were soaked in pine resin diluted with water. It was a very strange cure. Sometimes Arkenel thought that Mavarius simply collected random things around the forest and used them for his purposes without really having an idea what would help and what wouldn't. In fact, today's dinner was an example of this. Remedor's companion sat next to him and steered some weeds into a pan over the fire. They were leaves of acacia. They had not encountered any fruits or animals they could gather or capture, so this was what they were left with.

"I think I'm going to turn into a cow if I eat grass for another few days," commented Arkenel, who was obviously in a good enough mood to crack jokes.

"Start mooing then," growled Mavarius. "Arriving to Kranium alive would be a miracle by itself."

Arkenel snuggled into his blanket. Perhaps the worst had passed. The symptoms of his abstinence were fading, and it wasn't the same nightmare of hallucinations it had been a week ago. But even though his suffering wasn't so intense, he still felt crushed by everything that had happened. He muttered, "I don't know if I wanna go back to Kranium."

"We can go somewhere else," Mavarius immediately suggested. He wasn't eager to see Rabolii anyway.

"I don't know if I want to be seen by people any more. It would have been best if I had died," Arkenel stated with pain in his tone.

Mavarius shot him a piercing glance, not giving away any sympathy, worry, or other shameful emotion, and replied, "The heck's wrong with you?"

"What do you mean, 'the heck's wrong with me'? Didn't you see what I've done over these last few days?" Arkenel cried desperately.

"I dunno what you're whining about," Mavarius replied dismissively.

"You know very well. I mean the whole mission. Those people were our brothers, Mav. I promised them a ton of stuff. I told them that they'd rise in society, that they'd be respected warriors with trophies and properties, and that we'd have a place under the sun, and look where I brought them! ... Look what I allowed to happen to my sister." Arkenel bit his lip and sat by the fire, clutching the blanket as a shield against all the evils of the world. "Aveus told me hundreds of times that he wanted to return to his family, and he died without having seen them for the last time or knowing how they were ... We left all our plans and ideas in Kranium. Our diagrams for the renovation of the forge and the sketches for our armour are still there ... We still have that money there which we gathered. We just accomplished nothing. We were getting drunk every day and said we'd start tomorrow. And now I'll return to all these things, but there'll be no 'tomorrow'. What can I do with myself after all this?! How can I face Rabolii and tell him that Salina is dead?! How will my family accept me? They'll just tell themselves that there never was a chance for me to do any better and that they don't know why anyone expected anything else from a drugged drunk like me."

Mavarius was staring at the fire in silence. He knew that

Rabolii would really react just as dramatically as Arkenel expected, but he seemed to be incapable of caring. He bit off a piece of dried deer that he had been carrying around for a few days and noted as he chewed with an open mouth, "Pff, big deal, Arkenel! Those weren't our brothers. Sure, it's a shame about Graz and Salina, but you wouldn't have been able to turn that scum into an army. They just followed you because you gave them the odd coin and booze. Rabolii can be mad about your sister all he wants, but it was he who sent us on this dumb mission. He could have looked where he was sending us, but he stuck us into an ambush. The mighty necromancer!"

"He knew exactly as much about this as we did, even less. I can't blame him ... I should have done more. I should have been more careful," muttered Arkenel.

"You survived. That's enough," Mavarius stated.

"Because of you! Again! I'm such a failure on my own ... Because of me, my friends and my sister are dead."

Mavarius shifted his eyes away nervously and stared into the darkness. He wanted for Arkenel to stop whining, and he felt utterly helpless to meet his emotional needs. He couldn't tell him that everything was fine because it wasn't, or that everything would be fine because it wouldn't. Eventually he just blurted out, "Come on. Big deal. There are more tossers in Aldur. If you miss them, you'll get some more from there. We can't cry about this forever. And screw Rabolii. Since it's just us, we can tell him what we want. Let's play dumb and say Salina wasn't with us. She hadn't told the geezer where she was going."

Arkenel raised an innocent glance at his companion and blinked. He replied, "I can't lie to him. I have to tell him what happened and to endure any punishments he subjects me to."

"You've suffered enough. Come on, get your strength back. We've got a couple more days till we're in Krumerus, and then we'll do what we want."

"No, we can't. My father sent me on this mission. I must go back and tell him what happened ... that Valenis was a traitor," Arkenel began to protest.

"Why do you care about Rabolii?!" Mavarius raised his hands in annoyance, asking the legendary question that had been bothering him for years.

Arkenel paused. He wasn't sure why he was so desperate for Rabolii's approval. Somehow it seemed to determine his own level of self-esteem, and right now, when he was completely destroyed, he would do anything for his father's love. He knew he had a better chance of achieving this ultimate goal if he stood up like a man and admit what had happened. He didn't know whether he deserved forgiveness or understanding, but if he did receive these things from Rabolii, maybe he'd manage to come to terms with what happened. He snuggled into his blanket and tried to get some sleep.

Evena would be fuming if she could see how comfortable he looked. In fact, she was feeling terrible at the moment. Once she was finally taken down from the tree, trying to get some rest in the evening, she felt sick. She sat all pale by the fire and didn't want to touch any food because she felt like she would vomit. The men walked around her with anxious faces and asked her, "General, are you well? Do you not like the food?"

Evena felt annoyed that they were talking to her, so she stood up and walked away to the bushes with an angry gait and yelled, "If you'll excuse me!"

The men exchanged glances. One said under his breath, "I told you a dozen times not to put in so much salt. Now she'll pout and refuse to eat."

Evena's problems weren't remotely connected to this. She squatted behind some shrubs and took off her underwear. She had prepared bandages to clean herself, but she was surprised she had still not bled. It had been too long now! At that moment she suddenly felt very sick and began vomiting unnecessarily loudly and hysterically. She began crying. She was struck by a terrifying insight. She would give everything for this not to be true, but all the signs were present: she was pregnant.

The whole of Vern was bathed in sunshine. Rose petals poured from the sky as everyone celebrated the triumph of life. The news that Valenis had been murdered by evil creatures and then revived by Vernara herself flew across the land like a flock of birds and spread incredibly fast. People were flowing in from all over to the Crystal Castle to see the wonder with their own eyes and to bring gifts to the precious prince. Valenis had always been a little mystery to the entire country of Vern. It was known that Krementa had a wonderful boy, but few people had seen him. This didn't change after these events. No matter how many celebrations, festivities, and merriment there was,

Valenis was the one person who didn't attend. He was the most miserable person in the country.

"Valenis ... Valenis, sweetie, how are you feeling? Do you need anything?" Krementa was looming over him, stroking his hair, and looking at him lovingly.

So far the prince hadn't had the strength to say anything. His broken throat was slowly recovering, and every attempt to speak was painful. Something in his chest tore him apart. But despite his sufferings, he opened his mouth again and barely said his words under Krementa's anticipating glance: "How ... how is Salina?"

That instantly wiped the queen's smile away. Her lips became thin with discontent, then she made a compassionate expression and said softly, "My treasure, I don't want you to think about that now, so you can just ..."

Valenis widened his nostrils and gave his mother a stern, demanding look, demonstrating that he didn't want to talk about anything other than Salina at the moment. Krementa was stunned. It annoyed her that this ungrateful boy wouldn't even ask how she was and how she'd felt while she was holding her dead son in her arms. She tried to answer as calmly as possible, "Darling, I don't want you getting upset, but ... she's dead."

Valenis gasped in shock. He tried to get up, but the pain in his chest tore him again, and he was forced to stay in bed. Pain and suffering spread across his face as he exclaimed, "But how? ... Why?"

"No one saw what happened; the guards in the whole shrubbery bed were slaughtered," Krementa replied compassionately. "We can only guess what happened. There is one possibility." Valenis looked at her expectantly. His mother sighed and finally replied, "Whoever freed Arkenel probably killed her, maybe at his command."

"That isn't possible!" Valenis groaned painfully and buried his fingers in his hair. "Arkenel is her brother. He wouldn't do it."

"I have no idea, sweetheart." Krementa shrugged.

Valenis felt his eyes fill up and grimaced as he clutched the tangled clusters of hair in his hand. He responded angrily, his voice trembling, "And why?!"

"I can only guess. Maybe they went to free her as well, but she didn't want to leave you? Maybe they were worried about the things she said to us while we were questioning her? Maybe they were angry at the fact that she was married to the 'enemy'? Or Arkenel, the less favoured son, thought it convenient to get rid of a sibling and blame the Vernians."

"He wouldn't!" Valenis cried.

Krementa sat on his bed with a compassionate expression and pulled him into a comforting embrace. She began to speak to him, "Darling, I don't know why they decided to do this either. But there's no one else who could have done it. I know it's horrible, killing their own princess. But they're not people like us. They don't think in the same way."

Valenis shifted uncomfortably and said hoarsely, "Mother, I'm a pure-blooded vampire now. My blood is the same as Rabolii's potion. We could ..."

For a moment that hope flickered in his chest, but Krementa was quick to eradicate it. "Darling, we burned her body a few hours after her death."

Valenis was shocked by this answer. Why hadn't anyone waited? Especially Krementa, who knew she was reviving her son with vampire blood. It was well known that the magic of life stopped corpses from rotting. They could have kept Salina intact for a while. Valenis felt a burning anger, realising that she could have been saved but that his mother just hadn't made the effort. He wanted to chase her out and tell her to leave him alone, but instead, even more people started to invade his space in this personal tragedy. Someone began banging on the door and shouting, "I have an important letter for Queen Krementa!"

"Can't it wait?!" the woman yelled impatiently in a very different tone from the one she'd been using to speak velvet words to her son two seconds ago.

"It's an urgent matter, from Eslir Falnir, King of Aslania," added the voice.

Krementa frowned and told the servant to come in. She wondered what had happened that made the Aslanian king write to her. She took the letter and tore the envelope with trembling hands. The expression on her face froze. She shrugged nervously. "I don't know what he's talking about! I never ordered for Soleya's border to be attacked! There must be a mistake. And why is he writing to me on behalf of Soleya anyway? I don't have time for such nonsense." She turned to the messenger and gestured impatiently. "Write him a reply in which we apologise for the inconvenience and tell him I'm not hostile. Right now finishing off Rabolii would be enough for me."

Then she returned to her blessed son and began shoving a

basket of fruit at him. "You haven't eaten for days, treasure. Take something!"

Valenis looked at her as if he were poisoned. He was wondering whether to blame her for not preserving Salina, but then he thought there was no point. Krementa would probably tell him Salina was the last thing on her mind. That wasn't difficult to imagine. She probably didn't think about anything other than Valenis. He sighed, forcing himself to answer normally, and stated, "I don't feel like eating this."

Krementa crossed her arms adamantly and said, "Sure, I know what you want to eat. Now you're a 'vampire', aren't you? But how do you want me to explain to the people if you start walking the streets and drinking blood? I'm convinced that something else will still sate your hunger. Now take an apple."

Valenis snapped angrily, "I told you I don't want it! Just leave me alone."

Krementa was shocked by such an answer. How dare he talk to her like that? She threw the basket of fruits demonstratively. They rolled across the entire floor. She yelled, "How dare you snap at me after all you put me through? These last days for me were a nightmare while I was wondering what would happen to you. Do you think you're suffering? All for a girl you knew for a month? How do you imagine I felt? You're my son. I raised you with all my love since you were a helpless little baby! All that I've ever done was for you. And after you put me through such indescribable stress, you dare snap at me and refuse to eat? Do you not care about your own mother and how she feels?"

Valenis began to shrink like a threatened cat that was crouching lower and clinging to the ground. He didn't know how to react when Krementa yelled at him that way. He just wanted to make peace and end the tirade. His mother shoved an apple in his face again, and he took it hesitantly. For the first time in his life, he felt a devastating force inside him, which screamed that eating an apple was a terrible idea and was just as mad as chewing moss. But the implacable look on Krementa's face forced him to take a bite of the apple. As soon as he began to chew, he realised that he hadn't eaten anything worse in his life. It tasted like tree bark, or at least how he had imagined it would taste. He tried to swallow, but he choked on it and began vomiting. Krementa gestured with annoyance and called a maid in to clean up the mess. She knew nothing about the vampires. How could it occur to her that their digestive systems couldn't process anything other than blood, and that giving a vampire solid food was just like poisoning him? Valenis wiped his mouth with a miserable expression and wondered which god was punishing him. As if it weren't enough that he had lost Salina, he'd also been turned into a monster. If he had the choice, he would have told Krementa not to revive him, but alas. Nothing ever happened the way he wanted it.

A mood of tragedy and mourning had settled over Kranium. No one dared to speak loudly or laugh; the whole city was whispering. No one stepped anywhere near Rabolii's chambers. People knew he had some outbursts and involuntarily emitted deathly energy which killed anyone nearby. Rabolii was sitting at his desk, looking so old, defeated, and miserable that he could break one's heart. When he saw a few green pigeons outside the window, a heavy feeling dropped in his chest. The long-awaited response had arrived, and the necromancer somehow felt he would get bad news. With trembling hands he took the letter from the dove and unfolded it. His eyes slid across the rows:

Rabolii Remedor,

How humorous it is for me to get such a letter with ridiculous threats and pathetic ultimatums! I see you have fallen so low, and you haven't even a fraction of your former boldness and strength since you've resorted to chiding me via letters.

I don't know what spy you speak of. However, I am aware of the fact that an army of your wretched men shamefully clashed with my troops and was defeated. I captured your son and daughter and held them for questioning. I think the girl had some common sense and was ready to cooperate. Unfortunately, your son turned out to be just as mentally unstable and disturbed as you, so he found a way to free himself a few days ago, and on his way out he killed his sister.

I don't understand your strange Krumerian relationships; I don't wish to learn more about them. We honoured the girl with a funeral. You know that traditionally we return our dead to the ground, but we were unsure whether your putrid race spreads diseases, so we burned her first. Do you want me to send you her ashes?

I have nothing more to say. I just want to address the way you speak to me, you helpless, cowardly man. I don't want you to forget that nearly three decades ago we had the chance to establish a much different relationship for our countries, and you are the culprit for the failure of that prospect. Now your threats change nothing. I hold your very existence in the palm of my hand, and the day will come when you'll feel all my wrath.

Enjoy your pitiful existence while you can.

Queen of Vern and daughter of Vernara, Krementa

Rabolii tore the letter angrily and smashed his fists on his desk. Nothing in that answer surprised him, except that it was Arkenel who had killed Salina. The necromancer believed he knew perfectly well why—because his son was fighting for power and had decided to eradicate his siblings at a convenient moment. And it would seem that things were irreparable because Krementa had burned the girl's body, so he couldn't revive her with potions like he had done for himself. Also, he couldn't get over the tone of this letter. He burned with anger and spite. Memories raced in his mind of the man he was twenty years ago. He had so much magical energy at his disposal; he was always so energetic and commanded his elements with extraordinary ease. The whole world was trembling at his feet; he was divine in the eyes of both his people and his enemies. All that power had been taken away from him now. If he could only be himself again just for a day, he would do so much. He felt robbed. Something so personal had been taken from him that he couldn't rest from anger. His very essence had been taken away, so he was turned into something that he wasn't. He didn't consider it to be just the result of reckless decisions, greed, and mistakes. No, instead he was furious at the whole world, for now he was so weak, so helpless. The feeling that he was no longer in charge of what was happening across the continent drove him insane. The bitterness of the whole situation poisoned him, burned in his veins, and boiled in his head, causing his heart to explode with anger again and again.

Usually when these thoughts grew heavy and melancholy brought him down, Rabolii would simply surrender to a silent depression. He'd hide away in his chambers and wail over his unfair life. But this time it was different. Now he felt robbed once again—his dreams for a better future were trampled, Salina was dead. And all this was decorated by Krementa's mocking grin. She dared to make fun of him; she treated him like a worm. Rabolii would stand it no longer. All his anger, all his bitterness, erupted like a volcano. With all his aggression and hatred, he blasted away the doors of his chambers. Enormous and heavy, they crashed down under the pressure of his destructive force field and fell to the ground. The necromancer walked over them and went outside, leaving behind a smoky trail on the floor. He was done being passive. He hadn't shown Krementa a fraction of what he was capable of. No, now he would unleash all his hatred, all his anger, and drown the continent in blood. He would become a monster, a nightmare, and feed on the deaths of hundreds, eventually venturing into the centre of Vern and personally driving a knife though Krementa's heart.

Evena was miserable and irritable. The only thing she eagerly did was argue with the soldiers and complain about everything they did. They still thought it was just because it was "that time of the month", but they began to wonder if she could be so hysterical just because of that.

"The tracks disappear here," said one of the men.

"Yes, the tracks that were not even left by Arkenel and which we follow, God knows why!" Evena snorted.

The men examined another vague mark on the ground left by Mavarius just to confuse them. One of them turned to Evena and asked her, "General, what should we do now?"

"What should we do?" she yelled like a mystic beast. "Can't you decide on one thing without asking me nonsense? Who raised you as trackers? Did you grow up in Soleya where no one has gone hunting once and therefore you can't follow any tracks? Why do I always get stuck with the most incompetent idiots?! I'm sick of you!"

Then she turned around and began crying. The soldiers exchanged glances. They couldn't understand this behaviour. She had never been like this before! They stepped closer to her, cautiously, like she was a dangerous beast. One of them asked her gently, "General Evena ... is everything OK?"

"No. Leave me alone!" she cried, continuing to turn her back towards them.

"Something seems to be bothering you."

Evena wiped her eyes, took a breath with a look of despair, and yelled, "Yes! I'm bothered by the fact that my worst nightmare has become reality. I'm pregnant ... by Arkenel."

This news caused gasps and disbelief. It was really a shocking statement, especially because, according to Vernara's laws, people who have conceived a child together should get married by all means. Otherwise it would be very shameful and disgraceful for both of them and the child. The soldiers knew this. One of them said, "But if your child is his, you must marry him!"

"No," Evena stated. "If Arkenel dies before my child is born, Vernara will still bless me and allow me to live as a single mother or raise the baby with another man. But if it's born first, I will no longer have the right to deprive it of a parent. So we have to find Arkenel quickly."

Nine months somehow seemed like plenty of time to catch up with a wounded Krumerian. The men shrugged and continued the search, while Evena occasionally burst into tears.

Valenis sat in front of his piano and tapped one of the keys. He thought that after he'd been separated from his favourite activity for so long, he would play all day, but now this somewhat repulsed him. Before he left, he had started reading a book which seemed so intriguing that he couldn't put it down. The book in question now lay open just a few metres away. Valenis felt rage as soon as he looked at the picture on the cover. People embracing each other. It was more than obvious how this book would end. The protagonist couple would appreciate each other, overcome all obstacles along the way to happiness, and begin a life together. Like there was a grain of truth to such stories. Suddenly, Valenis felt like reading a book in which days after the wedding, the woman was killed by her disgusting brother. That would bring a much more realistic feel to the story. At least he wouldn't be so alone in his suffering. He still felt that the very fact he was alive was a terrible misunderstanding. He was no longer Valenis. His teeth were changed, causing him some discomfort in his mouth, which he was aware of at every moment. His fingernails grew every passing minute. They were sharp, thick, and ugly, so his only occupation was to file them all the time. Overall his body felt much lighter for some reason. He felt as if he wasn't walking but floating instead. Also, he was starving.

"Sweetie, I brought you dinner!" Krementa popped her head

into his room. A servant next to her held a large dish with roasted hare and potatoes.

Valenis wrinkled his nose because of the smell. It was too intrusive and somewhat nasty.

"I can't eat that," Valenis said.

"You must eat *something*! You used to love hare before. Why don't you at least try it? I can't feed you ... you-know-what," Krementa exclaimed trying not to give away anything in front of the servants.

"You should have thought about that before you injected me with this damned poison!" Valenis bared his elongated canine teeth, which flashed ominously.

Krementa looked at him sympathetically. It was hard for her to see her sweet boy changed and tainted by evil, but she could only be grateful to Vernara that at least he was still alive. She said, "Well, then I'll just leave this here. You can have it later."

Valenis clenched his teeth. He would rather starve to death than humiliate himself by eating this carcass. Krementa left his room, and once again he stared at the piano keys with a blank expression. He wished he had the power to trade his own life for Salina's. Surely she would find a way to exist happily in the form of a vampire, but he couldn't do it. Since she was gone, he didn't see the purpose of his own life.

Devastated by his suffering, Valenis spent all evening engrossed in dark thoughts. He had yet to discover that when vampires spend some time without eating, they become lethargic and have no energy for anything. Well, he felt that way now. He was almost asleep when he suddenly sensed a tantalising smell. He stood up as if hypnotised, and without realising it, he floated weightless in the direction of smell. He barely touched the floor as he walked through a dark corridor illuminated only by the firefly torches. He went in the direction of a terrace where he could hear voices: "Mommy, it hurts so much!"

"I told you not to climb! You're always covered in bruises. Get up now. We'll go to Grandma, and she'll put a bandage on this."

Valenis towered over a woman, probably a servant in the castle, who was now helping up her child who had hurt herself. She looked up, startled, then a light smile appeared on her face. She said, "Your Highness, I didn't see you there! I'm sorry if we bothered you. My daughter slipped and ..."

Valenis lowered his eyes to the dripping blood on the knee of the child. His pupils shrank like a predator's, fixing his eyes on the victim. His heart pounded so loudly in his chest that he felt his pulse throughout his body. And at that moment something monstrous took over him. He shoved the woman to the side, grabbed the child, and sank his teeth into her neck. It didn't matter that he was Valenis, son of Krementa, the prince of Vern, and a child of Vernara. When hunger took over, he was no different from those vampires with no souls who hung from Rabolii's ceiling.

With each following suck his sanity returned slowly. Valenis began to realise what he was doing. Until that point his senses knew only the compelling smell of blood and its indescribable taste, but now he realised he was sucking a dead child's neck. Shaken, he let go of her body and stood up, shocked by what he had done. He looked at his hands as if in disbelief that what was happening was real. The mother he had struck earlier now began to come around, rubbing the spot on her head where she had hit the wall.

"My child ... my child!" she screamed. With her whole body shaking, she clung to the dead girl, then looked up at Valenis. "You killed her! You killed my daughter!"

The prince wasn't in a position to deny it, when his whole face was smeared with blood. Valenis stepped back and began mumbling, "This ... it was a horrible accident. Please don't make noise!"

"Don't make noise? ... You killed my child!" she continued screaming.

Voices were heard in the corridor. Lights of lanterns lit up. Valenis realised that all this put him in a very bad position. The last thing he needed was for the whole of Vern to know him as a cannibal. Nothing would save him then. He felt a chill to the bones and made a last attempt to plead, "Don't scream ... We'll clear up this ... misunderstanding ... please. Nobody should know."

The woman was shaken by her weeping. She looked up at Valenis hatefully and yelled as loudly as she could, "Help! Murderer!"

In his horror, he could only do one thing: he grabbed her head and twisted her neck. Her body fell next to her daughter's, silenced forever. But was it too late? Valenis heard a yell from behind him: "Don't move! You are surrounded. There is nowhere to run, you butcher!"

Valenis stood in dismay. The guards had found him. But it was unthinkable for him to just surrender. Though he had been wishing for his own death over the last days, now that he was threatened, he'd defend himself. His back was turned towards the guards; they hadn't seen his face yet. He realised there was only one way to escape—the outdoors. Without thinking twice, he threw himself from the balcony. A membrane of light blue energy appeared between his arms and body, extending out and growing as wings. He hovered over the air currents and disappeared into the night, still shaken, scared, and heavy with remorse. He never should have touched that vampire potion. Now it had become his punishment, his curse.

Mavarius and Arkenel advanced slowly eastward. Remedor felt better now. He had regained some of his strength, and the symptoms of his abstinence had faded even more. However, the symptoms of the other man were unfolding in all their splendour. It was as if he had completely lost his mind. He couldn't be bothered to leave false tracks any more. He lost caution and could only pluck random weeds from the ground and chew them aggressively because they somehow resembled miner's. Arkenel felt like an orphaned kitten who couldn't survive on his own. Now he had to carry his own luggage. The worst thing was that he didn't know how to survive in the forest, how to get water or food. He decided to set up camp in an out-of-sight place in a ravine that resembled a dry riverbed. He left Mavarius by the rocky wall, then began to stack branches on the fire. He was trying to mimic the type of pyramid his friend would make.

"Man, do you hear me? We have to eat something," Arkenel muttered. "Give me that thing for setting fire."

Mavarius was nodding his head with a wandering look. He didn't seem to understand what was happening. The shapes in front of his eyes looked twisted. Everything looked like a beastly mouth full of teeth. That's how he perceived Arkenel's hand as well, so he attacked it aggressively.

"Thanks." Arkenel used this closeness to get the metal rod out of his friend's belt. He started rubbing it on the dull side of his sword. That created lots of sparks, but since everything had to be difficult, the sticks simply would not catch fire. "Mav, for how long are you gonna be like this? Tell me, are we going in the right direction? Tonight I slept through sundown, so I've lost track of where west is."

"Shut up, idiot. My head's gonna explode," Mavarius grumbled aggressively.

Arkenel bit his lip. He realised that not long ago he was in the same state, but his friend had somehow managed to take care of him until he got better. Well, Remedor didn't know if he would be capable of returning the favour. He continued hitting the metal rods against each other in a noisy way. The robins identified him and began to announce his presence. Arkenel had even learned to recognise this particular style of chirping, so it made him nervous. When he finally lit a fire, he poured a little water into the pot and began to throw into it leaves of chicory, acacia, and cedar and anything else he had noticed being eaten in this camp. While he was poking the green mass with a spoon, Mavarius reached out for him with a shaking hand and grasped him. Remedor was a little surprised at this attempt at communication, so he instantly tuned in, all ears.

"Listen to me now," said Mavarius with utmost effort. "No one has left fake tracks or covered ours for two days now. The Vernians are probably on our trail. If I'm right, the nearest village with Krumerians is about fifty kilometres away. Dump everything here except for your weapons and some water, and run as fast as you can. You should be there by sunrise."

"Can you run fifty kilometres?" Arkenel asked innocently.

"I said dump everything," Mavarius repeated hoarsely.

"Not happening."

"Go on. They're looking for you, not me."

"They're not gonna be nice to you either when they find you. I'm not leaving you."

"I left you in Krumerus for the Aslanians. Do me the same favour so one of us can live," Mavarius blurted out.

"Shut up or I'll hit you with the pan!" Arkenel threatened.

"What then? We'll sit here and wait for them? You know they move three times faster than us."

"Let them come then! I'll kill them," Arkenel answered confidently.

That was hilarious. Mavarius had the feeling that he would vomit his kidneys out, but he didn't have the luxury of doing so and then crawling into a hole. Instead, he tried to get up, pale and wet with cold sweat, trying to ignore all the distorted images his mind was drawing for him. He said through his teeth, "There'll be more of them, and tey'll be in better health. You'll have to catch them out. Take my bow and climb somewhere where you can watch the path we came from."

"Understood. As for you, just hide away," Arkenel instructed him.

Mavarius gathered their belongings and luggage and stuck it all in the bushes so it wouldn't be spotted. He leaned on the trunk of a tree where he would squeal in pain and misery. Right now he'd sell his soul for a single leaf of miner's, but unfortunately there wasn't a suitable vendor around to execute such a deal. He felt even worse when he saw Arkenel trying to climb a tree and make a lot of worrying movements, seemingly losing his grip or stepping the wrong way. He was far from a full recovery. He was a tough bastard, but how much hunger, cold, and beating could a man endure and still function normally?

The red robins were settling on the birch twigs, puffing their feathers to keep warm. They jumped up and down, occasionally diving towards the ground to check if something was food. Every once in a while they chirped to announce the presence of people, which they rarely saw in this part of the forest. Evena was annoyed by the sounds. She couldn't move undetected while all the birds were giving her away. She sneaked like a tigress. For the first time everything felt right. The tracks made sense, the smell was exactly what she was looking for. They all led to the enclosed valley of the ravine where the victim would be trapped. The impatience she felt at the thought of burying her knife in Arkenel's flesh again brought her delight, making her shiver with anticipation. And now that she was so close, she felt it. She wasn't surprised when something whooshed nearby and the man beside her collapsed with an arrow in his chest.

"Ambush. Take cover!" Evena yelled.

More arrows were shot, taking down another man while the others were ducking behind tree trunks. The gorge was narrow; there weren't many places to hide.

"We know you're here, Arkenel! You make things harder for yourself by resisting. Come out!" Evena called to him, preparing an arrow in her bow.

Arkenel stretched the string, holding an arrow. He wasn't making a single sound or giving away his location in any way. He had to aim very carefully because the bow had never been his favourite weapon. And the fact that he had just one eye wasn't helping him. Once one of the Vernians dared to peek out from his cover, he was struck down. Evena saw where the arrow came from and raised her head. She saw her evil enemy in the bare branches of the tree. She aimed and released the string. Her arrow found him. Arkenel grabbed the arm that had been pierced, lost his balance, and fell from the branch. He lived through a painfully long fall, hitting lots of branches before he finally dropped on the ground, as heavy as a rock. He felt like he had fallen apart and couldn't move any more.

The Vernians rushed out of their hiding places and charged towards their helpless victim. Arkenel had to think fast. With his healthy arm, he pulled his sword out of his belt and stuck it in the ground right before one of the bastards threw himself on top of him. The man collapsed on the sharp blade, impaling himself. The other one attacked him and began to choke him. Arkenel ended up buried beneath two heavy men—a dead one and a very much alive and aggressive one. Rabolii's son didn't know how to save himself from this disaster. Two hands were wrapped around his neck, threatening to break it at any moment. The world began to blacken. With the last of his strength, he broke the arrow that had knocked him down, took the sharp piece, and stuck it in the eye of his assailant. The man released his grip and, whilst screaming, went farther out somewhere to die. Arkenel grinned and relaxed his head. For a moment he thought he had won that fight. But he'd completely forgotten about his biggest problem. Evena appeared and overshadowed the sun as she stepped with one foot on the chest of her nemesis.

"Going somewhere, monster?" she hissed at him hatefully.

"Ohhh," Arkenel groaned, not even bothering to say more. He knew that bargaining wouldn't do him any good.

"You're making it so hard for me! Now that my soldiers have been killed, I can't drag you to Vern alone. Maybe I'll just have to kill you here," she stated with a bloodthirsty spark in her eyes.

In fact, she didn't really want to kill him. He had already ruined her life. He had befouled her, given her an unwanted child, and killed Valenis, at least as far as she was aware. She could just end him here, but that wouldn't fix any of his evil deeds. She wanted him to suffer, to burn in agony until old age, and let pain take him away. At that moment of hesitation, she lost invaluable time in which she could have acted. The next thing she heard was a broken twig behind her. Evena gasped quietly and raised her sword, turning around just in time to block a strike from Mavarius. He kicked her under the knee, and she stumbled and fell back, twisting her ankle. The man stepped over the collapsed Arkenel and went to finish her off. She tried to get up, but her ankle was painfully twisted. Her weapon had flown out of her hand, so she couldn't defend herself. She felt the wall of the ravine at her back and began to scream, "You can't kill me! You can't! This goes against Vernara's laws. I'm a mother!"

"Like I give a damn," growled Mavarius with a predatory expression. He continued advancing towards her.

Arkenel leaned closer to see what was going on. He felt mixed feelings. This was definitely one enemy he didn't want appearing in his life again, and he thought he hated her for all she had done, but now when the actual opportunity for her death presented itself, he wasn't too eager. Evena continued to drag herself away from Mavarius and screamed, "No, you don't understand. I'm pregnant with *his* child!" She demonstratively pointed at the culprit.

Mavarius and Arkenel exchanged glances, equally surprised by this announcement. The former grumbled, "Hey, you didn't lie with just one man. You really gonna pretend you know whose it is?"

"You mean that dozens of men under his command defiled me, but *he* was the first. But still, Vernara forgives. That's why he's the only one who remained alive. It happened so he can atone for his sins and do the right thing at least this one time!" Evena continued screaming.

Arkenel was left speechless. He had no idea what to do now. He had never really been a guardian of virtue, and prison had made him even rougher. Evena had lots to answer for. But could he really blame her? He was the first to kill her soldiers. She was the first to suffer torture by her enemy.

"That's so much crap. Bitch, just die." Mavarius took the impossible decision and swung his sword to decapitate Evena.

"Wait!" Arkenel yelled as he tried to stand up. He felt dizzy and weak, blood leaking out of his arrow wound. "Mav, there's no need. She can't chase us in her state. We can just walk away."

"In her state? And what state are you in?" Mavarius snapped at him. "She's insane. She'll keep coming back for you. Who knows if she's pregnant? She might be just saying it."

"We've almost reached Krumerus. She can't follow us there," Arkenel stated firmly.

Mavarius cast one last hateful look at Evena, then slowly turned towards his friend and walked over to him to inspect his wounds. He replied, "If that's what you want."

Evena stood up and stumbled farther from them with great difficulty. She had no intention of abandoning this hunt, but she had to retreat for the time being.

Mavarius cut Arkenel's damp sleeve and wrapped it around

his friend's arm. Stitching and bandaging wounds had become such a common part of the day. While they did that, Remedor noted, "I can't believe you managed to intervene in time. Mav, you were so weak just moments ago. What happened? How did you pull this off?"

A rare smile appeared on the man's face, definitely the first one in days. He pulled a bunch of a very familiar plant from his back pocket. Arkenel's eyes... eye widened. He asked with astonishment, "Where did you get that from?"

"While you were up the tree and I was hiding, I noticed it right next to me. It's best when it's fresh. Have some!" Mavarius handed him the bunch.

"Yes, but ... tosser, do you think we should?"

"What are you talking about now?" Mavarius replied, uninterested.

"I'm not sure if this thing's good for us. At some point we grew to need it, and we become wrecks when we don't have it. It's not like with drinking. We can't sober up. We just need to keep taking it. I don't want this constant need. Now that I have gone without it for a while, I think I can just stop."

"Fine, I won't force-feed it to you." Mavarius shrugged as he was chewing the plant's leaves.

"That's up to you as well, I guess. I just don't wanna be this helpless again. Getting beaten by enemies is bad enough without the symptoms of abstinence to deal with." Arkenel raised his hands... his hand. Now that it was wounded and bandaged, he couldn't move his left shoulder much.

Mavarius, looking at him as if he were an imbecile, just shook his head and went to pick more of the plant. The onward journey would be much easier.

Traneya strode nervously around the castle, looking for Rabolii. She really wanted to know what was going on with her brother and sister and why the necromancer had organised a nationwide search for Salina. She found him on his way out of his throne room while he was instructing Dunevir and Halena about something. "I think it's very clear what both of you need to do. I don't know why this is still a problem."

"I understand your strategy. I'm simply not satisfied with the prospect of such humiliation," Dunevir mumbled in his deep unearthly voice.

"Like you're one to speak," Halena said, also voicing discontent.

"Stop complaining. Mortelion loves humiliating us, and you love Mortelion, don't you? Just do as you're told." Rabolii shone this wisdom upon them.

Traneya walked up to them, disinterested in what they were talking about, and said directly, "I've been looking for you all day. I want to talk."

"I don't have time for that. Go away!" Rabolii banished her with annoyance.

"Then I'll be quick. Tell me what's going on with Salina! If she left with Arkenel, why are you so panicked about finding her? Wasn't it a casual mission? And we haven't had bad news about its outcome. What aren't you telling us?"

"Your sister is dead. Now leave me alone." Rabolii dropped the bomb in the hall.

He should have known better that after telling Traneya something like this, she wouldn't just calm down and be on her way. Her face froze in shock as if she couldn't understand what she had just heard. Then she started hurling other questions: "What? When did you find out about this? What happened? And what about Arkenel?"

"Who cares about Arkenel?! I'm busy! Now leave!" Rabolii croaked at her like an angry raven, then walked away so he could chat with Dunevir about Mortelion.

Traneya just stared at them in silence, then dragged her feet towards her room. A chaos of confusion blasted in her head, but one couldn't tell by her stiff facial expression. When she opened her door and walked into her room, she looked like the statue of some tragic character. Estrella was mending one of her shirts. She raised her emerald eyes and asked immediately, "What is it? Has something happened?"

Without answering, Traneya flung herself on her bed. She crossed her fingers on her chest and stared at the ceiling as if she were observing a whole new universe. Eventually she just muttered, "I hate him."

"Whom, Rabolii?" Estrella had spent enough time in this city to understand how things were.

"He did it on purpose." Traneya gasped. "Just as he did with Malior. When he heard that Vern was causing trouble again and attacking villages, he sent my husband on some vague mission with a handful of people so he'd die there."

"Why?" Estrella asked casually, not wanting to show how curious she was about the drama of the Krumerian royal family.

"Because he envied him. Malior was at his peak. He was very strong, and he was trying to do something good for this country."

"Did they argue a lot?" Estrella asked.

"My father loved him only while he obeyed him. They had more and more disagreements recently. Rabolii wouldn't leave Vern alone and would constantly attack them even though we got no loot from them. They're primitive. There are so few places where the people actually use coin! Malior had a different vision. He wanted to charge at the south and restore Krumerus to its former glory. He was gathering armies and support, so my father felt threatened by him. Rabolii has always been such an illogical madman! He'd complain about always having to do everything in the country himself, but when Malior tried to take some control, he killed him."

Estrella put the shirt she was stitching in her lap and turned her curious gaze towards Traneya. Never had she suspected that such dirty betrayals happened in Kranium!

"I take it you've found out for sure now?" the sorceress asked. Judging by the hopeless shock which was written on Traneya's face when she entered the room, the Soleyan knew the answer would be yes.

"He did it again," Traneya said. "He hates Arkenel. He stuffed him into that filthy prison when my brother was only seventeen, and ever since he was released, our father has treated him like a plagued rat. Arkenel takes some initiative and organises people under his command, just like Malior did. Rabolii thinks everyone's trying to steal his precious throne. That's why he threw my brother into a suicide mission, just as he did with my husband. And Salina paid the price for it."

"So you've had news from Arkenel and Salina? Has something happened to them?" Estrella raised her eyebrows.

"No real news that I've heard. I don't know what happened. Basically Salina ran away with my brother and his people because her beloved was amongst them. And as soon as Rabolii realised she was with them, he completely lost his mind and sent all possible patrols after her. If there is one person in this world my father cares about, it's her. And since he was so panicked, we knew Salina was in danger and also that he knew it. Whatever horrors they experienced on the western border, they were meant for Arkenel, not for my sister. But she became the innocent victim. Rabolii told me she's dead."

Estrella gasped with compassion. With each day spent here, she was more and more convinced that this necromancer was a dreadful monster like in the Soleyan legends. She asked softly, "What about Arkenel?"

"Who cares about Arkenel!" Traneya imitated Rabolii's squealing voice. "If tomorrow we learn Arkenel's dead, that corpse will celebrate!"

Estrella could only blink innocently and feel indignation about the terrible story. Traneya sat on the bed and slammed her fist angrily into the wall. Her hands were shaking. She said through her teeth angrily, "Salina was the last person in our family who deserved to die. But no wonder. Just look at who's in charge of us. Our biggest enemy sits on the throne."

"What are you going to do?" Estrella tilted her head and looked at Traneya.

"I don't know. If Malior were still alive, we'd take up arms and take over this country. Like anyone amongst the common people would oppose us in dethroning this idiot! But now I'm alone. I can't talk to the crowds the way he did. I can't rule a nation. But I also can't turn my back on everyone and leave my mother alone with that monster."

"We can only hope you're wrong." Estrella shrugged. "It would be better if Rabolii were just incompetent rather than malicious."

Traneya doubted that very much. There were just too many signs, and she believed she wasn't the only one to see this conspiracy. A sad smile appeared on her face. She turned to Estrella and put her hand on her shoulder, saying, "You know, we're both prisoners here. Being Rabolii's daughter is a trap of its own. Estrella, I don't know what to do."

The Soleyan looked at Traneya with a concentrated look, getting a strange feeling. She was in enemy land surrounded by people she once considered abominations. But right now, when the two of them were sitting together, stricken by the difficulties of life, she felt that Traneya was a very close friend, like none she'd ever had before. She took the Krumerian's hand and said resolutely, "You can't just sit here and let Rabolii do what he wants. If you do see him for what he is, you have to save yourself and your family. Whom would your mother stand for if all her children wanted to distance themselves from him? Perhaps she would come with you."

"What, you think we can just pack our bags and move?" Traneya gave a sad, curved smile. "Do you have any idea what a horror my father is? He'll take it as an insult and treachery, and he'll start chasing us so as to kill us."

"He's already doing it," Estrella noted. "It seems he is paranoid that everyone is trying to steal his throne. How long will it be till he sees you as a threat? Or your brothers?"

If the situation weren't so serious, Traneya would have laughed heartily at the prospect of someone feeling threatened by Regel and Dregel. However, she realised Estrella was right. She couldn't just stay idle in Kranium and wait for her time to come. She stared at the floor and began slowly, "I could travel west to find out what happened to Arkenel and whether he's alive. However, no road is safe. I'll have to pass either by the holdings of stupid Morelii, whose father loves Rabolii so much, or by the Skeletal Wall, where we have cousins. But they're bootlickers, and they'll definitely snitch on me."

"Maybe wait a few more days for more news from Arkenel and start planning a trip to someplace safe in the meantime," Estrella suggested. "If he's alive, he's headed this way. If you set out at the same time, you might miss each other."

Traneya kept staring at the floor, realising this was a good point. Rabolii had been the bane of her existence since forever. The thought of finally opposing him somehow and taking her life into her own hands was liberating.

The news of Salina's death scattered around the city like pestilence. Most people were in shock that something had happened to her as she seemed like the type of person who didn't get into trouble. Ravena learned the news from some random servants who had been cleaning Traneya's room and whom Estrella had told. At first Ravena didn't want to believe the rumours, so she went looking for Rabolii to see if he knew anything. When she found him, he was busy. He was in the courtyard of the castle, inspecting a number of homeless people and beggars who had been caught that night being very drunk and causing disarray. The commander of the guards was surprised that Rabolii had involved himself. The necromancer just laid his cold eyes upon the men in front of them and noted, "We have around a hundred people here. This is wonderful. They'll make a fine squad for my army. Kill them!"

The guards just exchanged glances like they were checking to see if they had heard right. The captives started crying and pleading: "My lord, please! I only stole because I was hungry!"

"Mercy, my lord!"

Some onlookers began yelling as well. "Hey, you can't kill my brother and take his body! His skeleton belongs to my family!"

"*Silence!*" Rabolii gave out a deafening scream and gestured towards the captives. "These skeletons will be seized by the state because of their crimes and will be used as soldiers. The families will not be entitled to compensation. Any protests or discontentedness will be viewed as treason and heresy, and the offenders will be publicly executed!"

All felt silent. Ravena watched with surprise, wondering what this was about. Her husband had never performed mass executions like that without even bothering to hear what the men were accused of.

The necromancer raised his hands, and all who stood before him fell dead and then rose up again with blank, expressionless eyes. Rabolii shuddered because of this energy-draining exercise. He'd need a lot more corpses, but he didn't have the energy to raise too many at once. Or did he?

"Bring out the sarcophaguses from the basement," he ordered his new skeletons. "They hold some energy I can use now."

Ravena thought she had watched him for long enough, so she stepped forward from the crowd of spectators. She began, "Rab, I heard something concerning. Some maids said Salina is dead. Where did they get that idea from?"

"How would I know? Traneya must have told them," Rabolii replied casually as he prepared potions to turn some of his corpses into undead vampires.

Ravena stared with shock. She knew her husband was legendary for his lack of tact, but this was too much even for him. She stood close to him, trying to meet his gaze, and asked, "Well? Is it true?"

"Yes! It's true! Are you happy? Have you satisfied your curiosity? Can't you see I'm busy?" he screamed at her angrily.

Ravena stepped back. It took her a few seconds to comprehend this statement. She asked in a weak voice, "But how ... when did you find out? When did it happen?"

"Ravena ... please," Rabolii snarled through his teeth with a boiling rage he was just merely containing and trying to keep from bursting out.

His wife realised that he was dangerous right now, so she just nodded and stepped back. She turned away and headed back to the castle. She covered her mouth with her hands, muffling her weeping. Over the last few days she'd been able to think about nothing other than how Salina was. The lack of information was suffocating her. Now it seemed the worst had happened, but she still couldn't believe it. It was just too awful. In retrospect, it seemed like she and Salina only lived for the purpose of keeping Rabolii happy. And whenever he became too much for them with his capricious nature and endless bad mood, they'd support each other and say it was all worth it. All this was over now. Ravena felt so alone and in the dark. She never fully felt like Salina's mother, so she hadn't really lost a child today. But she had lost her best friend. She didn't know which hurt more.

Rabolii watched his wife as she left, feeling a lump in his throat. It was hard for him, but he couldn't afford to share this moment of grieving and pain with her. He didn't have time for it, and he thought it was pointless. Grieving wouldn't change anything. The only thing he could do was to slay his daughter's killers. That would partially snuff out the anger and the pain. Revenge was all he could think about. Arkenel was going to get it.

CHAPTER 14

THE SON OF MORTELION

Eslir walked amongst tall, golden houses, contemplating that he had never been anywhere so sinister before. The white marble walls were stained with soot and dust. No one knew where it came from. Many of the windows were shattered; ragged curtains waved out of them. The tidy paving stones were stained with blood. Completely dried plants were sticking up like twigs from the gardens. Shaken by the wind, they were shedding their black petals. The trees spread their bare branches like a dead man's hands.

The oracle of light who accompanied Eslir stumbled, fell to his knees, and remained like that. The Aslanian king bent down by the man in white robes to help him stand up.

"Never have I felt anything like this. This whole town ... all its people ... Who could be capable of such a thing?" the oracle said with a shocked face.

"Rabolii Remedor," Eslir stated with all the certainty and contempt of this world. "He's been here. He's unleashed a storm of death energy, destroying everything around. We find no corpses because he's reanimated them and taken them to Krumerus with him."

"There was no way we could have predicted that." One of the Soleyan generals stepped forward and nodded towards the horizon, where the trees of the Thorny Woods stood shrouded in thick mist. "The forest is impassable there. The tree trunks are entwined in such a way that no man or beast can sneak through. We thought this region would be safe."

"Apparently you thought wrong." Eslir shook his platinum forelock with discontent. "We don't know where they'll strike, so I'll gather the troops and make sure we decide what battles to have."

The oracle stood up, still dizzy and pale. He said with a dry mouth, "Your Majesty, what could soldiers possibly do against such a devastating magical attack? We need to pray to Flalirion for protection. The seers clearly feel the return of Ardor the Magnificent."

Eslir groaned with grand annoyance. He turned unceremoniously to the oracle and snapped, "Do you know what the problem is with you Soleyans? You never try to actually solve a crisis yourselves. You just pray to Flalirion to send you Ardor. Didn't you have a very definite prediction twenty-four years ago that Ardor would return, and didn't you organise hundreds of fire festivals all the way to the White Beaches? Listen, I'd love to have a godlike man drop from the sky who'll slay all our enemies while we're drinking tea, but it's not happening. It's up to us to fight, and I'll be damned if I'll allow your helpless country to just collapse after my father died for you."

The oracle remained silent. The Soleyan general cleared his throat. "Of course we'll fight. I will gather whatever soldiers are brave enough to get closer to the Thorny Wood and have a closer look as to where the enemies came from."

"I'd like to participate in that," Eslir replied instantly.

The general wondered if he would mention that it was dangerous for the king of all of Aslania to go anywhere near this damned place, but he knew it wouldn't change his mind. Accompanied by several soldiers, they approached the forest. Eslir saw where the dried grass had been trampled by a lot of people going straight to the woods.

"I don't think the Thorny Woods are as impenetrable as you thought."

"Just look further." The Soleyan general nodded towards the murky woods.

Eslir narrowed his eyes and went on, striding bravely ahead of everyone else. He arrived by some really thick stems of thorny plants which were wrapping around each other tightly. All the footsteps were around that area, but Eslir couldn't see where they had gone. He turned around and yelled at the Soleyans, "Can anyone explain this? Where have they all gone?"

The men shrugged. This mystery had plagued people for generations. Eslir continued looking around stubbornly, refusing to just walk away. He found no possible gap through which anyone would be able to pass. However, as he was glancing around, he noticed something else. There were some different tracks in a muddier spot. The Aslanian paused for a moment and investigated them with a frown. They looked like the prints of a horse's hoof, but these were three times larger. The Soleyans also gathered to look at them. What kind of beast could have left such a print?

Meanwhile, another country far to the west was also having monster problems. Krementa tried to keep the story about the dead mother and child from spreading. Few people knew about them anyway, and they thought the queen was doing it to stop panic from spreading. That was actually one of the reasons. She was furious when she found out what had happened. She was giving orders to some of her guards and servants when she noticed that Valenis was sneaking through the castle with a guilty look and was trying to get into his room unnoticed. However, Krementa was standing in the corridor in front of his room, so she instantly lunged at him, pulled him in, and slammed the door behind them. Valenis was feeling too miserable and defeated to be worried about getting shouted at.

"You! When I heard someone killed people to drink blood, I knew it was you!" She yelled at him, "What were you thinking? Are you going to be a *murderer* now? Is this how I've raised you to behave?"

"Mother, you might as well hang me rather than tell me all this," Valenis snapped. "It's stronger than me. I can't control it, and I'll probably kill again."

"You have to learn to control this, darling. Things can't go on like this!" Krementa gripped his shoulders with a face like she'd cry at any moment.

Valenis rolled his red eyes. He was supposed to be a prince, and everything was forbidden to him—his books, the piano, the opportunity to live with the woman he chose. Now everything escalated to the point where he was forbidden food. However, they couldn't keep quarrelling right now because someone began knocking on the door and shouting in a loud, rustic voice, "Your Majesty, are you there? It's very important."

Krementa grunted and turned to the door. "Can't I have a moment of peace?!"

"But, mistress, General Evena has returned!"

The mother and the son exchanged glances. Valenis jumped towards the door immediately, his long leap facilitated by his new wings. He was really hoping he'd hear that Arkenel had been captured so he could interrogate him. And if he did have something to do with Salina's death, Valenis would dismember him personally. Evena stood alone in the corridor.

"Well, what happened?" Krementa also appeared at the door with a face emitting supremacy and importance. "Has the monster been captured?"

"My lady, I'm so sorry, but Vernara didn't let me kill him!" Evena announced with theatrical drama.

Valenis groaned. He was so tired of people always excusing their failures by attributing them to Vernara. He asked angrily, "Why, did she tie your hands? What stopped you from capturing Arkenel?"

"No." Evena sniffed. "But I found out something terrible. I am pregnant with his child. That's why Vernara didn't let me kill him."

"And how do you know it's from him?" Valenis asked as ruthlessly.

"I am absolutely certain the child is his. I'm a mother, so I can feel it," Evena said, raising her voice with unshaken certainty.

"That makes things very difficult. You can't raise this child alone while the father is alive. Otherwise Vernara will despise you!" Krementa exclaimed.

Valenis gave out a very heavy sigh, wondering if he was the only one who found this to be ridiculous. He muttered, "There's a statistical chance of 2 per cent that the child is Arkenel's."

"Valenis, behave more respectfully!" Krementa scolded him.

"And why would Vernara despise her if she's a single mother?" Valenis continued to protest since he was in such a great mood. "She wouldn't be the only one I know."

"Are you hinting something?" Krementa quacked with a quarrelsome voice.

"It just occurred to me that you never told me which Krumerian is my father or how you killed him before my birth to legalise me." Valenis casually dropped this topic of conversation.

Krementa and Evena gasped like two witches whose very important potion had spontaneously gone bad. The former stuttered, "How did you learn he was a Krumerian?"

Valenis gave his mother a long, unimpressed look. It was ridiculous that someone would bother denying something like this. Krementa sighed heavily and replied, "Your father was a bad man. We accepted him in Vern when he was sick, lost, and helpless. I accommodated him in the castle because the weak, feeble Krumerians can't live outside. They are too accustomed to their houses and buildings. He had lived with us as a friend for months. One night he slipped into my chambers and forced himself upon me. I was terrified, but I was able to defend myself with magic and kill him. Unfortunately, the irreparable had already happened, and I fell pregnant. Vernara was merciful and blessed me. She told me that you are not to blame for the way you were conceived and said that I should appreciate and love you. And so I did."

"Excuse me?" Valenis raised his eyebrows with a shocked look. "How could that even happen?! If I know you, you can sweep away dozens of people all at once before they even come close."

"I haven't always been as wise and powerful." Krementa raised her head bravely. "I've made mistakes in the past, but that doesn't matter since I'm working for the best for you and Vern. And I achieve it."

"Oh, my queen, I had no idea! I am truly sorry!" Evena told her sympathetically.

"It's OK, General. Now it's important for us to find a way to preserve your honour. I would recommend that you find a real husband and present the baby as his. If Vernara sees you're trying to be a good mother, she will bless you."

"Thank you, Your Majesty!" Evena bowed to her and walked away.

Valenis stared at the floor for a few seconds, then muttered, "So was that it? Was it so hard? Couldn't you have told me about this before?"

"Treasure, I did it to protect you!" Krementa exclaimed in such a tone as if it were the most obvious thing in the world. "I didn't want you to feel like an undesirable fruit of violence, as a memory of an event that ruined my life. You are very valuable to me. That is the only thing I want you to know."

Valenis felt like he'd been shot by such a statement. He had always felt like a shameful thing which should remain behind closed doors, not bothering anyone with his existence. Looks like things were even more dramatic than he'd imagined. It was good thing that he had died so that Krementa would appreciate him more and show some tenderness towards him. He nodded stiffly and stepped back. "Um, I need some rest now."

There was one upside to all this. It had distracted his mother from the talk they'd been having about him being a child murderer. Maybe no one would raise the issue till he killed again.

When Arkenel and Mavarius returned to Kranium, they weren't sure whom to visit first or what story to tell. Naturally, Ravena was the first to greet them as she was always busy around the city and knew what happened in it. She welcomed her dear boy with kisses and hugs. She was overjoyed to see he was alive. Arkenel felt unworthy of such a welcome. He thought he'd be stoned as soon as he set foot in Kranium. He tried to squeeze out of Ravena's grip as he mumbled, "Mom, don't get happy too quickly. You don't know what happened there."

"We'll talk about that later. I'm just happy you're back. I was very worried about you! Come on, let's go in. You look starved." Then she turned to Mavarius and told him, "Thank you for keeping my son safe. I can never repay you!"

The man nodded with an expressionless face. He didn't seem glad to be there.

However, they weren't given the chance to rest after their endless perils. Right on the stairs in front of the castle stood Rabolii, tall and majestic, like a colossus which held the heavens up; his mantles and cloaks were blown back impressively by the wind. He was gazing over the city with a predatory look, monitoring what slaves were passing by and determining if there was anyone worthy of becoming a vampire. He did choose one, when he realised he looked somewhat familiar and was accompanied by Ravena. At this fundamental moment Rabolii remembered that it was Arkenel. His pupils shrank like those of a shaggy, ill-behaved cat someone had just kicked. The necromancer charged at the culprit for all his trouble, wrathful and deadly. Arkenel started backing off when he saw who was coming for him. He felt this was his end. Even the slavers and the chained people they led halted for a moment to watch the apocalypse.

"Oh, look who decided to come back!" Rabolii's voice cracked like a whip. "I know what you've done. How dare you show your face here again?!"

Ravena gave Rabolii a questioning look and stood as a human shield in front of Arkenel to save him from beatings and death. Mavarius was quick to do the same. He felt very courageous and energetic now that he had treated himself with miner's. As for Arkenel, he felt crushed by guilt and his perceived failure. He had had a faint hope his father would forgive him, but that disappeared in an instant. His son's weakness was apparent and made Rabolii even thirstier for blood and revenge.

"Rab, what are you talking about? Calm down!" Ravena tried to speak with the raging evil man she had married.

"Don't tell me to calm down! *This* pathetic stain on my family tree killed our daughter! Now get out of my way!"

After saying this, Rabolii grabbed Ravena by the shoulder with a grisly, monstrous hand with stiff fingers and long, curved claws like those of a vulture and flung her to one side, sending her into oblivion. Then he shook his head like a bull and headed towards Arkenel. His son tried to step back but stumbled over something and fell to the ground. Mavarius reached out for the dagger on his belt and stepped forward to kill Rabolii, but Arkenel pulled his leg and said under his breath, "Please don't get involved. You'll make it worse."

"You!" Rabolii yelled at Arkenel. "I've always known you were worth nothing. I sent you on a simple mission, and this is how you return?!"

"Father, I swear, I did all I could," Arkenel whimpered. "But it was an ambush. We ..."

"I'm not talking about an ambush, you idiot!" Rabolii growled, his voice doubling, sounding demonic and nightmarish. "You killed her on purpose. It was you."

"What? No, I ..."

"Who else could have done it, you wretch?" the necromancer roared. The edges of his robe began to smoke like they were burning. "Come here, stand up, and face me like a man. Look me in the eye and dare to tell me the truth!"

Shaken and destroyed, Arkenel stood up before Mortelion's champion. Ever since Evena had slaughtered his friends, he felt like the most useless and pitiful being ever. Right now he felt even more that way. The only thing he could see in his father's eyes was contempt and burning hatred. Arkenel felt he deserved it. The necromancer's right hand shot forward like a viper, his fingers digging into his son's skin and tightening around his skull. Light blue energy glowed around his fingers. Arkenel could only gasp; he couldn't even properly scream. His eyes rolled back and turned white. His whole body began to shake like he was having a seizure.

"Hey, what the heck? What are you doing?" Mavarius yelled at Rabolii and started circling the necromancer aggressively.

"I'm reading his thoughts to see what he knows about Salina," Rabolii snarled fiercely.

Arkenel was writhing in pain as if he were in agony. Mavarius felt his friend wouldn't survive this in his weakened state. He clenched his teeth and pushed Rabolii back, interrupting his ghastly spell. The necromancer blinked and fixed his gaze on this insolent disgrace, giving him such a look as if he couldn't believe what he saw.

"Do you realise you're begging me to kill you?" the necromancer exclaimed, his eyes brightening and beginning to glow just like Dunevir's.

"You wanna read thoughts? I'm up for that," Mavarius replied breathlessly as he was trying to wrest Arkenel away to check if his tongue was in place or if he was choking. "I was conscious when they caught everyone. He had no idea what was going on half the time. You'll kill him with this. He's already been hurt by, like, everything."

"What a shame. In this case I'll kill you instead." Rabolii bared his teeth and grabbed hold of Mavarius's head. His palm was glowing again. The man fell to his knees in pain, feeling like his whole head was exploding. He gritted his teeth, trying not to scream, and forced himself to remember everything he knew about the death of Salina. Those days of his life were heavy and stressful. He had spent an eternity hiding and sneaking, moving like a ghost without making a sound, without leaving a trace, even when he was right by the Crystal Castle. He had seen where Salina was accommodated, but he didn't watch her much. He only cared about what they were doing to Arkenel. He had watched them humiliate him and spit on him. It had made Mavarius burn in anger and contempt as he was torn by contradictory urges to jump down there and fight with everyone, possibly resulting in his own death, or to escape a million miles away from there and just tell himself nothing better was possible.

His motivation to act was the quickly approaching execution. It was hours away. On that night there were almost no guards in the corridors, so he acted. When he did free Arkenel, his entire being was just screaming for them to run as fast as possible. That's why he really wanted to break the little idiot's melon when he proposed they look for Salina. When they found her dead, neither of them knew what had happened to her or why. Mavarius didn't care anyway. All he wanted was to get away from there with his helpless friend who wouldn't have lasted another day in the Vernian prison.

Rabolii pulled his hand away from Mavarius's head. The two of them just stared at each other. The necromancer observed him with arrogant superiority. Then a thin, mocking smile stretched across his lips. Mavarius clenched his teeth and shot Rabolii a hateful glance like he wanted to kill him. Shaken and unstable, he stood up, pushed away the crowd, and ran off to somewhere. Arkenel shuffled painfully, gazed after his friend and muttered dizzily, "Come on, what did you do to him?"

"Go soothe him, Arkenel. I just saw in his thoughts that he's planning to kill himself," Rabolii answered in a low voice to mask its mocking, ironical tone.

Arkenel stood up on his shaky legs and replied, "No way, he's not like that. *Tosser!* Wait up!"

Arkenel stumbled after his friend. The crowd was still staring at what was going on. It was so rare for them to see Rabolii. There were people who had lived in the city for decades and had never even seen the necromancer. And when he did come out, he'd cause a spectacular scene like this. Ravena stepped forward and stood by Rabolii with an annoyed look on her face. She asked him, "Well, what happened? Did you see their thoughts? Did they kill Salina?"

"No," the necromancer mumbled with an indifferent look on his face.

"You don't say!" Ravena raised her voice. "How could you come up with something that insane in the first place? You may dislike Arkenel all you want for not being the heir you wanted, but he's not an evil person."

"He's not. He's the kind of person who has completely failed to protect his sister." Rabolii shrugged. "He's a man unable to achieve victory, unable to fend for himself." He glanced at Ravena and said, "I'd rather he were a murderer than a useless failure. He lost an important battle in such a ridiculous way. Now leave. All of this has caused me a headache."

Ravena couldn't believe it. She had always known that Rabolii could be a bit disagreeable and not overly sensitive, but this was too much even for him. However, she couldn't be mad at him, not even now. She was able to recognise that he was hurt and that the death of Salina was making him bleed poison, which made the lives of everyone around him even more difficult. So she pulled him in a heartfelt embrace and just held him like that for a few seconds. Rabolii stood stiff like a wooden log in her arms, a supressed look of outrage frozen on his face as if he was suffering something unspeakable and had refrained from killing everyone because of decency alone. After letting him go, Ravena said with a painful smile, "Of course, my dear husband.

Rest now. Let me know if I can help you with anything. I don't want you overworking."

Rabolii had been reviving vampires all day long, and he had drained souls of degenerates, which must have felt unpleasant. To Ravena's utter surprise, however, he replied, "No, I plan to continue with my pursuits here. I'm developing a new kind of undead monster, assembled from combined skeletons. As soon as Dunevir comes back, we will build it and reanimate it."

Ravena blinked with surprise. She didn't know skeletons could be combined and function as a whole. Still, she wouldn't argue with the great Rabolii Remedor. She left him to his work.

A little farther into town, away from the crowd, Arkenel walked, hobbling along and pressing the bandages on his aching arm, which was now bleeding. He looked around and called out, "Tosser! Mav! Where did you go? Come out. It's over."

Arkenel passed a hole in the castle wall. He recognised it as the fire exit of the abandoned kitchen where he had lived with his buddies. Without much thought, he stepped in there and found the one he was looking for. Next to an overturned table, Mavarius sat with a large red spot on his forehead. He looked like he had been burned. Who would have thought Rabolii's touch could be so devastating!

"Hey ... What happened? Why did you run off like that? I know my father is kinda repulsive, but you're used to it, right?" Arkenel came closer and sat down next to his friend.

"That was so crappy. It's like he shoved that magic up my ass," Mavarius replied with a traumatised look as he hugged his knees to his chest.

"Ya, I know what it's like. There's not a single person in this family whose thoughts Rabolii hasn't read." Arkenel shrugged. "This time it hurt more because he was angry. The trick is to just let him see what he wants. Or if he goes digging, who knows what he'll find!"

"Ugh." Mavarius looked away and stared at the floor. "Let's not stay here. Your father's a curse. I won't stand him treating us like trash."

"It's not like we're not used to it." Arkenel sighed.

"You just came back home after torture and captivity, wounded at that! And what does he do? He tortures you as well in front of the whole town." Mavarius spread his arms. "And what do you say? 'It's not like we're not used to it.' Geez, Arkenel, you're like one of those dumb girls whose boyfriend beats her but she doesn't break up with him anyway."

"So what do you want? Where else can we go?" Arkenel replied, irritated.

"We can go back to Aldur. You set all those tossers free. They'll listen to you."

"Enough. You know very well that's not true." Arkenel groaned. "They all put a lot of effort into making this happen. I wasn't the only organiser. And what good am I as a leader anyway? After last time ..."

"Enough already. I'll smack you. What do you want me to do, tell you all about what a great leader you are? I'm still following you. What does that say to you?"

Arkenel looked away. He didn't know how it was possible for his friend not to see the problem here and to carry on as if nothing happened. Or maybe he was sick of Arkenel's complaining and was trying to kill that kind of conversation. This thought struck Remedor like a stone from a slingshot. Without saying a word, he got up and left the kitchen. He wanted to be alone.

—◊—

Too many responsibilities had fallen on the shoulders of the Aslanian king. What happened on Soleya's northern border was inexplicable and disturbing. Eslir wanted to believe that it was Rabolii's doing, but the huge prints of hooves remained unexplained. Soon local Soleyans began to send letters to him describing a huge horned four-legged demon which was spotted near the Thorny Woods and resembled a horse.

Eslir had to find out more about this enemy. He summoned the Aslanian oracles and dug through old fragile tomes but found nothing. There were legends about various ghostly horses, but they were related to a rider and held no importance on their own. However, the Reverend Elerya responded quite differently when Eslir told her about the unusual creature. The supreme Soleyan priestess was very sensitive to the energies of darkness, and Krumerians terrified her. So once something so evil and powerful was mentioned, she turned pale She sneaked by Eslir, who was talking loudly in the throne room about the unusual beast, and nudged him. "Your Majesty, please come with me for a moment."

"What, do you have information about this horse?" Eslir asked her.

"I beg you, don't call him that. You'll anger him," she whimpered. "Come to the temple."

Eslir followed her. Elerya had always seemed strange to him. She was a sorceress of light, was constantly carrying around lanterns and torches, and didn't remain in the dark even for a second. Every time a cloud passed through the sky, she'd become extremely disturbed. Still, he went with her to Flalirion's temple on a high hill which was always illuminated by the sun. The interior of the building was littered with torches in all shapes and sizes as well as with cascades of fire and sparks. Eslir looked around, feeling like this place was too warm for his liking. He'd always preferred the calm serenity Glacera's icy temples held.

"I hope it's not what I think it is," muttered Elerya as she strode around in the library of the temple and then climbed on two chairs stacked one on top of the other to each the higher shelves. Eslir felt uneasy watching an old woman do that. He felt she'd fall off at any moment. "Flalirion is now resting, unable to protect us from such a catastrophe."

"It won't be a problem. That's what I'm here for," Eslir replied casually.

"Here's the book." Elerya picked up a very thick, heavy volume bound with rough black leather.

"What manner of book is that?" Eslir wrinkled his nose in disgust.

"It was stolen from Krumerus a century ago," the priestess stated, looking equally revolted as if she were being forced to touch guts. "I never wanted it kept in the holy temple, but my teacher convinced me that it was important enough to store it where it's safe and that it had a lot of information about our enemy and the monsters."

"Have you read it?" Eslir asked.

"No, I've barely even touched it before." Elerya shook her head. "However, when I was still a student here, the supreme priestess at the time was very interested in legends of foreign peoples, and she often told us about Krumerus. I remember her having mentioned a four-legged demon, but he is one of the most heinous, nightmarish creatures Krumerus ever birthed. I sincerely hope it's not what we're dealing with."

A weight was forming in Eslir's chest. He felt like he was going to be unlucky enough to need to be protecting two countries alone right when the worst of beasts decided to make a comeback after being gone for centuries. With trembling hands, Elerya opened the book. She ran her finger down the contents. Something in Eslir's stomach turned when he saw her finger stop at a title which read "Children of Mortelion". She turned to the page in question and began to flip through numerous pictures of deformed, unspeakable monsters until finally she paused where the beast in question was drawn. His scaly body was a bit like a horse's, but his legs were somewhat too thick with very wide hooves. He had a long, sharp tail, and his head resembled a skull with two pairs of curved horns pointing downwards.

"They call him Stronius Mortre. He is a demon capable of drawing energy from his very creator. He knows no love or compassion; he's a being of pure hatred and is guided by a raw need for annihilation and lust for blood. He exists just to bring glory to Mortelion and nothing else. Evil as he is destructive, he is also …" The priestess paused for a moment, her breathing wheezy and uneven.

"He is also?" Eslir prompted her.

"He's Mortelion's son," Elerya finished. She looked up at Eslir with big protruding eyes full of terror. "He'll stop at nothing until he's levelled us to the ground."

"I don't think it'll come to that," Eslir said bravely. "If he really has been alive for the entire century after this book was found, someone must have been able to fight him off."

"Fight him off, maybe. Your Majesty, some scholars believe it was he who killed holy Ardor."

Eslir frowned, realising how ancient this creature was, and stated, "I want to learn more about this Stronius. Can I keep this book for now?"

Elerya nodded stiffly. Eslir took the huge volume that was so sinister and threatening that it seemed to be about to start casting curses on its own. The king shook his head, still in disbelief that he had to fight something like this. He wanted to meet Ilinar again and have another conversation about how Krumerus was so innocent and wanted peace so much.

In the meantime, not too far to the north, Ilinar walked through the Thorny Woods. He kept stumbling over roots, and his cloak got caught on most every thorn on the way. Halena walked beside him, silent and pale as an apparition. The Soleyan was trying very hard not to look at her because today she wore a dress with cleavage so deep that it would be considered vulgar in Soleya. Ilinar had never seen so much female flesh before, and he felt a strange mixture of embarrassment, excitement, and discomfort.

After them followed the other cultists, cloaked and gloomy, shrouded in mist. Ilinar was casting stealthy gazes at them. They made him feel restless. When they all reached an impassable wall of entangled tree trunks, the group stopped and one of the cultists stepped forward, raising his hands to the sky. He yelled, "Almighty Mortelion, lord of our souls and our lives, please accept me in your domain and grant us access to the vile southern land so we may bring you glory as my fathers have done before me!"

Ilinar didn't realise what was going on when said cultist just stabbed himself and collapsed to the ground. The Soleyan was shocked and lunged towards the man to help him.

"He surrendered to Lord Mortelion so we may pass," Halena explained with an emotionless voice. "It's a very honourable way to go."

Ilinar gazed with astonishment at the tree trunks as they suddenly reshaped themselves and turned into slimy tentacles. They moved out of the way so the group could pass and then once again turned into trees, standing still and motionless. The forest ahead was nowhere near as dense.

"We have almost arrived," Halena said softly and peered behind the black trunk of a tree.

Ilinar stood beside her, still feeling a bit shaken. They had reached Soleya. This made him feel uneasy. He didn't know if he could succeed with this. Tonight he would either regain his kingdom or lose his life along with those of many other people who'd fall victim to Stronius. He shook his head, turned to the darkness of the forest, and said, "This is a mistake. I can't take such a responsibility. I should have warned Soleya."

Halena stood in front of him and put a finger under his chin, lifting his head so their eyes met. Ilinar felt blood flow up into his face uncomfortably and began to shuffle in confusion. The girl said, "You'll make it. I believe in you. This is the will of Mortelion himself."

That was a confusing statement! Ilinar exclaimed, "How can Mortelion want peace with Soleya? I thought he was only interested in chaos and bloodshed!"

Halena gave him a mysterious smile and stroked his chin while saying, "That's true. However, Mortelion is fascinated by the fire element of your nation. It is no secret that this sphere has always made him envious. Fire can be so destructive, chaotic, and uncontrollable, so our god feels as if this element was supposed to be his. In a certain way Mortelion likes you."

Ilinar didn't know whether he should feel offended by the sympathies of Mortelion. He stared at the black ground, trying very hard not to look at Halena's cleavage, and mumbled, "So, we have to stand by and wait here until Stronius appears. Are we sure he'll attack that city in the lowlands?"

"It is possible to predict the beast's movements if you know him well enough," Halena responded quietly. She handed Ilinar a strange-looking sword. The blade was dark, but it was smeared with some phosphorescent liquid which made it glow. The young woman explained, "We tried to make one of our weapons look more Soleyan so that your countrymen won't realise we've given it to you."

Ilinar took the sword and cast a stealthy glance at Halena. He just nodded stiffly and prepared to camp.

The day and the night somehow merged into one in Krumerus because of the constant darkness and silence that gripped this place. Even at the border, where the energies of darkness and death were not so dense, the feeling was much the same. The cultists sat in silence, as still as statues. Ilinar sat by the trunk of a tree. He cuddled his backpack full of provisions and glanced at Halena from time to time. He felt strange. She was very beautiful but somewhat cold. He wanted to get to know her, but he was afraid to approach her in any way. He was tense around her, overthinking whether he had said anything wrong, whether his posture was good, whether he'd eaten anything stinky recently, and so on. Ilinar promised himself that once this whole ordeal with his throne was settled, he would pluck up the courage and talk to her. But for now he just took out his favourite book from his backpack so he could distract himself from the horrors of this world. He was rereading the part just after Felis had barely escaped the monster Lethius and regained consciousness after collapsing.

Felis awoke in an unfamiliar location. He was accommodated in one of those mystical houses. The warm cosiness was soothing; the atmosphere was light and pleasant. The boy shifted in his soft bed, ran his hand through his hair with the colour of ripe rye, and looked around.

"You are in good hands, young man. Relax and rest," said a tender female voice.

The exhausted boy glanced anxiously around and stared at a young girl. Her skin was quite dark and contrasted with her stunningly green eyes. A gentle smile rested on her lips.

"Who are you?" Felis said.

"My name is Kalia." She gave him a friendly smile. "We discovered you near our village; you were unconscious and exhausted."

Felis shook his head and hurriedly declared, "It's a pleasure, miss. Unfortunately, I have terrible news. An indescribable threat rises from the south, a monster of inexplicable origin. I participated in a march with other Flemitrians and accidentally discovered him. They attempted to slay him, but he possesses godlike might. I barely survived."

Kalia's smile darkened. The girl lowered her clear green eyes and said, "Unfortunately, I know who you speak of. Lethius has been a bane upon these lands for centuries."

To Felis it was unimaginable that other people knew of this terror and that Flemitris had no information on it despite the vile acts it performed in its territory.

"You know about him here?" Felis exclaimed with astonishment. "You should flee at once! Save yourselves! You are so close to the lands it has captured, it will destroy you!"

"Escape is not the way, dear Felis," Kalia told him serenely. "Lethius is an ancient creature and exists to feed its creator, Eratius."

"Eratius has been dead for centuries!" Felis contradicted her. "The wars between his pawns and Flemitris were heavy, but with fire and steel we overpowered and destroyed this evil. I have heard the ancient legends of Ardor's victory over the monsters!"

She shook her head and said, "Eratius is a god, Felis. He will not perish. You can disturb his cults and countries but he will always find a way to return. The appearance of Lethius testifies to this."

"We cannot withstand that!" Felis exclaimed. "Flemitris knows not what it's faced with. We have no weapon against such a scourge. We would all perish if Lethius wills it."

"That is precisely why we are here." Kalia smiled. "We are a people unknown to most. We call ourselves Equilitatem. We make an appearance when disproportionate magical energy rages across the lands and threatens the balance. With our unique magic, we are capable of suppressing anomalies and securing the natural order. We are not murderers. We are not saviours. We simply bring order."

"What's your element?" Felis asked uncertainly. He had read about all the nations and the spheres they used, and this one didn't correspond with the description of any of them. It would be hard to imagine that there was a ninth kind of magic that no one had ever heard of.

"It is not a sphere but just a sacred human characteristic," Kalia answered softly. "We are not special. We are not sorcerers. We use this which shines in our chest, the very same thing you possess as well—our souls. We are taught how to utilise this energy to fulfil our mission."

"You claim to be sorcerers who control no elemental sphere?" Felis was quite surprised. "Is this a craft which can be learned?"

"Although it's possible, it's a very lengthy process," said Kalia. "The initial progress is arduous and slow. The majority of the Equils, including me, began learning before we could stand on our feet. The rewards, however, have been worthwhile. The wisdom that opens before us illuminates our horizon and gives meaning to our lives."

"What kind of abilities do you acquire?" Felis asked, settling more comfortably into the soft bed. He was intrigued by this incredible culture and the secrets that were unfolding before him.

"We are able to touch the depths of human nature," Kalia replied. "We can see one's true self from one glance alone. We can cast our minds into the future. If necessary, we could also extract the essence of magical spheres, but we rarely do it. We are capable of possessing the human mind and healing it. Sometimes we are able to break the barriers of time and travel through it. However, using our powers irresponsibly could cause great cataclysms, even our own death, so we are extremely careful and don't perform a spell unless we've been preparing for years."

Felis watched her as if he were enchanted himself. Everything he heard excited him. He had not suspected the existence of these people. With skills like theirs, Flemitris might stand a chance. Perhaps together with them he would discover a way to protect his people and defeat the monstrous Lethius. He would set off at once to tell the prince and his father about all this. It was important to act quickly. Eneya's life might depend on it.

Ilinar sank into deep thought again. Could all this be true? As Agelik had said, how could our souls contain energy that everyone possesses and yet that no one uses? Perhaps it would remain a mystery as no one had ever heard of Equilitatem. Perhaps they existed only in this book.

Meanwhile, close by in the valley, Eslir stood behind the stone wall of a yard, clutching his sword so hard that his knuckles had turned white. The soldiers around him were restless. It would have been their first time facing such a monster, so they were seriously hoping it wouldn't show up for yet another night. The oracles had felt the intense energy of death in this area and had assumed that Stronius would hit the largest city there. This was the third night Eslir had set an ambush and was waiting for Stronius.

"Your Majesty, are you sure you want to be here? We don't know anything about the demon. It could be dangerous," one of the generals said. He was an Aslanian with eyebrows so light, they looked like silver.

"Someone needs to give a positive example to the infantile Soleyans," Eslir replied with a frown. "I keep telling them to take up arms and prepare for war, but they won't take me seriously if I speak that while hiding in castles."

The general didn't say anything more. He gazed at the misty outlines of the forest. It seemed as if it had become darker. The cold wind brought the smell of death. From the grim depths of Krumerus came a creature that few had seen for millennia. He was a four-legged beast with a tail like a whip. The heavy energy of death flowed from his eyes and mouth like thick glowing smoke. His very presence was crushing like a heavy rock, inspiring horror in the soul, the kind of terror one would feel in one's worst nightmares. It was a creature so unique and evil that it seemed somehow unreal. Eslir stared at Stronius. He had come across demons before, but this one was very different. Even though it wasn't as grotesque as other creatures of Mortelion, with its presence it carried an aura of panic and death. The soldiers were numb in shock. Eslir turned to them and whispered, "It is well known that if you break the concentration of a sorcerer, he won't be able to attack successfully. Perhaps the same applies to this being. Remember the plan, and try to confuse the beast."

A battle horn sounded over the silent city. At its sound, hundreds of soldiers charged out and attacked the demon. When the yelling and fighting was heard, Ilinar realised he had to act. He rose stiffly and began to look around nervously. Halena gave him a rare smile, grasped his hands, and said, "I know you'll succeed. It's meant to be."

After these words, she leaned forward and brushed her pale lips against his cheek. It was Ilinar's first kiss, so this overexcited him and dazzled him. As it was time for him to embark on the mission of his life, he stumbled and became entangled in some protruding roots. He tried to stand up, but he couldn't. His whole face turned purple with embarrassment for having done something so stupid. He tried pulling away but couldn't break free. Halena stared at him with no expression on her face while the other cultists began to wander around him and try to help him. His foot was stuck. This was a nightmare! Something really important depended on him, and he had gotten entangled in a plant!

There was a terrible battle in the valley. Fire burned, and beams of light magic were shot around the place. Soldiers attacked Stronius. He was throwing them around with his horns as if they were rag dolls and treading upon them with his huge hooves. It was complete chaos. No one could break through the solid scales of the creature with a sword attack. Eslir noticed this, and it occurred to him that if managed to get on the beast's back, he might be able to stab his blade between the scales at the demon's neck and inflict a fatal wound. He waited for an opportune moment. He approached Stronius from behind and threw him on his back. Eslir passed a steel rope through his mouth to keep himself mounted while the demon was jumping around like an untamed horse.

"The son of Mortelion, huh? What a joke!" Eslir told him smugly. He pulled out the same dagger which almost took Arkenel's fragile life. The blade found a gap between the scales, and Eslir thrusted the weapon with as much strength as he had.

The legendary Aslanian steel, famous as being the highest quality in these lands, crumbled like an icicle. Eslir couldn't believe his eyes. Stronius bounced again, managing to send his rider flying to the ground. He cast out a devastating field of death energy, smiting every soldier who was still on his feet. They dropped dead like poisoned flies. Eslir survived as he was on the ground and the blast missed him.

"Do you find humour in an encounter with Mortelion's son? This is a confusing statement," Stronius said without moving his mouth. His voice was hissing and echoing as if coming from every direction. "The only one who will laugh today will be our magnificent master, Mortelion, while your blood soaks these foreign lands, Aslanian."

Stronius swung his hooved leg and struck a heavy blow to Eslir's chest, bending his brilliant shiny armour. He spat blood and tried to twist and grip his other sword, which had fallen a bit out of his reach, when the hoof slammed down on his arm. Eslir gritted his teeth painfully while his bones were cracking. Stronius continued speaking: "Know that on this day, because of your monumental arrogance, I will feel pleasure when tasting your blood."

People peeked out of the windows of their houses, trembling and terrified. Many of them had left the city, but those who remained were regretting their decision. They were the first to notice that someone else appeared in the square where the battle was raging—and it wasn't Ilinar.

"Lethius? I've been searching for you. I'd say 'well met', but ..."

The demon lifted his head and cast his deathly gaze at Agelik, who stood a few metres from him, looking at him with curious eyes. A heavy silence fell, disturbed only by Eslir's groans as he assumed out breath-taking gymnastic poses to reach his sword despite the fact that Stronius was still standing on his hand.

"Remove yourself, child. I don't know you," Lethius snapped with a low-pitched, unfriendly voice.

Agelik walked towards him, ignoring all the desolation around. The surviving soldiers stopped attacking. They only stared at the scene in shock. Soleyans and Aslanians alike prayed to Flalirion that this was the reborn Ardor coming to save them.

"No, you know exactly who I am. Lethius, I saw you in my dreams. I couldn't understand whether you were a friend or a foe. I just felt your pain," Agelik continued to explain as if the two were sitting down discussing this at a tea party.

"The name Lethius is not familiar to me. Stop communicating with me, or you will force me to destroy you," the demon threatened.

A triumphant smile appeared on Agelik's face, and he pointed at the beast and began chattering, "Here, that confirms my suspicions. We were in fact friends with you! You came here with the intention of killing innocent Soleyans, so why would you warn me that you will destroy me? You are reluctant to hurt me. Lethius, you don't have to kill people. Let's just walk away to a more peaceful location and spend the night in conversation."

Even the wounded Eslir with broken ribs had to turn around to see if this was a joke. Surely, Lethius wondered the same. He stepped away from his victim and headed towards Agelik, standing in front of him, terrifying and deadly. He breathed light blue air and growled sinisterly. "I am capable of deleting you from existence with a single thought, and you offer me conversation? What manner of sick and deluded child are you? No matter. On this day you will either cry blood tears in honour of Mortelion or perish painfully."

After these words, Stronius swung his horned head and sent Agelik flying to one of the nearby houses. Then he turned around to finish his victims, but he faced his most dangerous enemy. In front of the beaten Eslir stood Ilinar, who had threateningly raised his sword, which was covered in glow juice. Stronius shook his head and said, "May there be more brave heroes amongst you who wish to attempt to slay me. What is your name, mysterious warrior?"

Ilinar was a little surprised by such a festive greeting. Trying

379

to be brave, he lisped, "I am ... my name is Ilinar Lumeris, and I am the king of Soleya. I will not allow you to hurt my people."

"How are you going to stop me when all the others have failed?" The demon laughed.

"I will destroy you with the blessing of Flalirion!" Ilinar gave a battle cry and charged.

Stronius tried to manoeuvre, but Ilinar's attack was simply too overwhelming. The glowing sword struck the monster on his well-armoured back. In order to protect himself, Stronius pushed Ilinar with his horns, knocking him to the ground. For a few seconds the demon seemed confused, and then he bent his legs and dropped to the ground, lamenting loudly. "This sword ... I've never felt such a combination of magical energies ... But how could Ilinar have known?"

When everyone saw the terrible monster wounded, various peasants and surviving soldiers were inspired and attacked him with pitchforks, brooms, shovels, and other devastating weapons. Although Stronius's face was little more than a bare skull, one could still notice shades of annoyance on it. The demon stood up, shaking his head to remove any people who were climbing on him. He fled a little further, stood up amongst the fires that had not yet burned out after the battle, and yelled, "You have not seen the end of this, Soleyans! King Ilinar will not be here to protect you forever. And when he leaves, my desolation will devour you!"

After these words, Stronius galloped away and disappeared into the night. As soon as he was gone, concerned, caring people gathered around Ilinar and helped him up while telling him how brave he was and how he had saved them. Eslir lifted his head painfully after having been trampled by hooves on the ground and spat out a ball of grass and soil.

"And what are you doing here!" the Aslanian yelled. "How come you left Father Erebius alone?"

"Well, I ... I heard about the monster attacking Soleya, and ..." Ilinar began mumbling as if he were apologising.

"Just go away from here. And don't you dare act like a saint!" Eslir roared and threw a ball of soil at him. "I bet the only reason you knew how to defeat the beast is because you share a house with him!"

"Or maybe because Flalirion gave me strength, but you wouldn't understand that because you're Aslanian," Ilinar told him. He walked past the fallen Eslir and knelt beside him. "I understand you were trying to protect our countries, but there's no excuse for some of the things you did. There is no excuse for declaring me dead and stopping me from returning to my own country, to my own people! But you just can't protect them like I can, Eslir. I'm not angry with you, and I don't want to start a fight, but I think it's best if you to go back to Aslania. We'll still be allies and friends, but from a distance."

Ilinar held out a hand to Eslir, who was still on the ground after Stronius had probably broken every bone in his body. But the Aslanian only pulled back and snarled, "You'll be the death of us all! As soon as you sit on this throne, you'll set such relations with Krumerus that you will bury us. Why do you want to feed this monster? How did you find something positive in the damn erebi?!"

"I see that your strategy to fight with them has already destroyed a few villages in less than a week," Ilinar remarked. He stood up. "I don't have to argue with you. I think tonight I proved the obvious: that I was right. And now I'm going to help the people pick you up and stitch and bandage you, but as soon as you're well enough to travel, you'll do exactly that."

Eslir glared at Ilinar with contempt and said, "I hope Flalirion will help you, though I don't think even a god can save you from what you're getting into."

While Eslir was prophesising disaster like an angry witch, Agelik approached them and stood by them respectfully, waiting for the opportunity to speak. The Aslanian turned his attention to him and pointed at him with the arm that hadn't been broken. "And where did this one come from? He just appeared out of nowhere and began talking about his *friendship* with that beast! I should have known Stronius had inside information from corrupted Soleyans. I want to have this guy executed at once."

Agelik didn't even have to open his mouth to defend himself since Ilinar instantly did it for him. "Do you have any idea who he is? Why don't you ever educate yourself on a matter before you start executing? He's not a corrupted Soleyan; he's just … he's traumatised and confused. Leave him alone."

Agelik stepped forward and introduced himself peacefully: "Hello. My name is Agelik. I …"

"Don't dare address me, demon lover!" Eslir roared in a hoarse voice, too loud for someone with broken ribs. "Warriors, get me away from here. We'll return to Lumis, where the sorcerers of life will heal me."

Ilinar rolled his eyes with annoyance. Some people were

impossible. He turned to Agelik and told him softly, "Are you OK? I got really concerned when that beast hit you!"

Agelik touched his waist and stretched his back. He noted, "I might have been bruised a bit. But it matters not! I believe this is the demon I have been seeking!"

"But, Agelik, this demon is called the Stronius," Ilinar pointed out this indisputable difference.

"Regardless of what he's called now, I feel it in my heart that he is the same creature. I need to find out more about him," Agelik continued to chatter.

The soldiers were getting Eslir unstuck from the ground, where his gorgeous armour had left an aesthetic imprint of all its ornaments in the mud. While this was happening, the Aslanian was listening to the conversation and spoke again: "Can you explain why your 'heart' longs for information about Stronius in such a disturbing way? What are you to him?"

Ilinar answered this question as well: "Eslir, this is Agelik, and he's a Soleyan who has lost his memory. He doesn't not know anything about his past and can't find any people who knew him. He had a dream about a demon called Lethius who may know him."

"That's nonsense, I don't trust him," Eslir expressed his supreme opinion.

"I think it's a good idea to learn more about the demon together so we will know how to defend ourselves against it. Perhaps this will be key to finding out more about you as well." Ilinar turned to Agelik, trying to ignore Eslir, who wouldn't bear that, and continued yelling from the ground, "This way he'll use us!"

Ilinar was getting sick of his cousin's voice and snapped at him, "Do you think before you open your mouth? If Agelik is malicious and is a friend of Stronius, why should he research him with us rather than just go and ask him what he needs to know? Just go get some sleep. Sure looks like you need it. Come on, Agelik, let's find an inn somewhere. Tomorrow we will return to Lumis."

The two of them, accompanied by the surviving Soleyan soldiers, walked through the city as many people left their houses to see what had happened. Ilinar and Agelik took a separate room for themselves, where the king of Soleya threw his backpack on the floor and said hurriedly, "I'm glad we met. I have a lot to talk to you about, but I have to do something else first."

Agelik tried to protest, saying, "As a matter of fact, I was hoping I could firstly speak to you about ..."

"I promise I'll be back quickly. Just wait a few minutes!"

It looked like Agelik had more to say, but Ilinar rushed outside. He sneaked through the shadows and headed back to the Thorny Woods. Remaining unnoticed, he slipped back into the darkness between the trees. The Cultists were still where he had left them. He stood stiffly in front of Halena and said, "I made it! I defeated the beast, and my people trust me again. Tomorrow I will return to my capital city."

Halena twisted her lips in a kind of a smile, though her eyes looked just as dead. She said quietly, "Ilinar, that's wonderful. I knew that you'd succeed."

He swept his hair back nervously and cleared his throat. "Yes, we succeeded. The plan was yours, and I'm really grateful to you. But, Halena, when I go back to Lumis, I won't be able to see you any more."

She tilted her head to one side, staring at Ilinar with her huge, pale eyes. She asked, "Would you like to see me in the future?"

"Well, I ..." Ilinar began to stutter, feeling the blood rush to his face again. "You're so different from everyone else I've been surrounded by. I'd like to learn more about you."

Halena smiled at him and stroked his hair lightly with her milky white fingers. She told him, "Maybe you will have the opportunity. I'm going to settle in Kranium more permanently, so when you visit your father, you can also pay me a visit. I'll see you soon, Ilinar!"

Saying that, she pulled him in her arms and hugged him. Ilinar breathed in her scent and melted in her embrace. He pressed her against himself and didn't want to let her go. He tried to make his wish come true by offering, "Halena, just come with me! I'll show you Lumis. It's wonderful, you'll see."

She pulled away from the hug, gave Ilinar another curved smile, and replied, "If I simply go and visit Soleya like this, the other Krumerians won't have me back and may even declare me a heretic. Our countries aren't such great friends yet. Maybe another time."

"Oh well." He lowered his head with an unhappy look. He hadn't expected that saying goodbye to Halena would be so difficult.

Then Ilinar had to return to the inn where Agelik was. Once there, he dropped on the bed, sighing deeply, thinking about how beautiful and incredible Halena was and how all he wanted was to go back to Krumerus to see her again. He did not believe that the day would come when he would feel a certain sadness for returning to his home town.

"Listen, I do apologise for interfering, but—" Agelik cleared his throat.

It was only then that Ilinar remembered Agelik was in the room and turned to him. He was irritated to see that his new friend was rummaging through his luggage and was investigating he almighty sword which had smitten Stronius.

"Hey, can you not touch my things? What's wrong with you?" Ilinar struggled to get his sword, but Agelik had the gall to pull it even farther away.

"The blade is smeared with mushroom juice," the young Soleyan stated in a critical, accusatory look. "Can you tell me what sort of a spectacle took place this evening?"

Ilinar, insulted, pulled his sword from Agelik's hands and said angrily, "It's none of your business."

A dangerous flame sparked in Agelik's eyes. He stood in front of Ilinar, trying to meet his gaze, and said, "You wish of me to simply shrug off the fact that I saw you 'defeat' a dangerous demon by wielding a tin sword covered in mushroom juice whilst numerous far superior warriors failed and perished? That simply will not happen. I invite you once more to explain everything now, or else I'll find myself in need of making some discoveries on my own. I may start by consulting Eslir on the matter."

Ilinar was shocked that someone would talk to him like that. He puffed up, lifted his finger in the air, and began: "Listen now! I am the king of Soleya, and because of my goodwill, you ..."

Agelik crossed his arms, looking at him adamantly. Without knowing why, Ilinar felt like a child who has been naughty. He felt like he didn't want to annoy his new friend, so he surrendered and mumbled tragically, "Agelik, this is a long story. Let's sit down."

Then Ilinar told him about his entire life, and especially the last few months, about how he had defended Krumerus, how Eley had betrayed him, about the murder, and about everything else. Agelik listened to this with growing discontent, and as soon as the story had ended, he rose from the bed angrily and said, "So I'm conversing with a murderer?"

"Did you not hear a word I said? I didn't have a choice! What else could I do? Just let Eley tell everyone that I'm an undead?" Ilinar exclaimed in his defence.

Agelik put his fingers on the bridge of his nose, as if trying to suppress a headache, and said, "Ilinar, we always have a choice. Our actions define us. You were not forced to do anything. Such an act will stain your soul forever."

Ilinar also stood up, planted himself in front of Agelik, and replied firmly, "Yes! It seems to me that having a stain on my soul so that my people could be safe is worth it."

"Do you call safety that which took place this evening?" Agelik waved his hand towards the window, gazing at the bloodstained square.

"OK, I'm not an ideal ruler. I get it!" Ilinar cried. "But what I did was because of my people!"

"The end does not justify the means." Agelik turned away coldly and looked away from him.

"How can you judge me? What would you have done in my place?" Ilinar snapped.

Agelik looked at him angrily and said, "Well, for instance, why would you not use the letter your teacher left you as proof against him? If you were dead indeed, he wouldn't have left you farewell notes. And the will by which he placed himself on the throne would have played a bad joke on him, especially since it was written by his own hand. His plan to dethrone you was simplistic and transparent. There were many ways to prove your innocence, but instead you killed him in his sleep. I understand that he wasn't a perfect human being, but nobody deserves something like that."

Ilinar stared at him with an open mouth. It had never occurred to him to use the note. He felt so stupid and ashamed that he didn't know what to say. Agelik stared at him reprehensively for a few seconds, then added, "And should we converse on the matter of the defeat of a powerful demon, which you achieved with the aid of a tin sword?"

Ilinar didn't feel talkative any more. He felt like he'd be told off regardless. He mumbled, "I told you, I had to face him so my people would trust me again."

"Though I applaud your bravery, I fail to see what made you prevail. You do realise this sword isn't magical?" Agelik stated.

"The Krumerians had weapons which could defeat demons. We just used the mushroom juice to make it glow as if it were blessed by Flalirion. My countrymen wouldn't support me if I kept associating myself with Krumerus on every occasion."

Agelik started pacing back and forth, wondering how to even voice everything which he disagreed with. Eventually he spoke:

"Every weapon is a 'demon slaying weapon' if you battle a lesser being. But in order to defeat something so powerful, you need a real enchanted blade, which you do not possess! To me this was all an obvious set-up. The demon allowed you to defeat him. He was a part of it all! And he murdered hundreds of people to reinforce the realism of your little spectacle."

Now Ilinar was furious. He refused to believe that his dear Halena had led him into something like this. He couldn't imagine she'd lie to him; she just seemed so innocent. He raised his voice, saying, "Well, wait just a minute! Are you accusing me of using the deaths of my countrymen to get my throne? I just learned about the demon and used whatever information I had on him to defeat him."

"How can you believe that? Are you truly so clueless? This was just a way for Krumerus to reinforce your return to the throne as you're a convenient ruler to them," Agelik stated, crossing his arms and looking for any sign of dishonesty on Ilinar's face.

The young monarch, however, continued to passionately defend his point of view: "You seem to express too many opinions on the subjects of magic weapons and politics for someone who lost his memory and is virtually a stranger in this world! You know nothing about me, and you know nothing about Krumerus, so I don't wish to hear your pointless speculations!"

Agelik remained staring Ilinar down for a few seconds, then turned around and stated, "I believe such disagreements are bound to make us unpleasant companions to each other. Apparently I cannot make you see reason, so I feel my presence here is unnecessary. I shall proceed on my way alone. I wish you all the best in your reign."

Having said that, he just walked out and closed the door behind himself. Ilinar wasn't going to chase after him. He felt infuriated by all this. He flung himself on the bed, thinking that his dear Halena wouldn't have orchestrated something so deceitful and lied. As he stared at the ceiling and contemplated all this, he remembered that Halena had told him that Stronius's weakness was that he couldn't face men who charged at him with bravery. Eslir and the soldiers did fight with courage, but it didn't seem to matter. Maybe their weapons were inferior, but Ilinar hardly even hit Stronius. It was just too easy for him. What if this really was a set-up? It still didn't mean that Halena knew the truth. Maybe someone purposefully passed the rumour about the monster to her. It could have been Stronius himself. Anyway, all this still meant that the demon remained undefeated. Ilinar could only hope he'd disappear now, because if he made another appearance, neither the glow-juice sword nor bravery would deter the demon.

Meanwhile, farther to the north, Arkenel sat in the blinding darkness of the night. The dungeon around him reeked of death. It felt as if the moisture was oozing through his clothes. He barely felt aware of where he was. He felt guilty for so many things. There was no trace of his confidence left; he had no idea how he could have trusted himself with the lives of all those people. He had failed with everything. He thought of how Evena could have been merciful to the Krumerians, but because of him she wasn't. He had neither killed her nor really saved her. He had left her besmirched and thirsty for revenge. Somehow he deserved what she'd done to him. The only ones who seemed to be innocent in all this were his poor friends who were slaughtered like animals right in front of him. He couldn't understand why he was alive at all. Was this his ultimate punishment for all the ways he had failed?

"Hey, tosser, are you here?"

Mavarius illuminated the dark corridor with the murky light of a torch which had all but burned out. He stood in the doorway of the dark room where Arkenel was sitting, not knowing how to approach the situation.

"Hi, Mav," Remedor answered him in a dead tone, staring at the nothingness.

"You been here for long? Have you eaten?" Mavarius approached this problem pragmatically.

"I don't wanna eat. Leave me alone," Arkenel spat inhospitably.

Mavarius remembered another pragmatic cause for his friend's bad mood, so he offered his help again. "Hey, I've got miner's. Want some?"

The very idea somehow disgusted Arkenel. His friends were dead because of him. How could he simply slip into the world of miner's and forget about it all? It wasn't fair, so he protested, "Get away from me with this miner's. I want to think with a clear head for once about what's happening to us."

"So what did you think up in the end?" Mavarius replied with irritation.

"All sorts ... I don't know. I don't know what to do with myself," Arkenel told him, his voice breaking. He was suffocated by the thought that he shouldn't be alive at all, that he should have just let Evena kill him.

"Well, I told you to get out of this messed-up city, but you're stubborn," Mavarius warmed him with wisdom.

"No, I don't want that. Just leave me alone," Arkenel snapped at him.

Mavarius raised his hands in a gesture as if to say he was done with this and went to find something else to do. He couldn't remember ever having seen Arkenel in such bad mood before, but he thought it would pass if his friend had some sleep, so he left him alone.

Remedor crouched in the corner, staring silently into the darkness again. His very existence was painful.

CHAPTER 15

THE ESCAPE

It was around six in the evening. The sky over Krumerus had dimmed. Kranium was silent. The lights were few; the brightest were in the dining room of the castle. The Remedor family had gathered there for dinner, but they were all silent and didn't say a word. The situation was extraordinary—Rabolii was present. Lately he had made so many public appearances that it was stunning. And now he had taken the honorary place at the head of the table, gauging everyone around him with a look of superiority. Ravena was afraid to ask him what he was doing there. Once he was sure that he had disturbed everyone sufficiently, Rabolii stood up and said loudly, "My dearest family, I have to admit that over the last few years I was somewhat passive and I ignored both you and Krumerus. Maybe I have seemed disinterested. Perhaps I was missing from your lives. But that will change. Mortelion opened my eyes once again and showed me how important it is to deal with the pressing problems in a timely fashion before they get out of hand. It is time to bring this country to its knees, and I'll do that efficiently without compromise." Rabolii thinned his lips proudly and flared his nostrils with an uplifted, inspired expression. "I wanted you to be the first to learn that I will once again take personal control of Krumerus's armies. Evidently, I can only rely on myself for the important things."

"But, Rab!" Ravena felt like she was going to choke. "How will you lead an army? You are ..."

"Silence, Ravena!" Rabolii bared his teeth like a rabid dog. "You've been treating me like a disabled cripple for far too long! I'm aware of what I'm capable of." He raised his head proudly and announced, "As soon as I stand in charge of my legions

389

of skeletons, I will remind this world who Rabolii Remedor is! And just so you don't feel useless, I will give you assignments; otherwise you'd be a disgrace to the country. You there, the two of you!" He waved his hand towards Regel and Dregel, who were so amazed that their father was addressing them that they started dropping cutlery. "You are appointed to maintain public order. I want you to round up all prisoners and execute them. I need their bodies as soldiers. They're more useful to me dead than alive."

"All of the prisoners?" Ravena emphasised. "Even the ones held for petty theft and drunken brawling?"

"Did I stutter?" Rabolii barked. "I have no use for dysfunctional members of society who are nothing but a burden. Why would I keep them alive and have them demand money and food all while causing problems, when they could serve the greater good of this country with no maintenance? And that reminds me, this city has become flooded with tramps and beggars who came from beyond the Skeletal Wall. Traneya, I want you to execute anyone who can't prove an income and submit the bodies to the necromancers in the temple. As for you, Ravena, just continue dealing with bureaucracy and the complaining nobles like you always do."

The orders were handed out, and no one muttered a word about it. Regel and Dregel were staring at their dishes, not daring to move. Traneya was murdering Rabolii in her thoughts. It was like the corpse wasn't sufficiently insane and unbearable until now, but now he had suddenly decided to execute half his citizens. She knew it wasn't the people's fault that they had to beg in the streets. As it was the skeletons who did all the filthy, miserable jobs, there was just no place in this world for poor people. They couldn't get any kind of work because the corpses would always do it for free. Rabolii had never bothered addressing this because he believed that anyone with half a brain could obtain skeletons and still function in society. Now apparently the necromancer didn't even see the point in having living citizens any more.

"There are too many useless people in this country who do nothing but leech off the resources we have and give nothing back," Rabolii continued talking. "Now that I think about it, I can't help but remember that rabble Arkenel freed from Aldur. I've been getting reports that they're being disruptive to the peace. I'll reverse my decision to spare them. They proved that they don't deserve it. I'll lead a force to recapture them and add them to my glorious army. And that includes the wretched creature which freed them to begin with."

Everyone had been hoping that Arkenel's name wouldn't be mentioned here since Rabolii was obviously in the mood for murder. Regardless, it had come to this. Ravena said calmly, hoping the sound of her voice would bring some reason to this rabid corpse, "Rab, I don't believe Arkenel's a danger to the peace at this point. I visited him earlier today. He seems a bit ... traumatised after what happened in Vern. He probably won't do much more than recover."

She had made a valiant effort to drag Arkenel out of the dungeons and give him something to eat, but she had been just as unsuccessful as Mavarius. Still, Rabolii didn't care, so he roared, "Recover, eh? So that he can gain enough strength to murder me like he intends to?"

"Dear, I can assure you, Arkenel has no such intention," Ravena tried to persuade him.

"There's no need to talk about this any more. After tonight, Arkenel won't be a problem any more," Rabolii said through his teeth with a stone-cold look.

Traneya raised her head with an angry look. To her this sounded like "I'm going to kill Arkenel after dinner." She felt on the threshold of her patience. Ravena didn't react to this line; she just continued to speak as if she weren't conversing with mentally insane individuals. "Rab, he's your son. I understand you have your differences, but it's time to put an end to it."

"Why is everything always about Arkenel?!" Rabolii roared angrily and waved his hands hysterically. "Everything I hear is all about how mean I am to him and how I should give him a chance. Let's forget for a moment that he destroyed my potion and he killed his sister. He's a human wreck, and I want him to have nothing to do with the work I do. He is not my son! He's the man who'll kill me according to the prophecy I received from Mortelion. And you want me to be *nice* to him!"

Traneya had her hand on the handle of her dagger under the table. She didn't know if Rabolii was a real villain or if he was just insane. He wasn't making sense any more and said things which were obviously untrue with all the certainty in the world. Either way, she didn't intend to stand for this a moment longer. Ravena gritted her teeth and tried to keep speaking calmly: "Yes, Rab. I understand you have problems with him. I see you're emotional tonight. Why don't you go upstairs to rest? We can begin work tomorrow."

"No, I'm going to do it right now," Rabolii snarled, got up, waved his cloak, and theatrically headed towards the exit.

Traneya and Ravena stood up, startled. They hadn't seen the necromancer behave like that before. He had never been a soft-hearted person, but his bloodlust right now was unreal. It didn't seem at all impossible to them that he'd just snap Arkenel's neck. The two of them walked after Rabolii, but he sensed that someone was trying to hinder him, so he sent out a devastating force field in all directions, sweeping the two women back, along with any nearby objects. Puddings, soups, and compotes flew in the air, spilling everywhere and making a mess, but only Rabolii remained clean, perfect, and wonderful as he walked boastfully towards the exit. Empowered by his own majesty and inspired by his power, he flew on the wings of righteousness like fate itself to bring order to this chaotic world. He walked down the stairs, planning to soil his soles in an extremely filthy and disgusting place, but it needed to be done. The necromancer barged into the abandoned kitchen, its rotten door smashing into pieces in front of him. He charged in and began rummaging around the place with an evil look, searching for a particular someone. He knew that Arkenel had probably heard him come in already and probably hid like a scared rat. However, nobody could play hide-and-seek forever with Rabolii Remedor! As he rampaged between the overturned tables, the necromancer was very deeply concentrated on what he was doing, so when he felt a movement behind him, he was startled dramatically. He turned around with a devastating gaze just to face the very person he sought.

"You!" Rabolii said through his teeth and walked forward like an approaching storm.

"I knew you'd come for me sooner or later," Arkenel murmured. He looked different, though not in any physical way. His very expression had changed. He seemed like one of those people who would become deeply upset if one was merely to raise one's voice in front of them. But if he was afraid, why would he dare show himself?

"How calmly you approach your own execution!" Rabolii's lips twisted in a mean smile. "Where's that disgusting man who always follows you around? Are you two setting a trap for me?"

Arkenel sighed tiredly. "Do I look like someone who's going to set traps? Just ... just finish me off."

Rabolii blinked in surprise then raised his head and looked at his son with superiority. "What? Have you finally realised how pitiful, useless, and wretched you are, and you've decided to make this easier for us?"

Arkenel sighed, stuck his hands in his pockets, and said, "None of your business."

"Well, that's splendid," Rabolii announced with a ruthless look, demonstratively removing the glove from his right hand. "But before I finish you off, I want you to know that I truly am sorry. You were my firstborn son, and I wanted you to have a more meaningful existence."

Arkenel collapsed onto his knees before the stern necromancer, waiting for his father's devastating touch to put an end to it all. The hand of doom was placed on the head of the young Remedor. He realised that this was probably the closest thing to tenderness he had received from his father for as long as he could remember. At that moment Arkenel could only feel relief. He had lived in pain and remorse for weeks and was so accustomed to the thought that he would die that he just wanted to have it end. As for Rabolii, he felt as if he were putting down a sick animal. But a moment before he would have let out his deadly magic into his son's skull, something surprised him from behind. A metal pipe slammed him across the back of the head, and Rabolii collapsed on the ground like a straw scarecrow struck by a lightning. Arkenel lifted an innocent gaze and saw the shabby silhouette of Mavarius rising behind the necromancer.

"Have you gone nuts?!" the man yelled.

"Mav, didn't I tell you to stay where I left you?" Arkenel mumbled.

However, Rabolii strong as steel, so he remained conscious after the strike. At first he was too shocked by the thought that somebody had committed assault on his precious self and thrown him to the filthy ground. He rose like a ghost from the grave, spreading glowing hands with an ominous expression, preparing to dash his abusers to pieces. He growled with a double-pitched voice, "Filthy wretches! Now I will ..."

"Shut up for a second!" Mavarius snapped at him and pointed at him with the pipe. After dealing with the champion of Mortelion, he turned to Arkenel and told him, "Can you stop acting like a grandma who's constantly crying about something?"

"Leave me alone!" Arkenel protested. He got up, crossed his arms firmly then tried to leave the scene.

"You think I don't know what all this is about?" Mavarius walked after him. "You've not touched miner's in weeks, so you're feeling like crap. What's this stubbornness? You prefer to die or something?"

Rabolii's eye began twitching from seeing this scene. He couldn't believe what he was witnessing. He decided to kill them both because they had caused him so much inconvenience, but he was also curious about why they were quarrelling.

"You think all this is because of some dumb herb?!" Arkenel shouted, seeming as if he would cry at any moment. "I just deserve to die here. If it weren't for me, Salina would be alive, Graz would be alive … Because of me, all those people …"

Mavarius bared his teeth and punched Arkenel, sending him to the floor. He stood over him and yelled, "And if you'd just gotten high as I told you, you would have forgotten all this drama. But you've given up on it all, drowning yourself in this crap, and you want to drown me as well. But I'm done with this, you hear me?!"

"Touching," Rabolii noted. He was still standing there as if he were watching a play.

Mavarius turned to him with a fierce look as if he didn't know at what to point his aggression, so he automatically switched to whichever target made the most noise. He walked towards Rabolii with a threatening gait and snarled, "What the heck are you still doing here?"

"I am not as easily distracted as your intoxicated self. I still remember I came here to send Arkenel to the afterlife with Mortelion. He does not mind, so get out of my way," Rabolii ordered powerfully.

Seeing that this battle was becoming impossible, Mavarius buried his fingers in his hair desperately. He could only ask one question about something which he'd never understood: "And why?! What did Arkenel ever do to you? You've screwed him over so many times. Do you have any idea what he's been through?"

Rabolii stepped forward, facing Mavarius up close, their gazes levelling. The cold, dead eyes of the necromancer stabbed the other man, and his words cut like ice blades: "And, if I may quote you, why are you drowning in his misery? Why are you tying a rock to your neck when diving into a pond? He's not even your real friend. You're simply useful and convenient to him. That's why he keeps you around. Such a shame Arkenel wouldn't do the same for you. He'll dispose of you as soon as he doesn't need you any more."

"What are you on about? This has nothing to do with it,"

Mavarius snapped as Rabolii stepped closer, approaching with his deathly breath like a terrifying mummy walking away from its sarcophagus.

"It has plenty to do with all of this. Because you're in my way again, and you're still in danger because of Arkenel. I wonder if you'd still do this if you knew him as well as I do," Rabolii continued to speak.

His gaze was piercing to the soul. Mavarius began backing off as the necromancer was approaching him, horrifying as death itself. Arkenel had shrunk in the corner with his bloodstained mouth and could only blink in fright. It didn't look like he planned to get involved. When Mavarius almost stepped on Arkenel, he realised he had nowhere else to retreat to, so he began pleading: "Uh, just listen to me for a moment. We won't be a bother any more. We'll leave the city. We'll leave the country if we have to. You won't see us again. Just ... just don't kill anyone, OK? I mean, just look at him!" He gestured towards the bloodstained Arkenel. "Does this look like a threat? Just leave him alone."

"Mav, you don't need to ..." Arkenel tried to speak.

"Shut your mouth!" Mavarius snapped at him and kicked him.

Rabolii had a disgusted expression. This was such a ridiculous scene to him. Arkenel seemed like such trash to him right now that he felt it would be beneath him to kill him. Obviously, the young Remedor was digging his own grave. When a man is defeated in his mind, no one can help him any more. Despite being seemingly young and healthy, he wasn't a threat any more. So Rabolii just smiled and stepped back, proclaiming, "I've wasted enough time with this. I'm convinced that Arkenel will find another way to kill himself. My intervention is unnecessary. Now get out of my city before I do decide to step in."

Mavarius gritted his teeth with supressed anger. Without looking away from Rabolii, he grabbed Arkenel and dragged him away. The necromancer just followed them with a cold gaze. He felt so powerful. This time he had killed someone without even laying a finger on them. He knew he was good at hitting with words exactly where people would be most hurt. Sometimes a single sentence caused more damage than a knife cut. That was just too easy. Anyways, Rabolii wanted to see how things played out. He took a dead bird out of his pocket. In the hands of the necromancer, it spread its wings and fluttered after Arkenel.

Shaking and overwhelmed by mixed emotions, the two men began leaving the ruined kitchen. Arkenel was hardly even walking; he was just being dragged along as if he had lost the will to use his legs. Mavarius kept dragging him, and after they found themselves on a deserted backstreet next to the castle, he threw his friend against the wall and crossed his arms. He seemed irritated and ready for quarrelling. He yelled, "Well? Now what are we going to do?!"

"I don't know ... you should have just left me there," Arkenel said powerlessly, propping his back against the wall.

"I'm so sick of your moods. You know that?!" Mavarius barked. "I'm sick of your problems. I'm sick of dealing with your crap. Just look at yourself! What will you do as soon as I turn around for a second?"

"What do you care?" Arkenel replied irritably. "It's as if you don't want me to just disappear and leave you in peace so you can go back into the woods with the savages."

"Gods, I can't stand you," Mavarius groaned. "Tosser, just get booze or something ... anything. Just stop being like this."

"Booze won't change anything," Arkenel mumbled.

"Sure, but letting the geezer kill you is a great decision, eh?!" There was no answer to this question. Arkenel only stared at the ground. Mavarius raised his hands and said, "You know what? Sort yourself out. I can't keep babysitting you. Go to Aldur, go wherever, but I won't carry you there."

"Is this how it's gonna be? You'll just turn around and walk away? Like you did at the siege?" Arkenel muttered. He didn't look disappointed or angry. He just seemed shattered and defeated.

"Why not?" Mavarius already had his back turned towards him.

A part of Arkenel was screaming for help in that moment. He couldn't bear being abandoned like this again. Still, despite being destroyed, he had some wrathful pride left in him, so he spat, "I'm not gonna beg you. Sod off if I'm such a bloody burden!"

Mavarius wouldn't wait to hear this a second time. Without turning around, he put his hands in his pockets and walked down the street, soon vanishing from sight. Arkenel stared silently after him. Now he was alone, without a single friend, without any reason to stay alive. He felt like he was bleeding from the inside. He'd been wounded in many ways before, but this was different. Something was ripping his chest. It was a pain like self-destructive hatred. It was something he couldn't bear any more. He pulled out the short dagger he always carried around. It was special to him; it was one of the first things he had made with Graz. It was strange that such a precious item would now take his life away. Without any concern for himself, Arkenel dragged the blade across his wrist. He stared at the black blood as it was flowing out. At that moment nothing else existed for him. The good things of this life were so distant that they were like memories of a dream. The only real thing that wasn't a hallucination in this cold world were the corpses of his friends and his sister's dead body. It was the hateful, disdainful gaze of Rabolii; it was Mavarius's turned back. Arkenel leaned his head against the cold stone wall. He could only think of the tragedies of his life. The street was deserted. There was no light around. Everything sank in a deafening silence and dazzling darkness. He sat there bleeding on the filthy street, shaken by the incoming cold. The shapes in the darkness took on a life of their own. They all resembled monsters with huge teeth, circling their helpless victim, ready to kill. Arkenel shut his eyes, shaking from the cold, trying to think that it was all over now and soon his suffering would end.

Soon after, Arkenel lost consciousness. Rabolii's bird was watching in the shadows, and when Arkenel stopped moving, it returned and landed on its master's shoulder. Rabolii had seen it all. Without any emotion appearing on his face, he turned and walked towards his room. If he were to find Ravena on the way, he would casually let her know that Arkenel had killed himself, and that would probably be the last time he would need to bother with this dreadful boy. He turned around to look at the demolished kitchen for the last time. He felt a weight in his chest. Throughout his life, his conscience and egoism had battled long and hard, the latter prevailing most of the time. The necromancer didn't always enjoy what he had to do. If he lived in a perfect world, Arkenel never would have set foot in Kranium, for his own good, and would have settled somewhere far away. However, he didn't do that. He messed things up for himself and forced his father to stain his soul with a murder. Rabolii felt as if he had no choice. He couldn't let the prophecy come true.

Ilinar quickly remembered that being a king wasn't as magical and wonderful as he had imagined in his innocent childhood. He was immediately overwhelmed by tasks. He had meetings with too many people and had to tell again and again his made-up story of how he found out all by himself about the dangerous demon Stronius and how he had defeated him with Flalirion's help. Of course, the magic sword used for this heroism had disappeared mysteriously before the sorcerers had a chance to take a look at it. That occurrence turned out to be a tragedy for two entire countries, because in fact Stronius didn't cease to appear. People still spotted him lurking around Soleya, but he didn't attack the villages there. Instead he turned his attention to Aslania. Ilinar was concerned about this outcome. He wouldn't be able to use the Krumerian weapons for protection. He was trying to distance himself from the land of monsters in the eyes of the people. And even if he did try, it would become obvious such weapons weren't very effective. He tried to spread the idea that courage helps against the beast. However, very soon afterwards he received reports that whatever brave Aslanians stood against the beast died just the same as the cowardly ones. All that worried Ilinar. He didn't know much about Stronius to begin with, and now everyone expected him to resolve the problem. And that wasn't even the only thing. Mountains of other issues awaited his attention. He felt crushed by his workload.

One night, Ilinar tried to save himself from the crowd, so he visited Eslir in the hospital ward, where he had stretched himself into his wondrous snow-white bed, covered in bandages from head to toe. Though it wasn't too late in the evening, the Aslanian was deep in sleep, snoring. Ilinar relaxed in one of the richly ornamented velvet sofas and stared ahead at the dimming landscape in the window. He contemplated the uncertain future. He missed Krumerus a bit. He had just begun to get to know his family and build friendships, and here he was again as if nothing had happened.

Something rustled in the darkness, silent and stealthy like the wings of a nightbird. Ilinar turned to one of the windows and froze, wondering whether to believe his eyes. In the large hospital room stood Halena, her pale skin contrasting with the darkness, making her look like an apparition. With an ungraceful, stumbling stride, the Soleyan walked over to her and opened and closed his mouth several times silently to start a conversation. Halena whispered softly, "I came to collect Her Majesty's cloak. She'll want it back."

Ilinar could barely comprehend this statement. He just stuttered, "You ... how did you get in here?"

"Windows." Halena shrugged casually.

Ilinar had the feeling that this was a meeting set by destiny itself. He began to move with trembling hands, as if he didn't know if he wanted to touch Halena somehow, and stammered, "You can ... you can stay over for the night. I don't want to send you off to the woods when it gets dark."

At this point, he realised that like every Krumerian, Halena deliberately travelled in the dark, so he began punch himself mentally for having said something stupid. To his surprise, her lips twisted in a smile, and she said, "That would be very nice. Your castle is magnificent."

Eslir began snoring more angrily as if he sensed in a dream that his evil enemies had gathered. Ilinar glanced at him and offered, "Let's get out before he wakes up."

They slipped silently out of the ward and sneaked through the deserted corridors. Here and there they came across guards who gave them strange looks, but Ilinar acted like everything was fine, so no one asked questions. The two of them reached the king and queen's chambers. There they could be alone. Ilinar ran a hand through his hair nervously and said, "By the way, we don't need to hide you. We can introduce you as an ... ambassador or something. I don't want you to feel uncomfortable here."

"It's OK. I don't think I'll stay for too long. I have work to do in the temple," Halena replied.

Ilinar had no idea what work there was to do in the temples of Mortelion, but he still tried to bargain: "At least for a couple of days? I mean, you can't leave before seeing at least one of our flame carnivals. It's so beautiful. In the evenings we ..."

While he was chattering, Halena did something unexpected. She grabbed him and began kissing him. Ilinar was shocked and started shifting, confused by this sudden assault. When Halena let him go, he opened his mouth to protest, but then he froze in place as he saw that she was unbuttoning her blouse. He said in a high-pitched voice, "Halena, we shouldn't do this. If people find out, you will never be able to marry!"

She gave him a faint smile and pushed him back onto the bed, saying, "That's not how it works in Krumerus."

Ilinar wanted to resist somehow because of the rules of decency his mom had taught him, but he was more excited than ever. He surrendered to Halena's lead. Over the next five minutes he became a man. Once he had finished, he could only hold her in his arms, perceiving her as the greatest treasure he had ever had. He never wanted to let her go. She lay silently, breathing shallowly. He was silent just for a few seconds, then began chattering, "That was ... amazing! Halena, I always liked you. You're just so beautiful. But I never imagined you could feel the same. You've made me so happy. I've never felt closer to anyone before. I ... I wish this moment could last forever."

Halena was blankly staring ahead as she lay in Ilinar's arms as if she were very far away mentally. She didn't reply to that statement. She was silent for a few minutes and then just stated, "I can't stay here for long."

Ilinar tightened his grip around her like a python around its victim and began protesting, "Why? What is it that you need to do in Krumerus?"

Halena paused for a moment, then replied, "You know about our fight with Vern, right? The cultists can't stay idle. My home town is in danger. That's why I left it. I'm trying to get help for the area."

Ilinar immediately suggested, "I could help Krumerus strengthen the border defences. That way you won't have to go back."

Halena shifted uncomfortably and replied, "Ilinar, you retrieved your throne a few days ago. Helping Krumerus openly can ruin you. You'll have to be discreet for now."

"What can I do?" he bellowed sadly.

"Do you have access to those skeletons that Rabolii Remedor left behind not too long ago?" she asked.

"No, the authorities crushed them way back. In Soleya we're very careful with any bones. We always destroy them."

Halena sighed, displeased, and asked, "What about gold?"

"How much gold would you need?" Ilinar asked with a frown.

"I heard from Rabolii that in order to provide a good defence for the west, we would need about a hundred kilograms."

Ilinar blinked with a troubled expression. He wished that Eley were here to tell him if that was a lot and how such an expenditure could remain hidden. He replied, upset, "I ... I don't know how I could bring so much gold to Krumerus in secret." Her expression barely changed. She just looked away from him without saying anything, and that immediately overwhelmed him, so he added, "But ... but I'll find some way. You can trust me."

She smiled at him and kissed him softly on the lips, then said, "Thank you, Ilinar."

He felt dizzy and buried his fingers in her hair. Paying a hundred kilograms of gold for such happiness seemed like a good deal.

It was hours before Ilinar was able to fall asleep. He felt incredible and couldn't believe that all this was happening to him. He could only stare at Halena, who was sleeping in the middle of the night for unexplainable reasons. He traced with his fingers every curve of her body and face. He caressed her and admired her. When the fatigue finally overcame him, he slipped into dreamland, where he could keep enjoying this wonderful woman.

In the morning, Ilinar found himself alone. As he was awaking, for a moment he couldn't tell if yesterday wasn't some beautiful dream. He started looking around for Halena when he saw a note on the pillow. He unfolded it with trembling hands and looked at the perfectly written letters arranged on the paper like beads on a necklace.

Dear Ilinar,

I'm sorry you need to wake up and find that I'm gone. I have a few urgent duties in Krumerus, and I need to go back before I can be with you again. As soon as my home town receives the necessary protection, I will find you again. Thank you for the wonderful night. You made me feel really special.

Forever yours,
Halena

Ilinar melted like snow in May as he hugged the note like it were the most precious thing in the world. He would immediately send the gold to Krumerus in hope that the west would be fortified as soon as possible and that Halena would return to him.

Once again, the familiar moment came when the darkness and the silence broke away so that pain and nausea could take their place. Arkenel woke up without knowing what world he was in. A memory flashed through his mind about what had happened recently, so he rose up and looked around. He felt dizzy. His aching sliced wrists were now bandaged. It was dark. Kranium stood in the distance like a shadowy silhouette outlined against the night sky.

"Careful, you'll get dizzy," Traneya said quietly, placing a hand on his shoulder.

Arkenel stared around like an owl at daytime; the very fact that he was in such a familiar setting suffocated him. How had he managed to survive this time?! He collapsed helplessly back to the ground and groaned, "Traneya, what's going on? Where are we?"

"Outside of Kranium, that's where," she answered. Behind her, in the background, Regel and Dregel were trying to pluck each other's eyes out. Estrella had also crouched beside the wounded. She had put a black scarf around her head so she'd look less foreign. Traneya added, "Rabolii tried to kill you, so we left the city."

Arkenel sighed angrily. He raised his hands in the air, nodding at his bandaged wrists. "If you mean this, Rabolii didn't do it to me."

"Rabolii has been treating you like a trash ever since you got back from Aldur, and that has had an obviously bad effect on you," Traneya replied sullenly. "He won't stop until he kills you, and I don't think either of us is safe."

Arkenel looked away with a dead expression. He didn't want to start explaining that Rabolii was the least of his problems. He didn't care much about living and dying; that didn't matter after everything that had happened. From the very beginning of his life, Arkenel had always been taught that he needed to earn his right to exist, to prove himself worthy, and to succeed in anything he did; otherwise it wouldn't matter whether he was in this world or not. What was the point of his existence if he couldn't protect the people closest to him? What was the worth of a man whose father was trying to kill him and whose best friend left him bleeding in some filthy alleyway?

Estrella barely listened to the conversation as she tried to unpeel her shoes from something sticky she had stepped in. At some point she said, "Well, I would offer to shelter you, but my husband wouldn't like you in the house. He has some very ... extreme views about your race."

"We can't cross the border anyway," Traneya noted. "The Thorny Woods passage is the usual place where enemies enter, so it's always kept under observation. Besides, it wouldn't be safe for us to head in that direction by ourselves with a wounded Arkenel and two big babies. We can't defend them if some beast finds us."

Arkenel turned his eye away with annoyance. Regel and Dregel weren't paying attention to what was being said. Instead they were stomping around some dazzled snake which was trying to escape from them. Estrella looked around and asked cautiously, "So, is it too dangerous for us to travel alone? But ...

but I was hoping that as soon as we escaped Kranium, you would allow me to return to Soleya! I thought we had grown out of being prisoner and master."

Traneya put her hands on the shoulders of the sorceress and gave her a sincere reply: "Of course we are. However, taking you to Soleya would be very difficult. The passages are monitored, and we are being hunted. And as if that were not enough, we also have the biggest gathering of monsters in the Thorny Woods. If we have the misfortune of encountering anything larger than a bat, we are all dead."

Estrella looked away, her emerald eyes filling with tears. She cried, "I ... I got married two months ago. I was still arranging all my things in my husband's house, and everything was exactly the way I wanted it to be. We were hoping I'd get pregnant soon. You don't understand what a comedown it is for me to be here after my life was perfect."

Traneya drew her in a comforting embrace and said encouragingly, "Now, now! You'll return there, I promise you. Perhaps it would be easier for us to cross the border with Aslania, then you can make your journey through there." Traneya lowered her voice and added quietly, "Besides, I really need you now. I must have one normal person around me so I can deal with my brothers."

Estrella wiped her eyes and nodded. Traneya was glad to have her around. She wasn't used to being the responsible person. So far, no matter what happened, she could rely on Salina and Ravena and Malior. People never depended on her. It was as if the sorceress felt what the other woman was thinking and asked, "Are we going to wait for your mother? I thought we were taking her with us."

Arkenel snorted and mumbled, "She won't come. If she finds outs what we have done, she'll try to reconcile us with our father, so if we'll be doing that, we might as well just go back to Kranium."

"He's right," said Traneya. "There's no way we can get Mom to see what an evil freak Rabolii is. She'll need to reach that insight herself. We're going to the east. Remedor has less control there. We'll stop in cities on the way to eat and sleep, but we'll need to use different names and try not to draw attention."

"Yes ... about that." Estrella turned her attention to Arkenel. "Aren't his scars a bit ... identifiable?"

Traneya laughed. "No scar is identifiable in Krumerus, believe me. Let's go now and use our lead before the corpse notices we're missing."

Arkenel stood up reluctantly and dragged his feet after his sister. Every movement, every breath, everything, was a pain to him. He couldn't live with himself. He couldn't imagine how he would live on after everything that had happened to him. His existence was agony, and no matter how much he wanted to get some salvation, he didn't think he deserved it. He was alone forever and destroyed.

It wasn't long before Kranium felt the absence of Remedor's blessed youth. Naturally, Rabolii was the last one to notice. He was having a great time in the courtyard while standing on a ladder. Demons and vampires fluttered around him and carried bones, sticking them together and building something which looked rather shapeless at this stage. The necromancer seemed very happy. He had widened, inspired nostrils like an excited horse, and he watched proudly as the work progressed. This was like a Saturday picnic to him. But of course his mad, hysterical wife barged in to ruin everything. She stormed into the courtyard and yelled, "Rabolii Vargnarii Remedor, where are our children?"

"I don't know. I'm busy. Stop ruining my concentration." He tried to dispose of this nuisance, but the very fact that he'd been called by his full name made him realise that salvation wouldn't come so easily this time.

"Listen to me for a moment. Look at me!" Ravena insisted, trying to meet his gaze, but Rabolii was perched proudly on his ladder like an eagle on a high cliff and was ignoring her. Angrily, she shook his ladder and yelled, "Where are they?"

Rabolii found himself forced to deal with this insignificance, so he caused himself the discomfort of coming down to the ground. He snapped, "Why are you asking me? You know I don't care. I'm aware that Ilinar is in Soleya, if that's what you're bothered about."

Ravena had never had such an irresistible urge to punch him in the face. She clenched her fists so painfully that her nails dug into her own skin. She said through her teeth, "Rab, yesterday you were very emotional at dinner. You announced that you would 'talk' with Arkenel and said he wouldn't be a problem any more. Traneya was furious at you. Now both of them and the twins are gone. Is there something I've missed?"

"How am I supposed to know?" Rabolii continued to behave in the same infuriating way. In fact, the whole situation sparked a slight curiosity in him. He thought someone would have found Arkenel's blood-drained corpse in the back alleyway, so at least this investigation would be over. He had no idea where the rest of his useless children were.

"And there's more. The sorceress is also missing. Mavarius is gone. I looked for them to ask them whether ..."

"Who?" It was as if Rabolii had dropped from another planet and had no idea what was going on. He was competent on hundreds of topics involving skeletons, carcasses, potions, Mortelion, magic, and whatnot, but anything regarding his family was much less interesting.

Ravena was losing her patience. She had no strength or will to be diplomatic any more and preserve the necromancer's unhealthy pride, so she snapped, "Do you think I don't know what this is all about? I know you're upset that your precious potion was stolen, I know you're broken by Salina's death." Rabolii turned to his wife with the devastating face of an owl which has been disturbed by a bright lantern in the night. That didn't scare Ravena, so she kept talking: "I know you're always in a bad mood, but ruining other people's lives isn't helping anyone. Right now you're destroying everything we've built. Rab, this is our children we're talking about. How can you not care what happens to them? How can you bear ill will against your firstborn son? I've always tried to understand you, but now I just don't know any more."

Rabolii stared at her, standing there like a tombstone and emitting just as much emotion. When the annoying tirade was over, he just asked coldly, "Are you done?"

Ravena stared at him in shock and shook her head. "I can't believe this, Rab."

"Staying here and moaning doesn't help anybody. Go back to the castle and deal with those annoying villagers who want help after the earthquakes. Two more people ruined my morning by mentioning this detail, and if I hear about it for a third time, I will acquire a new skeleton! I'm going to find the little traitors myself, and I'll make sure they get what they deserve for turning their backs on me and running off." Ravena felt like she was living in some nightmare. She tried to oppose this somehow, but Rabolii was incapable of refraining from speaking for two seconds. "If you insist on finding Arkenel, I can advise you to search the backstreets behind the castle, I think he killed himself there yesterday, after I informed him he was garbage."

"Rabolii, what's wrong with you?!" Ravena yelled at him.

"How can you talk like this? Have you lost your mind?! I don't know who you are any more ... If you don't plan to take your responsibility as a parent, then I'll do it. I'm going to gather soldiers. I'll find our children myself."

But when she turned, her path was blocked by vampires and skeletons who watched her adamantly. She took a step back. The terrifying Rabolii put his bony hands on her shoulders and hissed viciously, "Are you now planning to run away as well and join the rebel camp of that disgusting one-eyed fool you call a son? I will not allow this, Ravena. I will not watch my kingdom fall apart brick by brick. You will return to the castle and deal with the earthquakes and everything else as a good wife, and I will fulfil the will of the holy Mortelion and destroy our enemies. Do you understand?"

"Rab, you scare me," Ravena muttered. "I can't believe it. We're talking about your own son here. How can you be so determined to kill him? If you just stop and think for a moment ..."

"I've been thinking a lot about it, Ravena!" Rabolii bared his teeth. "I have no room for sympathy. It is prophesied that he will kill me. I can't afford for that to happen."

Ravena looked at him angrily and said, "I don't know about you, but I would die for my children. I'm sorry to tell you, but did it never occur to you that you won't live forever? For how long will you support yourself with potions and magic? How long do you have left? Ten years? Fifteen? What do you want to leave behind?"

"You don't understand!" Rabolii croaked. Now he was probably frustrated. He was always very emotional when someone mentioned his death. Ravena was rarely the one to do it, but this was a special event. "I can't die."

"Everyone thinks that," Ravena murmured.

"That's not what I meant." Some hints of pain appeared on the face of the necromancer. That was rare since his eternal pride was too strong to let such emotions show. "I mean, I mustn't die."

"We're all trying to prevent it, Rab, but you're creating enemies everywhere, even within your own family!" exclaimed Ravena.

Rabolii grunted gravely and said with a miserable expression, "You still don't understand ... I can't blame you. Death is an enigma to all of us." Ravena could already recognise the tone with which Rabolii would begin one of his regular long monologues which made sense only in the last two sentences. "It's not clear what happens with us. We can but guess. Maybe we wander like ghosts on the earth for eternity. Maybe we move on to Mortelion's domain, or perhaps it's the end of it all, just the end of our existence. But one thing is certain: death's the same for all of us, so there is no reason to fear it. It's natural. That would be what I felt had I not been burdened with something only I know of. Most of the time I try not to think about it, but this ugly secret keeps plaguing my thoughts. Over the years it has awakened me from my sleep ... when I did sleep." Ravena called upon her endless patience. She hated it when Rabolii dropped such surprises. Just when she thought she was informed of all his crimes, all his bastard children, and the ugly details of this past, something new would come up to cause panic again. "Decades ago I was confident. I was young and arrogant. I thought I could get involved with anyone and get out safely. I thought there was no situation I couldn't handle and that there was no magic I couldn't dispel. I found strong allies whom I'd use for my purposes and never intended to return their favours. I didn't even think that someone might be more powerful and cunning than me. I fell into a trap I didn't expect, and I became captive of something I couldn't fight against. When I realised what had happened, I tried to break free and get out of my mess somehow, but the deities didn't accept that." Rabolii sighed with a tragic face and added dramatically, "They didn't allow me. They chained me to themselves until the end of eternity."

Ravena failed to see how this was a real or relevant issue or in what way it justified Rabolii's desire to kill Arkenel. She saw that she was now expected to gasp, make a move to hug him, and ask him additional questions, but she was too annoyed for such displays of affection. She asked him, "Well? How did they chain you? I see you here in front of me now, and there are no chains or ropes."

"There's an amazing number of things you are blind to, Ravena!" Rabolii yelled at her. He wouldn't have people belittle his problems. "Psychically I managed to escape, but a part of me will always be there. My soul has been claimed. So when I die, I won't go to the lands of Mortelion. I won't be a ghost. I'll be a toy for my enslavers forever. I'll suffer one torture after another, along with humiliation and pain. They'll do anything they can to hurt me. My existence will be an endless agony. All

I'll be able to do is beg them to destroy my soul and release me, but they won't do it.

"Do you remember the day I was killed? I was shaken by panic, petrified by terror, for I could feel them pulling me towards them. If that were not the case that day nineteen years ago, I would have just closed my eyes and passed away in peace without fear, but I couldn't. I couldn't do something as simple and natural as dying."

Rabolii ran his hand over his purpling face. He looked miserable and desperate. Ravena gazed at him sympathetically. It was unreal how he would just always pull the sad face on her and, regardless of what he had done, get her to forgive him or at least sympathise. Ravena wanted nothing more in this world right now than to save him. She asked softly, "Why didn't you ever mention this before, Rab? If we would have known ..."

"Why? Would you have been able to do anything?" he snapped at her. "Neither you nor anyone else could help me. I wouldn't be able to bear the pity you'd display for me. I'm Rabolii Remedor, not some wounded baby. I can carry this burden alone."

"Is there no way for you to be saved? Who are the people who will claim your soul once you die?"

Rabolii gritted his teeth and said hatefully, "Vernian deities. It's rumoured that they are immortal, but at times like these I have no choice but to test the truth of this legend. I'll confront them with my armies. I'll slaughter every last one of their nation and free my soul. I have no choice."

Ravena stood and gazed at him. She said, "Was that the real reason to attack them this whole time? Was it just for your soul?"

"Well, is it a small thing? I don't trust my subjects to understand how important this is to me. I am afraid that if I don't give people a better reason to fight, they won't support me in this. Many of the nobles would choose to sacrifice me if that would mean peace for them. However, we'll never have peace. Mortelion wants blood. So I will do whatever I need to, no matter what the people think, no matter what the soldiers think, no matter what Arkenel thinks. His ambitions will be the death of me, and I will not allow that."

Ravena groaned. They had reached the Arkenel topic again. She noted, "That prophecy definitely came from the mouth of someone who hates you a lot and knows the whole story of your soul. It's probably a set up, which aims to ruin your family. Why do you insist on listening to those who hate you?!"

"I don't know exactly what I heard that night, but the speaker didn't know I was listening," Rabolii said. "They couldn't have lied to me. I am certain Arkenel will be my killer. Think about it, Ravena. Who else could it be? Ilinar? Either one of the twins? I regret having to do this, but ..."

"You mustn't die," his wife finished drily.

"Exactly. And now that you are aware of this, go deal with the earthquake problem," Rabolii commanded her coldly.

Ravena could only nod stiffly. She turned and walked towards the castle. She understood she wouldn't get through to Rabolii and that he wouldn't assist her. She was on her own and didn't know what to think any more. She had fought back against her husband's ridiculous behaviour for so many years, but now she felt powerless. She didn't know what the right thing to do was; she didn't know how to help. Everything was too vague to her, but she knew one thing for sure. She knew things between her husband and her son would go from bad to worse. She even began to think that maybe Arkenel would be inclined to kill Rabolii for no other reason than self-defence as he wouldn't want to be hunted like an animal. And who could blame him? The necromancer had made this a matter of life and death, leaving no choice for his son. Ravena couldn't defend her children, not openly. She'd try to gather her own information somehow and undermine Rabolii's attempts to find them, maybe even plant false information about their whereabouts to confuse him. It wouldn't be an easy task since the necromancer had millions of eyes and ears everywhere.

Rabolii looked grimly after his wife, feeling that he didn't have her support as before. He didn't know why he even cared. It wasn't like he was unaccustomed to being hated for doing what must be done. And come to think of it, it had been a long time since Arkenel had died on the backstreet. Someone would have found him already. This could only mean he had survived somehow. This was becoming painful. It was the same thing as killing an animal with a dull knife. You just want to get it over with, but the creature pulls itself away and screams, wounded, prolonging its agony. Rabolii would put Arkenel out of his misery himself, but at times like these, there were too many things he was responsible for. He would need to resort to getting help.

The temple of Mortelion was a bleak and sinister place inhabited by cultists, sorcerers, and oracles—all sorts of people who felt best amidst darkness and bones. Rabolii didn't know everybody there, but when he entered the gloomy cloister, everyone fell silent and stared at him with awe. For them, only Mortelion stood higher than their magnificent ruler. The necromancer walked amongst them, staring at them with piercing eyes. He was looking for someone who could locate and exterminate Arkenel, but most people looked too lame even to deal with a depressed drunk. The necromancer slowed as he walked past a more unusual individual. He was a man in his forties, his eyes covered by a metal mask which resembled fingers grasping his face by the sides. He sat beside a table on which there was an open book. A mummy of a young woman who stood by the man was gazing at it and occasionally turned the pages. One could see very little of her. She was dressed from top to bottom in white-beige lace clothes with a rich decoration of stones and pearls. Only a few strands of her hair were coming out from under the veil. It looked almost white. Her eyes were also uncovered, and they could almost trick a person into thinking that she was alive. At some point, the mummy turned her head towards Rabolii, and the blind man exclaimed, "Master Remedor! To what do we owe the pleasure?"

"I'm looking for a person whom I may entrust an important mission with," Rabolii replied, almost like he was boasting. "I have an enemy who I need to be discovered and killed. I don't mean to offend you, but I don't think you're capable of finding anything."

The blind man chuckled and said, "Why would you say that? I have more eyes than anyone else who's not a necromancer. I think that of all people, you would understand me best."

Rabolii inspected the mummy with interest. The body was well preserved even though it looked as if it had been dead for a long time. He asked him, "Does she actually see?"

"Of course. She admires your richly ornamented silk garments. This is rare cloth, I have not seen it since 11532. Dark blue becomes you," stated the man. It was strange how he had not even turned his head towards Rabolii. This was relatively rare. It was true that all the corpses had some magical senses with which the necromancers were able to perceive the environment, but nothing could compare to real, well-preserved eyes. It was almost impossible for flesh to be protected from rotting forever, but when it came to such a small part of the body, there were ways.

"All right, so you can see," concluded Rabolii. "So how physically capable are you? Could you kill somebody?"

"I am just as capable as the skeletons and vampires I bring along," replied the blind man.

Rabolii smirked and announced, "I am inclined to believe that you are a more skilled sorcerer than most people here since you have to control corpses for your very survival, not just as entertainment. I will give you the mission. I hope you can handle it. It is of vital essence. What is your name?"

"Morakai, at your service." The blind man reached out to shake hands with Rabolii. "Whose head do you want me to bring to you?"

"Arkenel Remedor's," the necromancer replied coldly. "It's unclear where he is at the moment, but I assume he's headed east, and it's likely he'll seek shelter in the fortress of Aldur."

Morakai remained silent for a moment, then asked, "Do you have other instructions, Master?"

Rabolii was pleased that at least someone wouldn't ask him questions and lecture him about how he shouldn't kill his son. Maybe this Morakai would get the job done, so then the necromancer could have one less problem to worry about.

———ᴍᴍ———

Valenis sat in front of his piano, his fingers running along the keys. If all his hunger, pain, and wrath were music, it would sound exactly like what he was playing. The tones were low and sounded angry. It was the voice with which he chose to curse this world and express his utmost resentment. He had been in such a bad mood all the time that he could no longer determine what it was that annoyed him—the fact that Arkenel was alive and free, the fact that he was a monstrous vampire, or the death of Salina. In days like these, the world seemed like it had turned black. But apparently someone thought that he wasn't suffering enough, so they came to bang on his door with more ridiculous wishes.

"Valenis, dear! Mommy's here!" a slavering voice came from the other side.

The prince stopped playing. He rested his fingers on the keys and turned his red eyes to the door. Of course, Krementa came in without waiting for an answer, followed by Evena. Since when had these two become such good friends! When the queen saw her son, she quickly grasped him and began annoying him. "Darling, when was the last time you slept? You have black shadows under your eyes. Let me fix your collar. You shouldn't look so shabby; you're a prince!"

As soon as she reached out to him, he felt the warmth and smell of human flesh. This made him dizzy. He pulled away so abruptly that he nearly fell from his chair. He stood up and stepped backwards, raising his hands. "I ... I'm a little tired. Could you please leave me?"

"But, Your Highness, we must talk to you about something very important!" Evena was staring him down like a hungry mutt, which was very disturbing. What could she want from him?

"Valenis, we wouldn't want to push you into making any rash decisions," Krementa began rambling. "We know you've been through a lot lately and that you need peace, but Evena and I were talking ... We concluded that her baby might be not be Arkenel's, but it was definitely fathered by one of her abusers."

Valenis rolled his eyes. Did anyone really need a few days of contemplation to come here and bring him this useless and obvious information? He replied, "Yes! Everyone knows this! Is there anything else you have to tell me?"

"Valenis, you will speak to me respectfully. I am your mother!" Krementa barked like a dog. "General Evena would like to try to start a normal life with a good man and present the child as his, but she won't be able to, because the child will be born grey-skinned. No one will believe her husband is the father."

"This is not my problem!" Valenis cried impatiently. He got up and started pacing around nervously. He failed to see why they were making him listen to this nuisance.

"Valenis!" Krementa scolded him again. She wouldn't tolerate such a tone. "It's truly dreadful that Evena got pregnant in such a way. And you know single mothers are excluded in this society. Do you know how difficult it was for me, even though I was the queen? I don't want her to live through all the shame and disgrace as I did. She'll have to marry a man capable of producing a grey baby."

Valenis suddenly realised why these two were ruining his peace. His eyes widened, and he began stepping back like he was being attacked. "Oh, no! I'm terribly sorry about the general, but how could you expect me to marry her? Salina died a week ago!"

"Actually, it was ten days ago," Krementa corrected him.

"I don't care!" Valenis snapped. "Any Krumerian could be used for this."

"I think it would do you good so you could get over this

whole Salina drama and move on." Krementa blessed him with this wisdom. "You will find personal happiness while helping this poor woman."

"Can I make just one decision in my life without it being enforced by you?" Valenis yelled. He pulled out from under his shirt the so-called "girly pendant" which marked his marriage to Salina. "Do you see this? I'm already married."

"Baby, what is all this drama? You barely knew that girl." Krementa kept talking.

"You can say what you want, but I'm not changing my opinion on the matter." Valenis gave his explicit answer.

So far he had said no, but only to Krementa, completely ignoring the third participant in this event. Well, Evena listened to all this with an upset expression. Her emotions escalated. Her face reddened and twisted, and she began to wail, "And why not? Is it because I am not grey like you and your previous love? Or because I've been disgraced? What makes me unfit for you?"

Valenis just felt awkward. It wasn't like he hadn't rejected women before. After all, the Violet clan's girl had suffered this disappointment more than once, but she had always taken it with a quiet humility. He stuck his hands in his pockets and wanted to turn invisible. Krementa began hugging Evena and comforting her. The two women hadn't even been close before this, but now that they had found something common they could both complain about, suddenly they were best friends.

"Valenis, I will not allow one of my strongest and best subjects to become a laughing stock about something that wasn't her fault." Krementa turned to Valenis with a stubborn face.

Evena stopped crying for a moment and stumbled towards the prince like one of Rabolii's zombies. Valenis stepped back to save himself from this peril, but his room wasn't as big as he wished. Eventually, the general grabbed hold of him and grasped him while wailing, "Valenis!" Oh no, she was addressing him by his first name. The situation was dire. "Please don't reject me! Just think about it for a moment ... We have both suffered a lot, but if we're in this together, we will support each other in difficult moments. I'm not doing this just to legitimise my child. I've always thought that you would be a good husband. We're a great match. While I'm out on the front line, you could stay here, take care of our children, and manage the country."

Oh, didn't that sound just like a dream come true? Krementa looked at them with satisfaction and then announced, "I'm glad to see you're getting along. Valenis, honey, you can be sure you're doing the right thing. I'm going to announce the engagement to the people and start organising the wedding."

And before Valenis had the chance to open his mouth and for the hundredth time object to this, Krementa left the room, majestically waving her long garments with a feeling of a job well done. Her son remained staring after her without being able to process the thought that his mother had somehow found a way to make his life even worse. Evena pressed herself to him and fluttered her eyelashes. "Yes, I know, everything's a bit sudden for me as well, but I'm sure it's for the best!"

"Oh, Evena, leave me alone!" Valenis pushed her aside. "Can you not see that I don't want to marry neither you nor anyone else? My wife is dead. Is this so difficult for you to understand?!"

The general gave Valenis a condescending look, as if she were dealing with some spoiled child, and replied, "Yes, she's dead. Nobody can do anything to help her. But on the other hand, I'm here, and I carry a child who needs a father. You can either spend all your life chasing ghosts and drowning in self-pity or pay attention to the people who are alive and need you. The latter would be more useful to you."

Valenis leered at her. He got the feeling that no one understood how miserable he was and how nothing they said could make him feel better. They expected him to just carry on as if nothing had happened. Not that he was the one to decide how to live anyway if Krementa decided to marry him off. And by the looks of it, that was what was going to happen.

"Don't look at me like we're feeding you poison with a spoon! Would you like us to present you with a very special wedding gift?" Evena nudged him.

"Do you think there is anything that could possibly please me?" Valenis mumbled.

"How about Arkenel's head on a silver platter?" suggested Evena.

Valenis glanced at her and mumbled, "You couldn't catch Arkenel while he was in Vern. Where would you possibly begin searching for him now?"

"We know he's in Krumerus, and the locals are probably aware of his whereabouts. Would you like us to send people to kill him? I wouldn't be able to hire top-quality assassins myself, but I'm sure together we could deal with this."

A faint smile appeared on Valenis's face. Receiving the head of his wife's murderer would bring him a shred of joy. He began plotting with Evena. Obviously, they'd need someone very talented who could carve his way through dangerous Krumerus, locate the target, and eliminate him. Evena already had some ideas as to whom she could send. She could already taste her evil enemy's blood, and this excited her no end.

CHAPTER 16

THE LIVING LEGEND

Eslir was awaking, stretching whatever limbs he had left and blinking with his sleep-covered unfocused eyes. He was slowly returning to this world, but he nevertheless noticed that something bleak and dark-haired was looming over his bed, so he quickly began waving his arms around, ready to smack erebi with his plaster. He was somewhat disappointed when he noticed that it was Ilinar. He greeted him drily, "Oh ... it's just you."

"Yes, Eslir. I came back after I endured all the tests and examinations by doctors and sorcerers until they concluded I wasn't dead," Ilinar stated with an accusatory tone.

Eslir rested his head on the pillow and replied, "Like it matters. You may be alive, but you're a pawn of Rabolii all the same."

Ilinar turned his eyes away from his cousin. Obviously, Eslir was aggravated by him. He tried to come up with a compromise because he wouldn't be able to live happily until they were friends again.

"Listen, Eslir. Soleya hasn't been in an open war for decades. Ever since my mother assumed the throne, she has always defended the borders, but she hasn't sent soldiers out to war. I don't see why things need to change."

"Yes, but your mother never stood in the way of Aslania's armies when they'd attack," Eslir snapped. Then he shot Ilinar a deathly glance and snarled, "Your actions killed all that was good between our countries. You're dead to me."

The Soleyan would have possibly felt hurt had he heard something like this a few months ago, but right now this only angered him. He snapped back, "That's a very extreme thing to say, Eslir! Maybe if you stopped stroking your ego for a moment, you'd manage to focus your attention on what's important."

Eslir hated it when other people spoke instead of him, so he interrupted, "The damned Erebi killed our parents and attacked your capital! How could you still be defending them?"

It was rare for Ilinar to raise his voice since he'd been properly raised to be polite, but now he just felt enraged by this statement. He yelled, "You want me to tell you something sad, Eslir? You killed our parents! Malior did threaten he would harm us and said that he would make us sorry. But you and your father just *had* to insist on imprisoning him. If he had just let him go, none of this would have happened!"

"Me and my father?? It was *your* mother who took the final decision to detain him! And I don't remember your voice of peace giving any sort of opinion!" Eslir roared angrily, sweeping with his plastered arm everything which was on his nightstand. A bunch of pots, pots, books and decorations flew all over the place.

The two kings turned away from each other, breathing heavily. Each of them tried to think how it had come to this. They could analyse all day what it would have been like if one thing or another hadn't happened, but it seemed impossible to find just one culprit for it all. Everything had gone wrong, and all sides of this conflict had suffered. Throwing around accusations wasn't helping anyone. Ilinar sighed and broke the silence, "What happened with our parents was tragic, but if we don't provoke Krumerus any more, nothing similar should occur again. There are other threats we need to focus on."

"If you say something about Vern again ..." Eslir groaned.

"Not just Vern. I won't deny that Krumerus is a threat, but tearing down their capital isn't going to stop demons attacking us through the Thorny Woods. How do you think I knew about the monster Stronius? He is a known menace in Krumerus, and the locals told me about him." That was in fact the truth.

"And you decided to use that and play hero," Eslir stated bitingly.

"And what else was I supposed to do?" Ilinar snapped. "You didn't have weapons to fight Stronius, and you wouldn't have listened to my warnings."

"Where did you get a weapon from anyway? From the erebi?"

Ilinar wished to stay true to his story, so he replied, "I prayed to Flalirion for help, and he granted me an amazing sword. Unfortunately after the battle it disappeared, and the demon escaped before I got a chance to deal the final blow. We need to come up with a more permanent solution to this."

Eslir nodded towards the books which lay on the bed next to him and noted, "This is all I have discovered about Stronius up to this point. It doesn't seem like he's very well known in Soleya, but he seems to be a creature that is impossible to kill."

Ilinar began rummaging through the books. He asked, "What have you discovered up to this point?"

"Well, basically it doesn't look like Stronius belongs to any of the documented demon species. Your priestess told me he's Mortelion's son. I hope she's wrong and that these are only glorified legends. I know what the children of Glacera are capable of, so I don't even want to imagine ..."

Ilinar was listening with a serious expression as he flipped though the books. He thought about what Agelik had said—that Stronius and the Lethius he saw in his dream were the same demon. Still, it was unclear whether the creature Prehorian described was the same Lethius. Despite being the biggest fan of those books, Ilinar didn't know whether he had enough evidence to suggest they were based on a true story. The answer to this question miraculously appeared before his eyes just as he was thinking about it. As he was flipping through one of the books, he found an added page which looked older than the rest. On it there were several highly detailed sketches of Stronius. His skull-like head, his scaly body, his sharpened tail—it was all very realistic. The book stated that these were sketches from the 113th century, drawn by an unknown artist. Ilinar carefully inspected the old paper. It seemed like the creator had only signed with his initials and the year: E. F. P. P., 11234.

When Ilinar saw this, something turned in his stomach. He announced, "Why, this is Prehorian!"

Eslir rolled his eyes and replied, "Of course it is."

"Those are his initials. Besides, I would recognise his handwriting anywhere. I have original manuscripts of some of his poems. Eleven thousand two hundred thirty-four is a year, isn't it? He must have been ... twenty-four when he drew this. But that would mean that ..."

Ilinar froze with the book in his hands. Lethius was real, and Prehorian had known it.

"Listen, kid, I know you love the writings of that old man, but I don't think that ..."

"What if everything did happen? What if Lethius and Stronius are the same demon and our ancestors led long battles with him?"

This thought excited Ilinar in a way that not even Halena's naked body could. This was his entire childhood coming to life! All those battles he had reenacted with his toy soldiers, all the characters from his favourite tales, it was all real! He always felt like he had grown up with Prehorian and had lived in his world. Could he now be battling the same Lethius whom Felis stood against countless years ago? This wasn't something a normal person would celebrate, because in the book *Between Fire and Death* Lethius was depicted as the worst thing which had befallen the world, but Ilinar just couldn't see things that way. He announced immediately, "Everything's coming together! This is the answer!"

Eslir looked just as indifferent. He asked with annoyance, "All right then. How are we expected to deal with this? What does your precious book say?"

Ilinar's face darkened. He replied, "As a matter of fact, I don't know. The book was never completed. The last thing mentioned was that Felis and Kalia were headed towards an ancient temple which possibly held a secret to the might of the demon. There was a lot of build-up which would make us think that a shocking revelation would take place, but that's when the book ended."

"Erm, is there a part two?" Eslir asked.

"That's just the thing. I've searched for it all over, but it's like it just doesn't exist! No library has even heard of it," Ilinar replied with a sad look.

The Aslanian replied with disinterest, "Well, it doesn't sound like we need it anyway. Obviously it doesn't end with them killing Lethius, because if it's the same horse, it's still alive and kicking."

Ilinar thought deeply about this and stated, "Perhaps there's one place which holds the answers. I've heard of a monastery far to the west, almost near the Aslanian border. That was the place where monks copied the original Prehorian books. Maybe ... maybe they have some draft of a second *Between Fire and Death*? Maybe one of the monks spoke to Prehorian and knew how the book ends?"

"Ilinar, you're wasting your time. How can you expect someone to remember what Prehorian said two hundred years ago? All the people who knew him are now dead," Eslir groaned. "Don't start dealing with this. You have a country to rule. Now you're responsible for the ..."

"I'll leave immediately," Ilinar announced spontaneously.

"Just wait a moment. This isn't ..." Eslir tried to protest.

"Eslir, this is important. It's the only way to learn how to battle the monster. I won't be long. My council will deal with my affairs while I'm away."

Having said that, he rushed out. Eslir groaned with annoyance. The stupid child and his stupid books! He couldn't understand how searching for Prehorian's books would help in any way. Even if one did assume the stories of that writer weren't completely made up, had he known so much about Stronius, he would have killed him a long time ago.

Left alone, Eslir got bored within thirty seconds. He began shuffling around and looking for something to do despite the plaster casts limiting his movement. The fingers of his good hand managed to get a hold of one of the books Ilinar had been rummaging through. With disappointment, he noticed that it was *Between Fire and Death*. He had no idea how it had gotten there. It was probably the Soleyan who brought it here and forgot it. He tried reaching out for another one, but the rest were too far away. He sighed and surrendered to this degradation of his sanity and began reading the book.

Arkenel was flipping between his fingers the filthy knife which had been served to him along with a portion of some cheap food in yet another inn which provided temporary shelter. Not too long ago he could do all sorts of tricks with blades. People were enchanted when they watched him. His movements had always been so smooth and flawless like they were magic. Today, however, it felt like the knife was a foreign object in his hand. He had already cut himself a few times. His fingers were numb and clumsy. Arkenel sighed with the bitter realisation that ever since he'd slit his wrists, his fingers had lost their dexterity. His hands didn't obey him like they used to. He had mutilated himself. Now he was disabled both mentally and physically.

"Hey, eat faster. We need to go upstairs and sleep," Traneya urged him. She wanted everyone to be up early so they would arrive in Aldur as soon as possible.

"This is gross. It tastes like slug slime," Regel complained noisily, poking his stew with a disgusted look.

"Yeah, I'm sick of staying in nasty inns. Can't we just go back to Kranium?" Dregel also began protesting. "Rabolii won't kill us. He hardly remembers we exist."

"Oh, he remembers you all right. He just doesn't bother with you, because if he were to witness your endless idiocy and nuisance, he'd kill you for reals," Traneya replied.

Estrella also thought that the food was disgusting and that the beds in every inn were smelly and full of fleas. It was as if every day was a punishment. Still, she was trying not to pout and complain since things were tense already. She tried to say something optimistic: "Come on, boys! I thought you'd be glad to be out of that old castle. This is like an adventure."

"I don't want that kind of adventure!" Dregel stated, nodding towards a few ugly prostitutes who were sitting at the bar and flirting with the customers. They looked so skinny in their ragged clothes that they resembled skeletons more than they looked like women.

"Unless you're accepting money." The other twin nudged Estrella and began grinning.

Traneya slapped him behind the neck then turned to Arkenel to tell him something. It was then that some huge, fat drunkard wobbled towards their table and began speaking with them: "You! You shrimps! What're you doing in a real man's pub, eh? I been drinking with me mates for fifteen years 'ere. Never seen yous before. We don't like you eastern folk here."

"Is that so? That's not what your mother told me last night," Arkenel replied bitingly.

Regel and Dregel cheered noisily at this brilliant statement and began applauding loudly. The drunkard started looking around in confusion as if he wasn't particularly sure what had just happened. Traneya tried to intervene. "Buddy, we're just staying here for a day. We'll be on our way tomorrow."

"Whatcha say about me mom?" The fat man turned to Arkenel.

Remedor began to grin and made a gesture with his hands, displaying what he'd done to the mother, and this angered the man. He slammed his huge fists on the table so hard that plates and tankards flew in the air. He attacked his new arch-nemesis. Estrella screamed; Regel and Dregel kept jumping and screaming like excited monkeys. Traneya was trying to stop the fighting, but soon she was pushed back by the gathering crowd, who wanted to watch the fight. Arkenel was pouring out all his feelings in the shape of punches. It was as if he took the pain of every hit he received with some satisfaction. His opponent was a much larger man, so he soon prevailed in this unarmed fight. He grabbed hold of Arkenel and slammed him on the table, which broke in half. Remedor could hardly move after this blow, but he still bared his bloodied teeth and grinned. "My grandma hits harder than you, you ugly pig!"

The drunkard flew into a rage and took a chair, ready to finish off his enemy. Estrella noticed this would end badly. She managed to reach out and lightly tap the fat man with life energy. This immediately made him feel horrible as if he'd been poisoned. He crumbled down like a chopped tree and proceeded to throw up all over the floor. The spectators were disappointed by this abrupt ending. None of them had seen what happened exactly, so they just returned to their tables. Arkenel shared their disappointment. He felt two hands grab him under the armpits and pull him up to his feet. Traneya snarled at him, "I'll break your skull! If you do something stupid like that again, I'll tie you up and I'll tell people you're a slave of mine if they ask."

"Nah, don't. It'll look kinky." Arkenel kept grinning. At least he'd won the admiration of Regel and Dregel, who were very impressed with him.

"You're unbelievable, you know? Because of you, we'll need to sleep outside now," Traneya snapped. "Let's get out of here before the innkeeper comes to beat us up as well."

Having said that, she almost had to drag Arkenel out. Then she began the search for shelter outside. It was so difficult for her to manage with this, but the thought that everyone here was still alive because of her gave her some strength. She had to keep protecting them.

Over the next few days Arkenel kept behaving just as badly. It was as if he was trying to get in trouble just for the sake of it by getting into fights and stirring up all sorts of trouble. Traneya didn't know if he was purposefully drawing attention. She was contemplating all of this while standing in front of a market stand. She could hardly see the goods for sale while she was thinking about what to do with her younger brother. Loud voices and screams pulled her out of her thoughts. She hurried towards the source of the noise. Her worst fears were that her companions were in trouble. Unfortunately that was exactly the case. A bit farther into the market, Arkenel stood on top of one of the stands, waving a sword around and yelling at the people who were gathering, "You'll speak to your grandmother with that tone, not to me, you freak! I'll peel your face off. I am Arkenel Remedor, your goddamn prince! So start treating me like one, or I'll ..."

Traneya died inside when she heard this. It was as if her

whole life was being demolished in front of her eyes. With all the anger she had in her, she threw herself on top of Arkenel and knocked him off the stand.

"What are you doing? Get off me!" he tried protesting.

Traneya felt his breath, which smelled of alcohol. She slapped her brother and reproached him, "When did you manage to get drunk? For God's sake, just come with me."

Once again the five of them had to escape and get as far away as possible before the consequences of Arkenel's mess could catch up with them. Even Regel and Dregel didn't find this funny any more. They were all in danger.

Aldur was nearby. It was probably about one night away for the young Remedors. They had to find another place to sleep since obviously they wouldn't be able to do so in the town they'd just left. Traneya pulled Arkenel to the side, away from the other three, and said quietly, "Before we set off, I want us to say a few things to each other."

Arkenel shot her a discontented look and mumbled, "Pff, what is it?"

"You know perfectly well what. You're acting like you're insane. It's becoming increasingly difficult to protect you and your brothers since you're constantly drawing attention to us. And you even announce in front of entire crowds who we are. Once we get to Aldur, you can't do that any more or we're all dead!"

"I never asked for your protection. And if I'm such an inconvenience, I'll be on my way," he replied with a tone in his voice which hinted he planned to behave badly again.

"Shut up. We're not separating. We can help each other much more by staying together, but please, stop making a mess in every city we stop in!"

Arkenel crossed his arms and replied with a quarrelsome tone, "I'm not making a mess. I'm just trying to have some fun in this idiotic situation we're in. What do you want me to do, just sit there pouting and bury myself?"

"Do you think you're having fun?" Traneya spread her arms. "Listen, I know it hasn't been easy for you over the last few weeks, but you're not the only one. Just take into account that over a very short period of time I lost my husband and my sister, but we don't have the luxury to mourn. We're all in danger, and you're not helping."

"I don't care," Arkenel announced, turning his head away.

"You don't care? About what? That we could all be killed?" Traneya was stunned by this attitude.

"I'm just sick of all of this!" Arkenel bared his teeth. "I'm just always in danger! I'm always in trouble! I always need to do something important, to fight someone, to protect someone, to break out of prisons, to be a leader, to manage stupid tossers— and I'm sick of it. If I'm meant to die, I'll die all right, and it'll be a relief to me because I'm so tired of being the runaway prisoner and wondering whether there'll be a tomorrow! Maybe you still have some drive and you think you'll find us shelter so we'll live for another year, but I'm tired of this. I'm tired of this goddamned endless battle. I don't give a damn how this story ends; I just want it to be over now. Either I'll find a place under this sun and get peace, or I'll die. And that's it!"

After this stream of words, he clenched his teeth and stared at the ground. Traneya paused for a moment, trying to stop her anger from erupting. She wanted to tell him he was behaving in a childish, egoistic way, that he had no right to give up, and that he owed that much to her, to his brothers, and to his mother. To her it was incredible to have him back after all those years he spent in prison, so she felt like slapping him for behaving like this. However, she knew that such an outburst wouldn't help him, so she tried to say something encouraging. She put a hand on his shoulder and began, "Arkenel, things aren't as bad as they seem. By tomorrow morning we'll be by Aldur. We'll find your old friends, and they'll help us settle in. We'll be able to hide there if you don't draw attention. We'll win some time, and we can search for a more permanent place for us. We won't let Rabolii ruin our lives. Just leave it to me; I'll make sure we're OK."

Arkenel kept staring at the ground. He snorted and replied, "Fine. However, I have no idea who our friends are in Aldur. You're forgetting that it is a place full of people who've seen me and know me, but not all are friends. I think that showing my face there is a terrible idea."

Traneya took his hood and demonstratively flipped it over his head.

"Don't forget that half the people on the streets hide their faces anyway because they love copying anything the nobility does at the masquerade balls. They turn it into fashion. You won't let just anyone know you're there. The people in charge are your friends, right?"

"I have no idea who's in charge. It could still be the Bloodred Skull family."

"We don't need to hide behind the very skirts of the lord of the province. It's enough to have a group of reliable people who will shelter us for the time being and dispel any rumours that we're there." Traneya simplified the situation.

Arkenel realised that his friends had immediately taken over some mansions in Aldur, so this would be convenient indeed. A faint smile appeared on his face as he remembered people he used to be close friends with. He said, "Dralus and Velior would help. We were inseparable in Aldur. Together we controlled it all, and no one dared mess with us and our friends. We would have never broken out if it weren't for them."

It was a good thing Dralus and Velior had stayed behind in Aldur so they weren't murdered horribly by Vernians. Arkenel really did need them now. Traneya grasped this fact and announced, "Dralus and Velior it is then! It looks like we have a plan."

For a moment Arkenel felt a bit of relief from the weight he had been burdened with over the last few weeks. He felt a pinch of excitement for the future. This unjust life had robbed him mercilessly many times, but it hadn't taken everything he had.

As the five of them went on, they found another miserable village that could shelter them. The people there started coming out into the streets and staring at the strangers with dead eyes. It didn't seem to be a friendly place, so the Remedors just went straight to the inn. Traneya was hoping that her brothers wouldn't make another mess and get themselves kicked out again. It wasn't helping that the twins had to be in a room separate from the others, which meant she couldn't supervise them.

"OK, just go straight to bed, you two!" she instructed them as they were sitting on their beds and exchanging mischievous glances. "I don't want to catch you climbing onto the roof or trying to catch bats or something else equally idiotic."

"Sure, Sis, no problem!" Regel grinned. No one knew if his intention was to say that in a way, conveying foul plans.

Traneya closed their door, rolling her eyes, and mumbled, "I don't even want to fight them any more. They're free to lose fingers in any dumb games they want, but if I have to sleep in the streets again, someone will get seriously hurt."

"How old are they again?" Estrella asked. She couldn't

discern how old children were; they all looked awkward and shapeless.

"Seventeenish. Too old to be behaving like baboons." Traneya knew their age just because the twins were the last children Rabolii had before he died—excluding Ilinar, that is.

"You have baboons in Krumerus?" Estrella asked with surprise.

"No, but Rabolii had some captured from Vern to see if he might use them for experiments." Traneya grinned. "It was funny, because once they broke free and ran loose around the castle for a few days!"

She kept telling the story while Arkenel was sitting way too quiet and peaceful in his bed just because he had a bottle of booze and was wondering how to drink it without getting noticed. Since that didn't work, in another half an hour everyone was asleep again.

—◆—

It was a bright day. The sun peaked through the clouds and chased the poor Krumerians from the streets. Few of them were out wandering at such a late hour anyway. Traneya slept lightly, ready to jump immediately if she heard her brothers wreaking havoc or Rabolii coming in to kill everyone. She sensed that Arkenel had started kicking too aggressively in his sleep. He mumbled loudly and at some point sat up in his bed. Traneya turned to see him sitting there soaked in cold sweat with a painful grimace frozen on his face. While attempting not to wake Estrella, she got up quietly, squatting beside the bed, and said, "Another nightmare, Brother? Everything is fine. Relax."

Arkenel kept breathing heavily for a few seconds, then threw himself onto his bed and covered his face with his hands. He cried, "Nightmare? I wish it was just a nightmare! I can't forget everything that happened."

Traneya looked away, wondering how to calm him. She was never good at conversations about feelings. She made a heroic attempt: "Well, I can't imagine what you've been through. Just give yourself more time. You'll recover."

"Screw me and my recovery!" Arkenel turned to his sister and lay on one side. "Those men were the only family I had in the last seven years. Throughout all the endless days in Aldur, they were there, and we supported each other. We constantly fought for our very survival. And now they're gone. They've disappeared just like that ... because of what I got them into."

"I'm really sorry about your friends, Arkenel. Though you should stop blaming yourself. This was the corpse's doing," Traneya replied.

"No, it wasn't Rabolii who marched the men into an ambush. If only I had ..."

"What are you talking about? Rabolii knew there was an ambush!"

Arkenel didn't seem to understand what she was saying and continued to groan, "I could have researched things better, but instead I ..."

"Arkenel, he knew everything. He knew that Valenis was a spy, and he sent you off to die," Traneya stated. Her brother looked at her in shock, wondering how she could have come up with something like that. She gasped, "What, you didn't know? The corpse was alone with Valenis a few times. He questioned him and investigated him even before he got close with Salina. During one of those meetings, he must have realised Valenis was from Vern. That's why Rabolii held on to Salina during the last few days before you left. Now that I think about it, he probably even knew she had the Mark of Mortelion. He felt she was in danger so didn't let her out of his sight. He did not want her to hang out with the spy. And when she escaped with you, Rabolii went mad. He did everything to get her back. He was sending skeletons, messengers, and whatnot. You were chased by a small army! So that was the moment it occurred to me that he knew perfectly well that he had sent you to die, and now he was terrified because Salina was with you."

Arkenel stared in shock. He couldn't understand what he was hearing. Eventually, he could only ask hoarsely, "Dad sent us to die? But why? I ... I did everything he wanted me to do."

"Why? Because he's a repulsive, hateful old man, that's why. Stop thinking that there's something wrong with you and that you need to prove yourself more. Obviously something is wrong with him. He's the one who has issues with the whole world. Nobody likes him, except for Mom, who must have noticed that he's an animal by now," Traneya said fiercely, no longer trying to be quiet. Estrella had awoken and started walking around.

Arkenel sat in bed, staring at his laced fingers in his lap. He said, "That makes no sense at all."

Traneya put a hand on his shoulder and said, "I know. There's no reason why we're punished with such a freak for a father, but all we can do now is try to sort out our lives and be happy despite his hateful, toxic persona."

Arkenel couldn't process the information that the greatest evil in his life had been caused on purpose by Daddy. Everything seemed so pointless and ridiculous that his brain was rejecting it. Traneya continued to talk to him, "It is a shame for the people who died like that. But you will overcome this. There are much better days ahead of you."

Estrella knelt beside Arkenel's bed and handed him a cup of tea as she said, "That's right. Now that the toxic people are out of the picture, things will get better."

He took the cup with trembling hands, realising that he felt some inner strength returning to him. Knowing that he wasn't the one responsible for burying his friends was a relief. He was not the incompetent one or the useless one. He was the same man as he was before this whole disaster. He could still be useful to others and pursue his goals. True enough, he was wounded and robbed, but he would recover and regain the things he thought were valuable. Two of those were already with him right now. He nodded to Traneya and Estrella with a faint smile of gratitude and said, "Yes, you're right. We'll survive this."

Shortly after everyone went back to sleep. Arkenel continued to sit in his bed, clutching the cup of tea. He stared at the blinding light, contemplating. A storm was forming in his aching head. It was all so absurd. He had spent so much time listening to Ravena, who explained what a good man Father was and that if Arkenel just tried to please him, the two of them would get along just fine. And Arkenel had tried and tried. Proving himself to Rabolii had become the purpose of his life, to the point where he became blind to the hostility he received as a response. Mavarius had warned him so many times that the necromancer was setting traps. He had pointed out what was wrong with their relationship, but Arkenel would have none of it. He just kept breaking his back to please a man who would never be content. Should he feel stupid for allowing his father to do all that? This naiveté had led to all sorts of terrible things. No. Traneya was right. The only one who was to blame was Rabolii. He was the cruel and illogical one.

Arkenel lowered his eyes to the cup he was holding. Because of all this drama, he had also lost Mavarius. What had his friend felt while watching Arkenel serving the man who wanted to kill them? No wonder he had left. Arkenel wished that he could see Mavarius again and tell him he now knew everything and was ready to completely change his life. But no one knew where Mavarius was. He could well be behind the border by now. Maybe the two of them would never meet again.

Ravena strolled through the abandoned kitchen, where her sweet little boy had been staying until recently. There were scattered blankets and empty bottles of booze, left behind by all those people who were now dead. She studied the place and felt her eyes fill with tears. How could she have allowed for her son to live in such a horrible place? She should have fought harder against Rabolii. Maybe there was something she could have done to prevent all the awful things from happening. She felt hurt and desperate because of the way her family had fallen apart. Was it too late for things to be fixed after everything that had happened?

"Um ... hi." She heard an awkward greeting.

Ravena turned around, startled, and saw a man in a long black cloak at the other end of the kitchen. She blinked and wiped the tears from her eyes, wondering if she knew him.

"Who are you? Are you one of my son's friends?" Ravena asked with some hope. She couldn't think of anyone else who would come down to a dreadful place such as this.

"I'm looking for Arkenel Remedor," the stranger said in the same stiff manner.

Ravena felt some sort of trust for this man. If this was a hireling of Rabolii, he wouldn't be asking her in such a blunt and straightforward way. She replied, "He's ... he's not here. I'm not sure exactly where he is. My husband believes that he might have set off towards Aldur. Maybe you can catch up with him. He left around four nights ago."

The stranger kept a confused silence, then asked, "Where's Aldur? In what direction?"

That was a strange question. This country had only three large fortresses, so it was ridiculous someone wouldn't know about one of them. She narrowed her eyes and stepped closer to the man, asking, "Who are you anyway?"

He kept silent, but when she approached him, she could see a bit of his chin and lips from under his hood. His skin was bluish and shiny. Ravena gasped in horror and stepped back. She stuttered, "You ... you're a Vernian!"

The man thought there was no point in hiding any more,

so he took his hood off. He was a Vernian indeed. His skin was pale blue. He had darker spots on one of his cheeks up to his eyebrow. His hair and beard were black with an indigo shine. He tried to calm Ravena, saying, "Yes, I'm a Vernian, but if you'll let me explain ..."

"Guards!" she screamed as loud as she could.

The Vernian snorted, pulled the hood over his face again, and fled. Ravena knew he was probably dangerous, but regardless she ran after him and kept screaming. She was mortified by the thought that Vernians were looking for her poor son and she had given them directions. Unfortunately the man could run faster than she, and as soon as he was outside, he merged with the crowd and disappeared. Ravena was shaking. She decided not to tell Rabolii about this. Under these circumstances it didn't seem impossible that he'd sign a temporary treaty with Vern until they captured Arkenel together.

Ilinar had never travelled east in such bad weather. Sure enough, he had visited Aslania before, just never in the late autumn. During the summer the lands by the border were wondrous. To the south lay a sea with lots of small scattered islands. His mother had a mansion on one of them. The region was called the White Beaches. Ilinar had spent lots of time there. However, he wasn't going to the south now. His road led to frozen peaks rising amongst dense woods. Ilinar rubbed his hands and shook atop of the horse's back. He was approached by a smiling sorcerer of fire, who offered, "Should we stop for a break, Your Majesty? I could create a fire dome for you."

"Not now, Freley. I just want us to arrive as soon as possible," Ilinar stated. He added, "It's still very kind of you to offer."

Ilinar knew that for a sorcerer to create a fire dome over an area and warm everything inside it was really exhausting and required a lot of energy. At least that's what he had heard. Freley swept back his fringe, wet from the tiny raindrops, and replied, "Cold isn't that bad. At least I believe so. It helps us appreciate the summer, right?"

At that moment Ilinar had a hard time appreciating the cold. The road was long. Sometimes it would turn into small footpaths where it wasn't safe to ride, so they all had to dismount and climb the frozen mountain. Some of the guards who accompanied Ilinar were Aslanian, and occasionally they'd nudge each other discreetly and grin as they watched the Soleyans struggle with the harsh climate which the platinum-haired men were so used to.

After a painfully long amount of time, the monastery finally appeared in the storm of tiny snowflakes which hid the scenery from sight. The warm yellow light of the windows was the most beautiful thing Ilinar had seen for days.

The monks knew that they were expecting important guests, so they welcomed Ilinar and his delegation with a modest dinner and small gifts. Everyone gathered in the main dining room, which had never been so crowded. The oldest of the monks turned to Ilinar and said, "It's a real honour for us to welcome you, Your Majesty. We hardly remember the last time we had a similar pleasure. We'll do our best to make you feel comfortable, but unfortunately I don't know if we'll be very helpful in your quest. Your letters mentioned you seek the second volume of *Between Fire and Death*. We're afraid, however, that such a book has never been brought to us."

This statement pricked Ilinar's insides, but he wasn't about to give up so easily. He kept insisting, "Yes, I know that the first volume was introduced to the public only after Prehorian's death and that he wasn't even alive to see the first published copy of his work. But I was hoping he left behind some ... drafts or lists with ideas as to what'll happen later?"

"We don't have any of Prehorian's drafts." The monk dropped the next heartbreaking statement: "He didn't write his books here. As a rule, whenever he had something completed, he'd ask his associates to climb up to the monastery, and we'd create copies."

Ilinar frowned, trying to think. He noted, "But *Between Fire and Death* isn't a completed book. In my opinion it always sounded as if the last few pages were just missing. There isn't a finale; the story is just cut off. I'm very familiar with Prehorian's work. He never ended a book like this. If we just presume he died and never finished it, how did you acquire it? I don't understand; this makes no sense."

The monk didn't know what to say. He smiled quietly and replied, "Your Majesty, all of this happened two centuries ago. It seems there's no way for us to know for sure."

"There must be *something* you know!" Ilinar exclaimed. "The people who used to live here knew him better than anyone else!"

"Not really. During the majority of his career, Prehorian

didn't appear in front of the monks. I've heard stories that he had some accident and broke a bone, so that made him incapable of climbing the steep paths," the old man explained.

"Hey, should we give him the books which that one boy asked for?" one of the younger monks said.

"Quiet, son. His Majesty hardly has time for such tales."

"What books?" Ilinar asked instantly.

"We have some old journals from a long time ago. They were written by one of the last people who knew Prehorian personally. They once belonged to Larii the Wise. We've all read them, but we believe old age was unkind to him and his wits, so eventually he stopped seeing things the way they were."

Ilinar wasn't even going to ask why the monks thought so. He already knew that nothing about Prehorian was exactly what one would expect. He announced, "I want to see those journals."

The monks exchanged glances and let out a sigh. They felt bad for the king for having come all this way when they couldn't offer him anything more useful than the journals of a confused old man.

After dinner they led him to the library. The young monk was chattering as they walked. "Larii is a distant relative of mine. His books were kept in my family. We kept them because they were full of very well-written thoughts and wisdom about life which has helped us over the years. There were also passages about Prehorian. It's strange for you to come because of this right now. Earlier today a young man appeared. He was asking the same questions."

Ilinar blinked. In his gut settled the feeling of who this young man was. He wondered if it was possible. He wasn't surprised when he walked into the library and found Agelik there. He was reading an ancient journal with a thick leather cover. The blond Soleyan raised his eyes and said casually, "Ilinar! I knew that we'd meet here."

The monks and soldiers started glancing around, wondering what sort of a strange meeting this was. Ilinar waved his hand, gesturing them to leave, and stepped stiffly forward. He didn't know what sort of a conversation to expect now. He cleared his throat and replied, "Yes ... I should have guessed."

Agelik moved the journal to the side and announced, "Ilinar, our last meeting turned out to be an unpleasant one." All right, it looked like he was getting straight to the point. "I would like to apologise for that."

Ilinar lowered his eyes and mumbled, "No, you were right. I

didn't think through the whole situation with Eley, and that led to many problems. Maybe there is some truth to what you said about Stronius too."

"I've been contemplating this situation," Agelik replied. He gestured with his hand towards the empty space on the bench he was sitting on. "I would sum up that you did make a mistake. However, it was unfair of me to judge you as I could not imagine the horror and confusion you must have felt when circumstances pressed you into making decisions such as these. Perhaps time and age will grant you the clarity and cool mind needed to react in similar situations and to do what's right."

Ilinar felt ashamed. He stood still in the middle of the library, his hands stuck in his pockets. He replied, "I ... don't even know what to think. I'm confused. I did spill blood to get my crown, even though I felt that I was doing it for a good reason. I'm not the same any more. I've tried to think about other things to distract myself, but it keeps creeping back into my thoughts."

Agelik gave him a kind smile and answered, "Plenty of people would state this is unhealthy, but I don't consider this to be the case. In my opinion it is wonderful that you attempt to concentrate on your work. If you do indeed grow as a ruler and make a positive change for everyone, this will give you self-esteem and will help you forgive yourself. Just give yourself time."

Ilinar felt gratitude towards Agelik, but he also had the feeling that he didn't deserve those words. Burdened by guilt and regret, he looked away and replied, "Yes, I'll keep busy. Since I killed a man for this crown and meddled with a monster, I'll try to justify the sacrifice. That was the point. I am here to investigate the same demon Lethius which you seek as well. I'm almost sure that he and Stronius are the same demon."

Agelik's eyes widened with excitement. He asked, "Have you discovered yet more information to confirm this? I ... just felt something when I stood before Stronius. On the one hand I did feel as if it was the first time I'd laid eyes upon him. My mind couldn't recall memories of his image, but in a strange way I felt the same pain in him as the one which struck me in my dreams."

Ilinar narrowed his eyes and noted, "Honestly, I don't know what you're talking about. I also faced him, and I didn't have a single thought about any pain. Do you have some sort of ... powers? Are you a sorcerer?"

"No, I'm not," Agelik denied that quickly. "I don't possess a sphere of any element. I suppose I just have good intuition. I pay a great deal of attention to my own feelings, and sometimes they reveal lots of information about our surrounding world which we are simply not taught to read."

Ilinar came up to Agelik and sat on the bench beside him. He replied, "I know I definitely haven't been taught to do that. OK, so about those books. If you've been reading these all morning, have you happened to ..." He gazed at the pages and noted with surprise, "What kind of a dialect is this? I can't read it!"

"Dialect? Is the handwriting difficult for you to read?" Agelik replied confusedly.

"No, it's just that these are not the same letters ... I should have remembered, two centuries ago the writing in Soleya was a bit different," Ilinar noted with disappointment.

"I have no difficulty deciphering this," Agelik stated to his friend's delight. "I do confess, I got a bit distracted with these books today. Larii the Wise has led a fascinating life. I spent hours reading of his journeys across foreign lands I can only imagine. But enough of his itineraries! Let's seek information about Prehorian."

The two of them began to browse the journals and to search for pages where the writer was mentioned. When they found such a passage, Agelik began reading out loud: "Prehorian wasn't what I had expected. I had heard of him. I had read his works, but meeting him was simply strange. There is no other word I can use to describe it, and it isn't because of the great respect I feel for him. He was but a child! He didn't seem older than my seventeen-year-old son, though he was supposed to be a man in his late twenties! He had no beard; he wasn't tall; his fair hair hung in front of his eyes, uncut, though it was apparent it irritated him."

Agelik paused, then he just stared at the paper for a few seconds. Then he continued, "There was a flame in his eyes. There was a certain firmness and rigidity which didn't become his young face. Whenever I'd gaze in those eyes, I saw great pain and bitterness which he had melted and crafted into a sword which he used to fight battles I knew nothing about. Though he was polite, he was always in a hurry to leave. We never had long conversations. I remember how one day I insisted on accompanying him down the path from the monastery, although he initially declined. I told him I admired his books, but I can't help but think that they were not his main occupation but merely the result of it. Emanrylii remained silent for a bit and then replied, 'The people find my tales amusing. But they're nothing but that, isn't that so? Just tales. Nothing of what I'm writing about has ever been seen or heard of. How could they be a result of my life?'

"'You are a mysterious man, Emanrylii. I can respect that, but I want you to know of my utmost admiration and fascination for you. I want to be your friend. I would accept your truth, whatever it may be.'

"Both of us halted upon the path. Emanrylii gazed at the ground, deep in thought. Perhaps he wondered how to tell me that which I so wanted to hear. Eventually he replied, 'The stories I write are not my own. I have never touched those events or personalities. However, I did collide with someone who did, who had participated. He gave them unwillingly. It was an accident. I write them for him, as he has forgotten who he is and I am desperately trying to return him to his life. I'm sure he's somewhere out there reading them. I hope I can touch something in him. Perhaps if he sees himself through another's eyes, he'll realise who he wants to be.'

"I was puzzled. I tried to think of a Prehorian character who appeared in all his books. Some did indeed make multiple appearances, but I was unsure who fit this description. Feeling overwhelmed, I noted, 'Most of your characters are demigods and heroes the likes of which this world has not seen, Emanrylii. Who on earth do you know? What kind of life have you lived?'

"He gave me a sad smile and replied, 'Not the one I dreamed about.'

"We didn't say much more on that day. I believe this was the last time I met him. He left me with so many questions, with a riddle I wouldn't solve in my lifetime. I knew that his books were special in a way, but it seems as if behind the fairy tales lay secret messages directed towards a being the likes of which I possibly can't even imagine.'"

That's where the passage about Prehorian ended. Agelik and Ilinar sat there staring at the pages without knowing what to say. Apparently, this was a riddle for them as well. In an attempt to make sense of those lines, Ilinar spoke first: "OK, so one thing seems clear—in Prehorian's opinion, his stories are based upon something which did happen. This helps us because whatever he wrote about the demon is a fact."

Agelik was still thinking about the beauty of the fact that Prehorian had dedicated his books to someone who needed to remember his life. He would have thought they were meant for him, because after all, how many people have completely forgotten who they are? The only problem was the pit of two centuries which lay between them. Ilinar was already digging in the book for more pages about Prehorian. He was mentioned here and there when Larii described his thoughts and reflections about the author's books, but there was nothing more specific. Ilinar was flipping through the last journal when he found something interesting again.

Agelik was shaking with anticipation. He knew that the open book in front of him might contain the secrets about himself which he was dying to learn. He tried to calm his voice as he read, "After we received the *Dark Flame* book, we didn't get any more Prehorian works for decades. We were saddened by this and believed he had ceased to write forever. The only thing left for me to do was to rewrite the same lines from his previous books which I knew by heart now. I thought about him rarely. He had left my life so long ago. It was on that blessed summer in the year 11290 when something incredible happened …

"The monastery was visited by a boy I never thought I'd see again. It was Emanrylii. He looked absolutely the same as on that day so long ago when we spoke on the mountain path. It'd been thirty-four years. I stood there as if I had been struck by thunder. I approached him and asked how this could be possible. He smiled politely and replied that his name was Agelik and that he was the grandson of Emanrylii."

When he read this, Agelik shut up in shock. Both he and Ilinar stared at the book. If a person could have seen them right then, he'd think they were realistic sculptures, depicting astonishment and surprise, as they remained like that for a long time, neither of them knowing what to say. Eventually Agelik started reading again because he just needed to know what else was being said.

"No one else in the monastery had ever seen Prehorian before. They could not confirm what I thought. I was older than any of them, and I remembered things which had happened before their time. Agelik announced that his grandfather had begun writing again and had tasked him with bringing his books to us. I had no explanation for what I was witnessing, but there it was before my eyes. They were the same person down to the tiniest detail! They both had that sun-kissed skin as if they had been out every day of the summer; the same blond hair, which casually hung in front of their eyes; and the same quiet wisdom which they kept but rarely shared … This drove me insane. I needed answers. One day I called young Agelik into my study and I asked him to write a letter on my behalf as I am a poor old man whose eyesight is failing him. The boy agreed and sat by my side. He wrote down the words I dictated. I followed the movements of his hand vigorously, feeling as though I'd been struck by what I was seeing.

"After writing a few lines, he realised what my intent was. I had been rewriting Prehorian manuscripts my whole life. I could recognise his handwriting anywhere. I was recognising it now. Agelik raised his eyes to me and gave me a calm look. He noted, 'You have always been too curious, my old friend. It's a quality I can admire even when it causes me difficulties.'

"I was shaken by excitement and torn apart by a kind of joy which cut me like a knife. I laid my hands on his shoulders and said, 'Emanrylii, I know not what secrets you keep, but you don't need to pretend in front of me. You know I would never speak to a single soul about this.'

"He smiled with sadness in his eyes and replied, 'It would be unwise for us to risk our lives just for the sake of a friendship and some books, Larii. Do you realise what this world would do to me if it were to notice I don't age? I would be declared a reanimated corpse, a vampire, a demon. Men are cruel when they're afraid. I wouldn't want to suffer such a fate. I wouldn't want you to be dragged into the dangers which surround me.'

"'I will not speak of this to anyone, I swear.'

"'It is required of us to be dishonest, unfortunately. Just call me Agelik in front of the others.'

"I knew not whether I was awake or dreaming. This really was him. I couldn't comprehend what he was. What was his real age? What kind of unearthly powers did he possess? What sort of life had he lived? I did ask those questions, but his replies were short and uninformative. I tried to read between the lines, and what I think I noticed was that he kept secrets and wisdom we are not ready for. Perhaps we are still simple greedy people. Perhaps we wouldn't understand. I asked him if I was correct in assuming this, and he confirmed I was. I pleaded with him to write down that which we needed to know in a book, to convey the wisdom which he kept hidden. This way those of us who were ready for his words would receive them, while the others would dismiss them as another fairy tale. He noted he'd need to write lots of books in this case, but he would consider it. Firstly he had other projects he needed to accomplish. Emanrylii was never one to write fast.

"He visited the monastery more frequently than ever, but

it was still months, if not years, until his next drop-by. I was unsure what he did during the rest of the time.

"It was autumn in the year 11299 when he appeared at the monastery again. He was carrying a new book called *Between Fire and Death*. He gave it to me personally and advised it was incomplete but said he would return to finish it. I forced myself not to read it in the meantime and just waited for him to come back. However, he never did. Emanrylii disappeared again, this time even more abruptly and mysteriously. Every day I just lived on with the hope that he would come back, but it'd been years. I just hoped I'd be alive when it happened.

"*Between Fire and Death* is an unusual book. It does follow the same structure as the rest. Most of them end with evil triumphing, but there is also a small seed of love and hope, and it's for us to dream that it sprouts. If I had to guess, I would think the ending of this book would be no different. However, the way in which he focused on some of the characters made me think this story was more personal to him. I wonder if this was his attempt to write that truth for the people who were ready for his words. I decided that I owed it to him to spread his last book in the exact state I received it from him. I had all the power to write my own ending, but I felt unworthy of doing something like that. Throughout my whole life I believed that his words would change the world. I hoped he'd left enough of them to achieve his goal."

The paragraph was over. This was the last page of the journal. All the other pages were blank. Ilinar and Agelik sat in silence yet again, trying to digest all this amazing information. The Soleyan king spoke first, "I ... can't believe it. You're Prehorian? But how?"

Agelik was thinking about how desperately he had wanted to get his memories back and to find out who he was, but now that he had these answers, he somehow couldn't accept them. He hadn't received a part of his life back; he had just read a text which seemingly described a stranger. He stuttered in denial, "No ... I couldn't be ... I have no recollection of this place, and the name Emanrylii does not sound familiar to me."

"Agelik, all the signs are there. The person Larii describes looked exactly like you. And that would also explain why we found you carrying a letter from the year 11299. That really was you. You're just ... eternal for some reason."

Ilinar had no worries that Agelik was a corpse or a vampire

or anything like that. He knew the pain of being mistaken for a corpse, and he didn't want to cause such misery to other people.

"I ... thought that I had suffered some accident and had forgotten the only sixteen to seventeen years of my life that I had," Agelik stammered. "I expected to discover my family, my home town, and instead this is what I came across! What am I?"

Ilinar gazed at him with awe and admiration. He put a hand on his shoulder and told him, "You're the man who inspired generations of Soleyans. You're a genius and an enigma who caught the attention of many scientists. You're the creator of dozens of books as well as the famous Prehorian cipher which contains hundreds of magical equations which have baffled entire nations. You've been a part of the life of so many people. The fact that I'm able to sit here and speak to you is ... surreal and is the best thing that has ever happened to me!"

Agelik smiled uneasily and mumbled, "Lovely. It seems I'll need to meet great expectations."

Ilinar was fluttering with joy and excitement. Larii had described a meeting with Prehorian as a "dream". There wasn't a more suitable expression for it.

"We don't need to tell anyone about this. You can just be known as Agelik. I promise not to tell anyone," Ilinar began swearing secrecy.

"Yes, just like good old Larii," Agelik replied. He lowered his eyes at the journal with secrets which had been read by ten generations of people. "These writings were probably discovered after his death. They couldn't have harmed me ... harmed Prehorian ... as he had already disappeared. And according to what I've heard, no one took them seriously anyway."

"I won't write journals," Ilinar declared instantly, and then resumed bargaining like a market trader. "Listen, if you come with me to Lumis, we'll read all of your books and poems, and we can try to find out who it was that you wrote everything for. I'll get sorcerers and healers to examine you and help you recover your memory. And in the meantime we'll look for information on Lethius. We'll be useful to each other."

Agelik shook his head and said, "I appreciate your enthusiasm, Ilinar, but I don't think sitting here and reading books will help us. It's what we did today, but it did nothing for my memory. I need to return to Krumerus and seek Lethius."

"And how do you know Lethius will help you?" Ilinar was quick to ask. "Even if he does tell you your story, it'll be just that—a story. There's no guarantee you'll remember. Besides, the thing with the memories isn't our only problem. Stronius is a menace to my country, and you obviously have some experience fighting against him. I'll need you, because if you do remember something, it'll be valuable to the whole of Soleya."

Agelik smiled sceptically. He almost felt as if he had visited the tailor to try on different clothes and for some reason they had made him wear exactly the ones which didn't fit him. He thought for a moment and then stated, "So be it then. However, I am still not convinced all this is accurate. But you're right about one thing. If I am who you believe I am, I would be more useful by your throne than in some Krumerian woods. If I do possess a rare knowledge which I may remember. It would be irresponsible of me to endanger myself. However, I cannot promise that I'll be useful indeed or that I'll remember my mission, but I could assist you in succeeding with yours."

Ilinar was gazing at him as he spoke, feeling enchanted. He memorised Agelik's every word. He was even trying not to blink so the mirage wouldn't disappear. He asked with a velvety voice, "How would you like me to refer to you when we're alone? Emanrylii or Agelik?"

"Agelik, please. I'm not sure why, but this other name just doesn't sound like it's mine. It might have been a writer's alias." He cast a glance at Ilinar, who was still gazing at him the way a hungry dog looks at the meat stand at a market, so he decided to add, "So far, you and I have had a very down-to-earth relationship. Let us not change that. I believe modesty is one of my virtues. I wouldn't want to be treated like ... a literature god or anything."

Ilinar chuckled. Literature god. He liked that. He tried to calm down, but it wasn't easy. This was literally the best thing that had ever happened to him. His entire magical world, his whole childhood, all those tales which had supported him through difficult times, all this had come to life in all its splendour. On this day the horrors of war and the uncertainty of politics disappeared the way shadows do when the sun rises.

Pink and bright was the next dawn for Soleya. It was like the warm sun promised new horizons, vastness of freedom, and opportunities. And though countless of demons hid in the darkness, they didn't matter on this day. Ilinar was so happy. He felt like he had everything in life. He undertook the secret sending of gold to Krumerus, believing that Halena would soon return to him. Then everything would be in its place. Everything would be perfect.

The same morning sun hardly managed to break the thick clouds over Krumerus. Pale rays slid through the mist and illuminated the jagged towers of Aldur. Arkenel was squinting against this unpleasant light, trying to see details of the scenery. Whose banners were those? In what state was the city? He told himself that it was all the same to him. Once he set foot in Aldur, he would either reunite with his friends or be betrayed and surrendered to Rabolii, who'd kill him. Both of those options had their charm, but Arkenel realised that his will to live was returning. He still felt like a shell of the man he used to be, but all the guilt and self-hatred he felt began settling down like sludge in water and tormented him less. He wouldn't be the man to lead armies, the pride of Rabolii, the hand to change Krumerus. But maybe he would find a way to live without being a burden or hurting the people closest to him, and that would be enough for now. It was all the same. Aldur would decide his fate.

Dear reader,

Thank you for sharing this adventure with me! I hope that as you're putting this book down, you feel like you've really lived through something epic.

And it's not over! Do watch out for the next book from the series,

On the Edge of Life
Uprising

And to give you a sneak peek...

As soon as Arkenel arrives in Aldur, he encounters the local militia and is apprehended. He's not happy to learn his friends aren't in control of the city. He knows he's worth more dead than alive. The future is uncertain, but he also receives a most welcome surprise.

Ilinar introduces Agelik to his court as a new advisor for the king. One would expect the two would resume investigating Stronius and ways to defeat him, but Agelik gets distracted by too many things and soon his presence causes conflicts. Ilinar doesn't know how to dispel disagreements and quarrels in his own court.

Rabolii gains more power through massacre and chaos. He has a score to settle with the Vernian queen and he'll kill every living person he encounters if that will increase the number of soldiers he has.

Table of Contents

Lightning Source UK Ltd.
Milton Keynes UK
UKHW010911200919

350103UK00001B/14/P